FOUR
BY
EGAN

FOUR BY EGAN

- *A Case for Appeal*
- *Against the Evidence*
- *My Name Is Death*
- *Some Avenger, Rise!*

by Lesley Egan

Nelson Doubleday, Inc.
Garden City, New York

CONTENTS

FOUR
BY
EGAN

A
CASE
FOR
APPEAL

"Truth is heavy, therefore few care to carry it."

—Proverbs of the Rabbis,
THE TALMUD OF JERUSALEM

ONE

Jesse Falkenstein came out of the smallish old building; the late-afternoon sun hit him like a physical blow there on the top step. This was September, and this was the great inland valley of California; at noon today the thermometer had registered one hundred and nineteen, and it hadn't dropped five degrees since.

L.A. and environs were bad enough; he wondered why anybody lived up here. Of choice.

He came down to the sidewalk and started up toward where his car was parked. Not much of anybody around now; the reporters had all gone, and the courtroom crowd dispersed.

Sure, he thought. Whole thing over as far as they were concerned. No use feeling bitter about that: natural; what else?

He ambled down the street, hands in pockets, suit jacket over one arm, hat shoved back, a tall, dark, lanky fellow, wearing his usual amiable, noncommittal expression. His own mother had never claimed he was good looking, what with his big, jutting, high-bridged nose, gauntly hollow cheeks, a jaw too long and a mouth too wide; what she had always said was handsome-is-as-handsome-does and Jesse was a smart boy, he'd go far. And he sometimes wondered if that had been just mother love.

There was someone waiting for him, leaning on the fender of his old gray Ford. Another tall man, another man in the early thirties, but much better looking than Jesse: mobile, clean-shaven features, a strong, straight nose, a long upper lip, square, strong jaw, square, high forehead under a shock of tawny-gold hair. He'd taken off jacket and tie, leaned there smoking, staring remotely across the sidewalk at the store fronts with their sale announcements screaming soundlessly.

"You might," said Jesse, "have made it January. I mean, adding insult to injury—another lost case on my record, and risking heat stroke besides."

The blond man's long upper lip twitched once. "Well, you can go home now. I'll buy you a consolation drink."

"That's a deal."

They left their jackets in the car and walked on half a block to the nearest bar. There were a few booths against the wall; in mutual consent they sat in one of those. The waiter who came over was fat and mustached. "*Ciao*, Captain Varallo—*come va?*"

"*Non c'e male*," said Varallo absently. "Brandy."

"Bourbon, straight," said Jesse. He looked at Varallo across the little table. Always struck you a little funny, remember he was Italian: big blond fellow: preconceived ideas—like, God knew, the preconceived ideas anybody named Falkenstein was always running into. Lodovico Varallo sounded like a fellow who ought to look like that waiter. North Italian, a lot of them blond . . . Hard to figure Varallo other ways. Smart boy, a good man all ways. So what the hell was he doing up here still stagnating? Different thing up to a couple of years ago or thereabouts, when he'd had the family on his neck. Which was the reason he'd had to leave the university twelve years back: father dead and a pack of younger kids still to be supported by somebody . . . Varallo had walked out of the Church a long time back, but he wasn't a man to walk out of responsibility. And it probably hadn't been so easy for him another way too, Jesse reflected: because the rest of the family had, of course, bitterly disapproved Varallo's leaving the Church and without much doubt had never ceased to work on him about it.

He and Varallo had kept up, as the saying went, the desultory way men do: a letter now and then, and a couple of times Varallo got down to the big town. Never said much about himself, Varallo; but it was possible to guess at this and that—since he'd apparently stayed at home only until a couple of the older kids were capable of managing alone. Domestically, not financially. Varallo's address for some time now had been the Contera Hotel. And possible to wonder, too, about a family who'd feel that way and still take his money. Well, necessity. And probably quite a lot of his money; Jesse remembered vaguely that there'd been five or six kids. But he remembered also that Vic had said something, a couple of years ago, about all the kids being on their own now. So what was he doing still here? He had a job he'd worked up in, sure, but it couldn't pay much and he'd never meant—so he used to say—to stay in Contera all his life. Do better down in the big city. Well, none of Jesse Falkenstein's business, of course.

"*Capitano—Signor!*" With a flourish the drinks set before them.

Varallo picked up his brandy and looked at it. "How'd she take it?"

Jesse shrugged. "How'd you think? She's got what it takes—she didn't go into hysterics, if that's what you mean. I'll appeal the verdict, of course."

"Think that's any good?"

Jesse swallowed half the bourbon and said, "Why, no, Vic, I don't. The judge knew his business, far as I could see. No little legal loopholes to make it a mistrial. Of course, I'm not one of those smart boys who've got all that business memorized—court steno sneezes during testimony, so one word left out, so hey-presto, it's a mistrial. I'll look. But on the face of it, there's no grounds there. Might do something on prejudiced witnesses. On that negative decision we got asking a change of venue. I don't know. But I don't think we'll get a new trial, or anything like that. Which I didn't say to her."

"Naturally. So what?"

"Else? Why, I can claim she wasn't fit to plead. Sanity. Obviously. You're going to say it's a democratic country, everybody treated alike?—"

"I wasn't, no."

"—If there was money to hire a couple of psychiatrists, I could put up a fight on that. Have 'em swearing she's got amnesia or something —double talk. She says no."

"I can't say I blame her."

Jesse finished the bourbon. "Life is life, even stashed away in Camarillo for a while."

"For how long a while? Five years, ten? And another hearing to establish sanity? Could she pass that one then?"

"And there's that," agreed Jesse. "Any case, she says no. She says she'd rather have it quick than slow, if it's coming and she knows it's coming."

They sat in silence for a while, until Varallo beckoned the waiter again. Over a refill he said, "There was that fellow Oscar Slater—back in the eighties, wasn't it?—he got off in the end."

"Sure. I've been doing a certain amount of thinking about Mr.

Slater too. Lot of time and work and money involved, fighting a thing like that."

Varallo looked at him. "Yes, money's important—I suppose—"

"Well, not so important as all that," said Jesse. "Sure, I'm going to fight it. What else did you think? Right now we've got about six weeks. The appellate court won't be sitting in Fresno until then. That's where and when it'll come up. The judge knows I'm going to appeal. She'll stay here until we get that decision. So I thought I'd use that six weeks to go on a little private hunting trip for the other one."

Varallo laughed. "Just like that! Planning any more miracles for later on? And where do you think you'll pick up the trail? You looked, I looked—"

"So we did. Look some more, that's all."

"*Diavolo!*" said Varallo. "It was the Inver one built it up—Teresa Zacchio, who the hell cared? And second degree, not first. They'd never have got the death sentence if it hadn't been for Inver. Two of them."

"That's about the size of it."

"And what the hell could I do? Seven witnesses swearing to her—"

"Well, you did what you could," said Jesse. "You sent for me. . . . Seven. Four second-class ones, three first-class—"

"How right you are!" said Varallo sardonically. "Four dirty stupid Catholics wth foreign names, and—"

"Now let's just leave the generalizations out," said Jesse. "By that I meant credibility and degree of certainty. Not an awful lot to choose, of course. Not very good light, any of the times and places. I said I'd been thinking about Mr. Slater too. One of the things I thought about was the witnesses there. In that case all but one of them was honestly mistaken and confused. You pay your money and take your choice about the last one—one of those pigheaded females who wouldn't admit she was wrong if she'd said it rained ink—but there's some hint she identified the wrong man deliberately, that she knew the real killer."

"That's not a new idea to me. I worked a little on it. Which one do you think might be doing that here?"

"Couldn't say. Haven't been able to get near enough, except in court. Prosecution witnesses. Now it's a little different. I'm going to work on them, and I may want some help."

"Anything I can do."

Jesse moved his glass around on the wet table. "Like to see your notes on their first interrogations, kick this around a little in private with you."

"Sure. You staying here?"

"Think I'll come back to your little one-horse burg with you, if there's anywhere to stay."

"We'll find a place."

"O.K., let's get going." They split the check and started back to their cars. Jesse looked over at the county courthouse as he switched on the ignition. The jail was behind, facing another street; he wouldn't see her face at any of those windows; but he looked, and sighed. He pulled the Ford out into the street and caught up behind Varallo's dusty black Chevy at the next corner.

He hadn't wanted the case to start with, had taken it on as a pure favor to Varallo. Not that Vic had given him details in that telegram: just said, in effect, come and take this case. He'd landed in this God-forsaken wide place in the road to face about the least desirable setup for an only moderately successful and affluent lawyer. A client with no money behind her; a case almost impossible to answer, on first glance, because there was so little to get hold of; and no time to do much delving, the calendar date fixed so soon.

And Vic Varallo, the senior police officer who'd seen her charged and arrested, said to him, "She's not guilty, and you've got to prove it. I can't, I've tried."

If he'd had any sense he'd have turned right around and gone home. Let her find some other fall guy to dream up some feeble defense to satisfy the letter of the law, for the two hundred and seventy bucks in her savings account.

Two hunded and sixty-four. They let prisoners draw on a little personal deposit for what they called sundries. He'd paid for the cigarettes he brought her himself, and those damned-fool crystal mints she liked. "You'll ruin your teeth," he'd said, and she laughed and said she never had anything wrong with her teeth, not a single cavity, and what did it matter now anyway? Takes a long time for teeth to get cavities, doesn't it, she said. Maybe it won't matter by then. Will it, Jesse?

And that was the first time he'd got her to call him anything but Mr. Falkenstein.

Well, any lawyer worth the ink on his diploma could always think of something to *say*. But whether it meant anything or not—

And Clarence Darrow himself might have found it just a little bit awkward to have seven live witnesses swearing in court that yes, sir, as God's my judge, that's the woman I saw.

Witnesses. Giacomo Tasso, salesman. Alice and John Price, housewife and merchant. Christine Inver, housewife. (These legal definitions!) Maria Zacchio, spinster. Francisco Zacchio, laborer. Antonia Cambiare, housewife.

Which lying, which mistaken? Any lying at all?

She looked at him, that first time, and she said simply, "I'm not a very religious person, Mr. Falkenstein, so maybe it wouldn't mean very much for me to say, I swear to God. And anyway, it'd be an easy thing to say, wouldn't it? When you come down to it, it's just my word against theirs. But I hope you'll believe me, though it's a lot to ask—against seven people—it wasn't me, I didn't do it."

And he believed her. No hard and fast rules about it. A lot of people hadn't. Most people.

Because, after all, seven witnesses—whatever there was to be said for and against them as individuals, *seven*—

TWO

"Mrs. Inver, you've told us that you had no knowledge of your daughter's pregnancy. That there was nothing, no hint, no suspicion in your mind—"

"That is true." Cold eyes hiding pain under their lids, unemotional voice. "The whole thing was a—terrible shock to me."

"I'm sure we all understand that. You first learned of this condition, perhaps I should say this former condition, when Dr. Burnett informed you after examining your daughter on the evening of March ninth last."

"Yes."

"So that approximately an hour before, on that evening, when, as we have heard, you daughter Carol arrived—or was brought—home by this strange woman, you had no idea what was wrong with her. You—"

"We have been over this." Taut voice. "I—she told me she was spending the weekend with friends—at a mountain resort. . . . Yes, three days. Nearly four, that is, it was the Friday morning when she—left. . . . Yes, her own car. . . . And Monday evening when she—came home . . . I was coming down the stairs—facing the front door, when it opened and—Carol—came in, or that is, I mean, she was—obviously ill, this woman helping her—holding her arm. . . . I believe the woman saw me but I couldn't be sure. She just—let go of Carol's arm and turned and went out—shut the door. . . . I don't know. I couldn't guess how long. Perhaps five seconds."

"Five seconds that you had this woman in view? But she was not facing you all that time, Mrs. Inver? She was helping your daughter in, supporting her—turned away from you, perhaps her head bent a little, as she—?"

"I—really couldn't—it was a short time, of course, but—"

"Yes. But the woman was *not* facing you for that entire estimated time of five seconds?"

"I—no."

"She came through the door slightly behind your daughter, and—"

"She *pushed* her, really—simply shoved her inside. Carol—stumbled on the rug, she—"

"Yes. And then this woman, whether or not she saw you there, dropped your daughter's arm, turned, and went out. Mrs. Inver, will you think back carefully—it's a long while ago, I know, and these little details are easily forgotten—and of course you were naturally a great deal more concerned for your daughter—but will you try to remember, did this woman actually cross the threshold at all? Did she come *into the light* at all?"

"I—think so. Yes—J-just into the entrance hall."

Entrance hall of the big Inver house on Sunset Drive. Place where money lived, you saw from a glance at the outside: sprawling Mediterranean-style cream stucco, manicured lawn, curving drive under Chinese elms.

"Yes. Now about the conditions of light, Mrs. Inver. It was dark outside; I believe you've told us that it was around nine o'clock. There is a ceiling fixture—an electric fixture—in this entrance hall. Will you describe it, please."

"It's—just a ceiling fixture. It's a large bowl-shaped—gray metal—with bulbs in the—the hollow, if you see what I—"

"Bulbs. How many?"

Hesitation. She didn't do her own housework, of course: how would she know? "I believe two. Lying crosswise. I'm not sure, so I won't answer that definitely." Honest woman.

Little flurry in the courtroom behind: female voice: "Excuse me, Your Honor, if I can interrupt—just to sort of have it definite-like—it *is* two, Mrs. Inver. Two hundred-watt bulbs."

Rap for order. And that wasn't in the testimony record, of course, but now everybody knew, including the jury. "Mrs. Inver, do you know the height of the ceiling in this entrance hall?"

"I b-believe it's ten feet, higher than— We wanted—well, that doesn't matter. I think ten feet. . . . I don't know, I suppose the fixture's, oh, perhaps twenty-four inches long—less. . . . Yes, the bowl part faces upward, of course. . . . There was enough *light*, if that's what—"

"Now, Mrs. Inver, you say you had this—er—*fairly* good look at the woman. How was she dressed?"

"I don't know, something dark—a long coat, something like that—I don't remember exactly. . . . No, I don't remember whether she wore a hat or scarf. You know how you look first at a person's *face*. I didn't—"

"But we have agreed that you had the opportunity for only a very brief glimpse of her face. You say you had a sufficiently clear view of this woman's *features* so that later—much later—one hundred and forty-nine days later, Mrs. Inver, on the fifth of August—you were able to identify her with complete certainty?"

Hesitation. "Yes."

And God damn Vic Varallo for so carefully making it an honest confrontation. Not just bringing the two of them together, *was this the woman you saw that night,* but noncommittal: parade of a dozen women, all the similar ones he could collect in this Godforsaken little one-horse town. *Pick out the one who might be.* So, skip over that: don't remind the jury.

"Upon what did you identify her, Mrs. Inver? . . . Her face, yes, but let's be a little more specific. The color of her hair?"

"Well, I—wouldn't say, it's just dark brown hair, nothing—unusual—"

"Not the color of her eyes; you had obviously never been close enough, observed so carefully—"

"I don't know. No. Just as a whole, that's all. Her figure—" a bit doubtful, there—"thin, oh, *straight*—the way she moved. Just as a *whole.*"

"Just as a whole—at a glance, a five-second or not quite five-second glance, all that time ago. I see. You had this sufficiently clear look at the woman then to remember her features one hundred and forty-nine days later. And yet, Mrs. Inver, if the prosecuting attorney is correct in the charge he is arguing here, in this interval of time you had seen this woman again, repeatedly. And had *not* so identified her. Can you explain this to us?"

"I don't know Miss Varney. I don't remember ever seeing her—until Captain Varallo—"

"Mrs. Inver!" (Implication in the tone, *really.*) "The official census of Contera is slightly over nineteen hundred persons. Miss Varney has lived there for over two years, and for all that time she held a position which brought her more or less before the public. Are you telling this court that you are *sure* you had never laid eyes on Miss Varney before you were asked if she *resembled* this strange woman?"

"I certainly don't remember it if I had."

"If you had. Yes, the mind plays us some odd tricks, we all know that—we look at things sometimes without realizing we're seeing them —but the mind registers it, of course. I believe you do bank at the Contera branch of the Merchants' National Bank? Yes. You have occasion to go to the bank perhaps once a week? . . . Well, once in two weeks? . . . Yes. You're familiar with the building, then, and I think we can take it for granted that the ladies and gentlemen of the jury are too. It isn't a very big building, is it, Mrs. Inver? You agree that there is just one large main office, with counters along two sides?—I can introduce competent testimony to this effect, but it will save time if you agree—that this main public office of the bank is just forty-four feet square."

"Yes. Very well."

"And on nearly every occasion when you entered this not-very-big place, Miss Varney was somewhere behind one of those counters, in her capacity as general clerk. You *never* noticed Miss Varney, just casually? . . . I suggest to you, Mrs. Inver, that on the night of March ninth, when this strange woman brought your daughter home to die of postabortion infection, you did not obtain as close a view of her features or person as you claim to have done—that at some later time you *did* see Miss Varney in the bank, very casually, as one does notice things and people without thinking very much about them—and that when you were confronted with Miss Varney and asked if she *resembled* this woman, you identified her *as* that woman because she looked familiar to you from the times you had seen her in the bank. That a perfectly natural confusion led you to connect her, quite erroneously, with another woman."

"No. I don't think so."

"—And Teresa is gone away, you understand, when I come home that night—she has told me, and I—it was very wicked of me to agree, but I did this sin, I gave her the money, fifty dollars it was to cost. I did not know where, what woman, no, sir, I did not—she did not tell me, I did not ask her. You understand, a little I am worried for her, this two days she is away—"

"Yes, Mr. Zacchio, we've been over this, don't get upset. Now you have told us that on the evening of August the first, you and your two daughters heard a car stop in the street outside your house. Your eldest daughter, Mrs. Cambiare, was expecting her husband to call for her, and assuming that the car was his, opened the front door. Did you go to the door at once?"

"Almost, sir. I get up from my chair, to greet Joe, you see, maybe pour him a little glass. I go—and I see the car, not Joe's car, a little car and light-colored—there is a woman helping another woman out into the road, and I see it is Teresa, and then we all run out—and the woman gets quick back in and drives away—I—it was very quick, yes, sir, but there is a street light—I—"

"Now, naturally you and your daughters were more concerned for your wife than with this woman in the car. You were intent on helping her up, into the house, and so on. You say—"

"Raving, she was—the fever so high—my poor Teresa, *Dio e Maria*, I—yes, sir, I am sorry, I try to answer what you ask—"

"You say you had a *fairly* unobstructed view of this woman. Only for two or three seconds, perhaps as she ran around the car—yes. Did you say anything at that time to your daughters about her?"

"Not just right then, sir. Later on, when we wait for the doctor to come, I have said to them I thought she looked like this young lady in the bank."

"She *looked like* Miss Varney. I see. Thank you. Mr. Zacchio, I don't think anyone in this court would blame you for feeling very bitter and resentful toward the person who caused your wife's painful death. You *do* feel angry and—vengeful—toward that person? You would like to see *someone* suffer for it?"

Silence. "Nothing like that—do my Teresa no good now, sir. It's bad to hold wrong thoughts like that—Father Piero says—"

Get rid of him, this good Christian. "Thank you, Mr. Zacchio, that's all for now."

"But what did you think about it *yourself*, Mrs. Cambiare?"

"I never been in the bank but once-twice. I wouldn't know I could *say*—right then—it was or wasn't. See, I mean, I hadn't seen her really enough to notice, *then*. This Miss Varney. *Padre* and Maria, they say so then—and—if you get what I mean, I'd seen this woman brought Mama back, so's when I took a good look at this Miss Varney in the bank, *then* I could say it's her. Sure it is. And *besides*, we all heard Mama say it *was* Miss Varney. The doctor asked her and she *said.*"

"That is not what Dr. Gannon says, Mrs. Cambiare, I remind you. He has testified that your mother *might* have spoken in answer to his question, but that no one could swear to that—she was far too incoherent."

"I know what I heard 'n' what I saw, that's all," said Antonia Cambiare sullenly.

And there wasn't much in that to play tricks with. He had a good idea that this witness was the one like that one in the Slater case—the stubborn one: the more you wooed her, coaxed her to admit the slightest confusion, the merest possibility of error, the more pigheadedly she'd go on saying, I am *too* right, I know what I *saw.*

He let her go without regret.

"Which of you mentioned Miss Varney's name first, Miss Zacchio?"

"It was *Padre*." Low whisper. Nervous, hands twisting together. Pretty girl, skin like magnolia. Eighteen, nineteen?

"And when he said—I believe we have his words on record here—when he said, 'That woman, she looked like that nice Miss Varney at the bank, did you notice, Maria?'—what did you reply?"

"I said yes, I'd noticed . . . the street light, it's right outside the front porch, I—we could see. . . . I—"

"That she *looked like* Miss Varney. I see. Now, you were all greatly troubled over your mother and the circumstances of her illness and death—very naturally—and there was, as we have heard from various witnesses, a good deal of discussion in the family. I—"

"We didn't mean nothing wrong, sir—I mean, about *talking*—"

"No, of course not, I didn't mean to imply you did, Miss Zacchio, it was only natural there should be talk about it, in the family. I'm not accusing any of you of a *deliberate* effort to throw suspicion on Miss Varney—I don't for one minute believe that any of you planned such a wrong action. But, you know, Miss Zacchio, when people talk about anything, and especially something important like this, sometimes they build up ideas into facts, quite unconsciously, in their own minds. Do you understand what I mean? Do you know that when the police question several people, all of whom have witnessed the same accident, for instance, invariably they hear a little different story from each person?—We're all human, after all, and each of us sees a thing a bit differently."

"Yes, sir. I know."

"I put it to you, Miss Zacchio, that during this very natural discussion of the circumstances surrounding your mother's illness and death, somehow that first small random thought of your father's—his remark, after this one very brief glimpse you all had of the strange woman, that she *looked like* Miss Varney—that somehow he convinced himself and you and your sister that it had *been* Miss Varney. That's perfectly possible, isn't it?"

Silence. Head down. "I—I guess. I don't know, sir. I thought so too, I mean, it *was*—I thought—and besides, *Madre* said her name! We all heard that—"

"Are you positive of that, Miss Zacchio? Your mother was not speaking clearly—she was in delirium. You agree to that? Yes. She was speaking not only incoherently but, very indistinctly?"

"Yes, I guess—mostly, sir—but 'Tonia heard her—she said—we all heard *Madre* say Miss Varney's name—"

"I suggest to you that because of your father's casual remark, that this other woman *looked like* Miss Varney, you all misunderstood some phrase your mother spoke in delirium—that you leaped to a conclusion for very little reason."

"Well, I don't know, sir—I *thought*—I mean, I really *did* think it was—"

"But in all this discussion, you could also have easily convinced yourself to agree with your father and sister?"

"I don't know." Wretched mutter.

"It is quite possible?"

"I—guess."

"—Even probable. I see. Thank you."

"—Always take our little walk in the evening, and it makes just a nice little circle, up to Sunset Drive and down Reade Avenue to our *own* street, Elm. Almost exactly a mile, and of course all nice residential district, perfectly *safe* . . . into the habit when we had our dear little doggie, and—"

"Yes, I understand, Mrs. Price. And you estimate that on the evening of March ninth you and your husband had arrived at the corner

of Sunset Drive and Woodlawn Road at approximately five minutes
past nine?"

"It would have been about that."

"From that corner, as you turned onto the east side of Sunset Drive,
was Mrs. Inver's house visible?"

"Well, the entrance to the driveway is, yes—Of course, the house
sets back quite a ways from the street. . . . Yes, a car, coming out of
the drive. Yes, I'm positive it was Mrs. Inver's driveway. It came down
the street toward us and passed . . . No, sir, going kind of slow—"

"Ah, I see, because of the poor street lighting along there, of
course."

"There's *good* light right there at the corner and we wasn't hardly
past. But the street *does* narrow down some there, which is how come
the car was pretty near when it did pass, and besides it didn't just
pass, it turned the corner onto Woodlawn. Naturally, because I suppose she was going home. I said to my husband, 'I didn't know Nell
Varney knew Mrs. Inver.' I was surprised. . . . How did I know? I
saw her, didn't I? And her car . . . I don't pay no notice to makes,
but it's one of them foreign cars, light-colored, not very big. . . . I
said that to J— my husband, and he said he didn't know she knew
Mrs. Inver either, so he saw who it was too *as* he's told you. . . . I
couldn't say how fast she was going. . . . No, I don't drive a car and
never have."

"Did you make any further remark to your husband, Mrs. Price?"

"I certainly did. I said I thought Christine Inver had better sense
and taste than to take up with Nell Varney. If it *was* a social call as
you might say and not just some sort of business, and the Varney girl
being there in the evening, it didn't look it'd be nothing like that. I
said I was surprised at Mrs. Inver."

"And why did you say that?"

Objection. Irrelevant. Overruled. You may proceed, Mr. Falkenstein.

"I said it because I know what Nell Varney's like, that's all. . . .
How *well* do I know her? I don't know her *socially* at all, of course,
but after all she's lived next door for nearly two years now, and a person can't help. . . . Well, when I say *she* bought the place, I daresay
it was the old man, her father, he was alive then, of course— They
come here together, and ask me, there was some reason for that too—
stands to reason—never said a word of why they'd all of a sudden

picked up and moved here, people like that from a big town. . . .
Drunk as a lord every night in the week, if you please, and *noisy*—
well, we had to complain to the police I don't know how many times.
And naturally you couldn't expect *her* to be any better than she
should be, coming from a fambly like that. I said—"

"Have you ever once seen Miss Varney intoxicated, Mrs. Price?"

"Well, not *intoxicated*—but it stands to *reason* . . . Just maybe
quieter about it than the old man . . . and *fast*, I mean, things no real
nice woman, a *lady*, does or says—I—"

"Let's hear about some of these things, Mrs. Price. These immoral
actions and so on that convinced you Miss Varney is—er—*fast*, and not
a lady."

"Well, she smokes cigarettes for one thing—and as for lipstick, well,
like the side of a barn—see it a mile off, that thick—and trousers—"

"I see. I believe you are a teetotaler, Mrs. Price? . . . *and* your husband, yes. Do you consider lipstick and face powder immoral of
themselves?"

Objection. Irrelevant. But a good judge. What exactly are you attempting to bring out, Mr. Falkenstein?—Prejudice. To a point, you
are within your rights. Overruled.

"Yes, I'm not ashamed to say I do, sir. Providence gives people the
faces they've got, and no call to tamper with it. . . . Is that *all* I can
say about her? Well, I should think—"

"It would be enough?" (Heavy irony.) "Well, we must let the ladies
and gentlemen of the jury decide that for themselves. Do you consider
cigarettes to be immoral?—the wearing of trousers by a young
woman?"

Objection. Irrelevant: this farce being carried much too far. A very
good judge. "I am inclined to agree, Mr. Burkhart. I think Mr. Falkenstein has made his point. Sustained."

"About your—er—guess at identifying this car which passed you,
Mrs. Price—you leaped to the conclusion that it was Miss Varney's car
on the glimpse you had of a small light-colored car?"

"Nobody else in town's got one of them little foreign things, as I
know of. I didn't leap to the conclusion—I saw—"

"Did you get *any* glimpse of the driver at all, in that light?" Subtle
incredulity.

"Who else'd be driving her car, I'd like to know! She never had any
friends *that* close in town, that I do know. You try to make out I'm

old-fashioned and strict and so on—not ashamed of it, I'm not—I grant you a lot of folks don't agree with me about your lipsticks and face powders and all like that—but if it's all in my head about Nell Varney being a bad young woman, you tell me why she never made any friends in this town, why folks didn't take her in! Found out soon enough what she's like, that's what it amounts to—"

"Mrs. Price, do you *know*, of your own first-hand knowledge, of any single moral lapse on the part of Miss Varney—beyond the fact, of course, that she wears lipstick?"

"Moral—well, I can't say I ever saw a *man* call at the house—"

"Mrs. Price, the word 'moral' does not refer exclusively to sexual matters, but to all aspects of personal principles. Do you *know* of any dishonest, dishonorable action Miss Varney has ever done? *Or* of any sexual lapse? . . . You admit you do not. Thank you, that's all."

"Callin' on a friend, that's all. Couldn't find a place to park then, see, and I lef' my car up the block a ways, so I had to walk past the Zacchios' house goin' back to it. . . . Sure I saw the car. . . . I know 's much about cars as the nex' fellow, I guess, anybody drives alla time and gets around to see things." This one, easy good nature, typical salesman gift-of-gab, unembarrassed, speaking up confidently. "I wouldn't want to say definite on the make, on account there's maybe three-four little foreigners look somethin' alike, see. I been kind o' thinkin' about one myself nex' time, account of being cheaper to run, but I gotta have space for all my stuff, samples, and so on—you know. I looked at some already, sure, down to Bakersfield and Fresno. . . . You wanna pin me down, it mighta been one o' those Renaults, or that thing it starts with V—no, not Volks—Volvo, they call it, that's it—or it mighta been one o' those Fi-atts, or it mighta been somethin' else that looks kind of like any of 'em. . . . It was white or tan, somethin' like that."

"Did you get any glimpse of the driver at all?"

"Sure. See, I'm walkin' up the sidewalk, same side, nearly to Zac-chios', and I see somethin's goin' on, couple of people out on the side-walk round this woman, like she's sick and they're kind of half carry-ing her up to the house. . . . Maybe twenny feet off . . . An' this other one just hoppin' into the car, gunning the motor . . . About fifteen, twenny m.p.h. when she comes past me, at a guess. The street light . . . Sure I seen. Just a little second like as she goes past, but I got good eyes. I got a pretty good look."

"You say you were able to recognize the woman from just this one very brief glimpse—into a *closed* car at night—at a distance of twenty feet or more?"

"That's what I said. Sure. Sure I did. Miss Varney's waited on me coupla times in the bank. . . . No, I didn't say nothing about it right then, no call to—didn't know what it was all about right then, acourse. I'm almos' down to my car, when Zacchio gives me a hail, see, and asks me will I call the doctor for him—they got no phone—if he gives me the dime. An' *then* I hear a little about what's wrong, see, Mrs. Zacchio sick and all. So I say sure, and I stopped at the corner drug store, called Dr. Gannon. . . . No, sir, I didn't go back. I know the Zacchios kind of casual, if you get me. I was sorry Mrs. Zacchio was sick, but I had business o' my own, long drive nex' day and I wanted get back to the hotel."

"When and under what circumstances were you asked if you could identify the woman you had seen driving away from the Zacchios' house?"

"I got a phone call two days later, down in Bakersfield—from Captain Varallo in Contera. Zacchio'd told him I was there, see. He asked me could I identify the woman and I said sure. So he asked me to come back. It was kind of a nuisance, put me off schedule on my regular calls, but we gotta help the law, I didn't have no choice. . . . Yes, I'm sure, I said it four different ways already, didn't I? It was Miss Varney that I knew from the bank."

Seven witnesses. But second-degree homicide, no malice afore-thought, and no evidence—or only very vague evidence—of direct guilt: only a strong circumstantial implication of involvement and most of that evidence after the fact. Yet they charged her with the direct crime and a jury brought her in guilty and set the death sentence on her.

The judge hadn't liked that, and it wasn't all because he grudged the jury this new right of fixing sentence, which the muddleheaded voters had taken away from the bench. He knew, as well as Jesse Falkenstein or Edward Burkhart (if Burkhart would admit it) that the evidence here didn't justify that; and he'd undoubtedly say so to the appellate court. He might even back up Jesse—cautiously—on a claim of local prejudice. Now, though they'd got a negative decision asking change of venue on those grounds before the trial.

But any court case, petty theft to murder—like an iceberg, only about a tenth of it above the surface to show. All the rest, the operative part, you might say, underneath. The things that didn't come out . . . *Irrelevant*, well, who was to judge yes or no? For also it was like the widening, joining circles in a pond when a stone was dropped in— one thing starting another. One thing leading to another.

THREE

Tasso had been calling on Gina Pozzo or one of her three girls, Vic said: that he knew because he'd asked, but a lot of people could guess where Tasso had been. And so what?

Nothing at all was said in court about Maria Salluzzo, who had nearly died of postabortion infection. Of the terrific excitement and scandal locally over Carol Inver. Everybody knew (motto of any small town, maybe, those two words) that Mrs. Inver had tried to get Dr. Burnett to hush it up, give out that Carol had died of pneumonia or something, but though he was an old friend he was also an honest man; he couldn't do it that way in law. There had to be an inquest and under oath the truth had to be told. Everybody knew too who had probably got Carol in trouble—she hadn't gone around with anybody but Jackie Bennett for quite a while. And you could reason that a nice girl like Carol, who'd been perhaps a little young for her twenty years—just on account of that, being brought up sheltered by money, in the conventional upper social brackets—wouldn't have known where to go for an abortion. So, what about Bennett?

"Sure I asked him," said Varallo. "First place to go. He denies knowing anything at all, and I think he's a liar, but what can I do about it? He would and probably will say the same thing under oath." (Which indeed he had.) "I think he knew where to send her. But there's no way to prove it, and he's just smart enough to be damned careful not to let anybody trip him up. He's also the son of our local state congressman, and he doesn't think much of me, but he knows I'm not a fool. And just because he maybe knew where to send her, that doesn't say he knew the actual people involved, you know. This kind of thing—the way it was, I've been told, in Prohibition. The word gets round. Somebody knows somebody who knows somebody. Go to the side door, knock four times, and ask for George."

"Like that. I know. Even in Contera?"

"Even Contera. You won't get anywhere with Bennett, unless you're better at scaring him than I am. He's got enough sense to know that if he admits any knowledge of it, he can be charged as accessory before the fact."

Maria Salluzzo, a much better bet. She had with very little doubt bought herself an abortion from whoever had botched up the job on Inver and Zacchio, and she'd almost died but not quite, and there she was back at the counter in Woolworth's, for anybody to question.

"So I'll introduce you to the facts of life," said Varallo. And this was an hour after Jesse had landed here, in Varallo's office at the rear of the little Contera police station, before Jesse had met the client at all. "There's no legal evidence whatever that the Salluzzo girl had an abortion. No doctor ever examined her. Her mother asked Dr. Gannon what to do for her, described her illness vaguely, and Gannon had a pretty good idea what it was. He went to the house to see her, though he hadn't been called, but they wouldn't let him in to look at her. Oh, Maria, she was much better now, just a little flu maybe, *molto cortese* of the good doctor to come, but not at all necessary! God knows why she didn't die. Scandal? Maria wasn't afraid of scandal, friend. Not as much as she was of eternal damnation. Which was what was in the minds of the family, and still is. I've got a very good idea of how it went there—because Gannon questioned her later, and what did she say?—probably what she told her family—with appropriate and becoming modesty—maybe a little infection she'd inadvertently picked up in a public rest room, something like that. And did they believe her? You and me, there's a line there for us, yes or no, but a lot of people, they don't look at a thing, so for them it isn't there. The Salluzzos took what she said at face value, because they were afraid not to—but they kept the doctor away, you notice. Talk about confused values, *Dio*—they were just as afraid as Maria. They knew, but you'd never get them to admit they knew, or Maria herself, of course. Because it would mean excommunication, a hard penance, and probably eternal damnation for her soul."

"But if they knew—if that's so, according to what they believe, how could it save her whether or not—"

"But you have the logical mind. People like the Salluzzos never reason that far. I'm telling you the facts of life, here and now, this place. That's how it is. Don't ask me to explain the theology of the Salluzzos—I can't. I'm just telling you, there's no evidence the girl had an abortion. What we've got there is a little whispered scandal between a couple of her girl friends, and we all know how gossip builds up. No evidence of pregnancy. What Gannon thought from the vague description Mrs. Salluzzo gave him of symptoms and so on. You go to Maria and ask her—I've been and asked, I tried it coaxing and I tried it tough. Ask her where she went for it, who did it, how much she paid. She'll look at you with big, innocent eyes and say, a nice girl like me, sir? I never did no bad thing like that, sir, don't know what you're talking about."

"Yes. What the hell if an innocent person is accused. Nothing to do with Maria. Like that? These good Christians. Of course, so what if Maria told me or you where she went, who did it—doesn't say it was the same place Inver or Zacchio went. Not for sure. Probability is it was, but that's not evidence. Prohibition," said Jesse thoughtfully. "Yeah. Word gets round. You don't tell me there's the business in a place like this for more than one abortionist. So out of nineteen hundred people maybe as many as a hundred'd know where to go—where to send the girl friend?"

"Go and ask," said Varallo. "I've been. Sure. I doubt very much that anybody knows a name or a face, and nobody'll admit to knowing even an address or a phone number. Not with all this razzamatazz over a homicide charge. Now I'll tell you something else you won't like." He sat up and lit a cigarette. "Business of that kind, no, it doesn't pay in a place like this. Too dangerous too, keep a permanent setup like that in a small town. It's big-city business. So, O.K., Mary Smith of Contera or some place like it gets in trouble, she asks around privately, or the boy friend knows, she goes into Fresno or Bakersfield for the weekend, innocent little shopping trip, likely enough with a girl friend to make it look better and lend moral support. Maybe even to Santa Barbara or L.A. I've been a cop in this town for twelve years, and while the police don't always get to know everything, to my knowledge there's never been a hint of anything like this in Contera up to about a year ago. I'm not saying how many girls went vacationing or visiting away from home and found a handy abortionist somewhere else. I'm just saying, in Contera."

"That's a nasty one. This woman's been here just two years, you said. Very nice if that point's brought up in court."

"It won't need to be. Everybody knows it," said Varallo sardonically. "And other outlanders—a few—have come to town in that time. I'm just mentioning it."

Jesse slid down even lower in the straight office chair and contemplated his long legs. "I don't like this case. Not one bit, what you've told me. I don't like your climate up here, and I don't like small towns. Why'd you pick me as the fall guy and what's your interest in getting her defended on a charge you built up?"

"She's not guilty," said Varallo. "Which is a private opinion and I've got nothing to base it on. Given the evidence presented to me, I couldn't do anything else but charge her."

"But not with premeditated homicide," said Jesse. He watched Varallo through half-shut eyes: Varallo nervous, jumpy, restless talker as always, gesturing, his mobile face wearing half a dozen expressions during one sentence. "And not such very definite evidence."

"You just don't know the facts of life, *amico*. Not outside city limits." Varallo was up, pacing where the crowded little office allowed. "I'll tell you one reason I sent for you. You're neither Catholic nor Protestant."

"You always were hipped on religion. What's that got to do with it?"

"I'm not the one who's hipped, for God's sake! There it is—" his hand slashed the air savagely—"line right down the middle—any place up here—some of it you get in big towns too, but a place like this it's right out plain to be seen. Sure, sure, it's a democratic country and these days it isn't like it used to be, when the Italians and Portuguese and Mexicans constituted all the cheap labor, the peasantry—some of them own their own places now, they've been to school and they own cars and they've got all the household gadgets, washing machines and T.V.—they've got jobs in a lot of lines besides farm labor—there isn't quite the economic gap all down the line. But socially, politically, it hasn't changed. There's the upper crust of superior-white-Protestant, and the rest, they know their place, they don't try to mix. *Comprehendere?* It's understood there'll be one Catholic on the school board, for the looks of it—for instance—things like that. It annoys the upper crust like hell that in county elections the Catholics have the say— more of them voting—not always so in city elections, because a lot of

Catholic voters live outside city limits. And the upper crust sees to it that most appointive positions go to Protestants. They can, and they do see to it—because they've got the money, and money talks all languages. No, *per Dio*, this isn't a crooked town, an open town!—or I wouldn't be on the force here. It's a collection of gentlemen's agreements, if you get me. The mere fact that I've left the fold of the Church wouldn't have made me eligible for promotion out of uniform. I'm still a Dago. A lot of people in this town don't much like the idea of a Dago cop. For one thing, obviously—to a lot of people—any Wop can be bribed damn easy. But Elgren happened to be mayor then and he'd appointed old Stoner chief of the force, and Stoner had some funny ideas about judging people on individual merit. He took me on and we always got along fine—I've had all my promotion under Stoner. Once or twice there was a little unpleasantness—that Shippey fellow muttering about taking orders from a Dago, that sort of thing—but nothing much, it never came to a head. Most of the other eleven cops on Contera's force I get on with O.K.—they know me pretty well and I'd say they respect me as a captain. I'd say most people do. Once in a while I run into the superior-white-Protestant citizen who resents getting arrested by a Wop, but not very often. And I know as sure as I'm standing here that most people in town—Protestant *and* Catholic—are convinced I renounced the Church to curry favor with the upper social crust, if you see what I mean."

"I get you. Why're you still here? You don't run into that sort of thing much any more in the big city."

Varallo had ended up at the window; he stood there a minute, back turned, in silence, and then he said, "So I'm not so damn bright. Especially since Stoner's dead and I've got Brant on my neck. I—damn it, all right, it's just *that*. He's not going to drive me out—I'll be damned if I'll let him think he could needle me into resigning. Which he's been trying to do every way he knows how since he's been chief."

"See your point," said Jesse, "but it looks like biting off your nose to spite your face. All that got anything to do with this case I'm supposed to take?"

"My God, of course it has—with bells on. Look—Christine Inver's one of the wealthiest people in town—land money—and her brother-in-law's the mayor. Me, I don't know them socially, but I'm given to understand that Carol Inver was the apple of her doting uncle's eye. He and his wife haven't any kids of their own. Our present chief of police,

Clare Brant, is the mayor's appointee, of course—old school pals—
Brant's got a finger in an automobile agency and an insurance company—promoter-type. Hail-fellow-well-met—*with* superior Protestants
only—and I wouldn't trust him any farther than I could carry him, and
he weighs two fifty. He got appointed chief just after I got to be a
captain—two years back—and he'd like nothing better than to get me
out of the way, force me to resign or catch me out in some legal
offense, to put Bob Lee at my desk. Lee's another one says Wop and
Dago. Technically my aide-de-camp, and when I want a place
searched, somebody questioned, Lee's the fellow I send. Rest of the
force, except Sergeant Sanders, who's desk man, out on traffic duty,
riding our two patrol cars. Brant takes every chance to needle me, and
I can't trust Lee to do any job thoroughly, he's a lazy lout without
much brain. So I go and do his jobs myself and that makes him mad,
he complains to Brant I don't trust him, don't give him opportunity or
responsibility. So there's that setup. Brant's very eager to oblige
Mayor Cardew any and every way he can, keep in his good graces,
and in any case we all had a fire-eating pep talk from His Honor
about finding and bringing to justice the foul dastard who caused his
niece's death. You'll gather that if I said the sun rises in the east,
Brant'd deny it—not just this background, Lee and so on—Dr. Fell sort
of business too—and in Brant's view I'm out of proper place, son of a
Wop carpenter who's got uppity ideas. So! Teresa Zacchio dies, there's
an inquest, and I ask questions, and this little remark of Zacchio's
comes to light, about Nell Varney. I'm surprised, to say the least. But I
start to follow it up, ask questions other places. I did *not* think there
was enough evidence there to warrant anything but questions, but before I've got much more to say yes or no instead of maybe, Brant's on
my neck. Why don't I follow up this lead hard and hot?—only smell of
a lead we've got! He goes roaring out to Nell Varney's house with a
search warrant, he rounds up Mrs. Inver and eventually the Prices,
and demands an identification parade. I tried to arrange it as fair as
possible, but—!"

"Yes. Find anything at the house?"

"Sure he found something at the house. Her father was a doctor.
Retired—polite name for it. Plain language, he was a lush. A very unpleasant old fellow—she can tell you more about that, it's got a bearing on this too. So Brant found all Dr. Varney's instruments put away
tidily in the spare-bedroom closet, and he was pleased as hell. She

says—and I remind him, why not?—perfectly natural they should be there. But Dr. Varney's been dead for six months, says Brant; why did she keep them? And now let's take a look at the district attorney. His name's Burkhart, he's a convert to Mother Church and just as fanatic and militant as converts usually are. He's also an honest man—as far as I know—but his religion prompted him to jump the gun here, because of the kind of crime it is—in law it's second-degree homicide, but to a man like Burkhart, or any really good Catholic, it's about the worst kind of murder there is, involving eternal damnation not only for the murderer but the victim. And by the time Brant went to Burkhart, of course, there was more evidence. Brant had the fingerprint then."

"Oh, dear," said Jesse. "Don't like fingerprints—awkward things to explain away. So incontrovertible. The Varney girl's print? Where?"

"To my mind it's the only solid piece of evidence there is. It's mainly the reason I couldn't stick my neck out any farther to argue with Brant. No, I don't think she's guilty, I think there's a perfectly reasonable explanation of the print, but there it is. Just damn-fool luck that Brant found it. He doesn't know damn-all about police work, you know—and I wasn't in on that deal, I was questioning Miss Varney at the bank. Brant went out to the Zacchios' with Lee and Sergeant Holgren, who's our print expert, and dusted everything he could see. I don't know what he expected to find. What Holgren found when he came to analyze the prints, eliminate the family, and so on was a print of Nell Varney's left thumb on a silver necklace sort of thing of Mrs. Zacchio's. It's a big medallion hung on a chain—religious medal, but bigger than most, about an inch and a half across. The family says Mrs. Zacchio used to wear it when she was dressed up, and they also say she was wearing it when she went wherever she did go for the abortion."

Jesse shut his eyes and sighed. "Where exactly was the print?"

"On the front of the medallion, near the edge."

"Where she'd take hold of it to look at, say, if the wearer said, 'Isn't this pretty?' Yes. What does she say about it?"

"More or less what you just said." Varallo shrugged. "First, she couldn't explain it— Then she remembered that one day when Mrs. Zacchio was in the bank, she—Miss Varney—had mentioned it, just being polite, you know, and she thinks she did take hold of it. That sounds natural enough. She can't swear what day, but is pretty certain it was sometime that week. It'd almost have to have been, for the print still to be there. But I don't think Mrs. Zacchio had it on her when she left home—I think the family's mistaken there. I think what happened is that very probably she took the thing off when she came home from the bank that day, and put it away, and nobody touched it until Holgren dusted it. Otherwise the print'd never have been preserved. But you see how it looked."

"Mmh. Awkward, as I said. Inclined to agree with you. But that's a long way from proving it."

"Which is just what Brant told me. He was pleased as hell about it, naturally. I argued with him, sure, I pointed out it's rather thin circumstantial evidence—" Varallo stopped, looking very grim, and then uttered a short laugh. "Maybe you can guess what he said."

"Suggested maybe the girl'd offered you something nice if you covered up evidence and kept her out of trouble."

"That he did. Look, friend, I'm not a coward, I'm not afraid of Brant, and I couldn't care less about leaving this force or Contera. But I'm damned if I'll be *forced* to leave under a charge of bribery and corruption. And, damn it, Jesse—it *is* evidence. It added up. Personally, I'd want a lot more, but it was enough for Brant. Off he went to Burkhart, as I say. Now, she's brought up on an information, not an indictment—"

"I noticed that. You don't keep a grand jury out here in the wilds?"

"Sure we do, at the county seat. And if it had been done that way, I don't think she'd have been charged with homicide. The evidence doesn't quite warrant it. But when a charge is filed in superior court on an information by a D.A., only two people are directly involved—the D.A. and the magistrate before whom he swears out the complaint—"

"I'm a lawyer," said Jesse. "That's why you brought me here, remember?"

"All right. And the D.A. brings the charge on the sworn complaint of a private citizen or citizens. Technically speaking. The magistrate in this case being a justice of the peace, Henry Richards, who's a pompous old fool with about as much legal knowledge as this desk here."

"You telling me she's been railroaded?"

"No," said Varallo. "Not consciously. Not deliberately. Everybody was just so anxious for action, they jumped the gun. There's evidence, of a sort. Some of it, in fact, awkward to get around—like Teresa Zacchio's remarks in delirium. I'll leave that up to you. But there's also local prejudice. And we're so close to the county seat that you can't count on getting jurors who don't share it."

"Why?"

Varallo hunched his shoulders. "Damn fool little things. Go and talk to her, Jesse. You'll see what I mean."

FOUR

Jesse had looked and listened, and believed her. Same time, he reflected in the first ten minutes there in the county jail, he didn't need chapter and verse to guess why the local prejudice. Even these days, with T.V. and cars to get to the big city and so on, the country and small towns old-fashioned, a lot more insular and conventional.

And she wasn't only big-town, Nell Varney, she was very much an individual.

"I don't know if you'll think it sounds silly, Mr. Falkenstein—but d'you know what Captain Varallo said? That I'm here in jail because I don't put my hair up in curlers or watch T.V."

"Sense of it not so silly maybe." He sat on the end of his spine, slouching in the hard, straight chair, watching her.

"I can't help it, I can't be *bothered*. Oh, it *is* my fault too, some of it, I know. I could help it— It wouldn't kill me to agree politely with people, seem to conform to their ideas and tastes—I'm not as silly as that, to go out of my way to—to show myself such a determined non-conformist. I haven't, I haven't meant to. Acting like a teen-ager proclaiming independence or something—you know—really, I haven't. But it's all been a combination of absurd little things—getting off on the wrong foot to start with. Just accidents, but in the most diabolical way happening the worst way they could—you know. Like the time—you wouldn't believe how trivial some of them are—like the time Mrs. Atchison was in the bank, it would be Mrs. Atchison of course, she's even worse than Mrs. Price—and I caught my stocking on a splinter on the counter, started a run, and said, *Oh, damn it*. I don't suppose I'd said damn for a month before or after, but to see the look she gave me, well! And then there was Ruth Cook and the Methodist Church lecture—"

"Mmh?" He studied Nell Varney. About five six, but she looked taller because she was thinnish, and carried herself so straight. Twenty-seven, twenty-eight. Individual: yes. Never cut her hair, and she was the one female in a thousand could wear it like that, pulled back smooth and straight to a big coiled knot: nice dark-brown hair, thick, with a suggestion of natural wave at the temples. Thin face, alive somehow, not much make-up to show except vivid lipstick: very interesting combination, the matte-white skin and long dark-gray eyes under rather thick pointed brows. Like little Gothic arches, her brows were. Not at all usual, any bit of her. Even the way she held a cigarette, between her thumb and forefinger. Deepish voice, quick, emphatic manner in speech and action. Kind of manner that struck some people as unwomanly—too decided. More often a cover-up for actual lack of confidence. She'd wear any kind of clothes well, with that figure, but evidently preferred tailored things—like this severely cut, lemon-yellow cotton dress, sleeveless, her jewelry big copper earrings, barbaric design, a wide copper bracelet. Colorless polish on well-shaped, long hands.

"The church lecture," he murmured, his own hands clasped across his flat middle.

"It wasn't long after we came here, we hadn't met many people. Ruth Cook works at the bank too, the same job I had—general filing, posting, and so on. She's about my age, and she was friendly. She's what's known as a nice girl, maybe not the quickest mind in the world, but all the usual virtues, and while I knew we'd never be bosom friends, you know, I was pleased she *was* friendly. It's not always easy to get acquainted in a small town, and it wouldn't hurt me to be bored a little listening to her, going out for coffee at the drug store with her. You know? And she asked me to go to this lecture with her—some dreary missionary telling how he'd converted the heathen. And I'd have *gone*, and been bored to tears, just to meet a few people and oblige Ruth, but I couldn't, and I couldn't tell her why— I made up some lame excuse, a headache or something—and I'm never any good at telling convincing lies, and she was offended. What with Dad proclaiming to all and sundry how childish orthodox religion is and how much wickedness organized religion makes—*which* I'm inclined to agree with, but having some sense I wouldn't have said so in public

—well, you can guess what Ruth thought. And said to everybody she knew."

"Mmh. Why couldn't you go?"

She sat down; she'd been walking back and forth, smoking nervously; now she looked at him directly. "It was my mother's birthday, and I knew how he'd be. . . . I don't want to bore *you*, Mr. Falkenstein, or waste time, but that's part of it too. It's why we came here. My father was a G.P. and a good one, up to the time Mother died five years ago. She died of cancer, and he couldn't do a thing about it but watch her die. They were very close—maybe too close, too dependent on each other—but people are made the way they're made, nothing to do about that. They'd been married nearly fifteen years before I was born, and while they loved me, didn't neglect me or anything remotely like that, well, I was always sort of the stranger within the gates to them. It was just the two of them, always. And he went to pieces when she died. He got to drinking, and he had to give up his practice, and he kept getting into trouble."

"Police trouble? Where?"

"Oh, Los Angeles. Hollywood, I mean. Yes, a lot of times. He was always rather impatient and very decided in his opinions, that kind of man—and when he got tight he wanted to argue, and when he got a little tighter he was apt to start a fight—"

"Takes some like that. True personality, they say. Awful thing to think—enough to turn anybody teetotal. Me, I just get more and more talkative—can't stop myself—but all very amiable and happy. What was your idea, wean him away from bad companions or keep a closer eye on him?"

"Some of both—the closer eye mostly. I thought in a small town there wouldn't be so many places he could go, and what places there were would soon find out he made trouble and refuse to serve him. Which they did. I didn't have a hope of stopping him. I just thought if he'd stay at home to do his drinking, he couldn't get into such dangerous trouble. And such expensive trouble. The year before we moved, it came to a thousand dollars and some odd in fines. Twice for drunk driving, and you know what they hit you for on that now, and being picked up on the street, and disturbing the peace."

"Tough. Disturbed your peace all right. What were you doing then?"

"Bookkeeping, general office, at a brokerage house. Yes, it did indeed. I hadn't any *hold* on him, you see— I'd never meant anything like what Mother meant to him. I'd try to talk to him, make him see sense, and when he was sober he'd agree with me—sometimes—and promise to try to pull up, get back on an even keel—and sometimes he'd just swear and say what the hell was the difference?—the sooner he killed himself the better it'd be. In a way, you see, it was because he *hadn't* any religion. I think if he could have believed he'd meet Mother again somewhere—that there was anything afterward—it'd have comforted him. But he didn't, he couldn't. She was just gone forever, and he couldn't stand it."

"Immature. 'When I was a man I put away—' Funny idea, Christian heaven. *Or* hell. Anything but orthodox myself, you know, but I think there's something afterward—only nothing we can grasp, maybe, way we are now. Like a kid imagining being grown-up means playing ball whenever you want to, and then finding out about *The Art of the Fugue.*"

She looked at him with more attention. "Yes, that's—a way to put it. I think that's the way I feel too. But—you see what I mean."

"Yes. And it didn't work out?"

"I'd never lived in a small town. Maybe I—romanticized about it? Getting back to grass-roots and so on. Anyway, that's one thing I'll never do again—if I have the chance!" She laughed sharply. "No, it didn't. I persuaded him when he was in one of his contrite, self-pitying moods. I picked Contera off the map, just at random—I liked the name. Funny to think—how casually you make decisions. I had a little backlog of savings, enough to last until I found a job, and I wouldn't be particular about that, if there wasn't quite as good a one as I'd had. We sold the house for fourteen thousand. That's what we bought the house in Contera with. And *that* was something else—another silly little thing. It's almost new, and it was built by some artist, a painter, who had more sense than I did, apparently. He thought he'd like a small town too, and he built this house, and then he got fed up and moved, and the real-estate man had been trying to sell it for him ever since. You see, it's not a nice, ordinary, ranch-type house with a picture window and an L-shaped living room. I found out afterward that everybody in town was quite prepared to find us *very* peculiar people because we'd bought that artist fellow's funny house instead of the nice little Archer place we could have had for the same price."

"One of those glass houses with a roof going up at a funny angle?"

She cocked her head at him. "I don't believe you about when you're tight. Do you ever say a whole sentence with a subject and verb?"

"In court. Judges like it. Says somewhere in the Talmud, *He who multiplieth words will likely come to sin*. Is it?"

"Heavens, no. It's a very handsome house—redwood and flagstone— but it's got a corner hearth without a mantel to put a clock on, and all vinyl flooring instead of nice hardwood to keep polished, and louvre windows, and concealed lighting round the ceiling. . . . Yes, fourteen thousand. I think he was desperate and told them to get what they could. But you see what I mean. I just got off on the wrong foot, you might say. I didn't *fit* anywhere." She put out her cigarette and looked up to meet his eyes. "They tell me one ought to be absolutely frank with one's lawyer. So I'll just say this, and—and I hope you won't misunderstand me and put me down as completely—hard-boiled. I knew it wouldn't be for too long, his heart was damaged, and the way he was drinking— I was thinking of the money, and keeping us both out of trouble. I didn't particularly like the idea of pulling up all roots, giving up a good job, and so on. But I knew he'd be easier to handle in a small place. I just wanted to make it as easy on myself as possible, *and* on him—if it was possible to make it easy on him. It seemed a sensible idea at the time, and of course in some ways it turned out all right—he did most of his drinking at home, and I didn't have to bail him out of jail again, that kind of thing."

"Yes. He died about six months ago? Why'd you stay on?"

"Oh, Lord," she said with a grimace, "I didn't want to—by then I'd had more than enough of the grass-roots, so to speak. But there was a little delay in getting the deed to the house transferred and so on, before I could put it up for sale, and while that was going on, I wrote to Mr. Stern—one of the officers where I worked in L.A.—and asked about getting my job back there. And he wrote and said they'd be very pleased to have me back but there wouldn't be a place for a few months, one of the girls was leaving in August to get married, and if I wanted to come back then I was welcome. Well, I haven't been making as good a salary here, you know, and there were a few bills outstanding, and I thought the sensible thing to do was stay on, to be earning *something*, and get the bills here cleared up so I could cut all ties, so to speak, when I left. . . . August fifteenth, I was to go back. That's next week. . . . I ought to write and tell them—I can't be there." She got up restlessly and went over to the window.

"What," asked Jesse, "d'you think yourself about some of this evidence sworn against you? Put it down to prejudice, or lies, or what? You know what most of it is?"

"Captain Varallo's told me, yes. I don't *know*—I couldn't guess, Mr. Falkenstein. As far as the—the actual identification goes, even when there are seven people, I can only suppose they're mistaken, that this other woman must have looked something like me. But about the rest—" She turned to face him, and now most of the spurious calm, the determined defiance, dropped from her; she looked white and tense. "It doesn't seem possible, I can't believe it even now. Why should Mrs. Zacchio say my name when she was dying? It doesn't make *sense*. I—" she put a hand to her temple. "I don't know if you'll believe me. I haven't any kind of—of story to tell you, truth or lie, about any of it— it's been like an Act of God, the sense the insurance policies use that— if you see what I mean—just coming on me out of the blue. How would *you* feel if the police came and arrested you and said they had all sorts of evidence that you were an experienced dope smuggler, for instance, and you heard people swear to it in court, chapter and verse? I keep feeling it must be a nightmare, nothing *real*."

"Of course," said Jesse thoughtfully, "you start out with a little advantage over Mr. Slater, because you're honest. On the other hand, Mr. Slater—being a smalltime crook—was a lot more experienced at thinking up lies."

"Who on earth is Mr. Slater?"

"Was. Fellow in Scotland in the eighties. Lot of witnesses identifying him positively—one witness in particular positive as hell—as the one who killed an old lady in the process of robbing her. He wasn't. Done other nasty things, but not that. Witnesses were confused, misled—the important one, stubborn female who wouldn't admit a mistake—or just maybe covering up for the real killer. Crooked policeman mixed up in it too. Quite a legal mess."

"I'm sure Captain Varallo's quite honest, he's been—"

"That I know at least. Don't say Vic's an angel—shared a room with him when we were both getting educated up at Berkeley, so I know him too well—wouldn't trust him with my best girl, but would with my bank account, any day. I don't think Vic comes into this. . . . You know the Zacchios and Mrs. Inver, of course. How well?"

"Mr. Zacchio comes into the bank to cash his pay check every month. Once or twice Mrs. Zacchio came instead, and it was usually

Mrs. Zacchio who came in to pay the monthly installment on their house. I don't—didn't—cash checks, but she'd pay the loan installment to me or Ruth Cook. Maybe—oh, a dozen times since I've been at the bank I waited on her for that. Sometimes the daughter, not the married one but the next youngest, the other one who identified me, was with her. . . . About three or four times, I think. . . . The other one, the married one, I don't remember at all. I suppose she's been in the bank, but either it'd be to cash a check—she'd go to Mr. Adamson for that—or just with her husband, so she wouldn't have any business with me. That was—that was how it happened about the fingerprint, you see. Such a silly little thing, really. I've done things like that dozens of times—hasn't everybody? Look, Mr. Falkenstein, these people—like Mrs. Zacchio—they're so used to being, oh, disregarded, patronized. You know what I mean—it's a pretentious phrase, but maybe the only one—second-class citizens. She was a shy little woman—I felt sorry for her. The way you do, I'd tell her she looked nice in blue, or some other little compliment—it wasn't just her, either, it was others like her who came into the bank, the same kind. You see what I mean. Isn't it, sort of, second nature with anyone who's been brought up with elementary manners, and deals with the public? A—a smoothing over of things. I said it that day off the top of my mind—*What a pretty necklace that is*— She was pleased, she held it out for me to look at closer. You know how these things happen. Wasn't there a song about it?—'Little White Lies'—"

"Mmh. Very natural. Yes, I know. You can't say what day?"

"I'm afraid not. I have the impression it was that week, but that's all I can give you."

"Which is only to be expected. Yes. O.K. Mrs. Inver?"

"I've seen Mrs. Inver, of course, but she wouldn't have any business with me either—she'd just come in to cash checks. I usually noticed her when she came in, you know— She's a pretty woman, looks young for her age, and dresses well too—rather surprising she hasn't married again, people say—but that isn't to say she ever noticed *me*, and I don't think I've ever exchanged a word with her."

"Tasso?"

"Or with him. His business'd be with Mr. Adamson too. I should think cashing checks mostly. He doesn't live in Contera, you know— he's a salesman for some farm-machinery company, goes all around the agricultural districts selling. I don't know much about him. I seem to remember someone saying that he came from Contera, or around there, originally, but I think he lives in L.A. or somewhere else anyway, now."

"He seems to've noticed you, enough to be sure of the identification."

"I don't know," she said distractedly, "I don't think I'd know him if I passed him on the street. He'd've *seen* me, I suppose, when he was in the bank—like Mrs. Inver—if not to speak to—"

"Maybe notice you," said Jesse, "where Mrs. Inver wouldn't, consciously. Maybe he's got an eye for a good-looking female."

And unexpectedly she blushed—slow and faint, at the little compliment. "Well, I don't know," she said in a low voice.

This kind, he thought: funny how people mistook them. The sophisticated, decided, confident manner—camouflage—the snap judgment, *unwomanly,* and actually they were the soft ones, the shy ones, without any self-assurance at all. . . . She'd have been a homely kid, gangling and plain, until she got to an age to use make-up, find out about clothes and smarten herself up. Very smart indeed, in the woman's magazine sense: type that unwittingly frightened off men, too smart, too tailored. A lot of men, that is. The ones who didn't realize, this kind the kind with all the dammed-up passion, the secret ardor, the urgent, inarticulate need. Sometimes they didn't know themselves. . . . A lot of men damn fools, going for the calendar girls, the obvious thing. This kind, burning themselves out with all this wasted, untaken passion.

"These Prices," he said. "They'd know you, of course—live next door, I understand—but couldn't've had much of a look at the driver in that car, at night—dark side street. Identified the car, and that isn't so sure either. You've got a Renault, I hear."

"The little one, not the Dauphine. The baby. It's cream-colored. . . . Three years old."

"Mmh. I can think of several cars might look like it—just seen in silhouette in the dark. Difficulty is the size—not so many that small."

"No, I know. I—none of it seems *real,*" she said again. "But it's all what they call circumstantial evidence, isn't it? I mean—"

"Lot of nonsense talked about circumstantial evidence. Best kind there is in most cases—short of eyewitness testimony."

"Is it? And I've got nothing to come back with, you see—I was home alone the night Mrs. Zacchio was brought back—like that—and I don't remember about the night in March, but probably I was then too. Dad would have been there then, but that's no good to me now. I—you know something, Mr. Falkenstein, a lot of use it is to say it, to you or anybody—but I wouldn't have any idea how to do an abortion! Just because my father was a doctor—! And what was so peculiar about my having his bag of instruments? I'd almost forgotten it was *there*. When we came here he'd been retired for over a year, and he sold the office equipment of course, then, but his bag— He just brought it along sort of automatically, you know. You can't sell that sort of thing very easily. Look, I've still got his watch, too, and some cuff links, and things like that—the minute somebody dies, you don't go weeding out every single reminder of them. I sorted out his clothes for the salvage people, of course, and probably when I was packing up here, when I got back to the city, I'd have done something about these other things. Maybe sold his watch, and I suppose there might be some young doctor who'd be glad to pick up some of the instruments second-hand, but— What was I supposed to do with it here? Offer the bag to one of the Contera doctors at half price or something? And I suppose if I *had*, they'd all have tut-tutted over my unfeeling money-grubbing, selling my own father's precious relics for what they'd fetch!"

"Sure—doesn't make much sense sometimes, way people take ordinary facts. I see that—perfectly natural the stuff still hanging around. But at the same time, well, it ties in very handy to the charge."

"Mr. Falkenstein—*do* you believe me? I couldn't blame you if you don't. There's nothing to get hold of, nothing I can say except, it's not true. I—Captain Varallo asked me about a lawyer, I didn't know what to say, I don't know any—and he said if I wanted, he'd send for you. But I couldn't blame you if you don't want to take me on. If you think I'm lying—and it's a sort of hopeless case, isn't it, to answer in court? If—"

"Oh, I believe you," said Jesse. "For some reason. Hopeless? Things to do here, things we can try. So let's get down to details. I've got copies of statements and so on here, from Vic—very helpful. Let's look at 'em. And I've got a lot of questions to ask you. . . ."

FIVE

Circumstantial evidence, and he'd done what he could about it, but—together with the eyewitness identifications—it was the kind of evidence to appeal to a jury as pretty straightforward.

The Zacchios, father and daughter-living-at-home, and Mrs. Cambiare, the married daughter, and Dr. Gannon, swearing that Teresa Zacchio had spoken Nell Varney's name as she lay dying, and possibly —fifty-fifty chance—in answer to the question, Who was responsible? Gannon: I couldn't swear that she understood me, she was in a high fever of course and delirious much of the time—but, yes, sir, I had asked her the question several times, the last time perhaps three minutes before she spoke Miss Varney's name.

Very awkward. Almost five months between the two deaths, and they hadn't had much to go on, on Carol Inver: nothing so definite as a name spoken. But when they had this on Nell Varney, then some of what Carol had said—also in high fever—before she died, tied up. Vic said it didn't tie up for him quite as definitely as it did for Brant and Burkhart, but there were points in it, all right.

Both women not returned home until they were in a dying condition. Dangerous for whoever had done the jobs to return them at all: they had both been capable of speech, if only just, and incoherently. What did that add up to? An amateur bungler? Who didn't have the knowledge to be sure they were dying, or conversely could speak? Dr. Burnett gave it as his opinion that Carol was aware of the questions addressed to her, was not simply rambling in delirium, but trying to give definite information. She had lived for an hour and a half after she was brought home. (Teresa Zacchio, two hours.) Conscientious doctor; sensible: he'd written down all he could get of her ramblings at the time, and Mrs. Inver was a witness there too. What had Carol said?

I always thought it was a funny house . . . long hair, it must be, or . . . such a big knot . . . didn't like her, I was afraid, sorry I'd let . . . She hurt me—and nobody else there, I thought a doctor but there wasn't, just her, just her . . . Such a funny house, thing on top like a cabin on a boat, looks funny . . . Saw her once at the bank, I remembered.

Not much in that then, but later, to tie up to the Zacchio identification . . . All the same, legally speaking, pretty slim evidence to base a homicide charge on, including Inver with Zacchio. But the kind of thing awkward to answer in court.

And the jury. He'd done his best there too, getting rid of some he didn't like the looks of, but that kind of thing was tricky—you just never could tell. Ask them whatever you pleased while a panel was being called, eliminate the ones who gave the wrong answers, and then this sensible-looking matron or that dignified male schoolteacher, who'd given all the right answers, turned out to be something different than they looked. Juries so very damned tricky anyway: he sometimes thought the combined sense of any twelve people, as expressed in a verdict, added up to less than the ordinary sense any one of the twelve would use in everyday life. He'd heard substantiated evidence, after the fact—as any lawyer had—about jurors who'd made up their minds this way or that because the prosecutor was bald or had a chronic cough, because the defense lawyer wore a red necktie, or because a character witness used bad grammar.

Well, for whatever reasons or no reasons, there it was: he hadn't got a change of venue; the jury evidently hadn't believed him or Nell Varney, and had swallowed all the evidence against her without much question. They'd only been out thirty-five minutes.

He didn't think the death sentence would hold: not for second-degree, and not on this evidence. He'd told her that. "We've got a breathing space, and we'll have more. They can't make that stick."

And she'd looked at him quite calmly and said, "I don't know whether I'd like to believe you or not, because if it comes to a choice between the rest of my life in prison, or even twenty years, and dying now—well, I'd rather have it quick than slow, Jesse. But I can't quite believe you, because this whole thing—the way it's happened—*nothing* on my side at all, like a kind of inevitable doom—I can't believe anything will happen right for me."

"Unflattering," he said. "You've got me on your side."

And so now he was thinking what else to do, where to start poking around looking. Most urgently for something for the appellate court, but while he was at it, for any lead on the other one.

The woman, who might look a little like Nell Varney—some way—who had brought those women home to die, and without much doubt had performed the abortions on them.

A number of vague ideas had been wandering around his mind as he followed Vic's dusty black Chevy the few miles from the county seat to Contera. As they passed the town-limits sign he had a more definite idea, and blew his horn at Vic and pulled up alongside.

"You still have the key to Nell's house?"

"Yes, sure, why?"

"Thought it might be a good place to stay. I don't think she'd mind. Nice quiet spot to brood in. O.K.? You go get the key, I'll meet you there."

It wasn't a house everybody would like, as she said. Also it could be said to conform to the house Carol Inver had talked about on her deathbed. He sat looking at it thoughtfully from the street, waiting for Vic. *A funny-looking house*, Carol had said. You might call it that, if you'd lived all your life in Contera, where even the new houses (and not many of those) were conventional ranch-type bungalows. It was built the length of the lot, not the width, so all the yard was at one side; the part facing the street was of vertical redwood panels, with a narrow but very long louvre window across it, in four sections. Down the real front, it was partly stucco painted tan, partly redwood, and at the corner, beyond that louvre window, rough flagstone faced it for a couple of feet each side, going up to a squat chimney. That would be the corner hearth. There were two more louvre windows along the front, beyond the slab door and the three little steps up to it; and squarely on top of the house was a second story only about a third the size of the ground floor. She'd said that had been intended for the painter's studio. You could say it looked a little something like the deck cabin on a boat, perched up there.

He'd brought his suitcase from the hotel in the county seat; when

Vic came with the key he got out of the car, held out his hand and said, "Thanks."

Varallo looked at him. "You want to brood in solitude? Two heads better than one, they say."

"Depends on the heads. There'll be questions I want to ask you, but I'll have to figure out what they are first. You'd better go and see if you can coax back your original notes from that chief of yours." Brant had grabbed those and impounded them for Burkhart, and Jesse had had to depend on Vic's memory of them.

"O.K. You know where to find me."

Jesse took his suitcase into the house. Stuffy from being shut up so long; he went around opening windows. Rooms not very big, but well planned: living room, kitchen with elongated area for informal dining, service porch, bedroom, and bath down here; up the stairs off the tiny entry hall, that biggish studio room, with a small but complete bath off it. She said she'd taken that, liked it for its privacy and better air. He agreed with her, and put down his suitcase in the one chair. Furniture throughout obviously not meant for this kind of house—the stuff they'd brought from the other place in the city. Conventional furniture, pleasant enough, a little shabby: the odds and ends people collected over a period of years. A good many of her clothes still in the closet: winter things; the police matron would have come here with her while she packed a few things, and probably cleared out the perishable items from the larder and so on. . . . Dressing table empty but for little things she wouldn't need often.

He unpacked and put things away in drawers, went downstairs and looked in the refrigerator, and methodically wrote out a shopping list for himself: eggs, milk, bacon, butter, bread, coffee. He went upstairs again, investigated, and found clean bedding on the closet shelf, and made up the bed. Then he took off his shoes and tie, lay down and shut his eyes, and thought about those seven witnesses, and what those two women had said.

Vic had been helpful, somebody who knew the town inside out, and the relationships, the private backgrounds. There were a couple of lines to follow up, and Vic had done what he could on them—somewhat hampered by Brant—but Jesse had been kept pretty busy preparing the case for court that three weeks before the trial came up on the calendar. He'd have had longer down at home: city calendars more crowded. Couldn't be helped. Now he thought there were several little things he'd like to know more about.

For instance, the little German dog, and Antonia Cambiare's best bedspread, and the picture in the paper, and the fowl. And *trust Mame* (or, *trust in the Name?*) and, *just for the money, a terrible sin, better you shouldn't have married him*. And, *ask Antonia*.

All of which had also been among Mrs. Zacchio's ramblings before she died—incoherent, disconnected. Besides some other phrases, which were easier to interpret and obviously irrelevant, such as the new curtains for the living room, and the names of her other children, and requests for the priest to come.

"You can see," Vic had said, "it doesn't all tie in with Nell Varney by a long shot, and I tried to get at the sense of it, separate what might be relevant—Gannon heard most of it, and the husband and two daughters were hanging around the room every minute, backed him up mostly, though about a couple of things one or the other of them had heard a little different or didn't agree just when she'd said what. Quite natural, in the circumstances."

Sure. Doctor working over her, family hovering around excited, upset, helping him—no hospital in ten miles, and she was pretty far gone when the doctor arrived. The younger kids, four or five of them, Vic said, kept out of the room, but probably underfoot nearby, as excited and upset—maybe the baby howling.

Teresa Zacchio, forty-four, her oldest child over twenty, youngest just eighteen months, six in between—dismayed to find she was pregnant again, at the prospect of another mouth to feed on her husband's wages as a laborer—buying an abortion for fifty dollars.

Damn cheap, compared to the usual prices. Some indication that Carol Inver had paid a lot more. Yes.

And what good was all that rambling talk as material for discrediting testimony in court?

"—Just wandering in her mind she was, 's all, when she said those things."

"Oh, I see, when she talked about this little dog she'd seen somewhere, and a fowl, and a picture in the paper and so on, she was *wandering*, but when she mentioned Miss Varney's name, *then* she was quite coherent?"

"Well, I guess must've been like that. I mean, looks like that one time she did hear what the doctor was asking, or *Padre*, and tried to

answer sensible—I mean, she did say the name, and right after the
doctor or *Padre* asked her again, who."

"Are you sure of that time interval? That it was just after? Dr. Gannon has testified that he could not say, that it seemed to him it was
several minutes afterward."

"He was kind of busy."

"You maintain seriously that when your mother, in delirium, talked
about these other quite irrelevant matters, she was simply *wandering*,
but when she mentioned—just *once*, and without adding any words to
it at all—Miss Varney's name, she must have been perfectly sensible
and coherent?"

"I guess, must've been. Sounded like that."

Unimaginative, the Cambiare woman. Stolid. And very stubborn.

"For anything it's worth to you," Vic had said, "Antonia Cambiare—
before she got married—didn't have too good a reputation. There was
gossip about her with several men. And at one time about her and
Tasso. This was two or three years back, and what I'm telling you is
strictly slander, gleaned from my sister, who goes around with the
daughter of the fellow who employs Zacchio—and of course the gossip
also got around to the church members by way of the priest's housekeeper. So you can take it or leave it. Tasso came from around here
but he's now, as you know, a wholesale salesman for farm equipment
and covers quite a territory, I believe, Stockton down to Bakersfield or
thereabouts. Hits Contera about once in three months. What the gossip says is that he was running after Antonia, and everybody knows
he's a married man—wife down in L.A.—besides which he's a good
twenty years older—and Antonia wasn't exactly turning the cold shoulder on him the way a respectable girl should. Her father went to the
priest about it and he spoke both to Tasso and the girl. I don't suppose it was the first time he'd tackled her about that kind of thing, by
what gossip says. What the ins and outs were, I couldn't say. Anyway,
about a year ago she married Cambiare. He has a little run-down
truck farm out of town, he's one of those amiable louts that just es-
capes the law—not quite moron level—probably the best she could do
for herself with the reputation she'd got. I'd never met her before this
business, but just from questioning her I'd say she's one of those
tough, strong-minded females who usually do acquire men they can
keep the whip hand over. . . . I've got no idea whether she's had any

dealings with Tasso since that time, or with any other man but her husband."

And nothing there for the court case, either. Irrelevant. With a question mark.

Vic had kept looking, as much as Brant let him; after Brant and Burkhart had jumped the gun, picked out the testimony they thought was significant, ignoring the rest. The rest, nothing much to get hold of, of course, really.

A little German dog . . .

Jesse sighed to himself and got up. It was getting dark. He reknotted his tie, put on his shoes, locked the door after himself—encountering the avidly interested gaze of Mrs. Price next door through her kitchen window, as he did so—drove to what Contera called downtown five blocks away, and went into the police station.

"My Uncle Malachi—very tedious old man sometimes," he said to Varallo, "fancies himself as a learned fellow. Always quoting at you from Holy Writ and the Talmud. One of the proverbs he's fond of quoting—*So say the most learned Rabbis, Praise the Lord for the evil as for the good.* Doesn't sound very sensible, but there's something in it, you know. Something bad comes along—but later on, when you look back, you see maybe if *that* hadn't happened, another thing would have had a worse outcome. You never know."

"I never was very hot on abstruse philosophy," said Varallo. "I got my notebook back from Brant—here you are. Just what's in your mind?"

"There's another one too—says, *It is best to study by night when all is quiet.* I've been in a kind of rat race since I've had this thing, getting the court business ready and so on—not much chance to sit down quiet and think about the little niggling details. A couple of things occurred to me when I started to. One of them—would the Zacchios use English or Italian at home? When these people quoted Teresa Zacchio, it was in English, but did they kind of automatically translate it for our benefit? And would the doctor know Italian?"

"Oh, English—almost undoubtedly. Zacchio himself, I think, is first generation—you notice he's got quite an accent—but the majority of Italians these days are third and fourth generation, up here anyway. You know how it is, the first-generation kids grow up bilingual, but they and *their* kids, nine times out of ten, are a little ashamed of the old-country talk and ways, try to be as American as possible. By the time you get kids whose grandparents and great-grandparents were born here, sometimes they don't know the language at all. Teresa Zacchio may have known Italian, but it wasn't her first language— She'd grown up speaking English, and you notice both the girls, the rest of the kids, haven't any accent. She was talking English all the while that night— As you know, I heard the tail end of it. Gannon's got a little Italian, just as he has some Portuguese and Spanish—a lot of those patients—enough to say hello, good-by, how are you, seem friendly to them."

"Um," said Jesse. "Well, that makes it a little easier. I wonder if Nell's got a dictionary at the house—should have looked. I just got to thinking, you know, that what the Zacchios and Gannon heard as *Nell Varney* might possibly have been something else."

"You plugged away at that line in court—were they absolutely certain? I don't know— What else could it have been?"

"Lord knows what a woman in delirium'd talk about, first to last. I just wondered about it. Right now I'd like to be introduced to Gannon. Socially. With a few helpful words like, of course, he wants to aid justice and won't mind answering questions. Suppose he'll be having dinner about now. I thought we might take some steaks up to the house and then go see him."

"Well, all right." Varallo lived alone in a room at the Contera Hotel: no family or landlady to put out by plan changing. Jesse watched him bang shut the desk drawer, reach down his hat.

They came out to the hall, and met the chief of police in his office door opposite. And there, Jesse reflected, was the big frog in the small puddle, all right. Typical. Give that kind a little authority— Brant was a big, paunchy fellow, fifty-odd, bald and pig-faced, with little shrewd pale eyes; they fastened on Jesse and moved to Varallo speculatively.

"Well, well, so I guess that's how come you wanted your notebook back in such a hurry, Vic boy. I took a copy, you know. Tryin' to dream up something to appeal on?"

Varallo said, "I'm all for justice," and smiled at him.

"There's a laugh," said Brant. "What you've been in a sweat about all along is to prove me wrong and prove you're the hell of a lot smarter. That I know, Vic boy. But there's nothing wrong with this case and you or nobody else can ever show there is. Straight evidence."

"There are other opinions," said Varallo, and walked past him.

"You sure are democratic, Vic," said Brant, heavily jocular, "consortin' with a Jew boy."

"I can always say I'm trying to convert him," said Varallo without turning.

They came out to the street; not any cooler for the sun being down, not this far inland in the valley—still sticky, muggy, breathless. "Always feel a little sorry for that kind," said Jesse. "Annoying, sure, but think how much more so to themselves. No self-confidence—awful inferiority complex—have to keep finding things and people to look down at, build themselves up. The way it says in *Through the Looking Glass*—running as fast as they can to stay in the same place."

"I've got no charity to waste on Brant," said Varallo savagely, getting into the Ford behind Jesse. "One of the damnedest odd things about this affair is Brant joining forces with Burkhart—"

"*The cat and the rat make peace over a carcass*," said Jesse absently. "Uncle Malachi—wise sayings from the Talmud."

"And very pertinent. Talk about irrelevancies—! I suppose you could say it's partly my fault Brant went off half-cocked in the first place. I didn't think much of the Zacchios' talk about Nell Varney, I said so that same night to Brant—so right away he jumped in on the opposite side and started out to prove she was guilty."

"So you said before. And that's part of an idea in my mind. Tell you how I see it, after the steaks."

SIX

"I've got a pretty good idea by now of how it got built up, this identification." Jesse had decided gratefully that her father must have been a tall man: the one big armchair in the front room fitted him fine. "And the hell of it is, nothing I can show the appellate court, you know. Nuances—obvious deductions—nothing legal. Just as I couldn't show real legal cause for a change of venue. No active concerted feeling against her—few people like the Prices, not too many—nobody knowing her much, that's all. Because she's not a regular churchgoer, didn't go spilling her personal troubles to everybody she did know—so, those getting the idea she's stand-offish, smarty. That kind of thing, all under the surface . . . You can see it as well as me, probably have, you gave me some of it before. That other Zacchio girl, Maria, could be persuaded of anything by anybody a little stronger-minded. And I read both her and Zacchio as the kind who more or less lose their heads in a crisis, skitter around aimlessly not thinking clear—or at all. I think how it went was this. Zacchio makes that little random remark about the woman looking like Nell Varney, as they're getting Teresa into the house—and I've got an idea why too. I think it was the hair. In that light, they'd have seen her more or less in silhouette, and I think what they saw was a woman who had her hair pulled back smooth to a big knot, and that's what reminded them of Nell. As confirmation, see Carol's remarks on same subject."

"Possible," agreed Varallo, who was stretched out on the couch passively digesting. "And that ought to make her easier to find, in a way. Very few women nowadays—"

"I tell you, you're stagnating up here. Not so. One of the latest chic fashions right now. Big false chignons, figure eights, made up to match different hair colors—fastened on with pins, but the same general effect. And so easily taken off too. Girl needs a permanent, maybe, or 's letting her hair grow, she wears it plain with one of these things pinned on, and then the next thing you know, maybe next day, she's got short curly hair in an altogether different style. Well, anyway. You take it according to the times things happened and were said—this little remark of Zacchio's, and then for a while they were all busy and excited over Teresa. Gannon wasn't in, his wife took the call, and it was about half an hour before he got there. Meanwhile, the Zacchios were rushing around trying to minister to the woman. I gather that, as you'd expect, Antonia the unimaginative was the one who kept her head, did most of the first aid. O.K., so when the doctor gets there—or a little later—for the first time, according to what all of them say, Teresa is asked about who's responsible, where she went and if she knows a name and so on. All they get out of her is this rambling talk, and some of it strikes me as pretty interesting, you know—the little German dog, and the picture in the paper. Yes. Pay your money and take your choice—might have been just casual things wandering through her mind—no relevance at all. Antonia says she'd admired her new best bedspread, wanted one like it—and that *ask Antonia* might have referred to that, or to the new place Antonia'd found to buy a Sunday fowl. . . . You find people still calling it *fowl* up here?— sounds a bit old-fashioned somehow. . . . Yes, well, Gannon heard most of that too. And presently Teresa says something that sounds like *Nell Varney.* I don't suppose she was talking very clear—"

"As both Gannon and I testified, sometimes mumbling and sometimes quite clear. I only heard the bit, as you know, about the dog— though Gannon said she mentioned that several times—and something that sounded to me like *Trust Mame.*"

"Which Antonia and Maria heard, all very pious, as *Trust in the Name.* Kind of highfalutin talk for a woman like that, but let it go. Now, I think it's quite possible, as I suggested in court, that this previous remark of Zacchio's had conditioned them into hearing a muttered phrase meant for something else as *Nell Varney.* And I seemed to get a suggestion out of both Zacchio and Gannon that there was a little gap between the *Nell* and the *Varney.* So. Antonia was chary at admitting it, but evidently it wasn't right then that everybody exclaimed over this so-called identification, *got* it so to speak and said to each other, *Goodness, she means the girl at the bank, that's who it was!* It wasn't until Teresa had died, and Gannon and you were asking questions—"

"*And* Brant, who shot over as soon as he heard about it. Around midnight. Yes. Zacchio and Maria had gone to pieces, the kids were standing around crying or asking questions too, the priest had got there by that time—he didn't get to her before she died, you know, he was out somewhere—and it wasn't an atmosphere very conducive to calm examining."

"No. But anyway, *then* Zacchio repeats his original remark, and the zealous Brant takes it as a hot lead, because he remembers what Carol Inver said about seeing the woman in the bank once. He then hears about Teresa's saying Nell's name—possibly in answer to Gannon's question—and he presses them right then for a definite identification, and they were confused, upset. They heard Gannon agree that it sounded as if Teresa had said Nell's name, so they said yes. All but Antonia, who was a little cagey—sounding honest, too—said she didn't know Miss Varney at the bank well enough to say. Now, one of the things that strikes me a little funny about this saga is the way Antonia went to pieces all of a sudden. They're all being questioned, not in turn but just as things come up, and evidently it all caught up with her—slow reaction times, some people *are* like that, of course—her mother's death and so on, and she broke down and had to be taken home by her husband. Who had also joined the crowd by then. At exactly what point in the questioning did that happen? I haven't asked you that before, it's only just struck me it might be important. After handling the female in court."

Varallo sat up and lit a cigarette. "I grant you she doesn't seem like one who'd break up in a crisis like that, but sometimes these hard-boiled, undemonstrative people are the ones who do. Lid of the kettle on too tight. Well, let me think— As I say, it wasn't the quietest spot in town just then. . . . Yes, this mention had come up of Nell Varney and Brant was pounding away at them all, mostly Gannon—I suppose on the theory that his testimony would be less emotionally colored. As I told you, Gannon didn't sound to me quite as definite at first as he sounded in court. You see that in the notes I took at the time, he said, *Nell Varney? Yes, that might have been what she said.* Later on he got surer. Now let me get it straight. . . . Zacchio said something about maybe the fellow who called the doctor for them had had a look, and that was the first we'd heard about him. Brant asked who it was, and that was when Antonia went into hysterics. We couldn't do anything with her, and the rest of them weren't far off it, and the priest kept saying it was inhuman to question these poor bereaved souls now, and in the end we gave up for the night. As a matter of fact, that was how come I was late getting on Tasso. Zacchio didn't know who it had been—they'd got Teresa up to the porch when one of them suggested the doctor should be called, and he saw a man on the sidewalk and just called, *Hey, mister!* at him. It was Antonia who ran down to give him the dime and ask him to phone Gannon. I went out to the Cambiare's place next morning to see her, and the husband told me she was *very, very sick in bed*—wouldn't let me in. And by that time Brant'd got his search warrant and was satisfied he had a case. I wasn't, by the hell of a long way, and I was just as interested as he was in hearing what everybody concerned would say about a possible identification. We went to the Zacchios' again— This was about three that afternoon, he'd spent the morning searching this house and then we had a little backchat about all this—and we found Antonia there. Seemed O.K., herself again. And it was then she told us who the fellow had been—Tasso—and, of course, he'd gone on his travels by then and nobody knew exactly where he was heading, I had a little trouble finding him. Caught up to him by phone next day in Bakersfield, and he said right away, sure he knew who that woman was."

Jesse had sat up straighter and straighter in the armchair, listening to that. "You don't say. Why didn't I hear all this before? I know, not important—irrelevant—didn't ask. I wonder. All that says a little something to me, but I'm not exactly sure what. I'll think about it. Yes. To go on, from what you've said, by this time Brant had taken over the whole thing and was directing the investigation. He'd also definitely made up his mind Nell was guilty. After all, she'd been named. Everybody was a little calmer by then, and he got more coherent answers— all four of them there told him yes, Teresa had said *Nell Varney*— Doctor a lot surer then, maybe he'd thought it over— Maybe they all had, or thought they had. That first little remark of Zacchio's taking on greater importance—all of them convincing each other. Like that Andersen story about the Emperor's New Clothes. If everybody else heard a thing, saw a thing, I must have too. People are like that. And so Brant went off looking for possible further identification on the Inver business. He didn't, if I know Brant's type, say to Mrs. Inver, we want you to look at a woman and say yes or no. He told her all about it, including Nell's name and where she worked, and he asked her some questions—which had been asked before, of course—about that woman who'd brought Carol home. Thus refreshing her memory, reminding her what she'd said then. Sure, I can hear how that went— I didn't get much out of Mrs. Inver on the stand, but enough to tell me —and that's another example of how irrelevancies get mixed up, send a witness this way or that way. Halfway intelligent woman, and she saw I was trying to discredit Brant and Brant's way of getting her identification, so she balked me at every turn—couldn't remember if he'd mentioned a name first, and so on. Business of standing firm with the home folks against the stranger in the gates. Though she didn't realize it consciously. But I know how *that* went. You say that woman was thin and had dark hair, well, by golly, it must be her because Nell Varney's like that— You say she held herself kind of straight and had her hair done up behind, that's right, Nell Varney looks like that! And by the time Mrs. Inver was brought face to face with Nell at the police station, all that was fixed in her mind. An honest woman, but she'd been honestly confused. Yes, I know, you tried to arrange it fair —rounded up some other young women between twenty-five and thirty, about Nell's size and build—but I'll bet you didn't find one with long hair in a knot, *or*, in this backward spot, one who keeps up with the fashions enough to have a false chignon pinned on. No. Naturally Mrs. Inver picked her out right away. And just as I said in court, she *must* have seen Nell in the bank, whether she noticed her consciously or not— Nell looked a little familiar to her, for that reason *and* Brant's gratuitous information, and the more she looked the surer she was. Yes, that kind of thing—human muddleheadedness—has been a big factor here. Like what I said about the Zacchios. Everybody in on this thing as a prosecution witness, they've been thinking vaguely—the law must have quite a lot on her to charge her this way, nobody could have so much against them if there wasn't *some* reason, so these other witnesses must be right, so *I* must be right. . . . The busybody Prices volunteered their testimony—"

"When she was charged, next day. Came in and offered a statement about what they'd seen that night. Of course, there wasn't anything in it, but Brant liked it. I'm the one asked why they hadn't said something before— All the fuss at the time over Carol, they must have realized that car they'd seen, at that time and place, was probably the one that had brought Carol home. Well, they said, they just hadn't thought about it *then*. Shows you how much they're worth. Said they didn't think much of that Nell Varney, but never connected her with anything like *this*. However, *now* they thought back, they realized the significance of it."

"Yes, two of the least credible witnesses. They weren't really sure, they probably hadn't thought much about it at the time, or obviously they'd have said something then. Price also very obviously meek, little, henpecked fellow who'd back her up whatever she said. Can we even say that car *did* come out of Mrs. Inver's drive? Might even have been Nell on her way home—she can't remember what she was doing that night. The Prices were just makeweight. Couldn't resist getting in on the act. . . . There's a story about a lost horse and an idiot boy."

"I've heard it."

"I've been thinking on those lines. During the trial, when I had a chance, and today. There's a funny mixture here, it looks to me, of amateur and pro. I mean, on the real guilty party. We hear about a lot more of these cases in the big city, you know—it is, as you say, big-city business—and a pattern emerges, as any city cop could back me up. When a woman starts to die on an abortionist, he or she's pretty damn careful to see she isn't found while she can still talk. I'd think they'd try to move her off the premises before death, but to some lonely spot where she wouldn't be found until she'd gone. Kind of place they find the bodies—now and then—empty lot at night, the beach, lonely stretch of park. Well, these women were returned to their homes—true, pretty far gone, but they could still talk—which looks like an amateur job, doesn't it? Also, of course, as if it was pretty certain they didn't know a name or where they'd been, exactly. But they must have had *some* idea. Carol Inver drove away from home in her own car—she must've known where she was going, if just to be met somewhere. Car found ten miles east of town, day after she died at home. No fingerprints anywhere on it. The pro touch? Funny mixture. And, yes, it *is* big-city business—not much market around here—even if there's the same, um, ratio of business to the general population, not nearly so much general population. Not one of the businesses I keep up with as to supply and demand, but from the cases in the papers I gather that the price runs high—inflated like everything else these days. Two, three, five hundred bucks. Or more. Seemed to be about seven hundred missing from Carol Inver's bank account which couldn't be accounted for in normal expenses. But Teresa Zacchio got it for fifty. Looks as if this woman was charging what the traffic would bear—anything she could get. . . . I suppose you could make me up a list of people who've moved into Contera and environs within the last year or so."

"There aren't too many, and I've looked, you know. On Carol Inver. I may not be the brightest cop in the world, but I do know, as I told you, that this is a new business here. I looked. And there wasn't a smell. Couple of new women in town who married residents within that time—nice, ordinary young housewives. One retired bookkeeper, male, who's opened up a little grocery, settled down to spend his declining years in the atmosphere of his youth. Two new schoolteachers hired by the Board of Education—both born old maids to whom 'abortion' is a nasty word in the newspapers, you can see. Not a smell of anything suspicious."

"No? Well, I wonder if you'd know about it, anyway. If that one would show. . . . Of course, a small town—and over a year, you said? —difficult. Groceries to buy, and so on—unless, of course—" Jesse was silent for a while, and then gradually he unfolded himself from the armchair and said, "Getting on for nine. Wife said the doctor'd be home by then. Let's go see him."

When he pulled up at the curb outside the house, he didn't move at once. "What about Gannon? Good doctor—people like him?"

Varallo didn't turn to look at him; in the light from a streetlamp a few yards away his regular profile stood out in handsome silhouette, hair touched to a gold glint above. "That really doesn't enter in. You notice there wasn't any discussion of which doctor to get. Please call the doctor for us, she says, and Tasso calls Gannon. Gannon's the Catholic doctor. I couldn't tell you how good a doctor he is." He opened the door and got out of the car. "So far as I know he's an honest, conscientious man."

Jesse looked at Gannon three minutes later and cautiously agreed, as he had thought before, handling Gannon from a little distance in court. Big, red-haired, freckle-faced fellow about forty—slow, almost diffident manner of talking.

"All I can tell you, Mr. Falkenstein, is what I know myself, for certain. Whatever you want to ask—" he spread big, freckled hands. "I'd never met Miss Varney, but she seems to be a nice enough young woman, if she's innocent I'd be only too glad to help you prove it. I *will* say, at this stage, I did think the whole—er—business was drummed up in a bit too much of a hurry. Perhaps Captain Varallo agrees with that." He glanced sideways at Varallo.

"Yes. So do I. I've just been looking over his original notes, Doctor, and it seems that that night, when you were first asked about Mrs. Zacchio's speaking Miss Varney's name, you weren't as definite as you were later. You said that *might* have been what she said."

"Did I?" said Gannon. "Well—I suppose so. Yes, I seem to remember saying that. Most of the time I wasn't consciously listening to her, you know—patients in delirium, you don't, it isn't important—Well, you see what I mean. She rambled on about a great many things, and I didn't bother to—er—tie them up, no reason."

"Yes, this little German dog, a dachshund that'd be probably, she'd seen somewhere, and Antonia's bedspread, and the fowl—"

"Patients come out with some funny things sometimes, but mostly it's ordinary things like that—just vague pictures, random thoughts wandering through their minds—you know. Yes . . . Well, I wouldn't care to say about that one. *Trust Mame?*" He shook his head doubtfully. "Might have been. She was going pretty fast by that time, you know. I couldn't say either, as I told you on the stand, whether she understood that we were asking her whether she knew who and where. . . . In between all this, that isn't so easy to get the drift of, you know; she was saying other things—asking for the children, and for the priest, and complaining of pain and feeling sick."

"She was in pain?"

"Yes, certainly. Her heart wasn't too strong and I didn't dare give her much sedation. . . . No, she wasn't nauseated, that isn't— After a while, when she went on complaining of nausea, I put it down to the delirium— That is, something she was remembering feeling, if you see what I mean. Kept saying that some smell made her feel sick—and there wasn't any particular—er—strong odor in the room at the time, so probably— I think the Zacchios could help you more on this, if that's what you're interested in, trying to decipher all that rambling talk. I don't see myself that there's anything in it, but—"

"Well, you never know. She said *Ask Antonia*. What did that refer to?"

"I really couldn't say. The new bedspread, perhaps—that's what Mrs. Cambiare thought. About where she'd got it, you know, or how

much it cost. . . . Well, as to *that*, what she said about Mrs. Cambiare's marriage, you understand, I don't know, just gossip, but I believe there was some talk that the girl had married him for his expec-
tations from his uncle. Cambiare's a good enough young fellow, but
not very bright or—er—prepossessing, as you'll have gathered." Gannon suddenly produced a rather charming shy grin. "But why her
mother should have said it was *a terrible sin* to have married him *just
for the money*, I can't say. A lot of very righteous people do that kind
of thing, after all—not exactly a sin."

"Isn't it the truth," said Jesse. "Tell me—if you remember—the order
of all this. I haven't got it quite straight. She repeated some of this
several times, I gather—did it come in the same order every time, or
all mixed up? Any two of these phrases always said one after another?"

"Oh, dear, I don't know that I could— I seem to remember that—
yes, one thing I can tell you there, because we all were a little misled
about it, when she mentioned the dog the business about the bedspread came right after, and I know at the time I got the picture of
the dog sitting on Antonia's best bedspread, and I think either Zacchio
or the other daughter exclaimed over it, wondered what she meant.
The Cambiares don't keep a dog, of course. Then she went on to this
other stuff, and we realized it was all mixed up in her mind. Later on
I think she mentioned the dog again and then the picture in the paper
—I suppose she'd seen a picture of it somewhere, you see."

Jesse digested that. "Well. You didn't do the autopsy, of course—but
did you form any opinion at all as to whether the abortion had been a
halfway professional job? That a doctor, or someone with medical
knowledge, had done it—or vice versa?"

Gannon drove fingers through his crest of red hair, looking per-
plexed, thoughtful. "That's hard to say. Dr. Burnett could tell you better, as he did the autopsy—being the coroner—of course, you asked
him that in court, didn't you? He didn't seem to want to say one way
or another. All I can say is, from the external condition there wasn't
any obvious—er—*butchery*. But it isn't a terribly delicate or difficult
piece of work, you know."

"No. For a doctor. Whole point. Burnett was caught between me
and the prosecutor right then—both of us concentrating on getting him
to say what was best for our side. I can't say I made much out of him
either. Well, thanks very much."

"Only too glad to tell you what I can, Mr. Falkenstein. If the poor girl *is* innocent, we must all do what we can to help. . . ."

"So?" said Varallo in the car.

Jesse fiddled with the headlight switch. "Think Burnett'll be up at this hour? You seem to roll up the sidewalks about eight o'clock in this town. Well, we'll try. . . . I wish I had an obliging pal who just happens to be a high-ranking police officer, who gives me all sorts of valuable information out of criminal records, just for the asking."

"You've got me."

"You don't count here—whole point—some friendly captain in the big city is what I want. But the trouble is, I don't know which city. And what a hunt, even if I knew—even if it's *there*. Not that I expect the L.A.P.D., or any other, 'd kick me out of headquarters for asking— but it'd be quite a job of research, on just a thin hunch. . . . What newspaper would Teresa Zacchio have seen?"

"I don't suppose they took one, if they did it'd be the Contera weekly, the *Valley News*. But she'd probably see other papers occasionally—as you've heard she went out doing casual housework sometimes, and some of the people she worked for would take a city paper. A Fresno paper, or Bakersfield, or one of the big L.A. papers. And quite likely, if she asked they'd let her take one home."

"Yes. Or, come to that, the picture she saw in a paper might, damn it, actually have been in a magazine."

"I don't think so," said Varallo, intellectually amused. "Teresa Zacchio would call a magazine a *book*."

"What I need is a dictionary of rural terminology," complained Jesse.

But he sat up with an ordinary dictionary, making notes in his small, finicky writing. Not that it would do much good now to be able to suggest what she'd said that sounded like Nell's name: everybody had it too firmly fixed in mind that was what she'd said. But it was a starting point, and he was curious.

Burnett hadn't told him much, in court or this time. Little too conscious of his own dignity, Burnett; and whether it was suspicion of the outlander or firm belief that the guilty party was found and reluctance to give her any aid and comfort, he wasn't committing himself definitely. May possibly have been some medical knowledge; may not. Difficult to say.

Jesse sighed over his notes. Another quotation Uncle Malachi was fond of: *Truth is heavy, therefore few care to carry it.*

Tackle the Cambiare woman in the morning, he thought, switching out the light.

SEVEN

But as a matter of fact he didn't. He drove out to their place, by Vic's directions, next morning, but he never got out of his car.

Joe Cambiare's farm was five or six miles out of town, and it looked dreary enough to Jesse, but most farms did. He couldn't have said whether it was prosperous or not. There was a narrow dirt track off the main road, up to the house, which was long and low, gray-weathered from lack of paint; at one side of the house and partly behind stood a big two-story barn even more dilapidated-looking than the house. The track took a little turn halfway up, and the other side of the house and part of the rear yard came into his view. He saw another ramshackle building, smaller; he also saw Antonia Cambiare.

She had her back to the car; she was opening a big gate in a wire fence there, balancing a pan on her hip. She went in and set the pan down, and was immediately surrounded by about nine dozen chickens.

Jesse stopped the Ford dead. He sat there for a full minute thinking, and then he turned around and headed back for town. On the way he did some more thinking, bitterly, about small towns and legal red tape. Down at home, he'd know people's backgrounds, and also he wouldn't have had every minute taken up with planning out some kind of court strategy for a trial scheduled so soon. Would have had a little leisure to sit and think about the details. Nine-tenths of a thing like this private, under-the-surface, which meant, at home: and he hadn't been in five miles of Contera until now, the trial, of course, being at the county seat. Backgrounds . . .

He walked into Varallo's office and said plaintively, "Nobody told me Antonia Cambiare raises chickens."

"Why shouldn't she?"

"No reason. But, so why should she be buying a Sunday fowl—at some place so good and cheap that it aroused her mother's envy so much she had it on her mind when she was dying?"

"Oh," said Varallo. "The fowl. Well, farmers aren't allowed to do their own butchering any more, of course, but that doesn't apply to the occasional pullet out of the barnyard. I do know that Cambiare used to sell eggs to the local dairy association— That is, the hens were kept strictly for eggs—but he got kicked out some time ago for below-par sanitary conditions. Maybe she's cleaned them up— Maybe she's selling eggs again, so she wouldn't take any of their own hens for the pot."

"Find out for me," said Jesse. "I want to know, right now. I also want to know what hotel in Bakersfield Tasso was at when you found him."

"The St. Regis—salesman's house. You're playing detective, not telling me why."

"I don't know why, yet. I'm just looking at everything all over again, a lot closer. After Antonia and her chickens—and her belated hysterics over her mother's death—I'm not taking anything for granted. Is there anybody in Contera who owns a dachshund?"

"There wouldn't be many. You could find out at the licensing bureau in the county seat. I can't think of any offhand."

"Yes, all right, I'll do that; I suppose they wouldn't make any trouble—unimportant thing. For something else we'll need your official rank. I'd like very much to know whether Tasso received any phone calls the night Teresa Zacchio died, when, and if possible, where from."

Varallo sat motionless for a moment, cigarette raised halfway to his mouth, his face blank of expression. "Phone calls."

"Because just maybe he was briefed what to say. Compare him with Mrs. Price—same kind of look into a passing car, same kind of light. I don't like Alice Price, but she's not a deliberate liar— You pin her down to definite facts, she admits, no, not a close clear view of the driver. Tasso's very damn positive. So maybe he was told what to say. For some reason. What time did he come back to the hotel that night, and did he have any phone calls or visitors afterward?"

"I see, yes. I'll have a look, try to find out."

"Say sometime today," said Jesse, and went out to his car again and started for the county seat. He was wondering what the appellate court might think of the way Gannon's first hesitant answer about the Zacchio identification jibed with his later definiteness. Very narrow line there: nothing much. Much more useful if he could get Mrs. Inver to admit that Brant had, in effect, briefed *her* to identify Nell. He wished he could do something like sending a persuasive gigolo with a hidden tape recorder to drink cocktails with the woman and coax the whole tale out of her onto the tape. Yes, and get into a hassle with the bench as to whether it was admissible evidence. In any case, he had a depressing suspicion that Christine Inver didn't drink cocktails.

He stopped at the first drugstore he came to, got ten dollars changed to quarters, and discovered that—as he had also suspected—there was no L.A. directory available. Sitting on the hard booth seat that was apparently designed for midgets, he got through at last to L.A. Information and felt homesick listening to the imperturbable voice from the big town. Information was rather short with him; this kind of thing wasn't her business at all. "I know," said Jesse, "but I'm marooned here in outer space, the sole representative of modern civilization, and nobody's got a directory for any place bigger than Fresno. Just a couple of names, please—won't take you a minute to look in the yellow pages."

"Well—" said Information. He got the names of three agencies, and called them all. The first refused all new business. The second asked suspiciously if he was a private detective and told him they specialized in theatrical clients. The third cheerfully accepted his commission and named a price that shot his eyebrows up.

"Of course, that's for putting a rush on it—call it a week, it's quite a job, you know. . . . Couldn't guarantee full coverage in less time, as it is it'll keep three girls busy."

"Yes, O.K., go ahead—I'll send you a check." He went on to the county jail.

When the matron shepherded her into the little bare interview room, she burst out before the door was shut, "I've been thinking. I can't possibly ask you to go on with this, whatever else there is to do—I don't know how lawyers charge, but all this time and work you've put in, I don't know how I could pay what I owe you *now*. I should have had the Public Defender—"

"Not knowing him, couldn't say if he'd have been better or worse. But I don't want to talk about money right now—just had a little shock in that direction— However, if it pays off it's worth it. I'm getting something out of you anyway, free rent. I've settled down in your house, hope you don't mind."

"What? Oh, no, certainly not—as long as you like," said Nell mechanically. "But why? What—"

"Looking into backgrounds. Looking—maybe—for the one who ought to be here instead of you." She was in the same dress she'd worn in court, plain tan cotton dress, tailored, with the copper jewelry; but she looked a little thinner than she had a month ago, and a little tired and drawn. "Don't fuss about the money. You seem to be experienced office help, you can always work it off keeping my books or something."

"Not if you d-don't get *me* off first. Which doesn't look very hopeful."

"And maybe you should have had the Public Defender, if you haven't any more faith in me than that. That's an incentive—I never would get paid out of what they let prisoners earn at Tehachapi. I grant you I've been a little late getting on some of this, but lawyers don't expect to have to be detectives—and you might say I'm out of my element up here. How I do *not* like little towns."

Nell leaned back in the hard, straight chair with a sigh. "If I ever get out of here and back to town, I'll never get out of sight of the Prudential Building again," she said in dreary humor.

"You're behind the times—couple of bigger ones up now. Real skyscrapers, thirty stories, promised. All of a sudden they've decided earthquakes aren't much danger after all. Tell me something. You didn't cash checks for people at the bank. You said you didn't recall ever actually waiting on Tasso when he came in. You sure you never exchanged a word with him, maybe that he came up and asked you *where* to cash a check or something like that?"

She shook her head. "That I couldn't positively say. I don't remember ever even noticing him, certainly I'm sure I never did any business for him—no occasion. The only things I'd actually be, you know, at the counter for, waiting on the public, were taking installment payments, interest payments on loans, things like that—and I shouldn't think he'd be coming in for any reason but to cash checks, not living there. But it might be he'd asked me something like that, said a few words— It'd be so casual I mightn't remember. But I don't think so. Why?"

"Well, just a little thing maybe—he said you'd waited on him a couple of times. Maybe meant you'd just answered a casual question. Maybe not—maybe he doesn't know you didn't cash checks. Yes. Let's see, what else did I want to ask you? Oh, yes—one of those little ordinary things so easy to overlook, I should have wondered about that after I'd read the statements the first time, damn it. I don't suppose the Contera bank is a very fancy layout. Big branch bank in the city, practically everybody working at the public counters seems to have a little bronze name plate—Mr. Grubb, Miss Whistlefinger, Mrs.— No, I didn't make it up, there really is a Miss Whistlefinger at the bank I go to mostly. Did you here?"

"Good heavens, no. I wasn't as important as that. Only Mr. Adamson and Mr. Forsythe—"

"Mmh. And, anyway, those things don't very often have a whole name. Seen some that do— Mary Smith, John Brown— but most of 'em very dignified with Mr., Mrs., Miss. And you never got on first-name terms with Mrs. Zacchio, the times she came into the bank?"

"No, of course not. After the first time, when I'd seen her name on the papers, you know, I'd say, *Hello, Mrs. Zacchio,* or something like that, but she'd only be there a few minutes and she was rather a shy little woman, we never exchanged much talk."

"Ever get your name in the local paper while you've been here?"

"I did not." She gave him a rather forlorn smile. "Don't you know about small-town papers? What you get into them for are Social Works. Church clubs, women's clubs, service clubs, bridge clubs, garden clubs, giving teas or dinners—working for the local Red Cross or P.T.A. or Scouts—political clubs—you wouldn't believe the number of groups. And I'm not a joiner, or very social-minded, even if I'd had the money. I loathe cards and gardening—"

"That's nice to know," said Jesse interestedly. "So do I. Awful waste of time. Yes, so tell me how come Mrs. Zacchio knew what your first name is? Zacchio knew the Varney, so there's that—if he mentioned it at home. How did he, by the way?"

"He's so polite," said Nell. "That's one thing about most immigrants and the first-generation Americans, isn't it? They're brought up with more formal manners, even the ones without much education. Some of them coming in asked me my name, but I seem to remember that Mr. Zacchio was there one day when Mr. Adamson came up and spoke to me by name—and he, Mr. Zacchio, I mean, always called me by it when he saw me."

"But so far as you know, neither he nor any of the Zacchios knew your first name?"

"I suppose they could have, but I don't know how—or why. There weren't many people in Contera who called me Nell, you know."

Jesse got up as the matron peered in the glass panel of the door. "Well, we'll see what turns up."

"Look—please," she said. "I suppose it's an automatic follow-up, so to speak, to make an appeal—but your fees— I'll never be able to—"

"Neither of us have much choice, do we? You might as well be hung for a sheep as a lamb—and, as for me, well, it doesn't do my reputation any good to lose cases. The Chinese have a system, I understand—if the patient dies, the doctor doesn't get paid. Very logical. You stop being so mercenary—crossing bridges. I'll probably see you tomorrow—maybe not till Monday. I'm going down to Bakersfield right now."

"Good heavens, in this weather. Why?"

"I'd better not say— It might not turn out to be anything."

He had a hasty lunch, got the tank filled and looked at a map. About eighty miles down there. It was just twelve o'clock when he left town. Call it two hours?

He wished he had an exact transcript of Tasso's testimony, but he thought he remembered the gist of it. First, the business about "had a long drive ahead nex' day, wanted get back to the hotel." Then, how he'd already left Contera next day when Vic and Brant found out they wanted to question him. And later still, in expansive and irrelevant answer to a question of Burkhart's, "I got an early start that morning, see, lit out for Bakersfield about seven, so's to get on the road before the worst heat. Didn't even hear Mrs. Zacchio'd died until Captain Varallo contacted me nex' day."

Traveling salesmen were usually fast drivers. And while this was a well-traveled highway—national road—and carried truck traffic as well as a lot of ordinary traffic, it was a good, wide, smooth highway, easy to drive.

It got hotter and hotter as he went south. He passed the Bakersfield limits at twenty past two, and he thought Tasso, who'd know the road better, would have cut that time.

He found the St. Regis Hotel: good second-class family place, probably had a lot of salesmen coming and going. He gave the desk clerk a hopefully friendly smile. "Afternoon. Hope you can help me out. I'm a lawyer, here's my card, and I'm trying to check up on a little evidence—"

"If it's *divorce*—" said the clerk coldly.

"Not divorce. Something a good deal more important. Now all I want to ask you is this. On the second of August a Mr. Giacomo Tasso registered here with you. He was here two days."

"Mr. Tasso, yes, I know him. He always stays here when he comes to town. What trouble is he in?"

Jesse looked at the clerk consideringly; did he detect a faintly eager note in the voice? "Don't *know* that he's done anything wrong— I'm just looking." Tasso—genial, hearty fellow on the surface, flashy clothes, the shrewd, cold eyes of the brash, high-pressure type—might very well be a cheap tipper, and also the kind to act lordly with hotel clerks and bellboys and waiters. "You know him, do you?"

"Oh, yes, sir, I know *Tasso*. What d'you want to know about him?"

"Do you have any record of what time he checked in?"

"Sure," said the clerk, reaching for the register. "You see, checking-out time's one-thirty P.M. Anybody isn't out by then pays an extra day. So we note down the time—approximate, that is, I don't mean it'd go down as nine-sixteen and a half, anything like that. So we kind of automatic put down *both* times, not that checking *in* 's so important, but you get in the habit. August second, you say? Here you are, G. C. Tasso, 307, two-fifteen P.M. What—"

"Thanks very much, very co-operative of you," said Jesse, and passed over a dollar bill with another smile, and went out unhurriedly.

Of course he might have called on some clients first. Playing detective was strenuous work: a lawyer just sat and thought, or did paper work, or talked—much easier job. And not much of the business day left. He looked up the Chamber of Commerce and said to the spotty-faced young clerk who came up to the counter, "If I was selling farm machinery wholesale, what firms in this town would I call on?"

"Beg pardon, sir? You're selling farm machinery? Well—"

He wasted half an hour there, but the list was encouragingly short. Sort of thing like buses or munitions, of course: not too many prospective customers, and a couple of sales would represent quite a commission.

By five-thirty he had seen someone in each of those five places, and had discovered that Mr. Tasso hadn't called at any of them on August second. He had made one sale on the morning of August third; the other places hadn't laid eyes on him since the last time he was through in April.

"All of which is very interesting," said Jesse to himself. He had a mediocre dinner at a cheap restaurant, and started back to Contera.

EIGHT

Varallo got up and stood at his office window for a little while after Jesse had left, looking down at the dusty, shabby main street of Contera. He didn't see it very clearly. There was a little more activity down there than usual, because it was Saturday.

His mind registered Gina Pozzo going into Barrett's drugstore down at the next corner; and the whole Reyes family dispersing out of Manuel Reyes' new Ford station wagon, youngsters toward the drugstore, Mrs. Reyes and two older girls toward Woolworth's or Hannum's department store, Reyes toward Johnny Novak's bar. He also noticed Cris Gonzales wandering down from the corner of San Rafael, steadying himself unobtrusively against the buildings he passed, smiling vaguely at everyone. And Father Piero's tall, thin, black-clad figure gliding at his usual swift walk under the office window.

What his mind was registering more clearly was, *Phone calls.* He stood there very still, looking into the street, and his face might have been carved out of rock.

After a while Lieutenant Bob Lee slouched into the office behind him and said, "Saw that Courtney woman about the nuisance complaint on the neighbors. Don't think there's much in it, but I took some notes. You want to look?"

"No," said Varallo. He turned around to Lee, to Lee's lazy-eyed, indefinable insolence. "Do what you want on it, I don't care." He took down his hat and went out.

Downstairs, in the street, the sun hit him like a fist; breathless, humid heat lay like an invisible blanket on everything. He turned right and walked down the block from the police station toward the little telephone building two blocks up. Past the gas company building, White's grocery, Sam's butcher shop, and the delicatessen at the corner of San Rafael; the men's store on the opposite corner, Mrs. Griffin's card-and-gift shop, the cheap chain furniture store. Saturday, and more people on the street than usual; they marked his passing with lifted voice and hand. "*Ciao*, Captain Varallo!" "*Come va*, Captain?" "How's it go, Captain?"

But he traveled a long way further than two blocks. A long way in time and a long way in another dimension.

Farther back than twelve years, because a long time before that he had started to be the questioner, the doubter. Before that, he'd often enough got the routine reprimand: *I did not see you at Mass on Sunday, Lodovico.* Away, up at Berkeley, anonymous, free. To think and do and doubt and be as Vic Varallo, this single entity, this one man in himself. But it had started before that. Long before he'd left the Church.

Let them think as they pleased about it—as he'd said to Jesse—that that had less to do with personal conviction than with the desire to dissociate himself from a social-class symbol. It hadn't, but let it go. If any of them stopped to think, even if it had been that reason, it'd never get him very far in Contera or places like it.

He was still a Dago. The Wop whose father had come over from the old country.

No, maybe you didn't find that brand of insularity so much in the big towns now. But places like this, it hung on. All his life, as far back as he could remember, those two unthinkingly insulting terms used—and sometimes not with any insulting intent, of course: the casual thing. The casual arrogance. The blind, unquestioned conviction of superiority—the bland, unquestioned acceptance that all these lesser-breeds-without-the-law were of one class, intelligence level, standard of honor, ambition, culture. Like that.

Not a thing a man could fight. Certainly not by cutting off one association that marked him. His name was still Lodovico Varallo.

But in a sense going back just twelve years too. To when somebody had to take the responsibility, when the old man died. The two youngest kids under twelve, Rita in last year high. No money. So all right, maybe more sensible to move them all into the city, more opportunity—better money. He hadn't. He'd taken it on here, and he'd marked *la fine* to it now: it was done.

Everybody had responsibilities he didn't much enjoy. Just one of those things. But it hadn't helped a great deal to reconcile him to the drain on his salary and his time and his energy all those years; even the kids throwing it up to him. Accusing him. Ashamed of his name and parentage and religion—trying to deny them all.

Non importa—never mind. It was not true, and what matter what anyone chose to think? There was a saying, *I pensieri non pagano dazio*—thoughts are free. Yes, and there was another newer saying about sticks and stones and names never hurting.

So, it hadn't helped; but he was a grown man sure of his own integrity, and he should not have let it matter so much. In any case, the accounts were closed now; it was done.

Not the way he'd have chosen for any of them, maybe, but there it was. *Peccato*—too bad; but in life these things happened. Rita dead at twenty-five, in childbirth. The other two girls married, both to local farmers; he saw very little of them any more. And Father Piero had got Stefano for the priesthood—fifteen-year-old idealist, going through that stage they all did, too young to know what he was doing. *Peccato!*—let it go. It was done; for two years his money had been his own to save or spend.

And Jesse asked very pertinently, What are you still doing here? What indeed? It was just, be damned if he'd give Brant or Lee the satisfaction of being able to say, We got rid of the damn Dago. Sure, so maybe it looked like just plain obstinacy; it didn't exactly feel that way—

But maybe it was, at that. Maybe—

He was wondering suddenly, savagely—some deliberate seeking of self-pitying martyrdom?

Jesse, he thought: Jesse and Brant's sneering glance yesterday. No new story to Jesse either, but it didn't get through to him the way it did to Vic Varallo. He could look at it, acknowledge it, cool and serene, for what it was—and go on his way: just another fact of life, and nothing to hamper Jesse Falkenstein from getting where he wanted to be, because it couldn't change what he was in himself. The mature way to take it, so it was. He couldn't come to it; he wasn't built that way. So, maybe, surface answers, easy and glib; but Jesse wasn't a first-generation American. He seemed to remember that there'd been an ancestor who'd fought in the Revolution; they'd been here a long time. Jesse didn't remember the old folks who never quite got the hang of English, kept to the old social ways, or the looks and conscious toleration from the upper crust who found them quaint.

But he stopped there, two doors away, and stared blindly into the window of Gordon's Insurance Agency, All Types of Insurance, We Can Serve You Better. Because he was a damn coward—all ways. Excuses. So easy to make. It could be that Jesse Falkenstein was just a bigger, tougher, better man than Lodovico Giovanni Varallo.

Knocking my head against a stone wall, he thought. For nothing but stiff-necked stubbornness and pride.

A man got into a rut. He also got a little cautious these days. Seniority built up—

Don't make excuses, Vic: seniority, hell. You wouldn't give them the satisfaction, by God. Brant or Lee or any of the rest of them. That's why you stayed here two years longer than you had to.

A coward, he said to himself; a damn coward. He could see himself in dim reflection in the plate-glass window—big, tough, experienced-cop Varallo, who had once taken on both Keane brothers and laid them out too, that ruction at Novak's bar—who had taken that kidnaper on the run after the city boys had missed him. Afraid now to climb a stair and walk in a door.

He turned and walked on to the entrance of the little telephone building. The two girls at the counter inside looked at him but didn't speak: Captain Varallo had a right to go where he wanted in this town. He went heavily up the stairs and down a little corridor past two doors until he came to one that said ASSISTANT SUPERVISOR.

He was wondering all over again why he'd stayed in this town two years after he'd had to. To die a little and go to hell whenever he saw her a block away in the street, heard her name spoken.

He went through the door, and this was the closest he'd been to her for two years—Laura Field sitting there at a desk inside the little wooden fence which kept the public out; Laura Field with her brown head bent over some papers.

"Hello, Laura," he said.

She raised her head quickly, startled, and they looked at each other.

Funny, he hadn't noticed her for a while after she came here to work; and for a while after that he hadn't got up nerve to approach her. Varallo, *Dio*, who'd never been known as backward with the girls; but this was Laura, who had a nice Anglo-Saxon last name and lived the other side of the fence.

And important, the most important, other ways. The only one he'd ever met who was everything he liked and nothing that he didn't. Just the twice they'd been out together, he'd discovered that; and he'd thought—he'd hoped—maybe she had too. They'd got to know quite a lot about each other on those two dates, for just a few hours of talk. He knew her birthday was in November; she'd be twenty-eight this year, and she had a married sister in Fresno, and her father had been a pharmacist; and that she smoked Parliaments and liked just a little cream in her coffee; and that she liked big dogs, and old-fashioned furniture instead of modern, and detective stories. That in some lights her eyes were blue and in some almost gray, and one of her eyebrows curved higher than the other, and she had a very small brown mole on her left cheekbone.

Two dates. They'd had fun; they liked being together, liked the same things. Spontaneous, nothing forced. He hadn't even tried to kiss her the first time, because this was Laura, the important one, the real one, and there was time—and time to make that important too. But he had the second time, and it had got a little out of hand for both of them. Because they were right for each other, somehow. He'd almost asked her right then, but in the end he hadn't— He'd kissed her a last time and watched her into the house, and he'd been feeling pretty fine about it. He might be sure, but no sense in rushing her—not fair, in a way. And a couple of other reasons too. Not that he thought it'd matter to Laura, but his name was Varallo; and the once he'd met her mother, she hadn't been very cordial. But Laura knew he'd left the Church, and she wasn't—she wouldn't—

All the same, don't rush her. It would all be all right.

And that was the night before it happened. Before Mrs. Field, coming back from the post box at the corner on a rainy, dark evening, was killed by the hit-and-run driver.

And a distraught, shocked Laura first clinging to him and then telling him, "It was that Kearney boy, Vic— I know it was, I just know it! He always drives like a madman, you must know that! I heard the car— I was— I was drying my hair, I ran out— No, I didn't *see* the car, but I heard it—just the way that awful little sports thing of his always sounds— I've heard it and seen it often enough, they only live four blocks up, you know, and he comes past— And in town too—"

Well, it was a thing to look into, of course. He asked her more questions, gently. He asked questions of the neighbors who had been at home. He went and saw young Francis Kearney. And he drew blank everywhere. There just wasn't any evidence.

He was an experienced police officer: about evidence he knew. What was or wasn't, what you could base a charge on or not. Sometimes you felt certain about where guilt belonged and still couldn't begin to prove it; but here, he wasn't even that sure.

Young Frank Kearney was a reckless driver; that much Varallo knew. The Kearneys were one of three families in town who were both Catholic and very rich, and thus, for the latter reason (he reflected sardonically), accepted in society circles. Mr. Kearney Jr. ran an expensive and powerful sports car, to the public danger, and on more than one occasion had tried to bribe traffic patrolmen to get out of fines for speeding.

That was a fact. But it was the only one Varallo got hold of. None of the neighbors had seen the car, though several had heard it—and what was that?—all Laura herself could tell him—a screech of brakes, and then a motor revved up and roaring off toward Elm Avenue.

That was on Wednesday night. Varallo went to see young Kearney at noon on Thursday, and Kearney told him his car was in the garage for repairs and had been since Tuesday afternoon. It was Holt's Garage downtown. Varallo went and looked at the car, questioned Holt. The car was clean: no evidence of an accident. Heavier metal in most of these foreign cars, and the impact of a body wouldn't necessarily have made a dent anywhere— That couldn't have been ironed out in the time, but of course any other evidence could have been cleaned up in short order. Holt swore the car had been clean when it was brought in; he'd looked it over himself, and it hadn't been out of the place since four o'clock Tuesday afternoon.

So, it was conceivable that Holt had taken a nice handful of change to say that. Who could prove it? His previous record was clear as far as the law was concerned. It was a dead end.

Varallo could see Frank Kearney doing something like that, but there was nothing to base a charge on, and that was what he had to tell Laura. Maybe Frank Kearney had driven that car; maybe he hadn't. You couldn't charge a man on his past record when there was no evidence here.

"You can see there's nothing to go on, Laura—"

"All I can see," she'd said tautly, "is Mother lying out there dead and a murderer getting off scot-free! I tell you, I *know* it was that boy! He comes past here like a— What? No, not any *regular* times, to set the clock by, I don't mean that—but often enough. . . . No, I didn't see the car, I said so. Oh, God, I wish now I'd said I *had*, because I'm sure as death—wouldn't matter—"

"Now look, Laura. If you weren't upset you wouldn't say such a thing, perjury— It's just that there's no—"

"What *would* it matter, if it meant he was caught up with? I *know* it was—" And right then she'd looked at him, white, shaking, angry, and she'd said, "Lying! Yes, maybe so—if one man can be bribed, so can another. He's got a lot of money, hasn't he?—or his father has, which comes to the same thing. How much did he give you, Vic, to keep him covered up?"

It was funny, just then he hadn't felt the terrible hurt; he'd only been damned mad. He'd said something about she ought to know better than to suspect— And she'd stepped back from him, and then he saw the contempt in her eyes, and her voice cut across his. "Maybe Mother was right—about taking up with—"

"Say it," said Varallo softly as she stopped. He didn't know how white and hard he looked; that minute, he didn't really feel anything— that came later. "Say it, Laura. A dirty Dago, with a funny foreign name. Different from us. Not worth—"

"I— I didn't mean—"

"But you did," said Varallo, and he smiled at her. "Isn't there a saying about it? What's bred in the bone, et cetera. Sure. Only natural, a Dago cop, he's easy to bribe—everybody knows that."

"Vic, you know I didn't mean— I couldn't—it's just that I feel so wild about this, I— Vic, I'm sorry—"

"Don't bother." He took up his hat; it was finished. "I'll just say this, for what it's worth—which is probably damn all. If there'd been any evidence, I'd have arrested Frank Kearney with pleasure, whether he offered me a million bucks or whatever. But I'm a cop, and I've got to go by the book. If I ever get any evidence on who was responsible, he'll be charged and he'll get what's coming to him. Meanwhile—we have to know a little something about the law, you know—maybe I ought to warn you that you're committing slander against both Kearney and me. Good-by, Laura."

Later, of course, there had been the pain. Yes.

He'd never seen her to speak with since. He'd seen her: that he couldn't help, in a town as small as Contera; and he knew this and that about her. She'd moved from the little house they'd rented to the three-room cottage behind Mrs. King's place on Oak Street. She had lunch every day in the drugstore on the corner down from her office. Sometimes in the summer when he saw her somewhere, he'd know she'd been on vacation because she was a little sunburned— She was so fair, she had to be careful in the sun.

That was it; that was all about it.

The worst, the very worst, but just another thing like all the rest: the prejudgment, the generalization, the casual secret weapon as subtle as steel straight to the heart—

And be damned if Vic Varallo would let any of them *drive* him any direction at all, by God!

Except into the secret martyrdom?

"Hello, Laura," he said again, a little numbly. He'd found out it wasn't a thing that got any better with time; however he might feel— intellectually. He'd found that out seeing her in the street, hearing her name spoken, reading the little article in the *Valley News* when she was promoted to assistant supervisor.

One of her eyebrows still curved higher, and the little mole was still there. Her hair was still a sort of light brandy color, and she wore it the same way with a side part and a deep wave over her temple the other side, and her hands were still slim and white and graceful, with just faintly tinted pink polish on the nails. But she dropped them into her lap, below the desk top, looking at him.

"Hello, Vic," she said quietly.

"I wouldn't have come," he said—abrupt now, wanting this over— "but I've got to ask you for some information. I could make it official— I'd prefer to keep it private. I want to know whether Giacomo Tasso had any phone calls after nine-thirty on the night of August first—he was at the Contera Hotel, room 312. And if he had, where they were from. Can you get that for me?"

She waited a minute, as if considering, and then she said, "Yes, all right, I'll try to find out for you."

"Aren't you—curious why I want to know?"

"It doesn't matter," said Laura, "does it? You have a right—to ask— for information. I'll find out."

"All right," said Varallo. "Thank you." He turned to the door; her voice stopped him.

"Vic," she said. "Vic."

"Yes," he said without turning.

"Vic, I— I've wanted to apologize to you— You didn't give me the chance. I don't mean to defend myself, but—you know I was upset, and I *was* so sure— I still am—about its being the Kearney boy. But I hadn't any business, any right, to say such a thing to you— I was ashamed afterward. You must know I couldn't ever really believe— Please, Vic—"

"All right," said Varallo. "I accept the apology, Laura. Thanks."

"Is—that—all?" she asked in a very low voice.

"Yes, that's all," said Varallo rigidly. "Because you wouldn't have come out with it in the first place if you hadn't—somewhere, just a little bit—believed all the generalizations. Would you? I—"

"That's not true—"

"Thanks very much, Laura," he said, and went on out quickly. He heard her say his name again, but he did not turn. He went down the stairs and into the street. He jaywalked across the street and went into Novak's bar.

"*Ciao*, Captain Varallo—*come va?*"

"*Non c'e male*," he said. "*Si tira avanti*—one manages to get along. Brandy."

"*E vero.* Right away."

He had taken the first bar stool he came to; as he waited for the drink he got out a cigarette and groped for a match. The man on the next stool leaned unsteadily toward him and proffered a lighter—a shiny new cigarette lighter, silver and black, of the windproof variety.

"Thanks," said Varallo, bending to it.

"'S a *good* lighter," said the man. "New. Cost two dollar. Light ever' time."

"That's fine," said Varallo inattentively. The man was Cristóbal Gonzales; as usual he was slightly drunk. He never made any trouble, drunk or sober: an amiable, cheerful fellow; and his brother Steve had a prosperous farm, didn't grudge him the room and few dollars a week, which was all Cris wanted out of life. Sober, he mowed the parish house lawn once a week, and spent loving care on crudely carved wooden toys for all the kids in town: kids he liked, and they liked him. Drunk, he sat in the bar or wandered the streets quietly—never any trouble with Cris.

"Got it at the drugstore," he confided to Varallo. "Two dollar. But I save the rest o' the money for Christmas. Buy nice presents for Steve and Mary and the kids. I give it to Father Piero, keep it for me safe, see?—an' ever' week I give him little more, maybe by Christmas have twenty-five dollar."

"That's a good idea," said Varallo.

"*Prendete, Capitano!*"

"*Grazie.*" He picked up the brandy as the waiter set it down.

"See, she give me ten whole dollar. She didn't need do that, just do a little something for folks—try act nice and polite like a fellow should." And then suddenly Gonzales drew away, clumsy and startled, knocking over his empty glass on the bar. "You the policeman—didn't see who," he mumbled. "The police fellow—"

"That's right, but I'm not planning to arrest you right now," said Varallo. Gonzales slid off the stool and scurried away, tucking his lighter into his pocket.

NINE

When Varallo left the bar, he walked back for his car and drove out San Rafael to Novallo Avenue, and all the way down it to the edge of town where the Zacchios lived. No zoning laws in particular: as he'd said to Jesse, just tacit gentlemen's agreements. Three or four sections where the residents with foreign names who went to St. Mary's lived; other areas where other people lived. Several much shabbier streets than this, districts needing a closer police eye, where the other people lived—but those, the lowest order of the others, the ones like Gina Pozzo (only worse), the drunks, the irresponsibles, the worthless ones.

These houses weren't anything fancy, but most of them were less than fifteen years old, cheaper copies of the ranch-type homes nearer into town. Zacchio worked for Harry Agrado at the lumberyard and made union wages: maybe eighty a week take-home pay. As most of the householders along here did—average wage. But with six kids still at home, the monthly payments on the house, and the prices of everything the way they were now, there wouldn't be much left over for luxuries. They were probably paying on time for furniture too; maybe a refrigerator, a stove, a T.V.

There was a patch of lawn in front of the house, and one of the kids was mowing it. Long, dry, brown grass; they'd be chary of the water bill to keep it green in the hot season, of course. One of the boys, looked about ten, weedy youngster, making heavy weather of pushing the old lawn mower.

Varallo walked up the cracked cement drive to him. "Hello there— you'd be Gregorio?" He tried to remember names when he could.

The boy stopped. "Yes, sir, Captain Varallo."

"Your father here? He doesn't work Saturdays, does he?"

"No, sir, but he's not here, he's to the church." Grateful for the little excuse to stop work, prolonging it: "He'll be home pretty soon, I guess. I—I'd be out on my paper route regular, but he made me quit." Bursting out with a vengeance on the first person handy, with what was in his mind, regardless of relevance. "Said on account I got bad marks at school, I wasn't studyin' hard enough, and I better not do the paper route any more, on account it took too much time. It isn't *fair*—is it, Captain Varallo? I had almost enough for a new bike, I mean I *would've* by Christmas—sixteen dollars I had. It's not *fair*, I do too study."

"Well," said Varallo. He sat down on the bottom step of the porch and pushed his hat back from his forehead. "Schoolwork's important too, Gregorio. Tell you what. It does seem too bad you shouldn't have that bike. I'd like somebody to wash my car once a week—job I don't like to do myself, you see. Could you do that maybe? On Saturdays? I'd pay you a dollar every time, is that O.K.?"

"Oh, gee, yes, sir, Captain Varallo. I do a real good job for you."

"Well, then, that's a deal. You come to the station Saturday afternoons. Come today after you've finished cutting the lawn, O.K.? Now, I've got a couple of questions I want to ask you, Gregorio. As long as your father isn't here maybe you can answer them. You were home the night your mother died, weren't you? Of course. I know it was a pretty bad time for all of you, but you know, somebody did a bad thing to her that made her die, and we want to find out who that was, so it won't happen to anybody else."

"Yes, sir," said the boy in a low voice, looking down again. "I know. But—but you arrested somebody—and—"

"Well, you see, we're not just sure that we arrested the right person, Gregorio. And you know, policemen are public servants—if you understand me— We're here to protect everybody from bad people who do things like this, not the way maybe some of your friends think, that we just like to boss people around and be mean to them. Good policemen aren't like that. It's like any other kind of job, we like to do it as well as we can. The way you just told me you'd do a real good job on my car—and the way your father tries to do an honest day's work for Mr. Agrado. You see?"

"Yes, sir, sure."

"You might say in a kind of way I'm working for your father, just the way he works for Mr. Agrado. Your father pays taxes on this house, and it's out of the town tax money I get paid for being a police-man. So your house doesn't get burglarized, or if it does, the burglar gets caught—and so whoever did this bad thing to your mother gets caught too, you see?"

"Yes, sir, I see."

"I know you don't like thinking about it, that time your mother was so sick and died, but I want you to try to help me, and remember. She had a bad fever, you know when people have a fever they don't talk very sensible, do they? Did you hear some of what she said, that time?"

"Yes, sir. I—and Lucia and Johnny was sort of round the door—to the bedroom. *Padre* wouldn't let us in to see her when she come home—"

"No. What did you hear her say?"

"About—about a little dog on Antonia's bedspread— That was sort of funny, wasn't it? Antonia don't like dogs—and—and she *wanted* to see us, sir, she said all our names— She kept saying our names, over 'n' over—and—about a smell that made her feel sick, somebody was paint-ing and the smell made her sick—and—how Antonia oughtn't to've done something, it was a sin. I—it was kind of scary, hearing—"

"Yes," said Varallo. He stood up. "You try not to think about it any more, Gregorio. *Grazie*, that's all I wanted to ask you. You come along to the station, two o'clock, O.K.?"

"I do a real good job, Captain," said the boy after him.

And, belatedly, the same thought had occurred to him that Jesse had had. The name. This little thing so ordinary nobody had thought twice about it. Of course, the other side would have a ready explana-tion: would there be anything useful to bringing it up at all?

It was eleven o'clock. Car back at the station at two, for the boy to polish. He drove out west of town, to Joe Cambiare's farm.

The farmhouse had been built about thirty years ago by a Swede from North Dakota, old man Swenson, and he'd built it the way they built farmhouses back there, for a different climate—a rectangular box, and originally the barn had been attached, so that in winter with the snow deep a farmer could get to his stock without going outdoors. Somebody—the Cambiare uncle?—had knocked out the room between, separated the big barn with its upper story for grain storage, but you could still see the outline of the foundation. It was a good-sized house, seven or eight rooms, because the Swede had had a big family.

Varallo walked around to the back. Cambiare was squatting at the foot of the three narrow wooden steps up to the kitchen door, nailing down a loose board; he dropped his hammer and stood up. "Why, hello, Cap'n," he said.

Another one very much like Gonzales, except that he wasn't a drunk, reflected Varallo. Weak, immature, willing and honest enough, but not quite grown-up, or aggressive in any way: needing the firm hand to push and guide him, and without much doubt he had it from Antonia.

"Mrs. Cambiare around? I'd like to talk to her."

"Oh, sure—sure, she's in the kitchen, Cap'n, jus' go right in—careful o' the step, sir, 'at's right, don't want the law suin' me for damages, do I— Go right in, sir—"

As he put his hand on the door, it occurred to Varallo absently that the few times he'd had any talk with Cambiare before this business, Cambiare had never bothered to call him sir. He stepped into the enclosed back porch; there was no door between that and the big, square kitchen, and he faced Antonia across an old-fashioned long trestle table, rough, unstained wood. She was stuffing a plucked hen, careless and hurried, with jabs of a wooden spoon. The Sunday fowl.

"Morning," he said.

She glanced up at him with no particular expression. "If it isn't Captain Varallo. What are you doing here?"

"Ask you a few questions, if you don't mind." He leaned in the doorway of the porch, watching her.

"Why should I mind? What about?"

"About this same business."

Her hands paused in their work; she was startled, surprised at that; her eyes narrowed on him. "Miss Varney and all? That's all done with, isn't it? I mean, they all said she was guilty like everybody knows and—"

"It's not all done by a long way. Because she's not guilty, and her lawyer's still looking for facts to prove it—and so am I. The verdict will be appealed, you know—the whole thing will come up again and be thrashed out in the appellate court—"

"What's that?"

"The court that hears appeals."

"I don't know nothing about that," she said, as if that disposed of the matter. "Jury found her guilty, nobody can change that—that's the law."

"Not always." Not a stupid woman by any means: ignorant, maybe, here and there. But a basic cunning, a certain shrewdness. This close, as he'd thought before, he could believe the reputation she'd had—one kind of crude, earthy appeal, though she wasn't pretty. Buxom female, and her waist hadn't thickened yet; coarse features, coarse, tangled black hair, but her mouth sensual under too much dark-red lipstick.

"You mean we all got to go to some court *again* and do it all over? What a waste o' time! Don't seem very sensible to me, when everybody knows—"

"Maybe, maybe not," he said. "Some questions."

"Go ahead, ask what you please, I got nothing to hide. Don't know what more I could say. I told what I seen and know before, it don't change now."

"You told this and that, yes. You said you heard your mother say *Nell Varney* when she was dying. She said it like that, both names?"

"I *said* so, yes."

"Had you known either of Miss Varney's names before then?"

"No call to. I wasn't in the bank much. I told about that too—I didn't like to say was the woman I'd seen this Miss Varney—like *Padre* and Maria said it was—until I'd gone and looked at her. Then I saw she was."

"Yes. How do you suppose your mother knew her first name? . . . Yes, the last one she knew from the bank, but not the first. She'd never have occasion to hear that."

"Look, she was *with* her two-three days, wasn't she? Getting rid o' the baby and being sick, until that girl saw she was going to die and wanted get shut of her—" Yes, of course, and that was the obvious answer they'd all have. But even so—could you visualize a professional abortionist, Nell or another woman, coming out all chatty and friendly, Just call me Nell?—or Mary or Kate or— A purely business relationship, after all . . .

"No, I don't think she was," he said pleasantly. "Are you and your husband members of the dairy association again?"

"What brings that up, anyhow? No, we're not— I can't be bothered, all their rules an' regulations."

"So this is one of your own hens?"

"Sure—" She was quick on the trigger; she got what he meant the next second, and laughed. "You're thinkin' about how Mama said, that time, ask me where I got such good fryers. No rule about it, Captain, times I take one of our old biddies, save money, and times I buy a better one, nice young bird, like for a special occasion."

"I see."

"Nor I don't waste no money on masses either. Me, I believe what I can see an' feel, don't know how nobody can find out or know any other way. Masses go up to heaven, they say—that I can't see—but the money, I see where that goes, all right! I don't just see how *my* doing this or that can help Mama now—nor I don't think God'd be all that hard on her just on account she didn't want 'nother brat to look after. The priests don't know everything—that I do know—don't know how it is bein' a woman with a dozen kids and no money. Change their minds quick enough if they could for a week, I say. Catch me filling this old barn of a place with kids— I got more sense. Day Joe's uncle gets buried and Joe gets his money, we're off for Fresno or Santa Barbara, somewhere in town—no more farmhouses for me!"

"And maybe you're using good sense at that," said Varallo. He looked at her a minute more and then added an abrupt thanks and went out. Cambiare was over by the chicken yard now, doing something to the wire fence; he watched Varallo, sideways, all the way back to the Chevy.

What did I come out here for? Varallo wondered to himself. And what did I get? He felt vaguely that he'd got something, but he wasn't sure what it was. Hens, he thought. Little dogs. Bedspreads . . . Nuances: sure, Antonia in hysterics, grieving for her mother—only an hour after the woman died. This was four weeks and four days later. People were like that.

Phone calls. Tasso.

Laura . . .

TEN

"Paint?" said Jesse. "*Paint*. First we've heard of that, isn't it? Somebody was painting something and the smell made her sick." He slid down lower in the one armchair in Varallo's bare hotel room and stared at the opposite wall.

"Look, that might have been six months before—impossible to link it up, if it means anything at all. I just mentioned it. What I *have* got is more—"

"Maybe. Maybe. Nice if we knew what's important and what isn't. As it is, it'd make a fine Dali mural— I can almost see it. Little German dog and the Sunday fowl cuddled up on the best bedspread, dog reading the paper with the picture, Antonia in background brooding over a paintbrush made out of the fowl's feathers—priest shaking a finger at her and holding copy of the marriage service, Cambiare cavorting around wearing collar and leash filched from the dog—all very spirited—"

"You need a drink," said Varallo, and slid off the bed, rummaged in a drawer and produced a bottle of brandy and two tumblers.

"Not that big a drink," said Jesse, eying them. "Your elegant gent's liquor is wasted on me—just a little one. Yes. *Paint,* of all things . . . Tasso didn't get to Bakersfield until later than he should have. He checked into the hotel at two-fifteen—they don't really care, apparently, what time you check in, but do keep a record of checking out because of the deadline, so there's a dividing line on the register, A.M. and P.M., and they note the time automatically. That is, he wouldn't pay extra for checking in before one-thirty, so he wasn't late for that reason. Salesman's stopping place—must have a lot who'd want to check in early, dump their stuff, freshen up to call on customers. Usually a full house, I'd say, and I'd also think he'd want to make sure of a room as soon as he hit town. He didn't. I don't know what else he was doing instead—not calling on customers."

"Really?" said Varallo slowly. "I wonder if that means anything. Now I'll tell you something else funny. He said he was on his way back to the hotel that night when Zacchio hailed him, and that was at approximately nine-fifteen. I don't know yet if he had any calls at the hotel. I just—started a follow-up—on that today. Tomorrow, maybe. But I asked Carlo—night desk man—if he'd had any visitors after nine-thirty, if he remembered. Carlo remembered because Tasso stopped at the desk to say he'd be checking out first thing in the morning, and paid his bill then. He further remembered the time, because he'd been keeping an eye on Ricky Blunt, the new bellhop, who evidently doesn't like to work very hard— He'd just sent him upstairs for something and was going to bawl him out if he was over ten minutes. This, I didn't ask for—he came out with it—it was just ten-twenty-five when Tasso came in, stopped at the desk and went upstairs."

Jesse sat up halfway. "You don't say. About an hour later than he implied. Wonder what he was doing. Why nothing on the phone calls? The switchboard operator here—"

Varallo shook his head. "No good. Sure, most of the rooms with phones, it's the usual arrangement, through a switchboard. But there are six or seven rooms like this one they rent by the month, and those have their own phones, separate numbers. And as it happens, Tasso had one of them that couple of days he was here— They were painting or something on the other two floors."

"Just by chance. I see. And funny as it looks, you know, I wonder if there's anything in this at all for me? Just one little discrepancy in testimony—one little mistake—*something* definite to give the appellate court, all I ask. I don't think I'm so hot as a detective—and even if I was, if I found the right female, ten chances to one there'd be nothing to prove she was, instead of Nell. Have to bully a confession out of her in front of witnesses to get anything legal to show the bench. Yes. In your little exchange with Antonia, all cozy over the trussed chicken—"

"Hen."

"—Did she at any time refer to it as a fowl?"

"What's so important about the fowl? No, as a matter of fact, I don't think she did."

"Um," said Jesse. "It's a long shot—a very long shot. . . . What? Well, did you ever stop to ruminate on names? All sorts of funny ones, and all sorts of names too we take for granted, think of as ordinary, without thinking where they come from and why. Take Falkenstein. Sounds better in English—Falconstone. Like a lot of others, dates from the time the law decided we all had to have legal surnames like Christians, and people named themselves sort of at random after all sorts of things—wild animals and mountains and rivers and so on. What's Varallo mean in Italian?"

"It doesn't mean anything, it's just a name— There's a town called Varallo somewhere—"

"Where some of your ancestors came from, there you are. And English names—Anglo-Saxon in general—a lot of them were trades originally, you know. Fletcher—arrow maker. Chaloner—blanket maker. Hunter—huntsman. Miller—miller. And so on."

"Are you just showing off erudite knowledge, or what?"

"Dropping hints to Watson, like all good detectives." Jesse stood up by degrees. "Or maybe woolgathering . . . Wonder where Varney came from. Odd sort of name— Norman, maybe. I'm going home to bed. A hundred-and-sixty-mile drive in this weather—"

When he got downstairs to the street he was mildly interested to notice that Contera was still up and about, as it had been at nine-thirty when he arrived. It was only a little after ten now, but by that time—judging from last night—the place would usually be dark and silent as the grave. However, this was Saturday night. The ordinary shops were closed, but the two drugstores, the bars, the movie house, a couple of sandwich counters were still open; there were a good many cars in the street and people on the sidewalk.

He'd parked across the street, the only space left then; he glanced both ways automatically—couple of cars coming a safe distance away in the next block—and stepped off the curb. He was halfway across the street when a car came down the side street behind him and turned onto Main; its headlights flashed brilliant white across the store front opposite him there, for just a second, as it made the turn.

Jesse stopped in his tracks and dropped his car keys. "Well, I will be damned!" he said aloud.

A car swerved desperately around him at the last moment and its driver yelled at him angrily. He pulled himself together, picked up the keys, and gained the sidewalk. A building standing alone here, it was, gas station to one side, empty lot to the other. Some kind of window display—cans stacked in a pyramid, a big placard. And streaming across the front, above the awning, white letters against a dark background—

WM. SATTERLEE—PAINT—WALLPAPER—VARNISH—STAINS
HOME DECORATING SERVICE

"I will be damned," he said to the window display. "Varnish. I wonder what it *does* smell like."

But the commission to the clipping agency, private deductions about Teresa Zacchio's ramblings, about the real setup here on the real guilty party—that was all extracurricular. He wasn't a detective, he was a lawyer; very salutary if he could solve the case and produce the right woman, but he was more urgently concerned with finding something to give the appeal judges. He could dream up something on the prejudiced-witness business, but not to hold water: not under examination.

The verdict hadn't been one very sensibly arrived at, but how many verdicts were? Hard to figure, for one thing, how the jury could have put much faith in Mrs. Inver or the Prices. When Mrs. Inver, as common sense showed, must have seen Nell in that interval between Carol's death and Mrs. Zacchio's, hadn't identified her, but was now so sure. When the Prices, also so sure, had waited all that time to make a connection between that car and the crime. Not at all logical, but that you couldn't count on with juries. Ever. And nothing in that to complain to the appellate court about: jury hadn't technically gone against the evidence.

Something to point to definitely, be able to show the trial—and by implication the verdict—invalid.

Mrs. Inver and Brant . . . He sat facing her, the next afternoon (Sunday morning worthless: practically everybody righteously at church), in her big, cool, conventionally appointed living room, and reflected that one of the nuisances about it was that most of the people concerned were honest, upright citizens. Just either confused or stubborn.

"Doesn't it strike you as just a little odd, Mrs. Inver—when you stop to think about it—that a young woman like Miss Varney should have been running an abortion mill for a year or so, in this small a town, without being suspected? Or haven't you thought about it?"

"Of course, I've thought about it," she said sharply. "Haven't I had reason? My only child—all I had—"

"Yes. But, you know, it doesn't quite make sense, looked at fairly. Ordinary sense ought to show that in that respectable a neighborhood, houses pretty close either side, and in one of them Mrs. Price—need I say more?—it'd have been a difficult business to carry on in secret. Miss Varney'd never been in any kind of trouble before—never even had a traffic ticket. It's the kind of business that does a lot better in a city—more prospective clients, you know—and yet all the while she lived down in L.A. she never tried it. Only when she moved to Contera—"

"How do you know? And I must say I find that a—an offensively flippant way of discussing such a— Just because she wasn't found out before! But I've thought too, perhaps it wasn't until after her father'd died that she—she started—"

"Oh, you *have* thought about it," said Jesse. "But not very logically, Mrs. Inver. You hinted in your statements, and said something to the same effect on the stand—as did Mr. and Mrs. Price—that perhaps Dr. Varney had been in it with her, or the other way round. That it wasn't until he died and she carried on alone that she got into trouble, not knowing enough about taking care of her patients. You can't have it both ways, you know. Either he was in it or not. And a couple of little things about both the cases suggest that it'd have been rather awkward for one person alone to handle. There was your daughter's car, for instance—driven out of town and abandoned. How d'you suppose she managed that alone? Walked back ten miles? Nobody remembers giving a ride to a hitchhiker at the time it must have been done."

"I don't know, and I can't see that it matters. After all, the evidence—"

"There's evidence and evidence. I've done some puzzling over that car myself—it's a suggestive point. Did you know the name of the person arrested before you were taken to identify her?"

"Yes, Mr. Brant—" She stopped. "You tricked me into saying that! You kept trying in court to— I—"

"So I did," said Jesse. "Let's use a little common sense here, Mrs. Inver. This isn't a game, and the trial wasn't a game, with points scored for me or Mr. Burkhart and added up at the end—opponents trying to trick each other about what cards they hold, and shaking hands and forgetting it when the game's over. You're not a stupid woman, and it must have crossed your mind that I had some reason for pressing you about that, besides showing myself to the jury as a smart boy. Now there aren't any witnesses here, and I can't do much with those three little words you just said. You're the one to do something with them, Mrs. Inver. Because I think you're an honest woman, and while it's understandable that you feel vindictive toward whoever it was who killed your daughter, on the one hand you want the right person found and punished, and on the other you've got nothing against Nell Varney if she isn't that person, no personal reason to dislike her, victimize her. If you'll think about what you just admitted, that you knew who was under grave suspicion of the crimes before you made the identification, I think you'll realize—looking back—that you'd been unwittingly briefed by Chief Brant as to what Miss Varney looks like. That you knew he was convinced she was guilty, presumably on good evidence, and that he more or less described her to you."

"That's an outrageous accusation! Really I cannot—" She stood up pointedly.

"Not an accusation. I don't for a minute think you connived with him to make a false identification. I just think he was a little less discreet than he should have been—because he was so firmly convinced himself—and confused you, which you didn't realize at the time. If you'll go over it in detail, Mrs. Inver, I think you'll realize now—if you're honest about it—that, for one little thing, you knew before you got to the station that day, to look at that parade of young women, that Nell Varney, the one accused, had long hair worn in a big knot— and there was only one of those women who did, so you knew her right away. That the brief look you had, last March, at the woman who brought your daughter home wasn't really a very good look, but that you did have a glimpse of a big knot of hair—*or* a false chignon fastened on—and that's what registered with you and largely prompted your identification of Miss Varney." He got up and looked at her thoughtfully: yes, nice-looking woman for her age, young-looking, pretty in that fair Scandinavian way. "I wouldn't say this if I thought you were dishonest, you know. You said in court you didn't know Miss Varney, hadn't ever spoken to her. I wish you would. Go in to the county jail and ask to visit her— Talk to her a little. And—"

"How you could *suggest*—! The woman who—"

"But she wasn't, you know. She didn't. Don't know if you're a very religious woman, Mrs. Inver—"

"I attend the Presbyterian Church," she said coldly.

"Yes, well, doesn't much matter—any religion you can name's got things to say about tolerance and charity and honesty. *And* slander. Things a lot of people forget all about the other six days a week. But if all that means anything to you, I'll just ask you to think about it. Examine your conscience, another thing all religions advocate. And maybe, if you will, just keep in mind a little proverb possibly not familiar to you—think it's from the Talmud, wouldn't swear to it—*To slander is to commit murder*. They did pass the death sentence on her, if you remember." He took up his hat and went out. She made no move to accompany him politely to the door; his last look, she was still standing there rigid, looking down at the thick-piled brown carpet.

He came out to the curving drive under the Chinese elms, the sweep of velvet lawn, and put on his hat, and got into the Ford. He thought, Well, done what I could, anyway. And what's that other one Uncle likes?— *Whether we accomplish much good or little good, the Almighty will reward us in accordance with our righteous intentions.*

Not altogether a comforting reflection. Rather have something concrete right now. Personally he felt more akin to old Omar than the sententious Rabbi Jochanan—*take the Cash, and let the Credit go.*

Well, time would tell. He turned out of the driveway and ambled along the curving street; he wasn't too certain of his directions yet in town, and presently discovered that he must have turned the wrong way, because he was going out into the country. Sunset Drive, the one exclusive residential street in Contera, ran north-south above the main town, and to get back there he should, he realized, have turned left. He wandered on for a while looking for a turn leading the right way, and got entirely out of town—fields with anonymous green crops, scattered farmhouses, little dirt tracks leading up to them, and—ah—a black-top road. He turned into it. This was rolling country, pleasant (if you liked the country) and green—in the dim distance northeast, on a clear day, a hint on the horizon of the majestic Sierra Nevadas, but closer, just rises and dips in the land contour.

About a mile farther on, the road took a sharp left turn. He came round it and saw ahead something that surprised and interested him so much that he stopped the car right where he was.

Off to the right there was a farm, and whatever little track led to it must be on the other side, because there were just ramshackle fences and fields leading up to it here. What was interesting was the house. Rectangular, no particular color—weathered gray—but at one end of it, or almost at one end, there was a kind of superstructure of upper story, and the whole thing looked remarkably like a boat with a deck cabin rising from it.

Always thought it was a funny house: Carol Inver.

And the other funny thing, there was something familiar about it. He had seen it before, but—

Revelations, he thought. He sat there in the middle of the road and slowly, thoughtfully, got out a cigarette and lit it, looking at the house. His day for revelations. A few breaks at last? A little luck coming his way?

That was the Cambiare farmhouse. It didn't have a second story, but seen from this angle, on this road, that big two-story barn so close to it stuck up behind and to the side, and unless you looked twice, you didn't see what it really was. Looked very much like the super-structure on a boat. *Thing on top like a cabin on a boat* . . . So Carol Inver had said.

Well, now, fancy that, he thought. Carol Inver, coming from Sunset Drive, coming along this road. Often? He'd placed where he was, vaguely, now: this road ran down to join the main highway, and along that, outside of town proper, were a couple of the more fashionable restaurants, the newest small shopping section, and the golf course. Carol—had she played golf? Never seen this house from another aspect, maybe: from the road where the farm track led off, up to the house. Glancing at it, around this curve, seeing a house with a thing on top like the cabin on a boat. Very likely if she *had* seen it from the other road, never identifying it as the same.

Carol Inver—oh, yes—nice conventional girl, growing up in Contera, belonging to the upper class of money and Protestantism. Nice, kind girl probably—like her mother, no violent, on-the-surface prejudices; honest, democratic American citizen—everybody due rights and privileges, *but*, our kind just doesn't have much to do with their kind—sure —so, would Carol Inver have known the Cambiares' name? So much as that?

Trying—vaguely, confusedly, the high fever slowing her mental processes—to answer a question penetrating dimly to her dying mind . . . Mumbling all she knew, remembered? Maybe more there to have come out, after that disjointed phrase about the house, about a woman's hair—maybe something about *Trust Mame,* a little dog, a fowl? But nothing wrong with Carol Inver's heart, and Burnett giving her a sedative injection . . .

Now I do wonder, thought Jesse. He finished the cigarette, contemplating this view of the Cambiare farmhouse, and drove on past it to town.

ELEVEN

But a couple of hours later found him back on Sunset Drive, the other end from Mrs. Inver's house, walking up the drive of a big, two-story, brick house. Halfway up the drive was parked a middle-aged MG roadster, and a young fellow in just khaki shorts and a nice tan was polishing it industriously. He looked up with a scowl as Jesse's shadow fell on him; the scowl deepened when he saw who it was.

"Afternoon, Mr. Bennett," said Jesse.

"And what do you want?" asked Jackie Bennett.

Jesse leaned one hip on the fender of the MG. "I don't know why everybody around here gives me such nasty, suspicious looks. I'm just trying to do my job. Far as I can make out, there isn't even the excuse that Nell Varney was actively disliked by most people— She never knew many people in Contera. No reason I can see why none of you want to give her the benefit of the doubt—or another chance. Unless, of course—if *I* had a suspicious mind I might jump to that conclusion— some of you are using her for a scapegoat."

"What the hell d'you mean by that?" Bennett straightened up, glowering. He was a hefty youngster, not quite as tall as Jesse but broad-built and well-muscled. Probably popular at home and at school, Jesse thought: football type. Be starting his third year at U.C.L.A. next week, he remembered; getting the MG in shape for the drive down. The kind of nice, healthy-looking young fellow everybody took pride in as typical American youth, the hope of the country. Athlete: not so hot at his schoolwork maybe—*or* the kind, a ball of fire at something mechanical, tangible, mathematics or engineering, and wouldn't know John Donne or Richard Strauss from a hole in the ground. Fine, rugged specimen: all that sissy stuff for the weak sisters. Very typical.

And what harm? Well, if the fathers who boasted about them stopped to think, they might admit that an ounce of understanding people (which meant imagination) was worth several pounds of brawn in getting along in life, and nobody develops much empathy practicing for track hurdles or spelling out the articles in *Popular Sports*.

"I'm just speculating," he said gently to Bennett. "Lawyer's job isn't finished when a trial's over, not always, you know. Right now I'm looking around collecting material to give the appellate court, and one very helpful piece of information—if I can get it—would be something to say who the other one was. The woman who's really guilty, you know."

"Look, I don't know anything about all this, damn it. I never did. I don't know this Varney woman, it's nothing to me if she's guilty or innocent— If she isn't guilty, that's too bad, that's all. But nobody can tie me up to any part of it. Varallo tried that before—maybe he's given you the same idea— Well, you can go peddle your papers somewhere else, see?"

"Didn't have nothing to do with it and don't know nothing," murmured Jesse. "Didn't get the girl friend in trouble, didn't know a name or a phone number to put her in touch with an obliging abortionist."

"I did not," said Bennett; he was still immature enough to flush a little. "Listen, I don't pretend to be an angel, but—but I'm about fed up with all this hinting and— Mrs. Inver not even saying hello to my mother on the street any more, and, my God, even Mother and Dad thinking— Just because I'd gone around with Carol some! So all right, sure I had! But—you want to *know*, one reason I've been so damn mad about it—*I* thought she wasn't that kind of girl, see. I kissed her a couple times but I never made another move at her—that's God's truth—because I just didn't think it'd be worthwhile, if you get me. And then I find out she's laid down for somebody else—and everybody says it's me! I can say no for the next year— I been saying it for six months—and I might just as well bat my brains out running at a stone wall! I—"

"That so?" said Jesse. "You know something, Mr. Bennett? Against all the evidence, I believe you. Thanks very much." He turned and walked back to his car. Backgrounds, he thought. Just facing people in court, the formal atmosphere, the set rules about relevance—you could never get the whole picture. And Varallo: a good man, an honest cop and no fool, but maybe very ready to think Jackie Bennett was a liar

because he was the son of the local state congressman and upper-crust
Protestant. Not a conscious thing, of course: Vic wouldn't realize that.

Clues to follow, fun and games, yoicks and away. Find the fellow
who *had* put Carol in the market for an abortionist, and maybe he'd
been the one to know where to send her. (But she'd paid for it.) Yes.
Seven hundred bucks. Damn the awful discretion of bankers: Carol
had drawn out that seven hundred in cash, but Adamson hadn't asked
her anything about it. Not that you expected a teller to ask what you
wanted cash for, but even for a young girl who had a more than generous allowance, seven hundred bucks in one fell swoop— And Adamson had known her all her life, was a friend of the family. He might
have given her a fatherly beam and asked, *A new car, my dear, or
some bauble for your mother's birthday?* But, no, he preserved the
discretion. Not, of course, that she'd have told him anything anyway. . . .

And absolutely nothing there for the appellate court. So, O.K., find
the right one; how could you prove it? A lot of abortionists here and
there, and this one might be in New York or Miami by now. He rather
thought, anyway, she wasn't in Contera any more.

It made a loose kind of pattern, an imaginative reconstruction of the
real setup—on the little indications they had. Somebody coming here,
about a year ago, and lying very low. Somewhere. For some reason. A
woman who wore her hair like Nell, and that was every last thing he
knew about her for sure. A woman who drove a little car that at first
glance looked something like a baby Renault. A woman whose name
might be— A woman, maybe, who had a little German dog? Keeping
herself to herself, could you say *hiding out?* Could you say, carrying
on an undercover business she'd practiced in more lucrative surroundings?

And that idle gossip about Dr. Varney; that might suggest another
little deduction. The talk that it wasn't until Nell tried to carry on
alone, after the doctor died, that she got into trouble and lost a couple
of patients. Could it be that not Nell but somebody else had had that
experience?

This woman. Oh, tempting—on such tiny nuances!—to think, on the
run from trouble somewhere else. No evidence at all, just vivid imagination, saying maybe—having lost a former partner in the business? Or
another undercover business. Lost him, her, or it to the police? Hiding
out. Why Contera? Just at random? And eventually getting into trou-

ble here (because she hadn't known quite as much as the partner?) and running on, after Teresa Zacchio had died. Place getting a little too hot for her then.

It made a nice, rounded story, and there was no evidence on it at all, and as for interesting the bench of the appellate court—well, go back to law school, my boy, he thought mournfully.

He drove back downtown and found Varallo's office empty; tried the hotel and drew blank there. So he retired to Nell's house and tried the radio. It might be, he thought, that one reason he hadn't showed much brilliance in this thing so far was that he was a hundred and eighty-five miles away from his automatic phonograph and all his records. He found Bach, for instance, very stimulating to the mental processes; in the course of working out a case for court he had been known to sit motionless listening to *The Art of the Fugue* for six hours straight, without consciously hearing a note of it.

All the radio offered him, gushingly highbrow, was a rebroadcast of the Metropolitan Opera and Wagner. He turned it off hastily and sat thinking in silence.

"Four o'clock Sund'y afternoon, you must be hotter 'n a firecracker, Captain," she greeted him from the dressing table. "*Che tipo*—what a man!"

"Don't flatter me, Gina," he grinned at her in the speckled mirror. "Official business."

Her eyes narrowed and she swung round to him. "What about?"

"*Non dubiti*—don't worry, nothing much. I don't think." Varallo sat down on the foot of the bed and considered her absently for a minute. Maybe the first basic problem for policemen, this business, and there just wasn't any set answer. Among the puritans and the passionate and the money-grubbers the other side of the law, and the law itself, and another thing they called human nature, what were you going to do about it? To some extent, like a lot of other things, it came back to the individual; and in this case, to individual places.

The compromise he made, as a cop in Contera, might be a good one or a bad one, depending how you looked at it. The point was it was a workable one; and he'd had differences with the two police chiefs he'd served under, but all of them had agreed on that. You had to live with realities here and now.

There they were, Gina Pozzo and the three girls who shared this ramshackle house at the edge of town. In a town like Contera, it was a different thing and they were different kind of women than you got in the cities: there, you couldn't compromise, because it was the syndicate thing, big-time, a lot of the women victimized and exploited, and all too often tied up to other big criminal businesses, dope and crooked gambling. No question there: a straightforward problem.

But here, nothing like that. Three of these women, including Gina, came from around here, probably hadn't been fifty miles away in their lives; the other one had drifted in from much the same sort of community. You could say, the old-fashioned kind: just careless, indolent women who made a scratch living the easiest way, didn't have very high personal standards about anything—but, so to speak, in business for themselves. No underworld connections, no dope, no number tickets. Just plain sex.

There they were, and in a town like Contera, wasn't it a hell of a lot better to know *who* they were and keep an eye on them? Chase them off for medical examination once in a while and so on? It made sense to him, anyway; and not just because he'd climbed the back stairs here himself and paid for some of the Dago red Gina liked.

"No trouble?" she said.

"No trouble."

"Well, in that case," and she got up, dropping the lipstick, and came to the table by the bed to fill a couple of glasses. He didn't want the thin, sharp wine, but he took it with a nod.

"This murder business . . . No, not all finished, until we get the right one. How much do you know about it—been following the papers?"

She shook her head. "Not much. I was kind of interested at first, you know—that girl, that kind of job an' all, right under ever'body's noses! Like I told you when that Inver girl died and you come askin' around—well, might think I'd be the first one to hear all about a deal like that, but I never. Don't think I ever even heard there *was* a deal like that to be had in town—and in a kind of way, why *would* I? Only girls around here'd be looking for *that*, they'd be the nicey-nice girls, wouldn't they?—like that Inver one. Little innocents—you know."

"That's so."

"You don't think that girl from the bank *was* the one? . . . Well, I don't know nothing about it," and she shrugged. "Like I say, I heard some about it, an' I seen one paper when the thing at the county seat

started, but I got better ways of passin' the time than readin' papers."
She laughed, refilled her glass, sat beside him on the bed. "Why?"

"Tasso," said Varallo. "Giacomo Tasso. You know him—"

"Sure I know him. From a long time back. Times he's passin'
through town, he drops in. Sometimes."

"Just sometimes? Well, he's pushing fifty, isn't he? When—"

"What's that got to do with it?" She grinned. "Tasso isn't ready for
the grave yet. But he's got a private girl in town, didn't you know?
Leastways, little bit more private than us here! Or so I understand, if
you get me. That Antonia Cambiare. Might call it competition, kind
of. . . . Oh, just talk, you know—fellows that come in, and we do go
into town now 'n' then, get to hear things. I figure maybe that one
married that fellow kind of as cover, you know?—talk there's been
about her— She took up with Tasso 'fore she got married, well, he's
got some money, and—while he's not ready to die like I said—he isn't
young as he was nor he wasn't ever no movie star, an' could be he's
ready to give out a little to a girl butters him up some—nice little presents an' so on."

"That could be," agreed Varallo. "The talk is he's still tied up with
her? Husband knowing or not?"

"Who knows?" She shrugged and finished her wine. "I just heard a
little something about it—from the oldest Reyes kid, I think it was. If
you're interested, now I think about it, must be the husband don't
know, because like I say Tasso does come here sometimes, see. Not so
often, but maybe the times he can't get at his own girl."

"Yes." Varallo looked down at the little red circle of wine thoughtfully. "Well, the last time Tasso was in town he did drop in here. I
know because I asked him, and he said so. It was the night of August
first."

"I don't pay no attention to dates."

"The night Mrs. Zacchio was brought home and died."

"Oh—that night. Yes, sure, I do remember. Ever'body talkin' about
it the next day. Sure. He was here that night."

"With which of you?"

"Me, matter o' fact."

"When did he come and when did he leave, or do you know?"

Gina yawned, set down her glass, and lay back on the bed. "Have
to think. That night . . . Mmh . . . Oh, do I remember! Sure—sure!"
She began to shake with laughter. "Per Dio, what a row there was!

See, Johnny Novak, he finds out his boy Rex is here— Why, Rex been droppin' in here two years, since he got into high school—an' you'd'a thought it was Judgment Day! Novak comes in roarin' like a bull, and *language*— Well, it was something! Hauled Rex out like a little kid caught smokin' behind the barn or something, an' callin' us every name in the book. An' the way I remember is, he kept sayin' to Rex—it was a scream, really, Captain!—*You're supposed to be in bed by nine o'clock, you young rascal!*—an' Cara she spoke right up at him an' says, Well, he *was!* An' Novak—"

"Yes, very funny. The time then—"

"It was five minutes past ten, I remember lookin' at the clock—kind of automatic, way you do when somebody says— An' see, Tasso'd been just on his way out, but Novak comes bustin' in like that—five, ten minutes before he dragged Rex off— I suppose it'd have been about a quarter past when Tasso did leave, an' he'd been here maybe an hour."

TWELVE

"So there's your something for the appeal—with a vengeance," he said to Jesse twenty minutes later.

"Oh, very nice—very nice indeed. This I like. He was so *damn* positive, you know—protesting too much. No finesse. So now it seems he was the little man who wasn't there."

"And you can't use it," said Varallo. He took the drink Jesse handed him and sat down on Nell's sagging old couch. "Or if you do, *amico*, you precipitate a minor earthquake in this town and throw me out of a job—and, of course, Brant. Probably. Look, it's common sense—you can't outlaw human nature entirely. The Ginas, in a town like this it's better to know who and where they are, keep an eye on them. We're not corrupt cops letting Gina and her girls alone for a kickback—it isn't the big-town thing. And you know all the jokes about little towns, everybody knowing everybody else's business—to some extent, *è vero*," and he shrugged, "but again you get right back to social classes. A lot of the people in this town, and the people who are pretty important too—like Mrs. Inver, and the Bennetts, and His Honor Mayor Cardew—they'd go straight up in the air if it came out that we've got, *Dio mio*, whores in our midst!—*and* that the police tolerate them! So many people look at these things in black and white, you know. You can fill in for yourself," and he sampled his highball.

"That serious? That important?"

"It could be, probably would be. Black and white, as I say. First place, any little town this far away from a big town, you can figure it on the average about twenty-five years behind in general social culture. More important, how many civilians in any sized town know much about the realities cops have to cope with? Like a bunch of idealistic teen-agers, not four cents' worth of common horse sense in the lot. Such things shouldn't be, it's against the letter of the law, so the cops who compromise on it are obviously crooked cops. You call up Gina to testify, friend, and that whole setup will come out in the open, a lot of these people will learn about it for the first time, and—*basta cosi!*—the lid blows off. Shake-up in the whole department, from the mayor on down through Sergeant Sanders."

"That's a nasty one," said Jesse. "Knife you in the back to get a new trial."

"Don't mind me," said Varallo. "I think I'm done with this town anyway. I should have got out two years back. And I'd rather do it the easy way, voluntary—for one thing I could take along a few honest references to show for twelve years' service—but I can't say I'd mind too much if I took Brant and the mayor along on the skids with me."

"Unnecessary vindictiveness. Well, I'll bear it in mind. It's just possible that that might not be the way to do it anyway." Jesse contemplated his glass. "The bench might not think an awful lot of Gina Pozzo. Girl like that, *was* she sure of the time, is she lying for money or just to keep in with a corrupt cop? And even if we called Novak up to substantiate it, is *he* sure of the time? All that while ago? Yes, this means we get a new trial— I think almost for sure—if I use it that way. Casts doubt on some of the testimony, at least. But I'd be a lot happier about it if we didn't have to stop there, with just this rather doubtful evidence. If we could say why Tasso wanted to get in on the act— what his interest was in the thing. Because I don't think—if I know Mr. Tasso—he did it just to oblige a part-time girl friend. And, of course, this also gives us Antonia Cambiare committing perjury—or does it—depending how the bench might look at Gina."

"She must have known who she spoke to that night—"

"But it's funny what people can get away with, even to supposedly learned judges. I don't say she *would* get away with it, but she might make a good try— I was *that* upset, sir, and it was dark right along there, you know, I sure thought it was Mr. Tasso, looked like him and all. . . . Not a very unusual specimen, Tasso, especially seen in poor light. Middle-sized, stocky, clean-shaven, ordinary clothes. And just why should Mr. Tasso say he *was* there when he wasn't, Mrs. Cambiare? Please, sir, I don't know nothing about that part of it at all, just trying to act honest like a girl should. . . . Yes, I can just hear— What's bitten you?"

Varallo had almost upset his glass, springing up. "*Per Dio*, but that's—it could be, it could be!—Cris Gonzales! My God, I wonder! Maybe we know who it was instead." He explained Gonzales tersely, walking up and down the room. "Said 'she' gave him a whole ten dollars. Antonia? If it was Cris who made that phone call to Gannon's house—but why would she—?"

"Because she needed," said Jesse softly, "to cinch the evidence pointing away from her. It could be."

"*Antonia?* You make it—"

"Not the principal, no. But she's mixed up in this, deep— I think. Did you know that from that back road, as you come round toward the highway, the Cambiare house looks a lot like the one Carol described? That big barn behind it from that side—looks like a second story at one end."

Varallo sat down again. "You don't tell me. No, I didn't know—or if I'd seen it I didn't notice. That's a funny one. How do you mix Antonia in? My God, her own mother—"

Jesse finished his drink. "I think maybe, you know, our Antonia's one of those people like—mmh—old Omar. *Take the Cash, and let the Credit*— And she'd been mixed into it for quite a while before her mother went hunting the local abortionist. For the money, Vic—the long green, the folding stuff—however it came, whoever provided it. I could tell you a nice little story about it, on no evidence whatever. About a woman named Mame—who's been lying low here possibly on the run from the city boys—and keeping her hand in by doing a little local business. Your guess as good as mine why she picked Contera, but I'm wondering now if maybe Tasso knew her somewhere else and either brought her here or—mmh—recommended it as a nice quiet spot to hide out in. And where do I think she's been lying low?— You take that one." He poured himself another drink.

"The Cambiare farm. *Dio,* I wonder. All this time!—but—"

"Nobody who matches the vague description known as a new resident—buying groceries, buying gas, getting to know people, et cetera. Inference, unless you're going to say that all of a sudden somebody who looks like an upright citizen, and 's always behaved that way, turned into a criminal abortionist—inference, she's been living in somebody else's household. You looked, after Carol Inver, at new residents and so on. Nothing. Loopholes there, of course—but another thing, you can't very well operate an abortion mill in one rented room,

when your landlady doesn't know a thing about it. Impractical, to say
the least. Not that I suppose she was doing such a land-office business,
a dozen a day—but even the occasional patient, you know, would pose
difficulties. I think the household the woman was in knew all about it,
and was being paid for sheltering her."

"Yes—yes. If all that's not just a dream, about her being on the run—
and another thing *I* can see about that, maybe, is the pay actually
being blackmail. But when Antonia's own mother—"

"I think," said Jesse, "Antonia thinks about Antonia a long way
ahead of anybody else. By the time Teresa Zacchio turned into a second victim, Antonia was pretty deep into the setup, you know. She
couldn't very well come out and denounce the woman, tell chapter
and verse, without laying herself open to an accessory charge *and*
quite possibly a joint homicide charge. Antonia wasn't protecting her
paying guest—if we can jump to a few conclusions and read it this
way—when she went to work to get Nell under suspicion that night.
She was looking after Antonia. And, you know, if all this isn't just a
fairy tale, and I don't think it is—it all ties in too neat—she grabbed
onto opportunity and used it with the kind of spur-of-the-moment
strategy many a general might envy."

"Zacchio said the name," said Varallo. "Just the name—and probably on account of the little glimpse he'd had of the hair— My God.
And *seven* witnesses—"

"Like the Andersen story, I told you. Sure. People are like that. And
now we know, or we think we know, where that solid-sounding, dying
testimony came from too. It's too late, probably, to untangle Zacchio
and Maria on it—but I'd bet you anything you care to risk that it
wasn't until you and Brant had come on the scene asking questions,
just before and after Teresa died, and heard a little too much that was
dangerous, maybe, that Antonia reminded them how Teresa had said
Nell's name. Antonia taking great care to hover over the woman, interrupting her or hushing her up other ways if she started to come out
with anything definite. But what she got out, in the hearing of those
witnesses, could be put together and prove dangerous. You noticed
that they all heard it at first as the little dog on Antonia's best bedspread, and only later—straightened out by Antonia—separated the
two. And, *Ask Antonia.* Inference, Teresa had said all she knew but
Antonia knew more. And, *a terrible sin, just for the money.* That one
Antonia explained away by linking it up to her marrying Cambiare for

his expected legacy. All the same, even though Zacchio and Maria weren't thinking very clear and Gannon wasn't paying much notice, maybe dangerous—when they thought it over, when they were asked specifically."

"I'll contribute this," said Varallo slowly. "That night, the one thing Teresa said that struck me as maybe important was that *ask Antonia*. Later on I swallowed their tying it up with the bedspread or the fowl. But I did—before Brant got there—ask her a couple of questions that might have made her think—"

"Mmhm-hmm. So you would. And then Brant comes and starts asking, did they get any kind of look at this woman in the car? And Zacchio repeats his little remark about her looking like Miss Varney at the bank. On account of the unconscious connection with the hair. And Brant probably says something like, What, Nell Varney? Which was when Antonia—they say imminent danger does stimulate the brain—seized on three little words her mother'd also said, and exclaimed excitedly, Why, Mama said that name! She didn't know Nell, it was just a name to her—a very handy name at the moment, too. She didn't give one damn who she got in trouble, so long as it wasn't Antonia."

"*Diavolo—diavolo!* It could be, sure, sure—everybody talking at once! It was—"

"*Smell of varnish,*" said Jesse pleasedly. "Smell of varnish made her feel sick. Somebody varnishing something. Could be?— It was, I'm telling you, it was. And Zacchio and Maria, confused and upset to start with, and Zacchio having Nell in his mind—taking Antonia's word, ditto Maria, convincing themselves that's what they heard too. Gannon saying at first, it might have been—later on, with the others so sure, getting surer. There's your four first-class witnesses who heard Teresa 'accuse' her. We know how Mrs. Inver was convinced to make the identification. We know what the Prices are worth. We can explain the fingerprint on Mrs. Zacchio's necklace— That's the solidest piece of evidence, and you say and I say that Nell's explanation is perfectly natural and plausible, but it can be read either way—depending on your prejudices. I'll bet Antonia had something to do with that too —because ten to one Brant didn't ask about the necklace until after the print on it was identified, and how easy for Antonia to say all very positive, Sure, Mama was wearing it!—and to convince the others to back her up. And when Carol Inver said she'd 'seen her in the bank,' she meant Antonia, not the other one. And you know something? In all that rigmarole there's not one damn thing I can put before the appellate court. There's no evidence at all. I can say I'm certain that's how it all happened, but there's nothing to prove me right. Just imagination working overtime. What I have got now is Tasso. And by inference Antonia, on *that* part of it—because, for ninety per cent sure, she knew who she gave that dime to for the call to Gannon. You think maybe it was this Gonzales. Could you get anything out of him for the court?"

"It's a chance," said Varallo. "Sure, I don't think it'd take much coaxing or bullying to break Cris. I'd guess his I.Q. at about eighty, maybe less. No guile. That, of course, is why and how they could pull this on us. I don't need to think twice to guess how it was done—if, as you say, all this isn't just imagination. She saw how Brant liked the Nell Varney business, and she didn't, no, give a damn who got thrown to the lions as long as it wasn't her. But she couldn't be sure Zacchio and Maria would go on backing her up definitely, and at that time Gannon wasn't very definite either. She wanted another witness, out of the family, who could speak up sure and certain. And for some reason she knew she could count on Tasso. But she didn't dare bring him in right then, because for all she knew he'd been seen somewhere in public at the time, couldn't claim to have been the witness. So she threw a fit to gain herself the time, and I'll bet if and when we find out, we'll find out that she called him at the hotel, soon as she could reach a phone—not the phone at the farm—and got together with him right then to dream up the story. Tasso could speak up because he knew Gina doesn't pay much notice to time usually. She'd probably never hear the details of what he testified, and if she did, would she bother to point out the discrepancy and who'd listen if she did? No trouble there. And so convenient that it had happened to be Cris, amiable, childlike Cris . . . Him she got hold of the next day and told him there was going to be police trouble, and she didn't want her good friend Cris to be dragged into it—the policemen might think he'd done something wrong—so Cris was just to forget about being there at all, she'd get a friend of hers to cover up for him. And meanwhile she wanted to give him a little present for being so obliging. Now remember, don't tell anybody it was you who made that call, or they might put you in jail! *E chiara*—don't I see it! Sure, I'll get Cris to admit it—and what the hell good is that? He's a lot less bright than the average ten-year-old, and he's apt to remember details wrong—he'll be scared to death—and how would he show up to a benchful of judges? The kind you can obviously bribe or persuade to say any God damn thing you want!"

"About ten points below Gina Pozzo," murmured Jesse in agreement. "With Antonia simply denying the whole thing—Tasso ditto, maybe. And Mrs. Gannon, who took the call."

"*Per carità!* Ten words over the phone four weeks ago? He didn't say his name or that we'd have heard about— She's not quite that scatterbrained—but I don't suppose she'd ever have spoken to either Cris or Tasso on the phone before. Couldn't say. Nothing there."

"No. It's something, but just as Uncle Malachi says, *A handful of food will not satisfy a lion.* Said lion being the benchful of judges. All the same, it *is* something. It is indeed. The story builds up. 'Nother little something occurs to me. Don't keep a dog myself, can't on account of being away all day, you know—and anyway, if and when I do, it wouldn't be one of those feisty little things that yap—but little dogs like that, they scratch things. Doors, asking to be let out and in."

"Well, so what?"

"Why, the varnish," said Jesse contentedly. "The varnish to cover up the scratches. Antonia doesn't like dogs, and she must have been getting a nice piece of change as room rent, when she let Mame's little dachshund sit on her best bedspread like that. She wouldn't like those scratches on the doors— She'd get Joe to varnish over them."

Varallo laughed. "You planning to hand that one to the judges?"

"I am not." Jesse sat up, eyed the bottle of bourbon, and cautiously poured himself another small one, offered the bottle. "I am absolutely ruthless and honorable as a professional man. Lawyer's first duty to his client. I'd throw you to the lions happily to win a new trial—but I'm not just that sure I would get a new trial with this. Want something a lot solider—legally speaking—to hand the judges. Did Carol Inver play golf?"

"And what brings that up? As a matter of fact she did, she played in the county tournament a couple of years ago, I remember."

"That's nice—and legally meaningless too. Yes," said Jesse to his drink. "I've got great respect for all the niceties of law, you know, but it's sometimes one big damn nuisance that judges can't—legally speaking—decide a case on common-sense reasoning if there's no evidence to back it up. . . . I'm going to let this lie where it is for a while. I may have to use this stuff about Tasso, on its face value, to base an appeal on—but I've got a little time. . . . Who'd have been Carol Inver's closest girl friends?"

"And where does that tie in?"

"I think you were wrong about Bennett. I saw him today—annoyed him a little. Somebody's said that the conclusions of passion are the only reliable ones. He told me among other things that he was damn fed up about the suspicion on him because he'd thought Carol was a pure and respectable virgin, consequently hadn't attempted her virtue, and then found out she'd been available to somebody else. Somehow, you know, that rang true to me—natural resentment—like getting a tip on a race run last week. Frustrating. I don't think it was Bennett. Might be interesting to know who it was—because maybe that one knows something to give us something more definite on Antonia."

Varallo shrugged. "I could be wrong. You can look. Her girl friends —well— I couldn't say who or which she might have confided in. I don't suppose she'd have told any of them anything definite, or they'd have said something at the time—"

"You think so? Nothing like a definite confidence about where she was going for the abortion—don't suppose she'd have let that out to anybody, no— What I'm after 'd be idle girlish speculation after the fact, as to who'd put her in the market in the first place. You think a nice respectable—maybe scatterbrained—twenty-year-old would realize that kind of thing might help the police in looking for her murderer?"

Varallo, who had been pacing up and down again, stopped and turned to look at him. "So, maybe not. Maybe not . . . That's so. She'd have gone around with the local girls in her own class, same kind of money and background. Sandra Wyatt, Shirley Grant, Linda Forsythe, Margaret Wallace. It came out at the time, I remember, that the Wyatt girl was her closest friend—Carol'd told her mother she was going off that weekend with Sandra Wyatt, winter sports at Arrowhead—and the Wyatt girl made a statement. Said Carol had told *her* some story about wanting an excuse because she was going to have an interview for a job and didn't want to tell anyone until she knew whether she'd got it or not. Which doesn't sound as if she'd have let out anything very confidential—"

"No. But her closest friend—girls going around together, double-dating maybe, going to the same places—and not many fashionable places, much choice of where to go, around here—seeing a lot of each other, in a place like this—" Jesse stared at the thimbleful left in his glass, drank it. "Where'd I find the Wyatt girl?"

"Somewhere in L.A. She left four days ago for the new term at U.S.C.—I remember seeing a little society note in the last issue of the *Valley News.*"

"That's nicest of all," said Jesse. "Excuse to go home for a couple of days. But it's a pity, in a way, I can't send you." He looked at Varallo and sighed. "You're so much handsomer. Better equipped to get on friendly terms with a girl all of a sudden. Me, they're apt to take one look and say, Maybe he's kind to kids and dogs and his old grandmother, *but*—! Often thought how convenient it'd be if all the generalizations were true, you know—people saying we've all got serpentlike cunning and charm—could have used some many's the time. Oh, well, have to do my best— No man can do more."

THIRTEEN

He showed up at the county jail next morning at eight o'clock, with two cartons of cigarettes and a pound bag of those crystal mints she liked. "Did I get you up?" he asked when the matron brought her in.

"Heavens, no. This place is as bad as a hospital, they think it's a sin to sleep later than six—bring you a loathsome hearty breakfast at some ungodly hour—"

"Ah," said Jesse, putting his burdens down on the table with his hat, "nice to know you're one of *that* half of the population. Science—it's wonderful—they've proved it now, with all their psychological tests. Half of humanity the kind likes to go to bed at sunset and get up with the chickens, other half night owls—not operating on all cylinders mentally until past noon. I belong to that half too, one of the reasons I picked law, you know— Court doesn't usually convene until ten, by which time I'm halfway alive at least. Get brighter and brighter as the day goes on—sometimes quite brilliant by midnight or so."

"I know what you mean," said Nell with a laugh. "Don't they say it's the very imaginative people? Don't like to go to bed, don't like to get up. My lord, you've got me talking like you. Thank you for the cigarettes, but you didn't need to— I can ask them to get me things, you know, and—all I owe you anyway—"

"I think it *must* be a Norman name, Varney," said Jesse. "Always understood they were a very mercenary tribe. All you seem to think about is money." He gave her a cigarette, lit it for her. "Don't look so serious. It's O.K., we'll get a new trial and a lot more interesting and pertinent facts are going to come out. I've got several irons in the fire on several lines, and at the very worst I think we've got enough to get you off with a short sentence—under any reasonable set of judges—but we won't stop there."

"Only t-twenty years, maybe? What irons?"

He told her. "On the face of it, even if I don't collect anything more on Tasso or Antonia, it's evidence—of a sort—of false testimony, and if the appellate bench believes it, it'll prove a mistrial. I'd like more to give them, because neither the one witness we've got nor the one we might get is the kind who looks very credible—law says everybody's equal, all very democratic, but it doesn't really work out in practice, you know. Much more useful if we had a couple of respectable, substantial people, with regular jobs and at least a high-school education, instead of Gina Pozzo and Cris Gonzales. But there you are—take what Providence sends and be grateful."

"Yes," she said. She sat across the little, bare, narrow table from him, her hands clasped on it before her; as usual, not much make-up to show except the vivid lipstick, and he thought she'd washed her hair, or had it done—it sprang up crisp and wavy at the temples, with chestnut lights in it, shining. "Is there—is there a *chance,* Jesse?"

"With me as your lawyer? That's an insult. Sure there is—more. We'll get you off, clear, vindicated—way the law puts it, without a stain on your character. You wait and see. We've got to."

"I—I don't know why," she said. Suddenly she put her head down, resting her forehead in the palm of one hand. "Isn't there some quotation about, you find out who your friends are when you're in trouble? I th-thought I had some friends—girls I know—people I know—down at home. You know, nobody's even written me a line—and it's been in the papers, I suppose—even to say, We're sorry, keep your courage up. . . . I *thought*— Of course, I never was the kind of person who had a lot of casual friends—acquaintances—and the last few years, with Dad the way he was, he'd—offended some people we know, you know the kind of thing. But I'd have thought *somebody* would have—taken notice, so to speak. Taken the trouble to say, We believe in you, good luck, we're pulling for you."

"Sad commentary on human nature—sure. People chary of associating themselves. Also, when you stop to think, a very complimentary implied judgment on the forces of law and authority. People unconsciously reasoning, They must have a lot of good solid evidence on her. You know? Country where everybody knows the police, the courts, the governmental setup are corrupt to start with, why, a lot of people who know you take just the opposite stand. That you must be innocent because they say you're guilty."

"Well—I suppose that's so." She lifted her head and looked at him. "I hadn't thought about it just like that."

"And it is, you could say, the exception that proves the rule. You interested in the etymology of words, by the way? That's an example. 'Proves.' Archaic usage—still meaning 'tests.'"

"D-does it?"

"As in automobile proving runs. Yes. But it's very much the exception in this country when somebody innocent is found legally guilty of any crime. Speaking off the record, happens much oftener the other way round— The written letter of the law leaves so many loopholes, you know, to provide leeway for the innocent—a lot of guilty people getting off, with the help of a smart-boy lawyer who's got all the fine print memorized. Not up on my homework, when it comes to that kind of thing— For better or worse I was raised with a few scruples about ideals of justice—my father's a lawyer too, you know, or did I ever tell you?—but you take it all in all, it's pretty damn exceptional in this country to get a really serious miscarriage of justice this way or that way. Eventually. In spite of all the legal rules and regulations— comforting to reflect—even judges are human, and sometimes possess a little common sense." He reached across and touched her hand briefly. "Don't you worry, it'll be O.K.—I think it'll be O.K."

"You—" she said, bending her head into her hand again. "You really think so? I—I don't know— You've been so good, all this time and—effort—at it. Don't know how I could ever repay—"

"There you go again. What a mercenary female you are. Of course, I do grant you that's pure human nature—first thought, what's in it for me? Not saying I'm so altruistic, or so interested in the two hundred and sixty-four bucks in your savings account. Fact is—"

"I d-don't know what else'd be in it for you," said Nell, attempting a smile at him.

"Well," said Jesse, "my Uncle Malachi's got some money to leave somebody—"

"That's the one who's always quoting at you, I know—you've mentioned him."

"Oh, have I?—very tedious old fellow, but it's only common sense to be polite and obliging to rich relatives, isn't it? And he's very hot on family and convention, you know— One of the quotations he's always throwing at me is that one—was it Rabbi Jochanan or Rabbi Simon?— don't remember— *He who lives unmarried lives without joy.* I've got an idea I might come in for a little more of Uncle Malachi's money if I acquired a wife he approved of. Done a little looking around, you know, but Uncle Malachi's pretty particular."

"Is he *indeed?*" said Nell.

"Little bit old-fashioned— I don't mean about things like cigarettes and lipstick, but he doesn't approve of married women working, or these newfangled ideas about wives expecting husbands to help with the housework and so on. In fact, rather difficult to find a female *I* wouldn't mind living with who conforms to Uncle's notions, if you see what I mean. And the minute I laid eyes on you, I knew he'd approve of you—mmh—unconditionally. Just the kind of girl he likes. Had a little vision of him saying to himself, Jesse must be a better risk than I thought, when a nice girl like that picks him—and putting me down for twice as much in his will—"

"Oh, *did* you?" said Nell.

"Mmh. You see what I mean. We have to think about these things, only common sense."

"*I* think," said Nell, "that your Uncle Malachi is a f-figment of the imagination, if you want to know—"

"He'd be insulted," said Jesse. "Of course, all this is presupposing that *you* wouldn't be insulted at the idea of acquiring a funny name like Falkenstein. I don't say it's got any aristocratic overtones, and I suppose we've got about as many thieves and traitors and general undesirables in the family tree as anybody else in this democratic republic—"

"How you could *think*—!" said Nell angrily, with a little involuntary sob. "How you *could*— Really, Jesse! *Really*— I know that horrible woman's staring at us through the— *Really!* I d-don't know *how*—"

"Well, I think it was something to do with your eyebrows," said Jesse. He reached across and traced the left one delicately with one finger. "Don't you ever pluck them. Uncle Malachi wouldn't approve— and in case you're interested, neither would I. And if that isn't just like a woman, accusing me of deliberately doing something I can't help. You expect me to show up, maybe, with a full orchestra—like those scenes in movies, couple out alone miles from anywhere in a canoe, and all of a sudden a symphonic background for 'I Love You Truly'?

Which reminds me, I'd better find out before I commit myself, do you like music and what kind?"

"I—I *don't* like grand opera," she said defiantly, helplessly. "It's just *funny*—"

"That's fine. The right instincts," said Jesse fondly. "Yes, isn't it? Corseted tenor being impassioned about True Love, facing away from his lady toward the audience—lady soulfully clasping her hands toward heaven, waiting her turn at the footlights. Very much like 'The Emperor's New Clothes.' You have the right instincts, you can be educated. I warn you, I like Bach. Very reassuring, Bach. Everything mathematical, precise, coming out even. Dovetailing. Makes me feel like the poem— God's in his heaven, et cetera."

"Yes," said Nell. *"The Art of the Fugue.* Isn't it? I— I don't know much about Bach. *Really,* Jesse—with that woman looking in the door—! But do you really think—*do* you think—?"

"Don't you know, woman, hadn't you heard, we're a hell of a mercenary people?" He reached one finger to stroke her cheek, gentle. "I said Uncle's got money to leave. Have to please him, you know—so he says, Jesse must be a good bet, worthy of being remembered. You know? He'd approve of you like anything. Tell you something else—"

"Yes?" she said. "Yes—Jesse?"

"Another quotation—*All the blessings of a household come through the wife.* Couldn't say—never having had one—but maybe so. Like to find out."

Nell bent her head to both her hands clasped on the table. "Maybe tw-twenty *years,*" she said limply, "or—! Really, Jesse, I don't see— And that matron watching! I can't—"

"Don't fuss," he said, and touched her clasped hands. "Not twenty years—or anything. It'll be O.K., Nell—don't worry. You think you might work up a little jealousy? I'm going down to the big city to make up to this coed—presumably a pretty one."

"I'll try," she said. "How much—has Uncle Malachi got to leave somebody?"

"Oh, quite a lot," he said. "Enough to put out a little effort on it, Nell."

"All right, I'll try. I'll be *awfully* jealous, Jesse."

"That's my girl."

For once he didn't do any bitter cursing at the traffic holding him up when he got into civilization again. He regarded it almost lovingly,

and even worked up a little sentiment for the three-way automatic signals, the used-car lots, and the straggling, scatterbrained pedestrians.
The country very nice to visit once in a long while, but no place to
live.

He'd taken three hours and twenty minutes to make the hundred
and sixty-odd miles down as far as San Fernando, where town began
(as far as traffic, signals, and people went), and it took him almost two
hours to make the other twenty-seven miles to his Hollywood apartment.

It was about twenty degrees cooler, too, this much nearer the
Pacific. He unpacked, starting a stack of records on the phonograph,
and lay somnolent in a lukewarm bath for some time, soothing himself
with toccatas. It then occurred to him that his next of kin might be
mildly interested to know where he was and what he was doing, and
he heaved himself out of the tub, shut off the phonograph regretfully,
and called his father's apartment. The affection between them did not
quite bridge the gap between the elder Falkenstein's disinclination to
listen to recorded concertos at midnight, and Jesse's disinclination to
live in a place littered with dismembered clockworks and approximately one hundred and forty-seven modern and antique clocks, concrete representation of the elder Falkenstein's single hobby.

"I—er—tried to reach you last week," said his father, "and assumed
you were still rusticating. Did you convince the jury?"

"Well, as a matter of strict fact, no."

"Pity," said his father. "Curious what damn fools people can make
of themselves when they get together to form a jury."

"Isn't it indeed. Rather especially annoying in this case."

"Oh, well, at least the appeal will be heard in, where, Fresno? Not
quite so rustic. You are appealing, I suppose?"

"I hope so, in one sense, and in the other, yes. It's a put-up job, but
I haven't got just a hell of a lot to prove it yet."

"That so? Interesting case otherwise? You just said, a case—I
haven't been watching the papers."

"Second-degree homicide. Bit reminiscent of the Oscar Slater business. Only seven witnesses instead of three."

"Oh, really? Dear me. Awkward. What are you doing back home?"

"Playing detective. Looking for something to make the appellate
court sit up and take notice. Keep your fingers crossed for me."

"Which sounds as if you're really working for a change. Seven
witnesses, did you say? Grateful client good for a nice fat fee?"

"Well, she's got two hundred and sixty-four dollars in the bank. Oh, and a house—quite a nice little house."

"Pure altruism. You can put it down on your income-tax return as charity."

"Not at all," said Jesse. "Quite a respectable dowry, these days. At least she's solvent."

"Oh, *really?* You don't tell me. . . . Seven witnesses. How very awkward. I suppose it's no use asking you if she's a nice girl and whether you think I'll like her."

"Not much. But yes to both."

"*Seven—* Dear me. Er—perhaps you can stop playing detective long enough to come along and have dinner here and—um—discuss the case. Not that I'm casting aspersions on your professional competence, but quite possibly in the befuddled state of the eager lover—"

"Befuddled hell, I am—"

"Thinking quite clearly and calmly, yes. They always are. *Seven—* You'd better come early."

"Say six o'clock." Jesse put down the phone, sighed at the stack of records, and looked up the number of the U.S.C. registrar. Get started bright and early tomorrow on this Wyatt girl . . .

FOURTEEN

Varallo had just got to his office on Wednesday morning when Sergeant Sanders came in with a special-delivery letter addressed in Jesse's neat, miniature, copperplate script. And before he had the tip of his letter knife under the flap, on the sergeant's heels Brant came in. Brant leaned on the desk and said, "Am I interruptin' any hard labor for the law, Vic boy?" He said it sarcastically.

"Not that you'd notice," said Varallo. He dropped the letter on his desk.

"I've just been wonderin' what tricks you're up to with your Jew boy friend. Understand he's been calling on a lot of people, asking questions. What's he doing still hangin' around?"

"The case isn't finished," said Varallo. "There'll be an appeal, you know. Mr. Falkenstein's looking for more evidence. It's a free country."

Brant laughed. "He's got a hope. Now I'll tell you—"

Varallo's phone rang and he picked it up. Her voice was calm and even in his ear. "Vic. I'm sorry I've been so long—getting that information for you—"

"Yes," he said steadily. "Let's have it."

"There was one call to that number, at twelve-forty-eight, just after midnight on August first—that is, it'd be the s-second by then."

"Yes, thanks." He noted it down on his scratch pad.

"It was made from the public booth at the corner of Main and San Anselmo, and it lasted one minute and four seconds."

"I see. Thanks very much."

"Vic," she said. "You don't give me a chance. And I ought to be ashamed to—to *crawl* to you, but you *won't* understand—you're just being obstinate, that's all. And—and stiff-necked. It's silly. I know you're sensitive over that sort of thing, and no wonder, but you ought to have better sense than to think I could believe—"

"All right, I'm not quite so bright as I should be," said Varallo. Brant shifted restlessly, close there, and drummed impatiently on the desk.

"Oh, for heaven's sake!" she said. "I was just wild that night, I hardly knew what I was saying. Later on, having some sense, I realized you were right. But if you're going to hold it against me the rest of my life—"

"There's no need for that. Let's both just forget it."

"—Obstinate," she said. "Obstinate! And I'm even more ashamed of myself now, to forget all my pride like this and— All right, then, we'll just forget it!" She hung up quickly.

Varallo put down the phone. "Look," said Brant immediately. "All I wanted to say to you, you keep out of it, see. None of your business. So a smart kike lawyer bitches up the police case some way, makes me look like a damn fool! *I* know what's in your mind! Look—"

"You're narrow-minded, Chief," said Varallo. "You think about yourself too much. Oddly enough, Mr. Falkenstein's more interested in getting his client vindicated than blackening your reputation." He slit open Jesse's letter with one slash of the knife and extracted the single sheet. For a moment it was only even lines of script, Brant's voice gabbling on at him, and then suddenly the sense of it penetrated his mind.

Small towns—won't take a chance on a phone call. Try one Francis Kearney, Jr.—presume you place him. The Wyatt girl says, under delicate questioning, a little talk about him and Carol last Christmas—speculation about parental approval, account of you-know-what. Affair apparently not serious, half a dozen dates and *finis*. Don't know when I'll be back—am on Tasso's track, faint but pursuing. And hoping.

"—You'd just love to see me thrown out, wouldn't you, Vic boy? I—"

"You should," said Varallo, "cultivate more objectivity, Chief. As I said the other day, I'm all for law and order—and if you want to take that as an answer, O.K." Well, well, he thought, with grim satisfaction. Young Frank Kearney. No cop within twenty miles of Contera liked young Frank very much—most of them having had some dealings with him. And, yes, maybe that had been Frank Kearney two years ago, in that hit-and-run car; who could say?— If so, they'd never catch up to him on that one now. But if this new thing was so, maybe they'd catch up to him this time.

"—Complaint," Brant was saying, "from the Bennetts. Coming around and asking questions—no reason to tie them into it. The Bennetts are important people in this town—"

"So they are," said Varallo pleasedly. And that was another thing. Young Frank Kearney was the nephew of the D.A., Burkhart— Often enough he'd tried to pull that one about important connections, and a couple of times Burkhart had used his influence to get Frank off the hook. The Kearneys—the Burkharts—important people. Kearney Sr. damning the police for being hard on the boy, vindictive; demanding that the police withdraw traffic tickets. He'd be a hell of a lot madder, the police questioning Frank about this.

He laughed. He said to Brant, "Excuse me, Chief, but I've got work to do today." He took down his hat and went into the next cubbyhole, where Lee slouched at a desk. "Come on," he said. "I've got some important questioning to do and I want a witness—you'll do."

Young Kearney—hardly college material, not for lack of brains but of ambition and self-discipline: September wouldn't find him leaving home. Varallo found him the first place he tried, at the Kearney house up on Sunset Drive, relaxing in the flagstoned, shady patio with a few cans of beer.

There wasn't much cunning in young Francis Kearney, and any there was had been nullified by years of having his own way with no effort—and, presently, by the beer. He began by blustering at Varallo's sharp questions, but when he found that didn't do him any good, he was about out of ammunition.

"You can't walk in here and start threatening *me*—"

"Who's threatening you?" asked Varallo. "I'm only asking a few questions, Mr. Kearney. You're known to have been out on several dates with Carol Inver— Were you—"

"What the hell does it matter now? Nearly a year ago—"

"Not quite. Around last Christmas, which was very probably about the time Carol Inver became pregnant. Perhaps you were responsible for that, and perhaps you knew how to get in touch with somebody to get her out of trouble. I'd like to hear all about it, Mr. Kearney."

Kearney wet his lips, looking from Varallo to Lee nervously. He was a good-looking youngster, the black-Irish coloring, fair skin, black hair, very blue eyes. "No, of c-course it wasn't me— Everybody knows it was Jackie Bennett—"

"No nice witnessed statement, you know, and Bennett has always denied it. I don't think so. I'm not interested in a blow-by-blow description of how you managed to seduce her—if that's not too old-fashioned a word for you— What I want to know is, how and where and from whom did you find out where to send her?"

"I didn't— I never—"

But Varallo was sure now: the voice and the look told him for sure. This had caught Kearney completely off guard: it hadn't crossed his mind that anyone would suspect him—or that anyone gave a damn—after all this time. "But you did," said Varallo. "You also started her on the way to the abortionist. That's what I'm interested in. How, what, and where did you find out, Mr. Kearney?"

"I didn't—it wasn't that kind of— I mean—"

"You're claiming you never knew anything about that part of it?" Varallo smiled, shook his head slowly, holding Kearney's eyes. Once in a while, policy to make it look as if you knew more than you did. "Don't try to pull that one, boy. It was you, and we know it was you. It will look a little better if you're co-operative—even after all this time —and tell what you know."

Kearney took a step back. "I— Look here, I don't know why the hell you're interested *now*—and you've caught that Varney woman—but— I mean, look here, you don't have to—to tell *who*, do you? If I—"

And Varallo wondered suddenly if he'd confessed it to the priest long ago: of course, inviolate: secrets of the confessional. He smiled slowly at Kearney and said, "Now just what d'you mean by that?"

"I—look, if you *know* I— We can make a deal on this, I mean if I tell you, you don't need to say how you—"

Lee, who had been standing a little behind Varallo leaning on the round, metal table, came upright. "Why, you damn, little, spoiled-brat bastard, you trying to bribe—"

"Now, now, Bob," said Varallo gently, "let's hear what the gentleman has to say, shall we?"

Kearney looked slightly relieved, edged a step nearer him. "That's right, Captain, you and I can get together on this, can't we? I mean, all this time after, it can't mean a damn, just the little details you're after, isn't it—"

"Oh, yes, I'm interested in all the details. And in what you started to say just now."

"Well, I mean—a little deal on it, see? I'm damned if I can figure how you came to— I didn't know anything at all really, or I'd've said so then, of course! See? I mean, Captain, well, look, you don't need to say who or—or where you heard about it from, do you? If maybe I slipped you fifty bucks to sort of forget it?"

And out of the corner of his eye Varallo saw Lee, covertly alert, watching him. Lee, hungry for such an obvious excuse to go tattling on him to Brant. "Suppose," he said, returning Kearney's smile amiably, "you tell me what you know, before we conclude the transaction."

"Well, O.K., I knew you'd be reasonable about it, Captain—only sense, way I said—" Kearney relaxed altogether. "You'll see it isn't anything, I don't really know a damn thing to tell you—and, anyway, it was all an accident to start with. I—but you said you didn't care about that— Look, you see nobody really knew Carol and I dated a little, except I guess a couple of her girl friends that she used for an excuse, said she was going somewhere with them—*you* know. Because her mother didn't like it, the couple of times we went out open, on account of me being Catholic—*you* know. Anyway, when she told me—*I* didn't want anything to do with it! Well, hell, it was kind of her own fault in a way— And I wasn't going to be dragged into a mess like that! All I knew for sure, she was just pulling a fast one, try to make me marry out of the Church—*you* know. So it was really kind of a joke, that's all, when I told her to—to go and ask that fellow at Tom Frost's garage. My God, I never took it very serious—I didn't think she'd *really*—!"

"What fellow at Tom Frost's garage?"

"I'll tell you how it was," said Kearney, expansive now. "I go there mostly for gas, see, and you know that guy he's got to just take care of working the pumps and so on, not his regular mechanic— I don't know his name, kind of a dumb guy, a roughneck. Well, I was in there one day getting gas, last January some time, I think it was, and while he was washing the windshield he kind of leaned in and said something like, you ever know a girl in trouble wants to get out of it, I can tell her where to go— See?"

"Well, well," said Varallo. "Did this interesting information come out of a clear sky? It doesn't sound exactly the sort of thing likely to come into conversation without some build-up."

"I don't care what it sounds like, damn it, that's what happened! Sure, O.K., I thought myself it was a kind of funny thing for him to say all of a sudden like that, but that's how it happened. I sort of laughed and passed it off—*you* know—and didn't think much more about it until Carol— Look, it was a *joke*, I never thought she'd really—"

"I see," said Varallo. And he hadn't known Carol Inver, only seen her around town, casually—a pretty blonde girl, she'd been, maybe a little scatterbrained and, well, young; but he thought irrelevantly how desperate she must have felt, how humiliated, approaching the fellow at Frost's garage—*a roughneck.*

"I didn't know anything about it, you can see that! Just a kind of joke, because I—" Kearney looked at him, suddenly a little nervous again. "So—so that's O.K., isn't it? If that's any good to you, why, O.K., but you don't need to remember who told you, do you?—"

"With fifty bucks in my pocket I didn't have before?" Varallo's smile tightened; and Lee was watching him like a hawk. "Rain check, Mr. Kearney!"—and he swung around, beckoned Lee with one savage gesture, and strode down to the drive toward his car, no back look at Kearney staring after them uncertainly. He backed the Chevy out to the street too fast, in one rush, and headed back downtown at traffic-ticket speed. *"Per l'amore di Dio!—che barbaro coraggio—giurinastro, canaglia! Questo arabo, questo gatto nero!* Fifty bucks, he says—fifty—"

"Hey, take it easy, for God's sake," said Lee. "I don't get this—" He looked faintly disappointed and eager at once. "What—"

"I won't kill us, I'm in a hurry," said Varallo grimly, taking the corner onto Main without braking, "to get back to the station and get a warrant sworn for this contemptible black bastard on a charge of offering a bribe to a peace officer. Sure, sure, so half an hour after he's locked in a cell, his father and the D.A. and a crew of lawyers will be on the spot with bail—so what the hell? But he'll answer that charge, by God, and he'll answer another one eventually, I hope—accessory before the fact to homicide! Let them try to buy him out of that!"

He got the warrant, he went back and arrested Kearney and brought him in just as he was, and saw him locked in—Kearney, a scared, blustering little boy, I'll have your badge for this, can't do this to *me*, my father, my uncle— He didn't wait for the lawyer and the D.A. and Kearney Sr. to show up for bail; he left Lee to do the honors to the rescue party, and drove down Main to the corner of Woodlawn, to Tom Frost's garage, to see the roughneck.

And he thought bitterly how muddled human feelings could delay and interfere and make things happen the illogical, wrong way. He had a little sense as a cop, even on an eleven-man force in the sticks— It had occurred to him at the time that whoever had got Carol Inver in trouble might have information to give, and he'd asked those girls, casually, if they knew anything definite. But when she'd made up a lie for her best friend, what would they know?— He hadn't pressed it; not indicated. The girls, if they had any conception of why he wanted to know, still feeling vague loyalty to Carol about the excuses they'd provided on those few dates with Kearney; maybe, my God, speculating among themselves even then, as to who—wondering about Kearney. No—not that Jesse was so much more persuasive; but this was six, seven months later, and he'd probably explained its possible importance: and out it had come, a little something that had lain dormant all that while. Young Francis Kearney and a roughneck.

He was that all right. Varallo surveyed him with cold distaste—the kind you found any place, wearing any kind of name and face. Just escaped the law mentally—probably never got beyond fourth grade if that—but a lot of good-hearted, simple people of that sort: this one, rudimentary amorality, you might say. Crude, yes; greedy, yes—and enough shrewdness to see the chance of a few bucks and try for it.

What it came down to, when Varallo pried it out of him—sullen, reluctant—was just another little something. A name, Anna Farber. A girl friend, sort of, he said; a girl who'd worked at Woolworth's once and got fired, and was now a waitress at that Dewdrop Inn joint out toward Santo Giorgio. A girl who'd got caught, and had an abortion, some time around last Christmas—he guessed it was—not *him*, my God, no, some other guy, but see, she'd broken up with him, and when she took up with the roughneck, little bit later, 'd told him about it. And he'd just had the idea—you know, no *harm*— She hadn't told *him* who or where, but he just thought, well, if he could help out any girl in the same fix, maybe get handed a couple bucks for giving her Anna's name so she could go ask Anna about it, where to go—you know, you could see how he figured—

Wanting to get in on the act. Varallo said he saw. He didn't think the roughneck was lying; he was too scared of the cops and too dumb. Another irritating thing: if all this had come out at the time, no trouble getting the information out of this one anyway. "All right. Do you remember a girl coming in here to ask you about it, in early March it would have been?"

The roughneck gave him another nervous, ingratiating grin. "Oh— sure, I remember that one. Only bite I had, it was— I don't pay no mind, dates, but she was the only one, see, 'at's how I remember. Sure. Along one morning she came in for gas. Open Buick roadster she had. A blonde. Sure. I tol' her Anna's name, ask her, see, an' she gave me five bucks. Lissen, you can see *I* didn't know nothin' really— I mean, I jus'—"

Varallo didn't waste another word on him. Really no use asking, hadn't he connected that blonde with Carol Inver, when it was in all the papers and everyone talking about it a few days later? Asking, didn't he realize he had a little valuable information? Let it go: he had the relevant thing.

He went back to Justice of the Peace Henry Richards again and got a warrant for the roughneck on the charge of accessory before the fact, and arrested him and saw him lodged in the cell next to young Kearney. It worked both ways; Richards a pompous old fool, but that was convenient for Varallo as well as Brant. And the roughneck wouldn't have the cash or the influence to raise bail right away, if ever.

That, Kearney was already negotiating. Varallo was buttonholed on his way out again by Kearney Sr. and the D.A., who demanded furiously to know how come—chapter and verse. And by Brant, asking the same questions. Strange bedfellows, Varallo thought sardonically: Brant didn't give a damn for either of the Kearneys—*or* the D.A.—but the charge on Nell Varney had been his manufacture, and if it wasn't at once apparent in this business of young Kearney, he knew that Varallo was hand-in-glove with Nell's lawyer to get her off on that charge, as he'd announced. He was protecting his supposed integrity and competence as chief of police.

Varallo didn't bother to answer Kearney Sr. or the D.A. He looked at Brant there in the doorway of his office, and he said, "Like any police officer, Chief, I'm supposed to proceed on sufficient evidence, whether it happens to be against the President or you or Mr. Burkhart or whoever. That I've got. Mr. Kearney Jr. admitted to me in the presence of Lieutenant Lee that he's the one who got Carol Inver pregnant and gave her information sending her to the abortionist—he also offered me the magnificent sum of fifty bucks to forget it—and by the book that's evidence for the charge on him. Ask Lee. Ditto this lout I've just brought in. I'll give you details later. Right now I'm going out after a third accessory."

"Extremely high-handed action," Burkhart was yelping. "The boy may have said something foolish, to mislead you—but it's unthinkable— You deserve severe reprimand for such impulsive— The chief—"

"I once told Mr. Falkenstein," said Varallo coldly, "that I thought you're an honest man. Now I'm not so sure. Out of the way, sir, I've got work to do." He left those two spluttering at him, Brant silent and watchful, and started out to find Anna Farber.

FIFTEEN

Jesse sat in his car outside the L.A. offices of something called Maxwell Wholesale Parts, Inc., and considered the magazine propped on the wheel. He glanced up every five seconds to look down the street at the doorway of National Machine Products, Inc., where thirty minutes ago Mr. Tasso had disappeared.

In the last three days, since a cautiously noncommittal phone call to his company had disclosed Mr. Tasso's whereabouts, Jesse had developed great respect for detectives in real life, as opposed to those fictional, who ran into almost constant excitement. The little problems facing a detective on a job of tailing were nothing compared to the abysmal boredom attendant on the job. He had sat outside an unreckoned number of places waiting for Mr. Tasso to come out again; he had gone to see two very bad movies with Mr. Tasso; he had picked up several very bad meals, catch-as-catch-can, in places near where Mr. Tasso chose to stop, in the last forty-eight hours; and he was now reflecting gloomily on those bright boys of fiction. When they referred to the leg work at all, they were so apt to say blithely, *The suspect was closely followed for several weeks, et al.*, and that was that. Probably all of those, of course, in much more rugged condition to start with than a sedentary lawyer; and, could one say, less imaginative and restless? If he'd had the money he'd have turned it over to a detective agency happily, but like everything else their prices were inflated these days. Which posed another little problem, because Mr. Tasso knew his face.

He sighed, stretched his cramped legs, and looked back to the magazine. While waiting for Mr. Tasso's reappearances he was improving the hours by trying to match up the cars: this was the big annual issue of *Sports and Economy Cars*, and full of photographs, most of them conveniently taken side-on. He had clipped out the one of the baby Renault, and was comparing it to every likely model, methodically, considering size and shape. The trouble there was, as Varallo had admitted, Mrs. Price had been nearly right in saying that nobody else around had one of those little foreign things, and what else could be quite as small as a baby Renault? And could you own a car in a place like Contera and keep it a secret? And all right, say Mrs. Price had leaped to a conclusion—just to get into the act—that that car she'd seen had *been* Nell coming home, and hadn't turned out of Mrs. Inver's drive. Mrs. Price might be nosy, but she had—just on account of that—sharp eyes. And Zacchio and Maria had also described a small, light-colored car—very small, they'd said—while Antonia, who ought to have seen it too, claimed she hadn't noticed, couldn't say. Fishy, since she was probably mixed up in it. It did look as if that little car, looking like Nell's, was in the picture somewhere.

Vic had said, sure enough, there were only a couple of foreign cars in town: the Great Schism hadn't reached the backwoods yet, quite. Bob Hannum, who owned Contera's one department store and ran over to Santa Barbara, down to Fresno, frequently, did own an Aston Martin, the Mark II model; but nobody could mistake *that* for Nell's baby Renault, even if it was a light color, which it wasn't. And this young Kearney who'd been mixed up with Carol Inver last Christmas —the Wyatt girl said, a lot of money, the father self-made lumber merchant—he had a Siata, that V-8 roadster, but even with the top up, on that one there'd be that long nose out in front; not even Mrs. Price could confuse them, seen in profile. There was Jackie Bennett's MG, but that wouldn't do either.

Jesse looked for Mr. Tasso again—not yet—and back to his homework, turned a page. And nobody either could confuse this sleek Maserati with Nell's humble transportation. Nor, of course, any model of a Mercedes-Benz. He ceased for a moment to think about the Renault profile, and—wistful child peering in the candy-store window—dwelt on that Mercedes hard-top roadster. Senseless, of course: hell of a lot of money for just a big sports car; much better, when-as-and-if he could afford it, to get that solid dignified town-sedan Mercedes made. But he could *look* at the roadster. . . . Well, there wasn't any MG model that might fit. Nor any Triumph model. But that Porsche was a distinct possibility, like the Volvo and Volkswagen and a couple of

Fiats. Little different angle of nose-downsweep, but seen in poor light— He checked it, and wondered what he was accomplishing besides killing time.

He looked up, and saw Mr. Tasso just emerging from the doorway of his home office half a block away. He put the magazine down and started the engine; Tasso's blue Pontiac was parked in front of that building. This was the manufacturing section of L.A., an old and rather squalid district, with few pedestrians or buses; he dawdled along half a block behind the Pontiac, lest Mr. Tasso begin to wonder about this Ford so constant in his rear-view mirror. Nerve-racking, this job: you had to be on the alert every minute. Good way to give yourself ulcers, watching and worrying at it all the time you were actually doing the tailing, and then dropping into boredom for long periods of waiting.

Enough traffic down here, but the Pontiac turned into Soto Street and Jesse swore, risking a ticket by sliding through a cross-walk, ignoring pedestrians, to catch up. Up Soto— Fifty-fourth, Fifty-third, Fifty-second, Fifty-first; apparently no more stops in this neck of the woods, bound for another area somewhere. Washington Boulevard— and *hell*, the Pontiac making it across on the amber light— Jesse sat fuming, interminably waiting for the green, nearly killed a jaywalker in the middle of the next block and severely frightened an out-of-state Dodge at the corner beyond—but there was the Pontiac ahead, still in the left lane, still going straight up Soto. On to Pico. Olympic. Eighth Street. Atlantic. Whittier. Sixth— Fourth— First. No offer to turn off at those main drags. Or at Brooklyn, or at Ramona; but at Marengo the Pontiac turned left and went up past the County Hospital to Mission, and up that to North Broadway, and left again up to Sunset, and right on that. Heading for Hollywood, then.

Jesse's hopes rose very slightly. Mr. Tasso lived (with a plump wife and three kids) in Huntington Park, and while it was possible that he had some business contact in Hollywood, it wasn't likely— Most of the business offices he'd have any interest in were down there where he'd just come from. A personal friend, then, or some personal business. Jesse was interested in both, as connected with Mr. Tasso.

He kept an anxious eye on the Pontiac as they approached the intersection where Sunset and Hollywood Boulevard joined—awkward spot to make a sudden turn—but the Pontiac kept left, stayed on Sunset. Past Vermont—New Hampshire—Berendo—Catalina. Edgemont, Kenmore, Mariposa—and a left turn onto Normandie, another main drag. Jesse hurriedly swerved into the curb as the Pontiac stopped and began to back and fill around, squeezing into a single empty slot there ahead.

Tasso got out, pocketing his keys, and walked two doors up to an apartment building, went in. Jesse slid up past the Pontiac, noted the address, luckily found a parking slot up the block, and added this address to the five he'd collected as possibles.

Just possibles, of the probably-personal, extracurricular places Tasso had visited these two days.

Because the long shot had paid off. Maybe he wasn't doing so bad as a detective, at that; that had been pure deduction, and, lo, he'd been right. In almost every detail.

When he'd finished prying delicately at the Wyatt girl (who hadn't, after all, been very good-looking) he'd dropped into the clipping agency to see if they'd come across anything yet, and the office manager welcomed him exuberantly.

"I was trying to get in touch with you yesterday, Mr. Falkenstein, so glad you came in!—that's quite the hell of a job you gave us, pawing through every edition of every city paper for the last year—and I must say, sir, we've all been mighty damn curious— However, I guess you could say it's spurred the girls on, something a bit offbeat so to speak! And something turned up yesterday I think you'll be interested in. Oh, Mabel!—get that Falkenstein file for me, will you? Now, sir. You told us to look for any news story about a woman wanted for questioning by the police—or who might have some other reason for, er, hiding out somewhere—who might have been mixed up in a criminal abortion case—and probably for a photograph along with the story, and you said it was just barely possible that her first name was Mame and much less possible that the last name was Fowler. That all shipshape?"

"On the nose. So?"

"And I must say it was a job, having to look for all those things instead of just a name—you know what most of our business is: actors, writers, and so on. I've had four girls ruining their eyes on it—but the point is—oh, thanks, Mabel—the point is, I think we've got it for you." He opened the manila folder and with the deprecating air of a modest miracle worker handed over a newspaper clipping.

Jesse looked at it and felt the proper awe—some of it for himself, for there hadn't been any real evidence to back it up. But here it was, and it was a very large part of the whole story, and even—as a kind of extra bonus—offered some evidence on two minor points.

Such a hell of a long shot, and it had come romping home lengths ahead—worth the original investment, a million to one.

From the L.A. *Times* of almost a year ago, last October thirtieth. A good-sized cut at the top, and by God, *by God,* there she was. Mary (Mame) Fowler, wife of arrested man. Three-quarter studio portrait, a woman in the late forties probably, blonde, and her hair pulled back smooth to a big chignon. And, by God, she had the dachshund with her, cuddled in her arms, a little red dachsie gazing up at her adoringly—Recent Portrait of Mrs. Fowler with her dog Fritzie.

"If I can ever do any little thing for you," he said earnestly to the manager, "like robbing a bank or committing a murder, just come and ask. Happy to oblige. Afraid I couldn't promise any miracles like this, but I'd do my best." He read the article greedily.

Dr. James Fowler, it seemed, had no longer any right to the title. He'd been struck off the medical register thirteen years back for unlawful dealing in narcotics, and had served eighteen months of a two-year sentence. Three years after his release—that would be upward of eight years ago—he'd been arrested on a charge of performing criminal abortions, and along with him his wife Mame. Her first arrest, so she was let off with a year and another year's probation, but he got another three. Came out five years ago, and apparently—reading between the lines—promptly went back into his old business, under yet another false name. Both his old businesses. A couple of years later they were both questioned in connection with the arrest of a dope pusher, but as was so often the case, there hadn't been quite enough legal evidence to charge them. Then, last October, the narcotics squad of the L.A.P.D. had caught up to the ex-doctor, but good. A lot of nice, solid evidence that he was dealing in drugs, and doing a brisk side business in abortions. They'd probably have thrown the book at him eventually—report of trial and sentence could be located in a later paper: this was the story of his arrest, and this detailed because evidently it had been quite an affair, nothing third-rate— He'd been supplying a couple of gangs the cops had been after for months; there'd been some patient detective work done on Dr. Fowler, to single him out and get him for a judge. A two-time loser, he couldn't have got off with much less than ten years, with the new stiffer penalties for dope dealing. However, he hadn't got his own supply through ordinary wholesale purchase of those drugs he could buy on the market as a physician. (These wholesale houses often careless; it wouldn't have been the first time a licenseless doctor had kept on signing the re-stricted-drugs register, not much danger.) But apparently he'd been a customer, for those as well as the outlawed heroin and marijuana, of some clandestine wholesaler his own side of the law. And that one not identified.

Well, so Fowler had been arrested, and now the police—so added the story—were anxious to pick up his wife, a lot of evidence on her too, who had skipped. Mrs. Mary (Mame) Fowler, five foot seven (an inch or so taller than Nell, but what was that?), one hundred and forty pounds (about twenty pounds heavier, but in bad light, with a loose coat—), forty-eight, bleached hair, fair complexion, blue eyes. She was presumed to have taken her dog, to which she was much attached, along with her. One Dr. Adam King, a veterinary-surgeon, had come forward to state that the dog suffered from chronic eczema, and had been undergoing a series of treatments. Possibly Mrs. Fowler, wher-ever she fled, would seek veterinary treatment for her pet again, and any veterinary-surgeon acquiring such a patient was asked to report it to the police. She was known to be driving a Nash car, license so-and-so, beige color.

All of which was extremely suggestive and interesting. Jesse uttered more gratitude to the manager, commissioned him to hunt out any follow-up stories, and departed to ruminate in solitude, with the aid of the *Fugue in A Minor*.

Not much danger that a follow-up story would report the trium-phant arrest of Mame Fowler. Without much doubt, Mame had ended up in Contera, at the Cambiare farm. Rusticating—for almost a year—*if* she wasn't still there. He didn't think she was; Teresa Zacchio had flushed her, on the run again.

Driving a Nash, then. Wonder if it had ever showed up—evidently she'd changed cars, if she was driving some little foreigner in Contera.

And why the hell Contera? Could be just at random, sure, nothing to say it wasn't, but— Money? Money always had to be considered, unfortunately. The ex-doctor probably making it hand over fist, but had they put any away, *and* could Mame have got at it easily on the run? Once she'd settled, by all accounts, she'd taken up the business herself—and bungled a couple of cases—so maybe she'd needed money. Yes. But how *had* she happened to land in Contera? Well, here was Tasso, who'd looked so transparently like the innocent by-stander, the outside witness, now revealed as in it up to the neck. What was in it for Tasso, of all people? Tied up with Antonia, yes, but it wasn't any immortal selfless love—not the only girl friend he had, probably— He wouldn't go to all that trouble just to do Antonia a favor.

And that Antonia would know. Shrewd young woman: no romantic love affair on her side either. She wouldn't, being in a little bind per-sonally—needing that false testimony—have asked Tasso to oblige just for her beautiful eyes, as the saying went. Was it logical to deduce that she'd called up Tasso because he already knew all about it *and* because it was also to his interest to lay a false trail in another direc-tion?

Because, when you used common sense, it was inconceivable that Mame Fowler—a big-city, pro crook—had sped sure and straight to the Cambiare farm outside Contera, just by chance. Please take me in as a roomer and don't tell anybody I'm here, the cops are after me. And Antonia: Glad to oblige, come right in. They knew Mame *had* showed up in Contera almost at once, by inference; Vic said the indications were the abortionist had been operating there about a year. Antonia, who'd probably never been fifty miles out of Contera in her life—what was the connection with a big-city crook? Well, of all the people An-tonia knew, obviously Tasso was about the only one with big-city con-nections. His home and his home office were in L.A., and he came and went— He was driving round and about Southern California most of the year.

A connection with Antonia. Did he have a connection with Mame at the other end— Was he the link? And it wouldn't have been pure al-truism there either— On the cards he'd had some reason to help Mame away safe.

Fowler buying dope from a criminal wholesaler.

A hell of a handy situation to be in—Tasso's—if you were running dope. Driving all around, passing through several cities on your lawful occasions, and always eventually getting back to L.A. It would be in-teresting to know how far south Tasso's territory went, if it brought him very near the Mexican border.

All up in the air, sure—tale spinning with a vengeance—and again no evidence, nothing to interest the appellate bench. This is the house that Jack built. Keep on looking. Keep trying to link things up; maybe someday there'd be some evidence. And this was a possibility, anyway.

Jesse got up, turned off the phonograph, and emptied the ash tray of a dozen half-smoked cigarettes. Even the most curious small-town operator or Western Union clerk couldn't make much sense of the dachsie business; he hadn't any hesitation in sending a telegram to Varallo—RIGHT PARTY IDENTIFIED BUT STILL MISSING EVIDENCE THAT DOG HAD CHRONIC ECZEMA ASK ALL VETS IN AREA IF TREATED STOP JUST AS WELL ON CHANCE TO SEARCH FARM.

He next manufactured a plausible tale for Tasso's company, phoned them, and eventually received the information that Tasso's route led him as far south as Chula Vista. Very handy to the border. Tasso was expected in L.A. today, and would be here for three days, through Friday: he would then take off northward, having just come from the opposite direction.

Another very long shot. If—if! Say this wasn't all a fairy tale; if he'd just been down by the border, might he have a supply to sell? And if he was followed around while he was here, would it be possible to collect some idea who he was supplying? Or even to locate Mame?

Because Jesse didn't think Mame was still in Contera, though he'd recommended searching the farm. Not only probably had she had her fill of rusticating, but she'd been scared out; and after a year, she might be reasonably sure that the heat had cooled a little on that Wanted listing. She might very well have run for home—anonymous big town—and probably too, of course, she'd changed her appearance as best she could. Unless she was a complete fool—which she might be, a lot of pro crooks were—she wouldn't start up in business again right away. (But she might need the money.) But ten chances to one, *if* all this was so, she'd still be in touch with Tasso, and he might go to see her while he was here.

Which postulated some leg work, because who could afford a detective agency?

SIXTEEN

So now he sat waiting for Tasso again, and reflecting that after all he might be wasting time with a vengeance. Say he was right about Tasso and Mame; it was very possible that any contact between them would be by phone, and he couldn't get close enough to memorize every number Tasso called. He couldn't go right in everywhere on his heels, and so at this apartment and two others Tasso had visited, he hadn't any idea which resident Tasso was calling on. As far as the hypothetical dope business went, it was possible that some of his contacts were in business places where he had legitimate reason to go, maybe even in his home office. And Jesse couldn't tail him twenty-four hours a day.

A compromise on that. Tasso was nobody's fool, a very shrewd customer, and it was almost certain, with that kind of man, that the wife didn't know anything about it. Also, he'd be very careful to behave ordinarily for other reasons, give nobody any cause to wonder: so he probably wouldn't be sneaking out in the small hours on the extracurricular business. Jesse had seen him home and watched the lights out these two nights before snatching a few hours of sleep at his own apartment and dragging himself out at five-thirty in the morning to wait round the corner for the blue Pontiac backing out of the garage: Tasso, damn it, was a go-getter; he hadn't been later than seven either morning. Thank God, this was the last day of the job. Tomorrow Tasso would be heading north; see him on his way, in case he stopped somewhere before he got out of town, and then what? Brood over these addresses, try to find out something about them.

Which would be quite a job. He had checked six, with this latest one, as possibles: places Tasso had gone for no obvious business reason—but that was only conjecture. Every one of these people might be just a personal friend, a relative, or connected with some innocent private business. . . . This apartment and two others, one in West Hollywood, one in Culver City. The office of one F. X. O'Mahoney, attorney-at-law, on Santa Monica Boulevard— That was a single building, an old house refronted into a business office with one tenant, so Jesse knew the name. The left side of a duplex on a side street in Inglewood. A single house, in a good residential district in Walnut Park.

Pay your money and take your choice. He had also been twice to the home office of his employers, and visited four other offices in that area, all of which could be allied in some way to his regular job. He hadn't gone to the same restaurant twice; he had taken himself to one movie and his wife to another; he had done a little shopping for the household at, of all places, a kosher delicatessen on Slauson Avenue. Any place at all he might have made the one casual, important contact. God knew how many phone calls he'd made.

And, chase around finding out what little he could, after Tasso had left—no guarantee there was anything there to be got.

But there it was. And he didn't, in this fix, think of any quotation of Uncle Malachi's, but of that funny old great-aunt of a second cousin— the cousin who'd married that Irish fellow. Great-aunt straight from the Old Country, not much English, and what she had she used in talking about her illustrious father, a rabbi if you please, a very learned man—otherwise, the incomprehensible Hebrew until you asked in self-defense what she was talking about. . . . *"Sheh'em lehv,* boy, *sheh'em lehv!*—put your heart into it!"

And here came Tasso again. Jesse switched on the ignition.

During the rest of that day Tasso took it easy. He revisited the West Hollywood apartment and drove home, and about seven o'clock he and his wife came out together. Jesse trailed them to the Church of the Holy Family, and was gratified to have time for dinner: both of them going to confession, probably; call it an hour at least. He was waiting round the corner when they came out again, but Tasso drove straight home and all the lights were out by ten-thirty.

And that doubtless meant an even earlier start in the morning. Jesse set his alarm clock and went to bed too.

He was waiting for the blue Pontiac by five-forty, and not long after six it emerged from the dead-end street where the Tassos lived, and headed west along Manchester. It was to be hoped that Tasso hadn't noticed his tail, though a number of times Jesse had felt nervous about it—hard to see how he could help it, but that was probably self-consciousness. There'd been enough traffic to hide in, most times and places; at this earlier hour, not so much, and he trailed a block behind.

Down Manchester to Inglewood, up Lincoln to Culver Boulevard and left down to the beach at Playa del Rey. Looked as if he was just heading out of town north, getting onto the coast highway the quickest route: but Jesse tagged along all the way up to Malibu, forty miles. The Pontiac set a steady sixty, once past Santa Monica on the Malibu road; and it could be that Mame, or one of Tasso's shady acquaintances, was to be found up in Ventura or Oxnard or points north, but Jesse couldn't follow him all over the state. He was out of the L.A. metropolis, his visit home ended. Let him go.

Jesse turned in at the next roadside restaurant, and over a leisurely breakfast debated his best move now. Those apartment houses. Difficult. Of course, there were brash, high-pressure salesmen (insurance, securities, encyclopedias, et cetera) who got a foot in the door by saying, I believe you're acquainted with Mr. So-and-So—implied recommendation, needing only a look at a list of club members or something like that. He could be one of those, and it was a common-enough device that it needn't rouse any suspicion—or would it?—the one resident in any of those buildings Tasso knew might have no open connection at all. . . . Maybe thirty apartments in each building; Jesse sighed into his coffee. But, of course, if one of them should say, "How'd you know I know him?" instead of, "Why, yes, Mr. Tasso's my wife's great-uncle," well, it might be a little helpful.

The apartments would be the worst and longest job; better get the single addresses out of the way first.

He drove back to Inglewood, to that duplex Tasso had visited on Thursday. Ten o'clock, a decent hour. He rang the doorbell and in-quired of the ordinary-looking, middle-aged housewife who answered whether Mr. Taylor was at home. . . . No Mr. Taylor here? But he'd been given this address— Was she *sure*? What *was* the name? Del Valle? Well, in that case, he must have been given the wrong— Thank you very much.

He went on down the street three or four houses and rang another doorbell, faced another housewife. Good morning, and apologies to trouble her, but he was an insurance investigator—very routine thing, but could she tell him anything about the Del Valles up the street? Solvent, respectable people?

"Well, I guess *so*, sir— We don't know them real well, but they seem to be nice, quiet people, he drives an old car, nothing flashy, so I guess— Where *does* he work, now? I think some aircraft plant, I'm not sure. . . . I don't guess he makes too much, they don't throw it around anyways. I know I did meet her in at the market a while ago, and she was saying how high everything's getting— Said she wouldn't hardly know how to manage sometimes except her brother slips her a little money now and then. Seems he's doing real well, salesman some kind, travels all around. He'd just bought her a new portable mixer, she said. . . . Oh, I couldn't tell you his name, like I say I don't really know them, just casual, you know, but they seem like nice quiet people. . . . Oh, you're welcome, sir."

So, ten chances to one, Tasso's sister, and a dead end. He noted down the information and proceeded to the house in Walnut Park to repeat the procedure.

That was an even deader end, by inference. A garrulous, lonely housewife greeted him joyfully, regretted that no Mr. Taylor was available, offered to help him look in the phone book, and managed to pour out quite a spate of irrelevant information at him, including the fact that her husband worked for National Machine Products and was at the moment on his vacation, but they couldn't afford to go away anywhere for a holiday.

So, a personal friend of Tasso's, fellow he worked with, and probably his call here quite innocent. Well, little by little— Jesse extricated himself and continued on up to Hollywood. He'd been so busy with Tasso that he hadn't checked back at the clipping agency; he stopped there now and was rewarded with two follow-up articles culled from the *Times* of early December. A little something in each one.

No sign of Mame up to then—she was mentioned as still on the Wanted list. And Fowler had been defended by one F. X. O'Mahoney, and that was very interesting indeed. He'd been found guilty and sentenced to ten years, and was now presumably stashed away in San Quentin.

O'Mahoney. Indeed. A link at last, if it meant anything: a lawyer's clients needn't all know each other, of course. . . . He had wondered what Tasso wanted with a lawyer. He was still wondering. He told the agency to carry on, and went on down Santa Monica Boulevard to the

old refronted house with the neat wooden plaque hanging outside,
F. X. O'MAHONEY, ATTORNEY-AT-LAW.

It had been transformed inside too—partitions knocked out to form
a good-sized front office, embellished with tweed carpeting, walnut-
finished steel furniture, and a voluptuous blonde at a typewriter. A
second glance, however, told it wasn't real class: the cheapest stuff
(probably including the blonde), a spurious front of prosperity. The
blonde, at the moment Jesse entered, was paying less attention to her
typewriter than to a man bending over it to kiss her. They broke apart
as the door clicked shut; the man gave Jesse a cold, disinterested look,
turned, wiping lipstick off his chin, and walked into an inner office
past a slab door bearing the legend F. X. O'MAHONEY.

But that ten seconds was all Jesse needed to spot him; here he was
on home ground. That one was the prototype of the cheap shyster, the
smart boy, the fast talker with all the answers and not many scruples.

The blonde was looking at him coldly now. "Did you wish an appointment?"

It wasn't any sudden inspiration; he didn't consciously decide to
take the chance at all, and surprised himself a little with it. "Well, not
exactly. You go and tell Mr. O'Mahoney he's got a visitor, and that
Mr. Tasso sent me."

"Mr.—Tasso, sir?" Well, well, so she didn't know the name; had she
just started to work yesterday, or had Tasso, possibly, used another or
just walked in past her as a personal friend?

"That's right."

The blonde minced through the slab door, and Jesse began to wonder how smart he'd been here. Oh, well, if he got the cold stare and
the questions he could always make up some tale.

He didn't have to. Four seconds later the blonde came out with
O'Mahoney behind her. He said peremptorily, "Come in here." Jesse
obeyed meekly. The inner office was more front: plastic-covered
chairs masquerading as leather, a big walnut (veneer) desk, a wall-
hung bar. "Higgins?" said O'Mahoney. "You're Higgins?"

"That's right," said Jesse. Really all he could say.

"I'll be damned, we didn't think you were getting out until next
week."

"They changed the date, sort of, see."

"Be damned," said O'Mahoney. He was a dapper fellow in the forties, polished, thinning black hair, a gold tooth, restless pale eyes, a

big diamond on one hand, onyx cuff links, one of those garish, hand-painted ties—fancied himself as quite the ladies' man probably, the charmer—gift of gab. Kind you always had to watch like a hawk for the little tricks on the jury, on the bench, on flustered witnesses. Full of tricks.

He said, "O.K., sit down." He went over and opened the door again. "You might 's well go out to lunch now, honey— Take an extra half hour, you want, O.K.?"

"O.K., Mr. O'Mahoney," said the blonde demurely. O'Mahoney watched her out, shut the door. "You—ah—done anything about seeing Tasso yet?"

Nobody had approached Tasso, obviously, these last few days—and if Higgins, whoever he was, wasn't *getting out* until next week, probably he was safe in saying— Getting out of where? "Well, uh, no, Mr. O'Mahoney." Subtle something in O'Mahoney's tone told him this Higgins wasn't entitled to a Mister, was expected to be low-class lout. "I don't know—" he let that trail off.

"No, I don't suppose— You wouldn't know Tasso, come to think. We just kind of used it for a, ha-ha, password, sounds melodramatic, but— Sure, I see. . . . They're so damn careful these days, the devil's own job to pass word in or out— I know—and delay, damn it to hell. Tasso's too damn cautious." And that was half to himself. "Well—*well?*" He stared at Jesse fiercely, hungrily.

And what the hell were they talking about? Jesse reminded himself hopefully of another Talmudic maxim—*If a word spoken in its time is worth one piece of money, silence in its time is worth two*—and stared back stupidly.

"The name!" said O'Mahoney. "What's the monicker he used? That's what you were supposed to bring out— My God, he *did* tell— But you wouldn't be here— What's the *name*, for God's sake?"

Monicker—so it'd be a man's name, not that of a place or a firm. "Oh—uh—it's—Jason, Jason Roberts," said Jesse, and held his breath.

O'Mahoney relaxed a little, let out an involuntary sigh. "Jason Roberts. O.K., got it. How's Jimmy doing, O.K.?"

"Oh, sure—sure. Like they say, well as can be expected." Jesse ventured a laugh; O'Mahoney echoed it too heartily.

Jimmy. Dr. James Fowler. Who had hired this smart boy as his lawyer. Yes?

"That's a good one—well as can be expected! Well, that's the breaks, isn't it?"

"Sure is," agreed Jesse. *The monicker he used.* False name for something?

"Yeah, well— Sure, you wouldn't know Tasso, just doing a little favor for Jimmy, but he asked you to see Tasso or drop him a note, I guess?" Casually sharp glance.

"Oh, yeah, sure."

O'Mahoney was suddenly expansive, friendly. He did it just a little too well. "My God, forgetting my manners, let me offer you a drink, huh? Scotch, rye, bourbon?"

"Bourbon's fine, thanks." Jesse took the drink gratefully; it might stimulate his wits in this little exchange. The phrase slid across his mind, *cross questions and crooked answers.*

"Yeah—well, damn nice of you to bring out this little, ah, message for Jimmy—not that it's very important, just a little something he wanted me to know, see? Let's see, he said you'd get ten bucks from each of us, didn't he?"

It was no risk to speak up on that one: Jesse knew O'Mahoney's type too well. "He did not, mister, he said twenty-five."

"Oh?" said O'Mahoney to his drink. "Well—sure, if Jimmy said so, O.K.—but—" another confident, flashy grin— "Look, friend, you care to make a little deal with me on the side? For maybe, say, an extra fifty bucks?"

Jesse finished his drink and asked cautiously, "What'd I have to do?"

"Nothing at all, see. I'll be frank with you—" Like the warning rattle, that one, from O'Mahoney— "This Tasso guy, he hasn't leveled all the way with Jimmy, which Jimmy naturally doesn't know, where he is—see? Just to protect Jimmy's interests, well, I don't want Tasso to get hold of this. Look, I suppose you got an address for Tasso, to send a note. You just forget about that part of it, see, don't do anything about Tasso, and you get the extra fifty. O.K.?"

"Well, O.K., sure," said Jesse.

O'Mahoney clapped him on the shoulder. "My pal, now you're the reasonable sort of guy I take to right off! 'Nother drink?"

"Well, I guess not, mister, I guess— I just got here, you know, I mean *out*—" Out of where, just possibly San Quentin? Could be?

"Oh, sure, I guess you got things to do!" O'Mahoney roared at his own wit. "Well, thanks again for the favor, Higgins. And Jimmy'd thank you too for obliging me in this other little business. O.K., here you are, as per agreement—twenty, forty, fifty, seventy, *and* five."

"Thanks, Mr. O'Mahoney," said Jesse, picking up his hat. "Glad to oblige." As he left the office, O'Mahoney was pouring another drink.

He got out of there fast, once he'd gained the car, with the vague feeling that the real Higgins might enter on his heels. That peculiar little exchange demanded rumination; he went home and started a stack of records on the phonograph. He had the distinct confidence that he'd got something related to this business—not just to some shady deal Tasso was mixed up in otherwise; but what was it all about?

Higgins. Sounded as if Higgins had just been *let* out—*devil's own job, pass word in or out*—prison, very likely—so, bringing out a message from Jimmy. Dr. James Fowler. What about? O'Mahoney double-crossing Tasso on it, anyway. A name, a name they needed to know; false name used for something.

And in addition to all that he'd collected seventy-five dollars he wasn't entitled to. He wondered what to do with it. Ill-gotten gains: by all accounts, the unknown Higgins wasn't very scrupulous either. Regrettable, but it might be bad luck to keep it. Another little maxim —several of them—about that kind of thing. Well, call it private charity: let it apply on the clipping agency's bill, divert it to a righteous purpose.

And what *had* O'Mahoney been talking about?

He got up and wandered around the living room restlessly. Presently he noticed that the little mail basket on the door—the apartment was on the ground floor and got mail individually delivered—bore several envelopes. Absently he extracted them. An ad. Another ad. An appeal for charity. And a letter postmarked Contera.

Varallo. Maybe Vic had got something too, and a clearer idea of what it was. Jesse ripped open the envelope eagerly.

SEVENTEEN

Varallo had had a busy two and a half days. Anna Farber was off on vacation; nobody seemed to know where she'd gone, but she was expected back at work on Monday. At least one thing the roughneck had told him cleared up a small point: Maria Salluzzo. The Farber woman had once worked at Woolworth's, where Maria worked: so that, probably, was how Maria had found out where to go.

It had come as a big surprise to the roughneck that he could be arrested for what he'd done: that, he hadn't known. When it penetrated his mind that he was being roped in on a homicide charge on account of Carol Inver, he changed his story a little. He had time to do some painful reasoning on it before they showed him Carol's photograph for identification, and he denied that she was the girl. No, sir, he remembered for sure now, hadn't been this one at all he talked to, not so blonde, older, kind of, somebody else. No, sir, not this Italian woman either, and now he came to think, it hadn't been March, more like some time in April.

Just enough cunning to understand that aiding and abetting an abortion wasn't nearly as serious a charge as accessory to homicide.

He did, unwittingly, help a little on Kearney. Kearney a bit smarter, and now *he* was denying the whole thing. He'd never told Varallo all that— He had admitted being out on a couple of dates with Carol, sure, but it wasn't him, my God, who'd got her pregnant, and he'd never said so or anything about knowing where to send her. Never tried to bribe Varallo. As for Lee's backing-up testimony, well, everybody knew cops'd always stick together, just liked to show their authority and bully everybody in their way; they'd always had it in for him anyway, handing out those tickets for no reason at all, jealous of his car probably; it was all a lie they'd dreamed up together. But he couldn't very well explain how Varallo had happened on the fellow at Frost's garage, right after, unless it was so that he'd told him. He blustered that they'd known beforehand, just wanted to tie him up to it, couldn't say why they'd picked on him except that they always were picking on him—harked back to the tickets, bitterly, to confuse the issue—denied everything all over again.

However, with Lee as witness he couldn't get out of it that way; Varallo thought the charge would hold. Burkhart didn't like any part of it, least of all his own position as official prosecutor, and would do all he could to delay getting it on the court calendar and to temper the charge.

Varallo got Jesse's telegram about the dachshund on Wednesday night; it sounded like a meager little thing, but true enough; those things were sometimes what built up a case. As for searching the Cambiare farm, just how the hell did Jesse expect him to do that? No reason to ask for a search warrant, and Antonia wouldn't let him set foot in the door without one; that was for sure and certain. He intended to start canvassing the vets on Thursday, but spent an hour in his office clearing up some paper work first, and just as he was leaving Mrs. Inver came in.

The *Valley News* didn't come out until tomorrow—Phil Baker had already been in to get the story—but it wasn't really necessary to put it in the paper; it was all over town now. Christine Inver would have heard it, probably, one of the first: some kind friend rushing in with the news. She looked drawn and tired. She sat down, at his invitation, in the chair across from his desk, and looked at him. "Captain Varallo, can you prove this about Frank Kearney?" she asked simply.

"I don't know, Mrs. Inver. There'll be a jury trial, and the verdict on Nell Varney shows that doesn't always guarantee justice. If you're asking me, do I know it's true, the answer is yes. He admitted it to both Lee and myself. He said he meant it as a joke really, telling your daughter about this fellow, because for all he knew she was trying to pull a fast one on him, and anyway it was sort of her own fault."

Mrs. Inver was silent a moment, looking down at her tight-clasped hands. "How could—could *anybody*— I don't understand such cruelty— Please, there are things I want to say, if you'll give me a minute—"

"This has upset you all over again, I know. Take your time."

She waited, steadying herself, drying her eyes, and said, "It's true—
I knew Carol had been out with him once or twice, but before—it
could have been . . . I did disapprove of it, but not so much because
he's Catholic as—as because of the kind of boy he is. Wild and irresponsible."

"Yes. We understand some of her friends covered up for later dates.
He's also, you know, quite good-looking," said Varallo noncommittally.

"And she was young. I know. I know. But—" she sighed, let that
drop. "Mr. Falkenstein came to see me on Sunday," she went on painfully, "and asked me—asked me to do something. It was a hard thing to
do, but—but I've always thought I was honest—and charitable—and I
did. I went to see Miss Varney. You know, I—I wasn't in court when
she gave her testimony— I don't think I'd ever heard her speak. . . .
And I tried to—do the other thing he asked me, too—to be fair. I
hadn't—some of it I just hadn't really *thought* about—they said, so
much evidence against her, cut-and-dried—and that woman saying her
name—"

"There's this and that kind of evidence. Most of this was brought to
light in a hurry, and nobody ever really examined it fairly or went into
it very deep, you know. And once she was charged, and it got first
place on the court calendar, there wasn't much time to find the right
answers, get at the truth. That, we're trying to do now."

"Yes, she said— She told me some of what Mr. Falkenstein—about
how you think it was something else Mrs. Zacchio said, not her name.
I— Captain Varallo, you'll think me very stupid, or—or dishonest, but
he was right— I've just realized that, really thinking about it for the
first time, you see. Maybe that's a dreadful admission to make, when I
knew I'd have to give evidence about it in court, and—as if I wasn't
that interested in my— But that was just *it,* in a way, if I can explain it
to you—"

Varallo sat motionless, afraid to interrupt, to steer her. The definite
something for appeal at last, if one of the witnesses voluntarily re-
canted, and such a nice respectable witness too.

"You see, I'd almost got *over* the—the first bad time about Carol's
death—and then there was Mrs. Zacchio dying, and the investigation
started all over again, and Mr. Brant came and told me definitely
you'd found the woman, Mrs. Zacchio had identified her—and—it was
just to charge her with Carol's death too, if *I* could say positively. I—

It was like living it all over, I suppose you could say I was—upset. Feeling vindictive and bitter—and he was so sure she was the one— It's the only thing I can say, that I wasn't perhaps thinking clearly. And at the trial, it seemed—you know those lawyers who try to make you *twist* things—it seemed he was just trying to call me a liar! But— it's so, I've got to admit it's so, when I've really thought. After I'd talked with Miss Varney. Mr. Brant *had* mentioned what she looked like before I saw her—and—it's queer, I didn't recall at the time, but the little glimpse I had of that woman who brought Carol home, she— she was just turning out the door, and I think there *was* a big knob of hair— I seem to— I must have connected the two, but it was quite un-conscious. I shouldn't have said either, so positively, that it was dark-brown hair—because I don't remember, I don't know, just that little look—she *was* almost out of the light, now I look back. But Miss Var-ney has dark hair, and I—I shouldn't have leaped to such a conclusion, it was—"

"Mrs. Inver, will you make a formal statement that you now find yourself mistaken in your testimony?"

"Yes. I will. I must. I—certainly didn't intend it as perjury, I hope you understand that— I haven't any defense except that I was—upset. And—and perhaps misled. I must do the honest thing. I don't know even now whether Miss Varney is guilty or innocent, she doesn't *seem* like a person who'd— But I see that I did testify wrongly about some things, and it's only honest to say so."

"We greatly appreciate your coming in. If you'll excuse me, I'll get a clerk and you can make the formal statement at once, if you will." Here was the basis for appeal; but there would need to be a lot more than this before they were sure of complete vindication.

And of course that brought Brant down on him, furious. Brant, from all Varallo knew of him, one of those people who stayed inside the law from fear of punishment, not any natural scruples. Brant hadn't intended to railroad Nell Varney; he wasn't mixed up in it that way; but he was also one of those who couldn't admit to a mistake.

He blustered at Varallo as loud as Kearney had, What the hell was this all about, trying to make him out a fool, working on witnesses to persuade them to tell new stories— That was an airtight case and the woman guilty as hell, and Varallo knew it damn well. Just because Brant was the one said so; and the same implication that anybody who thought different was trying to get her off just to show Brant up as wrong.

When Varallo got away from the chief, he was caught by the priest, telling him he was wrong about Kearney, he must be wrong.

"Are you accusing me of making a false charge?" asked Varallo. "The first story was that both Lee and I *misunderstood* something he said— Now the claim is that we deliberately railroaded him. Why should either of us do that, Father?"

"I could not say," said the priest icily. "Doubtless you can examine your own conscience, Captain Varallo. I know this, that Francis has assured me that he is innocent of the accusation—and he would not lie to *me*."

"There I think you flatter yourself," said Varallo.

There was, however—considering religion—at least one passage of Holy Writ you could admit truth in, and perhaps absurdly it was in his mind right now. *In the midst of life*— Jesse said, let it lie for a while, this thing about Tasso, until they got more on it; but, damn the quality of the witnesses, there they were. Now. It might be a very good idea to get it all down in black and white, signed and sealed, just in case. Cris Gonzales, now—you could visualize him staggering into the path of traffic some Saturday night. . . . And there were other aspects. Force the issue? Varallo thought vaguely: Damn it, not to jump the gun on whatever was in Jesse's mind; all this should have been done, should have come out, five weeks ago. Too much delay already.

So he took Sergeant Sanders off the desk, substituting a patrolman— just as well to have a witness other than Lee on this one, and besides Sanders took dictation—and ran Cris down at his brother's farm. Just as he'd surmised, it didn't take much cunning to get the truth out of Cris; but what the final statement was worth in law, that was something else again. Cris, terrified and confused—he had trouble in the ordinary way remembering the details of anything that long ago, and the fright turned him stupider than usual. Varallo was patient, but didn't get as many details as he'd have liked.

Yes, Cris had made that call to Dr. Gannon's house, obliging and friendly like a fellow ought to act, somebody sick and people in trouble— Antonia, sure he knew Antonia, she give him the dime, said to call the doctor, so he did. Didn't never pay no notice to times much, couldn't say. Sure, she talked to him next day, told him not to say nothing, he might get in trouble, and she give him ten dollars.

That was about it, and it came out in a jumbled spate of stuttered words between tearful protests of never meaning nothing bad, and fearful questions about going to jail. But whatever it was worth, Varallo wouldn't take any chances on it; he brought Cris back to the station, had Sanders type up the statement, and got Cris's shaky initials on both pages and his round childish scrawl of signature at the end. Nothing really to hold him on; if and when this came before the bench formally, maybe they'd decide to prefer a charge, and ten to one also decide he wasn't fit to plead, and where did that put his testimony? But— When he let him go, Cris scurried off thankfully, probably to head for Novak's bar; and Sergeant Sanders coughed gently and said, "Er—excuse me, sir, but—"

"Yes?" Varallo was standing at the window, didn't turn.

The sergeant ran stubby fingers through his hair. "This is quite a thing, isn't it, Captain? You never said a word— Ought to've come out five weeks ago, ask me. I don't claim to be a Sherlock, sir, but I can see this kind of ties that Cambiare girl right into the middle of it, and shouldn't you have told Gonzales to keep his mouth shut, not go blabbing to her that you know—until you can—?"

Varallo grinned. "Think twice. Sure I could have. He's so damn scared of the cops he'd keep quiet if I told him, too. But Antonia's a lot smarter than Cris, and if I sprung this on her all official, she'd know enough to keep her mouth shut, or just say he was lying, didn't know what he was talking about, and you know what Cris is— Who'd take his word unsupported? We wouldn't have much more than we have right now. . . . Cris went down the street to Novak's. I give him about half an hour there, and maybe three or four glasses of Dago red to steady himself, and then he'll think about Antonia—that maybe it'd be a nice obliging thing to do to tell her the cops know. Who's out front besides Whitsun?— Brad'll do. You go tell him to keep an eye out for Cris, and as soon as Cris has got to Antonia—*and* it's going to worry her like hell because she won't be able to get many details out of him, he's too scared, she won't be sure exactly how much we know —then we watch Antonia like a hawk, and it might just be that she'll take some action to tell us something else."

"Oh— I get you," said the sergeant. "Yeah, that might just be. I'll send Brad on his way."

Before he came back Varallo's phone rang. A severe female voice informed him that His Honor Mayor Cardew would like to have a talk with Captain Varallo at once. . . . Brant running off to complain to his old school pal. Varallo said, looking at his watch, "I'm afraid I won't be free until four o'clock, if that's convenient." The voice agreed, thinly disapproving of this casualness; and Varallo picked up his hat as the sergeant returned. "I'll be back in fifteen minutes with another witness. Meanwhile, better warn a couple of the men—that watch on Antonia, round the clock. Maybe not long, of course."

He drove out to the edge of town and collected Gina, and spent awhile persuading her to make a formal statement about Tasso. She didn't clearly understand the ins and outs of the political situation, the danger inherent in the compromise the police made here, but instinctively she was shy of any authority. He convinced her at last, brought her back to the station, and got her signed statement.

It was twenty to four. He went through the slim county phone book and copied the names and addresses of all the vets within twenty miles. Then, without bothering to put on the tie he'd taken off or his jacket, he went up to the little one-story, frame City Hall to see the mayor.

EIGHTEEN

"—Must say I did understand Chief Brant's point of view," said the mayor mildly. "It doesn't make for efficiency, Captain, when two—um —officials on the same staff don't pull together. Whether it's petty jealousy, or dislike—"

"I can guess what Chief Brant said to you, sir, and I won't waste time on that. I'll just outline the situation as it really stands—and hope you'll listen with an open mind. Though I'll say first that whatever you or Chief Brant or I do or don't do, I think a lot of unpalatable truths are bound to come out, and very soon— It's gone beyond the time of covering up, and Miss Varney's lawyer would see there wasn't any more of that, if I was fired off the force in the next hour. *Or* Chief Brant. I've made no accusation that the chief's been dishonest in any way. But up to the time you appointed him chief of police—I'll ask you to remember—he'd had no experience or knowledge of police work. He hasn't much more now, and he acted both hastily and indiscreetly in this case. Nobody really examined the evidence against Miss Varney logically and calmly, went into it to see just what it was worth—or wasn't worth. And, for one reason and another, the case was brought to court within a very short time, so that her lawyer had barely time to prepare the defense on what little material he was afforded. After the chief preferred the charge, against my argument, it was out of my hands legally—and his. As you know, the trial occupied only two and a half days, and a lot of details didn't come out.

"Now I'll tell you what some of those details have led to, sir. You'll recall that there were seven witnesses against Miss Varney. Two of them never were worth much—the Prices. I don't know what the jury thought, but it's obvious to anyone with common sense that the Prices couldn't have identified Miss Varney, or anybody else, in a closed car in that light at that distance. Let that go. Of the other five, Mr. Falkenstein and I now have proof that two were lying in their own interests, and that one of them was not present, could not have been a witness at all. A third witness—Mrs. Inver—has only today made a formal statement withdrawing her positive identification of Miss Varney—"

The mayor looked up sharply. "Mrs. Inver? I'm afraid I don't— Do you mean to say she's admitted perjury?"

"No, sir—an honest mistake. Chief Brant was indiscreet enough to describe Miss Varney to her, and tell her there was no doubt of guilt, before she identified her. She was convinced before she laid eyes on Miss Varney that this was the woman she'd seen. Now she isn't at all sure. The two witnesses left, there's evidence that they were innocently persuaded into backing up one of those who lied. Dr. Gannon, who testified that he heard Miss Varney's name spoken, was not at all sure of it at the time— He said so, because he took the word of others who said so. The evidence against Miss Varney is a house of cards—only nobody troubled to knock it down. The kind of investigation that should have been made would have brought all this out right then, and—" Varallo shrugged—"there'd never have been a trial. Since Mr. Falkenstein and I have been investigating further, a second look at a lot of things has begun to turn up the truth. This wasn't a local business, sir— I don't know yet what sort of evidence Mr. Falkenstein's come across in L.A., but I understand he's got another piece of the truth down there. I wouldn't be surprised if the whole thing broke open in a short time now, and you might give some thought to the fact that when it does, a lot of people are going to be saying that the Contera cops are either a bunch of fools or a bunch of gangsters—and none of us'll like that very much, will we?"

The mayor looked down at the pen he was rolling between his fingers. "You're not—ah—very tactful, Captain."

"No, sir," said Varallo, standing up. "I don't feel very tactful about this. I'm a police officer, and Mr. Brant is an insurance salesman, or was. If I went to work in an insurance agency, I'd take the trouble to find out something about the job, and I'd ask questions of more experienced men. Mr. Brant may have personal reasons for disliking me, and, God knows, I don't claim to be the smartest cop in California, but with twelve years of experience behind me, I do at least know enough to examine evidence objectively before I go running off to get a warrant. Mr. Brant outranks me, and I couldn't get through to him with any common sense on it. So he's put an innocent woman through a rough experience, cost the county the expense of a trial, and incidentally made a fool of himself. Nobody can stop the truth coming out now, and if he doesn't like it that's just too bad. And if you'll forgive me, sir, there's still a lot of work to do on this—work that should have been done five weeks ago—and I'd like to get on with it."

"I see," said the mayor quietly. "Like that, is it? All this new evidence— I see. All right. Yes— I suppose it would make quite a little—er —scandal."

"It's a homicide charge, pretty important. It will. And if *you* don't like it, sir—because it reflects on you as having appointed Mr. Brant— maybe you can see how I don't like it either, because it reflects on every man on the force here, including myself."

"Yes. I'd be obliged to you for details of this new evidence—"

"You understand I can't do that now, not yet. I think—"

"I was going to say, when you're ready to make them open. To Mr. Brant as well as myself."

"And the appellate court," said Varallo, "and various other interested parties. I think fairly soon, everybody'll know."

And very likely the mayor—who might not be the brainiest politician in existence but seemed to be a reasonably honest man—would get Brant in and ask him chapter and verse, and give him more reason to dislike his senior officer. Varallo was feeling what-the-hell about it: burned bridges.

He stopped in at the station and was informed that Cris Gonzales had headed for the Cambiare farm about half an hour ago, with Sergeant Bradley unobtrusively on his heels, and a couple of other men were primed to relieve him on the watch over Antonia if she didn't do something interesting right away.

If she was going to take some revealing action, it probably would be right away: unsure how much they knew, hoping they were still looking around for more evidence, before they approached her, she'd seize the moment's chance. And be very careful about it too, not being a fool. But if he wasn't smarter than Antonia Cambiare, he didn't deserve to catch her out.

He went back to his hotel room and wrote a brief letter to Jesse, to tell him the glad news about Kearney, the roughneck, Anna Farber,

and Mrs. Inver. Maybe a waste of time— Jesse might not be still in
L.A. by the time the letter was delivered; but if he showed up here
first, no harm done. The post office was shut now, and Varallo hadn't a
special-delivery stamp, but let it go. He mailed it, and had a scratch
meal in the hotel restaurant, and drove out toward the Cambiare farm
by the back road, to look at that view of it Jesse had discovered.

Funny he'd never spotted that one before: it did look like a second
story, that barn, sticking up behind. . . . And where would Brad be?
Not much cover, and it was still light. Varallo ruminated along the
lines of the lost horse and the idiot boy, and eventually came across
him in plain sight at the intersection of the two roads just down from
the farm, sitting in his brother-in-law Adam Wray's old Buick, half-
screened by the clump of old live oaks there.

"I can see her coming from here, so I just pretend to be fooling
with the engine or something, opposite side, and she'd know Addie's
car, never think it's a cop, see, Captain."

"Very good idea. What's happened so far?"

"Cris was in there about half an hour. I saw him in, and went and
borrowed Addie's car—got back in time to see him come out. About
twenty minutes ago. All quiet since— I guess they'll be eating dinner."

"Probably. You take my car, go and get yourself something and
come back, I'll sit on it awhile."

"O.K., thanks, Captain." Bradley went off in a hurry, and Varallo
got into the Buick and lit a cigarette. . . . Daylight saving was still
on, and it was barely six-thirty; but dusk a little earlier at this end of
the year, and in half an hour, before Brad got back, the sun was on
the horizon.

About ten minutes before Brad came back, the rear door of the
farmhouse opened and Antonia went out to feed the hens. And back
into the house again. When the sergeant drove up in Varallo's car,
Varallo slid out of the Buick and said, "Try to call in if she moves."

"O.K."

Not much chance that Antonia or Joe had seen that little exchange
from the front windows. Would it make any difference if they had?
She might guess, when she knew Cris's story had come out, that they'd
have a leash on her. No fool, Antonia: would she move at all? Had he
handled this the right way? Maybe better to go up there right now
and tackle her, not give her more time to think up a better lie?

Hell, play it out a little farther. More rope . . . He went back to the station and fidgeted around, waiting, smoking too much. Nobody else was there now except the night desk man: one patrol car out, cruising, as per usual. About six drinks left in the bottle of brandy in his bottom desk drawer; he had two of them, treated the night sergeant to another.

At ten minutes past nine the phone rang, and it was Brad. Varallo snatched the receiver from the sergeant. "Yes?"

"They've come into town, to the Zacchios'. I'm calling from the corner drugstore. I think there's a suitcase in the car."

"*Che diavolo*—you don't say!" Going on the run? "I'll pick you up, with luck— If I don't, call in when you can." He delayed long enough to get the tank filled, and headed for the Zacchio house in a hurry.

The famous street light just outside the house showed him Joe Cambiare's car, an old black Dodge, sitting in the narrow drive. Lights on in the house. A car parked on the wrong side of the street a little way down: Varallo slid up beside it, and a shadowy figure moved up to the offside window.

"Don't take too many pains about this," he said to the sergeant. "We'll run a double tail. If they notice you, O.K., but don't make it obvious. I'll tag along behind."

"O.K., I got you."

Varallo went on up to the corner, to the shabbier street where Gina Pozzo's house sat cater-corner to the intersection: switched off his lights and waited. While he waited he thought about Cambiare. Another weak reed, like Cris. He must know most of the story, and he'd break a long time before Antonia did. However, very nice—as Jesse would say—to have something more concrete than mere deduction to confront both of them with. Of course, what they had—Gina and Cris —the Cambiares wouldn't realize the third-rate quality of those witnesses, as the bench might look at it—that might break both of them. . . . Well, *fate il vostro gioco*—stakes down and wait for the throw.

Half an hour. Forty minutes. Fifty minutes. And the house door opening, and people coming out. Car doors slamming. Engine on, lights on. He started his own engine under cover of Cambiare's. The Dodge backed out and came in this direction, past Gina's house. Thirty seconds later Brad in the Buick passed. Varallo swung in after him, close enough to memorize the license plate, and then dropped back. He reflected that it was going to be an awkward tail, if it went

on long, at this hour. So little traffic out of town—or in town, come to
that—three cars the equivalent of a full-dress parade. Of course, not
much danger of losing Brad, or Brad's losing them—there was that.

All the way out of town now, heading south, empty dark all around,
occasional distant lights showing from farmhouses. He kept well back;
a pair of headlights out here would show up blinding bright: Brad's
taillight looked big enough. Right turn where the secondary road to
Santo Giorgio cut in. Through the outskirts of town there, five miles
on, and five miles past that, and up ahead the Buick's taillight hesitated and swung around left.

He accelerated, and came to the intersection: a stationary stop signal and two standard signs on tall posts, one of them outlined in shiny
reflecting buttons: the black and white shield of the national-highway
markers—99. The other one, bigger; he knew how it read, just noted it
as his lights went across: arrow right, FRESNO, MADERA, CHOWCHILLA,
MERCED; arrow left, SELMA, KINGSBURG, TULARE, BAKERSFIELD.

Well, at least they'd have plenty of company on 99. Not only a
major truck route, but a lot of people who had to travel by car inland,
up or down the state, at this time of year, sensibly drove by night.

The taillight ahead, illuminating just the first two letters of the plate
number, MX-, held steady at fifty. Varallo settled down to a long job,
reaching for a cigarette, shoving in the dashboard lighter. A big trailer
truck loomed up in his rear-view mirror, stayed there awhile until
Varallo gave him the safe signal, and pulled out to pass, blaring brief
thanks. A big yellow sign flashed past—ARE NOW ENTERING TRAVER . . .
35-MILE ZONE . . . And fifty seconds later, empty dark country again,
the taillight drawing away ahead.

Ten, fifteen minutes.—ARE NOW ENTERING GOSHEN. An even smaller
town, the highway skirting it. Yes, and they might go on all night, all
the way down to L.A. *L.A.?* Tasso was in L.A., as far as Varallo knew.
Hadn't Jesse said something about tracking him? Well, the die was
cast; he'd set this thing up, he'd see it through, whether anything
came of it or not.

It had been about ten when they left Contera; for nearly three
hours they kept steady on 99, through dark space, only the lights of
passing traffic to show briefly the wide fields, occasional hills, to each
side—the military line of telephone poles, twice the long, noisy rattle
of a freight, a passenger, alongside the highway. Past the dark, sleeping, little towns—Tulare, Tipton, Pixley, Earlimart, Delano, McFar-

land, Famoso, Lerdo, and into the city of Bakersfield, not much less dark than the little towns, a few neon lights left on along the main drag. Varallo was thankful he'd got the tank filled. Slower getting through town; and then country again, and little town signs . . . Greenfield . . . Slower; stop: he jammed on his brakes, shaking himself from the hypnosis of highway driving at night, the concentration on the white line and the taillight ahead. Left turn. Bumpy secondary road. Five miles, ten miles. Slower, dropping back as far as he dared.

Another intersection, another national-highway marker: 466. Well, well. And faster, a little, until suddenly out of the dark, lights sprang at him from off there to the right. A pavilion of some kind, modestly outlined in lights—tall gateposts—shadowy outlines of other buildings, fences, ranks of cars. A wide sweeping turn of dirt track leading off the highway; and between the gateposts there, as he flashed past, snatching a curious glimpse, a garish yellow streamer suspended—
WELCOME TO THE KERN COUNTY FAIR!

NINETEEN

"*Un milione diavoli da inferno!*" exclaimed Varallo. "So we take a little holiday to visit the fair!"

"Well, it looks like it was kind of on the spur of the moment, don't it?" said the sergeant, stifling a yawn. "I mean, the trouble they had finding a motel. If they'd planned it, they'd've made reservations somewhere—you almost got to."

"Yes, of course— She's come here to do something, but what a hell of a job to tail them here!" It was nearly three in the morning; Varallo yawned too, and swore again. Antonia and Joe had Maria Zacchio with them: nice little holiday for the kid sister. They had tried four motels before they found one with a vacancy, and Varallo and the sergeant were standing outside it now, having watched the lights out. "No point in trying for a room—if we found one we couldn't use it. Let's get the cars off the street, up there by the gas station— A lot of people sleep in their cars, a night or so, at fair time— I don't suppose they'll move much before eight anyway, they'll want *some* sleep."

"If I'd known what you was letting me in for, Captain—oh, well, I guess it's all in the game," said the sergeant philosophically. "You didn't happen to bring an alarm clock, did you? After that drive, I'm like not to wake up till Sunday, even in the back of this piece of junk of Addie's."

"I'll get you up in time," said Varallo grimly. He was tired, but not sleepy; when they'd got the cars up on the black-top paving by the station, he stretched out in the back seat, as far as it would let him, and finished the rest of his cigarettes before dozing off in a series of cat naps.

He woke finally at six-thirty. Joe's car was still in the port beside their half cabin. He woke the sergeant, who was snoring peacefully, and found that the gas station owner had hospitably left the rest-room doors unlocked. The sergeant yearned aloud for a razor. "You don't show hardly at all, Captain, you being blond-like, but I must look like a gangster. I wonder if there's a barber open. And I've only got four-something on me, damn it, and I oughta get gas—grace of God, she was filled up, but I just about made it, there's not half a gallon in her."

"Same here. Do that first, and then we'll take turns snatching break-fast. Let's see what I've got— Here, you'd better take a five, there'll be admission to the fairgrounds too."

They had both breakfasted, and the sergeant had himself shaved, before the Cambiares and Maria emerged from the motel at eight-thirty. "How do we work it?" asked the sergeant.

"The girls'll probably stick together mostly. But she might have given Joe instructions for something— As I said, I'd bet money she wants to get a phone call through, and either of them could do that. You stay with Joe, I'll take Antonia."

A stream of cars heading for the fairgrounds, but not as many as there'd have been five or six days ago, the first week of the fair. A hell of a job it was, too, to keep on the Cambiares' car close enough with-out being spotted, and find parking slots near enough to get after the three of them up to the gate. Once inside the grounds, with all of them still in view, Varallo breathed easier. But their troubles weren't over by a long way, as the sergeant was pointing out.

"I wonder is there a booth somewhere selling fake mustaches, Cap-tain. I mean, they all know us, and in this crowd we'll have to keep pretty close."

"All right, I know!" The three of them were still together, ambling down the main walk toward the central pavilion. "We can develop hay fever, keep a handkerchief up—"

"Tell you one thing, you'd better keep your hat on— She'd know that yellow thatch of yours anywhere."

"Teach your grandmother," said Varallo rudely. "They'll probably have breakfast at the restaurant counter before they split up."

They did, sitting in a row on the high stools. Antonia had on a black sun dress with thin shoulder straps, flat black sandals, and carried a big black patent-leather bag; she was hatless. The other girl was in black too, a plain short-sleeved dress, and had a black and white printed silk scarf tied over her hair. Cambiare's shirt, to make him easy to spot, was a bright blue-and-white stripe.

"Have a nice time," said Varallo as the three rose from breakfast and the girls took leave of Cambiare. He strolled after them, keeping an eye on Maria's scarf, Antonia's free-swinging black curls. They wandered along chatting, pausing at each exhibit for long looks and more talk. Past the fruit and vegetable exhibits, the packers' association booths, the national-cannery exhibits, and finally about ten-forty-five into the other side of the pavilion to the Great Home Show. They stopped and fortified themselves with soft drinks at another lunch counter before plunging into the wonders spread before them there. The newest thing in sewing machines, synthetic drip-dry yardage, stainless steel kitchenware and flatware, stoves, refrigerators, washers and dryers—dishwashing machines, steam irons, portable and standard mixing machines, intercom systems, TV, automatic phonographs and transistor radios—furniture, hardware, linoleum, carpets . . . They looked at everything thoroughly, while Varallo propped up walls and pillars, suffered frequent coughing spells with his face buried in his handkerchief, and began to wish he'd had more breakfast. At twelve-forty-five they wandered back to the biggest restaurant counter to meet Joe for lunch.

Varallo bought some packaged sandwiches from another counter and offered a couple to Sergeant Bradley, who had trailed up after Joe wiping his brow. They sat down on a hard bench behind the counter, a convenient thirty feet off.

"You got anything else but a pork sandwich?" asked the sergeant. "I never did like pigs much, Captain. Horses I like, and cows I can take or leave alone, but I never did much cotton to pigs, and I seen so damn many in the last three hours— That's all he looked at, pigs. Hundreds of 'em, all colors."

Varallo exchanged the pork for cheese. "No phone calls?" There were public booths scattered all around the grounds.

"Never made a move toward one. I'll tell you one thing, Captain. It's awful damn lucky I'm not married yet, or I'd have one big job explaining this jaunt to the missus. As it is, I expect my mother's callin' in to the station every fifteen minutes asking where I am. Come to think—this is my day off this week—I told her I'd drive her into the county seat this morning. Hell of a thing."

"Never mind, think what a hero you'll be, helping to crack a homicide case. . . . And off we go again."

During most of the afternoon the two girls covered the rest of the exhibits, ending up at three-thirty at the livestock pavilion, where they joined Joe in ambling past long lines of the big Percherons and Clydesdales, the cattle stalls, the goat pens. They watched some of the judging of sows with litters. About six-forty-five they went back to the restaurant counter for dinner.

"So it's just a day at the fair," said the sergeant bitterly, "and I can hear the chief jumping all over us for morons."

"All *right*, the day's not over," said Varallo.

"I wish to God it was. I wish to God I'd stayed in the army. I feel like I haven't had a bath in weeks, and my feet hurt. I never did like county fairs much. A lot of ballyhoo and advertising."

"They can't be figuring to stay over tomorrow— She didn't ask anybody to feed the hens for her," reasoned Varallo. "So far as I *know*. There *is* a phone, she could have called Reyes, he's nearest. . . . Hell."

Cambiare ordered a second cup of coffee, lit another cigarette, and went on sitting there; the two girls got up and walked purposely down the side aisle of the pavilion to a door at the far end bearing the legend LADIES. Varallo leaned on the wall twenty feet away and kept a casual eye on the door.

He had smoked a cigarette through when they came out, their backs turned to him at once, and went on toward the side door of the building. He strolled after.

Where the last cross aisle met this one, they stopped and then separated. The hatless girl, curls swinging free, turned up that aisle toward the Home Show; the one wearing the black and white scarf went on across, toward the door.

"Ah," said Varallo to himself pleasedly. There was a little row of phone booths there, three of them, just inside the big door. He watched the black and white scarf disappear into the middle one. Both the others were occupied. It was darkish along there, against the wall away from the big ceiling lights; he drifted up from the side, and two minutes later by his watch, the door of the end booth opened and a man came out. Varallo slid in, took down the phone, depressing the hook unobtrusively, leaning against the partition between this booth and the next. Had to be a chance he could hear something, these ramshackle little plywood enclosures. But a lot of noise outside, the crowds, the kids—

He heard her say, sharp and quick, "The money, the money! You *said*— Not till *next week?* Mother of God . . ." and a hiatus; and then: "I tell you, they *know*. I'll tell them I . . . Then you could . . ." A long silence then, and: "Listen, how can I say— Listen, if you don't get that cut to me by Sund'y, I'll blow it open— I don't have no choice, if I'm— All right, all right!" He heard the phone slammed down, and the door of the booth open.

He let her go; this was more important. He left his booth and shut himself into the middle one; he found a dime, dialed the operator. "Let me speak to your supervisor, please. . . . This is Captain Varallo of the Contera police. I'll come round at once and identify myself if it's necessary, but I want to know the number called on this phone just three or four minutes ago. . . . Yes. No . . . Contera, it's up-country about a hundred and twenty miles. . . . Yes, police. City police. I'll be glad to come to your office and give you identification, but it's imperative that you check the number at once, it's important evidence. . . ." He had quite a little argument with her, and waited while she consulted with some higher authority. Waiting, he leaned tiredly on the wall, shutting his eyes, and thought of Laura. Laura slim and cool and graceful there at her desk inside the little wooden fence to keep the public out, Laura looking at him, Laura saying— He started at the voice on the line.

He got it out of her in the end. A Los Angeles number. He copied down the number of this phone, that one, and the time of the call. He left the booth and sought the nearest lunch counter, got a bill changed into enough quarters. He went back to the end booth, avoiding the middle one not to confuse the calls, dropped in the money, got the operator, got long distance—heard a phone ring at the other end.

On the second ring it was answered by a man's voice. He thought he knew the voice, but wasn't altogether sure. "Hello—hello?" He was sure then: this was Tasso. "Hello! 'Tonia, is that you again?"

Varallo put the phone back gently, smiling to himself. It was getting tied up. They were getting it straightened out now, with some nice, solid evidence to prove it.

"A nice little try," he said to the sergeant as they came out of the telephone building. "Simple, but the kind of thing that works. She borrowed Maria's scarf—probably had a black cotton jacket in her bag, to cover those bare shoulders. They're much the same height. But she couldn't do anything about the shoes, and Maria had on closed pumps— I spotted that. . . . No, Maria didn't know anything about it —innocent bystander. 'Tonia'd know she'd be wearing black still for the mother—no difficulty there. In the rest room just now, I'd bet you she made some plausible little excuse for borrowing that scarf, producing the jacket. Maria's a docile little thing, she wouldn't think twice about it. . . . Let them come home their own time. They won't stay over, she's done what she came to do. We'll go home now."

Before he started the drive back, however, he tried to reach Jesse in L.A. All this was jumping the gun on Jesse with a vengeance, but there was enough objective evidence now, about this thing on Tasso and Antonia, to outweigh the quality of the two direct witnesses. He let the phone ring a dozen times, but got no answer. Jesse on his way back to Contera, or trailing Tasso somewhere? Couldn't be helped; try again tomorrow.

The sergeant had got away before him. It was about nine when he started back, and he was too tired now to try to make fast time. He got home at a few minutes before one, bribed Carlo at the desk to conjure up a sandwich for him, had a couple of drinks with it, and fell into bed thankfully.

But he'd remembered to set the alarm; he was up at seven-thirty on Saturday morning, and by eight-thirty, decently bathed and shaved, interrupting the justice of the peace at breakfast. There wasn't any choice, really, now: better jump the gun to get this out in the open once and for all. Quantity versus quality, on evidence. And he was counting heavily on Joe Cambiare.

He had the warrant on Antonia by nine-thirty, plus a search warrant. They wouldn't have been so extravagant as to waste another night's motel bill: had probably driven home a little later than he and Brad. He stopped in at the station and collected Whitsun and Keating, and went out to the Cambiare farm.

No sign of life about the place, but Joe's old Dodge parked at an angle in the yard. Too tired to put it away in the makeshift garage: that figured, two long drives inside thirty-six hours. He pounded on the kitchen door and went on pounding for some minutes, until there was a shuffle of footsteps and Cambiare unhooked the chain inside, pulled the door open a crack.

"What the hell, what you want this time o'— Oh, C-Captain Varallo, sir!— I— I—sure don't mean sound mad, Captain, but we took a li'l time off, go down see the Kern fair, jus' got back awhile ago, an' you know how 'tis, sir—kind o' tired like, we— What can I do for you, Captain?" He was unshaven, bleary-eyed, clutching an old flannel bathrobe around him.

"Let me in," said Varallo, grinning at him. "Where's your bedroom?" He brushed past Cambiare, beckoning his men after him, through the kitchen to the dark narrow hall, down to a musty room where there was a stir of movement. He groped inside the door for the switch, flicked the light on, looked at Antonia sitting up in a swaybacked double bed, black hair tumbled around her shoulders, staring at him. "Antonia Cambiare," he said in the formal ritual, "I have a warrant for your arrest on a charge of perjury. Get up and get dressed —you're under arrest. And—off the record—don't think it'll be the only charge, Antonia. When we get the legal red tape unraveled, accessory to homicide too, and enough on you to put you away for twenty years."

She lost ruddy color gradually, to dirty gray. "You—you can't—you haven't got—"

"The money won't do you any good, 'Tonia, stashed away in Tehachapi. Get up and get dressed— We'll finish this at the county jail."

She stared at him rigidly for a full minute, gripping the sheet around her; and then she said, with a slow, sensual smile, "I dunno what you're talkin' about, Captain, I never done nothing wrong. Maybe somebody's been tellin' lies about me, but I sure never done nothing like— What'd you say, *perjury*, what's that?—I come in with you, Captain, sure, whatever you say, but I don't know what you'd have against *me*, never done nothing at all. . . . You don't expect I get up 'n' dressed with a lot o' cops lookin', do you? I be with you, ten minutes, if you—"

"No treat," said Varallo sardonically. "You're not my type. *And* no promises, my girl, not if you laid down for all three of us in relays— You're not that good. Get up! And make it snappy." Cambiare was uttering frightened incoherent protests in the background; Varallo swung on him. "And you, *silenzio!* Get dressed— You're coming in too, for questioning at least."

"You got nothing to arrest Joe for!" she screamed at him then, forgetting the sheet, scrambling out of bed. "You bastard—you—"

Varallo laughed. "Don't you know it, he'll spill all he knows at the first question!"

"Neither of us done nothing— Somebody telling lies, that's all—*imbecile, seccatore!—che barbaro coraggio!* You can't—"

"*Finisca!*" said Varallo. "*Zitta là, bugiarda!*—liar of a female! Did you hear me? Get up and get your clothes on, we'll finish this all official at the jail."

She didn't stop talking, but she got up; the bathroom had no window so he let her in there alone, but couldn't say he appreciated the prior view of overbuxom haunches and breasts under the sleazy rayon nightgown. . . . Another little something, just by inference?—Antonia in hysterics after her mother's death, but keeping her head cool and calculating here— When she came out she'd taken care to plaster on the make-up, and the blue sheath sun dress showed off her buxom figure to best advantage. He eyed her coldly, and her tight-lipped return look was insolent.

He took them both in like that, straight to the county jail, and saw her locked in, and borrowed the little bare interview room to question Cambiare, with one of the sergeants taking it down in shorthand. Brant or nobody else would be able to say this hadn't been done according to Hoyle, by God.

They all missed lunch. As he'd hopefully surmised, Joe Cambiare came apart in the first fifteen minutes, and he got the whole story. He wouldn't have called himself a sentimental man, or even a particularly moral man (for a cop); but it shocked him a little.

And that, maybe, was an indication of how it might strike a jury. Any cop anywhere had run into the sordidness, the lewdness, the incredible amorality, and the appalling greed; but once in a while it shook even a hardened cop, hearing something like that. . . .

TWENTY

"*I* never had nothin' to do with it, Captain—I never—wasn't none o' my doing! 'Tonia— 'Tonia, she—see, it turned out—a lot o' money maybe, an', hell, Captain, you know 's well as me, *somebody* was goin' to get it, why not us? I mean— *I* never really had nothin' to do with it, you'll see that, didn't know nothin' really—"

(Questions, leading and otherwise, not appearing in the final formal statement.)

"Well, *hell*, Captain . . . *I* never figured do nothin' wrong, but, I mean, devil himself couldn't outtalk 'Tonia—*you* know— Tell you how it was, an' you can *see* I didn't have nothin' to do— Look, Captain, I didn't *like* it, see? I didn't like no part of it, but 'Tonia—"

(Questions.)

"Look, I show you how it started, see. This Tasso, you know him, you know who I mean. Ol' friend of 'Tonia's, see, an' he come round— maybe last November some time 'twas— He says—he says, there's this woman he know down to the city, havin' a li'l trouble with her husband, see, wants to get away like, for a while, where nobody can bother her. Says she'll pay fifty a month, take her in an' not tell nobody she's here, see. Well, you can *see*, a good deal it was, none o' our business what her trouble was down there. . . . Yes, sir, 'long about first week November las' year, she come. Mame her name was, she said. Smith. She had a car, she come in a car, after dark one night— Tasso brought her, lef' his own car in town, I drove him back. . . . She didn't go for the country, alla time complainin', nothin' here, nothin' to do. We say t' her, All right, go on in town, go to movies, go round the stores—but she never, she just stay in. I guess I was dumb, not see right off she was hidin' from the cops. 'Tonia said so right

then, when she— An' that damn dog, we hadn't figgered on no dog, a
nuisance it was, scratchin' an' whinin' around—an' you'd'a thought it
was this Mame's baby, way she talked to it an' all. . . . 'Tonia said,
hafta charge extra for the dog— 'Tonia, she already guessed how it
was, woman on the run from the cops, see. How it was, this Mame,
she said O.K. about the money, but she didn't pay. 'Tonia was mad
for sure—she— But then—but then— She goes in town, see her fambly,
you know, sometimes, an' once she come back— I guess about three
weeks after this Mame come, it was— She comes home awful pleased,
Captain, see, she—she seen something in a paper about this Mame, a
paper her ma had it was, somebody her ma worked for'd give her
somethin' an' this paper wrapped round it, see, an' 'Tonia jus' happened— Told how this woman, she's in bad trouble, cops after her an'
all—her husband in jail already—for, you know, fixin' up girls in the
fambly way—"

(Question.)

"I guess, a pitcher, yeah, I guess there was. Anyways, 'Tonia said to
this Mame, she's like get *us* in trouble, stay here, an' if she stay she got
to pay higher 'n fifty, seventy-five a month—an'—they was kind of a
row, know how women are. *I* didn't have nothin'—been just as pleased
have her gone, tell the truth—but 'Tonia— Well, Mame says she got a
lot o' money, money her husband put away somewheres only she don't
know where, can't get at it right off—an'—an'—upshot *was*, see, first
thing *I* know they got this girl here—this Anna, girl 'Tonia knew—she—
I didn't *like* it, Captain, but nothin' I could do, an', hell, you got to
figger, she'd'a paid for it somewheres, why not here? That one was all
right, see, she was O.K. and went off nex' day, an' it was a hundred
bucks, all 'Tonia an' Mame could get outta her. *That* one was
O.K. . . .

"I dunno—this Mame—made out she knew a awful lot account her
husband was a doctor. I dunno about that part of it, it was the
women's business, I never paid no— I never counted, I dunno, Captain, maybe four, five, six, alla time she was here. Maybe seven. I only
knowed one—before 'Tonia's ma, I mean—that Salluzzo girl. They
were scared about her, on account that was after that Inver girl, the
high-class one—an' the Salluzzo girl was sick, we heard, after she went
home. . . . Listen, Captain, you don't do nothin' to me when I tell you
all this, do you? I don't make no trouble about tellin', I see you got the
goods on 'Tonia, but *I* never was mixed up in it— I'm tellin' you

anythin' you ask, sir, 'at's the smart thing to do— You ain't arrestin' me, are you? . . . Sure, sure, I tell you all about it, so's you can see *I* never—

"That one, that Inver girl. Said as Anna told her—just where our place is, not the name, see— She come an' asked, an' come back couple days later, I guess when she'd kinda set up cover for herself—high-class girl like that. . . . Anyways, when she got sick, it put them kinda in a spot— Mame said, get her off the place, that was how the doctor allus handled it—alla time talkin' about *the doctor*, she was, her husband in jail, you know—on'y not till you could see she was really goin' to die, or she might talk—see? Well, acourse that was on'y sense. But it was 'Tonia made Mame take her right home, 'Tonia, she's smart, she says Mame don't know how things is in a place like Contera, comin' from the city—says, dump the girl jus' anywheres, she gets found right off an' maybe talks too much—not that she knew a awful lot, I guess, she was pretty sick most o' the time she's here, but she knew the *place*— Anyways, 'Tonia says, high-class people like that, they want to keep it all quiet, about the girl, see, they don't let it come out, so's nobody know anythin's happened, if she's took right home like that an' nobody else sees her. . . . That's how come— On'y Tasso, I meant to say, he was awful mad, about this Mame an' 'Tonia doin' business with girls that way— He says they're God damn fools, jus' make trouble for theirselves. 'Tonia says O.K., him or Mame pay a hundred a month, they don't need do it—but Mame, she's got no money, an' catch Tasso layin' any out. . . . Nossir, I don't know nothin' about the money. The money she said she had. Jus', Tasso say, he's workin' on it, on gettin' it, see, she's got to be patient. An' when he does, 'Tonia'd get a cut too, maybe five thousand—see. They was kind of a row about that, about 'Tonia knowin' about Mame— I figger Tasso never thought nobody would, an' he was mad when 'Tonia found out, seein' that paper. . . . Well, he says O.K., he'd see she got this cut, but meantime, for God's sake, don't go on so crazy, bring the cops here down on— But you can see it was easy money, Mame doin' the work if she *did* complain a lot, an' 'Tonia never let her keep much— That Inver girl, seven hundred bucks it was. . . .

"She made Mame do that too, take her home, case they got picked up on the way, you know. An' I had'a take the girl's car out a ways an' leave it. 'Tonia she trailed me in our car, picked me up—but that's the on'y part of it I ever did my own self, sir! Mame, she didn't have no choice, kinda stuck here, you can see. She talk a blue streak at Tasso ever' time he come, wantin' get out, but he jus' say, stick it awhile longer, till the money— She kep' her car in the barn, Captain, she on'y had it out four-five times alla while she was—an' after dark, she was scared some cop'd spot the license, I guess—Damn dog was sick a couple times, she took it to a vet'nary somewheres—an' like this time with the Inver girl, she—

"Oh— 'Tonia's ma. Sure, I tell about that, all I *know*, you can see I hadn't nothin' to do— 'Tonia brought *her.* Tol' her she's got no sense, put up with another brat when it's easy got rid of, see— An' then she hadda go an' get sick like that Inver girl. Reckon Mame don't know 's much 's she make out— Alla time she's sayin', You just trust Mame, honey, she have you outta this fix—but it all went wrong, alla same. . . . Sure, Captain, 'Tonia was awful sorry, her own ma, she seen she done wrong bringin' her, account maybe she wasn't in good shape to start, been doctorin' some—but you can *see,* even *so,* it was a spot— I mean, well, hell, woman goin' to die anyways, you could see, nothin' to do about *that,* there it was—an' like the other one, couldn't let her give nothin' away. That Inver girl, they hadn't covered it up like 'Tonia'd figgered they would, it all come out, an' it said in the paper it'd be a—a—*homicide,* did they find— That means *murder,* don't it? Why, hell, it wasn't nothin' bad like that—nobody did any murder! I never knew nor 'Tonia either they'd call it *murder!* But anyways, here was another one, an' we— I mean 'Tonia—couldn't let— See, she tol' her ma not say one word to anybody where or who, rest o' fambly never knew nothin'—but way her ma was then, after I mean, why, she's like to come out with ever'thin'— You can see how it was. An' 'Tonia figgered, was she right there when her ma was took home, she could take care o' her, see she didn't say nothin' to give nothin' away, see what I mean, or she could pass it off like—you know. That's how it was, sir. . . . I dunno about how it went, I wasn't there— Things kinda went wrong, I guess, her ma said too much, she couldn't— An' after, you come askin' things, an' she was awful nervous for fear . . . I mean, we didn't know *when* this money o' Mame's 'd be comin' along, might be awhile—an' till it *did,* there she was at our place, her car an' the damn dog an' all. An' if you come lookin'— Anyways, when you an' the chief let us go off that night, 'Tonia she made me stop, first phone we pass, see, an' she calls Tasso—"

(Question.)

"Nossir, I dunno what she says to him. I dunno nothin' really, none o' my doing, none o' this here—you can see. All I know is, I guess Tasso's in for a cut o' the money too when they get it, got reason not to want this Mame caught, see, an' help her 'n' 'Tonia out. *He* was jus' wild too, when he come to our place— Right away he come, 'bout one-thirty that night. He kep' sayin', *I tol' you so, get in trouble, keep on like that!* Says Mame got to get away right off, an' I tell you no lie, we was glad see the last o' her, an' *was* she glad get away! Didn't like the country noways, she didn't, that one. Tasso, he went with her—made her 'n' 'Tonia go all over the place, be sure she hadn't left nothin' to give it away, case you came lookin'—an' he said, he see her settled somewheres else safer— She didn't like the idea, drivin' right out open, but it wasn't light yet when they left. I dunno where they went, where he took her— Don't know nothin' else to tell you, Captain. . . . I guess 'Tonia'll have seven fits, me tellin' you all *this*, but I ain't so dumb, I can figger, smart thing to do, tell the plain truth long as you know so much, or you go thinkin' we done a lot worse 'n we really did, like maybe murder or somethin'. Ain't that so? You can see I never had much to do with it, women's business it was—an' 'Tonia, well, look, Mame owed her all that board 'n' keep, had'a get it some way, 'Tonia on'y took what was *owed* her. . . ."

(Question.)

"Yessir, I'd been doin' some varnishin', how'd you know that? What's that got to do— Doors, see, the damn dog scratchin' the doors, an' 'Tonia don't like it— I got to sand 'em off, an' varnish. . . . Well, sure, it was funny how it happened about that woman, kinda her bad luck, but it just kinda happened like, nobody figgered it. . . . We didn't know her anyways, never heard of her before, not till 'Tonia's Pa said her name that night, an' some reason— I never got it jus' straight in my mind, I wasn't there then, see—some reason, 'Tonia saw it was a way to pass off somethin' her ma'd said. That was all, really. . . . I dunno nothin' about any o' the rest of it, what her 'n' Tasso fix up for the court business nor nothin'. You can see, wasn't nothin' to do with *me*. . . . Can't say any of it was *my* idea, sir, I jus'— 'Tonia, she—"

Required course in the public schools, civics, workings of government and law, but wasted on a lot of people. Just as it had been a surprise to the roughneck, it was a surprise to Joe Cambiare that he could be arrested on an accessory charge. And accessory to homicide, at that. The legal definition of the word he didn't know, and he yelped all the way down the corridor to his cell that nobody had done any *murders*.

So they had plenty to confront Antonia with. She looked at Varallo stonily and said nothing at all to his questions, his rehearsal of the facts they had from Joe. He couldn't get anything out of her; but it didn't matter. On what he had from Joe, he got another warrant executed on her for the accessory charge, and a blank one for Mame, second-degree homicide. He saw the Zacchios, waited until they'd calmed down slightly after hearing about Antonia, and got confirmation from Maria of her innocence in the whole matter of the telephone call yesterday. He didn't think there was any point in being subtle about it: Antonia hadn't been; and he told them his reading of Teresa's ramblings, including the naming of Nell Varney, and asked them to think it over and make up their minds that that might be right, because they'd be testifying about it again.

He'd sent a couple of men back to search the farm, though he didn't expect much to show up there.

And about that time, at three-thirty on Saturday afternoon, he had time to remember that she had warned Tasso; and in any case, if possible, Jesse ought to hear how things had broken. He called the Hollywood apartment, and this time got his man. . . .

"Oh, very nice," said Jesse happily. "I said I wasn't a detective, should have left it to you in the first place. The professional touch. I've just had your Thursday's letter, so you needn't go into that background. . . . Presume you'll pick up the Farber girl *and* Maria Salluzzo—curious how ignorant people are of the law—going to be quite a shock for them that it's a criminal charge on the one who has the abortion, well as the one who performs it. . . . Yes, this does it all right, with actual charges preferred against other parties, and all those pretty details from Joe. Very nice indeed. Is the county paying for this call? . . . Well, then, reverse the charges if you like, but just read me that bit of Joe's statement in detail, would you?—that part about the money. . . . Yes, I'll hang on. . . ."

He listened, and said thoughtfully, "I should have remembered that— *The root of all evil*. Yes. That explains something I've been beating my brains out to— Oh, yes, I *see*. . . . Naturally, he'd have it stashed away under a false name, and nobody else knowing what it was or where it was. Very awkward indeed, as my father'd say. And he didn't dare trust his lawyer with the full information—he was *quite* right there, nobody else would ever see a dime of it if he had, and I suppose like any responsible husband he wanted to see his wife provided for while the state prevented him from earning a living. . . . Yes. Where does Tasso come in? Maybe he trusted *him*, though I don't quite— Maybe he owed Tasso some pay. . . . Anyway, he owed him something for rescuing Mame, didn't he? Tasso the altruist—I don't think. Two of them, three of them maybe, with bits of information, and none any good without the other bits. Smart way to play it, sure. Very awkward indeed, all the delay—sending information out with released prisoners— Higgins—somebody else with the name of the place—probably before Higgins, because O'Mahoney was so anxious. . . . My God, of course, of course! A safe-deposit box, and what Mame knew was his handwriting—samples of it, so somebody could forge— Yes, I see. . . . This is all very helpful."

"I haven't the least idea what you're talking about," said Varallo.

"No, well, I won't run up this bill any higher telling you, you'll hear all about it soon. Yes, this does it. I'm *not* cut out for a detective. I should have seen how to use that business— All I saw was the dubious looks a judge'd give Cris and Gina, you know. All the same, it'd be just a little nicer—more personally gratifying to both of us, too—if we could round the whole thing out, orderly—way the real detectives explain every little niggling point at the end of the book. . . . You *did* say that phone call she got through to Tasso was at about eight on Friday night? Yes. He'd just got home from church—confessing his sins to be pure for Sunday communion. . . . I do wonder how he's planned to cope with this. And where he's put Mame. Did you find the vet?"

"Listen, damn it," said Varallo, "how much do you want, you Shylock? If you've been listening, you'll have gathered I've been too damn busy to go chasing around the country after a vet."

"So you have. Very grateful for your kind help. I have," said Jesse, "great faith in our wonderful police. More of them like you than like your chief, fortunately. Think I'll cultivate some more of them right now—convenient acquaintances. No idea when I'll be back, but I'll keep in touch."

TWENTY-ONE

By half past four Jesse had negotiated the traffic into downtown L.A. and found a parking lot which deigned to accept the car after severe inquiries as to how long he'd be gone. He walked into the big new police headquarters building, scanned the directory in the lobby, and debated with himself as to whether he wanted Narcotics or Vice.

Tasso dipped the scale toward Narcotics, and he took the elevator up to the fourth floor as directed, found the right office, and went in, to be confronted with a uniformed sergeant at a large typewriter desk bearing several phones.

"Yes, sir, what can I do for you?"

"I want to see somebody," said Jesse, "fairly high up, who's got time to listen to a story. I think it'll be worth his while, though in the end he might rope the Vice Squad in too. You might tell whoever'll see me that it's in regard to James, once Dr., Fowler, who's at present rusticating in San Quentin."

The sergeant didn't look surprised or very interested. "Your name, sir?" Jesse gave him a card. "I'll see if one of the lieutenants can talk to you." He disappeared into an inner office, and when he came back held the door open. "The lieutenant'll see you, sir."

Jesse went into that office, a square cubbyhole decently but not fancily furnished. The man at the desk was rather like his office—square and darkish. He was in plain clothes, and he needed a shave; he had friendly, shrewd blue eyes under John L. Lewis eyebrows. "Well, Mr. Falkenstein, what can I do for you? Sit down, won't you? You've got some information for us?"

Jesse sat down in the chair beside the desk and looked at him earnestly. "Not to insult you, are you a reasonably intelligent fellow,

Lieutenant? Because there are what you might call ramifications to this thing, and you'll have to follow me through some—mmh—apparently irrelevant details to get to what might be business for you."

"Well, I guess I'm about as smart as any lieutenant on the force. My name's Silverberg, by the way."

"That doesn't necessarily say you're smart or dumb, but I'll give you the benefit of the doubt," said Jesse generously. "Now I'll begin by saying this. I'm not a detective, I'm a lawyer. All I'm interested in is vindicating my client. All very salutary if I can get the really guilty parties charged in her place— Some of them already are, and we're going to have quite a lot of legal red tape to unwind. But the main thing is to get her off the hook. Only the way the thing was, you see, I had to start playing detective to get something the appellate court could understand—er—legally. Damn fool rural jury didn't listen to me, you know."

"Juries," said Lieutenant Silverberg, and sighed. "I know. What was the charge?"

"Second-degree homicide. For one thing, I stand no chance of getting paid if she's put away. Me, very altruistic fellow, never expected to get paid in cash, you see— She hasn't got any— No idea what kind of cook and housekeeper she is, but I'm figuring she can work it off that way, life term in a manner of speaking."

"Now that's tough," said the lieutenant, looking concerned. "She didn't do it?"

"Of course she didn't do it. I know who did it. Mrs. Dr. James Fowler did it, with the help of assorted rural accessories, most of whom are now under lock and key—thanks to some energetic detective work by my friend Captain Varallo of the Contera police."

Lieutenant Silverberg sat up a little. "Don't tell me you know the whereabouts of Mrs. Dr. Fowler?"

"I don't. I wish I did. But I know where she was up to the early hours of August second, and I think I know somebody who knows where she is."

Lieutenant Silverberg got up and went to the door. "Ted, if Captain Lesley or the chief happens along, give me warning. Otherwise, no interruptions." He came back and slid open the bottom drawer of the desk. "We're very moral around here," he said to Jesse apologetically, "but once in a while something happens to call for mild celebration.

Let me offer you a drink. Apologies for the paper cups. Tell on, tell on— I'm all ears."

"Thanks very much. Well, it's like this. . . ."

The lieutenant listened raptly, and when Jesse finished talking, refilled the cups. "Mr. Falkenstein," he said fondly, "you underrate yourself. That deduction about the Sunday fowl—pure genius. Masterly. You fill in very conveniently— You'll recall that hampering Supreme Court decision about wire tapping—we've been doing our poor best on Mr. Tasso, but—excuse me—this God damned legal red tape, all the finicky rules about evidence—"

"Oh, I agree with you in principle," said Jesse hastily. "Very annoying. You know all about Tasso? I'll be damned."

"Not all. We've had a long leash on him for a while. Off the record —no solid court evidence for the D.A.—he's a wholesaler, sure. Linked to a syndicate agent in Tijuana. A dozen customers in L.A., and we've gone around the long way, after he led us to some of them, and got evidence, and picked them up. We hope and trust Mr. Tasso doesn't know we know about him, but he's coming to the end of his usefulness, if you take me. Fowler was one of his customers. Fowler, we surmise, had evidence on him besides his personal verbal testimony, and sold his silence for Tasso's services to the lone, lorn, temporary widow. I'm letting out official secrets, but fair exchange is no robbery. We've been rather hoping that Mr. Tasso might lead us to the Mrs. Doctor, but up to now it's been N.G. You've just told me why. . . . Sure, Fowler must have had quite a nice little pile tucked away somewhere, it's a damn profitable business. That, we knew. We're reasonably smart these days. We've had men at every bank vault in the city for weeks, watching for Mame. As Smith, Brown, Robinson, or whatever."

"Could be he's kind of old-fashioned," said Jesse. "Women don't need to know anything about business affairs?"

"Could be. Also, we caught him with his pants down, he didn't have warning. No time to tell her."

"He was smart not to trust O'Mahoney," said Jesse.

Silverberg grinned. "These Irishmen. How true. My sister married one. Nice guy, but so damn irresponsible with money . . . Yes. We didn't especially figure Tasso in on Mame's getting away. On the cards, maybe Fowler still owed him money—or Mame trusted him enough to ask for help—or he figured it as a good investment."

"I wondered about the car, as a lead. Did it ever turn up anywhere —the Nash she was driving?"

"Not a smell. And you said, some indication that she was nervous— even out in the sticks—about driving in daylight. Because she knew it was a hot plate number?— Why else? I don't think—"

Vague memory stabbed Jesse. "A *Nash*—what model?"

"It was one of those babies, what the hell did they call them—Metropolitan, American, something— Little bit of a thing, you've seen 'em, looked like one of these baby foreigners, and I think it *was* British made—"

"My God, of course! Why didn't I— Discontinued model, the last couple of years. Sure—"

"A safe-deposit box, that we figured," said Silverberg. "We kept an eye out, as I say. Never found anything. Now you tell us why on that one. She didn't know where or under what name. And there's Fowler under guard up in San Quentin, all incoming and outgoing letters censored. Difficult . . . This Higgins. Yes, I think you read it right, he'd sent out the name of the place first, with some other con getting out— to O'Mahoney. And Tasso too. Higgins—" He got up, went to the door. "Ted, get on the wire to San Quentin and find out when a guy named Higgins is due for release. . . . Next week, O'Mahoney said? To bring out the name he rented the box under. And it wouldn't do either Tasso or O'Mahoney one damn bit of good, knowing, because Mame's the one has samples of his signature, to coach one of them in forgery."

"Probably he didn't go to the box very often— I can see that—and probably a big place, so the clerk on duty wouldn't know every box holder by sight."

"Oh, definitely, that's the setup, sure. And I think O'Mahoney'd be the one to do the job. He looks just a little bit more like Fowler than Tasso does. Of course, we don't know what name Fowler used; it might have been something like Furaccio and Tasso'd look the part. . . . What was that one you told O'Mahoney again?"

"Jason Roberts."

"Um. I'll make a small bet, Mr. Falkenstein, that O'Mahoney is busy right now sending himself some envelopes addressed to Mr. Jason Roberts, getting a library card as Mr. Jason Roberts, et cetera, just in case he's asked for identification. *And—*" Silverberg got up and went to the door again. "Ted—oh, damn, he's on the phone—excuse me—" He went out, and when he came back three minutes later, said,

"Started a round-the-clock watch on O'Mahoney. Just in case he knows where Mame is, and goes to get the promised samples of writing. Bet you that's how they worked it. Bet you something else— Mame's been primed not to give anything away until Tasso's on the spot, to keep an eye on O'Mahoney. When O'Mahoney goes to clean out the lock box, Tasso'll be lurking right around the corner from the vault, to make sure he gets his cut—at least that's the way he's figuring. I don't *think* O'Mahoney knows where Mame is— Or does he?—"

"Tasso took off toward Ventura and points north this morning—*after* he knew from this rural girl friend that the put-up perjury job has been uncovered. What's he figuring on that?"

"Don't fret about Tasso," said Silverberg dreamily. "To confess it, Mr. Falkenstein, we've been rather wondering about you for the last forty-eight hours. There's been a leash on Tasso, I said, for some while —they spotted you, ah, tailing him from Wednesday night on, and were intrigued."

"To think of all the time and labor I wasted," said Jesse sadly. "I said I never claimed to be a detective."

"I rather think Tasso figured to stay invisible until Higgins got out and contacted him and O'Mahoney with the name—"

The sergeant opened the office door. "Excuse me, sir. There's an Albert Logan Higgins up on a three-to-five for armed robbery, getting out on parole on Monday."

"Ah. Thanks very much, Ted. . . . He maybe figures the rural cops won't reach out as far as the metropolis within such a short time. Figures to land back here sometime Monday, contact O'Mahoney, lead him to Mame, superintend O'Mahoney's practice at forgery perhaps, escort him most of the way to collect the money. Higgins might not show until Monday night or Tuesday—the real Higgins. But you said O'Mahoney offered Higgins a bribe not to contact Tasso at all. Now wait a minute—wait a minute. On second thought, that sounds as if O'Mahoney knows where Mame is, doesn't it? That he's in a position to pull a fast one on Tasso, get to Mame, persuade the handwriting samples out of her, before Tasso's in town. . . ."

"Just little nuances, you know," offered Jesse, "but it looks as if Mame—like me—hasn't any use for the country. Awful dull hole like Contera. I'd risk a little bet myself that when she had to go on the run again, she deviled Tasso to bring her back to home field. It's a big town, she could hide here without much trouble, after a year. Vic didn't think to ask Joe about it, but probably she couldn't keep up the bleach job on her hair, it may be gray or mostly gray by now— Was that one of those false chignons, or all her own?"

"Couldn't say."

"Yes, well, even if it was her own, she could've cut it—dyed it when she got back to civilization. But I'll bet you she's here somewhere. And strapped for money—this rapacious, rural female'd chiseled her out of most of her earnings, evidently."

"So it seems. Yes, it looks as if O'Mahoney knows where she is—no point in trying to keep information from Tasso unless he did, so he could get in first."

"Not to butt in," said Jesse, "but doesn't that sort of imply that Tasso, or Fowler, or somebody has got Mame primed not to give away the samples of handwriting to either O'Mahoney or Tasso singly? I mean, Tasso wouldn't be in it to act altruistic toward anybody but himself, but you see what I mean— Fowler, probably—wanting to safeguard her portion."

"We'll have you on the force yet, Mr. Falkenstein. It does indeed. . . . If O'Mahoney knows where she is, he won't waste time getting to her— Damn it, yes, probably he took off ten minutes after you left him— But, on the other hand, there is the fact that he won't be able to get into a bank or any other place with deposit vaults until Monday, and also he may have a little trouble persuading Mame. . . . Yes. He'll show at his apartment sooner or later if we don't pick him up at his office. And let's hope Mame's smart enough to hold out on him, so he goes to see her again tonight or tomorrow. . . . Another small one? You've done us quite a favor, Mr. Falkenstein—very helpful indeed."

"I don't want to interfere with your schedule," said Jesse, "but if you *would* just keep in mind the fact that there's my client sitting in the county jail out there. If, as, and when O'Mahoney does lead you to Mame, I'd be grateful if you—mmh—delayed outside the door long enough, maybe, to overhear a little damaging testimony—or asked some questions about Contera, *et al.*, when you've got her. And what about Tasso?"

"There's a saying about not muzzling the ox which treadeth out the corn. Don't worry, we're all for justice here, we'll remember your client. Should get the daily call-in on Tasso pretty soon now. There's a tossup as to who'll get him first, the rural cops or us, of course. There'll be a warrant out on him by now—"

"Yes, Vic probably got around to that after he called me."

"—I'll bet he's lurking up in Ventura or somewhere, waiting for the time to make a quick dash back to meet Higgins— Not a bad idea to tail Higgins down here, excuse me, I'll brief Ted. . . . Yes, *and* contact Mame, and another thing I'd risk a little money on, he's got some scheme in mind to double-cross O'Mahoney—maybe Mame too."

"Honor among thieves. I wouldn't doubt."

"—And with the money in his hands, go on the run—new name—cut his losses. Wife, kids, job, and all. No choice."

"All because a country girl happened to see an old newspaper," said Jesse. "Makes you think."

"Doesn't it," agreed Silverberg. "But the kind of thing we see happening oftener than you'd imagine. Speaking of wives, I'd better call mine and tell her what she already knows, I'll be late for dinner. Matter of fact, I'll tell her not to expect me at all—I'll treat you to a steak, Mr. Falkenstein, you deserve it, and by that time we ought to have some word on Tasso. Not usually done, to let civilians in on things like this, but I'll stretch a point for once— Very gratifying to get Tasso out of our hair, and if we can pick up Mame as well—"

He had quite an argument with the matron, but he was persistent, and quoted her precedents of prisoners' legal rights until she gave up. And then he hung on for a long while, the phone humming emptily in his ear, before Nell's voice reached him.

"Jesse? Jesse—"

"That matron's awfully mad at me," he said. "Hope she doesn't take it out on you."

"You've upset the whole routine. All respectable people go to bed about nine o'clock, didn't you know?"

"Never mind. Just a little while, you can get back on your own personal schedule. Correction. My personal schedule. I hope. Called to tell you it's O.K.—case broken, all but a few minor details. We know who—the L.A. police are in on it now as well as Vic— Vic's been busy arresting accessories left and right—whole thing coming unraveled all at once. All we want to know now is where, and when we do, I think we'll get what the law calls Damaging Admissions—already got some, from Joe Cambiare. Quite a lot, in fact. And that'll wind it up for all practical purposes. See?"

"Jesse," she said limply. "Jesse—"

"It's O.K., Nell. . . . Nell. Darling. One time in my life I don't see any sense in legal rules and regulations. Lot of red tape before you're free to walk out of that damn cell—but we'll make it quick as we can, I promise. Nell? You haven't fainted or anything, have you?"

"No," she said tremulously. "I'm here. Jesse—for sure?"

"For sure, Nell. Soon."

"Jesse . . . The matron's right *beside* me, trying to— I can't— What d'you suppose she thinks you could do over the phone?" A half-tearful laugh. "So silly . . . Jesse—"

"Unfortunately, not much. My father says to tell you, not an awful lot to choose between—county jail or me. Sends sympathy and best wishes. I never asked you if you can cook."

"Of c-course I can. Unless you're awfully particular. Gourmet recipes and so on."

"Don't claim to be an aristocrat— I said so, didn't I? No telling when I'll be back— Don't think later than Tuesday— Depends on a couple of things. If you don't hear from me, don't worry— Everything's in hand, it's just to clear up the legal mess. . . . I'll come soon as I can. . . . It's all over, Nell, just the red tape to unwind. Not all my doing— Vic Varallo did a lot of it."

"Yes," she said. "Yes. He got you to take the case. Jesse— Jesse? I really l-like to cook. . . ."

"That's fine," he said. "Nell darling. I'll come soon as I can."

TWENTY-TWO

On Monday morning Varallo got the warrants for Anna Farber and Maria Salluzzo; he arrested the Farber girl himself, sent Keating to pick up Maria. That put the finishing touch on a weekend of the most exciting gossip Contera had had in years. Garbled versions of the story had got out, even in the twenty-four hours since Sunday afternoon when Jesse had called back to give him the breakdown on the L.A. end. Varallo didn't discourage the men talking publicly about it: just the opposite; and that wasn't mere vengeance on Brant. The people who exchanged this news were also the people who might be giving legal evidence or sitting on a jury someday, and the more they knew and thought about this, the better.

He spent most of Sunday locating the vet, getting his deposition—clearing up the details: also on some paper work to do with this and other matters he'd been neglecting lately.

He had seen nothing of Brant on Saturday or Sunday, and couldn't say it worried him. Late Monday afternoon, as he came in from hearing the Farber girl's sullen, reluctant statement, he met Brant in the doorway of his office.

"Think you're pretty damn smart, don't you, Vic boy?" said the chief with an ugly grin. "Show me up all over the place—regular Sherlock Holmes—and I don't need telling that's what you were out for all along, my scalp."

"I wouldn't know what to do with it," said Varallo. "I don't need telling His Honor gave you a little lecture on caution, and maybe recommended that you study the rules-of-evidence chapter in the official handbook for peace officers. You're welcome to borrow my copy if you haven't got one."

Brant jerked out an involuntary obscenity at him. "You— Listen, Varallo, you're getting too big for your breeches around here—one more crack like that—! In my book that's what they call insubordination, if you—"

"I've heard the word. I can spell it too, which is probably more than you can."

"I said, one more crack. That does it. Thought you'd maybe talk fast enough to Cardew so's he'd kick me out, and just maybe too put you across the hall in my office!—I wasn't born yesterday, Vic boy, I know your kind—tattler and climber! Get quite a kick out of sitting at my desk, wouldn't you? You won't have the chance, that I can promise—"

"I wouldn't give one damn to sit at the mayor's desk in this town," said Varallo. And he had a little more paper work to do, but not with Brant in the same building. Let it go: what the hell. He went out, and across to Novak's bar, and spent the rest of the afternoon drinking a little too much brandy.

He wondered how Jesse's end was turning out down there; whatever happened, it was cleaned up now, this end of the case. Come to look at it fair, not a very important case: exciting to Contera, but the kind of thing you found in big-city newspapers quite often. Except, of course, the mistaken-identity part of it; that you could say, whatever else—all the faults of the system, innocent people didn't as a rule get charged and found guilty of a crime.

He supposed Jesse had called Nell Varney to tell her. She'd know soon enough, anyway. Nice girl, but she didn't mean anything to Vic Varallo—except, maybe, as a kind of abstract symbol of justice—and it was a damn funny thing, come to think, that it was over her Vic Varallo had come to an important end.

And maybe an important beginning. Yes, maybe so. Because all of a sudden he found he was thinking instead of just feeling about it. Damn the reason—if there was a reason—maybe just; he'd grown up enough to get here, where he was now. To use a little sense on it. Because, sure, you ran into the insularity, the prejudice, now and then; even these supposedly enlightened days, you ran into it. But come to think, look at actual facts, not really very often.

He'd said to Brant, narrow-minded: you think too much about yourself. Pot calling the kettle black. What else had Vic Varallo been doing? For this reason and that, the thing getting magnified in his mind, so he was always looking for it, expecting it. And nobody to blow off to, so it just festered there, hidden. And look at it square, Varallo, maybe more than a little self-pity involved, too.

It was just, right now, over this thing, he'd got to the end of something. He felt that one stage of his life was finished.

He took a new bottle up to his room that night, but gave himself only one drink. He felt both restless and tired; he couldn't settle to anything or make up his mind to go to bed. When the phone rang at twenty minutes to one he was still up.

"Reporting in," said Jesse. *"Better is the end than the beginning thereof.* It's all over. All tied up. These L.A. fellows very nice—let me tag along at a respectful distance. Tasso came back to town late this afternoon, but it was about all over then. O'Mahoney did know where Mame was—cheap apartment down by Echo Park—led us there last night and again this morning. Wouldn't recognize her as the same woman—short black hair, et cetera—and the experience has aged her. We figure it once bit, twice shy with Mame, there was quite a lot of argument about letting loose of those handwriting samples. So we heard some very useful things, including a number of forceful sentiments about the rural atmosphere *and* a certain crooked, chiseling, Dago girl."

Varallo laughed. "I'll bet you did. Everybody locked in nice and cozy?"

"Just now. To tie the last knot, we waited for both Tasso and Higgins to show. You've heard the one about when thieves fall out. When Tasso heard about the double-cross projected by O'Mahoney—not just my word, Mame could back me up because O'Mahoney'd told her he'd already seen Higgins, of course— When Tasso heard that, and it penetrated his mind that there was enough on him on the dope charge to put him away for a while even without this one—friend, he talked. At length. Loud. Half in Italian, at O'Mahoney. I surmise not very polite language."

"Wouldn't he," said Varallo. "Who gets him first, us or L.A.?"

"Lieutenant Silverberg offers to toss you for it. He'll probably be on the phone to you tomorrow, settle the details. . . . Yes, Nell knows, I called her Saturday night. I'm going to get a little sleep right now and start back early. Lot of legal mess to clear up, you know. I'll see you."

"Yes," said Varallo. "I'll see you, boy—if not here, down in the big city."

"What? You—"

"The big city," repeated Varallo. Suddenly he was utterly and beautifully relaxed and sleepy. He fumbled the phone back on the hook, rolled over, and went sound asleep with the light on.

He came into his office at eight-thirty, hauled out the ancient, seldom-used portable typewriter and rummaged for carbon paper. It took him just two minutes to tap out four lines; he ripped the copies out of the machine, separated them, signed them all, folded the last one away in his wallet and addressed envelopes for the other two.

As he rose from his desk Brant flung open the door. "Morning, Vic boy. *Sergeant* Varallo. Here's your official demotion papers, make it all shipshape, see? I been—"

"You're just five minutes too late," said Varallo. He held out the second envelope. "Formal resignation from this force. You may be getting a request for references, and I couldn't care less what you answer —good, bad, or indifferent. It won't make much difference to me or whoever reads the reference. Because this whole affair, thanks to a couple of circumstances, will get a little spread in the papers, and it isn't going to sound very complimentary to Chief of Police Clare Brant. Even in Contera, I don't think anybody's going to take you very seriously as the big brain from now on. Get out of the way— I'm leaving now." He took one brief, unsentimental look round the office, picked up his hat, came out, and then turned with a shrug. "Here, you can deliver the mayor's copy, I can't be bothered."

Brant never said a word after him.

He came out to the street, and turned right, and walked down the block from the police station toward the little telephone building two blocks up. Past the gas company building, White's grocery, Sam's butcher shop, and the delicatessen at the corner of San Rafael: the men's store on the opposite corner, Mrs. Griffin's card-and-gift shop, the cheap chain furniture store. He didn't hesitate or look in any windows. He went into the building, past the two girls at the counter, up the stairs, and down the hall to the door marked ASSISTANT SUPERVISOR.

"Hello, Laura," he said.

She raised her smooth brown head, startled, and looked at him.

"I've come to say I'm going away. I should have gone a long while ago. But then I told you I'm not so bright, maybe. I've tried to think about it, just lately, and I think in a kind of way I've been enjoying myself as a martyr—you know? We do these things sometimes—being human. Once you said to me, not trying to defend yourself—well, that's a thing we do too—so I'll just say, things haven't always been so damn easy for me. This way and that." He made an angry, unfinished gesture. "Never mind it—it's all done now. But—it's just to make you understand, Laura—so, all right, I'm *sensitive*, as you said— I've had reason, but not so much as I thought—that, I can see a little clearer now. I—"

"I understand that, Vic," she whispered. "I always did. I— I was so ashamed, afterward, coming out with a thing like that. Not as if—as if Mother had ever said anything *much*—just, she was a little old-fashioned. You know. I never meant, I never thought— I never could think— But you wouldn't listen, you wouldn't give me a chance! You just—went away."

"Well, you told me I'm obstinate. I guess I am, Laura. Very damn obstinate." He was silent, and then he said, "I know how it was— I know you were just half out of your mind, didn't know what you were saying. Just one of those things. And a little thing. But I— It looked a hell of a lot bigger to me than it should have. I know that now."

"Yes," she said. She looked down at her hands in her lap.

Varallo took a breath. "Laura— I'm finished here. I was a fool to stay so long. I've resigned from the force, and I'm going down to L.A., I think—probably try to get on the force down there. It'll mean starting all over again, from almost the bottom—though with the experience I've had, maybe they'd give me preference— I don't know—and of course I've passed the lieutenants' exam once. Probably I'd get promotion quicker, anyway. But there wouldn't be as much money, for a while at least, even though a city force pays more. I haven't any right, Laura, I haven't any business at all asking you— But you're the only one I'd ever want, I've known that for a long time now. It's a lot to ask —that you'd come right away with me, and marry me now, and start out somewhere else a long way from here—"

She looked up at him at last, and her eyes were wet, but she didn't move or speak. And he let go of the little railing and stepped back.

"It's too much to ask you, I know," he said. "All of a sudden. You don't really know me well enough. Not long enough—to be sure. The way I am. I'm sorry—"

"I guess," she said in a low voice, "I *know* you— I mean—"

"Look," he said desperately, "maybe if we could write to each other —so you could get to know me better, and—"

"Maybe you're obstinate," she said softly. "You're also an awful damned fool, Vic Varallo."

"So I'm a fool. That I know too. I'm sorry, Laura— I shouldn't have come. I shouldn't have asked you." He took another step back and started to turn for the door; and she got up, fumbling blindly at the little wooden gate.

"Don't go without me, Vic—please, Vic—please, I want to come with you—"

When the matron brought her into the bare interview room, she just held out her hands to him. Jesse took them, looking down at her solemnly. "You know, this is damned awkward," he said.

"Wh-why?"

"What's called ambiguous. Here I've saved your life, in a manner of speaking, and naturally you're grateful. But I don't want anybody to marry me just out of gratitude—feel it's a duty, because she owes me something. So she says to herself, He's not much of a catch, and I don't really like him much, but what else can I do, when he's been so kind and helpful? You know? And the thing is, how'd I ever be sure it wasn't on that account?"

"You don't think," said Nell, "I could *convince* you, some way?"

"I'm told women can be damn convincing without meaning anything at all. You see what I'm driving at. I'd feel uneasy about it— bound to."

"But a clever lawyer like you—you m-must have thought of some way around it, Jesse?"

"Well, I tell you. I could put in my bill right now for the two hundred and sixty-four bucks in your account. And you pay it. And then we're quits, aren't we? Even."

"Quits," said Nell. "So we are. Consider it done."

"You don't owe me anything, I don't owe you anything. O.K.?"

"O.K."

"You just hired me as a lawyer, and paid me off."

"Yes. You've been a *very* satisfactory legal representative, Mr. Falkenstein, I'll recommend you to all my friends."

"So that's that, and we can start out all over again from scratch. You can have the money back for a trousseau or something. And— You're not crying, are you?"

"No!" sobbed Nell into his shoulder.

He let go of her hands and put his arms around her; after a few minutes he said into her hair, "Now listen, stop that—there's no reason to cry now. Nell, stop it—you'll be getting me in trouble, go on like that."

"Wh-what d'you mean?"

"If Uncle's got the quotation right— *A man should be careful lest he cause women to weep, for God counts their tears and holds him to account.* Not a word about any difference between tears of grief or joy, so to speak. You see?"

"I'm sorry. I'll s-stop. I am stopping. I *have* stopped," said Nell, blowing her nose and wiping her eyes.

"Then I guess," said Jesse, "it's legal to kiss you."

AGAINST
THE
EVIDENCE

The righteous is delivered
out of trouble,
and the wicked cometh
in his stead.

—Rabbi Meir,
the Talmud of Jerusalem

ONE

The bathroom door was pushed open and the doorbell rang at the same moment. "Nell!" shouted Jesse.

"Just a minute, darling, the door." Nell's voice floated back down the hall.

Jesse regarded the intruder bitterly, heaving himself upright in the tub and reaching for his towel. "And they say cats are curious," he muttered to himself. Must definitely fix that latch somehow, though it might not do much good—the firmest-fitting latch might prove a weak reed with something over a hundred and fifty pounds leaning on it.

The intruder sat down on the floor, entirely occupying the space between the bathtub and the opposite wall, and watched interestedly as Jesse toweled himself. "No modesty, no sense of shame," said Jesse.

Nell came down the hall and looked in. "Oh, dear," she said.

"Which you may well say. Not that I'm so damn modest," said Jesse, "but once in a while we do have guests, and they use the bathroom. Very disconcerting to have the door shoved open and an interested observer stroll in. As happened, you recall, with that Manders woman and my sister Fran, not to speak of old Mrs. Forsythe. Reason she took her business elsewhere—nice staid, solid firm like Peabody and Sparkle, instead of an erratic fly-by-night like me. And," he added, gesturing with the towel, "it's all your fault."

"Yes, I know," said Nell. "Fran didn't mind, she thought it was funny. There's a woman to see you. Darling, come out—"

"Like this?" said Jesse. "What d'you mean, a woman to see me? Tell her to come to the office in the morning. I don't see clients at home. Especially in a state of nature."

"I didn't mean you," said Nell. "At least, not right away—you *had* better put some clothes on, or she'll think you're starving to death so you can't be a very good lawyer. It's maddening, I feed you well enough, but you stay so *bony*. Come out now, darling, let Jesse out of the tub to get some clothes on." She tugged the intruder by his collar, and got him up to his feet.

"The office," said Jesse. "I'm hungry, and I want to relax after the day I've had. Never saw old Botts so difficult. Maybe he's got ulcers."

"Well," said Nell, "I wish you would see her—if just to tell her to come to the office. She needs somebody, that I can see, poor soul, and it's a casserole and various other things that'll keep hot and still be all right. Now come out, Athelstane. Give Jesse some room."

"*Athelstane*," said Jesse. The intruder, excited and pleased to hear his name spoken, rose up and attempted to wash Nell's face; she dodged him expertly, still tugging. "I am not so very damn Anglophile that you'd notice, and why to God I have to be stuck with— You ask me, he's what the head doctors call a *voyeur*. Pushing into the bathroom when the door's shut—"

"He doesn't like closed doors," said Nell. "He's gregarious."

"Now that you can say again. The typical extrovert. And if there's anything more obnoxious— Why the hell should I see this woman here and now?"

"Jesse, she's desperate. You can tell—not that she's trying to cover it up. You know. Please do. Just to see what she wants, what's wrong."

"Oh, hell," said Jesse. "Between you and Athelstane and the climate—"

"Among," said Nell. "Among, for more than two objects of comparison."

"It is written in the aphorisms of Jeshu ben Shirah in the Torah," said Jesse, "*An evil wife is a yoke shaken to and fro.* Since when does a virtuous woman criticize her husband? What kind of desperate? Is she a beautiful statuesque blonde with a jealous husband she wants to divorce?"

"Would I be urging you to see her if she was?"

"Were."

"Was," said Nell. "No, she's not. I just felt awfully sorry for her, the little she said. I shouldn't think it's anything like that at all. It won't take ten minutes to say you'll take her on, or shunt her off to somebody else. And maybe you'd better take Athelstane into the bedroom with you, he might scare her."

Jesse draped his dressing gown around him and said, "For the first and only time. I did think once, well, when we acquire a proper house and settle down to raising a family, at least he'll be a hell of a watch dog. You say he's gregarious— I say he's undiscriminating. He just likes everybody. Any amateur burglar he'd welcome with open paws. All right, all right. Ten minutes."

Shut into the bedroom, he began to dress, muttering to himself. Whoever the woman was, she could take him as she found him; he wasn't going to put on a clean shirt at this time of day for anybody, when he wasn't going out anywhere. In such weather. Very little rhyme or reason to Southern California seasons at the best of times, but it looked like being a bad summer when the first hundred-degree temperatures arrived in June.

Athelstane, belatedly aware of a stranger in the apartment, was now leaning against the bedroom door, which fortunately opened inward. He turned an anxious expression on Jesse.

And no wonder at all that Mrs. Forsythe, though a personal acquaintance, had taken her damage suit elsewhere; even without the bathroom incident—

He remembered another of old Jeshu's aphorisms about women. *Watch over an impudent eye: and marvel not if she trespass against thee.* Only too true.

The trouble was, bridegrooms were apt to be too indulgent. Eight months ago, he could still have been called a bridegroom, a month married; and also he'd had half his mind on that Cotter case when Nell called to report on the latest apartments she'd been looking at. No, none of them would do; there was no sense moving out of Jesse's bachelor flat until they found something really nice—but there was this puppy. The people who'd had this apartment she'd gone to see, it seemed, a nice young couple (so the manager said)—planning to buy a house and looking around—they'd been killed together in a freeway accident, and no relatives or anyone. His company had taken care of the funeral and so on, but they'd had this puppy. Nobody wanted him or knew what to do with him, and the manager had been feeding him —he said it seemed a shame to send him to the pound when he'd heard the young fellow say they'd paid over a hundred bucks for him —but his wife didn't like dogs much and—

"Whose wife?"

"The manager's, dearest," said Nell. "He's a lovely puppy, and the man says he'll be glad to let anyone have him who'd give him a good home."

"What brand is he?"

"I think he must be a boxer," Nell had said rather doubtfully. "Only his ears and tail haven't been cropped, and he's a little different color than any boxer I've seen. The manager doesn't know either. Yes, I know it's really too big a dog for an apartment, but he's *sweet*, Jesse— I couldn't bear for him to go to the pound, and the man says he'll have to get rid of him somehow. . . . Oh, yes, he's advertised, tried to sell him, but no luck. . . . Well, he looks more like a boxer than anything else. His name's Athelstane, and he's ten months old, that's all the manager knows—not really a puppy, and all housebroken and so on— Jesse, *would* you mind if I took him?"

And with his mind on the Cotter statement, and reflecting that Nell would be the one to take this oddly-come-by orphan out for exercise, Jesse had indulgently given permission. And come home that night to be confronted with something incontestably canine but very dubiously a boxer. Or if he was, a much outsized one.

"I know he's too big," said Nell anxiously, "but isn't he beautiful? He's got a marvelous disposition."

"I see he has," said Jesse, as Athelstane attempted to climb into his lap. "He doesn't look much like a boxer to me. His nose is too long, and he's got dewlaps."

"Maybe he's not a very good one, and they were cheated on him," said Nell.

At that date, last November, Athelstane had stood a bit over two feet high at the shoulders and tipped the scales at some ninety pounds; they had consoled each other that at ten months he must have practically all his growth. But as time passed and he continued to grow, and to look less and less like any common garden variety of canine, they had begun to wonder. And then there came the day they found out—the knowledgeable woman Nell met in the park, who admired her nice young mastiff.

"I went and got a book at the library, and it's *so*. It might *be* him, in the picture. What's called a dark fawn-brindle English mastiff. Not a bull mastiff, they're smaller. And it says—"

"I can see what it says," Jesse said dismally, looking at the book. "Full growth attained at approximately two and a half years. Minimum standard thirty inches at the shoulder, a hundred and forty pounds. Good God. And he's only a year old now and eats three pounds of meat a day. I don't know how you get into these things. In a three-room apartment, and we had a hell of a hunt for it after you saddled us with this monster, too."

"But we couldn't let him go to the *pound*. The woman said they're quite rare and valuable. And we won't always be in an apartment."

"Go on, tell me we're lucky to get such a specimen free. He's so valuable, we sell him and get back some of his upkeep."

"Darling, he doesn't mean it," said Nell to Athelstane. And perfectly aware of this, Athelstane had leaned over the arm of the chair and applied a long pink tongue to Jesse's ear.

Athelstane had not yet been banished to the pound or elsewhere. At this moment, leaning on the bedroom door watching Jesse dress, Athelstane stood nearly three feet high and weighed slightly more than Jesse. He had sad black jowls, long black ears, a long snaky black-tipped tail, melancholy brown eyes and a large wet black nose. And a congenital dislike, as Nell pointed out, of closed doors. He made an impatient whuffling noise and Jesse said, "All right, let me get my pants on, can't you?"

Women. Wives. Why she couldn't have told this female politely to come to his office in the morning—

It was still up in the nineties, and he'd been looking forward to a leisurely drink before dinner, and dinner, and a restful evening thinking about the Blackwell suit while the phonograph soothed him *via* Bach.

"Hell," he said, and opened the bedroom door.

"Mrs. Nielsen," said Nell *sotto voce*.

Yes, trouble, thought Jesse. Bad trouble, some kind. A plain middle-aged woman, dowdy, shabbily dressed, what the statistics would call lower middle class. And very frightened. He had seen a lot of frightened people; some took it one way, some the other. Nell's word for this one was right: desperate. She looked at him out of pale china-blue eyes through thick rimless lenses that magnified her slow tears, and said on a little gasp, "I'm awful sorry to break in on you like this at your home, Mr. Falkenstein, but I just *had* to. The policeman said, a lawyer—"

"That's all right. Don't be afraid of the dog, he's very friendly. Suppose you tell me what it's all about." Jesse sat down opposite her.

"I got you outta the phone book." She had a handkerchief wadded in one hand, dabbed continually at her cheeks. "I never had call to know a lawyer. And I went to the address it said, but the lady there, she was just leaving, she said you'd be going right home when you got outta court, and when I said how important it was, she told me— I hadda come on the bus, it took awhile—"

Yes, muddle-headed, sympathetic spinster Miss Williams. Never mind. "A policeman," murmured Jesse. "Something criminal? What's the charge?"

"Oh, sir, he never done it, he never done such a thing! It's cruel, come and arrest him—my Harry!—say he done that! He never, I know, he couldn't've! I don't rightly understand what makes them think he did, but it's not so. A lawyer could show them it's not so, that's what you—" The handkerchief came up again.

"Your husband, your son?" asked Jesse patiently. "What's the charge?"

"He never. My son Harry, sir. My husband's dead these ten years. It's so, I can't rightly say it isn't, Harry's not—not just like everybody else. They didn't let him go to regular school after the first couple years; he went to a special school for the ones like him—it cost a little bit, whatever you could pay, you know, but they said he ought to. And he liked it, he always got along good, he's always been a good boy, everybody likes Harry. They taught him more'n you'd think he could take in—he makes change good, if you give him time—and I raised him to be honest and polite too, acourse. He's just *slow*, they said—backward, you know. But everybody likes Harry, he's always nice and friendly with everybody—way he was raised. Lots o' people stop by his stand regular for their cigarettes and papers and magazines. He's got the little newsstand in the lobby of the Ames Building, he's smart enough to do that—if he isn't just as bright as everybody—"

"Mmh," said Jesse, absently fondling Athelstane's ears. "The charge?"

A little gasp. "Oh, Mr. Falkenstein, it's *murder!* This girl that got murdered—and I guess, *you* know—she worked in the building, right there, and— But he never! It's a wicked lie, say it was Harry! Cruel— he couldn't even rightly understand why they was taking him away, he was scared. Harry gets scared awful easy—and what they're doing to him at that jail, I just can't bear to— Oh, please, sir, you go and find out what they think they've got against him, and show it isn't so! Harry'd never in this world do such a thing."

Jesse glanced at Nell, quiet a little apart from Mrs. Nielsen, and back to Athelstane. Athelstane's perennially sorrowful countenance mirrored his own feelings. Harry, he thought: one like that. He supposed that "and I guess, you know," meant rape. A nasty case: considering the quality of the L.A.P.D. as a professional force, probably a straightforward case. He opened his mouth to tell Mrs. Nielsen about the Public Defenders' office, and shut it again. Not that he expected Mrs. Nielsen would be good for a nice fat fee, but that office was always pretty busy: not even the newest of those eager young lawyers could be spared to run over to the County Jail just to hold the hand of a backward boy.

"I don't know what lawyers cost," she said nervously, "but I got enough money to pay you, Mr. Falkenstein. I—I own a little rental property. We always saved as we could and Sam was kinda lucky on a couple of deals. And Harry's little stand—well, it don't bring in much, but something—and it's something for him to do, not much a boy like Harry *can* do, and it's not good for anybody, sit around all the time. But— Oh, please, sir, if you'd just go and find out—show them it can't be so—"

"You don't want to worry about the police, you know," said Jesse. "Not monsters. Quite humane and reasonable these days. He's not being mistreated." She just went on looking at him, dumb and frightened and pleading. "Look," he said, "suppose I go down after dinner and see what's going on, and let you know. That O.K.? And then we'll see where he stands. If you'll give me your phone number—"

"Oh, thank you, sir, if you just would—but I haven't got a phone."

"Your address then," said Jesse with a mental sigh. He needn't take the thing on. Tell her where she stood, shunt her off to the Public Defenders' office.

"Oh, I do thank you, sir— I don't know if you want any money now—" She made a gesture at opening her shabby plastic bag.

"No, I don't know that it'll be a case for me. Maybe they've just taken him in for questioning, you know." In all probability, the sensible course would be to plead him guilty, get it over. One like that wouldn't get the gas chamber; they'd tuck him away safe, that was all.

"Oh, d'you think that's *so*, Mr. Falkenstein? Oh, if only it was—"

He got the woman out at last, still stammering incoherent gratitude and defense of her poor Harry. Nell vanished into the kitchen, unprecedentedly silent, to put dinner on the table. Jesse made himself a drink and set a stack of Bach fugues on the phonograph as background, but the expected sensation of relaxation did not follow.

"Damn," he said to his drink. Why had he said he'd do even that much? A cut-and-dried thing, probably. Time wasted on a very uninteresting case. And that poor damned woman, he couldn't morally put in much of a bill.

When Nell called him to dinner he asked her plaintively why he'd done it. Nell looked at him sidelong with her nice dark-fringed gray eyes and said, "You shouldn't have got her hopes up like that, saying maybe they'd let him go."

"I know, damn it. Had to say something. It looks cut and dried, from the little she said. The police don't make an arrest without some good solid evidence. And one like that— What she wants is the Public Defender, a nice quiet plea of guilty-as-charged, and stash the fellow away in Atascadero, where he can't do it again."

"Well," said Nell, pouring coffee, "there was a time I might have ended up with the Public Defender, if you'd acted all so disinterested as that then."

"Don't remind me. I aged ten years. Not exactly the same sort of thing."

"It won't hurt you to go and see. Even the police make mistakes— they're only human."

"I'm going," said Jesse. "I said I would. But I don't think it's anything for me. . . . And you know better than to beg at the table," he added to Athelstane, who was watching every mouthful he took. Athelstane sighed. "What impressed you about her enough to make me see her?"

"It doesn't mean anything," said Nell. "It's just irrational, I know. She reminded me of Mrs. Giddings. You know my father was the complete atheist, but Mother'd been raised *very* strict Methodist, and she sent me to Sunday school for a while. Until Dad got violent about filling innocent minds with nonsense and snatched me out. And Mrs. Giddings taught the Sunday school class. So all right, say any religion has got corrupted by senseless ritual and greed for power and all the rest of it—but ordinary people, a lot of them, they take it so—so serious and earnest. You know. Good people, who really believe what they've been told is so, and try to live that way."

"Oh, granted."

"Like your Uncle Malachi. All very innocent and solemn."

"The disappointed rabbi. Yes. Very tiresome old fellow, always quoting at you out of Holy Writ. Sure, a lot of nonsense in it—and some common sense, of course. Of course our branch of the family are the renegades. But what's it got to do with Mrs. Nielsen?"

"She's like that, don't you think? If her Harry was guilty, she'd try to take all the blame, she'd make excuses and feel awful about it—but she wouldn't deny it, Jesse. Not when she knew. She couldn't be that dishonest."

"Um. Mother love. And what I gather, she doesn't know much about it. Not yet."

"Yes, I know, but— She ought to know him, what he's capable of— or not. After all."

"Woolgathering. Sentimentality. So do the cops." Jesse looked at her severely. "Are you climbing up on a bandwagon over this? Just on the word of that poor devil of a female who says, My Harry never done it?"

"Not really," said Nell. "I just want you to go and see, Jesse. Just in case . . . I like your Uncle Malachi. Even if he is always quoting sententious maxims at you. I got a copy of the Talmud at the library so as to come back at him with some."

"I know you did. Showing off."

"And one of them I can come back at you with," said Nell, "is *Answer not before thou hast heard the cause.*"

"Don't know that it's very à propos," said Jesse. "I kind of think I have. Short and not sweet. But I'll go and see. You and your Mrs. Giddings."

Nell smiled at him. "I'm going to wash my hair tonight anyway." Which was a little project, since she'd never cut it—her nice dark-brown hair, just a bit of a wave in it, halfway down her back when she loosed it from its thick chignon. "It won't take you long. And I'll do the dishes by myself, I don't approve of men helping with housework all the time, as I keep telling you—so you just run along and see Harry."

"Well," said Jesse, finishing his coffee and groping for a cigarette, "to please you. You know something? In spite of all your faults—

saddling us with this Loch Ness monster to feed, and monopolizing the bathroom, and so on—on the whole I'm not sorry I married you. Virtuous woman brimful of charity. They say charity to the poor balances out our sins. About all the return I could expect from Mrs. Nielsen, because when she says she's got money I suspect it's represented by a couple of run-down shacks rented at thirty a month."

And presently he kissed her, told Athelstane he couldn't come this time, and started for the County Jail.

TWO

He was denied immediate access to Harry; the sergeant was questioning him. Jesse had no burning desire to see Harry, but asked if the sergeant could spare him a few minutes. In due time Sergeant Clock of Homicide emerged from the inner cells, and Jesse presented himself.

"Can't say I'd want the case, you know, even if the woman could afford a private fee. Shove her gently on to the Public Defender. But I did say I'd find out the general case and tell her where he stands. Be obliged for a brief rundown. Have you charged him?"

Sergeant Andrew Clock looked rather more like the Hollywood version of a gangster than any standby screen tough, a big burly man with a craggy face mostly prognathous jaw and brow. Surprisingly, his voice was very soft and bore traces of a Boston accent. "He's been charged, yes. Mind if we step outside?—never have liked this damn place. It gives me claustrophobia. Ought to be a little cooler outside."

It wasn't, much. They stood on the top step of the broad flight leading up to the entrance and lit cigarettes. This was the oldest piece of North Broadway along here, though the jail was a fairly new building; the street was narrower and twistier here than farther down. And nothing much around here but the big parking lot, warehouses, the great dismal cavern of the freight yards: it was dark and oddly silent for a place within a mile of the center of L.A. Jesse remembered suddenly that before it had been North Broadway it had been the Avenida Doloroso, the road of sorrows leading to the old Spanish cemetery. Very appropriate.

"You don't," he said, "lock them in all official unless you've got some evidence to satisfy the bench. Not on this force you don't, under this chief. That I know."

198 FOUR BY EGAN

"Or most other city forces these days," said Clock. "The mother think he's being railroaded?"

"Don't think it occurred to her. Just shocked and incredulous. Couldn't be my Harry, he'd never do such a thing."

Clock let out a long stream of smoke on a sigh. "It's standard reaction. People—sometimes you get it with perfectly sane, competent adults—the family's always the last to suspect. But you always get it with this kind, the nuts. Whatever kind of nuts they are—just missing some marbles like this one, or the ones bright enough but turned wrong some way. Because they're the lame ducks, and it's a damn funny thing, you know, for every lame duck there's somebody to mother him and take care of him and make excuses for him. And it always comes as a big surprise to them that their poor darling could run amok. . . . This one wasn't very hard to crack. He showed up almost right away."

"It was a girl who worked in the building where he has this little newsstand, Mrs. Nielsen said."

"Lilian Blake. Miss," said Clock, emitting another long stream of smoke. "Ordinary sort of girl—not even very pretty, not very anything. A little bit of a thing—just five feet, a hundred pounds. Blonde. Twenty-seven. Never been married. No steady boy friend. She was a dental assistant—worked for a Dr. Friedlander in this Ames Building. You didn't notice the newspaper stories today?" He sighed. "Well, just a run-of-the-mill, sordid little killing, no malice aforethought. She checked in at nine every morning. Harry usually opens his stand about the same time. Yesterday morning she didn't reach Friedlander's office, and eventually he got worried about her—and a little annoyed. Called her apartment to see if she was sick, got no answer. Then, about ten-thirty, the city refuse truck came along and the men on it found her, in the alley behind the building."

"Mmh?" said Jesse encouragingly.

Clock sighed again. "Friedlander's office is on the ground floor, at the back of the building—one twelve. There's a back door giving on the alley, just a couple of feet from his office door. She was about six feet down from the door, in the alley, behind a couple of big trash barrels. Actual cause of death was strangulation, but she was marked up— she'd put up a fight. She'd been dead about an hour. It looked as if she'd come into the building, started down the hall to Friedlander's office and been caught there. Not too surprising nobody saw her—that rear cross hall just leads to two back offices, Friedlander's and an eye doctor's who's never there on Wednesdays. Anyway, she was caught there, and attacked—dragged out into the alley."

"And raped?"

"Well, no," said Clock. "It looked as if that's what he intended, all right. Her dress was torn, and her underwear—she was sprawled out on her back—but the odds are he got scared off, or just plain scared, and ran. Or got confused. One like Harry—" he shrugged.

"What put you on to him?"

"I said it was an easy one, Mr. Falkenstein. Half a dozen people told us that Harry'd admired the girl, always said hello to her when she came by, offered her free candy bars and cigarettes—like that. Like a kid making up to a grownup he liked, they said. Giving what he had to offer, you know. Hell, that kind—well, he's twenty-four, you can read it he's just started to discover sex, maybe? I wouldn't know— let the doctors thrash it out. It's obvious he's not competent, I'd say an I.Q. of about seventy-five. Anyway, he'd singled the girl out for attention, in a way. Both the elevator operators said that, and other people. Her roommate mentioned it—she shared an apartment with another girl, up on Bronson Avenue. A Ruth Myers. She said—and we got some corroboration on that too—that Lilian was afraid of him. You know how a lot of people feel about the Harrys—a kind of combination of disgust and fear. She'd evidently let him see how she felt, too. Never took anything he wanted to give her, always hurried past his stand not looking at him."

"Oh," said Jesse. "And?"

"And," said Clock, "so eventually we took a look at Harry. And Harry's stand. After we'd poked around other places—the roommate, and Lilian's latest date, and so on—and come up with nothing. No reason for anybody to want her out of the way. She evidently got on O.K. with Ruth Myers, and the couple of fellows she'd been out with recently are just ordinary fellows, not much interested in her. Her only relative was a married sister. She hadn't much money, but she wasn't in debt or in any kind of trouble. She was efficient at her job, Friedlander liked her. Just that—he's got a wife a hell of a lot better looking than Lilian was. The only little thing we got at all was this stuff about Harry. So we looked, and this afternoon we found the evidence we wanted. Her dress had been torn, as I say, and a gold pendant necklace she'd had on was broken. We found part of the necklace—

about three inches of it, very fine chain—on the floor behind Harry's counter. We found a bigger piece of the lace trimming off her slip there, too. Better yet, we found his fingerprints on her handbag. It was a cheap plastic bag—shiny finish, you know?—and there was his thumbprint on one side and four fingers on the other, clear as day, where he'd grabbed it and tossed it away when he got hold of her. That, of course, we got after the first evidence, when we got his prints to compare."

"Very cut and dried," said Jesse sadly. "I see. As you say, never can predict, with one like Harry. Hypothesis being that in the first fine careless boyish rapture of love he went after her, she fought back and he got mad. What does he say?"

"Oh, for the love of God!" said Clock disgustedly. "You ever try to get any sense out of one like that? He can't remember a question thirty seconds. I ask you! I said he's not competent. Any judge'll see that, and sign the commitment order ten minutes after the case is called. All I've got out of him in six hours isn't worth a damn. He says yesterday morning—he thinks it was yesterday morning—he had an awful bad headache, like he does sometimes. He didn't come to open the stand at the regular time, he stayed home in bed. Like Mama could say. I needn't add, Mama does say. But she works at a Woolworth's out on Figueroa. She left the house at eight o'clock and can't swear to anything after that. So what?" Clock shrugged. "He usually opens the stand between nine and nine-thirty. He can tell time—he's real proud of that, Harry is. He says he didn't get there until about ten-thirty, he guesses, yesterday. Well, most of the people coming into the building to work get there around nine, and all those we've contacted say, no, Harry's stand wasn't open—also say, it isn't always at that hour. They weren't surprised at that. And what does it say? Lilian Blake died between nine and nine-thirty. So Harry was busy with Lilian, and then maybe cleaning up a little in the rest room before he opened. Or just wandering around in a daze after his big moment. I mean, he isn't so damned dumb that he wouldn't notice a few blood spots on his shirt, or something like that. Not," said Clock, "that we found any. But it was the day before—he could have got rid of the shirt."

"That smart?" asked Jesse.

"Hell," said Clock again, "I don't know. It's a kind of no man's land, with the Harrys. They surprise you sometimes. And then again— I'm just a fair-to-middling cop, Mr. Falkenstein. I go by evidence. Evidence we've got. And also, you know, the whole setup looks like Harry —it could hardly be anybody but one like that, you look at it. People coming into the building at that hour—nobody but a Harry would have attacked her in that public hall, even if it is out of sight of the main lobby. And while she was a little thing, as I say she put up a fight, but she didn't get a chance to scream—whoever it was was big and strong, like Harry. Didn't get a chance to mark him up where it showed, except for one little scratch on his arm. He says that was a cat, of course. Well—" Clock fell silent. He dropped his cigarette and stepped on it. He said, "They talk about the sanctity of human life. Me, I'm a realist. I don't figure the ones like Harry have much sanctity about them. If you ask me, it's a waste of time and energy—and when they pull something like this, a waste of public taxes—taking such good, loving care of 'em. Not doing any good to anybody—and always so apt to do harm. More harm. These sentimentalists, trying to abolish the death penalty—and the damn-fool legal quibbling, if you'll excuse me, about sane or insane. Splitting hairs . . . She was just an ordinary girl, sure," said Clock rather savagely. "Not even a very pretty girl. An ordinary nice girl, working at an ordinary job. Saving dimes in a piggy bank to buy an imitation-mink stole she'd seen in a catalogue. Paying her half of eighty bucks a month for a three-room apartment on Bronson Avenue. Writing letters to her married sister in Illinois. Going to the nearest Presbyterian church most Sundays. Coming home after work to mend her underwear or write letters or read a paperback love story—after fixing the scrambled eggs or the lamb chop—most nights. Once in a while going out to a movie, down to the beach, with a date. Not a very interesting girl, Mr. Falkenstein. But a hell of a lot more valuable human being than Harry. Can't we say?"

"You're a philosopher, sergeant," said Jesse. "Thanks very much for the breakdown. I don't know that I want to take on Harry. Just on the surface, seems it'd take a smarter lawyer than me to get him off— which doesn't look like a very bright notion anyway. No. Not much sense trying to dream up a defense."

"It was," said Sergeant Clock softly, "quite a messy little kill. Which was another thing pointing to Harry—more violence used than was necessary, if that's the word. . . . Just an ordinary girl, but she had rights, after all. The right to go on living." He was looking across the strip of lawn in front of the jail, to the floodlights and the big

black-and-white sign, LOITERING OR SPEAKING TO PRISONERS FORBIDDEN.
"So she had," said Jesse. "Thanks very much, sergeant."

But being there, he went in to see Harry. And got a little surprise.
Harry didn't, at first glance, look like what he was. He was a very big
young man, fresh complexion like a baby's, oxlike brown eyes, a slow
shy smile. No, not all there; you talked to him two minutes, that
emerged. But it went back to feelings, and the feeling Jesse got from
Harry was, first, bewildered innocence, and second, a complete lack of
aggression.

He sat there on the iron cot in his cell, neater and cleaner than you
might expect, in pressed brown slacks and a brown-printed sports
shirt, and he was polite, calling Jesse *sir*. "I don't know why you all
think I done something bad," he said. "I do things wrong sometimes,
sir, like when I ain't sure, but I never mean to. Like I got to look real
careful not to mix up the quarters with the half dollars. But I never
mean do things wrong, I'm extra careful."

Not much sense trying to question him. That job would be turning
Sergeant Clock gray; and what would there be to get, anyway? Obviously the bench would say unfit to plead, whether or not Harry was
represented by somebody from the Public Defenders' office.

"It's those things. I guess. They showed me. A little piece of goldy
chain, and—and—a sort of piece of cloth. I guess they think I stole
those things? And a lady's purse—I never steal anything like that.
Stealing's bad. I'd never do nothing like that." Not emphatic, protesting: just saying it, trying earnestly to explain. "I never saw those
things before, honest. I don't know why they think I'd do something
bad like that. I never mean do nothing bad, sir."

Jesse looked at him, feeling sad and rather annoyed. "You know
Miss Blake, Harry?"

"Oh—uh—Miss *Blake*, sure I know her! She's a pretty lady." His
brown eyes lit up, smiling. "She works there—some place in the building. Ever' day she comes in. She's got pretty goldy hair and she wears
red clothes a lot, I like red. I like to give her things—but—but—" His
heavy cherubic face clouded suddenly.

"But what?"

"Oh, well, she—she—she won't take nothing, 's all," said Harry. "I
guess she don't like me, but Mama says, Don't take no notice if folks
are like that, they don't mean no harm. . . . Please, why I got to stay

here, sir? I want to go home. I won't have no clean shirt tomorrow, if—
I want to go home. Please—"

"They think," said Jesse, "that you hurt Miss Blake, Harry. Did
you? They think you hurt her—very bad, the worst anybody can be
hurt. Did you, Harry?"

"I—I—I—hurt Miss Blake?" The brown eyes widened, not in denial
or surprise but in pain. "I never—I never—hurt nobody, I never! The
other man said—but I never! I'm allus careful—you got to be careful
not to hurt—I never do, I'm allus extra careful. Because there was
Spotty." And suddenly he began to cry, awkward and snuffling, unself-
conscious. "I ain't *ever* forgot. I never would."

"Spotty, who was that?"

"She was just the prettiest little kitten, sir. I loved Spotty—Mama
said we could keep her—it was a long time back but I never forgot.
You patted her and she purred just so loud, and rubbed against you.
She'd sit in my lap and purr, and she was so soft and nice, I loved
Spotty." He was still crying; the words came out in gulps. "I never,
ever, meant to hurt her—I never would! But Mama, she'd put wax stuff
on the floor, and I slipped, and I fell right down on Spotty—and she
was hurted bad some way, she cried and cried—it hurt *me*, hear her
cry—and after a while Mama called some place on Mis' Wilson's telephone and a man came in a truck and took Spotty away and I never
saw her no more. I felt so awful bad, and it was all my blame if I
never did mean do anything wrong—*hurting* her like that— Little
things, you got to be careful, they hurt awful easy. Sir. You got to be
careful, Mama says, when you're big like me. I always *am*. I don't
never want to hurt nothing noways, I never would."

That was what he heard from Harry, and it was pure impulse he'd
gone in to see Harry at all, after talking to Clock. Why should he? Cut
and dried.

He didn't ask Harry any more questions about Lilian Blake or his
staying in bed yesterday morning. As Sergeant Clock had discovered,
it would require great patience and a lot of time to pin Harry's mind—
such as it was—down to any one thing. And as Clock had implied, the
head doctors were in a sense broken reeds: they'd say this, they'd say
that, and offer a lot of precedents and double talk. You had to use a
little judicious common sense, listening to the head doctors.

Jesse stood again on the steps outside the jail entrance, and asked
himself if he was using common sense. And the only answer his sub-

conscious mind dredged up was a dimly remembered quotation from Uncle Malachi—was it from the Ethics of Solomon?— *For the bewitching of naughtiness doth obscure things that are honest; and the wandering of concupiscence doth undermine the simple mind.*

Applicable?

He had said to Nell, Woolgathering.

But there was another consideration, of course, aside from Harry, aside from pure justice. Call it a one-hundredth of a percent chance; still, there it was.

Jesse told himself he was likely being a fool. He walked down to where he'd left the Ford and drove out west to Albert Avenue this side of Santa Monica Boulevard, a shabby narrow street lined with old California bungalows. Couldn't tell much at night, but some of them would be kept up neatly, some just let go; from what he could see, he thought Mrs. Nielsen's little two-bedroom white frame house was kept up. He had a brief vision of Harry mowing the lawn on Sundays, watering the little bed of ivy geraniums by the porch.

He told Mrs. Nielsen what the police case was. And of course all she had to say was, "He never done such a thing. It's a wicked lie."

It was a small, shabby living room. Overstuffed furniture from Sears Roebuck twenty years ago. Hand-crocheted antimacassars. A worn flowered rug. A cheap, highly colored lithograph of a bad seascape, in a cheap gilt frame, over the davenport. And everything very neat and clean. She'd apologized for her apron, whisking it off.

Jesse said, "He mentioned a cat—Spotty."

She stared, and then said, "Oh, yes, sir. Quite a while back it was. Harry was only fourteen, around there. All broke up over it, and I felt awful bad too, if it was just accidental-like. A pretty little kitten, Spotty, and he thought the world 'n' all of her. Just an accident, over and over I told him, he didn't mean any harm—might've happened to anybody—but seemed like he couldn't get over it. . . . Harry's always been awful good and gentle with animals, like that, and Mis' Wilson's baby, he sure was taken with that baby, and gentle as could be with the little thing. Why, even I ask him to go 'n' cut a bunch of flowers from the yard, he's just so careful, as if they was alive."

"They found those things," said Jesse, "the piece of Miss Blake's necklace and the lace from her slip, there behind his stand. Where I don't suppose anybody would be except Harry."

Her hands were roughened and red from a lifetime of hard work;

they twisted together agonizedly. "I don't know nothing about that, Mr. Falkenstein. The police, I guess they're good honest men nowadays—they wouldn't lie. I don't know how those things got there, unless it was somebody put them there to make it look like it was Harry done that. But it isn't right, it isn't so. . . . Why, I— I—" She reddened a little, went on determinedly, "I don't guess Harry knows enough—or anything at all, about—I mean, you know, to want to—to— I don't figure he ever thought about such . . . And, sir, the way they tell it, it makes out that was the only day in his life Harry was late opening up his stand. That's not so. He gets these headaches, something-grain they call them, the doctor said—every so often, maybe once a month, twice, like that, he gets one, and stays on at home after I leave for work. They can ask those fellows run the elevators, anybody. They can say it wasn't the only time it ever happened. And anybody could've put those things there—"

Well, thought Jesse. It was possible, of course. And of course, the girl hadn't been raped. . . . A no man's land, one like Harry. Maybe just beginning to feel that way—as Clock said—and still ignorant, so even after he caught her— Who could say?

"Why, I remember once, I asked him to go and cut a couple nice roses—this one bush out in back, it's a Golden Autumn and doing real well, the soil's good and sandy for roses here—and he says, Mama, I don't like cut them, kill them so cruel when they look so pretty just growing. He says, Can't we just leave them where they belong, Mama, standing up nice and looking pretty?" She dabbed at her eyes.

"Yes," said Jesse unhappily. "I see."

"And they say he done a *murder*. Killed that girl. It's a lie, Mr. Falkenstein. I know, maybe it's hard for you to believe me—or Harry. It's awful easy for anybody to say bad things about somebody like Harry, on account they're not just like the rest of us. I know. And like that policeman said to me this afternoon, it's awful easy to think, just because I'm his mother I'd right away say he never done such a thing. But I know my Harry, Mr. Falkenstein, and he *never*. Why—you know how children are, sir, you got to teach them the right way to do, they don't understand about some things—but from the time he was a baby, Harry was always so gentle. Other boys, they scared him when they played rough. And he was always so careful with things, not to do any hurt. I remember, after it rained, he was always so careful walking, not to step on the worms left out. He used to say, Got to be careful not to hurt the poor little worms, till they get home safe. . . . And they say he done a thing like *that.*"

Jesse looked at the old-fashioned, eight-day mahogany mantel clock (which informed him that it was five minutes past ten) and he had a horrid little vision of himself talking about Harry's solicitude for worms to His Honor Justice Botts of the Superior Court.

"You got to show them he never in this world done it," said Mrs. Nielsen.

THREE

When Jesse got home Nell was sitting up in the big double bed, reading a Penguin reprint of Margery Allingham. Her hair was just dry, but she hadn't yet braided it for the night, and it lay in heavy loose waves over her shoulders, above her plain blue nylon nightgown. Athelstane had climbed up beside her and was whuffling in his sleep, solidly established on Jesse's side of the bed.

"I could sue him for alienation of affections," said Jesse.

"Don't you think there's enough to go round?" asked Nell.

"Bad policy to hand out indiscriminate compliments to a lawful wedded wife—give her ideas about her station. But what the hell, for once. You look very nice—very inviting. It's a pity you've got a damn fool for a husband."

"Well, there could be two opinions about that," said Nell. "What kind of damn fool, darling?"

Jesse shoved Athelstane over and sat down on the edge of the bed, stripping off his tie. "I'll tell you. The kind of overimaginative damn fool who tells himself fairy stories beginning, If it could be. Because I don't suppose there was ever a handier scapegoat than Harry Nielsen. His mother says, Awful easy for anybody to say bad things about one like Harry—and isn't it God's truth." He got up, hung up his jacket and began to unbutton his shirt. "About a thousand to one. They've got some nice straightforward solid evidence—kind a jury likes—always supposing it comes before a jury, which it probably won't. That Sergeant Clock, a good man. Knows what he's doing—an experienced cop, honest." He hung up his pants and stuffed his shirt into the clothes hamper. "Things don't happen like in the paperback detective novels. Evidence, it means just what it looks like." He got out a clean pair of pajamas and stared at them.

"Yes?" said Nell. "I expect so."

"Damn it, you put it in my head. Is that why my imagination got to working? Bright young lawyer convinced X is innocent, against all the evidence? . . . This kind of kill, spur-of-the-moment, crude lust, crude attack. Or was it? Or was it? Because— It looks as if it's got to be Harry. That kind, living from minute to minute—forgetting so easy. And irresponsible—not able to look ahead to logical consequences. All I've got to come back on that is, they're also unable to make up clever lies, to put on the convincing act."

"I could discuss it with you a lot better," said Nell, "if I knew what you were talking about."

Jesse got into his pajamas and stood staring absently at his reflection in the mirror over the bureau. To be hoped the girls they might have would take after Nell: he wouldn't want to inflict his overlean height, the high-bridged nose and equally disproportionate long jaw on a girl. Wouldn't matter so much about the boys. "Damn it," he said, "I'm no Don Quixote. I just figure to earn a decent living on run-of-the-mill legal business. Never wanted to be another Darrow." He took off his wrist watch and began to wind it.

"Didn't he do it?" asked Nell.

Jesse laid the watch on the bureau and turned to look at her. She looked very nice, very inviting indeed, his lovely Nell, and he wished there wasn't anything else on his mind. "I don't know," he said. "A thousand to one. I'd trust Clock as an honest man any day in the week. It's sound evidence—circumstantial, but that's often the best kind. All the bench would want. I'd just like to know if Sergeant Clock has heard about the worms. And if he's got the imagination to make it mean something to him. And what's that against the evidence? No, Harry's not putting on an act, but does that necessarily mean anything? You get people like that, whatever kind of brains they have. Look at that German Jack the Ripper, the Düsseldorf Monster, didn't they call him? Going around ripping up women, and sentimentalizing over his canaries and his garden. I don't know. . . . All right, so here's the story, such as it is."

Nell listened and said, "I see what you mean. It just might be that he's not the one. But if he's not—well, doesn't that say right away that he's being deliberately framed for it? The piece of lace, and the necklace chain—and his prints. I don't see how, about the prints—but—"

"Yes, the prints," said Jesse. "Don't like fingerprints. Such incontrovertible evidence. But a fingerprint once convicted you, when it was all innocent as day how it came to be where it was. . . . This kind of case, a little unusual to enter a not-guilty plea, drum up a defense. And that'd be quite a trick. . . . I think I'll have a drink, want one?"

"Just a small one, if you're going to."

Jesse wandered out to the kitchen, made two weakish highballs and came back. He said, "I don't want anything to do with it. A case like this. Impossible to work up any plausible defense. What does Harry matter? *Worms.* He's not important, is he? What the hell if he sits behind a newsstand in the lobby of the Ames Building, or does so-called therapy pruning rose bushes in the grounds of the state lunatic asylum? The worst that could happen to him, and why should I give a damn?"

Nell looked at him with sleepy affection and said, "There's a statue up over the Hall of Justice, with a blindfold."

"I've noticed it," said Jesse. "But I'm not thinking about the lady with the blindfold right now, so much as I am about Lilian Blake. Because if Harry didn't kill her, somebody else did. And if somebody else did, and is also framing Harry for it, then that wasn't a spur-of-the-moment kill, for crude lust. There was a reason. And somebody who's done one murder very often goes on to other murders. In which case, Harry is a kind of side issue, isn't he? . . . Just one helpful factor in the whole mess."

"He's got you on his side," said Nell.

"Well, no. Don't know that I'm committing myself yet. No, the helpful factor," said Jesse, finishing his drink, "is that Clock is a reasonable man. I think. Which being so, he's quite apt to be right in the first place. I could wish Mrs. Nielsen's blind stab in the phone book hadn't hit me. . . . And that's quite enough of Harry, for tonight at least. Let's get this usurper into his own bed where he belongs—you push and I'll pull."

He didn't have to appear in court again until Monday, on the Blackwell business; he took the morning off and went down to Police Headquarters to see Clock.

Clock listened to him and said bluntly, "I think you're crazy. You're as bad as the head doctors, reaching that far. He likes kittens and worries about the poor little worms, so he can't be guilty of murder. Whatever the tangible evidence says. In my book, Mr. Falkenstein, it doesn't add up so easy. Or rather, it does. On evidence. The ones like Harry—"

Jesse was getting very tired of that phrase; but he foresaw that he was going to hear a lot more of it. Yes. The standard answer. Of course. The evidence was good evidence against anybody; but not such tight evidence that the accused-as-charged couldn't put up a defense—if he hadn't been one like Harry.

"It's just," said Jesse slowly, "that that's a rather basic thing, isn't it? That kind of empathy for feelings. The feelings of anything—a kitten, the worms, other people. You're built this way or that, whatever brains you've got."

Sergeant Clock sighed. "Are you? Feelings are fine, Mr. Falkenstein, but as a lawyer you ought to know how much they're worth against solid evidence. This isn't an amateur force, you know—we looked into this thing. We've got this nice evidence, it's all very straightforward. And if you *are* Harry's lawyer, I've got no business talking to you like this."

"All true," said Jesse. "Not much criminal experience myself. I think I'd be very smart to tell Mrs. Nielsen about the Public Defender and wait to read the outcome in the *Times*. Which I may do. But thanks very much for listening, anyway."

Back in the Ford, he didn't start the engine at once. There were things he could be doing. Monday should see the Blackwell case finished, and there were continuances running on the other two court cases he had at present; he wouldn't have another court appearance to make for two weeks. But not all a lawyer's business was courtwise, fiction and TV to the contrary: not by any means. Always a lot of sedentary paperwork to do.

Even if there wasn't, say he was at loose ends, it'd do him no good to go home. Nell would be out house-hunting again. No telling where, because the only suburban area Jesse had put a firm veto on was the San Fernando Valley, so she might be looking at houses anywhere between La Habra and Culver City.

Which of course was not so irrelevant as it sounded, because with the price of real estate what it was these days (and also furniture) it behooved Jesse to cultivate clients with more money than Mrs. Nielsen.

He started the engine, reminding himself sententiously of another ethic of Solomon's: *He that maketh haste to be rich shall not be innocent.* He ambled up Main Street to Beverly Boulevard against the usual traffic, and on up Beverly to the Ames Building, two blocks from where Las Palmas crossed it.

It was a fairly busy intersection. Along here, not so much retail business as small manufacturing, this kind and that: a couple of wholesale film processors, manufacturers' representatives, also small clinics, a good many smallish office buildings.

He went round the block and got on the right side, found a place to park.

The Ames Building had been new about thirty years ago. It was of dull red brick and stucco, four stories high. The lobby was narrow, about forty feet long, with two elevators on the left side at the back, as you came in. Harry's little stand was on the right, beginning just inside the door and running perhaps twelve feet down that side. A folding grillwork enclosed it now, padlocked. Behind the grille was the usual counter, bearing displays of cigarettes, cigars, candy, chewing gum. A magazine rack below, with dozens of current issues on display. No cash register: Harry couldn't be expected to work one. There'd be a drawer for cash. Probably Mrs. Nielsen did his ordering for him.

He wandered back past the elevators. The building had a wider frontage than the lobby; behind the elevators was a cross hall, very dark, with office doors on both sides. On this side, the front side, around from the blank wall of the elevator housing was a suite of offices with two doors. On Jesse's right, to the front, was a discreet sign, PUBLIC REST ROOMS, and two doors side by side with appropriate signs.

He turned left down the cross hall. About twenty feet down, past the first office opposite, was a short hall leading toward the rear of the building. He went down it. It was perhaps twenty feet long, and at its end was a door with an opaque glass panel in it, undoubtedly the door leading out to the alley. Two doors faced each other across the hall, farther toward the end of the corridor than the middle. He contemplated them. Frosted-glass panels, neat black lettering. DR. F. S. FRIED-LANDER, D.D.S., OFFICE HOURS 9 A.M.—12 A.M., 2 P.M.—5 P.M. CLOSED

SATURDAYS. That was Room 112. Across from it, Room 114: DR. D. M. MACDONALD, M.D., OPHTHALMOLOGIST. OFFICE HOURS, 10 A.M.–1 P.M., 3 P.M.–5 P.M. CLOSED WEDNESDAYS AND SATURDAYS.

Jesse opened the door at the rear of the hall; he had rather expected to find it locked, but it wasn't. Down one shallow step with no guard rail was the alley. It was a fairly wide alley and ran behind these buildings from street to street the whole block. Somewhat to his surprise, it wasn't bounded on the other side by other buildings—apartments or office buildings. Some twenty-five feet away from this door, there ran for the whole length of the block a thirty-foot-high chain-link fence, and beyond it was the great dusty expanse of a public-school playground. He could see the middle-aged red brick of school buildings, the clean glass-and-stucco of a new addition.

"Well, well," he murmured to himself. The alley was just anonymous—lined at regular intervals with refuse barrels sitting beside rear doors. Nothing else. He turned and went back to the lobby of the building, and studied the office directory on the wall opposite Harry's stand.

The usual collection: doctors, dentists, a law firm, two tax consultants, a notary public, a dispensing wholesale optical firm, a psychiatrist, a loan company, somebody calling himself just A.P.B., Agent.

"Need some help lookin' for somebody?" asked a friendly voice. Jesse turned. Recent slam-crash of elevator doors: the first elevator returning to base. The operator was a fat fellow in late middle age, with a moon face and a cheerful expression; his uniform was ancient, a little tight and frayed at sleeves and neck.

"No, matter of fact I wanted to see you. And/or your mate. You know Harry Nielsen."

An expression of eager, excited interest slid over the moon face. Jesse had the notion that if the man had been, say, forty-five years younger he'd have come out with, Oooh, gosh, is it about *that*? "Sure, sure I do—you a cop?"

"No. Lawyer."

"Oh. Well, I guess he's got to have one o' those, but good gosh almighty, mister, what a hell of a thing! I mean, Mac said the same thing too—you know—a guy you know, always seemed so ordinary—if he isn't bright—and then find out he's done a thing like that! I mean—"

"Yes. Nasty. Obliged if you'd answer a few questions."

"Anything I can tell you, Mr.—"

"Falkenstein."

"Mr. Falkenstein. Sure thing. Tell you what, it's about the time I go off for lunch anyway—here's Mac—" Another slam-crash: the second operator was lanky and thin as Jesse, long melancholy face, bald head, about sixty. "Mac takes it alone while I'm gone, see, and then ditto for me while he goes out. Lawyer fellow about Harry, Mac."

Mac's expression didn't change much. "Awful thing," he said in a reedy voice. "But you never do know what that kind'll do."

"Look, I usually go downa block to Georgie's Grill, have a beer with my lunch. O.K., Mr. Falkenstein? We can talk there."

"O.K.," said Jesse. The operator stepped out of his cage, slammed the door and dropped a bolt across it, and led the way.

Georgie's Grill was small, dark and faintly odorous, its jukebox mercifully silent. "My name's Rance, Mr. Falkenstein—Jim Rance. Same as usual, George."

"Just coffee," said Jesse. "Nice to know you, Mr. Rance. Now, the first thing I want to ask you is this. Harry's mother tells me he has migraine headaches, say maybe twice a month, and consequently's late opening up his stand. You said he was late on Wednesday. Was it the first time you remember, or is Mrs. Nielsen right, it happens maybe once or twice a month? Do you know about his headaches?"

Small reluctance showed in Rance's eyes. "Yeah, I guess that's right. He was usually regular, but it *had* happened like that before. Maybe not that often. Yeah, he'd said something once about his headaches. He didn't— Well, he wasn't so easy to talk to, you know. Like a kid."

"Yes," said Jesse. George brought his coffee, half of it in the saucer. He drank some, considering. "It was about ten-fifteen when he opened Wednesday. Did you see him come in?"

"No, acourse not, on account he was already here," said Rance. "He must've come in at the regular time, that's how it looks, to catch Miss Blake, see. Only Mac and me was both upstairs or on the way then, and didn't see him. All the office people coming in at that hour, see. No, way it was, I remember—I'd just come down to the lobby again from taking some people up to four, and there he was just opening up. First I'd seen of him, see. It was maybe ten minutes past ten. They figure, I heard one o' the cops say, he was in the rest room or somewheres—afterward."

"Yes." Without surprise Jesse recognized that Rance (like others who'd be in on the fringes of this thing) was enjoying his contact with real excitement for a change: reluctant to see any of the excitement belittled. Kind of thing that colored statements. And that, Clock would know as well as he did.

"Big surprise to everybody, though, wasn't it?" he asked casually. "You never thought Harry was the kind to do a thing like that?"

"I sure never did!—and most anybody'd say the same. . . . That Miss Blake, she seemed like a nice girl. Always said good morning nice and polite, even if she didn't take the elevator, on account she worked for Dr. Friedlander on the ground floor, see. Little bit of a thing, and kind of—you know—trim. Neat. Not exactly pretty, maybe, but a nice girl. . . . I tell you though, guess I shouldn't say it, because, good gosh almighty, you gotta be fair and tolerant like they say—we can't all be alike, Mr. Falkenstein—and it isn't, I guess, anybody wants to go back to the time they stuck loonies in cages and whipped 'em and all—but I guess most people who're, you know, all *right*, they feel kinda queer with Harry's kind. You know? The ones not *right*. I mean, it's nothing you can lay a finger on, just a feeling. Sure, I got to say— and I'd have to say so in court, if they get me up there and ask" (brief anticipatory gleam) "there's never anything I could point to, Harry said or did, know what I mean." George came and set before him a thick club sandwich and a tall glass of lager carrying too much head.

"I know," said Jesse. "An uncanny feeling, you mean." Only human: sympathetic as you might be, rational as you might be. An entity outside the herd: not like the rest of us.

Rance picked up the beer and took a long swallow. "No, I got to say honest, he never acted like he might be—you know—violent. Just to look at him, on the surface like. It's just, with that kind, you never can tell, can you? Yeah, just a funny feeling. There I'd be, coming on at nine o'clock, and Mac too, and there he'd be, goin' in behind his counter. I'd say, Hello, Harry. Like to a neighborhood kid. What you took him for—you know? And he'd say, Hello, Mr. Rance. He was always polite. I will say, his mother always saw he was dressed clean and neat. But maybe that was Harry, at that—you know, he was fussy as an old maid about them magazines and boxes of cigarettes and all, always straightening 'em out where customers'd put 'em back crooked. He liked things just *so*. Like my wife can't stand a paper left around when you're done with it, got to put it away."

"That so?" said Jesse. He looked at his half cup of muddy coffee.

"Me, I've always thought that's a thing like an ear for music—you come equipped with it or you don't. Nothing you learn."

Rance was silent, eating. He swallowed, put down the sandwich and took another long drink of beer. "That's about right," he agreed. "I guess you do. But, tell you something funny, Mr. Falkenstein. Harry was like that, sure, and he used—once in a while—kinda complain, like to himself, about customers who'd stick magazines back crooked, and like that. But he never minded that brat of Reynolds', nor his dawg neither."

"Who's that?"

Rance finished his sandwich and caught George's eye. "'Nother beer, George. Well, Reynolds got the gas station catty-corner to us, corner o' Los Olivos. You noticed it, I guess, a Union Station. Him and his wife split up, and he got the kid, and the kid hangs around all the time after school, Saturdays and like that, see. Well, we get kids coming in sometimes, sure, but always with their mothers or somebody—goin' to a doctor or dentist in the building, see—and Harry was always kinda nice to them when he noticed, friendly. But they wouldn't be messing round his counter. The Reynolds kid, he'd come in lotsa times, running in and outta the lobby. I guess he's a good enough kid, Stevie, but you know what a kid nine years old is *like*." Rance grinned. "Good gosh almighty, barrel o' monkeys nothin' to it—I remember my two! He'd come in the lobby with his damn dawg—but Harry never seemed to mind, not even the dawg wettin' up against his magazine rack. He used to give the kid candy bars, sometimes."

"You don't tell me," said Jesse slowly. "Well. This Blake girl. He—liked her?"

"Sure. I told the cops, and so did Mac. See, I guess we're the ones'd see more *of* it, bein' on the elevators and a lotta the time in the lobby. Though I unnerstand she'd said something about it too, and a couple other people'd noticed—when she was coming in and out, you know. It was like he—sort of admired her. He'd always say her name, Hello, Miss Blake—like that, when she went through the lobby. And a lot of times he said things like, Wouldn't you like a chocolate bar, Miss Blake, or a package of cigarettes?—like that. She—well, she couldn't abide him. Like some people are about Harry's kind, you know—sensitive. She said something about it to me and Mac once, called him a loony. Said she couldn't understand why he was allowed to run a stand like that, in public. You see what I mean. . . . She wasn't maybe an awful pretty girl, just sorta cute and neat—but I guess Harry thought she was, way he acted. . . . Hell of a thing," said Rance. "I tell you, when they found her like that, it just didn't seem it could be—right here, in our building, a murder. And then when they found it was Harry—"

"Yes," said Jesse. "Well, thanks very much, Mr. Rance. . . ." Nothing much more he could think of to ask right now.

And he still didn't know why he was wasting the day like this. It was a very long chance indeed that it hadn't been Harry. But if it hadn't been, there didn't seem to be much to get hold of on it to say it all legal. Nuances. A kitten, a baby, the worms and the pretty Golden Autumn roses.

Hell and damnation. He was a lawyer, not a detective—as he'd complained before, on Nell's business last year.

When he left Rance, he found a little better place than Georgie's and brooded over his own lunch.

He didn't like the feel of this thing at all. Harry was so obvious, and yet— But Clock would have looked for anything to point a different direction (*had* looked, before he got onto Harry) and Clock was no fool. It didn't necessarily say that there wasn't anything to be found; it just said, if there was, it was buried pretty damn deep.

If he climbed on the bandwagon and said it wasn't Harry, right away he committed himself to the stand that Harry had been deliberately framed.

And Harry would, of course, have been very damn easy to frame.

The only trouble with that was, it sounded too much like a half-hour TV crime drama. Just a little farfetched . . . Of course, Harry, well, it was always easy to rouse suspicion of the Harrys, wasn't it? In a sense, people expected the worst of them. But—the head doctors didn't know everything, no, but it was reasonable, what they said about the ones like Harry: that they were more predictable than normal people. That they didn't deviate as much from established routines and thought patterns. That figured. And by what Mama said, Harry had a nice record of nonaggression. (Look up his school records, something to show the bench.) On the other hand, that old debbil Sex . . .

In the ordinary way, this would get shoved through in a hurry. Guilty as charged, and a psychiatric examination ordered, and the bench saying, Take him off to Atascadero.

Evidence. Good solid evidence. And he wished he had a dime for every guilty party found with incriminating evidence on him who yelled indignantly, Planted.

About that, nothing to say one way or the other. Harry or X. And there were the fingerprints, too.

Jesse said to himself, Hell, finished his coffee and went back to the Ames Building to see Dr. Friedlander.

FOUR

The office was closed. Inquiry of Dr. MacDonald's receptionist across the hall elicited the opinion that Dr. Friedlander was at home by now; he had volunteered to make the funeral arrangements, in lieu of any relative. Jesse was reminded that he'd like to see the autopsy report; he probably wouldn't get to. In the little carpeted anteroom, Dr. Mac-Donald was present as a deep voice beyond the wall, saying faintly, "Now read me the top line, please. . . . Now tell me when the vertical lines come together. . . . Ah, yes, that's fine. . . . Now—"

The receptionist was about thirty, homely and freckled, a no-non-sense sort of girl. He asked her a few questions. Yes, she'd known Lilian; sometimes they went to lunch together, or with another receptionist from upstairs, a Margaret Perry. It was just terrible, they could hardly believe it had happened. She'd been such a nice girl.

"Go to lunch with her on Tuesday?" asked Jesse.

The receptionist, whose name was Ann Walker, said, "Why, yes, all three of us went together. To the Thrifty up the block."

"Um. Did she seem her usual self? What'd she talk about?"

She eyed him curiously. "The police sergeant asked that too. Why? I mean, she didn't know she was going to be murdered. . . . Well, I think she was worried about her sister, was all. She was quieter than usual, and once when Margaret made a little joke she didn't seem to hear it at all, didn't laugh. I know I asked if she felt all right, and she said sure, she was just thinking. The day before, she'd been talking about her sister—she's going to have a baby, the sister I mean, and Lilian was a little worried because it's her first and she's thirty-five, you see. I think that's what it was. But—"

"Well," said Jesse, and thanked her. What did that say? Very probably nothing.

He looked up Friedlander's address. Rather an intriguing address: Swallowtail Road. It was, when he got there, a quiet, oddly suburban-looking, dead-end street in West Hollywood. The houses were not new, but solidly built and well maintained; mostly Mediterranean, Spanish design—neat, manicured houses (the adjective *well-bred* occurred to him) sitting behind neat manicured lawns and flower beds. The one he wanted bore an equally neat FOR SALE sign on its lawn.

"Well, well," he said to himself. Very good-looking house, too. Mediterranean, beige stucco, a little balcony on a second story—probably just one dormer room at the front. Red tile roof: so practical. And as he'd come up, he'd seen that the back yard, this side anyway, was enclosed by a chain-link fence. He wondered idly how much they were asking and what the taxes ran in this area.

He parked the Ford, went up the curving line of red-tile stepping-stones to the generous red-tile porch, pushed the doorbell. There was an ornamental aluminum screen door, and inside the slab door stood open; he looked into a square tiled entrance hall, and beyond to the right had a glimpse of a vaulted, dark, cool-looking living room.

"Hello," she said. She had materialized there on the other side of the screen door; he hadn't heard her come. She stood there smiling at him, leaning on the doorpost. But, he thought, it was the wrong background entirely; it should be a ramp leading off the stage, and the background music was lacking too—the raucous yell, *Take it off!*

She was maybe five seven, and—in a phrase—put together. Twenty-six, twenty-seven. Black hair in a tumbled, fashionable short cut, casual; and she was a warm olive tan all over, easy to see because all she had on was a yellow two-piece bathing suit. A triangular kitten face, little full mouth and big brown eyes under heavy arched black brows.

"Hello," she said again. She should have had a warm contralto voice, but it was thin and metallic, childish-sounding.

Jesse asked for Dr. Friedlander. He got what Clock had meant: there wouldn't have been, with Dr. Friedlander, any personal involvement with that nice ordinary girl Lilian Blake. Not when he had this at home.

"Oh, you want to see Fred?" she said. "I guess you'd better come in. What's your name?"

He told her, coming into the entrance hall as she held the screen door open. Passing close to her there, he got a waft of musky scent, and something else intangible: a feeling. A feeling that surprised him, for no emanation of sex came from her at all. She smiled up at him as unself-conscious, as unaware, as a child dressed up in Mother's high heels.

"I'm never any good to remember names," she said. "I guess I should say, I'm Fred's wife—I'm Mrs. Friedlander. You sit down, I'll go find Fred." She smiled at him hopefully. "Is it about the house?"

"Well, no—"

"Oh. I hope we sell it pretty soon, you know. I never did like it much, it's so old-fashioned. It belonged to Fred's father. Imagine." She looked around the living room, where she'd led him, as if she'd never seen it before. "And no room for a decent-sized pool. Only Fred keeps talking about the insurance. Something about, a different kind for people's kids falling in. I don't know. I'd rather—oh, some place like Playa del Rey or Emerald Bay. I mean, that sounds nice and classy, you know." Her smile was vague and gentle. "Oh, you wanted to see Fred. I'll go find him." She drifted out.

And Jesse wondered if possibly there *had* been something, with Lilian Blake. Clock was a good cop, but had he enough imagination to—? Mrs. Friedlander was quite something on the surface, but Jesse could see any man with an I.Q. over ninety getting just a little bored with her as a steady diet. Or could he?

He looked around the room. It could be a nice room; the proportions were good. It was nearly square, with windows front and back, the latter looking out on a pleasant brick-floored patio. The furniture was unimaginative, too modern for the room: a black plastic sectional, a couple of violently modernistic chairs in turquoise plastic, one of those obnoxious lamp-pole gadgets. No bookcases. But an expensive stereo phonograph in a teakwood cabinet and a long shelf of record albums. He went over to look. Very expectable, he thought sadly: Tchaikovsky, *Carmen,* Chopin, Dvorak, a little Stravinsky. And then Belafonte, Cole, Peggy Lee, Glenn Miller. Well. He was astonished to note, carefully filed on the lower shelf, some rather rare old Louis Armstrong and the whole of *The Art of the Fugue.* His curiosity shot up to fever-pitch. Who in this house had the delicate perspicacity to file those two great artists together?

"You wanted to see me?" It was a sharp thin voice. Jesse looked up. "Dr. Friedlander?" As he introduced himself, explained, Jesse looked at the man with more interest than he'd had before seeing those record albums. Friedlander looked a most unlikely husband for the brunette bathing belle. He was about five eight, thin and weedy, a sandy, unremarkable fellow in the late thirties. Nothing to mark him off from any other man in a crowd: ordinary features, ordinary blue eyes, regular teeth, nose, jawline. Just a sandy youngish man, in ordinary Southern California clothes at home, gray slacks and open-necked blue shirt. If anything, it was a rather intellectual face—the thinker, not the doer.

"Oh—" he said. "Oh, yes. Sit down, Mr.—Falkenstein? This has been such a shock—well, you can understand. Murder—the ordinary citizen doesn't expect to run across it, you know. She was such a nice girl. . . . Of course, anything I can tell you—that poor devil of a lunatic—"

And what the hell was he doing here, wondered Jesse. Clock, the efficient cop, had been and asked and looked. And found nothing. Not likely that the amateur would find anything. But he asked the questions Clock would have asked before; and Friedlander was patient, obliging.

Lilian Blake had worked for him, as receptionist and assistant, for only about six months. Since last December. The woman he'd had before had quit when she got married: very nice woman, Amy Gibson, middle-aged; she'd been with him for nearly ten years; she'd married a widower and they'd gone to Florida to live. So he'd gone to an employment agency and they'd sent him Lilian Blake. She'd had two good recommendations from dentists she'd worked for: one who'd gone into the Navy from private practice, one who'd retired. Both local, yes. He had found her very efficient, as expected. He hadn't known much about her personal life—she hadn't been one to volunteer things—but she'd been a nice girl. Very reliable and cool-headed in any little emergency. It was a terrible thing to have happened, but one like that Harry Nielsen—

"Yes," said Jesse. "She wasn't—mmh—friendly, forthcoming? I mean, just the two of you in the office a lot of the time—she didn't chat about boy friends, hobbies, et cetera?"

"Well, in the intervals between patients," said Friedlander stiffly, "she'd be working at the books, or— No. No, not to any extent, Mr. Falkenstein. Why do you ask? Well—you understand, there wasn't much time for—er—personal conversation; I have quite a heavy practice, and neither of us— Can I explain it to you?" He gestured help-lessly. "I liked her, poor girl, I think she liked me, but it wasn't the, ah, personal relationship it had been with Mrs. Gibson, who'd been with me so long. It was simply— That police officer asked, too." Fried-lander produced a rather shyly charming smile. "Meaning, had I any personal interest? Of course that's absurd." His long, square-fingered surgeon's hand was vague on gesture. "My wife—as I told that ser-geant—perhaps it'll give you the picture better—Berenice liked Miss Blake, was sorry for her. She—Berenice—was a model, you know, be-fore we were married, and she tried several times to, oh, advise Miss Blake, show her how she could make more of her looks and so on—you know what I mean. In a friendly way . . . Well, I felt responsible, in a sense, there being no relatives here, and—" He shrugged tiredly. "The girl she roomed with—they hadn't known each other long. There's enough money in her bank account—it was just, someone had to take charge and make the arrangements. I've been in touch with her sister back East, of course. They told me they'll release the body tomorrow, after the inquest, and I've arranged with Forest Lawn— Poor girl. It just doesn't seem possible, murdered—a thing you read about in the papers. . . . No, I don't recall her ever mentioning any—er—dates, anything like that. I do remember her saying she was born in Chicago —her sister still lives in Illinois, of course. I think she came to Califor-nia about eight years ago. I know she'd been with this one dentist two years and the other one four, after she'd taken her training, and that about covers—"

And what else was there to ask? The names of the other dentists, addresses. Damn all. It didn't say anything.

Not a very pretty girl, Clock said. Just little and trim and neat. Re-luctantly Jesse absolved Friedlander of any personal interest. There were men (he'd be one of them) who'd get tired very easy and soon of strip-tease model Berenice of the bird brain; but he didn't figure Fred Friedlander would. A very conventional stick of a fellow: probably a good dentist. The little mystery here was how one like Berenice (shades of E. A. Poe) happened to be stuck with him. But women you never could figure.

That was brought home to him as he left. Dr. Friedlander correctly shepherded him to the front door, coming out with more conventional phrases (but the overtones of sincerity in them, at that); and she drifted up the hall to them, still in the yellow bathing suit, still incongruous in this staid house. "Freddy," she said fondly, taking his arm.

"Er—my dear, don't you think something a little more—yes, I know it's a hot day, dear, but—" Friedlander didn't altogether like the bathing suit. Her mouth drooped like a child's under his gentle criticism.

"Oh, all right, Freddy, I'll put on something else."

"—This dreadful thing, about Miss Blake. Mr. Falkenstein is representing the m—that Harry Nielsen."

"Oh," she said, her small mouth drooping further. "Oh, yes. That poor girl. I told her to go to Rico's, for her hair. Nobody to touch him really. And she would wear red, all wrong for her. But she was a nice girl, it was an awful shame she had to be . . . Freddy darling, I just thought of maybe Emerald Bay? I mean, when we sell the house. You said— But it sounds awful classy, doesn't it?"

She was leaning on his arm, looking up at him. And it wasn't false, the naked adoration in her eyes. For some reason, thought Jesse, God knows why, it was the Miltonian thing here: *He for God only, she for God in him.* Very damn peculiar, but then human people were. This all-for-glamour pin-up, and an ordinary, sandy, unhandsome dentist. Well.

"We'll see, darling," said Friedlander absently. "Well, Mr. Falkenstein—" he offered his hand and a small chilly smile.

Jesse thanked him and went away.

When he got home at six o'clock he found Nell had come in just before him, in a state of gloom.

"Six houses," she said, "and all impossible except one, and that they wanted thirty-five thousand for. It's no use, Jesse. We'll just have to be one of those smart modern couples, all gay and forever young, who never dream of having a family or anything so old-fashioned as a real house. Just a succession of convenient apartments, and a madly merry social whirl entertaining your wealthy clients at cocktail parties and the best restaurants."

"Since when have I had any wealthy clients? We've both had the same sort of day, I gather. Let's console each other by going out to dinner."

"That's the first nice thing that's happened to me all day," said Nell, and kissed him again. "Athelstane ate one of the real-estate woman's gloves, and the man who owns the thirty-five-thousand house looked down his nose and obviously expected me to talk Yiddish at him and try to walk off with the silver, and then we looked at a horrible house on a hillside and I got runs in both stockings from their prize cactus garden. Give me fifteen minutes to make myself look human and I'm with you. You might feed Athelstane."

Jesse did so, fetched her a mild drink as she sat at the dressing table and sampled his own as he watched her apply new lipstick. "It is written," he said with a sigh, *"The lot is cast into his lap; but the whole disposing thereof is of the Lord.* Proverbs of Solomon. Which is to say that I've definitely taken on Harry. Don't ask me why, Nuances . . . Did I ever mention Foulkes to you?"

"Not that I remember."

"Funny—Sergeant Clock knew him too, slightly. Mentioned him to me. He was in my senior class, Foulkes—passed the bar at the same time. Very devout Episcopalian—literal-minded, poor devil. He used to suffer tortures of conscience over clients he knew were guilty of this or that. They *would* tell him such obvious lies, you know, and repeat 'em under oath—and Foulkes couldn't bear it. Fellow was a nervous wreck in the end. Just couldn't take being thrown together with all these sinners and whited sepulchers. He finally quit practice and went into Civil Service. Very sad case."

"And what has the poor man got to do with you or Harry?"

"Law says everybody's entitled to legal defense. I'd rather speak up for innocent clients, when I get a criminal case or otherwise—but the others have the same right under the law, after all. . . . And of course there's time. A little time. He won't be arraigned, probably, until next week, and even then I can plead him not guilty and still have a chance to change the plea later on."

"Is he?"

"That's just the point," said Jesse. "I don't know. But I don't think so. I really don't. It's a case in a thousand, looked at like that, you know."

Nell stood up, took a last critical look in the glass, tucked powder puff and lipstick into her bag and said, "All the publicity over a murder, you mean?"

"I don't mean. No. Because this is a crack police force, they don't arrest innocent citizens once in a blue moon. And Sergeant Clock's a damn good man. Brains *and* some imagination. It's just that what's on Harry's side is all imagination—and what Clock has, it's nice tangible evidence." He laughed and finished his drink. "Clock's got half an idea I'm another Foulkes—have to convince myself the client's inno-cent as day before I take him on. He's a good man—but I think he's wrong."

They took Athelstane downstairs and staked him out in the yard on his chain (the manager liked dogs), reassured him that eventually they'd come back, and got into the car. "The Fox and Hounds," said Jesse.

"Can we afford it?"

"Mercenary. We both need cheering up. Oh, by the way, *I* saw a house for sale today. You might go and look at it—the sign said Multiple Listing so I suppose your Mrs. What's-her-name could take you. Out in West Hollywood. On Swallowtail Road."

"What a lovely address," said Nell. "I will. Is it nice?"

"What I saw of it—could be, anyway. Unless," said Jesse, "you'd be nervous about psychic influences."

"Is it haunted?"

"Could be, if they've lived there long. Her, about six years old men-tally, adoring the obviously superior male whose word is law. Like that. Him—I don't know. Funny customer, or is he? Anyway—"

"Four bedrooms?"

"I don't know. And that's too many, as I keep telling you. What with taxes and inflation. Two, one each sex. Quite enough."

"Two of each," said Nell. "A much better chance that one of them at least will make money and support us in our old age. Your father agrees with me."

"He is not going to be responsible for their upkeep," said Jesse, "meanwhile. He can mind his own damn business."

"I'll ask Mrs. Alton about it. Swallowtail Road—*what* a nice address to have on stationery."

They handed over the car to the lot attendant, were received by a dignified headwaiter and settled at the blessedly quiet privacy of a wall table. Nothing obnoxiously modern here, but old-fashioned serv-ice in the best of tradition. A suave brown waiter brought Martinis. ("We can't *afford* it," said Nell. "Don't be so damn mercenary," said Jesse. "All you think about is money.")

"So why," asked Nell after a reflective sip, "isn't he guilty?"

"Go on and laugh at me. Because, first of all, he isn't the type. There's no violence in him. Laugh—Clock did. I don't blame him. But he's not, you know. I just can't see it. . . . But there's not much to get hold of to prove it. A couple of funny little things—I don't know. . . ."

FIVE

He had seen Lilian's roommate, and the place where she had lived. He had canvassed all the offices in the Ames Building, and found half a dozen women who had known her, none well; he had asked questions. And he had gone back to see Clock. He had a handful of little things, but whether they meant anything or not, who could say?

Two little things he had got from Ruth Myers, the roommate. She was a big bouncy blond girl, Ruth, boundlessly sentimental and talkative. She told him everything she knew about Lilian, without asking why he wanted to know; all he had to do was listen. He learned that they'd met each other at a wedding shower for a girl they both knew, and had liked each other right away. Well, they said about opposites and all, you know. Lilian was sort of quiet and reserved, "just opposite to me, I guess." He learned that Lilian was a pretty good cook; she'd liked spaghetti and breaded veal chops, and chicken salad in summer and she was real particular about the brand of coffee. She liked red, had lots of red things, and being a blonde—well, she had used a little rinse but just to keep the color—being a blonde she looked good in red. She'd been a fine roommate, never borrowed without asking and always right on time with her share of the rent and all. A real lady, Lilian was, she even went to church most Sundays. . . .

Out of the welter of facts a couple emerged. Last Monday, Lilian had forgotten a bracelet at the office and gone back to get it after hours; she had a key, because a lot of times she'd get there before the doctor, if he didn't have an appointment early. It was a "good" bracelet, a real gold bracelet, had belonged to her grandmother, so she'd been worried and gone right back to get it. Ruth couldn't say what time she'd got home; Ruth had had a date. Of course Lilian had been there when she came in. No, she hadn't said anything except that she'd found the bracelet just where she took it off and left it, on her desk. And Ruth guessed she had been sort of worried for a couple of days—had something on her mind, anyway. But Lilian was like that, it might've been almost anything; she had something on her mind, like it might be planning to buy a dress she'd seen, or worrying about some bill, or even if she just had a toothache, well, she'd be all quiet and moody, not saying much, and you wouldn't know what it was until she said. Like that. Sure, it might've been she was worrying about her sister that was having a baby.

Well, it wasn't so much that she wasn't, you know, attractive to boys; she was just particular. She'd gone out with a couple of real nice fellows, like Tommy Hamlin and Stu Walsh, but she kind of turned her nose up at them because they liked movies and popular music and had just ordinary jobs—"You know. Like Stu works in a garage. She was too particular. Well, I mean, you just gotta take life—*and* men— like it comes." Ruth giggled and then sobered. "I'll bet she's sorry now, poor dear. I've been awful upset, I was real fond of her really, reason I stayed home from work today." Ruth was a salesclerk at Robinsons'. "It just didn't seem like anything so awful could happen, you know—getting murdered like that—that awful boy— Yes, sure, she'd mentioned him to me. I told the cops that. She was scared of him, even before. Well, no, I never heard her say he'd, you know, *done* anything, like grabbing for her or anything, before, but—"

As Jesse was leaving, Ruth's current (or steady?) boy friend arrived, and was introduced. Mike Orde. Jesse hadn't much criminal practice, but he was used to sizing people up. He hadn't liked the smell of Mr. Orde. Mr. Orde—a broad young man, blue-chinned, sullen-mouthed, a little too sharply dressed—smelled just faintly wrong to Jesse.

There was also Mr. William Jenner, of the Acme Loan Company in office 224 in the Ames Building. A decidedly fishy eye, and he'd ordered his receptionist to mind her own business, she didn't have to talk to this guy or answer questions, nothing to do with her. "Damn cops snooping around bad enough," he had said; and added to Jesse, abruptly, "Well, sure, of course, a murder—hell of a thing to happen, they got to— But you unnerstand, Mabel's got work to do, I can't have her yakking to every—"

Jesse had got out of Mabel that she'd known Lilian, gone to lunch with her sometimes.

228 FOUR BY EGAN

There was that A.P.B., Agent. Who had turned out to be one Al Byerly, a paunchy, cynical-eyed fellow in the fifties, bald and red-faced and astonishingly noncommittal. He'd heard about the murder, but apparently hadn't much interest in it. Nothing to do with him. No, he didn't have a receptionist; he was all there was, mister, and so what? Agent, well, Jesse could read, couldn't he? Meant just what it said. Mostly TV actors. Fixing up jobs. That was it, and he didn't know nothing about the murder or have nothing to do with it.

Well. Was he seeing ghosts because he wanted to here? Jenner, maybe his loan business just over the line of the usury laws? And Byerly just maybe running a call-girl service on the side? The Ames Building wasn't one of the new, big, classy office buildings, but it wasn't in the middle of a slum either, naturally collecting shady tenants. Not by any means. Forty offices, all rented: could you say, two shady ones out of forty a natural ratio, in any big town? He didn't know.

You started to build theories here, what did you come back to? Could you say, the Ames Building? Not necessarily, but—

Another thing that made it look like Harry was the time and place. A very chancy time and place to do a deliberate murder. You couldn't be sure you could keep her from screaming, and there were people all around, nearby. But, so say it had been a deliberate kill: maybe one of the few places and times Lilian could be caught alone. She had a roommate. She went to and from work on the bus. She was with people all day in the office. Sunday afternoons (with, probably, Ruth out)? Wait for a night when Ruth had a date and Lilian was home alone (but how to be sure of that)? If that chance had been deliberately taken, what that seemed to add up to was—haste. It had not been possible to wait for a safer opportunity.

Why?

The easy answer was, she knew something and had to be stopped from passing it on. But—!

And that still sounded too much like crime on TV.

Damn it, he thought, if the record showed that Harry had ever biffed another three-year-old over the head to steal his rubber ball, I'd believe Clock. But—

He went back to Headquarters and apologized for taking up any more time. "It's just, I wondered, sergeant, whether you'd heard that she came back to the office after hours on Monday night. Or knew that Mr. Jenner of the Acme Loan Company doesn't like cops snooping around talking to his receptionist. Or that that fellow who says he's an agent doesn't like anybody coming around asking questions about anything. Or that Ruth Myers has a boy friend who smells a little like a small-time pro crook. Or that Lilian had acted worried for a couple of days."

Clock said patiently, "We don't like to arrest the wrong people just to be arresting somebody, Mr. Falkenstein. We've been there before you, yes. Before we dropped on Harry, we took a pretty good look at her associates and so on. You're conscientious, aren't you? What d'you suggest, she surprised a nest of spies maybe using Friedlander's office out of hours, and got taken off before she could tell the F.B.I.? Or maybe Mr. Jenner's playing footsie with his secretary when she works overtime, and Lilian found out? And he did a murder to keep the secret from his wife?"

"It's a very efficient force these days, I know," said Jesse. "Don't tell me I watch too much TV. I don't. But I think you've swallowed bait, sergeant. I think it was a frame. I *think*. I want to talk to Harry again, but—"

Clock sighed. And it was then he had mentioned Foulkes. "So," said Jesse, "all right, if you want to read me like that. Maybe I've got a tortuous mind."

"And what's that about Ruth Myers' boy friend? New to me."

"Is that so? One Mike Orde. Sharp-boy chalk-stripes and iridescent tie. Smart-boy talk. I'd take a small bet he's been in police trouble, this or that sort."

"You don't say. Well, just for fun let's find out." Clock phoned an inquiry down to Records. "And so what? If it was a planned thing—just *if*—I can think of a dozen safer places to get at her, and a dozen safer times."

"If you were in a hurry?" murmured Jesse. "She wasn't alone very often or very long."

"Oh, for God's sake!" said Clock. "This is ridiculous. We know who killed the girl. A little more evidence came in awhile ago."

"Oh? Mind saying what?"

"Yes," said Clock, and then laughed and offered him a cigarette. "I've got no business telling you, but—for some reason I kind of like you, Mr. Falkenstein. I'll pay you a compliment and say I figure, if you came round to thinking Harry did it, you wouldn't try to get him off—which it's a thousand to one you could do anyway. If—"

"Thanks very much. Retain a few scruples about justice, yes. Don't know if you know a Lieutenant Silverberg upstairs in Narcotics? Yes, well, I know him slightly; he'd tell you I don't go round talking a hell of a lot. *In the multitude of words there wanteth not sin.* What's the new evidence?"

"It's not much, and we won't use it," said Clock. "A bunch of kids—little girls, eight and nine, in the school ground across that alley. They have summer classes, to keep the kids busy, you know—aside from regular summer school. Arts and crafts, that kind of thing. There were about twenty little girls there, down at the end of the playground, Wednesday morning, doing what they call leather work. Learning to braid bookmarks and belts and so on. It was the teacher came in, nice young woman, a Miss Regina Shipley. Said some of the kids had seen something. So we asked them. Four of 'em said—I spare you the roundabout questioning—they'd seen a man come out that door into the alley and throw something on the ground. Two of 'em said they saw him bend over and look at something. Pretty vague on time, of course, but they thought it was about fifteen or twenty minutes after the class started, which puts it at ten-fifteen or ten-twenty."

"Something," said Jesse. "Not the body, they'd—"

"No. The only reason the kids noticed at all, probably, it was something a little unusual, see one of those back doors open. And probably the ones who did notice were bored with the class, looking around instead of paying attention to teacher, you know. If they got it right, I figure it was the handbag. If he caught her at the end of the hall, there, just as she was going into the office, the bag was dropped there. It could be the murder was done there, not in the alley, and he shoved the body out afterward. Or in the struggle she got out to the alley and was finished there. In either case, he may have picked up the bag and tossed it after her. He evidently kept it awhile and then decided to—"

"But—" said Jesse, and was silent. Well, it could be. But if she'd struggled free enough to get away from him, wouldn't she have screamed? Of course, some people, fear turned them dumb. And if she'd got away from him, wouldn't she more likely have tried to get into the office, where Friedlander was? Or was he? Of course, in panic she could have mistaken the door—the two doors were close together.

"Was Friedlander in his office then?" he asked. "I forgot to ask him."

"No. His first appointment was ten o'clock. He came in about ten to and was surprised she wasn't there."

So. And yet, he didn't like it. He thought suddenly, the handbag. Those damn convenient fingerprints. It could be—what those little girls saw—somebody tossing the handbag near the body after having got Harry's prints on it. How?

And how tortuous could you get? The other way, it was so open and shut.

"Had she got her keys out?" he asked. "Ready to unlock the door?"

"Well, funnily enough," said Clock, "the keys are missing. I think she had—I think she had them in her hand when she was attacked. She might've just dropped them, but we've been all over that alley—no keys. So it looks as if he picked them up for some reason, and probably later on just tossed them away somewhere on the street. Because they weren't on him, and they're not in the house."

"Oh, really," said Jesse. "Any description from the little girls of the man they saw?"

"From kids that age? Nothing usable. They seem pretty sure it was the Ames Building door, that's all you can say. And we've got enough evidence otherwise—not a very nice case to bring kids into." One of the phones on Clock's desk rang and he picked it up. "Yes? . . . You don't say. . . . Mmh . . . He just showed on the edge of something, thanks." He put the phone down. "You'd win your bet. Michael Orde has a modest little pedigree. Two arrests as a juvenile—car theft and petty theft—one charge after he turned eighteen: unlawful possession of narcotics, a year's term."

"Well," murmured Jesse. "Fancy that. I wonder if Ruth Myers knows. I don't think so. I wonder if maybe Lilian found out. And—"

"For God's sake!" said Clock again. "You're really reaching, aren't you? Look, Mr. Falkenstein. We've got I.Q.'s over a hundred nowadays. As a cop with some little experience, I can tell you that what a thing looks like is generally just what it is. We don't get the fancy plots out of books. So we missed Mr. Orde, here, but he's just one of the irrelevancies that show up sometimes. Small-time pros—if he is—don't do murders to keep their records secret from girl friends. And, in passing, I didn't like the smell of that agent any more than you did, and I passed his name on to Vice, they're looking into him. We

worked this case, Mr. Falkenstein. We covered it. And on the evidence, Harry's our boy. You're not likely to turn up anything different
playing private eye."

"Last ambition I'd have," said Jesse, unfolding himself from the
hard office chair. "No private eye has the equipment, system or usually the brains available to the regular force. But it looks as if I'll have
to turn up something new, sergeant. If I'm going to get anything to
back up my feeling about Harry, I'll have to locate the real guilty
party for you. If possible."

"We've *got* him," said Clock. "And I've talked a hell of a lot too
much to you."

"Very cooperative—appreciate it."

"I'm also a busy man," said Clock. "So if you get into trouble with
this Orde or Byerly—a lot of pros are kind of hair-trigger—or otherwise, don't yell for help to me. I will be damned. Just on a feeling.
You—"

"Entirely," said Jesse. "I won't. *His own iniquities shall take the
wicked himself, and he shall be holden with the cords of his sins.* Forget whether that's Job or Isaiah. Thanks very much, sergeant."

"Wednesday morning, Harry," he said.

"I—I—I had a headache. Like I do. And I told Mama, and she give
me a pill outta the doctor's bottle. And I—"

"Yes," said Jesse. He looked at Harry tiredly. One like this—how did
you reach that childish brain? Make him understand? Get at any
memory he might have?

Friday night he'd dropped Nell at home and gone to see Mrs. Nielsen. To tell her definitely he'd take on Harry. And got a little surprise
there, too. He'd asked her for a hundred bucks' retainer, prepared to
take less; and she had gone into the bedroom and come back with it,
five new bills, no question. Nice crisp green cash. Well, that kind—
stashing it away under the rug, behind the picture. Having a little
more common sense himself, he'd given her a short lecture on the folly
of keeping so much cash around. . . . "Oh, well, it's a kind of safeguard," she'd said. "You know. Just in case. Like nineteen-thirty over
again, when Pa lost the farm and all. I just like to have some on hand,
in case."

And that kind, usually if they had a twenty tucked away they were
rich. But no question; she had it. . . .

"—Almost forgot," said Harry. "I liked to look at the picture—it was pretty. And—and it said under it, *soft as a kitten's fur.* I could read it, I can read pretty good, sir. But I did remember, how Mama said, put it out for the man, so I did. You gotta be honest. You know. And I—and I—"

Jesse reached over and touched Harry's arm. It was on his right arm, midway between elbow and wrist—a long angry red scratch. "Where'd you get that, Harry?" It was quite fresh, no more than a couple of days old.

"He didn't mean nothing bad!" said Harry, jerking away. "Honest he didn't! He's an awful nice cat, Mis' Wilson's Sammy. It was all my fault—I shoulda known better, sure—trying make him stop catching the bird. I don't like see him catch birds, I was trying sort of make him change his mind to something else, was all—they don't know no better, cats don't—but acourse he'd scratch when I pick him up like that, he's did it before. Only—only—I *hadda* get him away—poor little bird. He don't mean nothing bad, Sammy don't. He's a real nice cat— only—he's just a cat, sir, and don't know better. I told him I was sorry, and then—and then—he told *me* he was sorry too. He licked me nice and friendly. You won't do nothing to Sammy—he didn't mean—"

"No, Harry," said Jesse. He wondered if all that would say anything to the bench: along with Spotty and the pretty roses and the poor little worms. A tomcat named Sammy. Well. He said, "Harry. There was a lady's handbag. A big shiny white handbag. Do you remember anything about that, Wednesday?"

"Lady's—" said Harry. And after a minute, helpfully, "They set them down on the counter, get the money out. Sure. Lots of ladies carry real big ones. All different colors."

"Mmh. Wednesday? A big white one, Harry. Remember?"

Harry looked vague. He said, "Once a lady dropped her bag down behind the counter, and I pick it up for her. I remember."

"Wednesday?"

"I—I—I guess so. Yes, sir. Maybe . . . I don't know what she looked like, just a lady. I—I—hadda headache that day, I guess, like I told you, it was real bad like they are. Sometimes I got to stay home all day, but I don't like that on account I get to thinking, where's everybody gonna get their candy and books and gum and all, I'm not there? So I went 'n' opened up—but I still kind of had a headache—I— Please, sir, I want to go home. I don't like it here, why I got to stay here? I won't have no clean shirt tomorrow if—"

"Your mama's waiting to see you, Harry, pretty soon, and she's got some nice clean clothes for you. If you'll just try to think hard and tell me what I want to know."

"Yes, sir," said Harry. "That's good, I like to see Mama. I'll try, sir. I'm pretty good to remember things, if it isn't too long. You know. Like I almost forgot about the book, how Mama said put it out, but I did remember. And I can tell time too—"

"That's fine, Harry." What this rigmarole was about almost forgetting what Mama said, he didn't know, but let it go: probably not important. "Harry, you ever have a girl friend?"

"I—I guess not, sir."

"You know what I mean? You know what boys like to do with girls, Harry—kiss them and hug them?"

Harry's brown eyes looked bland and then timidly embarrassed. "Like in the movies," he said. "I guess."

"Like getting married. Do you know what that means?"

"Oh, yes, sir! Sure. I seen that in movies too. And once real. You get up in front of the minister and say answers when he asks. Like the Reverend Kallman where we go to church ever' Sunday. He's a nice man, he came to see me today, you know? Mis' Gracchio's little girl got married like that—she wasn't a real *little* girl, but—you know—and Mama said, even if she isn't like us she's Christian and she give her a present, a nice vase for flowers it was. And I see it in our church once, a wedding they call it, like in the movies. The minister asks questions and they say yes and all."

"Mmh. Do you know what that means, Harry? What—" Damn it, how could you put it to him?—"what it means they can do afterward?"

Utter blank in the soft brown eyes. "Well, I—I guess maybe they can kiss each other all they want, just any time, not just in cars or the dark—like in the movies," said Harry. "You know how they do. You like the movies, sir? I—I—I like go to movies. Only some, there's people hitting people and shooting, I don't like that kind. I—I— Please, sir, can I see Mama now? I don't know why I got to stay here—"

"O.K.," said Jesse, defeated.

He waited for Mrs. Nielsen on the steps of the jail. So he wasn't a head doctor; he didn't know the questions to ask, the reactions to watch for. But that said to him, Harry was genuinely ignorant. Sure, he'd read the books; he knew that they said, nobody ever is entirely. Instinct, et cetera.

And of course the girl hadn't been raped.

But—

Those little girls on the playground. Anything to be got? A possible description?

And Mike Orde. A record. If he was mixed into something—a pro job, maybe a big job, and his girl friend's roommate somehow suspected—

How, for God's sake?

Or that Jenner, maybe running a bookie shop on the side, and Lilian finding out through his receptionist? But, murder—

And a fairly elaborate murder, too, with somebody framed for the job. If.

Friedlander, well, what?—an abortion mill?

Talk about TV drama.

Talk about reaching for it.

But there was Harry, rescuing the poor little bird from Sammy the tomcat.

Hell.

He didn't like criminal cases. He thought he'd have been very smart to go in for corporation law like his father. This kind of thing—

The law was supposed to be a cut-and-dried thing: established. The whole trouble was with lawyers, who kept having feelings.

Like his about Harry.

"Damnation," said Jesse, and (after ferrying a tearful Mrs. Nielsen home) went home himself to Nell and Athelstane.

SIX

"So on Wednesday you saw this man open the door at the back of that building," said Jesse.

"Sure," said Stephanie Liebman. She sounded half reluctant, half eager. "It was the time Miss Shipley was handing around things, before we, you know, started work. I mean, it wasn't as if we weren't paying *attention*." She giggled nervously and looked at her mother. And both the Liebmans stared at Jesse, alert for every word.

Jesse reflected uneasily that this sort of thing wasn't going to be so easy. Four, Nell said. My God. What did you say to them, how did you talk to them? How much could they take in at this age or that, and how did you *know?* Of course, probably easier when you'd known them from the diaper stage. He'd never known any of them like that; his sister Fran wasn't married yet. More of a proposition than it sounded; it just came home to him now, trying to question them. Made him feel incompetent, out of his depth.

To be hoped Nell was a little more knowledgeable about them.

"Yes?" he said encouragingly.

"Stephanie was asked all this before, Mr. Falkenstein," said Mrs. Liebman. "The police came. Quite a nice young man."

"Well, I know. But you see, I can hardly ask them for their notes," said Jesse humbly. "I'm just—checking. For anything, you know." And what would there be to get? And what would it mean legally—the word of a nine-year-old—if there was anything?

"*I* didn't like him," said Stephanie contemptuously. "He was silly. He talked to me as if I was a baby or something."

"Now, dear," said Mrs. Liebman.

"Oh, did he?" said Jesse. "Very annoying. I can see that. If I'd been you, I might've been tempted not to tell him anything, when he acted like that." And he was only going by experience of adult witnesses there.

She gave him a swift, secretive side look around the heavy dark curls falling across her cheek. "Oh, well—" She giggled again.

"Stephanie, if you didn't tell something—that's very wrong—the police, dear—" It had, of course, been necessary to let the parents sit in.

Jesse's hopes rose very faintly. He felt as if he'd spent several weeks, though it was actually only since one o'clock, talking to little girls in the presence of mildly hostile parents. He'd got the names from Clock —and just to be thorough about it, he had gone to see not just the little girls who'd spoken up, but the whole class who'd been at that end of the playground braiding leather or whatever on Wednesday morning. Stephanie was the last one.

He hadn't heard much of any interest. The teacher, of course, hadn't seen anything. What the little girls remembered wasn't of much help to him. A man had opened the door in the red brick building, and come out to the alley there. Maybe tossed something on the ground. Maybe looked at something. Not the sort of action little girls (or anybody) would notice except vaguely; ordinary. Probably the only reason a few of them had, it was something to look at besides what they were supposed to be doing: typical of kids?

"Oh, well, it wasn't anything much," mumbled Stephanie. "Not really. It was just, he was so *silly*, talking baby talk to me—I—"

Jesse had the sense to keep still then. Mr. Liebman got up, tall, dark and grim, and went over to his daughter. Mr. Liebman was a highly respectable and conservative public-school teacher, and quite obviously he ruled in his own house. "Stephanie," he said sternly, "do you mean to say you didn't tell the policeman something you know?"

"Not azackly, Daddy, not really, only you know how I remember things, but he—but he— Well, I mean, Sally and Joan said so too, I guess it was the same policeman asked them. Like we were *babies*. He wouldn't tell us why they were asking about it like that, 's if we didn't *know* about that lady getting murdered there—you know—*I* read it in the newspaper," she said to Jesse. "I mean, like we were about three years old. It sort of made me mad—"

"Don't blame you," said Jesse. "I'd've been mad too, Stephanie. So you didn't tell him about something. Something you saw?"

She sat up a little straighter, with a sense of importance, and giggled. "Sure. I—"

"So you'll come out with it right now, young lady," said her father, "and no nonsense! You know it was wrong, don't you?—and you'll be punished for it! Telling lies to the police—"

"I didn't either! I just—"

"Oh, well, Ben, maybe she was frightened."

"*Mother!* I wouldn't be! It was just—"

"Nonsense," said Mr. Liebman. "If there's any truth in I.Q. tests she knows better than that. Let's have it, Stephanie. What was it you didn't tell the policeman?"

"It wasn't anything really!" she said, goaded. "Just, I saw that man, and you know I *remember* how things look, Daddy. I would've told him, I started to even, but I saw he wasn't going to believe me, he thought I was a baby! I—I—it was just, I saw him real good—"

"Really well, dear," said Mrs. Liebman.

"—Really well, what he looked like—I mean, Sally and Joan and Dorothy and all of us were sort of talking about it after—I mean after we knew about the murder and Miss Shipley heard about some of us seeing the man and said, well, you know, we ought to *tell*. I did see him good. I was sitting on that end of the bench nearest to the fence—"

About thirty feet away, but Stephanie's brown eyes looked sharp.

"All right," said her father, "take it easy." He looked at Jesse. "I'll just say, speaking objectively, she seems to have a photographic memory. Very strongly visual. As you probably know, it's nothing relative to the—ah—interest involved. The mind just records pictures. All right, Stephanie. What did he look like, what did he do?"

She gnawed a thumbnail. "He pushed the door open and came out, I guess down to a step, like. He looked over at the ground a ways from the door—there was a big trash barrel there, a light-colored one— and then he went over that way and dropped something, like he was throwing it away. But I don't think he dropped it in the barrel, just on the ground. I—I think it was something white. He—I don't know—I mean, if I *saw* him again I could say right away it *was* him, but just to say how he looked— Well, he was sort of old. He was sort of fat. He had a red face. . . . I don't *know* how old. . . . He had on a gray suit and a red tie. He didn't have much hair, but some."

Which certainly wasn't Harry, thought Jesse. But what was it worth?

"Color? Was he short or tall? How did he move, quickly or slowly?" rapped out Liebman. Jesse made a small gesture; Liebman looked at him. "Prompting the witness? Well, if we're to get anything—! Speak up, Stephanie!"

"He had a fat sort of face," she said slowly. "You know. He moved sort of quick, Daddy. He—it was almost gray hair. Sort of in between black and white, like Aunt Grace's. He—he—reminded me— He looked like Santa Claus."

"Well, really, now!" said Mr. Liebman. "How?"

"I don't know, he just *did*. I'm sorry I didn't say before, but you see it wasn't *much*— I—"

"He looked," asked Jesse, "like which Santa Claus?"

"Ah," said Mr. Liebman thoughtfully, "a shrewd question, sir. The way they scatter them all over in every store. Stephanie?"

"I don't know. Just like Santa Claus. Like at Walters' or Kress's."

And that was definitely all. Mr. Liebman made a little speech to Stephanie in which good citizenship, responsibility and the moral teachings of her religious mentors figured; and started another to Jesse, which Jesse interrupted.

"Yes, well, just one of those things. Grateful for small favors. It's something. Thanks very much."

"By the way," said Mr. Liebman at the door, "there is a Mr. Joseph Falkenstein I know slightly, who attends our temple—perhaps some relative?"

"Couldn't say," said Jesse absently, still thinking about Santa Claus. "A lot of us around. Me, I'm not very religious—brought up very sensible and modern, you know."

Mr. Liebman's eyes went cold and disapproving on him; he said a few more formal words and shut the door on him rather too vigorously.

Jesse said sadly to his car keys, "Nobody loves me. *Santa Claus.* Now what in hell could have made her think of Santa Claus?"

All the little girls had left him feeling more tired than he'd ever been at the end of a hard day in court. He went home, found Athelstane staked on his long chain in the back yard, rapturously pleased to see him, and took him upstairs. He put a stack of Bach fugues on the phonograph and sat down to think.

He didn't get very far. Odds and ends: little things. Nothing conclusive. Probabilities and improbabilities.

Santa Claus . . .

Chase round, play detective, investigate everybody associated with Lilian Blake? When the police had done so already and hadn't found anything? Of course, they hadn't looked long or far; as soon as Harry showed up, and the evidence, they'd stopped.

Look at it from the other end: who else? No handle to get hold of. That showed very plain.

Santa Claus.

Well, all right, damn it, what distinguishing marks did Santa Claus have? A long beard, a red suit. He was fat, he was jolly, he said ho-ho-ho. He had twinkling eyes in a round red face. He asked little boys and girls what they wanted for Christmas—or probably, in some situations (so confused had things got these days in matters of social culture) what they wanted for Hanukkah. What else? Nothing.

And Nell must be having a Roman holiday of houses; it was nearly six.

She arrived presently, however, and said she'd seen the place on Swallowtail Road and liked it. "It could be nice. There are two bedrooms and a den, and the dormer—it's not finished, they use it for storage, but you could make another big bedroom and half bath there, it's a good size. . . . Twenty-three thousand five hundred, but Mrs. Alton said she's sure they'd come down, maybe to twenty-two. They seem quite anxious to sell. At least she—Mrs. Friedlander—followed us all around, breathing down my neck and making inane remarks. She's a funny one, isn't she?"

Jesse said he could think of other words.

"Oh, well, of course, quite something—in a lush sort of way," agreed Nell. "Somehow I can't see her as a dentist's wife. It's such a nasty sort of job, which is irrational, I know, but— She'd remembered your name, that you'd come about the murder—how she put it."

"She would. Was she wandering around in a bathing suit again?"

"Red shorts," said Nell. "*Quite* something. And don't tell me it's sour grapes, but I feel sorry for that kind, you know. In a way. The really beautiful women. They never have to be anything else—never have to use whatever minds they have. . . . It's quite a nice house.

And it could be a bargain, Jesse, if they do come down, because it's a good neighborhood and single-residence zoned, and a lot better built than most of these new ranch houses they want thirty thousand for. One reason, Mrs. Alton pointed out, that they can't ask as much— everybody wants new houses in the suburbs now. It's one of the few possibilities I've seen."

"Well, you'll be in it more than me, it's up to you. We could manage that, I guess. You want to start dickering for it?"

"We just might. Ask Mrs. Alton to offer a lower price, anyway, and see. It could be a nice house, if," said Nell dreamily, "you got all that awful pink chintz out of the biggest bedroom, and different curtains in the kitchen. . . . She's got a horrible big whatnot shelf in the living room, and it's probably left marks on the wall so we'd have to paint right away. But there *is* that chain-link fence all around the yard, you know what they cost, and it's a nice big kitchen and at least the tile isn't lavender or some other ungodly color. Yes, it would *do*—I liked it."

"That's fine. You and Mrs. Alton see if you can get them down to twenty-two. I'll come and look at it myself if they consider the offer. What comes to your mind when I say Santa Claus?"

"Nothing—you asked me too quick," said Nell. "Santa Claus, for heaven's sake! Are you expecting him to buy us the house for Christmas?"

"Nice thought. No. Like a word-association test. What occurs to you?"

"Long white beard. Red suit. Fat red face and a big stomach. And a jolly laugh. Why?"

"You're no help," complained Jesse. "That isn't Harry, is all I can see."

"I suppose I'll hear all about it at dinner, which I'd better start to see about," said Nell.

"It isn't," said Jesse to Athelstane, "anybody I've heard of in this business at all. How could it be?" But Athelstane was no help either; he was more interested in what Nell was doing in the kitchen, and deserted Jesse precipitately.

"Or is it?" Jesse asked himself suddenly. Fat red face—fat all over— jolly twinkle in the eyes. What small detail, what general overall appearance, might nine years old fasten on to remember? . . . Very vaguely indeed, that could just be Jim Rance, the elevator man.

And that ended the first phase of the thing, because there was time in hand; Harry wouldn't be formally arraigned until next Monday, possibly even later. Jesse would like to plead him not guilty, but he wasn't justified in it with what he had—or didn't have. Hopeless to prove it. In any case, he'd made up his mind to waive a jury, whatever plea he put in; sad comment on the ideals of democracy, but mostly you were better off putting trust in one reasonably intelligent and experienced judge, with a mind trained to use logic, than in a random collection of sentimental and/or prejudiced laymen.

There was a little time to mull it over, and he had other business.

He spent Monday in the office, keeping Miss Williams busy, and cleared up a lot of paperwork. By then he knew that Harry wouldn't be arraigned until Wednesday. The Witherspoon business erupted into life late that day, and he managed to get it sandwiched into the calendar on Tuesday: scarcely another hour's worth in court, matter of getting missing testimony on record, but so much red tape that he was there the better part of a day.

In the meantime, at odd moments he did a little thinking about Harry and reached a few conclusions. The very small start he'd made on going back over ground covered by the police had yielded him nothing but Santa Claus, really. That he had, which ten to one meant nothing at all. He'd only waste time, probably for nothing more, going on with that line. Wrong way to go at it. Because who would pay any notice at all to Stephanie Liebman's description of the man she saw? Nothing said that had been the murderer of Lilian Blake, so what did it matter that it wasn't a description of Harry? Himself, Jesse was pretty sure it had been the murderer; and later on, a lot later on, when-as-and-if-he got to that one, the description might be valuable. But not now.

No use at all to put probabilities before the bench, produce character witnesses and so on. Against the police evidence. Not in a murder case. If he was going to find anything to answer the prosecution, he'd have to get at it from the other end—sniffing round to see who it might have been instead. And in ways the police hadn't tried. The police were very efficient these days and he didn't flatter himself he was any brighter, though he hadn't done so badly playing private eye last year, to get Nell off, out there in the sticks. However! Maybe at that he had a little advantage over Sergeant Clock in this business.

Because he didn't think Harry was guilty, so he was convinced there was another X to be found. And that said a couple more things, too. If you postulated a frame on Harry, right away logic said that that hadn't been an impulsive kill. It had been planned. There had been a reason for it. Somebody had had the bright thought of framing Harry. Those fingerprints. The lady who dropped her bag behind the counter? If that had been that day, which Harry wasn't sure of . . .

He'd talked to Harry again, and Mrs. Nielsen, and Jim Rance, and it had come out (a very little useful thing) that Lilian Blake hadn't been the only one Harry had tried to be friendly with, in the Ames Building. There were maybe half a dozen people, both young women and men, Harry had especially liked, offered his little presents to. One of them, a Lester Smart (tax consultant, third floor) had even said he thought Harry was being railroaded, because, "Well, you know, what he *is.* I don't think he'd ever have done a thing like that—he's a real gentle sort, Harry."

Well. How to show it all legal to the bench? Find X and get some nice legal evidence on him. Easier said than done, sure.

Some other way to get at it than the straightforward routines of the police. A gimmick—a shot in the dark? Unfortunately, you couldn't pin it down to people Harry knew—even to the tenants of the Ames Building. A lot more people would know Harry and his little stand, casually, than Harry knew as individuals. It didn't narrow the circle very much. Did it come back to the Ames Building? Just maybe. Others than those who worked in the building would know about Harry at second hand. But—know that he admired Lilian, that Lilian was scared of him?

Nothing very difficult about dropping the evidence behind his counter, the piece of lace, the piece of necklace. That lobby was darkish; just wait around until Harry left for a minute, to visit the rest room around the corner, and both elevators were upstairs. And then what? Wait for people to come out with the inevitable—that Harry had made up to her, that she had been scared of him. And it could be, too, that X hadn't known about that: hadn't needed to know. People like Harry were always among the first choices in a thing like this. It could be that X had just seen Harry as Harry, a convenient scapegoat—the one everybody would find it easy to suspect. Sure.

At that point, which was on Tuesday night, he became vaguely aware that Nell had said something, and asked, "What?"

"I said, aren't you coming to bed at all? I don't like to interrupt—

live and let live—but that's the third time round for the Toccata and
Fugue in D Minor, and it's nearly one o'clock."

"So it is—apologies." Jesse shut off the phonograph, got undressed
and into bed.

But not to sleep; and not on account of Athelstane's nearby snoring.

Who might know about Harry, see him as the handy scapegoat? He
saw it neatly outlined in headings, that being the way his mind
worked.

    A. Occupants of the Ames Building
    B. Acquaintances of Lilian's (apart from the building, private)
    C. Acquaintances of Harry's (private)
    D. Everybody nearby the building, who frequented the same lunch
counters, bus lines.

A list that might run up into the hundreds. You could imagine, for instance, the waitress at the café across the street mentioning to a boy
friend, "That's the guy keeps the newsstand in that building, he's a little off, not right, you know"—casual talk—Reynolds the gas-station attendant mentioning him to customers, something bringing up some related subject. Quite a lot of people might know about Harry.

And of course X would know now that the frame had worked, that
Harry had been charged and arrested. . . . A lot of people, of course,
still had the idea that cops were dumb, didn't look beyond the ends of
their noses.

All the same, thought Jesse sleepily, there had been a hell of a lot of
luck floating around. Good luck for X, bad for the lady with the blindfold. . . .

He went to sleep. But he woke earlier than usual, when Nell got up,
and astonished her by appearing in the kitchen at eight o'clock. Neither of them was markedly human before ten o'clock; she poured his
coffee silently and handed him the first section of the *Times*. Jesse
brooded over both.

There had been another race riot in South Africa. Gasoline was
going up half a cent a gallon. The weather-report box said, unsurpris-
ingly, Smog Today. The British Prime Minister had made a speech.
(Reading the resumé, Jesse was irresistibly reminded of Mr. Coo-
lidge's précis of the sermon about Sin: "He's against it." But poli-

ticians—) A Senator had made a speech. Two men had been rescued by helicopter from a cliff in Angeles forest.

They had finally selected a calendar date for the Killeen trial, after all this time. Full-dress affair, that would be: high union boss charged with misappropriation of funds (polite term: in plain talk, theft of around half a million) and no less a personage than Adam Leibowitz hired for the defense. Very smart boy, Leibowitz. Maybe a little too smart. But he'd be bucking a pretty good justice, Cunningham. People said: people Jesse knew. He'd never tried a case under Cunningham himself, but the man had a good reputation. . . . Human-interest story about a dog in the pound. The governor had made a speech. There'd been a tornado in Kansas.

He finished his coffee, handed the first section back to Nell and went to shave and dress. Feeling very slightly more human, he came back to the kitchen where she was still buried in the paper. She put two more slices of bread in the toaster and shoved over the second section.

Its first page spoke of death: another freeway collision, and two teenagers dead in a stolen car. The Board of Education was engaged in a private fight; there was a cut of an indignant-looking stout woman, CHARGES BOARD DISCRIMINATES AGAINST MINORITIES.

Jesse turned past the second page (Inter-Valley Horse Show and D.A.R. Meet) and discovered with joy that this was one of the days when Mr. Morrie Ryskind's column appeared on the editorial page. He read it with appreciative chortles over a third slice of toast, and went on to Letters to the Editor. There ensued a long silence broken only by Athelstane's hopeful demands for buttered crusts. Eventually Jesse asked, "Where you bound today?"

"Mrs. Alton. Marketing. And if I can find a skirt just the right shade of brown to match the— I thought I'd try the May Company."

"Not taking the monster, then."

"Heavens, no."

"That's fine," said Jesse absently. He folded the paper neatly, got his hat and briefcase, kissed her good-bye and left. It was ten past nine. In the garage he looked at her baby Renault and thought it might be three-quarters of an hour before she emerged.

Gave him just nice time to see Harry through the formal arraignment.

Not that he expected any of them, except possibly the sullen-eyed pro crook (was he?) Mike Orde, to threaten him with mayhem. But—

All easy and casual. The careless talk . . . As he backed out the Ford, he was trying to remember the chemical term, from one semester in high school a long time back. A catalyst, would it be? Something you added to a lot of other ingredients, and it wasn't affected but it set everything else off having reactions. . . .

SEVEN

He put in a plea of not guilty, adding nothing about incompetency; the formalities were over in ten minutes, after (of course) a three-quarters of an hour's wait. Afterward, he bought Mrs. Nielsen a cup of coffee at a nearby lunch counter and said honestly, "I don't know," when she asked him if he thought he could prove Harry hadn't done it.

"Against the evidence," he said, "quite a trick. About the only way, find out who really did. And prove it. Which would also be quite a trick."

"You just got to show them he never," she said fiercely.

"Oh, well, I don't want to say too much," he said to Rance vaguely. "A lot of—er—ramifications in this thing, once we looked into it. Police on their side, me on mine, you know. Harry, well, he makes a very handy sort to pass the buck to."

Rance looked at him uncertainly. "I don't—you mean he might not be the *one?* Good gosh almighty—"

"Oh, early to say. Shouldn't have said that. Just little things showing up, you know," said Jesse. He lit a cigarette, looking at Rance sidewise. The other man had stepped out of his elevator cage to talk. This broad and unexpected hint worried him, you could see: his round pink face drew into a frown, and the little pale blue eyes looked puzzled. But was it any different than the worry he might feel innocently, to hear that his contact with newsworthy excitement might not be a real one, that an innocent man had been mistakenly accused? Impossible to say. But he would tell Mac, and—almost undoubtedly—let out something to most regular elevator users in the building. You could hear him—"Lawyer fellow, he said it wasn't Harry did it after all—maybe, by what he said, the cops have got something—it kinda sounded like they got something more."

Asking questions now, of course. "You mean, somebody else? But good gosh almighty, Mr. Falkenstein, they found those things of the girl's right there under his counter! And I unnerstand there was finger-prints, too—how could—"

"Shouldn't have said anything," mumbled Jesse as a smartly dressed matron tapped briskly into the lobby. "Forget it." He drifted back toward Harry's stand, and she stepped into the elevator.

"Four, please."

Rance cast him another uncertain look, joined her reluctantly and banged the door.

So the news was passed to Rance. Rance with his round pink face and twinkling eyes like Santa Claus. Woolgathering?

Before starting through the building on today's errand, Jesse took a look at Harry's stand. He had had the key from Mrs. Nielsen. It turned smoothly, the grillwork rolled back; there was a flap at the end which lifted to let you behind. Too narrow for wall shelves behind the counter; all the storage space was underneath. All the shelves filled; so many different brands of cigarettes and candy bars these days. A few cartons of chewing gum, breath lozenges, the little dental sticks guaranteed to remove tobacco stains. On the counter, more of the same, plus about half a dozen Japanese-made lighters and a card of cheap ball-point pens. All the magazines were on the rack outside. There was also a nondescript old kitchen chair with padded seat and back, and one drawer in the counter. It was locked, but the second key she'd given him fitted it. As he turned it, Jesse knew the drawer would be empty; she would have been here and cleared out the cash take left.

It was empty, except for an old newspaper clipping about a cat who'd adopted a baby squirrel to raise with her kittens. Jesse looked at it thoughtfully and put it back.

No trouble about dropping those two small items on the floor behind the counter. Might even have been done when Harry's back was turned. And even though Harry was very neat and clean, and probably swept the floor here fairly often, he wouldn't necessarily have noticed such small things. Only the police had such eagle eyes. And they wouldn't have been here long. Lilian Blake killed on Wednesday morning, nine to nine-thirty; the evidence found and Harry arrested Thursday afternoon.

Rance had been up and down a couple of times while Jesse examined the stand; each time he hit the lobby he threw a curious look at Jesse. Now he and Mac were unoccupied at the same moment, and he'd stepped over to talk to Mac; both of them gave Jesse covert glances.

Jesse pulled the grillwork back over the stand, locked it and made for the elevators. He went up with Mac to the top floor, and Mac cleared his throat and said, "Say, Jim was just saying—you mean, it looks as if Harry isn't the one?"

"Shouldn't have said so much," said Jesse, sounding uneasy and secretive. "Kind of early to let it out."

On the fourth floor he visited only one office, that of a G.P. whose receptionist, Janet Andrews, he had marked as a nonstop talker. He needed an excuse, of course, to start a conversation and drop his dark hints; he had made up a couple of mysterious questions to ask. What he asked Janet Andrews was whether she had ever seen Harry smoking. (Harry didn't smoke.) She was properly mystified and curious.

"No, I never have, why?"

"Oh, well, just—it's beginning to look as if he was framed for it, you see," said Jesse as if absently. "The police think—" He stopped rather abruptly, and added, "Shouldn't have said that so soon. Thanks very much."

That should take care, he thought, of the whole fourth floor; and also of everybody Janet Andrews knew elsewhere in the building. It would be fatal to overdo it; X would smell a rat at once. And he didn't, of course, have any guarantee that this artful little performance was going to worry X at all. If X was really smart, he'd just go on sitting tight and making like the Tar Baby, and he'd never be smoked out. Also, if a couple of lines got into the papers (which they probably would) about Harry's arraignment, X would know there wasn't any truth in the rumor that the cops had scented a frame.

It was a long chance that, hearing that rumor, X would be sufficiently alarmed to do something else, trying to cover up. Something that might, just possibly, point a direction to look. But it was a chance.

Jesse went on building it. As artfully as possible. He visited two offices on the third floor: Byerly's and that of the tax consultant,

Smart. He asked both whether they ever smoked Turkish cigarettes, and went on to let out his absent-minded information about the frame. From Byerly he got (assumed?) profane indifference; from Smart, eager questions which he didn't answer.

He skipped the second floor. He must be very careful not to over-play it.

On the ground floor, he went to Friedlander's office first. The little anteroom was empty; in the inner office he heard Friedlander talking, apparently on the phone.

"But, my dear, it's simply silly to spend the whole amount in one place. Don't you see— Lots in Emerald Bay begin at five thousand, and to build a house according to the specifications the association there asks— The taxes alone . . . We can't discuss it on the phone, dear, really. . . . I know you do, but— I'm sorry, my dear, someone's just come in, I'll have to—"

When he came to the door, he looked slightly harassed; Jesse felt a twinge of sympathy. Evidently the glamour girl had set her heart on some place classier than Swallowtail Road, whether or not she was talked out of Emerald Bay.

"Oh—Mr. Falkenstein," said Friedlander. He said it noncommittally, neutrally. "Yes? I have a few moments before an eleven o'clock appointment."

Jesse asked him whether he'd known that Lilian had come back to the office on Monday evening to retrieve a forgotten bracelet.

"Oh, did she?" said Friedlander. "No. Does it matter? And why?" A slight frown creased his forehead. "My assistant always has a key—I had duplicates made of both keys, office and building, because sometimes I haven't an early appointment and don't— It was quite all right that she should, for something like that, but of course in the ordinary way I shouldn't care to have— No, I didn't know, why?"

Jesse said his piece. Just asking. (Sounding cryptic.) Some new evidence, which said to both the police and him that just maybe Harry was being framed. Oh, shouldn't have said anything, really early to—

Friedlander's eyes narrowed. "Oh?" he said after a moment. "Oh, really? I don't— From what that sergeant said, it seemed pretty much cut and dried. I can't imagine who else would— Do you mean—"

"Sorry, shouldn't have let that out," said Jesse. "Thanks very much, doctor." He let himself out into the hall.

He thought that would take care of the Ames Building. And he was, call it seventy percent sure, that it was connected with the Ames Building in some way; but just in case, he spread it around a little more. He went into the lunchroom across the street and did his act there. He went down to Georgie's Grill and repeated it.

That brought him up to twelve-forty. Nell must be gone by now. He drove back home and found Athelstane staked out on his long chain, as expected, and went upstairs to find the short leather-and-chain leash the pet shop had recommended for a big dog. Athelstane recognized the general meaning of the command *Heel*, and was obliging about *Sit* and *Stay* because he was sedentary by nature; he didn't like the short leash, but would put up with it for the sake of being in human company instead of alone. Clipping it to his chain collar, Jesse inevitably had his face washed by a loving pink tongue, got out his handkerchief and said resignedly, "The complete extrovert. But you don't wear a sign saying *I love everybody*. In fact, just on surface appearance, quite formidable. Yes. A pretty pair we make, to anyone who doesn't know us—the brilliant private eye with his police-trained, all-but-human hound to protect and aid him. If I'd remembered not to feed you this morning, maybe you'd look fiercer."

Athelstane was delighted to be going somewhere in a car; it didn't matter where. Lucy Street, when they got there and found a parking place, did not repel him. In the police records, Jesse had learned from Clock, Mike Orde's last known address had been the San Cristofero Hotel on Lucy Street.

It stretched drearily down a few blocks, the other side of Main, bordered by flea-bitten hotels (Men Only, 50¢ per Night), dubious-looking bars, a few pawnshops, a penny arcade with a shooting gallery, a couple of frowsty movie houses. The San Cristofero Hotel was another flea trap, ancient, dirty, sagging on its foundations. The desk clerk, resembling the hotel, disclaimed all knowledge of Orde, but in such a tone that Jesse surmised that he was cautious rather than truthful. Seeing what Orde's business probably was, natural. . . . Rather funny that one like Orde had taken up with an honest, nice girl like Ruth Myers?

He tried all the bars in that block, emphasizing the fact that he was a lawyer. Funny, but few people could resist the mysterious efforts of a lawyer, to contact them: the eternal hope of an unexpected legacy. In the sixth place he struck lucky; the barman, wooden-faced, said he didn't know anybody by that name, but almost at once vanished through a door at the back of the bar. Jesse waited around hopefully, finally gave up and sought the street again. He walked half a block toward Main, and at the opening of a narrow alley between buildings was accosted by a low voice.

"What you want with me?"

"Hello, Mr. Orde," said Jesse pleasedly.

"You're that lawyer fellow was asking Ruth about the dame got knocked off—"

"That's right," said Jesse. "I just wanted to ask you where you were on Wednesday morning a week ago, Mr. Orde. When Lilian Blake was killed, you know."

"What the hell—" said Orde. "What you mean? They got the guy did that— I didn't have nothing—"

"Well, you see, we're not just sure it was Harry after all," said Jesse. "Not now. A few things showed up, and it begins to look like a frame. And by the description we— Well, never mind. Just where were you on Wednesday morning, between nine and nine-thirty, Orde?"

"Description? What the hell—" The cold eyes closed to slits on him. "You got nothing on— What the hell you mean?"

"A couple of little things've shown up since Harry was arrested," said Jesse. "The way they do sometimes." Athelstane was pulling on his collar, interested in investigating a new human and making friends; Jesse held him hard, close to his side. "Way it looks to me, Harry was framed. The cops have talked kind of free—in fact, I got the idea they're still looking around too—and you've got a record. I'm thinking of my client, Orde. Where were you last Wednesday morning? Got an alibi?"

"What the *hell!* You don't make sense. Why the hell should I've taken that dame off? Trying to frame *me* for it, sounds like—" Orde was eyeing Athelstane with concealed nervousness.

"Does Ruth Myers know about your record, Orde? What kind of a job does she think you have?"

"You go to hell! I don't—"

"Sure, you could hire witnesses to give you an alibi," said Jesse. "But you know about lawyers, Orde? Smart and dumb, they come. The client comes first with the smart ones. The cops gave me a little, and I've looked around. I'm still looking. You could be X, on what I've got."

"You been drinking third-rail stuff," said Orde. "Brace me, mister—

go on 'n' brace me all you want—you're talking Greek. You're maybe fronting for Mawson, play like the Double O on me—"

"A spy? Not nearly smart enough," said Jesse. "Just smart enough to pick up a hint from a cop, Orde. I want my client off the hook, and that means showing that somebody else ought to be on it. You won't answer questions, but I'll find out what I want to know. I've got ways and means, Orde."

The man took a sudden step toward him, one hand groping, lips back in a snarl; and Jesse relaxed his hold on the leash and said, "Watch the dog, Orde." Athelstane surged forward, and Orde stepped back hastily. "That's better. I'll be looking at you a lot harder. You made a mistake dragging Harry in, friend—it doesn't look that way, but there's money behind him, to buy him off—and somebody else in."

"You don't reach me," said Orde, poker-faced.

"I'll be looking at you," said Jesse. He turned and walked on, down toward where he'd left the Ford. Very helpful, he reflected—yanking Athelstane away from a decayed tennis shoe in the gutter—all those old movies and recent TV dramas. Not to speak of the hard-boiled school of mysteries. Gave you some idea how to act with them, anyway. He wondered who Mawson was. Rival hood, probably; Clock would know.

And as he'd surmised, Athelstane had been helpful too. Also funny how people who'd stand up to a human threat (and God knew he'd never claimed to be Mr. America or the all-round athlete) would back down before a big, dangerous-looking animal. Personally he thought the L.A. force had been wrong in deciding not to use dogs to make up for the man shortage. Just as a psychological factor, so useful—aside from other aspects. Of course, those dogs, the ones Scotland Yard and other forces were using, were really intelligent trained animals.

Athelstane nudged him and proudly presented a very ancient and damp piece of cardboard which, by the label, had once held a pound of prime bacon. Jesse took it and tossed it back into the gutter. "Come on, here's the car. In, that's a good boy. According to Solomon, *The way of a fool is right in his own eyes.*"

As he turned the ignition key another quotation occurred to him and he sighed over it. *For the thoughts of mortal men are miserable, and our devices are but uncertain.*

One could only hope.

He thought he'd covered the possibly fertile ground. You couldn't work nice and straightforward like the police, from this end. Detective-story plot as it looked, you had to use the gimmick sometimes.

Because people talked. Especially about anything like this. Give it twenty-four hours, amazing how many people could have been contacted with the story. . . . People didn't read Kipling any more. Which was a pity. Some very pithy and pertinent remarks in the *Jungle Book*, about the Bandar-log. The monkey folk; yes, eternal chatterers.

He sat back to wait and see what might happen. If anything.

He waited through Thursday, and nothing did. But about eight o'clock that night, he remembered vaguely and belatedly that there had been some talk about a house. He laid down the latest issue of a catalogue of L.P. releases and said, "That house you liked. What about it?"

"There were three," said Nell, looking at him with affectionate amusement, "altogether. Out of about fifty I'd seen. That is, several others I like, but impossible prices and taxes. Don't you remember anything about them? I took you to see them all, the third one just last night—the Friedlanders' place. You must remember that one, the way that woman followed us all over and kept talking about Harry and how it's really better for these crazy guys to be shut up somewhere."

"Oh, yes," said Jesse. "Of course." He did remember. Friedlander hadn't been home. The glamour girl Berenice, in yellow shorts and halter, had been reluctant to let them in, even shepherded by Mrs. Alton. . . .

"Quite hopeless," said Nell. "You, I mean. That's a lie—you don't remember the house at all."

"Yes, I do—wallpaper with peacocks on it in one room. And it's unnatural, a normal American wife complaining that her husband doesn't interfere in domestic affairs. What about them?"

"I've had Mrs. Alton submit offers, the prices we agreed on that you said we can afford—which you've probably also forgotten. I don't know anything definite yet. These things take time."

"Don't they indeed," said Jesse. And he wasn't thinking about houses. If something was going to happen, it should more or less right away. Well, continue to hope. . . .

EIGHT

In spite of good resolutions, Nell felt a little exasperated with Jesse. These single-minded men. When he had something on his mind, you could set off a cannon under him and he'd never hear it. After all, whatever house they bought he'd be living in too. Not that he was obnoxiously particular, but she would like to be reasonably certain that he didn't mind his den overlooking the neighbors' drive (in that house on Vizcaino Avenue) or the rather cramped main bath (in the house in View Park) or the peacocks on the wallpaper (in the house on Swallowtail Road). You didn't buy a house every day.

Of course it wasn't only Jesse, but a lot of men. Most of them. So considerate and accommodating, and never knowing how maddening it could be. You finally gave away that very smart blue hat to the salvage people, as past reclaiming, and he'd say, "I never did like that hat." Those casual acquaintances you'd rather liked moved back East, and he said, "Thank God we needn't listen to that fool woman's chatter again." You never knew where you were, little things like that.

Naturally, for the rest of it, she read him like a book. Part of it was quite genuine, his not being awfully particular which house so long as she was satisfied and the payments wouldn't break them; but partly too it was just that he had his mind on something else. Nell had cast her mind over what she knew of his current cases and unerringly reached the conclusion that it was Harry. Because he'd stopped talking about that one.

Usually, anything on his mind emerged; he'd talk it over with her. But when he suddenly stopped, and went into long silences with *The Art of the Fugue* stacked on the phonograph, it was a symptom that he was worried.

Nobody was perfect, and he came by it naturally. Nell had a vivid recollection of her father-in-law, one evening, absorbed in examining the inward parts of an antique clock and taking no slightest notice of the appalling crash of a traffic accident outside the open window, or the consequent screams and sirens.

But at times she could have wished that Jesse was not quite so much like his father. It wasn't that she was so meek and overconsiderate as not to intrude on his silences; she had talked about all the houses, and asked him how he liked this and such. And he had said yes and no and all right, and she was resignedly aware that he wasn't paying much attention.

She'd just like to be sure that six months or a year from now he wouldn't say, "Why did we ever buy a place without a proper entry hall?" or "I never did like pillars on a front porch." (The Vizcaino Avenue house was colonial.)

Well, that was Jesse. Heaven knew she had done her best.

She didn't (most of her attention being on the houses) give much thought to what was worrying him. Eventually it would come out; she'd hear all about it.

Personally she rather leaned toward the house in View Park, but the chances looked dim that they'd come down to anything possible, and it would probably be one of the other two in the end. Rather funny, Jesse being the one to come across the place on Swallowtail Road. You could do a lot with it—quite an attractive house. . . .

One advantage to living in a multiple-zoned area near a business district was that the mail came early. On Friday morning she went down to get it before Jesse left, about nine-thirty; as usual, a lot of ads, no letters, but also that catalogue she'd sent for. Nell handed over the rest of it and sat down to look at the catalogue.

"Ah!" said Jesse, sounding pleased. "How gratifying."

"A check?" asked Nell without looking up.

"Not exactly, but almost as nice. Yes, indeed. How does old Jeshu put it? *Many have fallen by the edge of the sword, but not so many as have fallen by the tongue.* I'm off," and he kissed her, snatched up his hat and left.

Nell finished looking at the catalogue, washed the breakfast dishes, made the bed and dusted, staked Athelstane out in the yard and departed to see Mrs. Alton.

Mrs. Alton hadn't been able to contact the Friedlanders, she said, since Wednesday night when Nell had taken Jesse to see the place, but she thought the Vizcaino Avenue people were definitely receptive to the offer of twenty-one-five. Only they insisted on the buyers' taking the living and dining room carpeting, and wanted another five hundred for that.

"But it's pink," said Nell. "I couldn't live with pink carpeting. Yes, I know it's only two years old, and nylon—I still don't want it. We all have foibles. That nice shade of gray on the walls, and a north exposure—it simply shrieks for scarlet or orange in decorating."

"You could take it up," said Mrs. Alton, "and have it cut to fit the bedrooms or—"

"I don't *like* pink. Anywhere," said Nell. "I'm not a—a pink person. If they'll come down to twenty-one-five without the carpeting, we'll think about it."

"Well!" said Mrs. Alton with a sigh. "I'll see what I can do."

"I know I'm difficult," said Nell apologetically. "I've been bothering at you for ages, and only these three I really like after all your hunting. It's just, I have rather definite ideas. And I've got all these odds and ends of family furniture in storage, you know—too good to get rid of, the price furniture is now—and you couldn't put mission oak in one of these new ranch houses. Or, come to think, on pink carpet either."

Mrs. Alton, who had grown a little tired of Nell's definite ideas (especially since Athelstane had eaten her glove), sighed and said again she'd see what she could do. Nell thanked her and went on her way, first to get the gas tank filled and then on a continued hunt for the brown skirt. In this she was entirely unsuccessful, and in the dozenth shop, at three in the afternoon, she found her patience wearing thin.

"We're not showing brown, madam," said the dozenth salesclerk. "It's not a color this year."

"It's still in the dictionary," said Nell. "I couldn't care less what's being shown in Paris or New York—who can afford to keep up with the Duchess of Windsor and people like that? In my ignorance, I'd always considered brown to be one of the basic colors. And I'm getting very tired of being dictated to by these autocrats. There must be hundreds of women just around here who want brown skirts, or navy cardigans, or shoes with round toes, and just because somebody in New York says they're not High Fashion, they stop making them and we can't buy any. It's ridiculous."

"I'm sorry, madam," said the clerk in a bored tone.

"Oh, I know it's not your fault. But I do think, in a supposed democracy, they might consider the minorities more," said Nell. She came out and walked up the street to where she'd parked the car and found a ticket for overtime parking on the windshield. The meter was obviously defective, because she'd put in a nickel not thirty minutes ago, but try to convince the patrolman! She used some unladylike language and started home. It was definitely not her day.

But it began to look a little brighter when she got home. She stumbled over a parcel in the dark hall, left outside the apartment door; and as she opened the door a note wedged in the jamb fluttered out. Nell put the parcel on the coffee table and opened the note; it was from Fran, her usual hasty scrawl. *You housewives, gadding around all day! Celebrations in order—think I've landed the editorial job!*

Nell opened the parcel, which was neatly wrapped as from a store, and a little card fell out which said primly in gold script, *With Compliments.* It was a fifth of bourbon. How nice of Fran, she thought, sorry she'd missed her: coming around to share her celebrations, and also bringing the wherewithal. It must be a special celebration indeed, for Fran didn't as a rule drink very much.

Nor did Nell, but after the day she'd had, perhaps she deserved a drink. Might make her a little better company at dinner. She opened the bottle, made herself a highball and tried to call Fran, without success. Oh, well, later on.

It was only a quarter to four. Sit here peacefully and finish her drink, relax a little. Dinner wouldn't take long. Ought to go down and bring Athelstane in, poor darling, he did hate being alone. . . .

Jesse had had nearly as annoying a day as Nell. He carried his treasure straight down to Headquarters to show Clock. "I've had an anonymous letter," he said proudly.

Clock said, "Not my department, Mr. Falkenstein. First you contact the postal authorities, and they'll work with our boys, depending on what it's about."

"Well, that's just the point. It's about Harry—as," said Jesse, "I was hoping it would be." He laid it carefully on Clock's desk. "Handled by the postman, of course—it was in the middle of a bunch of mail so I don't think my wife's prints'd be on it, and when I spotted it I handled it very carefully by the bottom corners. Isn't it pretty?"

Clock sighed at it. The envelope was an ordinary letter-size one, of cheap white stock. Dime-store variety. The postmark was the main Hollywood office. The address had been carefully made up of separate letters cut from a newspaper. Some of the cut-out letters in the body of the thing were also from a newspaper, some from a slick-paper periodical. In fact, the standard anonymous letter. It said, *Dont try to put someone else in Harry Nielsens place or youll be sorry this is a warning theyve got the right man youre just a crooked meddler.*

"Yes, very nice," said Clock. "I suppose now you're going to tell me this proves Harry isn't X because somebody thinks you're going to get him sprung and we'll be sniffing around again."

"More or less."

"Why, Mr. Falkenstein? What produced this little love letter?"

"Me," said Jesse. "I cast my nets in every direction—last Wednesday. All around the Ames Building and that whole area, and at Mike Orde. I was indiscreet—I hinted. I said Harry was framed and you knew it, and maybe I had more evidence to say who instead of Harry. I meddled, in other words. And somebody doesn't like it—somebody's scared."

"I don't doubt that. It's a long way from saying that somebody is X instead, on Lilian Blake. Tell me what you said. . . . Yes, well, that'd worry people a lot less open to a possible frame than Orde or anybody in that building. I can see any one of a dozen people putting this thing together, for any of several reasons. Because I'll tell you something else. In almost any kind of crime, where a good many people are questioned, you always run across the ones with innocent little secrets they're sensitive about. Big things and little things, serious and otherwise. The extracurricular lady somewhere, the illegitimate kid ten years ago or Uncle Bill's little peculiarity of putting away a pint of whiskey a day. They're so damn conscious of it themselves, they think everybody who comes around asking questions suspects it."

"Lawyers run into it too," said Jesse. "But—"

"But, the mention of Harry? Sure, you stepped on somebody's toes," agreed Clock. "But it needn't have one damn thing to do with Harry. That's what you were talking about. It could be that you or anybody else poking around, here or there, might come across some irrelevant little secret somebody's keeping. You covered quite a lot of territory there. Sure, people talk. I'm inclined to think somebody's just worried about any further poking around at the Ames Building or the adjacent area. For all we know, maybe Reynolds at the gas station sells numbers tickets, or one of the receptionists you talked to does a little hustling in her spare time. Or almost anything. People, in case you didn't know, are funny."

"That's one way to look at it, but not the only way. Don't you think it's a little funny that I'm warned off trying to help Harry just after I've been dropping hints I've got evidence on someone else?"

"Sure, you can read it that way too. But let's be objective, Mr. Falkenstein. Let's look at the probable possibles before the improbable ones."

"Just because you're convinced Harry is X, you call this improbable?"

"On the evidence. Is this evidence for Harry's innocence to lay in front of the D.A.?"

"There you have me. Very presumptive. But I thought you'd be a little more interested."

"Oh, I'm interested," said Clock. "For one little thing, if it was Mike Orde who sent you this, it could be he got nervous because he's got a major caper coming up and doesn't want anybody fooling around. I'll keep this, and we'll have a look. Sure." He looked at the letter distastefully. "You annoy me, Mr. Falkenstein. Go away. I'll let you know what we come up with, if anything."

"Our efficient, upstanding police—yes—every faith in you," said Jesse, and went away.

He went out to Albert Avenue and called on all of the Nielsens' neighbors he found at home. And this was, damn it, an elementary thing he ought to have done the first day he took Harry on—so busy deducing complexities he neglected the obvious; maybe that hundred bucks' retainer was all he was worth, at that.

He found nine housewives, several husbands and assorted kids at home, and put his question. Had anybody seen Harry leave the house that Wednesday morning, and if so at what time? Inevitably, here too the police had been before him.

Yes, Mrs. Gracchio had seen Harry walking up the street that morning, toward the bus stop on Santa Monica. She'd been washing her front windows, how come she happened to be in front, and as she'd told the police, it'd have been about a quarter of ten because she hadn't started until after she'd listened to that morning's episode of *The Career of Wilhelmina Bradley* on the radio and that was nine-fifteen to nine-thirty and she'd done the left window and almost finished the right when Harry came by.

That hour, most women would be in the kitchen or back yard, wouldn't notice, of course. Kids in school, husbands at work. But another one nearer the Nielsen house thought she remembered seeing him too. Mrs. Thomas, just setting out for market. She couldn't swear to the time, except that it was a few minutes before ten or maybe not so late, about a quarter of.

Which said very little. Because, as Clock had said to him, Harry could have come home after doing that kill. Maybe to change his shirt, if he'd got a little blood on it. (And try to find a witness to seeing him on the bus!) Harry, very neat and clean. And Mama not noticing a stained shirt in the laundry? Clock would say—had said—that Mamas lean over backward defending the Harrys. And if there had been a stained shirt, he could have thrown it away in the trash, of course. Plenty of time after the murder to get home and be seen on Albert Avenue. And to get back to open the stand at ten-fifteen. . . . What Jesse had hoped for was someone who could corroborate Mrs. Nielsen that Harry had stayed in bed with a headache that morning. Someone who'd come to the house, seen him. And you couldn't expect that. Ask Harry, and get some vague answer that said even less: ten days ago was a long time back, to Harry.

All that brought him up to nearly one o'clock. As he'd left the Johnsons' house, before finding Mrs. Thomas, he'd seen Mrs. Nielsen plodding up the sidewalk ahead of him; she didn't work on Friday afternoons, was on duty Friday nights when the stores were all open, downtown. He wanted his lunch, but as long as he was here, he should get from her the names of any doctors who had treated Harry, any psychiatrists, the name of the school. When he left Mrs. Thomas he went up to the Nielsen house.

Going to be a bad summer, all right; only June twenty-first, and he'd bet it was ninety-five degrees in the full sun. . . . The front door was open, but the outside screen obscured his view of the living room; he rang the bell, and was a little startled at her nearby voice: "Yes—who is it?" Dull, tired.

"Mr. Falkenstein."

"Oh. The screen's open—"

She was sitting in the overstuffed chair that matched the couch. Tired, yes: on her feet all day at her job, and when she relaxed it was

ungracefully—she didn't think any more of how she looked, except to
be clean and tidy. Her feet in their sensible black oxfords splayed out
at an unbecoming angle, and wisps of hair escaping from the hair net
the law required waitresses to wear. But something more than
tiredness in her expression: fear.

"What is it, Mrs. Nielsen?" Because for that moment, she had
looked up at him with the terrified expression of a trapped animal.

"It's not—!" she said. And then she leaned back and shut her eyes,
as if she'd just now come to the end, where there was nothing any
more.

"What's the trouble?" asked Jesse.

"I suppose," she said in a dragging voice, after a minute, "you got
to see. And I don't know for sure what they are—except not mine or
ever around here before—but I can guess, something else to make
Harry look bad. It's no use, I guess, tell you I know they wasn't there
a couple days ago. On account I was looking for them old school reports of Harry's, I'd saved 'em all, only not things you keep close at
hand like, and they were in my mother's old trunk in the garage."

"I see," said Jesse.

"I found them," she said, eyes still closed. "Only that policeman, he
said it wasn't needful, the school had records too and they'd got them
there. For the trial, like, you know."

"Mmh." Jesse sat down opposite her. "What are you talking about,
Mrs. Nielsen? You found something?"

"They wasn't there, then," she said. "They wasn't! I wouldn't lie
about it—not even for Harry, I wouldn't. If it *was* him did such an
awful thing, well, it don't bear thinking about, but I wouldn't lie. Anybody who'd do such a thing, it's right they should be shut away. And
it's no good to say it, everybody'll just say I'm trying to cover up. . . .
It's this, sir." She opened her hand and showed him.

A bunch of keys. Without much doubt, the keys missing from Lilian
Blake's handbag. Three Yale keys, a tiny one which might belong to a
suitcase or jewel box, and a couple of old-fashioned straight steel keys.
They were on a fancy gold chain, with two cheap ornaments dangling
from it: a pearl-encrusted heart, and a gold-filled disc engraved
Lilian.

"How and when did you find these?" he asked. "And where?"

She didn't open her eyes. "Just now," she said almost indifferently.
"I went out to see to them ivy geraniums. Awful woody and untidy

they get this time o' year—need clearing out. I went into the garage to get the trowel, and they was sitting right there on top o' Mother's old trunk—where they wasn't before. I know. It's my garage, isn't it?"

"So it is," said Jesse.

Suddenly she sat up and opened her eyes. "I shouldn't've showed you. I shouldn't. I—I reckon you're an honest man, Mr. Falkenstein— like the police nowadays. I know how it looks, sir. But it's not true! I swear it isn't. I know Harry. Wouldn't I know, sir? I birthed him, I raised him. It was a grief to us, I can't say any other way, he wasn't— right. Sam was good about it—and no other children either, we'd hoped a nice family—but Sam was a good man, he was kind. He said, Nobody's fault, just God's will, and we got to do best we can by him. We did, sir. The best anybody could do. Do you think I don't know him, what he'd do or not do, after twenty-four years? It's not true!"

Jesse stood up, dangling the keys from his forefinger. "I don't think so either, Mrs. Nielsen," he said soberly. "Because, aside from my own opinion, I'm backed up by my wife's. Can't deny it—most women get nuances about people easier, don't they? She says you wouldn't lie even for Harry—my own conclusion, if arrived at a little later. Yes. But, *All iniquity is as a two-edged sword,* according to old Jeshu— comforting thought. Maybe somebody's been a little too impulsive. Tell me, after they arrested Harry, the police came and searched here, didn't they?"

She nodded. "Two of them came, right after. They tried to be nice about it, I could see even if I was upset—and they put things back where they was, careful. Mostly in Harry's room they looked, but they didn't find anything they seemed interested in."

"And then they looked everywhere else, including the garage?"

"No, sir. That was all. I was here all the time, and it was just in here they looked."

"Hell!" said Jesse between his teeth. Clock had slipped up on that one—more likely, the two underlings given the job had been dumb or inexperienced. So now nobody could say positively that the keys hadn't been in the garage all along. And while it was a little point to make—that surely if Harry had just left them out in the open like that she'd have seen them before and been curious—it didn't mean much; such a small thing, she wouldn't necessarily have noticed. Hell and damnation. "Do you keep the garage locked?"

"No, sir," she said, staring at him. "There's no car. Only odds and ends, you know. Things that back east you'd keep in the attic, but out here you don't have attics. I sold the car after Sam died."

"Yes, I see."

"Mr. Falkenstein—you going to tell the police about this?"

"Not," said Jesse dreamily, "until I've visited the newspaper offices, anyway. But eventually they'll have to know. . . . You never know, something may show up. I can't tell you not to worry. Early to say how it'll come out. And Clock's no fool, but this isn't going to help unconvince him. However. *A two-edged sword.* Let's hope so. When were you last in the garage, to notice whether these were there or not?"

"I couldn't swear," she said. "I know they wasn't last week, a week ago today it'd've been, on account they arrested Harry on Thursday afternoon, and I— I was in there late Wednesday, but I might not have noticed. How come I did now, the trowel was on the shelf alongside the trunk. But I don't think they was there last Thursday or Friday."

"Mmh," said Jesse. "No, I can't tell you I like it. But sometimes— this making assurance doubly sure—it shows the machinery in the flies. We can look, anyway. And hope. Don't give up too soon, Mrs. Nielsen. Never know what'll happen tomorrow."

She looked up at him almost timidly. "I—I guess I was lucky, just picking you outta the phone book, Mr. Falkenstein. If it makes any difference, I—I can pay you *good.* I never like people to know, on account they rook you and like that, if they know—none o' anybody else's business—but we did pretty good in real estate, Sam and me. I—I—I own that Ames Building, sir, and a couple others like it. I got the money to pay you good."

Jesse couldn't say it came as a surprise to him. With this kind. Still working at a slavey's job: all she knew. Living close to the bone like this. Still scrimping and saving. If you asked them, this kind, what they were saving it for, they couldn't tell you. They said, fearful and cautious, you never know—maybe 1930 all over again, someday. And he wondered how much of that nice crisp green cash she had stashed away under the rug or behind the pictures; he hoped nobody would knock her on the head for it some night. Because inevitably these things got known.

He said, "That's all right, Mrs. Nielsen, needn't think about that now. I'll let you know whatever I come up with. In the end this just might help Harry a little."

He went to the public library, on second thought, instead of the newspaper offices, and looked at all the stories about Lilian Blake and Harry. Satisfactory: the *Herald,* the *Times* and the *Citizen* had all published Harry's home address.

Not that that would go far, by itself, in convincing Clock. Or the grand jury. But it was something.

He had a lot of ruminating to do. He did some of it over a belated lunch, and then went to his office and did more there. A lot of interesting theories occurred to him, but nothing immediately helpful.

At five o'clock he roused himself, said good-bye to Miss Williams, locked the office and drove home. He ran into a lot of traffic, as usual at that hour, and it was twenty to six when he turned into the apartment-house driveway. He slid the Ford into the garage beside Nell's baby Renault, and got out. And heard Athelstane's rapturous whuffling bark of welcome.

"Well, hello, boy. What're you doing still out here?" Funny— Nell usually brought him upstairs when she got home. "All right, come along."

NINE

Nell thought dimly, But I don't *want* any more black coffee. So tired. Just want to sleep—a long while.

"Come on, that's my girl—one foot in front of the other—'s all right, lean on me—come on now, walk."

Husbands, thought Nell. Always at the most inauspicious times. When she was so tired—

But there was someone else, then. Another man, strange voice. "That's fine, Mr. Falkenstein, keep talking to her, and if you can get a little more coffee down her— Nurse, you help him hold her there—"

"That's my girl. Come on now, drink just a little more, Nell—just for Jesse, just to please Jesse—"

Really, thought Nell. Of all the maudlin things. Even when they were first married, they'd never degenerated to baby talk. Jesse, of all people . . . And she never drank coffee black. Did he think she was getting too fat, trying to put her on a diet? A thick cup held to her mouth; she tried to protest and heard only a mumble. She was suddenly conscious of an iron-hard grip on each arm, holding her upright.

"My girl. Just for Jesse, now. That's right—swallow it. Come on, keep on walking, darling—one foot in front of the other."

Somebody said very distinctly, "Stomach pump, doctor."

"My good girl. Come on, I'm holding you, just keep on walking. . . . Doctor . . . For Jesse, Nell—Nell darling—don't let me down now, don't give up so easy—fight for it, Nell—come on, lean on me, keep moving."

Jesse frightened about something. Funny—never knew him frightened about anything. Must help him. Make an effort. Somehow.

The only sensation she felt was the awful hard grip on her arms, holding her up—her head so heavy—so sleepy—but she made the effort, must help Jesse, and she said, "Darling—maddening—they want us to buy—that awful pink carpet." Her voice wasn't her voice at all, a thick croak.

"It's all right," he said. "We don't have to. That's my good girl. Talk some more."

"I meant to call Fran—" A sudden sharp needle thrust into her arm and she screamed. She felt she screamed, at the suddenness and coldness of it, and was immediately ashamed. She forced her eyes open, and saw close above her a kind, absorbed, homely, middle-aged face—rimless glasses—deep worry lines from nose to mouth—thin receding hair. A doctor. She said apologetically, thickly, "Sorry—I never mind hypos—silly—"

"That's all right," said the doctor soothingly. "Don't you mind."

But Jesse there, asking—frightened. She tried to turn, to see. Somebody said, "Pulse more normal, sir." That was good. Somebody was ill; *she* was ill; how silly, she never was, but anyway, *Pulse more normal.*

"Jesse?" she said faintly, worriedly.

"Right here, darling. All O.K., don't fuss."

. . . *Be all right. Oh, yes. Unquestionably. Very odd indeed . . .*

Nell thought suddenly, Did I drink too much of that whiskey? They think I'm drunk. Disgraceful. Of course not—absurd—if I could sit up and tell them— Because now she seemed to be lying down.

"Jesse," she said clearly. "Jesse. It was awfully nice of Fran, wasn't it? I was sorry—I wasn't home. Leave—a present."

"Yes, darling."

"Because—had such a—horrible day. Parking ticket. Only a dollar, but—it adds up."

"Damn it, all you think about is money," he said, and he sounded—well, she'd never heard Jesse sound like that.

All right, someone else said. *All right now. . . .* And, *whiskey.* They did think she was drunk. Come to think of it, she felt rather drunk. Incompetent. "Jesse?" she said. "I'm not either drunk. Only—one."

"No, we know. Everything's all right now."

And that was very nice to know.

Jesse came out to the hospital corridor and said briefly to his father, "O.K. They got it in time. Did you get hold of Fran?"

"God be thanked. I did. She was there about one-thirty, and left a note, but no present."

"Yes. As expected. Coincidence taking a hand. And," added Jesse, "it's about time you showed up!" Clock, emerging from the elevator down the hall, looked as stolid and unhurried as ever. "Now tell me, just go on and tell me, friend, I'm chasing a wild goose! And why to God I listened to the damn woman—even thought about taking on this case—! Go on and tell me, sergeant!"

"You're upset," said Clock placidly. "No wonder. Your wife?"

"She'll be O.K., but you think that makes me feel any better? You think that makes me ready to agree, accident—or maybe some disappointed client I didn't get a settlement for three months ago? I—"

"Well, no," said Clock. And introduced himself to Falkenstein senior, who surveyed him shrewdly and said that everybody made mistakes.

"As any lawyer knows, sergeant."

"And any policeman," said Clock. Whereupon Fran descended on them from the elevator, no less darkly svelte than usual for being distraught, and demanded news.

"She'll be O.K.," said Jesse. "*Why* I ever listened to the damn woman—! All my own doing. So smart, I had to be, oh, sure! Dropping hints. Casting nets. The biggest goddamned fool—"

"Oh, well, I wouldn't say that," said his father mildly. Clock didn't say anything at all. He just looked at Fran, and he looked a little stunned, for some reason. As if somebody had just used a blunt instrument on him.

"But what *was* it, Jesse, what happened? I was there at one-thirty, at your apartment, and nobody was— What happened?"

"You left a note. Somebody else left a bottle of bourbon, all nicely wrapped with a little card saying Compliments. I saw it while I was waiting for the ambulance. So I guess we can take it that Nell naturally thought you'd left that too, and had a drink. And somebody had spiked the whiskey."

"She *is* all right? They're sure? Well, really," said Fran, "I suppose she had her mind on something else, but after all—! If I'd intended to bring her a present, I wouldn't think of a bottle of whiskey, Jesse! You, possibly, yes, but not Nell. What on earth—"

"I don't approve of women drinking whiskey," said Clock suddenly. They all looked at him blankly. "I like old-fashioned girls," he added.

"Er—my daughter, Miss Falkenstein, Sergeant Clock—Headquarters," murmured Falkenstein senior.

"How do you do, Miss Falkenstein," said Clock enthusiastically.

Fran threw conventions at him hastily, tossing off her scarlet knitted stole; Fran, West Coast correspondent for a fashion magazine, unprecedentedly looked more like one of its models than a newly promoted editor. "But what was in it?"

"They're not sure yet. Some narcotic. Quite a lot of it. They knew, a narcotic—even I knew that when I found her—I called you then," Jesse shot at Clock. "Not that I thought you'd believe it's Harry's business. Oh, no, I'm just an overimaginative nuisance with a tender conscience. Every day some client who's lost a five-hundred-buck damage suit sends his lawyer a bottle of poisoned whiskey in revenge—oh, sure! Our efficient police force!"

"Ann Harding," said Clock absently. "Sorry. I was watching an old movie on TV. Ann Harding. Pretty girl, she was. I like nice old-fashioned girls—blondes," he added a little resentfully. "These damn career women, all four-inch heels and magenta nail polish and dyed hair."

"If you're looking at me," said Fran coldly, "I do not dye my hair, sergeant."

"You look," said Falkenstein senior, "like a reasonably intelligent man, sergeant—er—that is, in a normal state. Sit down and stop looking at the man, Frances. You are, um, inhibiting him. Yes. I gather that whatever argument Jesse gave you was not—er—logically conclusive to your mind."

"My God, no," said Jesse. "Improbable possibilities. These educated cops. My God."

"What d'you mean, a normal state?" said Clock. "I haven't been drinking any whiskey."

"That's all," said Jesse. "That's quite enough. Say she's an alcoholic, guzzling whiskey all alone in the middle of the afternoon."

"Now you be quiet," said his father. "Let the poor devil alone a minute. Nell's all right, we know that now. . . . You're not the only one, sergeant. She's just too damn particular."

"Is that so?" said Clock.

"You can try, of course. Don't much approve of career women myself. Prefer some grandchildren. . . . A narcotic. Yes, well, it is attempted homicide, whether Jesse's leaping to conclusions or not. I daresay you'll want to look at the whiskey. And the wrapping, the card, et cetera."

"What?" said Clock. "Oh, yes, sure. Also question various people."

"I don't suppose they'll let anyone in to see Nell tonight—"

"No, she's sleeping it off now, the doctor said she'll be more or less herself tomorrow, she can probably come home. And he said he'd have to send in a report to the police, so I expect he'll want to talk to you, sergeant."

"Or our surgeon. If you're going home, then, I'll tag along and send for some men and have a look. Get the whiskey for analysis and so on. What's your address?"

Jesse told him.

"Er—yes, seeing there's nothing more we can do for Nell at the moment," said his father, "suppose we all adjourn there and discuss the matter." Clock looked pleased, said he'd be right with them and made for the nearest phone booth to summon his minions.

Fran turned on her parent. "Grandchildren? With that—that fugitive from the county museum?"

"I—er—don't follow that."

"He's the Neanderthal man come to life. Thank you, I'm not quite so hard up as that. Just because he looked at me."

"Your usual effect. Not his fault."

"Oh, certainly not—nobody would *choose* to look like that. I don't suppose he's ever been within ten feet of a female much higher class than *Tobacco Road,* no wonder he stared. Really, Father, you are tiresome. And at such a time and place!"

Jesse, who'd gone back to see Nell again and have a word with the doctor, rejoined them as Clock emerged from the booth. "My car's in the garage," said Fran. "I had to take a cab, I'll—"

"Very glad to offer you a lift," said Clock hopefully.

"Thank you, I'll ride with Father. She *is* all right, Jesse?"

"Sleeping very peaceful now. Yes, you'd better. This thick-headed cop here, he'd be apt to get lost driving eight blocks."

"Now listen," said Clock mildly, "am I supposed to come equipped with telepathy? Naturally you're annoyed, but don't put it on me, friend. I didn't spike the whiskey."

They went downstairs in silence, got into their respective three cars and drove to the apartment. Here they met an ecstatic welcome from Athelstane, who had decided he'd been abandoned, left there din-

nerless all that time. Clock eyed him with respect and said, "Now I
see why poison. Nobody'd dare try the direct attack with that
around."

"Don't believe it. He'd just think it was a nice new game. . . .
Well, there you are. The bottle, with one shot out of it—a brand I
never buy, incidentally—wrapping and card on the coffee table. No, I
didn't touch them. Excuse me while I feed the monster, he's starving,
apparently. . . . I didn't see Fran's note, it must be here somewhere—"

"Here."

"Where'd you leave it, Miss Falkenstein?"

"Stuck in the crack of the door. . . . Well, I don't *think* there was a
parcel, but I might have missed it—not looking down at the floor, you
know, and the hall's so dark."

Clock grunted and went to let in his two minions as the bell rang.
They clustered round the note, the bottle and wrapping and muttered
at each other. One of them carefully folded up the paper, string and
card in another sheet of paper, swathed the bottle in a second, and
Nell's empty glass in a third, and departed—bound presumably for the
police laboratory. The other one went out and began to knock on adjacent doors. Clock sat down on the couch and stared fixedly at the
brass trivet on the coffee table.

"Well, all right," said Jesse, "not your fault. Of course. All comes
back to my damned smart meddling. Sorry I jumped down your
throat. I guess we could all stand a drink."

"Thanks very much," said Clock absently. "I take it you haven't any
personal enemy on your heels right now who might be responsible for
this?"

"My God, what else have I—"

"Give him time," said Fran. "Nothing can penetrate that thick skull
all at once."

"Look, what have *I* done?" asked Clock. "Give me a chance, will
you? What'd I ever do to you, Miss Falkenstein?"

"Never mind, sergeant, I'm on your side," said her father encouragingly.

"I am not," said Jesse, handing around the drinks, "the kind of lawyer in books and movies, always mixed up in some sensational case involving beautiful actresses and syndicate hoods and mad scientists.
Divorces here and there, the damage suits, the odd wills and con-

tracts. That's all. No sworn blood vendettas that I can recall at the moment."

"Well, I had to ask. And don't swear at me again when I say this doesn't say Harry isn't X. Because you stepped on the toes of at least one chancy customer that we know of, and maybe more. You passed around the idea that there might be a framing job set up to get Harry off—in effect. And besides Orde, there's that Byerly—Vice has turned up a few interesting little things on him, by the way, just what you might expect—and as I said before, no telling what side businesses a few people there might be mixed into. There's Jenner—I think we might take a look at him too—"

"I can just see that small-time crook Orde taking the trouble to fix up a bottle of poisoned whiskey! Instead of— Look, that kind of pro crookedness doesn't exactly square with poison, does it?"

"Just where you're wrong," said Clock. "Not a very complicated job. The seal cut with a sharp knife, afterward stuck together again with Scotch tape. Not noticeable. About five minutes' work—providing you had the stuff at hand. And these days a lot of people use sleeping pills. They all knew your name, and you're in the phone book. Right now, pending any definite evidence, I'm betting heavier on Orde or Byerly than anybody else who might have got jittery because you might come close to a secret of some kind. Because attempted homicide—well, you get all sorts, and like any cop I've seen murder done for three cents or a row over a bottle of beer—but usually you don't get a thing like this over, say, the threat of somebody's finding out about the extra lady friend or Uncle Bill's whiskey. That little hood Mike—and Byerly, well, he did a stretch for enticement back in forty-seven and won't want to do another."

"Jesse," said Falkenstein senior, "what have you been up to?"

"Keeping low company, obviously," said Fran. "Probably introduced by Sergeant Clock."

"Now I'll take just so much," said Clock. "You keep quiet."

"That's better," said Falkenstein senior. "That kind of thing they respect."

"I'll keep it in mind," said Clock. "And that Jenner— Just bad luck your wife got it first, it was intended for you, of course. And excuse me, but you asked for it, you know. For something. Meddling. Know something? Nine times out of ten—well, seven or eight anyway—what touches off murder is just plain fear. Fear of something coming out—

fear of losing money—a job—a woman—a man. You scared somebody, Mr. Falkenstein. Not necessarily in connection with Lilian Blake's murder. Maybe—probably—something right outside. It's very easy to scare somebody mixed into something the wrong side of the law, you know. . . . What'd you draw, Dale?"

"Damn all," said the minion who'd been covering the other apartments. "What'd you expect, sergeant? If the women don't work, they're out shopping or gadding around. Woman next door was home all afternoon, but didn't see or hear anything."

"Yes, well, there it is. We'll see what the lab turns up, but I don't hope for any prints. The detective-story writers have briefed even the amateurs on that. We'll be looking, don't worry. Everywhere indicated. I'll keep in touch with you." Clock stood up.

"If you don't, I will with you," said Jesse. "And I hate like hell to hand you anything else, but for better or worse I was raised honest. Mrs. Nielsen found those missing keys this afternoon. Here they are. She'd handled them, of course, so there won't be any prints. And it's no good to tell you she swears they weren't there last Thursday or Friday. And you slipped up there, Clock—how to hell I wish you hadn't! Because your boys didn't search the garage when they looked around there. And that's where the keys were, out in plain sight. If they had, they could have backed up Mrs. Nielsen that the keys weren't there— after Harry was arrested."

"You don't tell me," said Clock slowly, looking at the keys. "In the garage."

"She found them today. Me, I believe her. You won't. No evidence to back her up—and that's some your fault."

"You don't tell me," repeated Clock. Without moving or speaking further, he gave the effect of somehow swelling in size. He looked at Dale and said gently, "So you didn't search the garage?"

"Well, I—well, no, sergeant, it didn't seem—a guy like that wouldn't—"

Clock just went on looking at him, and Dale took a step backward. "You didn't search the garage. I see. You can go back downtown, that's all." Jesse felt academically sorry for Dale, escaping wrath only temporarily. "Thanks very much. And I suppose you think somebody came along and planted them there?" Clock sighed. "More gospel according to Mr. Falkenstein."

"Well, it could be," said Jesse. "I think so, yes. And if you do come up with anything to point to who spiked the whiskey—"

"Oh, we'll be looking," said Clock. "Whatever there is to find, we'll find."

"Whatever it is, you seem to have missed it before," said Fran sweetly.

Clock sighed. "These things happen. Every man on the force isn't an Einstein." Hat in hand, he looked at her. "Er—if you're ready to be going home, Miss Falkenstein, I'd be glad to give you a lift."

Fran looked back at him, head cocked, and suddenly gave him her pixyish one-sided smile. Both the other Falkensteins recognized the symptoms, and Jesse said, "That's right. You take him but good. He deserves it."

"Er—my sympathy, sergeant," said Falkenstein senior. "And a word of warning. *She is loud and stubborn; her feet abide not in her own house.* Not—um—in exactly the sense Solomon meant that, but quite literally."

"Well, I guess Solomon ought to've known," said Clock.

Fran got up leisurely and adjusted her stole. "I haven't the slightest idea what you're talking about, but it doesn't sound very polite. I'd love a lift home, sergeant, if it won't put you out—*so* nice of you! Darling Jesse, I'm so glad Nell's all right, I'll be around tomorrow to see her. *Good* night, Father," and she made a graceful exit ahead of Clock, who looked a trifle dazed all over again as her perfume hit him when she passed so close.

"That's a pity," said Falkenstein senior thoughtfully. "Seems a very good fellow. Like to see her settle down. . . . Now let's hear all about this business, Jesse, and I could do with another drink."

TEN

Jesse was wakened at nine-thirty by the phone, and staggered out to answer it, swearing. "There were," said Clock, "no prints on the bottle, the paper or the card. We are asking the wholesaler, but the chances are the stuff is all packaged the same way, by machine, and the card enclosed—gift-wrapped merchandise. Approximately two thousand seven hundred liquor stores roundabout would stock it. There was quite a dose of stuff added. I won't trouble you with c.c.'s, but that's what the lab said—not in the report—quite a dose. It was mostly codeine—a standard sleeping capsule, popular prescription. Usual dose, one capsule, and there were about ten dissolved in the bourbon."

"That's a lot of help," said Jesse. "Anybody who has insomnia. And I understand a lot of people do. Sleeping pills very popular these days. I take it this was a very usual prescription? Yes. Well—"

"You needn't tell me. I'm just reporting. It was, of course, delivered by hand. When your wife is able to answer questions, I'll want to ask some."

"Obviously. I'll let you know. Hospital said she could come home this afternoon. Thanks very much."

When he got to the hospital he found Nell sitting up drinking bouillon and looking rather pale but otherwise herself. "She's fine," said the nurse. "She asked for lipstick the first thing she woke up."

"How do I feel?" asked Nell. "Just the way you might think I'd feel when I've had my stomach washed out and a lot of injections and people prodding and poking at me. And I must say, the maddening thing is that I got it for nothing—I gather it was all your fault. Not that anyone's told me anything, but I can add two and two, and I've grasped that something was added to the whiskey. So it wasn't Fran's whiskey?"

"Well, no. Coincidence, her note. You leaped to the conclusion. No, it was me all right. Looking for whoever framed Harry. As if it matters a damn what happens to Harry."

"You seem to have struck pay dirt, anyway," said Nell.

"Clock doesn't think so," said Jesse gloomily. Then they chased him out while they got her ready to go home.

He took her home, saw her settled propped up in bed in a fresh nightgown and said of course Clock wanted to question her but later would do, she'd better get some sleep. "Don't be silly," said Nell. "I want to hear all about this. You can't expect me not to be curious, after nearly getting murdered. I knew you were worried about Harry's case, but you haven't told me any more about it. And seeing that the whiskey was probably intended for you, I think I'm entitled to know what prompted it."

"Look, you ought to rest—"

"I am resting. I'm in bed. I feel all right, as long as I don't have to rush around getting dinner. Tonight, anyway. I'll be quite all right tomorrow, the doctor said. I can't just sit here, devoured by curiosity. I'm all right to answer questions, but I'm going to ask some too. Don't fuss, Jesse."

"Well, if you must," said Jesse, and sat down to tell her all about it. "I only wish I had the least notion who I managed to scare."

"Whom."

"I'm not so sure of that either. But— A lot of territory, how right Clock is. And it looks open and shut, just on inference, that this very definitely centers around Harry—but it's not evidence, or even very usable as implication in court. You see what I mean. All up in the air . . . I had to be so smart."

"It doesn't," said Nell, "seem to me that you'd go to so much trouble trying to murder somebody unless you had an important reason. I mean, I don't see what he says about someone being a bookie on the side, or one of the receptionists being— That wouldn't be big enough."

"Mmh," said Jesse. "Fran's note was unlucky coincidence. Without it, would you or I have accepted an anonymous bottle left outside the door?"

"It's hard to say. Wouldn't we? All nicely wrapped, with that little card inside? Wouldn't we, either of us, have thought naturally, somebody we know, who forgot to enclose a note? You don't *expect* a thing like poisoned whiskey. . . . But somehow, I can't see whoever killed Lilian doing a thing like that. It's a different kind of—of plot, somehow."

"You'll get on fine with Clock," said Jesse.

"It's a different sort of thing," said Nell obstinately. "It doesn't fit. Committing that kind of murder. And then doing the whiskey. I don't see it."

"So it wasn't X. Oh, no, because they've got him—Harry—sitting down there in the County Jail."

"I didn't say that," said Nell. "Conceivably it could be both ways."

"Well, you can't be a much worse private eye than I am. You go right on thinking about it and maybe you'll be inspired. The doctor said beef bouillon. I'll go make some."

Clock came around later and asked her questions. All that emerged was that whoever had rewrapped the bottle after adding the codeine had been neat-fingered, producing as tidy a job as the machine wrapper. Which said nothing at all.

Nell submitted meekly to another of the doctor's pills and later on to the bland meal recommended; when Jesse asked her if she'd like a magazine or a book she said, "I'd rather see those police files. Or your notes, if any. Because I quite see that, as you say, if you're going to get Harry off, you'll have to find the right one instead. Just the same sort of thing it was with me last year. And they say two heads are better than one. I can't honestly say I'm awfully concerned about Harry, but I do have a personal interest in this now. Because they might try for us again, you know."

"You think we're smarter jointly than the whole Homicide Bureau of the L.A.P.D.?"

"Just possibly. I don't know," said Nell vaguely, "sometimes—how shall I put it?—Well, you want to find a murderer, and they mostly think in lunatic ways, so maybe you have to look for him in a sort of lunatic way. A special way. Not just routine, the way the police would. I mean, in a special sort of murder like this, that isn't just the ordinary straightforward thing."

"I can just hear what Clock'd say to that. You're welcome to my notes," and he produced them. "But the doctor said another pill at nine and early to bed."

"Mmh," said Nell, reading.

When he brought her the pill at nine o'clock she was sitting up straight, staring at the opposite wall earnestly. "What it comes to," she said, "is that there must have been a reason for someone to want her out of the way. A logical reason, I mean. You say nothing's showed up in a—an emotional way. A jealous boy friend or something. And of course the fact that she was killed in the building sort of points to—well, a business reason, if you see what I mean." She took the pill absently, accepted the glass of water he offered to go with it. "I could make a guess about it."

"Yes?"

"She'd found out something," said Nell. "Some important, dangerous secret. *I* think on that Monday night when she went back to the office to get her bracelet."

"Jumping to conclusions."

"Well, but it fits, Jesse. It makes the times fit. What time did she go back? . . . Well, find out. All of those offices would be closed at night usually, wouldn't they?"

"Maybe once in a while not," said Jesse. "The tax consultants, they'd probably have a lot of rush business around the tax deadlines, and be working overtime. I suppose the doctors might take an evening appointment now and then to oblige an old patient. But usually, yes, they'd all be closed."

"Yes. Suppose when Lilian went back for her bracelet that night, she saw something. Heard something. In one of those offices. And—"

"Such as what?"

"How should I know? I'm not psychic. Almost anything big enough. Important enough. Somebody blackmailing somebody. Two people plotting a murder. A—a Communist cell meeting. A couple of spies talking. Anything, you know, dangerous enough. But something she couldn't be quite sure about—that it was what it looked like."

"Why?"

"Because he—or they—had time to plan the murder. All of that night and Tuesday, you see? I think it must have been something very suspicious but not certain, at least in her mind—and you know, Jesse, that's very likely in a way, because she'd have known the people there in that building, and just at first it'd seem impossible to her that Dr. Smith could be a blackmailer or Mr. Jones a murderer."

"You," said Jesse, "have been reading too much blood-and-thunder stuff. Spies, yet. And talk about jumping to conclusions! Yes, well?"

"But don't you see, if she'd seen a light in one of the offices, after hours, she'd have been curious. Maybe it was an office where the receptionist or a secretary was a friend of hers, and she thought she was working late and just innocently dropped in. Like that. Or—is there a night watchman?"

"No idea."

"Find out. Anyway," Nell was warming to her story, "she saw or heard something, then. And either she let them know it, asked for an explanation, or they saw her and knew she knew. I think she let them know, and they gave her a drummed-up sort of tale that'd convince her for the moment while they planned how to be rid of her. And then they thought of Harry—the convenient scapegoat. And that's why she was killed in the building, that way."

"Very lucid."

"Don't belittle. It's quite logical. She wasn't just sure about whatever it was, but once she'd thought it over she would have been, and they knew that. You see? They knew she had to be—shut up. So they did. And to forestall any awkward detailed investigation, set up the frame on Harry. One of the ground-floor offices, Jesse."

"Oh?"

"Don't be stupid," said Nell. "Of course. Dr. Friedlander's office is there. She wouldn't be going upstairs. So."

"Yes," said Jesse. "I see that. You build nice stories. Maybe you ought to try your hand at fiction. There's not one iota of evidence—"

"Oh, for heaven's sake!" said Nell. "Lawyers. I'm just trying to help."

"Yes, darling," said Jesse. "I'll bear it in mind."

"Go and ask her roommate whether she said anything, that Monday night. Ask—"

"Yes, darling," said Jesse. "The doctor said early to bed."

"Men," said Nell. "All right. But I'll make a bet with you—"

In a quiet sort of way, he was feeling desperate enough about this damned case to take any long chance, even to riding Nell's hunches. He did want to see Ruth Myers again, and he'd even ask her Nell's question as well as his own. And he wanted to see the couple of fellows Lilian had most recently dated. But also—

Well, it intrigued him. Admit it. Santa Claus.

Why the hell had Stephanie been reminded of Santa Claus?

Sunday he spent somnolently ruminating, and getting no place. On Monday morning he stood over Nell to see she took the last of the pills, admonished her all over again about following doctor's orders as to diet. "Yes, yes, all right," said Nell. "I'm all right again now, don't fuss. Go and collect evidence." She sounded absentminded; she had just opened the newest Charlotte Armstrong. . . .

Stephanie Liebman, pressed about Santa Claus, had said vaguely, like at Walters' or Kress's. Jesse visited both the Kress's branch Stephanie would be most familiar with, and the large independent department store, Walters'. He gave the managers a manufactured reason—undefined legal business, oh, no, nothing to do with the store, not a damage suit, anything like that—and asked where the Santa Clauses had come from last Christmas.

The manager of Kress's referred him to an employment agency downtown; that was all he knew, hadn't even heard the men's names. Two men. It was a package deal; the head office made arrangements for all the stores.

The manager at Walters' smiled and said, "Oh, that'd be old Mr. Walters. . . . Yes, sir, the owner. He's retired now, of course, his sons have taken over, but he comes in quite often, as he shouldn't do. High blood pressure, you know, and it worries Mr. Edgar and Mr. Jack—and I might say all of us, a fine old gentleman—but what can you do? It isn't as if he'd ever had any hobbies. The Santa Claus business, well, the first time it was the employees' Christmas party, and he was such a success at it and enjoyed it so, why, nothing would do but he must try it out in the store—and it's got to be something of a tradition, the last few years."

"Enterprising old fellow," said Jesse.

"And stubborn," said the manager with a grin. "He's got no business doing it, it worries his family. After all, he's eighty, and it *is* a full-time job. In fact, we usually used to keep two or three Santas on duty, to spell each other, with the store being open evenings for Christmas shopping. But he looks forward to it all year, just like a kid himself, and he won't hear of having another Santa. Upshot is, we make it a rule, our Santa is on duty, so to speak, just two hours afternoon and evening. It pleases the old gentleman, and I can't say it's affected business any—after all there's plenty of other Santas for the kids. . . . What exactly was it about, sir? I mean, we wouldn't like old Mr. Walters upset—"

"Oh, I won't upset him," said Jesse. "Give him something new to think about. If I could just have the address—"

The manager parted with it reluctantly. A call to the employment agency, after some delay, supplied him with the names of Charles Fortescue and Thomas Meadows, address given as the Bessie Cochran Home for the Retired in Culver City. Since old Mr. Walters lived in Mar Vista, Jesse took in the Home for the Retired on the way.

It proved to be inhabited almost exclusively by retired actors. Mr. Meadows had departed this life two months ago, but Mr. Fortescue was still available. He was a spruce old fellow, delightful company for the first fifteen minutes, thereafter a deadly bore. All Jesse wanted to do was look at him, and he did so under cover of the excuse of asking if he'd witnessed an imaginary accident in the store last Christmas. Naturally Mr. Fortescue had not, but he tried to make up for it by retailing several incidents involving long-forgotten silent stars. He was perhaps eighty, valiantly well-preserved. His silver hair might be a toupee, but his rather luxuriant mustache was all his own; his suit was old, but clean and originally good. Jesse detached himself and sought out the stubborn and enterprising old Mr. Walters.

He liked Mr. Walters; probably everybody did. Chiefly because Mr. Walters liked nearly everybody. It was a rich man's house, view of the Pacific from the modern window-walled living room, flagstone hearth, the latest Danish-modern furniture. Mr. Walters was the only anachronism. He was short, fat, untidy and bald, with a straggling grayish-white handlebar mustache, a round red face and little shrewd dark eyes. In one essential at least he reminded Jesse of Athelstane; he was pathetically pleased by human company. He offered Jesse a chair, a drink and his undivided attention before he heard what his business might be. Jesse accepted all of them, feeling that he'd come home, and unburdened himself to Mr. Walters of the entire story.

Mr. Walters planted his elbows on his knees, his chin in his hands, and listened. At the end he said, "And the little girl said the fellow looked like me. Be damned."

"Or one of those Santas at Kress's. Or just any Santa."

"There isn't another one like me," said Mr. Walters simply. "I make 'em believe it. Too damned much cynicism around these days. Little kids four and five saying, Santa Claus, *that* old stuff! Bad. You know something, Mr. Falkenstein? People underestimate youngsters. Have another drink. Spite of what I just said. You take an ordinary normal kid—hey?—and maybe he believes in magic and some o' this damn silly science fiction stuff on TV and so on, but I tell you, most o' the time he's a damn sight better judge o' what people are like than his parents."

"Well—" said Jesse to his drink.

Mr. Walters renewed his own drink. "I tell you—" A handsome middle-aged matron looked in the door and said, "Oh, Father, you *know* what the doctor said about *alcohol!*" "You go away and mind your own business, Betty," said Mr. Walters not unkindly. "I've enjoyed myself for eighty years here, and if I've got to give up everything that's a little fun just to stay around awhile longer, well, it's not worth it. *While* I'm here I'll do as I damn please, and to hell with the doctor. I tell you," he went on to Jesse, "grown-up people, we're so damn busy thinking about what impression we're making on other people, we never see 'em. Any more than they see us. If you get me. You want an objective view, and that's just what you get from any kid. Most of 'em are smarter than people think. It's just, they haven't got a common language with grownups to get it across."

Thinking of all the little girls, Jesse agreed with him in heartfelt tones.

"This Mrs. Nielsen," said Mr. Walters, and made the sound usually spelled "tchah." "Poor silly dreep of a female—plenty of money, and no notion how to enjoy it. I know the type. And Harry. Damn shame, victimize 'em. What it amounts to. You say he's not the one, hey?"

"I'll be damned if he is," said Jesse. "Just a feeling. I know there's no evidence, my God. But— He's not all there, no, but he's the kind who's careful about the poor little worms left out after the rain. Empathy, they call it. And I don't think any more conscious of sex than the average two-year-old—hell of a lot less, according to Freud and company. He didn't do that kill. But no evidence."

"Now I believe you," said Mr. Walters. "I don't think much o' the law. Fiddle-faddle. Got to have this and that, black 'n' white, all signed-sealed-and-delivered, and so on—that I see. But feelings, usually they're a damn sight more important. I'm sorry for that fool woman."

"So am I." Mr. Walters was a man after Jesse's own heart.

"I'll tell you what's to do. We've got to—"

"Well, all I wanted was—"

"You listen to *me*," said Mr. Walters energetically. "I'll tell you what's to do. Now you're too busy—got other cases, and all the red tape on Harry—I see that. That little Liebman girl, she's maybe not the only one didn't tell the police something. We don't know. All sorts o' reasons—way it was with Stephanie, because the policeman treated her like a baby. Kids are sensitive about things like that. Now I think it might be a good idea if I was to go and see all these little girls over again. Principle of killing two birds, hey? If this character does look something like me, well, it might jog their memories, see."

"Matter of fact, I was going to ask if you'd come and just let Stephanie look at you."

"You needn't bother yourself, I'll go round on my own. I'm good with kids—they like me, and I'll bet if there's any more to be got out o' Stephanie or one o' the others, I'll get it."

"Well, it's very good of you, but I couldn't ask you to go to so much trouble, just—"

"Tchah!" said Mr. Walters. "No trouble. Give me something to do for a change, something useful. Everybody seems to think, minute you hit seventy or seventy-five, all of a sudden you lose interest in everything, all you want is your meals and no worry and a comfortable chair. They'll find out when they get there themselves! They took away my license five years back, but there's Bob Martin next door, nice young fellow compared to some college kids, he's always glad to ferry me around for a little extra gas for that sports car he's got. Don't you trouble, Mr. Falkenstein—just let me have the names 'n' addresses. I'm interested in this business, and it'll keep me occupied awhile. I'll just bet you I'll find out something—and I'll let you know soon's I do."

ELEVEN

About eight o'clock that evening Clock put in an appearance. He sat down opposite Jesse, on invitation, and looked at him with dislike. "You've got no idea how much you annoy me," he said. "I wish to God I'd never laid eyes on you, Mr. Falkenstein. Because before I met you I thought I was a middling-smart detective—and also I fully intended some day to marry a nice docile little old-fashioned blonde and settle down respectably."

"I've upset all this?" asked Jesse.

"You have. And as I'm going to be doing my damnedest to get to be your brother-in-law, I guess I'm entitled to begin finding fault with you now. They tell me everybody does with in-laws, though I'm bound to say your father seems like a reasonable man."

"Does Fran know about your intentions?" asked Nell interestedly.

"The last man," said Clock, "she'd take seriously. That little harpy. She needs taking down, but good. Thinking she can make eyes at me and get me smack under her thumb with no trouble at all."

"And hasn't she?"

"Not under her thumb," said Clock. "You wait and see, that's all. Four-inch heels and red nail polish. She needs a lesson. And I suppose it's very damned late, because probably every man she's met since the age of five has fallen all over himself with gratitude when she so much as looks at him."

"I've noticed she has that effect, for some reason," admitted Jesse. "Often wished somebody would take her down a bit. Sympathy and good wishes extended."

"You want to ignore her, sergeant—condescend to her, patronize her all lordly—like that. You know. She's not used to that kind of thing," said Nell, basely betraying her own sex.

"Do I need telling? And as if that weren't enough, you come and give me the double talk about Harry. A feeling you've got about this and a feeling about that—just worth damn all, and I say you ought to know better. Me, the middling-smart detective."

"I think the man needs a drink," said Nell.

Jesse sat up slowly. "Are you going to tell me your lab came up with something contrary on those keys?"

"I might have known you'd guess without being told. I tell you, it's not anything to send me rushing over to the D.A.'s office to say, Hold everything, we've got the wrong man. It's just a funny little thing that I'd like explained." He took the drink with thanks. "Oddly enough, even after Mrs. Nielsen and you had handled them, there was a print showed up on those keys. On the back of the disc engraved with her name. About three-quarters of a print, actually, but the boys are pretty smart these days, you know. They tagged it. And if you can tell me what it means—"

"Identified?" asked Jesse. "In your records?"

"It's the print," said Clock, "of one Stephen Belawonski, who was charged with assault and battery and involuntary homicide in August of 1947, and served a one-to-three sentence. Model parolee, and since vanished—from our ken at least. Tell me what it means."

"Now that's a very peculiar thing indeed," agreed Jesse. "I do wonder. I can't make any sense out of that at all."

"I don't like anything about this," said Clock. "All of us committed now—and if the lieutenant knew I'd chased right around to the defense lawyer to tell him about this— But we don't *like* to railroad people. Even the Harrys." He finished his drink and stood up.

"*Whom the Lord loveth He correcteth,*" murmured Jesse. "You going to do over some homework?"

"We *looked,*" said Clock. "Everywhere we went was a dead end, except Harry. Sure I am. Check as far as I can, where I can."

"Yes. I too have a—er—minion in the field," said Jesse. "Don't be surprised if you run into Santa Claus in—um—civilian dress. And many thanks for sharing the evidence. Very interesting."

"Santa Claus!" said Clock blankly. "Maybe I'd better ask him for the truth for Christmas."

"Just be a good boy and see what the fairies will bring you."

"They've brought me a hell of a lot too much already—via you," grumbled Clock.

Jesse saw Ruth Myers again the next morning. This time at one of the lingerie counters in Robinsons'. She eyed him a little distrustfully and said she couldn't talk here, she was supposed to be working.

"And what're you after, anyway? I told you all I could. You're just trying to get him off, that crazy fellow who killed her. So's he can go and kill somebody else—"

"Well, I don't think he did, you know," said Jesse. "I'm just looking for the truth, Miss Myers. And some facts to show what the truth is. Do you have a coffee break? Could you talk to me then?"

"Well—" she said reluctantly. Twenty minutes later she met him at a sidewalk sandwich bar down the street, and he bought her a cup of coffee.

"That Monday night Lilian went back to the office for her bracelet—"

"Well, what about it?"

"D'you know what time she went back?"

"I guess it'd've been about seven-thirty she left. I was waiting for my date, see. She'd fixed herself dinner, and first she thought the bracelet'd be O.K. and she'd get it in the morning, and then she said no, she'd just worry all night, she'd go back and get it."

With the bus service what it was, call it half an hour to get there—if she'd been lucky and got right on a bus, maybe twenty minutes.

"She was home when you came in. Did she say anything about—well, anything?"

"I don't know what you mean. She said Hi and had I had a good time and so on. . . . Well, I guess I probably asked, did she find her bracelet O.K., and she said yes. She was kind of quiet—she was sitting up in bed reading the newspaper, see. So I didn't bother her with a lot of yakking," said Ruth Myers virtuously. "She was a great one for reading, Lilian was—me, I'm not, makes me awful fidgety, I can't see what anybody gets out of it, but we can't all be alike. So when she was reading something, I let her be, didn't bother her."

"I see. Reading the newspaper."

"Every night the newspaper," said Ruth, nodding. "She took the *Herald* regular. She'd sit down with it right off after dinner, go all through it. It was a habit, like."

"She didn't say anything to you about her trip back to the office?"

"Not that I remember, just that she'd got the bracelet."

"Mmh. Say anything to you about it next day either?"

"No, why? I don't get this. I mean, what's that got to do with—"

"Maybe nothing," said Jesse. He looked at her. Not much education and not the brainiest female in town, but an honest girl and with some elementary shrewdness. "Did she ever say anything to you about her boss? About liking or not liking him?"

"About Dr. Friedlander? You mean, like he was maybe making passes? Oh, gee, no, I know there wasn't anything like that! All she ever said about him was, he was all business—way she put it—you know, no personal talk or like that. You trying to put it on *him*, make out—"

"I'm not trying to put it on anybody. Just looking," said Jesse. "Ever say anything to you about other people in the building where she worked? The other receptionists and so on she knew there?"

"I don't remember anything much. No. Except her mentioning this nut at the newsstand there, how he tried to make up to her. Anyway, I know for sure there wasn't anything with this doctor she worked for. On account of she did say, I remember, the doctor was just crazy about his wife. Her, Lilian didn't like. She came in sometimes, and Lilian said she's one of these clothes horses without a brain in her head, and tried to make her—Lilian, I mean—go to a beauty parlor, and fancy dress shops. You know. Kind of condescending. Well, gee, *as* Lilian said, nothing she'd like better, but who could afford it?"

"Yes." Jesse looked at his empty cup.

"I got to get back—"

"Just a minute. Do you know anything about Mr. Orde's business, Miss Myers?"

She looked very surprised and very angry. "Mike? *Now* what're you getting at? What d'you mean, his business? He's a wholesale salesman, works for an outfit downtown, that's all. What's Mike got to do—"

"That's what he told you?" asked Jesse. "Close enough, maybe. I think you're a nice girl, Miss Myers, and you ought to know you're apt to get into trouble running around with Mr. Orde. He's got a police record, you know, and the odds are good he's a dope pusher."

"*Mike?* You're just *crazy*—I won't listen to such—"

"Ask him," said Jesse; but she was gone, angrily, almost running. Well, he'd passed on the news.

He went and saw the two fellows Lilian Blake had dated most recently. Tom Hamlin was a salesclerk in a men's store, and obviously too devoted to his regular profile to be seriously interested in a girl like Lilian—an ordinary girl. His reaction to the murder seemed to be chiefly gratification at getting his photograph in a newspaper (Recent Escort of Murdered Girl). He didn't recall that she'd ever mentioned her boss, or the place she worked, or her roommate or the roommate's boy friend. Stuart Walsh, on the other hand, had really "sort of fallen" for Lilian. She was, he said wistfully, "cute. So little, you know. And a nice girl." But she hadn't had much time for him. . . . She'd never said anything to him either, about her boss, roommate, et cetera.

Both of them had been demonstrably at their jobs that Wednesday morning. Of course.

Jesse felt frustrated. He felt he was clutching at straws. Nothing, but nothing, to point any direction to look.

He thought about Nell's hunch. Well, he'd look at almost anything right now, and there were a couple of points—

He went up to the Ames Building and noted down all the tenants on the ground floor. Thirteen of them. Following Nell's hunch, you couldn't eliminate any of them, because Lilian, coming into the office after hours, could have seen a light, heard voices, from any office there. At the end of the lobby, she would have had a view down the corridor to her right; and turning left for Friedlander's office, she'd have passed the other six doors.

Thirteen tenants. Neither Byerly nor Jenner among them.

R. D. Matthews, notary public and tax consultant. Adam Hyde, D.O. Robert O. McIlheny, optometrist. A. G. Gilbert, Rare Coins Bought & Sold. H. A. Anthony, D.D.S. R. L. Wilder, chiropractor. D. M. MacDonald, M.D. The Meredith Escrow Company (that had two offices, 108–109). The Alert Detective Agency (A. S. Fox and H. W. Stern) at your service 24 hours a day. W. George Kaufman, M.D. Armand Sylvester, D.O. C. C. D'Angelo, D.D.S. H. Franck, Exports & Imports.

Just anonymous names. Some of the receptionists had known Lilian, but— The detective agency, might be something there? Ask Clock about its reputation. But—

Still feeling frustrated, Jesse elicited the information from Rance that there was no night watchman. And departed, to have another hopeful try at Harry.

"You told me about a lady dropping her handbag behind the counter. Was it that day that I'm asking about, Harry? The day you'd had a bad headache?"

"I dunno," said Harry. "I ain't had a headache in a long time. Days 'n' days."

"Yes. This was the last time you had a bad headache. You remember? You opened up the stand late. Went to work late."

"Oh—yeah." Harry brightened a little. "I do remember. . . . When Mama left, I was in bed, and—and—and she told me not to forget. It was a—a book, like."

"A book?"

"I hadda remember—put it out for the man. He was coming, get it back. They don't give it away, see. There was this picture in it I liked —a picture of a pretty lady with an awful pretty little kitten, it was brown 'n' white and all soft hair and a pretty face and all, and it said under it—I remember—it said, Soft as a kitten's fur. That's what it said. Such a pretty soft little kitten, like—like—Spotty. I liked to look at it. And Mama said all right, but be sure—put it out on the mailbox for the man. I did. I'd've liked to kept the picture, but—"

And what was this? A book they didn't give away; did anybody give away books at all? Or did Harry—probably—mean a magazine?

"And then—and then—when I put it out ready—"

"All right, let's go on to something else," Jesse interrupted him gently. It was sufficiently uphill work questioning Harry about anything; better concentrate on the important things. "Do you remember looking at the clock when you left home that morning, Harry? What time it said?" No, Harry hadn't. "Well, did you talk to anybody on the way to work? . . . Mrs. Gracchio, I know about her. Anybody on the bus? Did you have to wait long for a bus that morning?"

"I—I don't guess I remember."

"You remember anything about the driver? When you got in and paid your fare?"

"No, sir—except he wasn't Jackie. I mostly ride with him mornings. Jackie's got a mustache. It wasn't Jackie."

Very helpful. Look up Jackie and ask if Harry had ridden with him that morning; because if Jackie could say he hadn't, that was pretty good evidence Harry was just where he said, at home in bed. But it wasn't an alibi. At that hour in the morning, the buses ran fairly close together. So, ask all the morning drivers on that route. Except for

Jackie, who presumably knew Harry as a regular passenger, all of them saying, Gee, mister, I couldn't say for sure.

"O.K. Now, that day. Was it the day this lady dropped her bag behind the counter and you picked it up for her?"

"I guess. I dunno. I don't remember. Maybe," said Harry vaguely; he was losing interest in this conversation.

Jesse reminded himself of an admonition from the Gospel of Luke: *In your patience possess ye your souls.* "All right. Do you remember what time it was when the lady dropped her bag?"

Harry just looked vaguer. After a minute he said, "I guess I hadn't eat my lunch yet."

"Do you remember what the lady looked like? Can you tell me about that?"

Harry looked down at his big, thick-knuckled hands clasped together. "I—I—I— She was pretty," he said suddenly, "even if she didn't have goldy-colored hair. She was nice. She said thank you real nice. Sir, is Mama coming to see me today? I don't like it much here, I don't know why I got to stay here. I—"

"Do you remember anything else about that lady at all, Harry? What did she buy? Had you ever seen her before?"

Harry just shook his head. "I don't guess so. I guess it was a package of gum or something. I guess. It was awhile ago. . . . Oh, yes, sure, I remember now, she had real long red fingernails. You know the stuff ladies put on, sir."

"Well," said Jesse. "Anything else?"

"No, sir. Why, sir? Why you ask if I remember all this stuff? Is it something about why I'm here and can't go home and all? I—I—they're nice, kind of—that fellow comes, lets me out to go 'n' have dinner downstairs—but lotsa the others, they're funny—not nice, you know. I wish I could go home. They think I done something bad, and I never. That I knew about, sir."

"I know, Harry."

"They could ask Mama. She'd say I never—"

"She already has," said Jesse with a sigh. "I'll see what I can do, Harry."

An empty promise if there ever was one.

Long red nails. Unlike most of the girls working in the building?— girls who did typing? Well, you couldn't say. The vanity of females—

"Now I told you," said old Mr. Walters. He beamed at Nell, at Jesse, and scratched Athelstane in that perennially itchy spot behind the ears which dog people reach for automatically. Athelstane, recognizing a kindred spirit, sprawled contentedly between Mr. Walters' legs and shut his eyes, looking blissfully drunk. "Nice to see people keeping a real dog, 'stead o' one of these imitations. Feisty little yapping things, like that Shy-wah-wah of Betty's."

"What a good name for them," said Nell, "isn't it? They are like that—back away as if you were going to kick them."

"Not that I haven't been tempted," said Mr. Walters. "But I guess I never could. Poor damn-spirited little thing, no guts. Now this is a dog."

"That you can say twice," said Jesse. "Three and a half pounds of meat a day."

"Oh, well, it's only money," said Mr. Walters comfortably. "What the hell?" He rubbed harder and Athelstane uttered a small whuffle of pure content.

"You'd like a drink," and Jesse got up.

"I won't say no. Damn doctors. You get past seventy-five and people don't treat you like a person any more. Just a geriatric case. You know? I told you there was more there to be got," said Mr. Walters.

Jesse nearly dropped the bottle. "You got something else? Already?"

"What d'you mean, already? Yesterday you talked to me, and I got busy right away. Nineteen names and addresses. I've seen 'em all. Thank 'ee kindly," and he took the drink and disposed of half of it in one swallow. "No trouble, driving around—Bob's up at Lake Tahoe so I took a cab. Now, kids like me—we get along fine. I guessed, from what you said—well, you take the police, good men these days, honest, conscientious—but that's a thing you can't buy or learn, getting along with kids. Hey? You do or you don't. They trust you, like you, or not. And right off too—like fellows like this one here," and he ran his free hand down Athelstane's spine. Athelstane moaned happily and collapsed against him, shamelessly exposing his stomach and adjacent anatomy. "They know, first minute you talk to 'em, whether you really like 'em or are just putting on."

"Which is why some people find them embarrassing," said Nell.

"Egg-sacktly," said Mr. Walters. "Now you take me. I look like everybody's grandfather—matter o' fact, I've got five grandchildren and'd like more, only Betty's so damn set on those clubs of hers and can't be bothered, and poor Sylvia, she can't have any more, after only two. Point is, kids like me, and I can get 'em to talk. You acting so damn scrupulous, going around asking the parents first!" He grinned at Jesse. "No way to get at it. Kids never talk much real in front o' parents. And I had a notion— Well, get to that in time. I caught 'em on the school playgrounds, at the civic swimming pools—such places. You know. We're lucky it's not a couple of weeks later, a lot of 'em leaving for summer camp then."

"Dear Mr. Walters," said Nell, "I'm bursting with curiosity. *What* did you find out?"

Mr. Walters beamed at her and finished his drink. "A couple of things, Mrs. Falkenstein. Sixteen times I drew blank, see. Nice little kids, and all forthcoming enough, but they didn't remember much. Now I'll tell you one thing I was after. When you talked to me," he said to Jesse, "it struck me as a little bit peculiar that even four or five little girls should take so much interest in looking over at that bare sort of alley the other side o' the school fence. Why were they, to see this character at all? I started out asking about that first, and right away I ran into a funny sort of reaction. They came out with things like, 'Oh, no reason I guess,' but they were embarrassed about it, see."

"Oh? That sort of struck me too," agreed Jesse. "And you know, if we put the little girls on the witness stand, it's a factor the bench wouldn't like. Why were they, how could they be sure of what they saw?"

"Egg-sacktly. Well, I got this reaction. It wasn't until I found one of 'em with a few less inhibitions or something that I got the answer. It seems that a couple of weeks ago there was a fellow picked up in that alley for indecent exposure. Matter o' fact, it was a teacher made the complaint—fellow the other side of that fence, see, coaxing kids down to him. Well, of course it had got around, and you know kids that age—"

"I *see*," said Jesse amusedly. "So they all had their eyes glued on the alley, hoping for more excitement. That explains it."

"It relieved my mind, in a way. Knowing that, it makes more sense that they did see all they did and remembered it, hey? Well, next I got to this Mary Ellen Foss. I don't suppose the police often have occasion to question kids, but they could use some lessons, at that. With Mary Ellen, I figure it was the same officer saw the little Liebman girl, because Mary Ellen says he treated her just like a baby. You know.

Kind of fellow's never known a nine-year-old, treats 'em—" Mr. Walters chuckled—"like an eight-year-old." He looked at his empty glass, rubbing Athelstane's ears, and Jesse got up and brought the bottle over. "Thank 'ee kindly."

"Don't keep us in suspense," said Nell. "What did Mary Ellen tell you?"

"Well, she saw this character come out that door and throw something away. And she says it was 'something kind of big and white.' She's pretty positive about it."

"The handbag," said Jesse.

"Egg-sacktly. It was the same sort of thing as with the little Liebman girl, the policeman putting her back up, and kidlike she thinks, Serve him right, not tell him."

"Stephanie Liebman remembered something white too," said Jesse, staring at his own drink. "I like this, one way—and another way I don't. Not the kind of evidence the bench is very fond of, from kids. But all this says—doesn't it?—that it was a frame, just the way we think. That Lilian was killed deliberately, and afterward somebody took a little trouble to get Harry's prints on her handbag, and then the bag was taken out and dropped beside the body. Making it look like a spur-of-the-moment kill. Yes. And I think I know how. There was a lady, Harry says, dropped her bag behind his counter—of course he can't say for sure it was that day, or what time—and he picked it up for her. She'd just have had to wipe it off beforehand, and be careful to handle it by the straps. That shiny plastic takes prints very nice. Harry says she was a pretty lady even if she didn't have goldy-colored hair."

"A dark-haired woman," said Nell.

"Well, something to keep in mind all right." Mr. Walters swallowed half of his third drink. "I kept on looking and asking. Just in case something else showed up, you know. And pretty soon, about four this afternoon, I ran across this Cheryl Wells. . . . These damn made-up names! Cheryl, sounds like an Oklahoma hillbilly. Don't know what gets into people. Enough nice old names to choose from, plain and fancy. Now my mother's name was Mary, and my wife was Deborah—perfectly good names. But d'you think Betty or Sylvia considered using either of 'em? Not on your life. I've got two granddaughters, and I almost blush to tell you their names. Darlene, for God's sake, and Lorie. You get even crazier ones than that, o' course. La Donna and Marlene and this Cheryl. And be damned if they don't even change the spelling when they do use some decent old name, make Debra out of Deborah and Lorie out of Laura. Damn foolishness."

"I do agree with you," said Nell. "It's awful. We're going to have four—"

"Two," said Jesse.

"—and I've got the names all chosen. Mark and David for the boys, and Judith and Jennifer for the girls, and in case it doesn't come out so even as that, possibly also Jonathan or James, or Sarah or Celia. Nice ordinary names, so it won't matter if they're handsome or homely, you know."

"I," said Jesse, "you notice, haven't a damn thing to say about it."

"Very nice," said Mr. Walters approvingly to Nell, and to Jesse, "Oh, well, that's wives, isn't it? I was telling you about this Cheryl Wells, who also saw this fellow. I tell you, like I say, kids are smarter than we think. They all knew about the murder, you know, and they'd talked it over, sort of comparing notes. Cheryl came out with this flat, right off—she said, 'He had a mustache. A mustache like yours,' she said. Which I take to mean not one of these little clipped things, all bristly. Kind of a long mustache. So I—"

"Oh," said Jesse. "That's what reminded Stephanie, maybe?"

"Sure," said Mr. Walters. "I didn't get a chance to ask Cheryl very much more, her dad came up to get her just then—it was at a public swimming pool I talked to her. Turns out they belong to one o' these funny puritanical sects, you know the kind. Practically everything a sin. He was awful damn suspicious of me. Cheryl'd said her mom and daddy hadn't liked the policeman asking her things, didn't think she ought to know about bad things like people killing people. I ask you, now. Don't look at it, it'll go away. People, they sure as God come all sorts, don't they? And I suppose the police, um, respected their ideas and didn't—you know—probe. My God," said Mr. Walters simply. "Like everybody else these days they've got infected with this crazy idea, mustn't offend anybody—mustn't maintain any standards, on account they might be different from somebody else's, which'd be a terrible sin. Got to be tolerant. Me, I'm all for tolerance, sure. Got no funny prejudices myself. All I say is, we ought to be awful damn sure what we're being tolerant *of*, because if it's something that isn't going to be tolerant of *you*, well, it's not exactly common sense, is it? Takes two to make a fight, they say. Also takes two—or more—to make brotherly love. But try to get it through the thick heads of those fellows in Washington."

"I told you he was a man after my own heart," said Jesse to Nell.

"That Cheryl. First thing she said to me, I'm praying for the poor lady got murdered. Now it was irrelevant, but I couldn't help it—I says, Why? You get told there's no better place than heaven, and you think the lady's there. So— Shouldn't have said anything. Just confused her." Mr. Walters poured himself a fourth drink. "It makes you wonder how people figure. No logic. If they really believed all that, they'd play jazz at funerals and have a hell of a time celebrating the dear departed's blessed release into eternal happiness. Well, anyway. That was Cheryl."

"Solomon warns us, *The instruction of fools is folly,*" said Jesse, renewing his own drink.

"And how right he was. *The simple,*" said Mr. Walters astonishingly, "*believeth every word, but the prudent man looketh well to his going.* That how it goes on? I got a lot of time to read lately. . . . Well, so I went back to see the little Liebman girl. Nice little girl. I said to her—she has that trick kind of memory like some people have— I said, Did this fellow have a mustache like mine? Was that maybe what she remembered, what made her say he was like Santa Claus? And she thought, and shut her eyes to kind of think back, you know, and said, Sure he did—she could see him plain as anything, remembering. He was bigger than me, she said, and had a redder face, but he had a mustache like mine only it wasn't so gray." He retired into his glass.

"I'll be damned," said Jesse. "And where does it get us? No place."

"Of course it does," said Nell. "Look at all the men on the ground floor of the building. Does any of them have a long mustache?"

"I got something else," said Mr. Walters, "that I don't know means the hell of a lot. Just kind of suggestive. All of 'em said it wasn't very long after the class had started, while teacher was still handing out stuff to work with. And the class started at ten o'clock. Well, I don't know—" he added bourbon to his glass—"you said, the police doctor said nine to nine-thirty. Looks like something funny there. Those fellows on the refuse truck found her about ten-thirty, and she'd been dead about an hour. If these kids saw somebody throwing the handbag beside her at maybe ten past ten—"

"He must," said Jesse suddenly, "have been worried as hell. I can imagine. . . . Harry's headache, yes . . . Because he'd have known approximately when the refuse truck would be along if he was famil- iar with the building, and it looks as if he is. And he'd want Harry's prints on the bag, to clinch the frame. And Harry was late that morn- ing. Very awkward for him."

"Oh, I see, of course!" said Nell excitedly. "He'd planned—"

"It must have been cut damn fine, on account of Harry's headache. The other evidence, the piece of necklace, the lace, could be planted at any time before the cops got around to a detailed search. But the prints on the bag— She was killed as soon as she got to the building. Call it nine, a couple of minutes before. And stashed in the alley then —or the kids would have seen that. Did X know about that class meet- ing so close to the end of the playground? I don't think so—or he dis- counted it. Yes. But Harry was late coming in that morning. It was after ten when he came. And right away, in a hurry, the pretty lady went up and dropped her bag behind the counter so Harry'd pick it up for her. Harry, raised to be so nice and polite."

"More than one X," said Nell. "Because it must have been a man who strangled her."

Jesse said yes, absently.

"You reckon this helps?" said Mr. Walters.

"I reckon it helps one hell of a lot," said Jesse. "But it's a long way from legal proof, and where does it send us to look? I don't know."

"Ground-floor tenants," said Nell.

"Maybe," said Jesse, and relapsed into silence, brooding over his drink. Nell told Mr. Walters how very nice of him it was to go to all this trouble for strangers. "Tush," said Mr. Walters, "not strangers now, are we? At least, this fellow here doesn't think so. . . . Just have to do some thinking on it and look some more. It's all kind of involved, but the more I think about it, the more I think your husband's right to say it wasn't Harry. I don't think so either. Hell of a thing." He finished his drink and reached for the bottle.

"We've got some suggestive things all right," said Jesse, "but tell me where to go from here. Just tell me. . . . Of course there's Stephen Belawonski too. I wonder where he fits in. . . . And still not one shred of legal evidence—"

TWELVE

Nell was in the middle of the breakfast dishes next morning when Sergeant Clock called.

"I just thought you'd better be warned. There's a female coming to see your husband— I wasn't sure what hours he keeps, gave her both addresses. No, not that kind—or rather she is, but not after him especially. Not that I wasn't interested in what she had to say—just a little bit—but I thought he'd be interested too."

"Well, that's very nice and cooperative," said Nell. "What kind of thing?"

"I think I'll let her tell it. Probably nothing but female imagination. Or wanting in on the act. And the lieutenant'd have me back in uniform tomorrow if he knew."

"It's very nice of you, whatever it is," said Nell. "Have you got anywhere with Fran yet?"

"Don't be funny. Set for a long campaign, you might say."

"She *can* be annoying, but she's quite intelligent, sergeant. She's bound to recognize your sterling worth."

"I don't doubt it," said Clock. "I am not unique. Not everybody wants to live with that sort of thing, when it hasn't got either looks or money besides." He sounded depressed.

Speculating, she returned to the dishes. She had just finished them and was applying hand cream preparatory to calling Mrs. Alton for the latest report, when the doorbell rang. She opened the door to be confronted by a blonde vision, voluptuous and graceful, covered to a minimum in very pink cotton lace and rather overembellished with costume jewelry. The vision shied back as Athelstane came hopefully up to meet a new friend. "Oh, dear, what a horrible big dog!" she exclaimed in a thin, high voice.

"He's very friendly," said Nell, bristling. "What is it?"

"Mr. Falkenstein. The cop said he might be interested. *He* wasn't, much. I could tell. Well, it's what they call a civic duty, I just thought I better tell them, you know. First he says why didn't I come in before and then he says well, it doesn't mean much. Well, I said to him, I was on *vacation*—you can't expect a person to drop everything, up at Lake Arrowhead, and come rushing back just to tell the cops something. And anyway I didn't know about it then so I couldn't've anyway."

"Well, my husband's in his office," said Nell. "But I'm sure he'd be interested in whatever you have to tell him, Mrs.—"

"Duveen," said the vision in a discontented voice. "Miss Duveen. Gloria. I haven't got all the time in the world to waste. Well, thanks. I'm just trying to do what's right, after all. Besides, of course, any publicity's good publicity." Suddenly she favored Nell with a dazzling white smile. "I'm a dancer—and actress—only not in the big-time yet, you know. I don't know anything about this kind of thing—maybe, if your husband's client's got money and what I have to say'd help him, there'd be a kind of reward?"

"I really don't know," said Nell vaguely.

"Oh, well, no offense. I just thought, take a chance on it."

Nell hung on to Athelstane, who was not at all offended by Miss Gloria Duveen's overpowering aura of chypre and would have loved to investigate her closer. "Well, you'd better go to my husband's office. I can call him and tell him you're coming, so you'll find him in."

"Well, thanks a lot, that's nice of you," said Miss Duveen. "On account I haven't got all the time in the world. I'd be real obliged—I got an appointment with my agent at one o'clock I couldn't afford to miss, see." She smoothed lace over one slim hip, absently displaying mandarin-length nails painted a bright pink. "See, I didn't know they'd got anybody for it, or I mightn't have come in. Just that she'd been murdered. So I thought I ought to go and tell. Now, I guess it doesn't matter much, when they got the guy. If he's the one."

Nell resisted the temptation to get the story out of her—she'd hear it tonight—started her off to Jesse, and called his office to warn him.

"I'd welcome anything new," said Jesse. "I'll be waiting for her."

"With open arms? Yes, and maybe I should have tagged along," said Nell. "She's a very statuesque blonde of the kind I understand gentlemen prefer."

"You mind your own business. You go gadding around looking at houses all day, why grudge me a little fun?"

"See, I didn't know about it at all," said Miss Duveen, settled in the chair next to Jesse's desk. "I was on vacation until yesterday. I live with my mother, and when I got home, it'd be about four o'clock yesterday afternoon, she says guess what, that dentist you go to, his office girl got murdered. Well—"

"I see, you're one of Dr. Friedlander's patients."

"Yeah, I had to have a couple front teeth capped after I was in an accident awhile back, see, and an actress's got to take pretty good care of herself, you know, I go regular for checkups. Well, thanks," and she bent to his lighter, gave him her dazzling smile. "Naturally I was interested, you can see, but Ma hadn't followed it up—neither of us much for reading, she'd just happened to notice the name, see, when it was in about the murder. So I didn't know they'd picked this guy up for it. And I got to thinking about what I'd heard her say that day, and that maybe it had something to do with her getting killed. I didn't know anything about the murder, see, where or how or when, but I thought I ought to tell about it. So I went to the cops and told them. This sergeant, down at that big police building downtown."

"Yes. And he suggested you come and tell me?"

"He said right off they'd got the guy did it. He wasn't just awful interested, I guess. Did I get it right, you're the lawyer for the one did it?"

"Well, I don't think he did," said Jesse. "I think he was framed for it."

"Gee," said Miss Duveen in sole comment. "That sergeant said it's the guy had the little magazine stand in the lobby there. He said he's kind of off, not right. I never noticed him much, passing through."

"Yes, well, what was it you heard that you thought might have something to do with it? Did you know Lilian Blake very well?"

"Didn't know her at all," said Miss Duveen promptly, crossing her knees the opposite way and pulling her skirt down primly. "I didn't even know her name, it was the doctor's name Ma recognized. It was just like usual, you know, going to see any doctor. She'd take the appointment on the phone, and when I came in she'd say like, 'It'll be a few minutes' and 'The doctor'll see you now.' You know. But that day—"

"Which day?"

"That was sort of it. It was just the day before she got killed, Mr. Falkenstein, see? Tuesday. I had the appointment for my regular six-month checkup at ten o'clock, and I was leaving on my vacation that afternoon. With Sandra—we went dutch. And the cheapest cabin, on account poor Freddy can't pay me any alimony, matter of fact I loaned him fifty bucks last month, and I never asked for any from Bill or Al. Well, that don't—doesn't matter. I'll tell you how it was. I guess you've seen Dr. Friedlander's office. There's a waiting room, and off of it a kind of little place—hardly big enough call it a room—where the office girl has a desk and the phone and all, and then off that there's two bigger rooms where all his stuff is. One of those chairs in each one, and the little bowl and all, and a place for his tools. You know."

"Mmh. So?"

"Well, I was a couple minutes early. Now maybe you'll think—" Miss Duveen was unexpectedly businesslike—"I guess that sergeant did, it's funny I should remember all this so plain, couple of weeks back, and maybe I'm just remembering more than happened, to maybe get my name in the papers, like that. But it was funny enough to make me remember it, see? And besides I got a good memory." She stubbed out her cigarette, looking at him earnestly. "Like I say I was a couple minutes early. When I came into the waiting room, the door into where this girl's desk was was open and she was talking on the phone, see. I saw her there. She said something like, 'Hold the line, please,' and came out and said to me it'd be a few minutes. And then she went back to her desk and shut the door between. Got that?"

"Mmh."

"Well, like I say I'm not much for reading and I'd seen the only *Glamour* there was lying there, so I just sat and waited. I could hear her talking, but not much of what she said, see. I heard her say, 'Yes, Mrs. Gilman,' and then I guess she hung up because a minute later the phone rang. It just went once, she must've answered it right away. And I didn't hear what she said just at first, only that she was talking, see. She'd stop, and wait, like the other person was saying something, and then I'd hear her talking again. But I guess the wall's just a partition like, not very thick, and soon as she started talking louder I could hear what she said." Miss Duveen got out another cigarette, leaned to his lighter and smoothed her dress over one admirable knee. "She was talking louder because she was mad, see. You could tell that. The first of that I heard, she said, 'I'm not such a fool to believe what you said. It just doesn't stand up.' And after a minute—when maybe the other person was talking, see—she said, 'It simply doesn't explain what I heard all of you talking about last night, that's all.' And then she said, 'What d'you mean, shouting? I'm not either.' Well, she wasn't, exactly, she was just talking a little louder than usual, see. And then after another little bit, she said, 'Well, I don't believe it, especially after seeing the paper last night. It was the same man, I know it was. And I could make a guess—' And then she didn't say anything for quite a while, and then her voice got lower and whatever she said I couldn't catch. And about five minutes later she opened the door and said the doctor'd see me now, and she looked just the same as usual. I went in and he found a little cavity and had to fill it, and— Well, you don't want to hear about that. You can see, it was sort of funny, and I remembered. What I thought, when I heard she'd been killed, all that sounded like maybe somebody had a reason to murder her. Like she'd found out something about some hood, or something like that. And I thought I ought to—"

"Quite right," said Jesse fervently. "How very interesting . . . talking on the phone . . . Was there another patient ahead of you?" He was thinking, to carry on that very interesting conversation so publicly, Lilian Blake must have closed the other door too, into Friedlander's actual workrooms; and Lilian must not have known that the partitions were so thin. Had Friedlander or his patient, if there'd been one, overheard any of that?

"Gee, I don't know. You see, there's another door from the inside offices to the hall, if there was somebody they could've left that way. Patients usually do. Just thinking it over, I thought it sounded—"

"Yes," said Jesse. "I'm very glad to hear this, Miss Duveen. Will you make a formal statement about it?"

"Gee, I guess so—it's the truth, whatever that sergeant looked like. Sure. You can see why it kind of stuck in my mind, can't you, Mr. Falkenstein? I'm not making anything up, honest."

"I believe you," said Jesse. He called in Miss Williams and encouraged Miss Duveen to repeat her story. While they waited for it to be copied he thanked her for coming in. "This might help a lot, if indirectly. Very suggestive."

"You really think this guy was framed? It's just like a TV show. I never thought— Well, I *didn't* make anything up, you know, it was all just like I said, but if I do get my name in the papers it'll be awful good publicity. You think I might?"

"Very possible," said Jesse.

She leaned back, smiling. "That'll be swell," she said. And a few minutes later, "My, it's warm for June, isn't it? Back home they'd call it good corn weather. That big police building, it's got air conditioning."

"Wish I had," said Jesse. He was mildly intrigued by an irrelevant discovery: underneath the bleached hair and long painted nails Miss Gloria Duveen was a nice, simple-minded, small-town girl; in the soil of Hollywood she had taken on a few native traits, but remained basically Irene Bergstrom or Greta Miller or whatever it had been from South Fork. After all, she had married Freddy, Bill and Al.

Miss Williams brought in the typed statement, and Miss Duveen signed it in a large careful round script. "Gee," she said, "just imagine, me helping in a murder case. But it's just the truth, Mr. Falkenstein, I wouldn't say it if it wasn't."

Jesse thanked her all over again. When she had gone, he called Clock, to thank him for the unexpected witness.

"What the hell is she worth?" asked Clock. "One like that? I ask you. Two-inch pink nails. An actress, my God. About as much as I am."

"Oh, a little closer," said Jesse. "Just a little. Let's not be prejudiced, friend. Perfectly honest woman, if she does bleach her hair."

"She built the whole thing up out of about five words she heard, just to sound important. And you'd be a fool to take it at face value. I don't know why I sent her to you."

"Don't you?" said Jesse. "Listen, Fran looks up to me, Big Brother and all. You behave nice and maybe I'll put in a word for you."

"Tell me another one. She goes her own way, I know that kind," said Clock darkly. "Probably do more harm than good if you did. And that's an attempt to bribe an officer."

"All right, come and arrest me. Don't know why I should wish you luck, at that. All your damn puritanical ideas, she'd probably walk out on you within a week, and I can't say I'd blame her. It *is* possible to have bleached hair and inch-long fingernails and also a pure heart, you know."

"All right," said Clock. "I suppose you believe all that rigmarole's gospel truth."

"You sound," said Jesse, "uneasy. She's not the kind would dream that up, is she? If she was making it up to get in on the act, she'd have made up something a lot cruder, more blood and thunder. Wouldn't she?"

"You go to hell," said Clock.

Sounding uneasy.

It suggested some very interesting possibilities. First and foremost, that there was something to Nell's hunch. That Lilian had seen or heard something (or both) that Monday night when she came back to the Ames Building after hours.

That it had been something—queer, off-beat; and that she'd been given a hasty explanation (as per what Nell said) to satisfy her for the moment, and accepted it. And then—something new added here—something she'd seen in a newspaper had made her doubt the explanation. ("Especially after seeing the paper last night," she'd said. Yes. It figured. Ruth Myers said Lilian had usually read the paper after dinner, but that night she'd gone back for her bracelet and hadn't got to the paper until later.) The *Herald,* on that Monday night.

He liked this. He liked it a lot. He thought fondly of Miss Gloria Duveen, helpful citizen.

He had intended to get on the trail of the bus drivers today, but now it seemed the more immediate move was a very thorough examination of that Monday's *Herald.* The public library would supply him. He stood up and reached for his hat, and the phone rang. It was his father. Jesse said, Yes, Nell was feeling fine, and (optimistically) that Harry's case was looking much healthier too. "Good," said Falkenstein senior. "This pawnshop on Second Street. One Abraham Teitel."

"What about him?"

"He looks out for old watch parts for me. Very obliging. Only way I can find some missing bits for the antiques, you know. He wants a divorce from his wife. I told him I'm on the corporation side, not private practice, and recommended him to you."

"Thanks very much, always happy to have new business."

"The thing is, he's afraid of publicity—perfectly honest fellow, but the wife, I gather, is a lush and promiscuous—and he's afraid if he tries for a divorce it'll all come out and everybody'll know. You'll have to reassure him. I explained about the police—she's been picked up several times—that they don't— What's bitten you?"

"My God, what a fool I am!" said Jesse. "Yes— No—I've got that, O.K. This is something else. Tell you later. Thanks very much for jogging the slow mind. A hell of a detective I make." He put the phone down and stared at it.

He had indeed explained about the police, himself. To Orde and everybody he'd seen that day. Casting nets, dropping hints. He'd said, or hinted broadly, exactly that: that it wasn't just J. Falkenstein who thought it a frame, but also the cops.

So how had anybody with elementary sense thought that getting rid of Falkenstein via the whiskey would prevent the frame being proved a frame?

Narrowing the circle, my God, didn't that put right out of the running everybody he'd contacted that day? Some comfort; he'd told Clock all about it, and Clock hadn't spotted the joker there either. But it must say that. And who else had been given any reason—deliberate or not—to be afraid of Falkenstein in this case? It wasn't—regretfully he had to admit—as if Falkenstein had the kind of reputation that anybody would automatically assume he'd get Harry off. Who else?

No, not a detective, God knew. . . . An elementary thing like that. But, damn it, he'd contacted everybody that might have anything to do with the case. Who the hell had he missed?

After a glance at that Monday's *Herald*, he knew he'd want to spend quite a while with it, making notes, and not at a library table. He dickered long with a librarian, finally got grudging permission to take it away with him overnight. Take a good leisurely look through it, with special attention to stories illustrated by cuts—because that little remark of Lilian's, "It was the same man," sounded as if she'd recognized someone. Taken in conjunction with her remark about seeing something in the paper—maybe a photograph? A fair deduction? Well—

He locked the paper carefully away in the trunk of the car and thought about the bus drivers. Just maybe a little evidence to be got there in Harry's favor. He sought the bus company headquarters and asked questions, went through a lot of red tape, explaining. Finally he located Jackie. Jackie's last name was Buchanan, and he'd be on his break right now, but taking over his other route at the corner of Beverly and Van Ness at two-ten.

Jesse had a late lunch and was waiting on that corner at the appointed time, having left the car in a lot. The aisle seat behind the driver was empty, and after ascertaining that the driver *was* Jackie, Jesse took it and talked to him over his shoulder from behind. A hampering position; and the fact that he was continually interrupted by passengers getting on, demanding change and asking questions, was not helpful either.

He told Jackie who he was, and that there were indications that it was a frame on Harry. So easy to accuse one like Harry. Did Jackie know who he meant? A big simple, good-natured lout, who got on the Fairfax bus every morning, about eight-thirty, at Albert Avenue.

"Him," grunted Jackie, who was short, stocky and aggressively mustached. "That the one they picked up for this murder? I'll be damned. . . . You want a Number Four, lady, be along about ten minutes. . . . Sure I know him. So?"

"So, do you remember him taking the bus two weeks ago Wednesday, on that run, or wasn't he on it?"

"Listen," said Jackie, "sometimes I get a chance notice things, sometimes not. How could I say? Maybe yes, maybe no. I don't remember. All I can say is, if he was, I don't think he talked to me special. One day's like another. Sometimes the regulars do talk to me, and sometimes, like any of us, they got things on their minds, just say Morning. I know the one you mean. He knows my name, sure, a lot of regulars do. But, two weeks back! . . . Ten cents, sir, not nine. Sorry, complain to the company, I don't fix the rates. This zone, it's ten cents. . . . Ask me something easy, mister. The lady with all the bundles and the ten-dollar bill, I maybe remember—or the drunk who wants to sing—or like that. But regulars who just get on and get off, how should I remember if they was or wasn't, a certain day?"

"I see that. Does he generally speak to you when he gets on? Say, Morning, Jackie, something like that?"

"A lot of regulars do. I don't think that one ever called me by name more'n once or twice, though. He knew it, sure—but, come to think, it seemed like he thought it might be kind of disrespectful, way a kid might feel, call a grownup by their first name. . . . Move back in the bus, please! Let's make a little room!"

"Typical." Jesse was now squashed into a minimum space by a very

large red-faced woman with a number of brown-paper parcels and an
umbrella. He was inevitably distracted by the umbrella. In Los Angeles, at the end of June. He had decided that she was either a newly
arrived Easterner or an Englishwoman when she turned to him with a
broad smile and apologized for discommoding him in a Texas accent
he could have cut with a dull knife. The mystery remained unsolved.

"Ten cents, lady. . . . Move back in the bus, please!"

"Well, thanks very much anyway," said Jesse.

"All in the day's work," said Jackie. "The things you run into, driving a bus!"

Jesse got out at the next corner, waited twenty-seven minutes for a
return bus and paid the lot attendant a dollar to redeem the car. The
things you ran into, being a lawyer. . . .

He spent the rest of the afternoon, dogged in ninety-degree temper-
ature, tracking down the five bus drivers who'd been on that Fairfax
run, in successive buses, between Jackie's eight-thirty bus and the
quarter-to-ten one. Eventually he succeeded in talking to all of them,
and of course none of them remembered Harry at all. Couldn't say
whether anybody like that had got on at Albert Avenue—or anywhere
else. Harry must, Jesse figured, have been on the quarter-to-ten bus, to
get to the Ames Building when he had. But there was no proof of it
here.

When he got home at six o'clock, he found Fran and Nell sitting
over sherry animatedly discussing interior *décor*.

"This horrible reproduction mahogany wall shelf— Hello, darling,
have some sherry—and a couple of cheap modern ceramic things on it,
no taste at all, like Woolworth's—and it's probably marked the wall, so
if we buy that place we'd have to paint. But very good proportions,
one of those solidly built older houses, the front room's about eighteen
by twenty—French doors. You could do a lot with it. I thought if we
could afford to have the couch reupholstered—the one I have in storage
—it's a good plain style, you know—in Naugahyde, beige or brown—
and beige walls—and one big chair done the same—and a plain tan
carpet—"

"*Not* broadloom," said Fran. "It shows every footprint. Something
with a thick pile, tweedy. And that brass lamp someone gave you for a
wedding present at one end of the couch. What's the mantel like?"

"Oh, not bad—quite plain and flat, Spanish tiles in brown and green, and just a narrow shelf. No niches, thank God. Maybe they've had it done over—they were putting niches in everywhere about the time it was built. I thought, if we do get this one, that big Chinese carving on one end of the mantel and a long narrow picture of some kind off center."

"Very nice. And—"

"I hate to interrupt this important discussion," said Jesse, "but it's six o'clock and I'm hungry. And I don't want any sherry, thanks—discreet drink for gentlewomen."

"*Six!*" said Fran. "Heavens, I must get home and make myself look presentable, your fugitive from the county museum is taking me to dinner at seven."

Jesse, making himself a drink, reflected that Clock hadn't been far wrong when he said that praise from Big Brother would take the opposite effect. Some reason, sisters were like that. So he said, "That thick-headed cop! I'll bet he'll take you to a Main Street beer joint. You shouldn't run around with the lower classes like that."

"You do not," said Fran, "reach me at all, Jesse. You and Father are hoping that Sergeant Clock will arouse my tender passions and settle me down with a brood of grandchildren and nephews and nieces. Though why you should want them all to look pure Neanderthal I can't think. You can go on hoping. He amuses me—I'm working on him to civilize him a little. We're going to Sardi's. Me in black chiffon and scarlet satin shoes and those black star sapphire earrings Father gave me for my birthday."

Jesse said, "Poor Clock. Give him my sympathy."

"Do have a nice time," said Nell.

"Oh, I fully expect to."

"Well," said Nell with a sigh when Fran had taken herself off, "I'd better see about dinner. And I'm dying to hear what Miss Gloria Duveen had to tell you."

"It was very damned interesting," said Jesse. "Tell you over dinner. Nell, what magazines don't they give away?" Because, irrationally, that little puzzle had just risen to the top of his mind.

Apron half on, she stared at him and said, "Nobody gives magazines away, except back numbers. What's this?"

"Harry. He said Mama told him, put it out for the man to pick up, because they don't give it away. I couldn't make sense—"

"Oh," said Nell, and finished tying the apron strings. "Fuller Brush man. They bring the brochure around and leave it—they sell all sorts of things now, you know, cosmetics and so on—and say they'll be by tomorrow to pick it up and take your order, if any."

"Well, I'll be damned," said Jesse to Athelstane, who was occupying his favorite chair. "Why didn't I ask her before?"

Athelstane woke up, pounded his tail on the chair arm, suddenly discovered that Nell was in the kitchen and departed thence hopefully. Jesse sat down with his drink and started his thorough examination of that Monday's *Herald*, with the Fuller Brush man at the back of his mind.

THIRTEEN

The *Herald* was not as big a help as he'd hoped, and that was natural, in a way. In the nature of things, what got into newspapers was very largely violence, death, tragedy—the kind of actions and reactions that might be somehow involved with a murder. He hadn't the slightest clue to tell him, for instance, whether the relevant column in that *Herald* had been the first-page one, MAN ACCUSES WIFE OF ATTEMPTED MURDER, or that sixth-page one, WANTED MAN BELIEVED IN AREA.

And it was probably a wasted effort to make a note of all the cuts, looking for men with long mustaches. Nothing said that the man Lilian had presumably recognized had been recognized from a newspaper photograph—that was doubtful inference—or that he'd been her murderer. For that matter, nothing said that the mustached man the little girls had seen in the alley had been the murderer. That was inference too. Nevertheless, Jesse looked and noted.

He could count out some things, of course, as almost certainly irrelevant. In the thirty pages of the *Herald* was this and that relating to society weddings, afternoon teas and dances, and a horse show. There was the double book-report page. (Although, just to make it interesting, one of the four cuts in the newspaper showing a man with a longish mustache was on that page—a rising young novelist. Jesse shook his head at it in doubt.) There were brief reports on women's-club meetings, a long article on a controversy among the board of water commissioners, several articles on the financial pages about new corporations, mergers and expansions, and half a page of beauty advice. He felt safe in counting all that out. Also a human-interest story about a runaway kid, the usual plea for contributions to the summer-camp fund for indigent youngsters, a description (with cut) of two

TV actors leaving for England by jet, and two obituaries, one of a famous socialite, one of an ex-Senator. When he had eliminated all that kind of thing, which for ninety-nine percent sure hadn't been what roused Lillian's suspicions, what did he have? Quite a lot. Too much.

The result of the appeal in a four-month-old homicide case, with cut. Two cases of child neglect, one with a cut of the charged parent. A new suspected homicide. The man who thought his wife had put arsenic in his coffee. Another truck running away down the Angeles Crest highway, brakes failing—HEROIC DRIVER RIDES RUNAWAY TRUCK, WALKS AWAY FROM CRASH! Three kids drowned in three swimming pools (he had a brief vision of beautiful Berenice talking about pool insurance). A near riot at a political rally. That had been the day the Killeen trial judge had been chosen, and there was quite a long article rehashing it in detail, with five cuts of interested parties. (A full-dress affair, you could say; the trial was still dragging on. One of the occasions when the law looked a little silly; almost a foregone conclusion, unless Leibowitz was very damned smart indeed or the judge was got to. The man was guilty as hell, caught out by a couple of minor union officers with facts and figures.) A grandfather (see cut) accused of rape. An ex-con, known deviate, picked up for enticing minors. A well-known local businessman arrested for drunk driving. A thirteen-year-old boy accidentally wounding his brother with their father's unloaded, safely-locked-away automatic. Two brothers picked up by the F.B.I. as (read between the lines) small-time spies; both aliens, scheduled for deportation. An ex-con, wanted for murder, believed seen in Gardena.

Well, maybe an average day for a big city? A very big city, of course, now. Upwards of six and a half million in the county. It was conceivable that the *Herald*, not one of the two big newspapers in L.A., had even missed mentioning some of the violence that had gone on that day.

But how to figure which of these vignettes of violence had been the one to attract Lilian Blake's special attention? There wasn't any way.

Mustached men. Well, a lot of men wore mustaches. Most men, at one time or another, grew one just to see what it looked like. Jesse fingered his upper lip, remembering the one he'd tried his last year in college. An almost too successful mustache, which had unexpectedly made him look so sinister and furtive, like a wolfish con-man; not the ideal impression an honest young lawyer wanted to make. After it had suitably impressed that girl named Louise (and what the hell had her last name been?) he had, a little regretfully, got rid of it. . . . But at this stage of social culture, not very many men sported what might be described as long mustaches. The preferred kind was what Mr. Walters called bristly: the hairline, toothbrush or Latin mustache. There were (he had counted) thirty-six cuts of men in this issue of the *Herald*, and thirteen of them had mustaches; but only four had long, or halfway long, ones.

The rising young author, one Aubrey Fitch. (He had, apparently, written a powerful and moving tale, titled *Out of This Burning Furnace*, about the involved passions, jealousies, loves and hatreds of a group of American technicians and their women isolated in the arid desert whence a benevolent government had dispatched them to aid a backward people.)

Number two was the heroic truck driver. One Bill Jacobs. He had an old-fashioned handlebar mustache, and the cut showed it as dark; but a newspaper cut would show most hair dark except outright white or platinum. That one of an actor Jesse had seen and knew to have sandy-red hair—he looked dark in the photograph.

Number three was one of the two lucky, if crooked as hell, union officials who had escaped indictment along with Dave Killeen. Harold Norman and Alex ("Tiger") Bennett. Bennett was the one with the mustache. Not enough legal evidence on them, but they'd both been subpoenaed as witnesses. The mustache was a thick, untidy-looking mustache, on a heavy square face, and it looked darkish; but the cut was a poor one.

Number four, the man (a neighbor) who had pulled one of the drowned kids out of a pool. Harvey Watson, a guard at Lockheed, fifty-six. That was a handlebar mustache too, and looked light—near-white, probably.

A very long chance, of course, that the real mustached man was pictured here.

And how to know which story had been the one that was somehow significant to Lilian?

No way.

Jesse took voluminous notes, in his neat copperplate writing, took down the names of the mustached men, copious details of all the stories it might have been. The library had insisted on having the paper back at nine the next morning. . . .

He dragged himself out early again, thinking of the librarian's grim and gimlet eye, and dutifully returned the back issue of the *Herald*. He then sought out the local headquarters of the Fuller Brush Company and asked which of their salesmen would have been covering that section of Albert Avenue that week. After a certain number of suspicious questions, he got hold of a sympathetic personnel man who was interested and helpful, and plunged into his files hunting.

"That would," he said at last, "have been our Mr. Barrett, Henry Barrett. Dear me, I'm afraid you're out of luck here, Mr. Falkenstein."

"Don't tell me he's been killed in an accident or something?"

"Oh, dear me, no. One of our most reliable men. No, not quite as bad as that, ha ha!" The personnel man showed him a gold-toothed grin. "No, he's off on his honeymoon right now—took his vacation early, you see. I believe he left at the end of the week you're asking about. He's not due back at work until next Monday, but it's quite possible he'll be *home* earlier—to settle into a new apartment or something like that—I don't suppose they could afford a long trip anywhere. I can give you his former address, perhaps someone there would know."

Jesse thanked him. It was an address in Highland Park. He drove out there and found Henry Barrett's mother just leaving the house and somewhat annoyed to be delayed. She told him briefly that Henry and Jane were expected back on Saturday, to get moved into a new apartment before they both had to be back at work, and with some reluctance parted with the address.

Nothing more to do on that until then. Well. What did he have, to send him where, looking further? Damn little. Those newspaper stories—

He thought of Harry down there saying *I want to go home*, and he hoped that because somebody had picked Harry to frame for this, some officious judge wouldn't order a psychiatric examination even if the frame was proved—as, by God, he would prove it—and Harry known innocent. Because ten to one the head shrinkers would say incompetent, and tag him for Atascadero or Camarillo. And what harm was Harry doing, enjoying himself quietly, being nice to people, looking at pictures of kittens? As long as Mama was there, Harry was getting along all right, doing nobody any harm. After she was gone, there'd be enough money to hire somebody to look after him in the same way, see he didn't get into trouble. Yes, and Jesse knew what could happen there, too. Without that money, who cared what happened to Harry? Stash him away in the asylum and forget him. But there was probably a very substantial little pile there: the Ames Building, "a couple others like it." How many greedy unscrupulous lawyers, bankers, seeing a chance to get some of it? What she ought to do, if there was some younger relative to be named guardian—or a trustworthy bank to take charge of a trust fund—but bank personnel changed, and Harry was only twenty-four. Better ask her about it anyway, offer advice if she hadn't made provision. A tiresome little responsibility, one way, taking on a guardianship, seeing about the motherly housekeeper, the monthly payments: but a little regular fee coming in, and at least, he flattered himself, it'd be a fair fee. Not very religious, no, he wasn't, but there were a lot of maxims about that kind of thing he adhered to. Solomon had been quite right in saying that *Treasures of wickedness profit nothing.*

He drove up to the Ames Building to see Friedlander. He wanted to know if there'd been a patient in before Miss Duveen, if maybe the patient and/or Friedlander had also heard a little of Lilian's phone conversation that day, on the other side of a thin partition. Of course, Friedlander hadn't said anything about it if he had, and probably—like Miss Duveen—if he had, he would have remembered it and spoken up. On the other hand, he'd be used to hearing his assistant talking on the phone in there, to shutting his mind to it as he worked; it might have passed straight over his head even if he had heard it. But the patient, if any—

He found Friedlander just arriving at the office. Questioned, Friedlander frowned and said he couldn't say, it was awhile back, but they could look at the appointment book. He was as always neutral, noncommittal. He looked at Jesse curiously but didn't ask questions; opened the book to him without persuasion.

On that Tuesday morning, the first listed appointment was Miss Gloria Duveen, at ten o'clock.

"Oh, yes," said Friedlander. "I remember now. Why do you ask, Mr. Falkenstein? It seems— Very probably I didn't come in until then, you know. If I haven't an early appointment, quite often I don't."

Which explained that. Lilian hadn't realized that she could be heard in the waiting room, and knowing she was alone in the inner offices— "Thanks very much," said Jesse, without further explanation, and left Friedlander staring inquisitively after him.

He was beginning to hate the sight of the Ames Building.

He arrived at his office to find old Mr. Walters sitting in the anteroom watching Miss Williams work. "Don't want to interrupt anything important. I just wondered if you'd got anywhere new on this business. Or maybe had another little job for me."

"Not at the moment, but you're not interrupting. Come in. Got a couple of other things, yes—one of them may be very helpful. But as to who it was instead, no more. Sit down."

"If," said Mr. Walters, "you got a couple of glasses, I've got a bottle."

"I have both," said Jesse, opening the bottom drawer. "For emergencies only. This is an emergency. I've got no line at all. Just nil. I think I know more or less what happened, but there's just nothing to prove it or point to X as an individual."

"Discouraging," agreed Mr. Walters. Jesse poured drinks. "What's the new thing?"

Jesse brought him up to date on Miss Duveen and the funny twist about the newspaper. And his brainstorm about the poisoned whiskey. "You see what I mean—it looks as if that eliminates everybody I contacted that day. Now who else did I see, what did I do, that gave X the idea I was dangerous? Can it be that X isn't among those people I hinted at? It's got to be tied up to this case. I don't collect enemies like that every day. . . . And then Miss Duveen—"

"Yes, and it's really no matter to you about catching X—police job—as long as you do your own job and get Harry off. But I get you—looks as if you've got to find him *to* get Harry off. Seems to me this female's given you a lot. Showed a definite motive—not a motive Harry'd have had. Well, if you can show there *was* a logical motive, that it was planned, that lets Harry out right there."

"Not legally. Clock thinks she dreamed it up. Halfway. Oh, he didn't like it, but he didn't go rushing right off to get a release order either. After all it's a negative sort of thing. Not positive evidence. Nothing says she didn't dream it up to get in on the act. No other witness."

"But it's awful suggestive," said Mr. Walters, and gave himself another drink out of his own bottle. "Acourse I see what you mean—no proof."

"And as for the rest of it, the hell I don't want to find X. I've got a score to settle with him too, you know. Right now I'm hoping for some more useful presumptive evidence to alibi Harry." He told Mr. Walters about the Fuller Brush man. "If this fellow picking up his brochure heard Harry inside the house—it was a warm day, doors and windows open—you see? Of course, it could be he didn't come around until after Harry left, but if it was in the morning—well, it's a chance, that's all."

"Sure. This stuff Miss Duveen heard—it looks like good evidence to me, that somebody had a reason to kill her all right. She'd seen something, heard something—"

"But where does it point to look? Any direction you pick! Just groping in the dark," said Jesse resentfully. He laughed. "Nell says it's the wrong way to go at it. She says—thinking of *Through the Looking Glass*, maybe—you want to find a lunatic, look for him in lunatic ways."

"Now that's what they call a profound remark," said Mr. Walters. "But then she's a smart girl. Acourse you could say Mr. X isn't exactly a lunatic. Been pretty successful in plotting, so far. But on the other hand, maybe nobody that does a murder is just as sane as you or me. . . . I tell you, I've got kind of interested in this thing now. Well, I haven't got just so much to occupy me these days. I'd like to find out the truth here. You mind if I go on sort of looking around?"

"Only too happy to have some help. But where? That's what I say— no pointer."

"Well," said Mr. Walters vaguely, "I got a couple of notions. Think I'll go to the library and take a look at that newspaper myself. Just a couple of little things I kind of wonder about, and'd like to check up on. You know."

"Such as?"

"Oh, well, maybe they sound kind of elementary," said Mr. Walters apologetically. "One thing, the way your wife built it up—Lilian coming into the building late that night, and seeing a light in some office, like that, and wondering, and going to see. Just occurs to me, would she have? Wouldn't she have just taken it for granted, somebody working late? Would she bother? She'd put in a day's work, she'd want to get her bracelet and go home and read her newspaper."

"Well—" said Jesse. "Does that point anywhere?"

Mr. Walters looked at him thoughtfully, finished his drink and poured another one. "You're a pretty smart fellow for a young man, Mr. Falkenstein. You don't think it does? Maybe not. . . . And then there's that doctor's appointment book. Acourse, it might just be coincidence—just that day."

"What d'you mean, Friedlander? I don't—"

Mr. Walters looked disappointed in him and said, "Tush. Should've thought you'd see. Never mind—I'll look into it. Best I can. Maybe nothing to it. But no harm looking, just in case."

"You," said Jesse, "sound as if you're talking to Dr. Watson."

Mr. Walters grinned and said, "Don't mean to. You're a smart fellow, sure, but only about, what, thirty-four?"

"Next January," said Jesse.

"Well, you know, if you got any kind of mind at all," said Mr. Walters, swallowing the last half of his drink, "and get in the habit of using it, it just naturally gets some better with practice. And I'm eighty-one come next March, and never a sick day—barring a little indigestion now and then—and I guess I've naturally got a little bit more experience with human people than you have, Mr. Falkenstein. They're awful damn predictable, some ways. And not—when you come down to it—awful damn complicated. Just a couple of little things here look sort of suggestive. So I'll have a look—'n' come and tell you if anything turns up." He got up.

"So, trot along and play Sherlock," said Jesse. "Making mysteries. You sound like *True Detective Tales*. Just take it easy."

"Oh, I'll be careful," said Mr. Walters, carefully stowing his bottle away. "You wait, maybe you'll laugh t'other side of your face yet."

Jesse called Clock, told him about the newspaper stories and asked if he'd like to make any guesses about which one it might have been. "Listen," said Clock, "that bleached blonde dreamed it up. Most of it."

"Don't try too hard for the convincing tone," said Jesse. "You know she didn't."

"Oh, hell," said Clock unhappily. "I don't like it, no. I damn well don't like it. Almost you begin to sell me, it wasn't Harry. And what you might call an unprecedented situation, all this cooperative contact with a defense lawyer."

"You decided you jumped the gun on Harry?"

"I have not," said Clock. "All I'll give you, off the record, is a kind of funny thing that showed up. Those keys. We asked around the Albert Avenue neighborhood, just in case. You might say it's helpful that it's not a neighborhood of apartments where a lot of the women are out at work all day. What we've got doesn't say anything definite at all, I'm just passing it on for you to build another dream on. Evidently on the afternoon before the day Mrs. Nielsen says she found the keys in her garage, there was a nice shiny big car parked in front of the Nielsen house for a little while. Two women across the street noticed it, and the next-door neighbor. One woman says she saw a woman get out of it. Couldn't say what she looked like or where she went—you know how people are about descriptions. Couldn't say what kind of car it was. Just, it was a dark color, and it wasn't there very long."

"Just long enough for somebody to drop the keys in Mrs. Nielsen's garage. Her unlocked garage," said Jesse. "A woman? Well, of course—" The lady who had dropped her bag.

"Damn it, it was somebody calling on somebody else quite openly and that was the only place to park. It doesn't make sense from any angle. Because X—if there is an X—couldn't know that dumb lout Dale had overlooked the garage on the search. No reason for us to go looking again, and find them—X couldn't be sure the keys would ever be found, except by Mrs. Nielsen, who'd probably keep quiet about it, seeing what they were."

"Yes," agreed Jesse, "but—" Much the same sort of thing as the poisoned whiskey, he thought suddenly. Was it? Muddled thinking on X's part. But everything else said that X had a mind very far from muddled. What the hell was this? He thought of Nell saying that she couldn't see Lilian's murderer doing the poisoned whiskey act. Two X's? Let's not, he thought, make it so complicated; one is quite enough. "Something else," he said to Clock. "And you—tut tut, the trained detective—didn't spot it. I'd told everybody I cast nets at that not only me but you suspected a frame. So why did somebody go all out just to get me? It'd just make you all the more suspicious."

After a moment Clock swore and said, "I laid myself open—say it—Elementary, my dear Watson. These little picayune things that we overlook— That *is* a hell of a funny one. Are you sure there isn't somebody gunning for you on some outside business?"

"Said I wasn't that kind of lawyer. Quite run-of-the-mill business, this last year. Ordinary. And so far as my father can tell me, I shouldn't think I'm the unsuspecting heir to a fortune or anything like that. Wish I were. As it is, I'm lucky to have acquired a mercenary wife. You won't. What'd she stick you for at Sardi's?"

"None of your business," said Clock, annoyed. "Who gave her those

earrings? I know a little bit about stones. She implied a kind gentleman."

"So it was. Father, for her birthday. He got a bonus from the firm
last year. Don't say I gave her away, we have to stick together. You
going to leave Harry sitting in jail?"

"You're damn right," said Clock. "I've got nothing but a lot of
maybes to say he doesn't belong there."

"You might think," said Jesse, "that a lot of maybes equal one
definite no."

"Well, I don't. Not yet."

"So, more information, please. This Stephen Belawonski. What's his
record, in detail?"

"I looked, naturally. Before my time, it was. He was twenty-four in
nineteen forty-seven when he got picked up. Employed by a trucking
firm, driver. He was also a very minor official in the local union, and
he got into a hassle with a fellow who crossed a picket line during a
strike. There was a fight, and he's a big strong fellow—six two, two
hundred pounds—he hit the guy a little too hard. Fellow had a thin
skull, fell onto a cement walk, *kaput*. So Belawonski got a stretch for
involuntary homicide. He came out in forty-nine, reported in very
faithful as a parolee until August of, fifty, when his term ended. At
that time he was working for another trucking firm, in Long Beach.
Unmarried. We haven't any record on him since. If you care, that
print is the biggest thing that worries me about this. How the hell
does Belawonski fit in?"

"I don't know," said Jesse. "He'd be about thirty-eight now? Yes.
Well. That Byerly?"

"No longer," said Clock, "in tenancy at the Ames Building. Picked
up about an hour ago by two Vice officers, for heading a call-girl service. I understand some nice evidence. You going to tell me Lilian
found out and he did that kill, and went to the trouble of framing
Harry?"

"I don't know," said Jesse. "You said you were going to look at
Jenner too. At the loan company."

Clock made a sound registering disgust. "He's keeping his secretary
—Mabel Webster. That's all. His wife's got money and he's scared to
death she'll find out. So, are you going to say that Lilian knew and
tried blackmail, and he killed her? Taking the time and trouble to

frame Harry? It's a usual sort of situation—comment on our modern morals."

"I don't know," said Jesse. "You puritan. That detective agency?"

"The Alert Detective Agency," said Clock. "Yes. Quite a good reputation. Nothing irregular. Both partners—regardless of the paperback fiction—happily married men, one with two kids, one with four. License all in order. Seven employees all have spotless records. They don't get so much divorce business in this state, a lot of absconding debtors and deserting husbands and runaway kids. Very little on the criminal side. They're competent. Good record."

"But you looked," said Jesse. "You've got it—as they say—at your fingers' ends. You're not so sure any more about Harry."

"I'm not saying it out loud," said Clock. "I rue the day you walked into my office, Mr. Falkenstein."

"Jesse. If you're going to be my brother-in-law."

"What a hope. That little harpy . . . We like to think we're a very top force. We don't railroad people. So, take it I'm still looking. Sure."

"Our efficient boys in blue," said Jesse. "That satisfies me. So am I."

FOURTEEN

He went out to lunch, and over it he told himself the story he'd built up. Gaps in it—too many gaps. The essential parts of it—the names of X and his lady friend—were missing. But he could see more or less how it had gone, though there was almost no legal evidence to show it. It had started the way Nell had said, with Lilian coming back to the building that night. (In passing, he had wondered belatedly how come she happened to have a key to the building door, and remembered what Friedlander had said about duplicate keys. It turned out that, because there was no regular manager or janitor—a bunch of women from a cleaning-service place came three times a week—each tenant was given a key, along with the keys to his office. Presumably whoever arrived first unlocked the door. And Friedlander had had duplicates made for his assistant. Evidently he was, like Jesse, not an early riser by preference and when he could liked to sleep late.)

And Lilian, coming into the building about eight o'clock that Monday night, had heard and seen something curious, unusual and/or suspicious. Pay your money, take your choice, there: might have been anything. And here Nell's theory broke down, because—on second thought—whatever it was couldn't be confined to the ground-floor offices. It might have involved any tenant in the building, because whoever it was could have been just coming in too—or just leaving. It was a very strong presumption if not a moral certainty that one of the tenants (or, of course, one of the employees of same) was involved.

At the time, Lilian was told some story that satisfied her. But when she got home, she read her newspaper, and something she saw in it definitely roused her suspicions all over again. She was "quiet" when Ruth Myers came in. Thinking about it? Wondering what to do? She was "quiet" on Tuesday. And early Tuesday morning she was demanding a better explanation of the—call it the incident. She was telling X (presumably X) that "it was the same man" and that she "could make a guess—" About the significance of that, or of the incident? On the phone. Could have been on the phone to any office in the building. She was alone in the inner office, didn't realize she could be overheard from the waiting room. Then, either X said in effect, I can't talk now but I'll explain everything tomorrow, prove to you it's all quite innocent—perhaps he promised to take her to "the same man" and let him explain—

Well, yes. When you thought it out, "the same man" must be somebody other than X. But the phone call might have been—probably had been—to the lady friend. (One of the receptionists she knew in the building?)

Either that, and she decided to wait and see, giving them the benefit of the doubt: or Friedlander came in (by the other door) and she had to hang up: or maybe she realized she might be overheard by Miss Duveen and cut it short herself. But apparently whoever she had been talking to had managed to satisfy her again, temporarily, because she didn't take any action about it—whatever the hell it had been—on Tuesday.

But the lady and X knew that they couldn't satisfy her permanently, that sooner or later she would—what?—go to the police, go to some interested (and deceived) party, tell what she knew. She had to be got rid of. It had been an important and dangerous secret then. And got rid of in such a way that suspicion would fall on someone else: someone framed for the job. Why? Why not just an anonymous kill, made to look like a mugging on a dark street maybe? Well, Lilian wasn't often alone. And— Because one or both of them was an associate of Lilian's and might attract suspicion at once?

Jesse stared earnestly at a forkful of baked Virginia ham. He had a glimmering of what Mr. Walters had meant by one of his little notions. But he didn't see that there was anything to it. The evidence they had didn't point that way at all. . . .

Well, and so they had thought of Harry. So easy to frame. And that again pointed to someone familiar with the building, who knew about Harry. And that was why it was done the way it was, in the building. By the male half of the team, who must be a big, powerful man, to catch her and keep her from screaming. Of course, strangling didn't

take long. . . . And then the hitch in the plan: Harry not there. And
the refuse truck due at ten-thirty. . . . And then Harry coming. And
all in a hurry, the lady going up, dropping the polished white bag to
get his prints. The man carefully dropping it beside the body, unwit-
ting of all those little girls the other side of the schoolyard fence,
watching. Later, the piece of necklace and the lace dropped behind
the counter.

The keys. What about the keys? Lilian had had them out as she
came up the hall, and dropped them when he grabbed her. You could
see them getting overlooked, in the excitement of the murder and the
worry over Harry's absence. You could see them not being found until
after the bag had been placed with the body—and then, too dangerous
to replace them in the bag, because the refuse truck might be along
any minute. So X had said, Leave it, they'll think he just dropped
them some place, like a nut might. Or—or—

Because the keys and the poisoned whiskey belonged together. In a
way: a rather nebulous way? The whiskey: why go just for Falkenstein, when he'd said the police suspected too? The keys: how to know
they'd ever be found, more evidence on Harry, by the police?

A muddled mind conceiving those two actions. Not the same mind
that had worked out the frame on Harry. Was that a fair deduction?
Quite possibly carrying out both actions without X's knowledge. On
impulse—getting scared. By Jesse's hints?

The lady friend? Maybe. Maybe. Picking up the keys in the hall
there, not mentioning them to X, and later on—

Well. On the whole, it had sure as hell been a successful plot. And
if they were now smart enough to go on lying low and saying nothing,
doing nothing, it looked like going on being successful.

Just nothing at all pointed to anybody. The cynical professional
pimp Byerly. The anxious Jenner with a rich wife and a mistress. Anybody else.

Jesse sighed, finished his coffee and looked at his watch. He had an
appointment with a new client at two o'clock, and that Brooks will to
dictate. . . . He removed his mind from Harry regretfully.

The new client turned out to have a damage suit in mind, and as it
was rather complicated business it took up most of the afternoon.
Jesse suspected that the physical damages incurred in the accident
didn't add up to quite the incapacity the client claimed, but she had
two useful medical statements and some X-rays, and the police report

laying all the blame on the second party—who turned out to be a young TV actor (loaded with money) Jesse intensely disliked. He went over the case with the client, got a satisfactory retainer and got through some of the preliminary paperwork on it before dictating the Brooks will to Miss Williams.

He went home, to an enthusiastic welcome from Athelstane and a somewhat abstracted one from Nell, who was still brooding over the autocratic dictatorship of the authorities on fashion.

"It's maddening," she said. "I should think it'd come under the trust laws or something. Try, just *try*, to find anything in between flat heels and four-inch-spikes! How anybody can walk in them I'll never know. And the salesman trying to tell me they're not really high because there's a platform sole. I'm not such a fool—"

Lilian had said that too. "I'm not such a fool to believe—" What?

Over second cups of coffee they talked about Harry, and came to no new conclusions.

Jesse set a group of toccatas on the phonograph and ruminated—ignoring the new Charlotte Armstrong Nell had pressed on him.

He was involved with a real-life suspense story of his own.

On Friday morning he proofread the Brooks will, a very complicated one, and received the venerable Mr. Brooks at ten o'clock to sign it. Mr. Brooks, who had brought his two witnesses with him, looked over the impressively blue-bound document and duly appended his shaky Spencerian signature; the witnesses signed; Mr. Brooks laboriously made out a check for twenty-five dollars, thanked Jesse and departed with his will.

Jesse told Miss Williams she could take her coffee break, rummaged out the relevant documents on that Scott business and stared at them gloomily. Scheduled on the calendar a week from Monday, and he'd better start thinking out his ideas on what to say to the jury. . . .

He was reading one of the witness's statements (it was another automobile accident damage suit) when the outer office door opened and crashed against the wall. Someone said, "Oh, dear! Oh—"

Jesse got up and opened his office door. "Hello, Miss Myers. What—"

"Oh, *dear!*" said Ruth Myers. She came into his office in one awkward lunge, banged the door behind her and looked at him, panting.

"Was it *true,* what you said? I was so mad—but—please, Mr. Falkenstein, you better—"

"About Mike Orde?" said Jesse. "Yes. Sit down, won't you? I just thought you ought to know, Miss Myers."

"Oh, my heavens!" she said. She didn't sit down; she held her big black patent-leather bag like a shield in front of her, and looked at him with scared round eyes. "It just didn't seem— Well, I mean, I was *introduced* to him, and the idea of Betty knowing a real crook—! He seemed like a nice guy, and he said— Well, gee, I was mad when you said— But it kind of stuck in my mind, you know, and I—and I—"

"Wondered about it, and asked?" said Jesse. "Look, Miss Myers, no harm done. I mean, it isn't as if you'd married him—just had a few dates, I gather? Sit down and relax."

"My *heavens,* me thinking I'm so smart!" she said. "You'd think I could *tell!* I mean—well, gee, I never— I'm not on, Friday mornings, see, on account they stay open till nine and I'm on one to five and six to nine. I—it kind of bothered me, what you said, even if I was mad—and I got so's I had to talk to him, tell him— Listen, Mr. Falkenstein, I guess he'd have to look up your address like I did, but— Oh, gee!"

"Now calm down," said Jesse. She was panting, almost incoherent.

"So I phoned him, see, number he gave me—said his head office, but it didn't *sound* like an office—and I said—and, boy, was he mad! He said— Gee, is he really a dope-pusher like you said? Honest? I can't hardly believe— He sounded— Listen, Mr. Falkenstein, what I come to say, I think you better lock the door."

"Why? Now you calm down, Miss Myers, not a tragedy—"

"You better," she said. "Honest. I guess. Because he said—he said, get even with you for telling me such things about him—get a gun and show you—like that. And I—and I— Gee, I still can't hardly take it *in!* But I guess he really meant—"

"Oh?" said Jesse. And he thought, a small-timer like Orde, would he—? Giving himself away like that? Of course, the sullen Mr. Orde might have a temper.

He was slow on the uptake. Thinking also that the girl might have warned him sooner, he took a step in the direction of the anteroom, and was too late. The hall door crashed violently open again and then the office door banged against the wall, and there was Mike Orde. A sufficiently big, broad young man, no longer sullen but wild-eyed. And tugging out, and waving around, what looked like a very big and businesslike gun.

"You goddamned bastard!" he shouted. "Telling tales to Ruthie— Goddamned cops just got it in for me is all—make Ruthie think I'm no good, you damned shyster, you— Spoil everything with Ruthie! Damn you, I'll get you for that, said I would and I will—you goddamned—"

"Now, Mr. Orde," said Jesse. Understatement, a temper. Very odd (said his mind, working independently of emotions), a cheap little hood like Orde really falling for honest, ordinary Ruth Myers. But, as Mr. Walters said, people came all sorts.

"Oh, *Mike!*" she said in a high, scared voice. "You can't—oh, *Mike!*"

"I'll—I'll— By God, you goddamned—get you for it if it's the last—"

The gun went off, but apparently not into Jesse, because he was still on his feet and moving. He thought (in something like slow motion) that it was also very odd, not once in thirty-three years did he remember hitting anybody in anger—very sedentary fellow, he was— hadn't a notion how to go at it— But quite involuntarily he shoved Ruth Myers roughly to stagger back toward the windows, and lunged for Orde and the gun. Heard the gun go off again, and the girl scream. He collided with Orde and they both staggered the other way, toward the door, and the gun went off again and ditto the girl. He was conscious of pain in his right shoulder, and heard the gun bark a fourth time—the girl was now screaming her head off—and he fell on something that squirmed and struggled and swore vilely at him.

Somebody else screaming, then. Miss Williams. And then shouting hysterically, "Give me the police! I want the police!"

Police already there, the woman was hysterical all right. Policeman bending over him. Jesse sat up. He was, now, very damned mad. He started to swear.

"Ambulance'll be here in a minute," said the policeman. "What went on here? Who's this?"

"If you can shut up these two females, I'll tell you," said Jesse. "Goddamned little hood!" He looked at the unconscious Orde resentfully. "Coming here and— For God's sake get that gun away from him, can't you?" He felt his shoulder and looked at the blood on his hand. "For God's *sake,* coming here shooting up the place—"

"Take it easy, now. Better lie down again, sir, you're bleeding quite a bit—here—" His jacket being eased off, something tied round his arm—

"For the love of God, shut up that girl," he said. A siren somewhere in the distance, approaching.

"Oh, Jim," said the policeman, sounding relieved. "Lend a hand here. Assault of some kind, better put the cuffs on this one, I haven't got it straight yet but— There's the ambulance boys, good—"

Why the hell, thought Jesse faintly, was I such a fool to take on Harry? Getting into all this—

"You're damn right I'll make a charge against him!" he said to Clock on the phone. "The damn little hood. Shooting me. Bullet hole in the window, bullet hole in the ceiling. Like a damned TV program." And to Nell, "You get away from me with that pill! I don't want any pills! You—"

"Darling," said Nell, "don't get so excited. The doctor said—"

"And a bullet hole in *me*. Well, on me. Just a crease across the shoulder, but it's the principle of the thing. This is turning out a damned dangerous case—why'd I ever take it on? Poisoned whiskey. Hoods shooting at me. Ten bucks at least for a new window pane—"

"Darling," said Nell, "you're supposed to have the pill. Please."

"And who's excited? Listen, I know it's got nothing to do with Harry, but— What? . . . Well, obviously, you thick-headed bastard, it's involved with somebody in the Ames Building—if you can't see that you ought to be back in uniform. Look—"

"Darling Jesse," said Fran. "You lost quite a lot of blood, you know —The doctor said—"

Athelstane, who was always fascinated by the telephone, was trying to climb into Jesse's lap.

"All *right*," said Clock. "He's been arrested and charged. I'm very sorry to hear about your bullet holes. Relieved to know you're not seriously hurt. But these things happen. Why blame me?"

"Damn it, I'm mad," said Jesse. "Why the hell hadn't you people caught up to that hood years ago? Just tell me—"

"Jesse, you fool," said Fran. "Of course they have rules about evidence. Which you perfectly well—"

"You shouldn't get so upset," said Nell. "Please. Just one pill, Jesse—"

"Now look—" said Clock.

Fran took the phone away from Jesse. "He's delirious, sergeant," she said sweetly. "We're looking after him. . . . He'll be quite all right. And I find I'm free on Wednesday night after all, I'd love to have dinner with you. . . . Mmh . . . See you about seven? I'll look forward to it, of *course*. . . . How very nice of you . . . Oh, of course not. . . . See you then, 'bye. . . . Now for heaven's sake, Jesse—"

"*And*," said Jesse, "a bullet hole in my newest suit, and even if they can get the bloodstains out—"

"Invisible menders," soothed Nell. "Now take the pill and stop swearing, for goodness' sake."

He condescended to stay in bed the rest of the day, but dragged himself out on Saturday morning, groaning and stiff, and shaved and dressed. "Listen," he said to Nell's protest, "if I don't make sense out of this thing and finish up the case in a hurry, what else is going to happen to us? And I'm all right—just stiff. . . . And I don't want a proper-breakfast-for-a-change."

Nell resignedly poured his coffee and handed over the first section of the *Times*. And about thirty seconds later was startled by a loud, "For God's sake!"

"What?"

"Did you see this? This—this unbelievable—"

"Oh, the Killeen thing. Yes. Only to be expected, wasn't it, the way everybody seems to—"

"I don't believe it," said Jesse blankly. "Acquittal. Just on what's been released publicly, which seemed plenty, it was an open-and-shut case—plain theft. This business about inadmissible evidence and suspicion of perjury and so on—a lot of double talk. It sounds— Of course I didn't hear all the testimony, it's *possible*, but—"

"Maybe the jury was bribed."

"Wasn't a jury. Defense waived it. Just the bench. And Cunningham's supposed to be a good man. But—" Jesse was silent for a while, and then he said suddenly, "I wonder. I do wonder."

"What?"

"Several things," said Jesse, and went to collect his briefcase. He kissed her good-bye, said again he was all right and, yes, he'd be careful and take it easy, and left.

FIFTEEN

"Oh, dear," said Nell. "How funny—and provoking. Both at once. I really don't know what to say offhand."

"Haven't you a preference?" asked Mrs. Alton wearily.

"Well, it works both ways. I liked the living room on Swallowtail Road better, what I remember of it, but the other kitchen was bigger, and no stairs. You know, I'd—"

"Hasn't your husband expressed a preference?"

"You just don't know Jesse. I suppose six months afterward he'll realize in a dim sort of way that we've moved, but that's about the extent of it. I'd like to go and look at both of them again. I suppose that's all right? I mean, a house isn't a thing you buy every day, you can't be expected to decide on just one look. Now I know definitely it'll be one of these two, I'd like to go back and check over closet space and so on."

"Very well, Mrs. Falkenstein. I'll phone them to expect you, shall I? Today, of course. As both offers have been agreed to, we'd like the whole matter settled—the sooner we get it into escrow—"

"Oh, yes, of course," said Nell. "I'll leave right away, if it's convenient to everybody."

"I'll ring back and let you know."

Bother—and the hottest day this month too. The car would be like an oven. Clear over to Highland Park and then back to West Hollywood. The Hollywood address would be easier for Jesse; they said wives ought to think about these things, heart attacks and high blood pressure being induced from the tension of driving in traffic. Poor Jesse—he really should have stayed in bed today. . . . On the other hand, that house had stairs. Not that they could afford to finish the dormer room, or would need to, right now. Still— And she seemed to remember that the other place, where they'd unexpectedly backed down about the carpeting, had larger closets. Really, how people expected you to look at forty houses once apiece and then decide without seeing the few possibles again—

Mrs. Alton called back and said someone would be at home in both places. "Of course, it will mean identifying yourself as the prospective purchaser. I hadn't mentioned any names, naturally. But as they have agreed to the offers—"

"Oh, certainly, that's all right. Thank you, I'll let you know definitely by this afternoon."

Mrs. Alton said unhopefully that she hoped so. Nell made the bed and washed the breakfast dishes, wondering if she was as difficult and particular as Mrs. Alton apparently found her. Over a big thing like a house, you wanted to be sure. A place you'd be bringing up children and living close with neighbors. She didn't *feel* awfully particular— she'd been quite willing to overlook that frightful wallpaper in the View Park house, when the rooms were such a good size—they could always paint. But evidently she'd been a difficult client. Oh, well.

Thinking over what she remembered of both houses, she dusted, straightened up the apartment. Washed her face and made it up. Unbraided her hair, thoroughly brushed and combed it, and put it up with accustomed swiftness into its usual smooth chignon. Chose the coolest of her summer dresses, the tan-and-violet voile, and the violet sandals on bare feet. Her toenails needed redoing but she couldn't stop now. She ran a white pencil under her fingernails, sprayed on an extravagant amount of cologne, screwed on the enameled pansy earrings and transferred all the necessaries into the tan straw bag.

"Come on, boy," she said to Athelstane. "Downstairs."

But when she started toward the stake and chain in the back yard Athelstane whined and balked. He sat down and looked wistfully from her to the garage, and Nell burst out laughing. He might as well have said it in plain English— Please can't I go too, wherever, and not be left out here all alone, nothing interesting to see or do or smell?

"Darling," she said, "you're too big for my car. Only a Cadillac could do you justice. And it'll be twice as hot driving. And I can't take you in with me, you'd have to sit outside."

Athelstane said eagerly with eyes, tail and tongue that he didn't *care.* "Oh, all right," said Nell, unable to deny him, and went back upstairs for his leash. "You be good, now. No leaning out of my window, to shove me into the dashboard. That's your window there. Settle down, you big lummox, I want to see the rear-view mirror."

Athelstane was supremely happy. He leaned out his window, tongue hanging to one side, and drank in the hot moving air. At stop signals, where people in other cars and on the sidewalk stared at him —in Nell's car he gave the effect of a lion in a Taylor tot—he grinned happily at them. Going somewhere in a car, with one of the Two Important Humans, was very near to Athelstane's canine notion of heaven.

"What?" said Henry Barrett blankly. "Oh, sure, I guess I was along there that day. What about it?"

Jesse surveyed him sadly. It was expecting quite a lot of Henry Barrett to hope that he'd remember something, quite an ordinary little something such as hearing human noise inside a house as he retrieved his company's brochure, three weeks ago. Not only no reason to remember one house (where he hadn't got an order) from another, but in between some important things had happened to Henry Barrett. He'd got married and gone on a wedding trip, and now he was in the middle of moving into a new place, and—doubtless—making the discovery that all females had some odd foibles about placing furniture. We *can't* put the TV there, quite impossible, Henry! Oh, Henry, can't you see the couch has *got* to go on the long wall!

He looked rather harassed already, here in the middle of a half-settled apartment living room, a cramped inexpensive apartment, cluttered with a few items of very cheap new furniture and better secondhand stuff. The bride, a rather improbable blonde, was tactfully busying herself in the kitchen. Jesse could not help twisting his head to identify the titles of a stack of records spread on the couch, and was saddened further: popular bands and—were they still called crooners? He could think of other names.

"I know it's asking a lot," he said coaxingly, setting out to explain.

Henry Barrett was perhaps twenty-eight, a thin, sallow young man with a perennially blue chin, unexpectedly Mephistophelian eyebrows and a savage nick on one side of his jaw where his razor had slipped. He also bore at the moment a small smear of lipstick on one corner of his mouth. He said, "Well, three weeks back . . . And when there wasn't an order. I mean, I ring the bell, you know, and sometimes they come, but mostly if they see it's me and don't want to order anything, they don't bother. It's funny how honest most people are, though—we don't lose many brochures. They leave it out for you. But you see what I mean, I've got no reason to remember special, a thing I do twenty times a day."

"Sure, I see that. I wish you could. A lot might depend on it. Proving a man innocent, maybe. Now let's just see if we can't jog your memory." Jesse sat back beside the stack of misbegotten records and lit a cigarette, and his host rose up, searched distractedly about, found a tiny glass dish, and deposited it neatly on the table at Jesse's elbow. After which he did not have to add apologetically that neither of them smoked. Jesse had never run across a nonsmoker who believed, apparently, that an ashtray needed to be more than an inch in diameter.

He thought fondly of Nell's many outsize modern ones with slots, and said, "Now, Albert Avenue—shabby middle-class street, old frame bungalows, working people. Some yards kept up, some not."

"I go down a lot like that," said Barrett.

"Sure you do. Might help if you look up your order book. If you got any orders in that block, you might remember clearer."

"That's so." Barrett brightened and went to get it. "I'd sure like to help you, Mr. Falkenstein. Can't say for sure, swear to anything unless I do remember, but if like you say the fellow's not guilty, I'd sure like to help. Let's see—week of the ninth to the fourteenth, that what you said? Last week before my—my vacation," and involuntarily he glanced toward the kitchen. "Albert Avenue . . . I was lucky that week, I got a lot of orders. . . ." He leafed through, glancing at addresses only. "Here we are. What address did you say? Seventy-six-twenty. Well, I got three orders in that block, that Wednesday. I'd left the brochure day before, see. Pretty good orders, too. Nearly ten dollars' worth of cosmetics, one place, and some floor wax and brushes and more cosmetics another—eighteen-twenty it came to—and some scouring pads, there's a special on them this month—" Suddenly he grinned. "Say, I remember *that* place! It was an Italian woman—seeing the name on the order kind of jogged my memory. Nice woman, but awful Italian—you know, accent you could cut with a knife, and she asked wouldn't I like to try some of her nice pizza just out of the pan."

"That's fine," said Jesse. "Keep it up."

"It's funny how one thing brings back another, isn't it? That was a good idea of yours, look up my orders, Mr. Falkenstein. See, I remember—looking over the orders I got that day—I started in the block just down from that one. These are the first orders that day. It'd have been about ten to nine I started. Some guys, they take it easy, figure women don't like to be interrupted doing the breakfast dishes and all, you know—but in my experience, if they're going out to market, which a lot do, it'll be around ten-thirty to twelve, and I like to catch 'em earlier, and take a break myself those last couple of morning hours. I think I get more of them at home, working it that way, than the fellows who don't start until maybe ten."

"Experience of human nature," said Jesse.

"I guess so. Anyway, that's one reason I remember this Italian woman, Mrs. Gracchio. She bought a package of scouring pads. And asking me to taste her pizza, at maybe nine-thirty in the morning! It was funny. I suppose she gets up at five or six. . . . Gee, yes, I do remember that morning now. It was just a couple of doors down from there I ran into the nut."

Jesse upset the tiny ashtray, and could have cursed himself. "The nut. Yes?"

But Barrett hadn't noticed. "Yeah. This one place, I went up to the porch and this fellow was just putting our brochure out on the mailbox. So of course I started to give him the sales pitch, had he noticed all the wonderful specials on this month and the rest of it—only in about two minutes I see he's not getting a word. When I say nut, I don't mean in that way—I mean just backward, retarded, you know. Like a little kid. He just stood there grinning at me. So I tapered off, and I took the brochure, but he took it back and opened it up to the page of cosmetics and pointed out one cut to me. Of a girl with a cat—part of the ad, see. He said, Pretty, ain't it? You see the kind I mean. So I got out of there fast. But about this address you asked about, I couldn't—"

Jesse put out his cigarette, and noticed that his hand was shaking a little. For Harry. What the hell did Harry matter? An interesting case, what had looked like (and God knew been) a difficult case. And now not even to get into a courtroom.

And Harry not very important, this way or that way? Well, there were never enough of the people who had that kind of what was called empathy. The people who felt the feelings of other animate beings as if they were their own. Smart or dumb, never enough of them. If the world was ever going to be made a little better place for all of the people in it, that was the kind of people you wanted. The most important kind—whatever their I.Q.'s were. And he thought on that basis, maybe Harry, with that kind of empathy and a low I.Q., was a more valuable human being than the smartest army general or head doctor or politician on the face of the earth.

"Mr. Barrett," he said to the stub of his cigarette, "what did the nut look like?"

"Oh, far as I can recall, just a big good-natured lout. Not very old, but big. . . . Dressed? Why, he had on pajamas, matter of fact, I remember. No bathrobe or anything. Sure I could recognize him again, why?"

"Look at Mrs. Gracchio's address," said Jesse. "Seventy-six-sixteen. Two doors down. The nut—he's my boy, Mr. Barrett. Because he isn't all there, he'd forgotten talking to you, or didn't have the sense to tell about it. No, damn it, I remember he started to say something once, and I shut him up. You've just alibied him but very damn good. Could you swear to the time within fifteen minutes?"

Barrett looked a little pale, a little excited. "Is that a fact? Sure— sure I could. I always start out about a quarter of nine, and I'd covered the block down from there and most of that one. Got two orders. A couple of places as usual nobody answered. It would have been, oh, between nine-twenty and nine-thirty I saw him."

Lilian killed between nine and nine-thirty. A twenty-minute bus ride from Harry. Even if you put it at nine o'clock or a few minutes before, he couldn't have been back in pajamas at his own door, telling Barrett how pretty the little soft kitten was, at nine-thirty. Let alone nine-twenty. That must have been just before he got dressed and left; he'd have got the quarter-to-ten bus at Santa Monica, which let him out a three-minute walk from the Ames Building. . . . Just in time to pick up the bag the pretty lady dropped.

This was evidence Clock had to listen to. It was evidence for the hurried red tape at the D.A.'s office, the dismissal of charges and a release order. And he could have had it a week ago, if he'd let Harry tell him about the Fuller Brush man. Damn it. Harry, not comprehending what bad thing they thought he had done, much less when they thought he'd done it.

"I want a statement," he said. "You understand that. You'll be swearing to this before the bench, Mr. Barrett. You're quite sure of the truth of what you've just said?"

"Sure—sure I am." Barrett looked excited, apprehensive, a little pleased at being so important. "I'll be damned! I never thought—you just said the address, I wouldn't remember an address— Well, that's something, isn't it? A *murder*. Oh, sure, I'll be glad to do whatever's right. Sure it's the truth. I remember all about it—at the time, just one of the funny little things that happen, you know—but naturally it stayed in my mind. . . . Jane! Jane honey, guess what? The damnedest thing . . ."

Gratifyingly imbued with a sense of importance, as most people would be in such circumstances, Barrett followed Jesse back to his office in his own car and made a formal statement officially witnessed by Miss Williams. Jesse wasted a little time talking with him, gave him a drink, thanked him repeatedly; finally Barrett left, to go home and talk it all over with Jane.

Jesse got on the phone to Clock. Clock made sounds of annoyance, regret and grudging congratulations. "Apologies," said Jesse. "I know this means you've wasted time and have to start looking all over again, but as you told me, you don't *want* to railroad innocent people. . . . You'll start the red tape unwinding so Harry can go home, I trust. . . . Yes . . . Cheer up, friend, think of the profit on the case. You've lost a murderer, but gained a prospective bride and a nice respectable family of in-laws."

"Respectable?" said Clock. "Red nail polish and four-inch heels she wears. And don't call me a puritan, you shyster. I'll live to rue the day you walked into my office."

"Comfort to reflect, so will Fran. She tells me you amuse her, and she's trying to civilize you. Little does she know our efficient police. My bet's on you, boy—it may be a long pull, but I think you'll make it."

"And I don't know but what I'm a fool to try."

"Don't say that. Quite intelligent girl, and her heart's in the right place. Comes of a decent family, after all. You might—in time—reform her into a good wife and mother. Both my father and me on your side. . . . You go and see about Harry." He looked up as Miss Williams opened the door.

"Oh, dear, I'm sorry," said Miss Williams. Over her shoulder old Mr. Walters peered in.

"All right, all right," said Clock. "As soon as I get a copy of that statement. We have to do things the legal way, after all. Red tape. I will be damned. So now where do I start to look?"

Jesse beckoned Mr. Walters in and said, "You really asking an amateur for advice? I'll give it to you. Both my wife and the volunteer minion working on this case, going on the theory that a murderer's bound to be a little abnormal, they say, You want to find a lunatic, look for him in lunatic ways." Clock uttered a long, loud snort like an offended stallion and hung up. Jesse grinned at Mr. Walters and opened the bottom drawer. "Before you tell me whatever you've got, I'll tell you my news. Harry's definitely in the clear." And he told him about the Fuller Brush man.

"Now isn't that the damnedest thing," said Mr. Walters over his drink. "All for nothing, if we'd only known. If it hadn't been one like Harry, sense enough to remember it and tell you—and the cops—right off. Makes you wonder. You going all round Robin Hood's barn like this, me getting interested and going out looking—and all the little girls, and all. Just for nothing, really. . . . But anyway, I've solved your mystery for you, Mr. Falkenstein." He grinned at Jesse, pulled his own bottle out of his pocket and renewed his drink.

"What? You mean—what've you got?"

"Well, I don't know *why*," said Mr. Walters, "I got to say that. But I know who. I had a couple little ideas, see. One of 'em was this. We said Mr. X had his head screwed on tight—not like Harry—so it didn't seem just very reasonable to me that he'd actually do that murder right there in that open hallway. Or out in the alley. I know the hall only leads to those two offices, but at nine o'clock when she'd be coming in, other people'd be passing out in the main hall, and could've seen. X couldn't be sure she wouldn't get a chance to scream. . . . And at the same time, why put up a frame on somebody, to make it sure? Because Mr. X was close enough to Lilian so he might be suspected—and investigated—right away, otherwise." Mr. Walters swallowed half his drink and looked at Jesse with his little shrewd eyes. He was pleased with himself.

"Well?"

"Well, and I kind of wondered about this Dr. Friedlander's appointment book. There were two times we know about when he didn't have an appointment before ten in the morning. He says to you he has a heavy practice, but does he? What we do know he's got is a wife who sounds kind of extravagant. Talking about a house at Emerald Bay and so on. And he's selling his house in Hollywood—house in a pretty good residential section, too. Good enough for anybody. I just kind of wondered if it isn't maybe they want to move to an even better place, but because he's not doing so good and can't afford it any more. You know, that Ames Building—well, it's not in a slum, but it's just an ordinary office building, not like those real classy new ones along Wilshire or Sunset. So I—"

"Look, nothing points to him at all. But nothing. Sure, I got a glimmer of what you were driving at there, but—"

"You just wait 'n' let me tell it my own way," said Mr. Walters, placidly pouring himself another drink. "I thought I'd like a look at the fellow. So I called up and made an appointment. He's got a new girl now, by the way. No trouble at all, fit me in any time tomorrow, she said—this was Thursday. Which doesn't sound as if he had just a hell of a lot of patients clamoring for attention. Point is, you know—or do I have to explain it?—a lot of people will do a lot of crooked things for money, if they need it and think they won't get caught. And you say to me, he's got a pretty wife he's crazy about, and her about him, and she's pretty good at spending money."

"But what—"

"*What*, I don't know," said Mr. Walters. "But we figured probably Lilian found out about something crooked, and that's why she had to be got rid of. All right. Just, here's a fellow might possibly be mixed up in something crooked. I just wanted to look at him. Let's take it in order. I got an appointment at two o'clock yesterday, and I went to see him. Spent the morning in the public library looking over that issue of the *Herald*. Damn frustrating, because there was no way to tell what was in it she—"

"How right you are," said Jesse. "And?"

"And," said Mr. Walters, disposing of the second third of his new drink, "I didn't cotton to Dr. Friedlander. Good dentist, though. . . . Got all my own teeth, barring a bridge with two on it. Just been to my own dentist, and Friedlander said just what he'd said—no trouble. But he's a cold kind of fish, the kind goes all out for only one or two people—you know. Calculating, too. Sees people like—um—on a chessboard. And this wife he's really crazy about, sure. She called him on the phone while I was there—new girl called him. You could tell, by the way his voice changed when he talked to her, 'n' all. The only actual words I caught, he sounded kind of harried. Was saying, 'Yes, darling, but that's a lot of money—' You can read it as well as me. He's hard up—she keeps him that way—and he doesn't like to deny her anything. Wants her to have everything she's got a yen for."

"Look," said Jesse, "this is all up in the air. I grant you all that. But it doesn't say— So maybe, just very much maybe, Friedlander might be open to a crooked deal of some kind. What kind, and what specifically? I don't—"

"You just wait," said Mr. Walters. "I read him, is all. And I got to thinking I'd like a look at his wife and the house and so on. Took a trip there yesterday afternoon, but nobody home. So I—"

"But," said Jesse, suddenly remembering it, "Friedlander can't be X. Because Lilian was talking on the phone that morning—"

"Oh, was she?" said Mr. Walters. He finished his drink and looked at Jesse blandly. "Was she for sure?"

"Of course, Friedlander didn't come in until—but—" Jesse stared at his own half-finished drink and said after a moment, "My God. Of course she mightn't have been. She might—"

SIXTEEN

Nell parked opposite the house, reconsidered—a dead-end street, nuisance to turn around afterward—turned around via a convenient driveway and parked in front of the house. It *was* a nice-looking house, with the upper dormer windows and neat ivy-bordered strip of lawn.

The dead-end street she liked. Nice for children and dogs. Less busy than Vizcaino Avenue. But stairs— And the other house had a great deal to recommend it. A larger living room, and a tub in both bathrooms, not just a shower in the second one; and that nice big service porch, room for a dryer too, always supposing they could afford one.

She said to Athelstane, "You be good now," and started to clip his leash to the robe-rail, and then hesitated. Such a short leash, and she'd be gone a little while. He wouldn't try to jump out the narrow window. She left him loose in the small confines of the car and walked up the flagstones to the house, pushed the bell.

When the door opened, Berenice Friedlander just stared at her for a moment. "Good morning," said Nell. "Mrs. Alton called you, didn't she, to say I'd be—"

"What do you *want?*" asked Berenice in a high, frightened voice. "What do you *want*, coming here again, snooping around? Go away!"

"Why—" Nell was taken aback.

"With your husband dead too," said Berenice. "Don't you *care?* Anyway, you weren't interested in the house, that was just an excuse to come snooping— What do you *want?*"

"What?" said Nell. "Jesse, d—? I don't—"

The whiskey, said her mind. But that's absurd, this—

"It was just an excuse, I knew that! He suspected something, I could see— Coming to spy on us some more—so's you'd find out about Fred. What did it *matter*? And ten thousand bucks—well, gee! You go away!"

"I don't understand," said Nell. "Really, it was just—"

"You don't kid me! You *suspect*— And they'd put Fred in jail—and me too." She was in yellow shorts and halter today. But now the pretty kitten face wore an expression of almost witless fright. "If they could prove—! What do you know? What did he know, anyway? Coming snooping— Steve said—oh, gee, I never do remember call him Alex instead, his middle name—Steve— It was awful about that girl, but she just walked in and Steve said— We were *sorry*, but—"

"I beg your pardon," said Nell. She thought her mind had never moved so fast in her life. Not exactly at putting two and two together, because that it didn't seem capable of right then, but at telling her what to do. Get away, fast. Out of this—whatever it was. "You're upset, I won't bother you now." She began to back away.

Berenice seized her arm in an unexpectedly hard grip. "No! You got to tell me—why'd you suspect us? What did he know? He— *Isn't* he dead? It wasn't any good after all? You don't *look* like he's dead."

Nell tried to pull away; Berenice's grasp hardened desperately, and she relaxed. "No, he's not. But we didn't really suspect anything, you know. It was just—" And what was all this?

"Then why'd you come back? Pretend to be int'rested in the house— that was just an excuse—I knew! I got—got what they call intuition about things."

Nell looked with something like fascination at the beautiful vacuous face, distorted now with fear. "It wasn't a lie," she said. "We were interested, really. Please, Mrs.—"

"What *did* it matter? Steve said— It was just to pick some safe place where they could pay the money, that old man was kind of nervous about it, Steve said. An awful lot o' money, so he'd say Mr. Killeen wasn't guilty. Steve's boss. It was a hundred thousand bucks, and just to make it all safe and so's nobody would suspect, if Fred let them use his office, and so if anybody ever—and Steve—" Suddenly she put a hand to her mouth, childishly. "I oughtn't tell you—I never meant—oh, my God, what'll I do now? I—I—Oh, if Fred was here, tell me what to do—"

"Mrs. Friedlander, please, I don't mean you any harm!"

"No! You can't—" Berenice held her tightly, pulling her farther across the threshold. "I can't let you go now—oh, if Fred was only here!" Sudden triumph lit her eyes. "I know! It's right here too—" She pulled Nell into the entrance hall, and fumbled one-handed, the other clenched on Nell's arm, at the drawer of a little table there. "On account of burglars, right here. Fred's old army gun, and I know he keeps it loaded—" She was panting, pulling things out of the drawer to fall on the floor, groping for what she sought. It was a big, heavy revolver, and she pointed it waveringly. "I never meant to— Listen, we were *sorry*, but she walked right in. And Fred told her some story, only afterward she got suspicious and he hadda tell Steve, and Steve said— Nobody liked it, but she was going to—and ten thousand bucks —a lot more to that judge—you can see— Oh, I *wish* Fred was here, or Steve, they'd tell me— But I know what I'll do. I'll call your husband and—and—I'll tell him I'll shoot you unless he says he won't do nothing—anything, I mean—about what he knows. To hurt Fred—put Fred in jail—I'd do anything, help Fred—"

But just a foolish, hysterical woman, thought Nell, insofar as she was thinking at all. "Mrs. Friedlander, you must see you can't do any good that way."

"I *would* too, shoot you I mean, unless he— When you *know*, and could say—Don't you move now, or I *will*! I—"

"Mrs. Friedlander, it's not only my husband, it's the police too," said Nell, hoping she told the truth. "You can't—"

"That's not so! The paper said—clear-cut case—I read it in the paper! What's it *matter*, a poor nut like that? They wouldn't do nothing to him—like they would to Fred and Steve— It doesn't matter! Besides, he's the kind *might* do something like that, isn't he? Fred said—"

Quite as Jesse said about the whiskey, the muddled mind. The ditherer. Why hadn't they seen it before?—the only mind like that remotely connected with the case. Farfetched. Just on the fringes of the case, after all. Nell found herself mesmerized, shamefully, by the revolver in Berenice's hand. She had no doubt—kept in readiness for burglars by the efficient Dr. Friedlander—it was loaded.

It was, of course, ridiculous. The front door was wide open; any neighbor who passed by could see them here, Berenice gesturing wildly with the revolver, still holding Nell's arm. But somehow she couldn't move.

"Steve said it was a good idea—one like that nut—and it went off O.K.—" She was fumbling with the telephone book now, and trying to keep an eye on Nell at the same time. Nell told herself she must just watch for the chance, when the other woman's eyes were off her, and grab for that gun. But it was loaded, and in the hands of an inexperienced, almost hysterical woman—it would undoubtedly go off, and who could tell where? Berenice was unexpectedly strong; she'd let go of Nell now, but she was still close, and—

"I was there, it was awful, but Steve said—on account of getting his prints after—and those keys, she had them in her hand when she walked in, and when Steve grabbed her she sort of dodged and put up a hand, awful quick, and he got hold— But it was funny, he dropped 'em and it wasn't until after I picked— You stand still, don't you move! I *will* too shoot, if— Nobody's going to hurt Fred! Fred laughed about it—your husband—saying he *knew*—but I got intuitions about things. And I thought it was a smart idea, people like lawyers always got a lot of people got it in for them. But Steve called me a damn fool and hit me. Nobody's going to put Fred in jail—I'll kill you before—"

Just watch for a chance, thought Nell. But the gesturing revolver hypnotized her, like a snake with a bird; she stood still.

"Now wait a minute," said Jesse. "The phone. So maybe she wasn't talking on the phone? She'd hung up—on an ordinary call, patient making an appointment. Which Miss Duveen didn't hear. And you say she was talking to—"

"The doctor. Sure," said Mr. Walters. "What she saw and heard that Monday night was right in Dr. Friedlander's own office. Likeliest thing, isn't it? Not likely she'd take the trouble, investigate somebody working late in some other office. Is it? She walked in on something there. Now I don't know what, but—like Lilian—I could make a guess. I haven't got to the clincher." He drank, and grinned at Jesse. "Just coincidence—luck—I got it. I said I wanted a look at his wife. I went up there this morning, primed with a tale I was interested in the house, see. Got the hell of a lot more than I'd hoped for. I went up to the porch, rang the bell. Nice-looking house, all right. The front door was open, and a little way inside, there she was. Hell of a good-looking woman, isn't she? But only about half as many brains as normal, poor girl. There she was, hanging on to this big fellow's arm and saying, 'But it's O.K., isn't it, Steve? You think it's O.K.?' And that one I recognized."

"You—"

"It was," said Mr. Walters, echoing Lilian, "the same man. In the newspaper. I don't know why, or what it's all about—but there he was. Big fellow with a kind of long mustache—mustache going gray but not very. Paper said, Alex ('Tiger') Bennett. Fellow mixed up somehow with that—"

"My God!" said Jesse.

"Well, seeing I'd got what I'd come for—*and* more—I made an excuse about a wrong address and— That say something to you?"

"My God!" said Jesse again. "Does it make sense? Cunningham— But the stakes high enough, anybody— I wonder. . . . And that fool woman—get her alone, get her rattled enough—she might let out enough—" He got up suddenly. "Let's go, right now!"

"Anything you say," said Mr. Walters, and drained his glass and took up his hat. "You can explain what you're talking about on the way."

"You can't dial the phone with one hand," said Nell. She felt absurdly as if she was reasoning with a child.

"I can too. I will. I won't have anybody hurting Fred! I—I'll say, if you ever, ever say one word, I'll come and shoot both of you! What did it matter, a nut like that? I won't—"

"Mrs. Friedlander," said Nell distinctly, "you know there's someone waiting for me in my car. He'll think it very odd if I don't come back soon, and he'll—"

"Somebody—" The childish mouth drooped.

Without turning her head, Nell shouted desperately at the top of her voice, "*Athelstane! Come!*"

Athelstane had been waiting, in his cramped confines, as patiently as he could, and was delighted to hear the summons. It was rather inconvenient that the One Important Human had not come to open the door, but it was—he discovered—just possible to get out the window if absolutely necessary, though awkward. He scrabbled out clumsily and fell into the new ivy in the parking, painful and ungainly; heard his name called again, picked himself up and galloped for the Important Human thirty feet away inside the doorway. There was a loud noise, startling him considerably, and a sharp fire in his side, but the Important Human had summoned him and must be obeyed. He galloped gamely, and collapsed against her.

And Nell, clutching the revolver wrested from Berenice, stumbled into the living room to the phone and requested the police in a shaking voice.

When the patrol car arrived the two officers found a beautiful young woman in shorts and halter leaning on the doorpost weeping hysterically, and a distraught young woman tearfully crouched over the body of a great big dog sprawled on the threshold. "Where's the assault, lady? The dog attack you? What's it all about?"

"She *shot* him. No. S-Sergeant Clock at Homicide knows all about it —I mean—you'd better call Sergeant Clock right away." Nell looked up and saw Jesse and Mr. Walters just getting out of the car behind the patrol car. Jesse took one look and started to run, and Nell ran to meet him. "Jesse, please get a doctor for Athelstane, he's been *shot*— she shot him—"

Clock came in as Jesse opened the door, and Athelstane growled at him. "There!" said Jesse, gratified. "It's made a watchdog out of him. An ill wind that blows, et cetera."

"He's just irritable, like all sick people," said Nell, patting Athelstane's bandage. "He'll get over it."

"Well, so what's the news?"

Clock didn't say immediately. He sat down and said to Nell, "Not that I expect she could have hit the side of a barn with a shotgun, but she was damned close. You were lucky—*and* had guts, to grab her arm like that."

"My darling Athelstane was the hero. You see, Jesse, *I'm* the one wanted to adopt him. Aren't you glad now?"

"He's earned his keep for once," acknowledged Jesse, making a drink for Clock. "But I'm damned glad the case is over. All of us winding up getting attacked. You've pinned it on them for sure?"

Clock took the drink with a nod. "On the three of them. The four of them, really, counting Cunningham. This is all going to make quite a legal stir, you know, on account of Cunningham. He had such a high reputation. . . . The woman came all to pieces—expectable. If Friedlander had been there to shut her up—but he wasn't, and we heard the whole story. In bits and pieces—she was kind of incoherent, of course. As you guessed, it was the pay-off for Judge Cunningham. He was being careful, wanted an answer for everything, in case he was ever investigated. As well he might want to be careful, on a pay-off like that. . . . Well, this Bennett—alias Belawonski—isn't talking, and

neither is Friedlander. I'll bet if they could get at Berenice, Belawonski anyway, she wouldn't last thirty seconds. But we've got the
story pieced together. Short and sad. There was a pay-off fixed for the
judge in the Dave Killeen trial. Reason they waived a jury—easier to
get to one man. But he was very damn cagey, Cunningham—wanted
to take delivery very secret, make it a foolproof cover-up. Well, this
Bennett character, you see—he'd changed his last name and used his
real middle name after the stretch he did as Belawonski—and he's this
Berenice's big brother."

"Oh, really? Oh, I *see*," said Nell.

"Mmh. It was his idea—knowing Friedlander was hard up—cut him
in. If the judge was ever suspected, investigated, why, it was all very
much on the level, so innocent—an evening appointment with the dentist. That was how the pay-off was set up."

"And," said Jesse, "Lilian walked in on it, just by chance."

"And Lilian walked in on it. After her bracelet. We don't know just
exactly what happened. As I say, Berenice is talking pretty incoherently. We'll find out. Anyway, they told Lilian some story to satisfy
her temporarily. But when she went home and saw her paper—I think
it was Belawonski she recognized, from the newspaper cut—or the
judge. Maybe both. Who can say? 'The same man' or 'the same men'?
She said she could 'make a guess.' No telling what she walked in on—
maybe the actual handing over of the cash. Anyway, you can see she
was dangerous. I mean, it didn't involve just the bought acquittal, the
hundred grand to Cunningham, the ten grand to the Friedlanders.
There was also Killeen's control of the union—which is worth fifty
grand a year in salary to him. Acquitted, he'd go on being re-elected.
By—"

"A purblind majority," said Jesse. "Sure. Refill?"

"Just half, thanks. You see what was at stake. It was Belawonski—
Bennett who did the job. It was, obviously, Friedlander who had the
bright idea who to frame. They—by which I mean Friedlander—put
her off with another plausible tale, maybe promising her a full explanation proving how innocent it all was—until Wednesday morning.
Belawonski's not such a fool to have done the kill in that open hall—he
was waiting inside the office. All three of them were—because they
needed Berenice to get Harry's prints on the bag afterward. She
hadn't been in the building often, and they figured Harry wouldn't
recognize her. And when Lilian walked in and saw Belawonski reach-

ing for her, she put up her hands—too scared to scream, probably—and he got hold of the keys first, dropped them, grabbing her with the other hand and— And Berenice picked them up, probably dropped them in a pocket or her bag, and nobody thought about them again. Until she got scared about maybe her darling Freddy getting connected to it. . . . It's funny how that print of Belawonski's was still there, after all that handling, but's the kind of thing happens. . . . It emerges," said Clock, "in a muddled kind of way, that your—hints, Jesse, were passed on by the doctor, who knew you must be bluffing, because Harry'd been arraigned. But Berenice didn't think so. She was afraid you had something. She was a little confused, didn't get the word that you'd said the cops were suspicious too. And I guess she watches the TV shows, has the idea that lawyers—like private eyes—are naturally mixed up with hoods, acquire a lot of personal enemies. We've got her prescription for sleeping pills—same stuff as in the whiskey. And she planted the keys too. *And*," said Clock pleasedly, "from what she said, big brother Steve told her off but good as a damn fool, when she let out what she'd done. And Friedlander too. But it was too late then."

"And the anonymous letter?" asked Nell.

"Well, she says not, and I don't think that was Berenice. I think if Berenice set out to write an anonymous letter, she'd use any paper handy and her own favorite ball-point. She doesn't, I suppose, read anything but the fashion magazines. Almost anybody who's read a few paperbacks, you know, you ask them to fake up an anonymous letter and they'd produce that kind of thing—letters cut out of newspapers. No, I don't know who sent you the letter, but my guess would be Mike Orde. It would be like him. Whoever sent it, you see, had just enough brain to be afraid you were getting close to dangerous ground, and not enough to see that the letter by itself would tell you there was something more to be found."

"Will Berenice—?" asked Nell. "I mean, she was only a fool. Only—"

Clock smiled at her briefly. "No," he said. "Accessory. And not Friedlander, probably. Accessory too. Terms, sure. Accessories before and after. What it comes to—in plain words—Belawonski's a violent man. Thinks in terms of violence. I don't say that Lilian Blake would have been open to a money bribe. She probably wouldn't have been—nice honest girl, serious girl—maybe, the way she had the habit of newspaper reading, very serious about politics and so on. And probably Friedlander knew her well enough to know that. But they didn't—for ninety-nine percent sure—try that on her. Because I think if they had, either Monday night or Tuesday, she'd have made a beeline for the nearest cop and told all she knew. That would have told her that what she'd seen wasn't innocent, you see. . . . They had to get rid of her. The easiest way—by violence. And I think Belawonski made that decision, and Friedlander let him. And he and Berenice aided and abetted."

"I do wonder," said Jesse, "if we could get an identification of her from Harry. Not very likely. The jury'll like her. Poor pathetic pretty little thing under her husband's thumb, under big brother's thumb. She'll get off with a short sentence."

"I wouldn't doubt," said Clock.

"I'm sorry for her," said Nell. "I am. I know it sounds wrong, but she's really not—not responsible. Rather like Harry, in a way. These just naturally beautiful women—they never have to develop their minds. Use their brains. You know. Oh—except a very few of them, like Fran, who're just naturally smart."

Clock laughed. "Smart up to a point," he said. "Fran—well." He finished his drink. "I won't say I don't feel sorry for her too, poor little fool—Berenice, I mean. But, these people. Bribing judges—and judges taking bribes—judges with as good a reputation as Cunningham had. There's something going on in the world today—all this juvenile delinquency, and a general lowering of standards—" He shook his head. "I don't know, it's—"

"The heart is deceitful above all things, and very weak," said Jesse. "Yes. All we can do is stay by our own standards, friend. . . . At least I didn't come out short." He was feeding Athelstane by hand with some of the salted cocktail pretzels he was so absurdly fond of. "Quite a nice little fee for getting Harry off."

"Congratulations," said Clock somewhat bitterly. "Me, I get told off by the lieutenant for jumping to conclusions, *and* told off by Fran for not paying attention to her clever brother in the first place."

"No! Did she say that? Never knew she thought so much of me," said Jesse, gratified.

Clock suddenly grinned at him. "We'll keep it a secret amongst us."

"I think," said Nell, "it's been a very profitable sort of case all round. Even if it did turn out dangerous. You've met Fran, and Jesse's made some money, and we've met darling old Mr. Walters. I've fallen in love with Mr. Walters."

"I'd better keep an eye on you," said Jesse. "He's got a hell of a lot more money than I have."

Athelstane crawled off his bed of pain and over to Clock, to offer an apologetic paw and a head to pat. "There, you see, just what I say— he'll never be a watchdog," said Jesse. "Why you had to saddle us with this monster—"

"Darling, don't mind," said Nell. "He doesn't mean it really, do you, Jesse? Kitchen, darling—I've got your nice dinner *all* ready."

Jesse said sadly to Clock, "Before mine, you notice."

MY
NAME
IS
DEATH

Poor little turtle-dove, setting on a pine,
Longing for his own true love as I did once
                                    for mine, for mine,
As I did once for mine.

I come down the mountainside, I give my horn a blow,
Everywhere the pretty girls said, yonder goes
                                    my beau, my beau,
Said, yonder goes my beau.

Walked down the street that very same night, in my
                        heart was a sweet, sweet song—
Got in a fight, and in jail all night,
And every durn thing went wrong, went wrong—
Every durn thing went wrong.

                                —American Folksong

ONE

Miss Williams half-opened the door and said in a conspiratorial tone, "The new client's here, Mr. Falkenstein—that Mr. Austin."

Jesse looked up from a copy of Mr. Godfrey's new will with a sigh. "All right, shoot him in." He had once cherished hope that Miss Williams might some day be turned into a halfway professional legal secretary, but hope was dimming; and, damn it, he hadn't the moral courage to fire her—a nice woman, and sole support of an aged mother. He stood up as the new client came in from the anteroom. "Mr. Austin? Sit down, won't you? What can I do for you?"

Mr. Raymond Austin advanced a little hesitantly. Jesse put him down as not much over twenty-six or -seven; he was a very neat young man, pressed dark suit, white shirt, discreet dark tie. Office job, thought Jesse. He wasn't much over medium height, but stocky; he had a thin sallow face, not bad looking, with dark eyes, and the shadow of a heavy beard showed on his jaw, at this end of the day.

"Well," he said, and sat down abruptly in the chair beside the desk. "Well, it's—I want a divorce from my wife."

"I see." Jesse concealed surprise; usually it was the woman who applied for divorce. But it did happen the other way round. Austin was nervous; he sat balancing a well-bred-looking Homburg on his knees, licking his lips. "Well, suppose you just tell me the circumstances, Mr. Austin. What grounds did you—"

"Well, I don't know," said Austin blankly. "I don't know much about what grounds there are here, I thought you could suggest— Lord," he added suddenly then, and passed a manicured hand over his thick dark hair in absent gesture, "what a mess! I never thought I'd get into a situation like this, but there it is. And I don't know if you could do anything about the rest of it either, but I've heard of—of lawyers getting injunctions, is that the word, to prevent a husband or wife from annoying—I mean, you know, the bank doesn't like it, Mr. Falkenstein." He was earnest on that.

"Let's just start from the beginning," said Jesse gently. "O.K.? Your wife's been annoying you—how? You work in a bank?"

"The Security-First National, branch on Olympic Boulevard," said Austin promptly. "I—you see, I did most of my military service here, and I like California—my mother's married again, I should say I come from Pennsylvania—Reading, Pennsylvania—and I like Bruce all right, but—well, you know how it is. So I stayed out here and got the job with the bank. I've been there nearly six years, I just got promoted to the trust department, that's what I'm really most interested in, and I was— Well, never mind that. Mr. Raglan's been very patient about it, but a few times Tamar's come in and made a little scene, and all the phone calls—"

"I see," said Jesse, suppressing a grin. Austin very obviously the typical young of the banker species; on the way to being a stuffed shirt. He sounded a nice guy for all that, and Jesse felt sorry for him. These females.

"It's—you see, it's a good job, a secure job, and I'm working up in it, but it doesn't pay all that high a salary. Since I—left her, I've given her a set sum every week, after all I'm still responsible, you could say, but she wants more, she doesn't understand—"

"Let's have it from the beginning, Mr. Austin. How long have you been married?"

"A little under six months," said Austin. He sounded ashamed on that. "Damn it, I never thought I'd—I don't want to sound like a—a prude, Mr. Falkenstein, but when I married Tamar I expected to stay married. Start a home. You know? I suppose I'm just one like that, way I was brought up and so on. But I guess I expected too much of her. She's only twenty-one, and she likes—oh, going out every night and all that. She did quit her job for a while, but she got bored—that's how she put it—she doesn't have any idea of housekeeping, she hardly lifted a hand—about meals and so on, you know. She'd never had to— and then I guess she hasn't got all that out of her system, dancing or something every night, all the—excitement." He stuck there. But he'd drawn the picture, and a familiar and sad one it was.

"Mmh," said Jesse, taking notes. "She go out with other men if you wouldn't take her?"

"I—she might have," muttered Austin, "and I didn't know. A lot of times she'd just say she was going to see one of her girl friends, and— But I don't know. I never thought I'd get to this point. But I—it got so I couldn't take it. It got on my nerves, so they even noticed at the bank. I couldn't concentrate properly. A man wants some peace at home—a decent place to live, you know. Half the time when I came home she wasn't there, and the place in a mess—dirty dishes all over, those trashy magazines— And then again she'd invite a lot of her friends in, they'd be there until two or three in the morning, and the manager complaining—"

Mr. Austin had got himself into something, reflected Jesse. And not the first one. And now the poor devil would be paying alimony set by some unrealistic judge. "You left her. When?"

Austin licked his lips. "About a month ago. I'd tried, I talked to her and tried to make her see how she ought to settle down, but it was no go. I guess she just hasn't grown up yet. Some people don't, do they? I guess I got myself hooked all right—" He laughed unhappily. "By the pretty face and all. How many of us do? And find out afterward— Hell. But there it is. She's—she's quite something to look at. Different. And I suppose you've heard all this from other clients before."

Jesse smiled at him encouragingly. "You're not the first, and you won't be the last, Mr. Austin. Is your wife still living in the same apartment where you left her?"

"Oh, I think so. Probably. It's an old place on Francis Street." He added the address. "I know I got her there last week when I phoned to ask her to stop bothering me. I've been giving her twenty-five a week, it's about all I can afford what with the car payments and my own rent. . . . Oh, I moved to a hotel on Sixth Street. Not very fancy, but I couldn't afford—"

"Yes. You're a California resident. Is she?"

"I don't know, I suppose so. Yes, I think so because she said she'd come here about two years ago. She was—is, I suppose I should say—a kind of amateur singer. That's how I met her, and, well she *is* something, you know. But damn it, I never thought I'd get in a mess like this." Austin looked at him, rueful, angry. "Just another fool, and old enough to know better too. I should have seen what she was like. And

I suppose I'll have to pay her alimony now. Have I any grounds to *get* a divorce?"

"California judges are pretty lenient," said Jesse with a shrug. "She refused to keep a home for you, technically—did she ever refuse you, mmh, conjugal rights?"

"Oh, well, yes, of course," said Austin rapidly, looking embarrassed. "She's—just as fed up with me, you see. I guess I knew it'd never work a month after we were married. I think she married me, actually, because I was different from all the other men she knew—a—a square, maybe she'd say. You know? And then pretty soon she got fed up. No, she'd hardly be likely to contest a divorce, but if I know Tamar she'll try for all the alimony she can get." One hand clenched suddenly on the arm of his chair. "Silly, shallow little fool," he said under his breath. "Why I couldn't see her for what she was at the start—sit around drinking beer and singing with those oddball characters at The Cygnet, and— I was a square all right, thinking it was all so damned—fascinating. 'Oh, careless love—' My God, yes . . . Nothing," to Jesse's raised brows. "But you can get me a divorce?"

"Not much trouble, I don't think. And yes, we can try to stop her bothering you at your work. Now, I need a little more information, Mr. Austin—"

Austin answered questions dully, precisely. No, not the first man to get himself into such a situation, but Jesse supposed it must always feel like a unique situation. . . . "Well, I'll do my best for you, Mr. Austin," he said when they'd settled the retainer and he had all the facts he needed.

Austin stood up. "Thanks very much." And he added to himself, "Why in God's name did I go with Elliott that night? I could have turned him down— I could have said—and I'd never have met her. Do you believe in fate, Mr. Falkenstein?"

"*All things come alike to all: there is one event to the righteous and to the wicked*. . . . Or does Holy Writ have all the answers? I don't know," said Jesse absently. And on that one, he was suddenly thinking that if he'd just ignored Vic's telegram, or been tied up on another case, seventeen months back, he'd never have met Nell. Destiny? "I don't know."

"Well—" said Austin. "Well, thanks. You'll be in touch with me, then." He went out.

It was six o'clock. Get Austin's business started bright and early tomorrow. Jesse unfolded his lank seventy-four inches and stretched; reached for his hat. In the anteroom, Miss Williams was agitatedly sorting through papers from a file folder. "Oh, dear, Mr. Falkenstein, I don't know how it came to slip my mind, but I *completely* forgot about that Bergstrom contract, and, oh, *dear*, you wanted it for to-morrow—"

Jesse sighed. "Yes, well, if you wouldn't mind doing some overtime, or coming in early—the appointment's at eleven."

"Oh, I know, I'll just slip out for a tiny bite and start it right away, I'm so sorry, Mr. Falkenstein—"

"That's O.K.," said Jesse. Maybe he was a fool to keep the woman, but who else would hire her? Quite a nice woman, and oddly enough an efficient typist at least; and then there was the fact that he needn't pay her the astronomical salary a really good legal secretary would demand.

He went home, to the house on Rockledge Road above Hollywood Boulevard, which they'd bought instead of the one in View Park they'd considered. It was a nice house, of Nell's favorite Mediterranean design, and its generous yard was enclosed by a chain-link fence, which was half the reason they'd bought it. Jesse slid his Ford into the garage beside her baby Renault, and Athelstane whuffled loudly at him through the fence. Jesse opened the gate and braced himself, and Athelstane rose up lovingly, front paws on Jesse's shoulders, and washed his face. "So you're glad to see me," said Jesse, getting out his handkerchief. "All right, all right. And on second thought, if I hadn't met her I'd never have got saddled with you. A mastiff, for God's sake. Three pounds of meat a day."

Athelstane followed him into the service porch eagerly. After the February-evening chill outside, the house was pleasantly warm, and there was a succulent smell—Jesse sniffed hopefully—of baked ham and candied yams.

Poor Austin.

"Is that you, darling?"

"In person. And on third thought," said Jesse, kissing her and holding her away for a fond look, his lovely Nell with her long gray eyes and neat dark-brown chignon and slender roundness, "in spite of your saddling us with the monster, I'm not sorry I did meet you. *Who is rich? He who has a wife beautiful in deeds.*"

"Oh really?" said Nell. "Beautiful in deeds. A left-handed compliment if I ever heard one. And if you want a drink before dinner you've just got time."

At approximately the same moment, Sergeant Andrew Clock of Headquarters Homicide was replacing the outside phone and doing some swearing.

"Why the hell," he demanded of his desk blotter, "didn't I go to work in a bank or somewhere I'd have regular hours?"

"Well, why didn't you?" asked Detective Peter Petrovsky reasonably.

"Because I'm a damned fool," said Clock, "obviously. Go get Dale or whoever's at loose ends. We'll have to go look at this." He picked up the outside phone again, a gloomy expression on his craggy Neanderthal face with its jutting brow and jaw, and dialed the number of Miss Frances Falkenstein. . . .

"Well, really," said Fran crossly. "There isn't a thing in the place but breakfast food and a couple of eggs—I was going to shop tomorrow—and I'm starving. I see you can't help it, Andy—"

"Don't call me—"

"—but it is a nuisance. Why on earth I condescend to go out with a *cop*—"

Clock, who often wondered about it himself with a kind of prayerful awe—Fran, West Coast editor for a fashion magazine, looked more like one of its models—clutched the phone tighter in one big fist and said desperately, "I'm *sorry*, but—these things come up, after all—"

"Oh, I know, I know—duty before pleasure, and you the stern dedicated puritan you are—"

"Listen," said Clock, "I—"

"I know, I'll go wish myself on Jesse and Nell for dinner," said Fran. "Nell won't mind. And in a cab, so you can come and take me home when you've looked at your new corpse, darling."

"And don't call me that either, damn it. When you don't mean anything—" These career women, thought Clock gloomily. Everything happened to him. Why the hell he had to fall for—

Fran laughed, sweet and high. "Puritan. Have fun with your corpse, Andy. See you."

Putting down the phone, Clock swore again. That little harpy. Red nail polish and spike heels. He didn't like that kind of girl. But Fran—

well, Fran seemed to be the one. If he could ever get her to take him seriously, which was doubtful.

Dale and Petrovsky came into the office. With an effort Clock shoved Fran to the back of his mind. Somebody had to look at the corpses as they turned up, and the L.A.P.D. was always undermanned. In spite of being the top force anywhere.

"O.K., let's go and see what it looks like," he said abruptly.

L.A. was growing fast these days, splitting its seams; to keep up, a lot of tearing down and rebuilding was going on. One of the many current downtown projects was the enlarging of one entrance to the Harbor freeway. A whole block of ramshackle old houses on narrow little Holland Street was being knocked down to make room for the new lead-in. And near quitting time this chill Wednesday afternoon, the foreman of the city crew working its bulldozers at one end of Holland Street had called in excitedly to report the body.

So Clock went to look at it, with Dale and Petrovsky, and said, "What the hell do they expect us to do with a thing like this?" But there it was, a homicide; they had to start work on it.

It had been buried under the earth floor of a garage: the tumbledown old garage belonging to 2808 Holland Street. It hadn't been turned up by the bulldozers until both frame houses on the property had been demolished—2808 and 2808½. The foreman said, typical cheap old shabby houses.

It was the body of a man, and at a guess the body was anywhere from a year to two years old. This was sandy soil, which helped in preserving bodies; maybe the surgeon could tell them more than what was obvious at a first glance at the skull, that the body had had a severe bang on the head which had probably been the cause of death: the skull was cracked deeply. There were clothes: remnants of gabardine slacks; a once-white shirt; what might be a sleeveless sweater, gray or beige; the wreckage of a pair of brown moccasin-type shoes and a corduroy jacket, gray or beige.

Fortunately, the bulldozer hadn't inflicted any new injuries: just turned it up.

There were, in the pockets, a bunch of anonymous keys on a dimestore key chain (not even, damn it, an initial); an anonymous cheap plain white handkerchief; a half-empty packet of matches from The Brass Hat in Florence, Arizona; three pennies, a dime and a nickel; a

packet of matches, with two left in it, from The Keg Inn, Santa Rosa,
New Mexico; a half-full pack of king-size Chesterfield cigarettes; an
unopened purse-size package of Kleenex; a paper-backed Spanish-
English dictionary and two cheap ball-point pens.

"I ask you," said Clock bitterly. "I just ask you. My God."

"All right, Sergeant," said Petrovsky soothingly. Clock was always
pessimistic at the start of a case. "We've got to look. And routine
might turn up something. Ask Missing Persons and so forth."

"And so forth!" said Clock. "I know, I know." He looked at the
corpse again. That savage dent in the skull—a spade, something like
that?—something fairly sharp anyway. Pretty obviously murder, and in
his territory, so he had to start the hunt. He sighed. What a hope.
They'd be lucky to get an ident on the corpse after all this time.
"O.K.," he said heavily. "Let's get moving on it. Get a full description
from the surgeon—contact Missing Persons—I wonder if we've got a
hope of prints off him. The lab can work miracles sometimes. . . .
And you boys," he added to the foreman of the crew, who was hanging around interestedly, "can go knock down houses somewhere else.
We'll be busy sifting through every square inch around where he was.
And, my God, how can we pin it down, anyway? I'd guess anywhere
from eighteen months to two years back—and I know these areas, all
rented places and people drifting in and out."

"Well, we've got to look," said Dale through a yawn. "It's our job."

"And what a job," said Clock, thinking of Fran.

TWO

That was always the toughest kind of case there was, the anonymous corpse. The age of this one just made it that much tougher. There were a lot of things to do on it, a lot of routine to set working, but Clock didn't think they'd turn up much.

He couldn't get the routine started until he had something definite from the surgeon. It looked a little silly to ask priority on a corpse that old, but he did; Dr. De Villa had a look at it on Thursday morning, and had quite a bit to tell him about it, but would any of it help?

The body wasn't reduced to bare bones—that was the sandy soil—and it told this and that even yet. It was the body of a Caucasian male probably between twenty-two and twenty-five years old; the right leg had been broken below the knee some years before it became a body, and there were still traces of an old appendectomy scar. The teeth were good, a full set barring one missing molar; there were three fillings. The man had been six feet one inch tall and judging from the apparent size of the clothes, about normal in weight, maybe one-seventy to one-eighty. He had had brown hair and probably (not certainly) brown eyes.

The probable cause of death was a skull-smashing blow delivered from in front, with some fairly sharp and probably heavy weapon. The surgeon suggested a shovel or the edge of a two-by-four.

The lab men were very pessimistic about the possibility of getting the corpse's fingerprints. Meanwhile, they were working on what was left of the clothes. There was a label in the corduroy jacket, but it didn't help much. It said briefly and uninformatively, "The Man's Shop, 110 N. Main Street." Wherever The Man's Shop was, it wasn't on L.A.'s Main Street; it might be on any Main Street anywhere in the country, but they'd take a look at all those in this area, of course.

Nothing found on him was of the slightest use either in identifying him or pointing to a possible murderer.

Clock set some men hunting carefully all around the disturbed earth which had been the floor of that garage, where the bulldozer had turned up the body, and went back to headquarters to see Missing Persons. The surgeon, apologetically, had said anywhere between eighteen and twenty-six months; he couldn't pin it down closer with anything like certainty— "Though if I had to make a stab at it, Sergeant, just a guess, I'd say nearer two years." So Clock went up to Missing Persons to ask who they'd had on their books since two and a half years back—give it that much leeway—who might correspond to the description and had never been located.

He got quite a little list there. Which was natural, because the dead man had been fairly run-of-the-mill in looks, and this was a big town with a lot of people to keep track of; and they got inquiries from out of town and out of state too, from, in fact, all over the country. When they'd sorted through all the records for those crucial months they came up with twenty-one names. Missing Persons groaned in sympathy with Clock and said he sure had a job on this one.

Clock went down to Records and asked for all the flyers they had since that far back, from the Feds and elsewhere, and the present Wanted list to compare. Because maybe the corpse had been on that side of the fence. Going by the description, he got fourteen more names there, mostly smalltime pros, a couple of elevator men, one known killer still on the Most Wanted list.

Dale, Petrovsky and Lindner came in, still grimy, at the end of the afternoon, with a carton of flotsam gleaned from the earth which had once constituted the fairly large area of the floor of the garage on Holland Street. Clock looked at it and groaned again.

"We didn't think you'd want the various pieces of rusty metal or the old tennis ball or the inner tube," said Petrovsky.

"I don't know why you bothered with any of it," said Clock. "I ask you." There were three jacks from the child's game, and a couple of little plastic sticks of the kind you put in to mark plants, and a twisted, broken plastic calendar, the kind used for advertising; you could just make out the begrimed date, 1954. There was a child's shoe, very ancient and battered; an old pocket knife with both blades broken; a frayed piece of electrical wire; half or thereabouts of what had once been a table-tennis net; an old yo-yo minus its string; a dog collar, dime-store variety; a newish-looking empty beer can; half of an ace of spades; a blackly-tarnished silver St. Christopher medal with about an inch of tarnished chain hanging from it; and about half of an old paperback book. "Now I *ask* you," said Clock. He produced his list of names. "Shall we say eeny meeny miney mo?"

"Funny how people can just drop out of sight," commented Dale, looking at it. "But we know they do."

It was and it wasn't funny; settled people with families, living orderly lives, didn't—or not for long. But it was a big country and there were a lot of loners and drifters.

The two houses and single garage at 2808 Holland Street had been owned by a Mrs. Helen Manfred. She was now living at an address on Ward Street just a few blocks away. Clock went to see her on Friday morning.

It was probably about the same kind of house as the one on Holland had been: a shabby little frame house, two bedrooms, put up cheaply forty years ago and not much done to it since. It had a narrow strip of brown grass in front, and from the side you could see there was a smaller frame house behind it, and another ramshackle garage looking ready to fall down.

Mrs. Manfred was about sixty, stout and rather dirty in a torn cotton housecoat also in need of washing. She let him in reluctantly. She held a cracked teacup in one hand; it was half full of sharp-smelling red wine. "Police!" she said bitterly. "Police, now. What you want o' me? Nothin' but interference alla time—damn gov'ment gettin' too snoopy altogether, ask me—*interfering!* Makin' me sell my house for *twelve* thousand dollars— My God, way real estate is nowadays, I coulda got fifteen easy, if I'd'a wanted to sell, first place. What could I get for twelve thousand dollars? That had a rental on it? This place not near so good as the old one. But just try complainin'! You don't get nowhere. Well, whaddaya want, anyways?"

Clock explained economically. She didn't seem much concerned or interested about the corpse; she finished the wine, said, "Well, whaddaya know, that's funny, all right. Mighta been there for years, I s'pose, before I owned the place." Probably, he thought, nothing made much impression on Mrs. Manfred any more, except her grievance against the county or, maybe, running out of *vino*.

And as he'd foreseen, she was vague about her tenants. There'd usually been tenants in the little rear house, but they came and went. Of course he'd be taking a look at Mrs. Manfred too; you had to look everywhere. . . . "Well, I didn't pay so much notice to givin' receipts or such-like, they paid up or they didn't an' that was that. Records? Lordy, why'd I go writin' it all down somewheres? I already knew they'd paid or hadn't, an' if they didn't, they got out." She wouldn't, of course, have asked any references. It wasn't the best section of town, down here; it attracted the ones who lived hand-to-mouth, and a lot like that never stayed in one place for long.

He got a few names. "Them Whites, they had it quite a spell. Maybe six months, it was. Oh, well, as to *when* exactly—I'd hafta think— I seem to remember it was around Christmas they moved in—"

"Christmas two years ago this last December?" It was that eight months he was mainly interested in, December to July two years back.

"No, come to think, it'd be the year before. They went some time that next summer, an' then, lessee, them Popes moved in. Funny woman she was, persnickety-like. Lordy, washin' on the line near ever' day! They wasn't there long. Whassay? Oh lordy, how'd I remember the man's name? I guess 'twas George, John, some common name. He worked for the city, I recall her sayin'—" Mrs. Manfred heaved herself up. "Offer you a glass o' wine, mister?"

"No, thanks," said Clock; she looked relieved. She came back with a half-tumblerful this time, sat down and sipped. The shabby living room looked as if it hadn't been dusted in weeks; the curtains were torn and grimy, and the stuffing was coming out of gaping holes in the sofa. There was a smell of stale food and unwashed dishes.

"Then there was some Mex fella tried to rent it—I got rid o' *him* in a hurry, I never rented to no Mexes or Dagoes, like that. And then that young fella and his wife had it, Boyle, Doyle, some name like that. They wasn't there long either. I'm easygoin', ordinary, 'n' I don't mind folk havin' parties and so on, but they carried on so—wouldn't believe the noise—I finally hadda ask them, get out. When? Lordy, mister, time gets away from you," said Mrs. Manfred comfortably. "Roundabout, oh, maybe that fall. And after that I didn't have nobody for a spell, I hadda put an ad in about it, and then who had it? —would it've been them Kellys, or the Hoffs? No, it was the Hoffs had the dawg, musta been the Kellys first, and I couldn't put up with all them noisy kids—not that the dawg wasn't as bad—"

He made up a list as well as he could, and what good it was going to do him he didn't know. Try to track down all these people, look at them. Look at the Manfred woman: though he didn't see her burying a body in her garage, not without help anyway.

He could foresee the end of this one. There'd be an inquest, an open verdict, a burial in potter's field. They'd break their hearts at all the slogging routine, and come up with nothing legally usable. Even if they identified the corpse, turned up somebody with a motive to want him a corpse, what evidence would there be after all this time?

And as an experienced cop Clock knew that—whether they identified the corpse or not—there might not have been any motive to show. He might have been accidentally killed in a fight, or killed for what he had on him. The job would be more interesting, he reflected, if homicide was more like the paperback mysteries—really mysterious, and complex. Only an experienced cop could know how depressingly uncomplex it usually was.

He could wish the city engineers had picked some other street than Holland to dig up. Just to present him with another headache.

Jesse was interrupted at four thirty on Friday afternoon by Miss Williams' announcement that Mr. Austin was here. "And he's got his wife with him, at least she doesn't look—but he *said* so, and asked if you'd see—"

"Oh?" said Jesse. "Well, O.K." Had the fastidious Austin, possibly, reconciled with his unwifely Tamar? Odd name, he thought. He stood up as they came into the office.

Apparently there had been no reconciliation. Raymond Austin looked flushed and annoyed. "I'm very sorry to come like this, without warning, Mr. Falkenstein. But Tamar doesn't seem to understand—she insisted—I *told* her—"

"This injunction thing he said you were getting," she said. "I never heard about a thing like that. He's my husband, I don't see why I can't go see him when I want." She looked around the small office with the fleeting open curiosity of a child.

"I *told* you," said Austin. "I can't afford to—"

"What'd they do to me?" she asked Jesse. Her eyes wandered over him as curiously.

Well, in a way he could see why Austin had got hooked. Tamar would never have hooked him, but the conventional, respectable, probably not-very-experienced Austin— But she wasn't the type Jesse had expected. He looked at her interestedly.

The first thing he thought was that her name suited her. She was —different, all right. Not beautiful: and not the chocolate-box-cover shallow prettiness he might have expected, either. There was something, oddly, a little wild about her—a whiff of, what, lawlessness. Something outside all the rules.

She looked older than twenty-one. She had looks, of the pocket-Venus type, but she wasn't doing anything about herself at all. She had a lot of wild black hair, past her shoulders, and she hadn't even tied it back with a ribbon—it fell carelessly down her back. Sometime today she'd put on lipstick, but not much was left. She was wearing a pair of knitted black capri pants and a tight scarlet sweater that showed off her small rounded figure; but the sweater was stained down the front, and her bare feet in black thong sandals were dirty, toenails unmanicured. She had, he thought, an actress's face: not beautiful, but good bones. High cheekbones, a narrow jaw, a wide mouth. It was her eyes you noticed first: large eyes set very far apart, a curious topaz color under straight thick brows.

"You'll know me again, mister," she said. "Would they maybe stick me in jail? On this injunction thing? I don't get it. I don't care about a divorce—shoulda had better sense than to marry Ray, first place, but I was mad at Dickie, then. But he's got to give me some dough. Would they?"

"Would they what, Mrs. Austin?"

"Jeez, don't call me that." She looked at Austin resentfully. A long lock of hair fell across her forehead and she swept it back over her shoulder impatiently. "Shoulda had better *sense*. Put me in jail, I mean?"

"If you ignored the injunction?" Jesse shrugged. "It'd depend on the judge. You'd be held in contempt of court—"

"Double talk!" she said. She raised a hand to her mouth, chewed at a ragged nail; her hands were stubby-fingered, dirty, the nails uncared for. He looked at Austin curiously; and yet there was an animal magnetism to her. She exuded a raw vitality that cast its own attraction. He remembered Austin saying she hadn't grown up; that might be true in a very special sense. She was youth, all the pros and cons of it: crude physical energy, sex, vitality, irresponsibility, selfishness, rawness. But also an unyoung wariness. And while there was this vogue for the deliberate carelessness of clothes, make-up, well, she carried it rather far, didn't she? But there was, he supposed, a kind of attraction there too—for the very much opposite Austin.

Austin—well, the animal magnetism; but they made a funny pair, all right. Austin was looking at her with something like hatred, frustrated un-understanding.

"Tamar, I told you that—"

"I don't care about a divorce," she said to Jesse, not looking at Austin. "Let him pay the lawyers. I don't give a damn. They wouldn't put me in jail? Look, I'll make a bargain, see. He gives me five G's and I'll forget any alimony. I don't care. That's fair, ai—isn't it? I said—"

"I couldn't raise five thousand dollars!" Austin sounded goaded. "It's crazy! I told you. I would if I could, God knows! I couldn't raise two thousand, cash. Well, maybe that. But—"

"Five," she said. "I'd make a deal for five. I'd level with you for that. Right now, see."

"I can't—"

"You got those things," she said. "Those stock things. Like on Wall Street, they talk about." Her voice was flat, emotionless.

"I can't—that's *savings*," said Austin, sounding shocked. "Besides, that would only realize about two thousand—God knows, to be done with it for good, I—" And then he said, "Why, Tamar? I don't understand. Why would you—"

The banker's mind, thought Jesse. Why indeed. The way judges allotted alimony, without stopping to think in realistic terms, she could take him for a lot more than five thousand, over a period of time.

She moved her shoulders impatiently. "A thing's finished, it's finished. I'm sick o' this burg. Maybe go back to Chicago, awhile. It was O.K. at first, but I get fed up with places. And Theo said—" She looked at Austin with dislike. "Turned it all on the blue, when I took up with you. Musta been out of my mind. See, you raise me the five G's and I'll be happy."

Jesse's curiosity rose to fever pitch. Oh, really, he thought.

"I can't—"

"Can't you make him?" she asked Jesse directly. As naïve as a child: as ignorant. And her extraordinary eyes wise in other ways.

"Well, if he hasn't got it—" said Jesse. He was unwillingly fascinated. He wondered what Andrew Clock would think about Tamar; he thought he knew.

"Oh," she said. "Well, it don't seem fair, all I can say." Austin suddenly looked murderous. Jesse thought, The little things. Austin precise, upright, educated: white-collar man. The unlikely glamour of Tamar dead for him, maybe the grammatical slips annoying him more than the greediness, the childishness.

"Damn it," he began, "can't I make you see—"

"I'm sick o' this burg, I want out," she said—still to Jesse. "That's all. He raises all the cash he can, I'll play it level 'n' get out. Hell with any alimony. I always got along O.K. I'm broke, and I owe Jimmy for them—those geetar lessons, an' the back rent. You raise a couple of G's, Ray, we call it square."

"I told you, I can't sell securities—*capital*," said Austin, outraged.

"You might find it a good deal cheaper in the long run, Mr. Austin," Jesse put in quietly. "If Mrs. Austin waived alimony—"

"That's right, you tell him," she said. "And I got to go meet Jimmy, you can drive me, Ray." She brushed back the wild mop of hair and turned to the door, turned back and flashed an absently seductive smile at Jesse. "You tell him. I guess I might try Chicago again awhile. He can raise the dough, tomorrow maybe. O.K.?"

Austin looked from her to Jesse. "It's crazy," he muttered. "I can't—" She went out into the anteroom, rounded hips swaying in the tight pants. "My God," said Austin. "I'm sorry about this, Mr. Falkenstein. You—see how she is. I'm sorry." He went out after her.

Ray Austin and his little problem had been rather ordinary business up to now. Now, Jesse found himself considerably interested.

He wondered if it would be worthwhile to ask Clock about Tamar. On the long chance. He might just do that.

THREE

The corpse wasn't Edward Bristow from the Missing Persons list. A check with his mother, who had filed the missing report, revealed the fact that Bristow had turned up hale and hearty about a year ago; he'd just got mad at his wife and left and got a job up in Alaska. "He never was much of a one for letter-writin'," said his mother. Nobody had thought of notifying the police, of course.

The corpse was equally not one Fred Clinton, wanted by the Feds since three years back on a couple of counts, a Mann Act violation and passing bad checks. Petrovsky, leafing through the list, had vaguely remembered reading something about Clinton recently and checked. The New Orleans police had picked him up last week.

Just to be thorough about the routine, they sent everything from that unsavory collection of flotsam down to Prints, to see if anything could be got there. It was doubtful. It wasn't likely that any of that was connected with the corpse; none of it had been found very near the grave.

By Monday, they were still hard at work at the routine; they probably would be for some time. They had located some of Mrs. Manfred's former neighbors, asked questions about her and her former tenants. It was hard to say whether what they got there meant anything, though some of the neighbors could tell them more about the tenants.

Mrs. Manfred had owned the Holland Street property for about fifteen years. Most people seemed to like her well enough— Oh well, everybody knew she was a bit of a wino, but harmless enough, they said, and easygoing. People down there tended to be easygoing, as a rule: live and let live. One thing that emerged was that around two years ago Mrs. Manfred had rented her spare bedroom. "It was some old gent," said a neighbor vaguely. "I remember people kind of kidded about it, called him her boy friend." Another neighbor remembered his name, Jack Battuck; so they had a casual look, and a little to Clock's surprise found him in Records.

He'd been picked up twice on a D.-and-D. count, and once for assault. Actually a brawl in a bar; but Clock looked at that record thoughtfully. He could see a man who had a hasty temper cracking that skull impulsively, getting stuck with a corpse. And the vague, easygoing Mrs. Manfred—

Still, "an old gent" and a big healthy young man? He could have been taken by surprise. But if Mrs. Manfred knew the corpse had been buried there, wouldn't she have shown some reaction? And if she hadn't known, she must have guessed when she heard about the corpse— Why the lack of reaction?

Well, she was a wino. In a pleasant haze most of the time, probably. Time didn't mean much to her; two years ago was an age back, she could have forgotten what she did know.

Clock thought in any case he'd like to talk to Jack Battuck. He put out a call on him.

They had found the Popes on Saturday, easily, because George Pope was a city employee, a laborer in the Parks and Recreation department. Beyond a violent denunciation of Mrs. Manfred as a dirty, disgraceful old woman—"I scrubbed that kitchen floor half a dozen times before I got it really clean!"—from Mrs. Pope, they didn't get much there. The Popes looked very unlikely as possibly connected with a mysterious corpse: a middle-aged couple, childless, nothing known against them. He had a clean record with the city.

They got a little more information from the neighbors about the other tenants, which might help in locating them. One couple who'd rented the little rear house within the significant times, a Mr. and Mrs. Royball, were believed to have gone back east to Cairo, Illinois. Clock sent out a request to the Cairo police on them. You just had to try everywhere, cover every possibility.

Always with the conviction born of experience that, barring some very lucky breaks, you wouldn't get anywhere.

On the whole, he wasn't sorry when a new homicide call came in just before noon on Monday. He took Detective Joe Lopez, the only man available, along with him and went out to look at it.

It was a middle-class apartment building on Francis Street, close in downtown: about twenty apartments. It had been in need of paint for some time; downtown dirt coated it thickly. The narrow front hall, with its row of wall mailboxes, smelled of dust. A little crowd of eager-eyed, interested people milled around there talking excitedly: other tenants. A scrawny old man in an ancient flannel bathrobe said avidly, "You more cops? It's the second floor—number twenty-eight. They told us stay down here, but they let Mr. Pierson go up—"

Clock and Lopez climbed stairs. It was an apartment door halfway down on the left side: the door was open, and people stood around. Two uniformed men (they'd be from the squad car first on the scene), a young man, a young woman, a big paunchy man in shirtsleeves. The ambulance boys had just got here: Clock could see a white coat past the door.

As they came up, the big man was talking. "Musta been her husband, right enough. He was here, I know that—about seven thirty it'd've been, I come up to dun her for the rent she owed, see, and he was here then. Sure I know him!—he lived here himself quite a while, didn't he? And they were havin' an argument then, you could hear her all the way from the head o' the stairs. Something about money—"

Clock introduced himself and said, "Let's have it from the start, but I'll take a look at the corpse first." He and Lopez went into the apartment.

An old apartment, but these old places with larger rooms could be made pleasant. This one wasn't. The funny thing was, Clock felt, looking around, that it once had been. The furniture was old but good, looked like carefully chosen secondhand pieces: a long plain couch, a pair of walnut tables, a walnut coffee table, a couple of upholstered chairs in neutral colors and a plain beige rug on the floor. The door at the left led into a small kitchen and dinette; he could see a confusion of piled dirty dishes on the dinette table. The door at the right would lead to the bedroom; that was apparently where the corpse was. There were a couple of pleasant framed landscapes on the walls; in one corner was a cabinet phonograph with several record racks alongside it.

The room was wildly untidy, but it was more than a day's or a week's untidiness. Dust lay in a thin film over everything—except the phonograph, he noticed. The furniture was haphazardly arranged, looking as if it had been pulled out of its usual places and just left. Lampshades were crooked. Something had been spilled on the carpet beside the kitchen door and made a dark stain. All the ashtrays were overflowing; a cardboard carton in the middle of the room was evidently in use as a wastebasket and was full of crumpled paper napkins, cigarette stubs, empty beer cans, oddments. The two windows had old-fashioned shades and thin glass curtains; one of the shades had come off one end of its roller and hung at a crazy angle; the other was rolled all the way up.

Lopez looked around and said laconically, "Somebody had a fight."

"Funnily enough," said Clock, "I don't think so." He went on into the bedroom.

The body was on the floor between the bed and the windows. He went closer and looked at it. The interns knew enough not to fool with it much, but he asked, "How and when do you figure?"

"Just at a guess, fourteen to eighteen hours," said the biggest intern. "Pretty obvious she was strangled. Knocked around a little first." He lifted the head by the hair—she lay prone on the floor—to show the face: Clock nodded. He had briefed De Villa and the other necessary men; at sounds in the other room he turned—that would be them.

"O.K.," he said. "You can have her in a while." He passed the surgeon, the photographer and the boys from Prints in the disheveled living room, went back to the corridor where the big man was still holding forth. "All right, let's take this in order now. Who found her?"

"I did," said the young man. "Leastways, Jeanie and me did. I'm Lee Davenport, sir." He spoke with something near a drawl; the "sir" was nearly "suh." Clock looked at him and the girl beside him.

He couldn't place Davenport at a glance. Not an ordinary young man, but what was different about him? A lanky fellow about twenty-eight, sandy coloring, long thin face, wide grave mouth. Not bad looking. His sandy-blond hair just a little longer than ordinary, not much. He wore pale green slacks, a lighter green sports shirt, a dark green cardigan, all very neat and clean; his gray moccasins were polished. He held a battered-looking guitar case in one hand.

The girl was younger, and scared and unhappy. About twenty, a pretty little blonde. In fact, thought Clock gloomily, exactly the kind of girl he'd intended someday to settle down with—before he'd met Fran Falkenstein. (And hadn't he told Jesse he'd rue the day he first walked into his office!) She had a pink and white complexion, and her long wavy blond hair was coiled back into a neat ponytail, with fluffy bangs across her forehead; her eyes were very blue. She wasn't as sartorially elegant as Davenport, though; she was wearing wrinkled white capri pants and a blue overblouse, with a tan car coat clutched round her.

"Oh, it's just too awful!" she said shakily. "I c-can't take it in, some-how! We just saw her yesterday afternoon—"

"And this is Miss Jeanie Carlson, sir," said Davenport. "We came on account we were all going to have lunch together. We were going on to rehearse some at my place. We'd set up to do the 'Fair Elinor' for the bunch tonight, and she needed rehearsin' on that one. Not my idea." He spoke precisely, gravely.

The girl turned on him. "You were down on her, that's all! You didn't really like her. She—"

"I don't like it insulted," he said softly. "You got to sing it right or not try."

The girl made a sound between a sob and a giggle. Clock said, "You had a lunch date with her—both of you. O.K., take it from there."

"We c-came," said Jeanie Carlson, "and she didn't open the door when I knocked—but we knew she'd be here, she was expecting us."

"You knew," said Davenport detachedly. "Far as I knew her, she might've forgot all about it, or just not felt like openin' the door. She was that way."

"But I had a key—you see, I stayed here with her for a couple of weeks, just up to last week when I— And I *knew* something must be wrong, and so I— We went in and f-found her—"

The big man broke in. "And they came and got me—I'm the man-ager here, Pierson's the name, sir—and I called the police, and then I goes up to see for myself. No *sir*, I never touched a thing, I know bet-ter than that! I just looked, see, and right away I says to myself, It was her husband did it. And maybe with good reason too, the poor bas-tard. What I seen—well, you can see how she kept the place—she wasn't no wife to him at all. They had a lot of arguments before he fin'lly moved out. Not that he was noisy about it, but she didn't give a damn who heard what. The times I had to complain about that pho-nograph, and her wild parties! And he was here last night, see? I saw him—I come up to dun her for the back rent, tell her if she didn't pay up she'd have to get out by the first—and they were arguing again, her asking him for money and him saying he couldn't give her any right away. That much I heard—"

"What time?" asked Clock.

"It was twenty past seven when I come up, I'd just looked at the clock before. And he was still here when I left, he told me he'd see the rent was paid. My God, as nice a young fellow as you'd want to meet, and a big cut above her kind, never any trouble when he lived here alone, it was all her—but I can see how he maybe just couldn't take any more off her, lost his temper and—"

It was a nice lead, anyway, thought Clock. The intern said, between six and midnight. De Villa would probably narrow it down further. That put a suspect on the spot at what might be the right time. And automatically you looked first at the husband or wife. It was a thing to check.

"You!" said Jeanie Carlson bitterly to Davenport. "You had to go off on some crazy kick! Last night—she wouldn't have *been* here, we were going up to Jimmy's to rehearse—she'd have been with us, all safe! If she hadn't been home alone—!" She started to cry.

Lee Davenport carefully leaned his guitar case against the wall. He straightened up and lounged against the wall beside it, head thrown back, hands in pockets; his eyes were half-closed. "There was a need in me for the blues," he said. "A cryin' need for the blues I had. I had to go down to Central after the blues—good blues. Whites can't sing the blues, and they all know me at the Ace-High. . . . Theo said, Let her in with you a few times, no hurt. But it was a hurt to sing with her. Last night I didn't want to listen to her. I had a need for the blues."

Clock stepped closer to him. Reefers? Or what else? Davenport's tone was dreamy, relaxed. "Mr. Davenport!" said Clock sharply.

He opened his blue eyes full. "Yes, sir?"

"What's your occupation?" Nothing to show in the eyes; the pupils were normal.

Davenport smiled slightly. "I'm a musician, sir. We don't always get appreciated financial-wise in the right places, but we've still got to eat. I also work a job at Lockheed, runnin' an infernal machine, sir. I did not like the girl, no, but it wasn't me who choked her to death. Not me."

"Well," said Clock. He felt a little bewildered, which was unusual and made him mad. He couldn't place Davenport at all. He asked, "What can either of you tell me about her? Her associates? You both knew her well?"

"She was—she was so *different*," choked Jeanie Carlson. "Not like anybody else! She was—sort of fascinating. Oh, everybody liked her. Who could've wanted to—? She was so kind to me— I just c-can't believe it—"

"Little Jeanie," said Davenport. He sounded unaccountably sad. "Little girl not grown up. Nice little girl. Neither was she, but not a nice little girl."

"She was a singer?" asked Clock. He continued to feel out of his depth, which made him madder. He looked at Davenport suspiciously.

"Yes, she— Oh, only amateur yet but—"

"She sang," said Davenport. His eyes were half-shut again. "The popular band bit, could be she wouldn't have hurt. That doesn't matter, that. Froth. But the real thing, she hurt. I heard it. She didn't understand it in the guts, which is where it's got to come from. Ah, she didn't understand it at all. She was one of those saw it like a thing— like any new fashion—the thing to do. The outside thing. She never felt it in the guts. More like that than the rest of us. And we can't help it. There it is."

"Oh, for heaven's sake!" said Jeanie Carlson. "You! Sounding like— making it a—a mystic rite or something! And we'd *arranged* it all—we were going to have dinner and then go up to Jimmy's— You had to go off just because you didn't feel like it, all of a sudden, so she was home alone and some *fiend*—"

"I had a need for the blues," said Davenport. "I didn't want to listen to her last night. She insulted the music, that one. She wanted to use it for herself. You can't do that and have it go along with you willin'. It's the only honest-to-God honest music there is. It won't stand for that."

"If you hadn't—"

"Honey," said Davenport, "it wasn't me. If she was meant to go that road, and it doesn't surprise me any, she'd have gone, yesterday, today, tomorrow. Whoever did it."

Clock felt that the situation was slipping away from him. He said, "Mr. Davenport, would you mind telling me where you were between six o'clock and midnight last night?"

Davenport gave him a slow smile. "No, sir, not at all. I got off work at four and I met Jeanie and—her," he nodded at the apartment door, "for dinner roundabout five thirty, at Giorgio's on Spring Street. The way Jeanie says, we'd meant to go on to Jimmy Antropus' place to rehearse, but it came over me it was a night to listen to the blues, and I went down to the Ace-High on Central Avenue. Benny Lovelace and a lot of others, they can tell you I was there until past closin'. I sat in for Eli on piano, but I didn't do much singin', though Benny asked—he did. Well, maybe I gave them a couple verses of 'Poor Boy,' but no white man can sing blues. And I went home and to bed, sir. That's all."

"Home being where?" And Davenport answered readily. Clock couldn't place Davenport worth a damn; an offbeat one. He let them go when he'd got the girl's address; he started, with Lopez and others, to poke around. See what showed.

What showed pinpointed the husband rather definitely. He was placed on the spot at the right time; there was evidence of quarreling between them. The neighbors on both sides of the apartment had overheard some of last night's argument. There was a nice torn-up check, dated and signed. At the very least, the husband was the first one he wanted to talk to. On what was in so far, it looked pretty open and shut.

It was two o'clock, only a couple of hours since the body had been found. Clock had a belated lunch and went to talk to the husband. And it started to look even more open and shut. The old familiar story.

In spite of that offbeat character Davenport, who had probably been exactly where he said he was, at a Negro night club down on Central Avenue. (And, what the hell! Those places, most of them, pretty exclusive about welcoming whites.)

The husband was staring at him like a rabbit transfixed by a cobra. "You can't mean—!" he said incredulously. "You don't think *I* did—that? *Murdered*— I can't believe—" He ran a hand over his hair, harassed. "My God," he said. "My God. It was a mess before, but this—!" And he added abruptly, "Can I call my lawyer?"

"You can call a lawyer any time," said Clock. "I just want to question you." But he had a little surprise hearing what lawyer Austin was calling.

FOUR

"—Born unto trouble, as the sparks fly upward," said Jesse unhappily. "I don't like criminal cases. Why do I keep getting dragged into them?"

"Well, I haven't charged him yet," said Clock. They both looked at Raymond Austin, sitting at the table in this interrogation room at headquarters, from where they conferred on the threshold. "But he looks like the number-one suspect."

"I don't know, Andrew," said Jesse. "Only met him twice, but he doesn't strike me as the kind apt to fly off the handle. Incipient banker, you know."

"Cross out the rules," said Clock, "when there's a female in it. But I haven't asked for a warrant yet. I want to poke around, see who else she knew. Just for fun. Just in case."

"That's my boy," said Jesse approvingly. "Association with me improving your intellect. *Teach thy tongue to utter, 'I do not know.'*"

"Who said that?"

"Forget whether it was Rabbi Meir or Rabbi Jochanan."

Austin had been watching them; now he got up restlessly and came a few steps toward them. "What's this all about? You're supposed to be talking to me, not him," he said a little fretfully to Jesse. "My God, all I know is they say somebody's murdered Tamar— My God, I can't imagine who'd— They can't think *I* had anything to do with it, can they? Well, I can see—but—"

"All right, take it easy, Mr. Austin," said Jesse soothingly. "Andrew just wants to ask you some questions right now. He's getting cautious, and time too. Awhile back he jumped the gun on another client of mine and I had to put in some overtime showing him he was wrong. Maybe he'll think twice here."

"So your clients are all automatically innocent," said Clock. "That ought to make it easy. Sit down, Mr. Austin."

"Oh," said Austin. He looked from Clock to Jesse. "You—know each other."

"For my sins," said Clock with a sigh, sitting down opposite him.

"That murder—last year," said Austin dully. "It was you found the murderer, wasn't it, Mr. Falkenstein? I remembered your name, it was actually the reason I came to you— I wasn't sure about the California divorce laws, I thought if anybody could—"

"Mmh," said Jesse. He'd rather wondered about that, his office being in Hollywood and Austin working and living downtown. Criminal cases of some practical use, at that: advertisement.

"But what—tell me about Tamar, how— What happened?"

"She was strangled," said Clock, watching him. "Last night, some time between six and midnight. We'll pin it down a little closer. Actually we know she was alive at around seven thirty, don't we, because Mr. Pierson saw both of you in the apartment then. You seemed to be having quite a fight about something."

"Oh my God," said Austin. "How did I ever get into this mess? Acting as if I was about eighteen—a month later I knew I'd been a fool, but—there it was, damn it." He looked at Jesse. "You saw how she was. Like a—an ignorant kid, about a lot of things. Yes, I was there but we didn't have a fight exactly. I just couldn't explain to her, she couldn't get it through her head. You remember what she said about the money?"

Jesse nodded; Clock said, "What money?" so Jesse gave him the background on that. "You don't say," said Clock, rubbing his jaw thoughtfully. "So she was anxious to get out of town? She didn't give any reason?"

"Tamar was like that," said Austin. "A thing came into her head, she'd do it the next minute. There probably wasn't any reason—just, all of a sudden she got bored here. I don't know. But when she said she'd take all the cash I could raise and be satisfied, I— Well, you can see it was a break for me. In a way. You pointed that out, Mr. Falkenstein. I mean, I wouldn't have to pay alimony. I suppose you'd have wanted her to sign something to that effect, or she could—"

"How right you are," said Jesse. "Women being unpredictable."

"She's—she was unpredictable all right," said Austin. "Well, about the only assets I have—had—were common stock. I've been saving as I can, and I've got an account with a brokerage downtown. It went against the grain to do it, I can tell you, but when she said that, I phoned my broker to sell out everything. I knew about what it'd come to, a little under two thousand. Actually it's eighteen hundred seventy-nine forty-three—I got the statement this morning. Well, I went to see Tamar last night to tell her, and say I'd have the check on Wednesday or Thursday. She didn't understand why they hadn't sent me the money right away. You see, there's a four-day gap between the actual sale of securities and the final settlement—you know that? She couldn't understand it, she wanted the money right then. I said as soon as I got the check she could have it, but it'd probably be Thursday. She got pretty worked up—like a child, you know how she was—" He looked at Jesse. "I guess she thought I was holding on to it deliberately. She kept talking about Chicago. I don't know, I can see how Pierson thought it was a fight—she was yelling her head off, and I was trying to explain—"

"There was a torn-up check you'd written," said Clock.

"Yes, sure." Austin was a little calmer, seeing that he was being listened to and not threatened with the third degree; he leaned forward, anxious to explain. "She was pretty incoherent, but I gathered that she needed some money right away, and I knew I could write a check up to a hundred and still be safe—my salary's due in a week, and by then I'd have the brokerage check. By then I was feeling—oh Lord, anything to pacify her halfway, you know. So I said I could let her have a hundred right then, and I wrote that check. Only then she got mad all over again and said she wasn't taking off with a piddling C-note, how'd she know I'd ever send her the rest, and she tore up the check. Well, I saw it was no use trying to get her to understand, so I cut it short and walked out."

"What time?"

"It'd have been—oh, a little after eight, around there. My God, why should I have murdered her? I didn't have any reason to— My God, I wouldn't kill anybody, reason or not! I—"

"Nobody's said you did," said Clock, and added, "yet. You might just have lost your temper at the way she was acting. Did you?"

"No," said Austin shortly. "I'd heard Tamar in a tantrum before. It was just—damned annoying. . . . *Yet?* My God, it'll be bad enough if it gets in the papers you questioned me—if you— Dear God, what Mr. Raglan would say! Look, Sergeant, I've got a—a position to hold on to. Banks are like Caesar's wife—you don't know—"

"Just don't borrow trouble," Clock soothed him. "What was she doing when you left?"

Austin laughed without humor. "Jumping up and down on that torn-up check and swearing. My God above, how I could have been such a fool—! But she had a—a kind of fascination, I don't know how to explain it, but—until you got to know her, what she was like—" His voice trailed off.

Well, that was Austin's story and he wouldn't change it for the asking. Jesse looked at Clock. "Quite plausible, Andrew. And a couple of points, aren't there?"

"Yes, well, early to say. Yes—she didn't want to wait three or four days to get out of town. Maybe it'd be interesting to know why?"

"Oh, that was just Tamar," said Austin wearily. "When she wanted a thing it had to be right now."

Jesse raised one brow at Clock, who sighed at him. Was Austin so naïve as not to see that Tamar's eagerness to get out of town could indicate that she was afraid of someone here? Or hadn't that meant anything, and was he underlining it that naïve way to emphasize it for them?

"Tell me about her friends," said Clock. "The ones you knew. By the way, that was your apartment, wasn't it? Your furniture?"

"That's right," said Austin. He massaged his forehead wearily. "I figured she could stay there until the divorce—it was easier than arguing at her to move out. I was giving her twenty-five a week, all I— Actually she was earning a living, you know. She'd gone back to work— in the coffee shop at the Plaza Hotel."

"I thought she was a singer," said Clock.

"Oh—that. It was—a fad," said Austin. "She was in with this bunch —a lot of different kinds of people hang around a few places like that. People interested in folk music. Types—and some professionals, too, of course. Elliott could tell you all about them. He's doing his master's thesis on folk music and he knows all the locals and a lot of others. It's— Sometimes they can be interesting, it depends on who turns up. I went with Tamar quite a few times, for a while. The Cygnet—that's one of the local places—I met her there. She was going around with one of that crowd then, that's how she'd got interested. Only I think it was just a passing craze with her—she took things up and dropped them, you know."

"By any chance was her boy friend Lee Davenport?"

"*Davenport*," said Austin in surprise. "Oh no. Davenport's a cut above the steady crowd there, he's a professional. I think he's made a couple of records. He's good, Elliott says."

"Who is this Elliott?" Clock was taking notes.

"Elliott Carey. He teaches in a junior high in Inglewood. We knew each other in the army, ran into each other again a couple of years ago, we're about the same age, and— He took me to The Cygnet the first time."

"Where is it?"

"It's a hole-in-the-wall club out on Western—way out. All the regulars are folk-music fans, a lot of them amateur singers themselves, and sometimes they provide all the show, sometimes there are professionals. People trying to break in, people still not very well-known. Like Davenport."

"Did she know him well?"

"I don't think so, no. There was Theo Grafton, I gather he owns part of the club—and the one she'd gone around with was Dick somebody, I don't remember his last name. There were some other girls—Betty Lewis and Rita Garcia and Pat, I don't know her last name either, and—oh Lord, I can't remember half the names, Sergeant. They weren't my crowd, you know. Maybe a dozen times after we were married she had a bunch of them in for a party, but they all knew each other so well, they didn't pay much attention to me. I wasn't their kind. Not to sound snobbish, but—"

"You didn't care much for them?"

Austin shook his head. "Some of them were O.K. Grafton's all right, he's a serious sort of fellow, really interested in music. But most of them are—" he shrugged— "I don't mean beatniks, anything like that, but—this folk music was just the latest kick for them, if you get me. The kind of—of immature people who think life's just—getting as much fun as you can. You know. They just sat around listening to records or singing, and getting tight, and a couple of times they got to singing—well, some pretty raw stuff. You know."

Neither Clock nor Jesse knew. "Folk music?" asked Clock. "Like—'On Top of Old Smoky' and so on?"

Austin smiled. "It's not all like that. Some of it's—there was even some of that stuff on *records*." He sounded faintly outraged. "Well, I don't think I'm a prude, but I didn't like it. And they'd get noisy— Pierson came up to complain a few times."

"Well," said Clock. "Let's go back to last night. When did you get home—back to your hotel? You left her about eight. Go straight there?"

Austin hesitated. "I—well, no," he said awkwardly. "No. I— The fact is, I—er—decided to have a drink. I don't as a rule, and I hadn't any liquor at the hotel, of course, so I stopped at a bar just down the street from the apartment. I didn't really notice when I got home— maybe the night clerk would remember—"

"Don't think we won't ask," said Clock genially. "More than one drink?"

"I—a couple," said Austin. He moved restlessly, avoiding Clock's eye. "My God, what Mr. Raglan would— Look, all this won't be in the *papers*, will it? My God, I can't help it if my wife gets murdered—"

"What, don't bankers take an occasional highball?" Clock was amused.

"Drinking isn't encouraged," said Austin stiffly. "I—now I remember, I don't think the clerk was on the desk when I came in. I went straight to bed, I don't—"

"Oh, you did?" said Clock. "Leaving your wife's place at eight o'clock, even if you nursed a couple of drinks along, it couldn't have been more than an hour, an hour and a half? You went to bed about nine thirty?"

"No, I—oh, damn it," said Austin. "It was a little later."

"How much later?"

Austin looked at Jesse a little wildly. "Look, I'm not a criminal, he can't treat me as if— Can't you—"

Jesse contemplated his cigarette. "*When the ox is down many are the butchers.* Wise sayings of the rabbis. It's just as well to get the truth on record, Mr. Austin. I'd like to hear it too." He raised steady eyes to Austin, and Austin flushed miserably.

"Oh, for God's sake," he said. "I feel like such a damn fool, that's all. Look, I'm not a—a prude or a—mama's boy. The conventions— Damn it, I got a Commended for sharpshooting in the army!—but it's just, well, my kind of job and all, people always seem to think office men are— And banks don't exactly encourage—roistering. I never did drink much—I don't smoke at all, just don't care for it—and, well, a little liquor *affects* me, you know. I was—upset—last night. The way she carried on. Childish. I don't like rows like that, and—well, I was just fed up. And then too, I knew I'd be rid of her pretty soon, and that was—something to celebrate, if you get me. I went into that bar, as I said, and I think I had about four highballs. I think four. Anyway, I—I got pretty high, you see. Enough so I had the sense not to try to drive. I left the car on the street and took a cab back to the hotel. I don't know what time it was." He was still flushed; he looked down at the table. "There was a parking ticket—when I picked it up this morning."

"Oh, really," said Clock.

"My God, you don't think I—"

Clock didn't say what he was thinking. "Mr. Austin," he said, "are you thinking of marrying again? Have you, in other words, found a new girl friend before or after leaving your wife?"

Austin looked up with what seemed to be genuine astonishment; his thin sallow face suddenly took on a lopsided smile not without its own charm. "No, Sergeant," he said. "A thousand times no. I'm not a queer either, but right now I'm feeling like that fellow in the folk song—'I've got no use for women.'" The smile twisted. "Always supposing you don't get me sent to the gas chamber for a murder I didn't do, could be I'll feel different someday, but right now, no."

"Well," said Clock again, and stood up. "I want to do some looking around, Mr. Austin, but—don't leave town. I'll be in touch with you."

"I'll bet," said Austin. "I can go now? I've read a few detective stories, Sergeant— I realize I'm your prime suspect. But I didn't do it. I really didn't."

"Suppose," said Jesse, putting out his cigarette, "you wait a few minutes while I have a word with our pet bloodhound here. Few questions I'd like to ask you, over a cup of coffee maybe. O.K.?"

"Well, O.K.," said Austin with a shrug.

"You can see he's the obvious one to tag X," said Clock.

"*Who gains wisdom? He who is willing to receive instruction from all sources*," said Jesse. "Way I read him, Austin isn't one to fly off the handle, Andrew. Not so easy. Kind that keeps it all inside—nurturing incipient ulcers. What did he do? He went and had a few drinks to settle himself."

"Which he admits is unprecedented," said Clock. "He might have been upset—more than he said—because he'd lost his temper and killed her, not meaning to."

"I don't like that much," said Jesse. "She'd thrown tantrums at him before."

"The last straw."

"Oh, it could be," said Jesse. "But I don't feel he's your boy, Andrew. I really don't."

"You and your feelings."

"All right. Said the same thing to you once before, and it turned out you were wrong."

Clock laughed and massaged his Neanderthal jaw. "Oh, I know, I know," he said. "*Ten measures of wisdom came into the world; the law of Israel received nine measures, and the balance of the world one*. Naturally, you've got to be right."

"My God, a literate cop," said Jesse. "Since when do you read the Talmud? Always thought that sounded a little bit prejudiced, myself. Special pleading. However. Don't claim to be infallible, but he doesn't feel right for that kind of murder, somehow. The banker type. Incipient stuffed shirt. Looking down his nose at the ribald songs. Such a sober, upright, cautious fellow. Crime of passion? Don't see it."

"Still waters," said Clock. "Just the type, ask me. I'll look, of course. Elsewhere—who else might have had a reason, and so on. But he's the obvious favorite. He's placed there at the right time, and—"

"You might," said Jesse meditatively, "take a little look for Tamar in Records. I'd thought of asking you to, just for fun. Or ask about her record wherever she came from. Because she came out with a couple of things—didn't you pick up that 'C-note'? When she was in my office, she said among other things that everything had gone on the blue since she took up with Austin. Suggestive?"

Clock said mildly, "Be damned. She did? The pro slang. Well, well."

"If we're exchanging quotations," said Jesse, "I'll remind you, *Two pieces of coin in one bag make more noise than a hundred*. You've got this and that to make Austin look like X, and sure, of course he's obvious. Maybe too obvious. If you delve a little deeper you might find another couple of candidates. Don't say yes or no. Naturally like to think so—he's my client."

"Sure," said Clock. "But he is damn obvious. And I don't run the homicide bureau. If I don't come up with anything definite otherwise,

Austin such an obvious suspect and some nice evidence on him, I'll have to charge him, you know. You don't convince me halfway, Jesse. We both know that the obvious answer is usually the right one. We've heard a story from him, without pressure. If he was really grilled— hell, you know how nice we are to suspects these days, but under sustained questioning, could be he'd break down and come out with something different. How she made him so mad he just went for her blind—everything went blank, et cetera. Homicide's generally damn uncomplicated."

"True," said Jesse. "Like this anonymous corpse-buried-in-garage you've got on your hands. Probably an impulsive fight over a girl or a poker hand, *kaput,* and the bright idea how to get rid of the body. You getting anywhere on that?"

"Damn all," said Clock gloomily. "You want to bet, we'll probably never know for sure. Nothing to get hold of—not like this Austin thing."

"Mmh," said Jesse. *"Whom the Lord loveth He chasteneth."*

"For somebody who claims not to believe in any religion," said Clock, "you know enough Holy Writ for a minister."

Jesse grinned at him. "Let's go looking. With open minds. You know, Fran was kind of mad at you before when you didn't pay any notice to my hunches."

"You leave Fran out of this," said Clock, glowering.

"But let's look," said Jesse. "Especially at our Tamar. She interests me quite a lot. Come to think, Austin adhered to one Talmudic maxim —*Descend a step in choosing thy wife.* Yes, I think if we looked at Tamar's past we might find it interesting. Odd sort of name, isn't it? Wonder where it came from?"

"You don't know it?" Clock laughed. "Advantages of a New England boyhood. It's a favorite old puritan name—it comes somewhere in the Bible."

"Is that so?" said Jesse. "New England? Funny—she sounded just a little bit Southern. Well, ask Austin if he knows. . . ."

FIVE

"It doesn't," said Nell, "sound like a terribly entertaining place. I can't think why I'm going with you."

"Look less conspicuous with you along," said Jesse, fumbling for a clean shirt. "Besides, you can protect me from Fran. She's kind of mad at me lately because I've pressured her about Andrew. They're meeting us there. He's too good a man for her to push around."

"Well, in a way it's not her fault," said Nell, brushing her hair vigorously. "Ever since she's been old enough to notice it, her looks and her charm have got her everything she wanted. And out of everything she didn't want, if you take me. She's spoiled, that's all."

"What Fran needs," said Jesse, buttoning his shirt, "is a regular weekly spanking. Been hoping sooner or later she'd come up against some immovable object, and maybe Andrew's it. She ought to know better by now than to tease at him the way she does, halfway making fun of him—"

Nell laughed. "That's why."

"Why, what?"

"Waving the red flag at the big dangerous bull, darling. A certain element of thrill to it. I don't know, it's none of our business, but—"

"Both Father and I'd like to see her settled down." Jesse knotted his tie. Nell coiled her long hair with practiced quickness into its big smooth chignon, sprayed cologne.

Athelstane, recognizing all too well these signs of a lonely evening, mourned in a series of deep whines. "Better leave him outside," said Jesse, "it's a nice enough night." They went out the kitchen door with Athelstane at their heels, and admonished him to be good. Athelstane whimpered sorrowfully. "We'll be back," Nell promised him. As Jesse backed the Ford down the drive, its headlights caught Athelstane, black-masked brindle face wearing a martyred expression, with his big black nose squashed against the fence, watching his Two Important Humans abandon him.

"It's *respectable*, isn't it?" asked Nell.

"Oh, eminently. After meeting Grafton, that I can say."

"You were just starting to tell me about him."

"Not much to tell," said Jesse. "Really. I went and saw him after I'd had a heart-to-heart with Austin. Poor devil. But of course the old saw is quite right, we do bring most of our troubles on ourselves. The funniest thing there is how a fellow of Austin's type was so smitten that he married a girl he'd known less than a month and knew hardly one thing about except her name. He didn't even know where she came from, if she had any family."

"Well, come to think, you didn't know much about me," said Nell. "*Or* vice versa."

"That was different," said Jesse. "At least I knew you didn't say ain't. And far as I remember, you didn't raise any objections."

"Oh, I knew it was quite all right as soon as I met your father," said Nell. "It's very reassuring to know exactly what your husband's going to be like in thirty years' time. Do you think Austin murdered her?"

He didn't answer for a moment, negotiating traffic, and then said, "I don't think so. Andrew said, Still waters. True enough, these quiet sober fellows sometimes have hot tempers, but I don't read Austin like that. I think he's just what he looks like, a nice quiet fellow—bit of a stuffed shirt. I think he's got caught in the middle of something else, and I hope to God the something else shows, or Andrew'll have to charge him. Reason I want to see all the people she knew, her crowd. Maybe it'll show up, somebody else had a real reason to murder Tamar. . . . Grafton's a funny one. He's part owner of this club. It's only been a going concern about a year, and got taken up, so to speak, by this folk-singing bunch. He's one of those desperately friendly little men—life of the party—determined everybody's going to be jolly old pals together. Shies off admitting that anybody ever disliked anybody else. But I got a couple of things out of him. This Jeanie Carlson who helped discover the body—"

"Yes?"

Jesse managed the left turn onto Western on the amber light. "Seems she's even younger than she looks, only seventeen. Just out of school. Lived with her older brother, one James. And he disapproves of the whole crowd at The Cygnet, tries to keep her away. Says they're a bunch of lazy bums, bad influence—tossed a couple of her friends out of the apartment once. Just the two Carlsons, parents dead —he feels responsible. Especially disapproved of Tamar, who I gather little Jeanie has—is that still the phrase?—had a crush on. So, maybe under Tamar's influence, Jeanie moves into an apartment of her own, and Big Brother's raising Cain about it."

"After what you said about Tamar, I can't say I blame him," said Nell.

"Maybe not. He seems to have a hot temper, anyway. Want to see him too. I'm also interested in Dick O'Riordan, apparently the latest of Tamar's boy friends before she married Austin. Don't suppose all of 'em both Andrew and I want to see'll turn up tonight, but we can sample the flavor of the place at least, get a look at the kind of crowd it is."

It was, when they found it out past 120th Street, a small place at the corner of the block; a neat blue neon sign outlined a preening swan and the name of the place below. There was a parking lot round the corner. As they walked back, Nell said, "A cygnet's a *baby* swan. Why didn't they just call it The Swan?"

"Silly question. Cygnet sounds a lot more elegant. Ah, thought I spotted Andrew's car." Clock and Fran were waiting just inside the door. As usual, Fran—slim, dark and svelte in charcoal-gray chiffon— was collecting a good many interested looks from all the males passing.

Here, it was light; the little entry was about ten feet square, paneled in knotty pine, with a counter and a cashier behind it—a thin dark woman in untidy peasantry-art clothes, who looked at them expressionlessly. Beyond a double doorway at the rear, partly open, it seemed to be darker. Two blended female voices in there harmonized on "Shenandoah."

"You do find interesting dives, you two," said Fran. "Had I better put my earrings and bracelet in my bag?"

"It's not that sort of place at all," said Clock. "Not by what I saw of Grafton."

"Oh, you saw him too?" said Jesse. "Did he tell you about Carlson?"

"Reluctantly," said Clock. As they moved toward the double doors, they opened full and Theo Grafton came through. He was a rather tubby man about thirty-five, balding, with a perennially determined smile on his mouth and worried eyes. He stopped short, and then welcomed them in effusively.

"*So* happy you decided to visit us for yourselves—must see you have a very jolly evening—I'll find you a really *good* table—" He backed before them, gesturing, rather a comic little man in his carefully matched sports clothes, all fawn and brown, hair brushed carefully across his bald spot, laughing a breathless little laugh.

"That's not the principal reason I'm here, Mr. Grafton," said Clock dryly. "Are any of Mrs. Austin's friends here tonight? I thought it might be an opportunity to talk to some of them. Is Miss Carlson here?"

"Ah, no—no, Jeanie wouldn't be here—she's felt poor Tamar's shocking death very much, you know. I quite understand, sir—yes, certainly, some of her friends are—"

"I'd like to talk to Mr. O'Riordan especially. If you'd—"

"Certainly, certainly. But I hope you'll enjoy our entertainment as well." He had them fairly into the larger room by now; it opened out to unexpected size. It was dark, but not as dark as most night clubs; its small square tables, each with a red-checked cloth, bore squat wrought-iron candle-lamps. Across the rear of the room was built a slightly raised platform; it was bare of microphone, props, or backdrop—only several ordinary kitchen chairs occupied it. As they sat down at the table, a big man with a beard mounted the few steps to the improvised stage and flourished a guitar. Whistles and catcalls greeted him; he struck a few chords and began to sing "The Cowboy's Lament" in a deep bass voice that filled the room.

"I'll send you a waiter directly," said Grafton, and skittered away.

"There's Davenport," said Clock. They looked. Lee Davenport was sitting alone at a table just under the platform; light spilled from the overhead lights there to his face. He looked withdrawn and curiously sad, his long mouth grave. There was a glass on the table half filled with red wine, but he was not drinking.

The Cygnet was licensed to sell only wine and beer. Clock looked even gloomier; he and Jesse ordered coffee, but Fran presently reported approvingly on the sauterne, while Nell made a face over it. The bearded man was superseded by a young woman, and instant silence fell on the room; evidently this performer was known and respected. She stood there quiet and poised, a thin girl in a plain white dress, and a gangling young man came beside her with an odd-looking stringed instrument slung across one arm.

Jesse sat up and said incredulously, "Where the hell did anybody find a *lute* these days? For God's sake, I didn't know—"

The lute spoke softly, in a faraway voice, and her clear soprano rose, astonishingly, on an air of Thomas Campion's.

> "Thrice toss these oaken ashes in the air,
> And thrice times tie up this true lover's knot,
> And murmur soft, she will, or she will not."

It was a finished performance; the silence held to the last lingering note—

> "In vain are all the charms I can devise,
> She hath an art to break them with her eyes."

"But that's charming," said Fran under the applause. "She's really good. What a queer foreign-sounding tune—"

"Post-Elizabethan," said Jesse. "No idea you'd get that sort of thing here. Is she going to sing another one?"

Apparently not. As quietly as she had come, she was gone; and the applause died reluctantly.

Jesse looked around the room, studying faces. For the moment the stage remained unoccupied. "You know something?" he said presently. "Two sets of people, Andrew. Pretty definite line."

"I've noticed," said Clock.

"*I* haven't," said Nell. "What d'you mean?"

"One bunch—in the minority—look at that party of four over there in the corner, girls in jeans and ragged haircuts, boys minus ties and so on. They weren't interested in our Elizabethan lady, hardly bothered to listen. Four-five little parties like that. Who applauded the beard. And then, in the majority, the ones like that elegant pair—" he nodded at a couple nearby, the woman well-groomed in black, the man looking vaguely like a professor—"who come to hear the good stuff, like that. And that pair at the next table—" Two men sat there, in neat dark suits, exchanging a companionable word now and then, sipping wine. "What do you say about them, Andrew?"

"Possibly—possibly not," said Clock, sounding amused. "You can't tell the fags from outside looks."

"Remember you have a couple of ladies with you," said Fran. Grafton came on tiptoe; two men threaded their way among tables behind him.

"Oh—er—Sergeant, is it? I have *such* a poor memory, excuse me— yes—you said you wanted to meet Mr. O'Riordan. I persuaded him— that is, well, here he *is*—" a nervous laugh—"and I'm sure you'll be tactful enough not to—er—start the third degree in our pleasant little place— We're in for a great treat this evening, you know, Davenport is going to sing for us—"

"No disturbance," said Clock. "Just a friendly little talk."

"Yes, I'm sure. Everyone who knew poor Tamar—only too anxious to give you any help we can—a dreadful thing, dreadful! Yes, well, this is Sergeant—Clock, is it? Yes—Mr. O'Riordan and Mr. York."

"I'm O'Riordan," said the shorter of the two. He sounded nervous and defiant. "Don't know what help you think I'd be, but—whatever you wanna ask—" He hooked a chair from the next vacant table, sat down. York brought another one and sat down astride it. He was a hefty fellow about twenty-five, very dark, and his eyes were watchful. O'Riordan was younger, slighter, with the black-Irish good looks— creamy skin, very blue eyes.

"Sure, I—we both knew Tamar," he said. "It's an awful thing, her getting killed like that. I don't know, but it seems to us—we've all been talking it over, you know—it must've been that husband of hers. No- body else'd have any reason—but he was always arguing at her, maybe you've heard—"

"Maybe so," said Clock genially. "Could be. How long had you known her, Mr. O'Riordan?"

"Oh, a couple of years. I guess you heard we went around together a little, but it wasn't anything serious—"

"Yes. Mind telling me what you do?"

"I— I'm not doing anything right now, looking for a job. I've worked around, different jobs, construction work and like that."

"What was Mrs. Austin doing when you first knew her? And later?"

"Oh, gee, lessee, I think she was at a restaurant on Main Street then —she got the Plaza Hotel job later on, that was better account of the tips."

"Do you happen to know where she came from? I understand she came to California about two years back."

"Oh—yeah. I don't know, don't remember her saying much about that— It was some place in Maine, I think. Maine or New Hampshire, way back East anyways. No sir, I don't recall her ever mentioning any family except she did say her and her stepmother didn't get along."

Jesse broke in gently. "You were all pretty surprised when she married Austin? Not one of your crowd?"

O'Riordan turned to him, smiling frankly. "Well, I guess we were. He was kind of a square, and different—you know—but he was so crazy about her, I guess that got her. You know, Tamar was really something when she was fixed up. If she was going to be singing here, or going somewhere special, she did her hair up real fancy on top of her head, and she'd have a long dress and a lot of make-up—really something, she was. I mean, if you just saw her when she wasn't dressed up, well, she was different but not—you know. But when she got dressed up—"

"O.K., they got the point," said York in a bored tone.

"Well, I was just explaining, Les." O'Riordan was anxious.

"When was the last time you saw her?" asked Clock.

"Oh, gee, I'd have to think—she was here Saturday night, wasn't she? Yeah. With Rita. That's the last time I saw her. Betty was here too but they'd had a fight, she came with Pat or alone, I guess."

"You, Mr. York?"

"Oh, I just got back to town," said York, "I hadn't seen any of the crowd for a while. Been up in Barstow on a job."

"What kind of job?"

"Construction. New office building. I work for my brother-in-law."

"It was sure a shock to everybody," said O'Riordan. "Tamar getting murdered! Don't seem possible. But I don't know anything to tell you, but what I have. Nobody here— Everybody liked her! We—"

"Except James Carlson," said Clock.

O'Riordan laughed, and it sounded genuine. "Oh my God, that isn't anything! I mean, enough for— He just likes to keep Jeanie under his thumb. But she's grown up. No, way I see it, it must've been that husband of Tamar's, all right. That's all I could tell you, Sergeant, I'm afraid." His eyes kept wandering to the stage. "Could you excuse us now? Lee Davenport's here tonight, he's going to sing—"

"You know Mr. Davenport?"

"I've just met him—a time or two. Tamar knew him a little, I guess. He's—it seems kind of funny, but he's sort of taken up with Jeanie Carlson. Well, I don't mean funny exactly, but Davenport—he could take his pick."

"What do you know about him?" asked Clock.

"*Know* about him?" O'Riordan was surprised. "Well, he's—on the way up, you know. He's had a couple of TV parts, and cut a couple of records, I think. He's really good— Brother, he can make that geetar talk seven different ways! Only he's kind of an oddball, he goes for a lot of different stuff—offbeat."

"Did he ever go around with Tamar?"

"No," said O'Riordan. "No, he'd only met her a while back, when Theo—" He stopped, his eyes on the stage.

Lee Davenport stood up casually and wandered over to the steps up to the platform. He swung a guitar from one hand. The sound of conversation began to die; as he was spotted, applause broke out. He turned and faced the room, smiling his oddly grave little smile.

"He's really good," said O'Riordan in a whisper. "He'll get places."

Davenport had slung the guitar round his neck; his fingers strayed over it, and the guitar began to talk. Soft in the utter silence it answered to his touch, from minor to major and back to a queer little harmonic minor, chords wandering imperceptibly into a recognizable melody.

"Only you never know what kind of thing he'll do," said O'Riordan absently, watching him.

The guitar was still. Then one compelling chord struck, and Davenport began to sing.

It was a strong tenor, not a great voice but a voice you had to listen to: a compelling, dynamic voice of personality. The guitar followed it, a beat behind; and it was an odd, halting minor tune.

> "As I walked out one morn in May,
> The birds did sing and the lambs did play,
> The birds did sing and the lambs did play,
> I met an old man, I met an old man,
> I met an old man by the way."

Jesse heard a smothered exclamation behind him and half turned. Grafton stood within touching distance there. His gaze was fixed on the stage, and his foolish mouth had dropped in almost childish dismay. "Oh no!" he whispered to himself.

But that dynamic golden voice, a trained, effortless voice, held the audience in spell.

"—I asked him what strange countryman,
Or what strange place, or what strange place,
Or what strange place he did belong.

"My name is Death, cannot you see?
Lords, dukes and ladies bow down to me,
And you are one of these branches three,
And you, fair maid, and you, fair maid,
And you, fair maid, must come with me.

"I'll give you gold and jewels rare,
I'll give you costly robes to wear,
I'll give you all my wealth in store,
If you'll let me live, if you'll let me live,
If you'll let me live a few years more.

"Fair lady, lay your robes aside,
No longer glory in your pride—"

Jesse wondered if O'Riordan was going to pass out. He was white as chalk, breathing deeply through his mouth.

The voice, and the voice of the guitar under it, were all that lived in the room.

"—Here lies a poor distressèd maid
Whom Death now lately, whom Death now lately,
Whom Death now lately hath betrayed."

The voice was silent. The room was silent, as if even applause would be somehow an affront. In the moment before the applause began, Grafton took a blundering step toward the platform, coming up beside Jesse's chair.

"Oh no, really, that was too bad of Lee!" he said to himself agonizedly. "He shouldn't *do* such things—such very poor taste!"

SIX

Muttering a disjointed excuse, O'Riordan got up and went away; York followed him silently. Clock let them go without comment.

"Well, quite a performance," he said mildly. Davenport was smiling, coming unhurriedly down the steps. Grafton met him; they saw him shaking his head earnestly, and Davenport's smile widening. "I'm no musician," and Clock looked at Jesse. Jesse, whose passion for the intellectual musical mathematics of Johann Sebastian Bach had at one time or another annoyed his less intellectual friends. "Is he good?"

"He's very damn good," said Jesse softly. His eyes were on Davenport, who was coming toward their table. Grafton had vanished.

"Evenin', Sergeant," said Davenport. And it hadn't occurred to either Jesse or Clock to introduce the women to O'Riordan, but as a matter of course Clock did the honors now. "Evenin', ma'am—Miss Falkenstein. Did you like my 'Death and the Lady'? Nice old piece—came across it in a collection of old English things. Roundabout seventeenth century, I'd say, by the music."

"Earlier," said Jesse. "The Elizabethans liked harmonic minor. It's—interesting. But maybe just a little bit too appropriate right now?"

Davenport smiled. "Perspicacious, sir," he said, and moved leisurely away.

"And at that," said Jesse, "probably only a few people saw the significance. Tamar's crowd. The jeans-and-levis crowd that's infiltrating."

Clock was silent; he was watching a woman who seemed to be making for their table. She came purposefully, and halted, and looked from Clock to Jesse. "I understand one of you's a police officer—wanting to see Tamar's friends." She had a throaty, harsh voice; she was about thirty, a brassy blonde with a voluptuous figure in a tight black sheath dress.

Clock introduced himself and she sat down in the chair O'Riordan had vacated. "Well, God knows I was no friend of hers, but I could tell you a few things about her, all right. Tamar Adkins was no good— plain no good. She was a bitch, if you'll excuse the term, and I can tell you right now that husband of hers probably had good reason to lose his temper and kill her. She—"

"You seem to be pretty sure it was the husband," said Clock.

She looked surprised. "Why, wasn't it? It looks like he must've been the one, and the paper tonight said about his being questioned and all. I took it for granted—"

"Well, maybe so, Miss—?"

"Lewis, I'm Betty Lewis. I never did like Tamar much, and after a couple of things she pulled—like getting that poor little Fielding kid drunk enough so she didn't know what she was doing, and Bob Price could— Tamar thought that was funny. That kind of thing. And—"

"We've heard that you had a fight with her just recently. Mind saying what about?"

"That's what I came to tell you," she said laconically. She got out a cigarette and Clock lit it for her. "Thanks. I told the other cops too, but they said I've got no proof who took it, it could have been a sneak thief. I guess so, but I know it was Tamar. She stole something from me last Thursday. She stole my gun, and—"

"Your *gun?*" said Clock. "What kind of gun and what do you want with a gun?"

"I work nights a lot," said Betty Lewis crisply. "I'm a waitress at the Crescent Club. And I don't have a car, I got to walk home from the bus stop, on side streets. After I'd had a couple of narrow shaves with muggers—*and* fellows following me, trying to get fresh—I got this gun and I took some lessons on using it. Yes, sure, I've got a license for it—show it to you."

"What kind of gun?"

"It's what they call a Smith and Wesson twenty-two Kit gun. And like I said—"

"May I see your license, please? We found a revolver like that in her apartment. Serial numbers'll show whether it's yours. You were sure she took it but hadn't any proof? I see."

"I know it was her. I'd seen it just that morning because I changed bags, see, put it with some other stuff in my navy bag, out o' the black one. And the only other people in my apartment all day were Pat Heffner and Stan—Stanley Brawley, he's my boy friend. Neither of them would do such a thing, and besides they didn't have the chance. But Tamar went to the john while she was there, and I was in the living room, she could've looked in all my handbags till she found it, see? And that's just what she did. Anybody who knows me knows I carry it and that it'd be in one of my bags. Tell you the truth, I was kind of surprised when she turned up—we weren't all pals together, if you get me. Afterward, I saw why—she came on purpose to get that gun. Like I said, I told the cop on the corner and he told me what station house to go to, to report it. You'll find it on their books."

"Well," said Clock. He handed the license back. "That's a funny one. Why do you suppose she wanted a gun? Was it loaded, by the way?"

"It sure was."

Clock nodded. "So is the gun we found."

"And how should I know why she wanted it? This I'll tell you. No matter what Tamar wanted, if she couldn't get it one way she would another. It didn't surprise me any—whatever she wanted she took. When can I have it back?"

"Well, maybe not for a while," said Clock. "I'll see you have it as soon as possible, if it is your gun."

"Oh damn," said Betty Lewis. "Trust Tamar to make trouble even after she's dead! Maybe—I've been wondering—that husband of hers had threatened her and that's why she wanted it? Well, anyway, I've told you about it and that's that."

"Just a minute, please. When did you see her last?"

"Saturday night," said Betty Lewis instantly. "In here. I talked to her in the ladies' room. I said what I'd said to her the day before—I didn't find out the gun was gone till Friday, see? And right off I knew she had it, and I called her on the phone and said so. Then when I ran into her here, I said it again. That I knew she's the one took it and she'd better give it back. She just said she didn't know anything about it. I was so mad I made a grab for her bag, see if it was in it, but she yanked it away and ran out. And when I went out after her, she was just going out the door with Dickie O'Riordan."

Clock sat up. "She left with O'Riordan?"

"That's right. I guess, since she and her husband split up, she'd taken up with him again."

Clock caught a passing waiter. "You know Mr. O'Riordan? Good. If he's still around I'd like to see him again, will you tell him? And that's the last you saw of her, Miss Lewis?"

"It was. I was going to the cops again, try to jigger them up some about getting my gun back. And then this afternoon Pat called and told me about the murder, she'd heard it on the radio."

"Thanks very much," said Clock. "That's interesting."

"I thought you'd like to know." Betty Lewis stood up and started away abruptly.

"The odds are it's the same gun, I suppose," said Jesse.

"Yes. Funny. I wonder why she did?"

"Somebody threatening her," said Nell thoughtfully. "But that wouldn't be Austin, would it?"

"Why not?" asked Clock. "We haven't heard all Mr. Austin could tell us, I'd take a bet. I'm going to have a long talk with Mr. Austin in the morning. I wonder if O'Riordan— Ah, here he comes. Looking nervous."

"You affect people that way, darling," said Fran. "It's all that jaw shoved at them. Not everybody as stolid as our Andrew."

Clock frowned at her, turned the frown on O'Riordan as he came up.

"You wanted to—?" O'Riordan was very nervous.

"You told me," said Clock, "that you last saw Mrs. Austin on Saturday night. You didn't tell me that you left with her."

"Oh," said O'Riordan. "Well—it doesn't matter much, does it? I mean, I just drove her home. That's all."

"Go in with her?"

"No. No, I just let her out in front of the apartment. She was in a kind of bad mood, said she didn't feel like company, so I just dropped her off. And that's the last time I saw her, honest. I didn't mean to hold anything back, it just didn't seem very important."

"Mind telling me where you were between six o'clock and midnight last night?"

"Well, I was home." He gave an address on 127th Street. "I got home about six and I didn't go anywhere."

"You were alone?"

"Oh, no." O'Riordan wet his lips. "No, Les was there— Les York.

He moved in with me when he got back to town. He could tell you."

"And I'll ask him," said Clock. "O.K., thanks." O'Riordan fled. "What's he so nervous about?"

"Nobody likes being connected to a murder," said Jesse. "But it's a little funny, maybe."

"Have you people had enough of this place?" Clock signaled a waiter for the check. "I'll tell you something else funny. We found the bar where Austin says he went. Talked to the bartender. He remembered Austin all right because he never saw anybody get so high on four highballs. When Austin left—the bartender says about nine fifteen —he went to the door, the bartender I mean, to see if he could make his car O.K., and so he saw which way Austin went. And he says Austin turned west. Back toward the apartment building. Though his car was parked a few doors down from the bar."

"He said he didn't drive home," said Jesse. He picked up the check, looked at it and laid a single on top of Clock's.

"Yes, but why didn't he phone for a cab from the bar? It's a little thing, but it says maybe he went back and killed her after he'd had those drinks. I'm afraid you're stuck with this one, Jesse. We've been through his hotel room, you know. We found a suit jacket with what looks like blood on it. The lab's got it now. That's one of the things I want to ask him about. We're also looking for the cabbie who drove him home."

"Oh dear," said Jesse dismally. "Could I be wrong?"

"It seems this time," said Fran, "the thickheaded cop is right, and not my brainy big brother." She slid her arms into the coat Clock held for her.

"If he was drunk, you know, you can get second degree," said Clock.

"Don't need you to tell me. It's just," said Jesse, "I don't like getting wrong hunches, and I don't like criminal clients. However, *Praise the Lord for the evil as for the good.*"

Austin didn't make any protest at being haled down to headquarters next morning; and he didn't demand his lawyer's presence. They found him at his hotel; he said Mr. Raglan had thought it better for him not to come in until all this was settled. He sounded resigned.

Clock took him into an interrogation room and started to work on him. Prolonged questioning, sudden unexpected questions, the demand to retell a story again and again, usually produces the truth sooner or later. It is tedious work for the questioners, but then a good deal of police work is tedious.

Detective Peter Petrovsky, in Clock's office next door, was swearing about people who left buried corpses in garages. He had now established that the corpse was not Louis Steiner from the Wanted list: Steiner had an old knife scar on one leg, which the corpse hadn't. Neither was it John Wilberforce Abrams, the missing college student who had unaccountably walked out of his classroom apparently into thin air one day three years ago. Abrams had never had his appendix removed. That left a list of twenty-nine people, from the two lists, to check out.

They hadn't found any of the other people who had rented that house during the relevant times. A newspaper appeal, of course, would (or might) bring some in; but it wouldn't bring in the ones responsible for the corpse, if any tenants had been.

The call was still out on Jack Battuck: no trace of him.

They hadn't heard from the Cairo, Illinois, police about the Royballs who had (a neighbor thought) gone back there to live. Of course, said Detective Joe Lopez with the scorn of the naturally superior L.A.P.D. man, Cairo was down in Little Egypt, and the force there was probably backward enough never to have heard of telegrams or teletype. If it had troubled to make any inquiries at all. Probably hear from them eventually, said Lopez, by dog sled or something.

But an idea had come to Detective Petrovsky, a tenuous sort of idea. He had, as a good detective should, been conscientiously going over every little detail of the case and had remembered two packets of matches. The matches found on the corpse. One bearing an ad for The Brass Hat in Florence, Arizona: the other with an ad for The Keg Inn, Santa Rosa, New Mexico.

He shared the idea with Lopez. "It says nothing for sure, I know. But it just struck me, had he maybe just driven west? And those were places he'd stopped? It might be a way to narrow it down."

"Could be," agreed Lopez. He rummaged and got out an atlas. "Well, neither town's on a main highway, but it could still be—sometimes people stray off to do a little sightseeing along the way. What else could it say? Maybe that he was a rock hound, went over to the desert to hunt rocks? Or a traveling salesman?"

"Hell, *I* don't know," said Petrovsky. He looked at the list again. On the Missing list were three men who had apparently disappeared while en route across country. One Wilbur Forstman, traveling salesman with a food-canning firm, had been on his way from Flagstaff to San Diego. He was a little old for the corpse, twenty-eight, but the surgeon had given them some leeway there. One George Edward Tice had never been seen or heard from since leaving his home in Wichita, Kansas, to drive to California; he had been a third-year student at California Poly-Tech. One Vincent Saluzzo of New London, Connecticut, had started for California in his car two years and three months ago; his parents had never heard from him again.

Those men answered superficially to the description of the corpse. But who could say now whether the corpse had been any of them? Who, in fact, could say for certain that they had the corpse's name on their list?

People did drop out of sight—out of life—without leaving traces. People alone, with no one to report them missing. People who didn't matter much to anybody, so those who knew them thought vaguely, So-and-So must have moved, and did nothing about it.

On the other hand, Petrovsky reflected, the corpse's clothes had once been of good quality, which didn't look like a drifter or a bum. The chances were he had been reported missing somewhere, some time. But they could hardly ask every police force in the country for its Missing list. The out-of-state Missing flyers they got in were relevant to those cases where it was known that the person in question was heading west. The corpse could be somebody who'd walked out on a wife back in New York; or an escaped con from Fort Leavenworth; or somebody who'd had a brainstorm in St. Louis and somehow got to L.A. The corpse, in fact, could be anybody.

"Maybe," said Petrovsky, "even if I'm right about those matches telling us something, he just liked the desert."

"Maybe he was a prospector," said Lopez. "Amateur, you know. Those are both small towns a bit off any main drag, looks like on the map."

"Yes, but the fact that they're pretty far apart," said Petrovsky, "still makes it look more to me like he was driving west. Look, maybe he *started* from Santa Rosa. No harm asking if anybody's missing from there."

"You'd better ask the sergeant first," said Lopez, but Petrovsky, fired with enthusiasm, was already at the teletype.

That was at eleven A.M. on Tuesday morning. Although Santa Rosa was a little hick town, a good deal smaller than Cairo, Illinois, a reply came smartly back from the county sheriff by two thirty. Nobody was missing from Santa Rosa, as of two years back, with the exception of one Sharon Berger who had rather certainly eloped with an itinerant ranch hand and wasn't being worried about. The Keg Inn was a small middle-class coffee shop on the main street of town, respectable and well-patronized.

"Well, it was just an idea," said Petrovsky philosophically. "It could still be he was driving west." He pored over the atlas. "Look, I say let's take all the big towns from Santa Rosa east, and query Missing Persons. Neither of these places is actually on a main highway, by what I can make out—wait a minute, Santa Rosa's on a railroad, the S.P., and the main highways usually follow those pretty close, don't they? Yes, and look—Florence is just a few miles off the S.P. line. What'd that be?— U.S. seventy, looks like. Let's backtrack and see if we can't come up with something." He had found a map showing national highways and was scribbling rapidly. "Amarillo—Oklahoma City—Fort Worth—Dallas—Memphis—even maybe San Antonio— Of course, it's a hell of a long chance because he could have been going out of a direct route, sightseeing, or if he was a salesman with a definite territory— But we can ask, just on the chance."

Clock called Jesse at three thirty. "Very sorry to stick you with this one, but we've got more. Quite a bit more. I'm charging him—waiting for the warrant now."

"Oh hell," said Jesse. "What more?"

"I've had him here since nine o'clock. You know the routine—"

"I do. I also know that a tired, confused, goaded man will say things that sound funny—and incriminating. And sometimes say what you want him to just for the sake of a little peace."

"All right," said Clock. "We're careful these days—we don't railroad people. We found a suit jacket, as I told you, with blood on it. Definitely blood. Rather unfortunately, both Austin and Tamar type O, but there it is. He says, of course, that he cut his finger accidentally awhile back, that's where the blood came from. Says he'd meant to take the suit to the cleaners', just hadn't. Naturally it wasn't the one he was

wearing Sunday night. But it's a light gray suit, and the only gray suit
he's got, and the bartender says he was wearing a light gray suit when
he was in there."

"Eyewitness evidence," said Jesse, "is not always what it's cracked
up to be."

"But we like it," said Clock. "Judges like it, juries like it. And we've
now got an admission from Austin that he hit her that night. In the
course of the argument. He says that's all—he hit her just once. Says it
didn't knock her down, she just swore at him."

"Now that does surprise me," said Jesse after a moment. "I don't
like that. On the other hand— What else does he say about that? Let
me tell you. Says he was so shocked at himself, hitting a woman—
never done such a thing before—he just bolted. Ran, feeling all upset-
like, and to settle himself went into that bar for a drink."

"You must be psychic. Just what he did say."

"Yes," said Jesse reflectively. "Just what he would do. Being the
type he is. He still denies killing her."

"Vehemently."

"Yes. Damn it. Why do I have to get them? I can see you've got the
kind of evidence the D.A. likes—circumstantial evidence, the best kind
a lot of times. So you're charging him. All right, I'll be down. Tell him
so."

"You can plead second degree."

"I could," said Jesse. "I still think you're looking up the wrong tree
for the right cat, friend."

"With all this on him?"

"With all this on him. My God, will I have to play detective again?
Well, we're told, *It is well that men should be afflicted, for their
distresses atone for their sins.* I'll be right down."

SEVEN

"All right," said Jesse, "is what you told Clock the whole truth? Don't keep anything from your lawyer, very good rule."

Austin sat on the jail cot in the rather bare little cell, and looked at him dully. "I didn't kill her," he said. "I know how it looks. I'm not a fool, and it was bad enough that I'd been there some time before she was killed—if I'd told you all right off I'd hit her—! But I didn't kill her. God, how did I ever get into this mess?" He beat one hand on his knee in sudden frenzy. "God, I'm tired," he said. "I didn't sleep much last night, and then that sergeant—the same questions over and over, tell it again, tell it again—I saw the only way to get any peace was tell all I knew, so I did. I know how it *looks*. Maybe even you think—"

"And maybe not," said Jesse. "Just want your assurance you won't lie to me."

"I'll tell you anything you want to know, but— I can't imagine who might have done it. Nobody had a reason so far as I know—"

"It might not have been much of a reason," said Jesse. "Way Andrew thinks about you—somebody just losing his temper and grabbing her by the throat."

"But that's crazy," said Austin. "Nobody but a lunatic—"

"Mr. Austin, you ever glance through magazines like *Police Cases* or *True Detective*? No? You'd be surprised. Ninety-nine out of a hundred murders committed are pretty crude affairs, done on the spur of the moment and often with a very slight motive if any at all. Man has a fight with his wife about which movie to go to, and she conks him with a kitchen chair—Mama says Junior can't go out tonight so Junior shoots her with Daddy's gun. Or somebody's hopped up on heroin, or

full of cheap whiskey, and before he knows it he's standing over a
corpse. Hardly believe how crude they can get."

"But that kind of thing, it's not—it doesn't happen to people like us,"
protested Austin. "Professional crooks, people in the slums, down on
Skid Row, sure, but—educated people—"

"People don't vary so damn much. It happens in Beverly Hills too,
Mr. Austin. And far as that goes, I didn't get the notion that your wife
was just so educated?"

"No," said Austin. He sat there limply, looking exhausted. "And in a
kind of way it's all my own doing. If I hadn't been such a—a *Goddamned* fool— I saw how you looked at her, I couldn't help it. But I'd
only seen her when she was all dressed up, before, you know. Her hair
combed and pinned up, and make-up on. I— Well, the only excuse I
can give myself, she was different. Naturally I realized she wasn't—"
He was silent and then said with naïve wonder, "You may not believe
this, but I think the reason she married me was, she actually thought
anybody who worked in a bank would have lots of money. She couldn't
get it through her head I just work there, I'm not the president.
When it penetrated that I couldn't buy her mink coats and so on, she
just—sort of went her own way, didn't bother about me any more. She
kept saying, that flat kiddish way, 'But I don't get it, Ray.'" He stared
at the floor. "You know, I can hear her saying it now. Last thing I ever
heard her say. Over and over, 'I don't get it,' and I can't explain how
damned irritating it was— Like trying to get some simple fact across to
a half-wit. 'Why can't I have the money now, I don't get it, Ray.' I— It
was then I hit her." Austin raised haggard eyes. "I wouldn't have
thought I could do such a thing, but she said it once too often. It was
a perfectly simple thing, I'd explained half a dozen times, and then
when she— It was like smacking a child that was being deliberately
naughty, like that. I didn't really hurt her, you know—just slapped her.
But I was horrified at myself—and it wasn't any good saying it all over
again, so I—"

"Yes. Now, I want to ask you a few questions. About this bloodstain
they've found on a suit of yours—"

"Oh God, that's nonsense," said Austin. "It doesn't mean anything.
But I can't understand that bartender saying— I had on the charcoal-
gray suit that night."

"How many suits have you?"

"Three. The charcoal-gray, and the light gray tweed, and the navy one. It was on the tweed jacket they found the blood, and I *told* them about it. I wasn't wearing the tweed Sunday night. Well, how it happened, I'd just been putting a new blade in my razor. This was maybe, oh, a week ago. I'd finished shaving, and took the old blade out and put a new one in. You know those double-edged blades, and especially a brand-new one—you can cut yourself and not realize it for a few minutes. We've all done that one time or another, haven't we? Sure. I came out of the bathroom and put on a clean shirt and pants, and just as I reached for the jacket I saw my finger was bleeding. A paper-thin cut like that, the blood doesn't start to show for a little while—and it was a deep cut, there was quite a lot of blood. That's how I got the blood on the tweed jacket. I did some cussing, and ran cold water over it till it stopped. That's all. And I'd meant to drop the suit off at the cleaners', but you know how it is—what with all this on my mind—and I never wear the tweed to work, so—"

"Yes. All right. When did you tell her you were going to get a divorce?"

"That Wednesday night. After I'd seen you. I thought I'd better—and I wanted to warn her about the injunction too."

"What was her reaction?"

"She was—puzzled about the injunction, but she didn't care about the divorce. She just said, Go ahead."

"She didn't mention alimony or make this suggestion about a lump sum?"

"She didn't say anything about money at all, and neither did I. We only talked a couple of minutes. I got the idea—well, she implied—that she was expecting some people in, and I hadn't any desire to meet any of that crowd, so I left." Austin was answering in a dull tone.

"Yes. When was the first time she told you she'd take a lump sum in cash and waive alimony?"

"It was Thursday afternoon," said Austin, resting his head on one hand. "She came to the bank—I was with a client, and she came right in, God, in that dirty sweater and pants—my God. I managed to avoid any scene, but— Well, she said she'd decided to leave L.A. and if I gave her five thousand dollars right away she wouldn't ask for alimony. Like talking to a *half-wit*," said Austin with something like a groan. "Said I could borrow it or something if I didn't have it. I got rid of her finally, and then she called the hotel that night, pressuring me some more. I know that damn switchboard girl listens in on calls, too—it was annoying. And I'm damned if she didn't come to the bank on Friday again. And I tried to explain how she'd get in trouble, when you'd got that injunction, but— Well, you heard her."

"Mmh," said Jesse. "When you saw her on Wednesday night, you got the impression the apartment was empty—she was alone?"

"Well, of course. She said—"

"What about Sunday night?"

"Yes, she was—" Austin stopped and said, "Well, the bedroom door was shut, but— Do you think there might've been somebody else there?"

"Always a possibility. Andrew's tame surgeon's pinned down the time of death to between eight and ten thirty. Kind of narrow margin. Helpful if we could show somebody else was there, but very doubtful. Her maiden name was Adkins? She have a middle name? When you filled out the marriage-license application—"

"It was Rebecca."

"Notice what she put down for place of birth?"

"Yes, I did, because—then, I was n-noticing everything about her," said Austin, "and besides I was curious because she'd never tell much of anything about herself. If you asked about her family, she'd just laugh and say something like, we don't get along, or what's past is past. She put down New York City."

"Well, well," said Jesse. "Ought to be able to get a record there. If. So on Thursday and Friday she was very anxious for you to raise the cash money for her so she could get out of town. What about Saturday?"

"She called me at nine A.M.," said Austin exasperatedly, "wanting to know if I'd raised the money. I told her I'd ordered the stock sold, and that as soon as I got the check— I said I'd be gone all day, so she wouldn't call again, and she didn't. And on Sunday, about noon, there she was phoning again—as if I'd have got a check by mail on Sunday, even if—! I tell you, some ways she was just a child. I thought I'd better explain definitely just when she'd probably have the money, so that evening I—"

"Mmh, yes." Rather a funny little story, thought Jesse, but did it point any way to look? "What do you know about her family, when she'd left home and so on?"

"Not much," said Austin. "She'd pass off any questions. And I knew after a month what kind of fool I'd been, the way she acted at home, I stopped— I do know she had an older sister, because she said once that Sally'd had sense enough to clear out before she did, and it came out Sally was the sister. Tamar claimed she didn't know where she was now. And there was a stepmother she didn't like—I think she'd been out on her own since she was just a kid. I know she'd lived in Chicago awhile, she mentioned that, and I remember her saying something about Baton Rouge too. I don't think she'd had much formal education, so maybe she left home when she was pretty young. Why?"

"Try anything," said Jesse, standing up with a sigh. "I've got a funny hunch that maybe Tamar's murderer came out of her past somewhere. Maybe quite wrong—may have been some quarrel that boiled up that Wednesday night after you'd seen her. But a girl like Tamar, off on her own since she was just a kid, she'd have been around a little. Working at odd jobs because she wasn't trained for anything, she'd have run across some not-so-nice people, maybe. And on the other hand— Well, I'll have a look round and see. Can't tell you not to worry, obviously, but I'll be working on it."

He left Austin with his head buried in his hands: probably reflecting all over again on his brief and unlikely thralldom to Tamar that had brought him to a cell in the county jail.

And of course he had been seven kinds of fool: but what man could say he never had been, at this time or that?

Jesse went home, to welcome from Nell and Athelstane, and told Nell about the arrest. He took off his tie, set a stack of Bach fugues on the phonograph, made himself a drink and sat down to brood. Recognizing the symptoms, Nell vanished discreetly into the kitchen.

He had compiled a little list of the people closest to Tamar in the last few weeks. ("She was changeable," Grafton had said. "She picked up new friends so easily, you see, and for a while she'd forget old ones, and then—poor child, poor child!" Grafton—something just slightly phony about Grafton? See him again, anyway.) First, James Carlson. Big Brother James disapproving of Tamar: just by hearsay, or did he know her? Dick O'Riordan. Rita Garcia. Betty Lewis had mentioned "the poor little Fielding kid," whom Tamar had obligingly filled up with liquor for some dishonorable suitor. Had the Fielding girl any relatives hot on revenge? Or would they have known Tamar's part in the seduction?

All such little things.

But—could you see a pattern there? On Wednesday night, Tamar had been indifferent about the divorce: uninterested. Had made no mention of wanting to leave L.A. or of a pressing need for a lump sum in cash. Had implied that she was expecting company, and had hurried Austin out. Then, on Thursday, first she went to see Betty Lewis with, apparently, the deliberate intention of stealing that revolver, and next was deviling at Austin for a large amount of cash so she could get out of town. Because she was bored with L.A.

Girls of Tamar's type got bored easily, but not quite as easily as that. Didn't that say, maybe, that overnight on Wednesday something happened, or she learned something, that gave her reason to, first, feel she needed protection and, second, want to get out of California?

And what the hell could it have been?

But it hung together, after a fashion. Find out who had been at Tamar's last Wednesday night, what had gone on—a party, or what. See what Andrew thought—and he might agree, but it was out of his hands now. He had the kind of evidence the law liked, and then there was the fact that any experienced cop was bound to get a little prejudiced. He ran into so much crudity, the motiveless, senseless murders, that he didn't look for subtleties. Andrew thought Austin probably was guilty, because he'd seen so many similar homicides. And now the charge was made and Austin lodged in jail to await arraignment and the convenience of the court calendar, he was out of Andrew's jurisdiction. Andrew was back trying to identify his anonymous corpse-in-garage (and hunting that mugger who'd already accounted for two women, and the gang of liquor-store robbers who'd shot the clerk, and whoever had assaulted and killed that doctor's wife in Leimert Park).

This list of Tamar's known recent associates. Add Lee Davenport. (Quite an extraordinary performance, that had been.) And a Dorinda Keller, whoever she was. (But no female had beaten up and strangled Tamar.) And a few other names: Louie Jackson, Helen Wells, Tony Rodriguez. Go and look at them.

Hell. He didn't like criminal cases.

Nell called him to dinner and, sighing, Jesse folded away his notes and shut off the phonograph.

The headwaiter at the Plaza Hotel was lugubrious. It was a middle-class hotel, catering mostly to traveling salesmen. "If the management would pay decent union wages," said the headwaiter, and shrugged.

"Oh, to key personnel like me, and the manager, and so on—but what kind of girls can you expect to get at minimum wages? Only the ones not good enough to get better jobs." No, they hadn't especially liked Tamar, she wasn't a very good worker, often lazy and impertinent, but so were most of the other girls. They were always changing; either got bored and quit, or—the good ones—found they could get more somewhere else. "It's a disgrace," said the headwaiter gloomily.

James Carlson, Jesse had discovered, was a civil engineer working for the city. Easier to catch him at home, in the evening; and there was somebody else he wanted to see before he started playing detective. He didn't think Austin was guilty; he had placed Austin's type and thought he read him, but he'd only seen the man four times after all.

Elliott Carey taught seventh-grade English at a junior high school in Inglewood. Over the phone he had sounded a nice fellow—shocked about Austin, forthcoming, helpful. He had, he said, a free period between eleven and twelve. . . .

He met Jesse in the staff parking lot. "You'll be Mr. Falkenstein? Nice to know you. I just can't take this in about Ray. I hope to God you can show they're all wrong— Ray'd never have done such a thing."

"What I want to talk about," said Jesse. "Can we sit down somewhere quiet while I ask questions?"

"It'll quiet down in a minute, they're just changing classes. We can use one of the teachers' lounges." He led Jesse into the main building, past streams of noisy children, to a smallish room at the end of the corridor furnished with old-fashioned wicker chairs. "We can smoke in here. Now, sir, any way I can help you to help Ray, count on me." Carey was a little fellow about five-four, slender and good looking, with a dapper black line of mustache and intelligent eyes. "Manner of speaking, it's all my fault he ever met that girl. If I hadn't taken him to that place—but how could I know he'd make such a fool of himself?"

"Before we get to that," said Jesse, lighting a cigarette, "you know Austin, Mr. Carey. Said you can't see him doing this—losing his temper that far. Just lip service to a pal or gospel truth?"

Carey surveyed him shrewdly. "You'd like to be sure," he deduced. "Well, all I can tell you is this: Ray and I did our military service together, and I guess you get to know a fellow in barracks. Ray's a very steady fellow. Not brilliant, but steady. Very much the cautious, con-

servative type. I've played a little draw with him too, and I guess
you get to know what a man's like that way. He never calls a shot unless he's absolutely sure of himself. I've known him for seven years
and I've never seen him lose his temper. He gets excited about politics, and you can guess what his are, but not much else. I wouldn't call
him a cold fish by any means, but he's—undemonstrative. I don't know
his family but I'd have a guess that he was raised pretty strictly. And I
know that woman trouble can send the best man off the rails, but I
just don't see Ray going that far off. He'd been—disillusioned about
her for four or five months, you see, it wasn't as if he'd still been—emotionally involved with her at all. We'd talked it over, I know how he
felt there."

"There is that," agreed Jesse. "Well, thanks very much for the opinion. Way I read him myself."

"Maybe I shouldn't have been surprised he fell for one like that,"
said Carey thoughtfully, stroking his mustache. "A very obvious type.
But then I don't think Ray'd ever got around much, and she was quite
stunning when she was dressed up. . . . Of course, you're apt to run
into all sorts of types in any crowd of folk-music fans. After a couple
of years' research, I know that. But it's an interesting subject."

"I heard Lee Davenport at The Cygnet last night," said Jesse. "Getting local background."

"Oh, did you? He's on the way up, that one—he's very good, I
think. It's an individual style, isn't it? Did he do 'Six Dukes Went a-
Fishing'?"

"No. Thing called 'Death and the Lady.'"

"Oh. I don't know that one. It's a tough field to break into, but he's
so good I think he'll go places."

"I don't know much about it," said Jesse. "Understand there's been
quite a revival of interest in folk music, last ten, twenty years."

"That's so," said Carey. "In all kinds of it. A few popular performers like Ives have made people realize that it's an important art
form that we should preserve. Actually it's extremely interesting how
much has been preserved by the people themselves. Up to the last
thirty years or so, very little folk music was transcribed at all—like leg-
ends, it's passed down from the common folk-memory. In time, you'd
think a lot of it would have simply vanished, been forgotten. But as it
is, even now that fresh interest in it has led to a great deal of it being
transcribed properly, you'd be astonished how old some of it must be.

Of course, you get different versions of the really old things. I've come across at least five versions of 'The Fox,' one of our best-known American songs, and when you consider a thing as old as 'The Elf Knight' or 'Hind Horn,' the variations are amazing. As a matter of fact," added Carey, "and it rather surprised me, too, Ray's wife gave me a new version of 'Young Hunting,' one I'd never come across. Said she remembered her grandmother singing it. Surprised? Well, not exactly that, but—" Carey paused, considering his words. "If I understood that girl rightly, she wasn't really interested in it— She'd happened to get introduced into that crowd, and found out that the top performers, the stars, are in the big money. She wasn't a musician herself. She was a funny one, some ways— I don't think she ever grasped the fact that there's more to being a top performer in that field than just singing the words."

"But she knew this folk song you hadn't heard?" Jesse sat up a little straighter in the uncomfortable wicker chair. "That an American one? New England?"

Carey smiled. "No, a good bit older than that. It probably dates in its original form back to sixteenth- or seventeenth-century Scotland. When you collate anything as old as that, there are bound to be a number of versions—names get twisted, melodies get changed. But it's amazing how relatively accurately such old ballads do get remembered, without being written down. You probably know that in this country a very great many of them were preserved by the various people who settled in the Southern hill areas, the Ozarks and so on. Most of them were Scots-Irish or English, the kind of stiff, proud, ultraconservative people who resist change of any kind. They'd preserved old ways of culture, really archaic, up to this century, along with the old music. But I mustn't lecture you on the subject just because I'm interested. Do you think there's a chance for Ray, Mr. Falkenstein? He couldn't have done it—I know that. And a girl like that—"

"'S what I thought myself," said Jesse. "She'd have been around, maybe picked up a few low friends."

"Or I suppose it could have been just a casual burglar," said Carey, "and she— Why on earth Ray ever—but in a way I can see why. He understands figures," and Carey gestured. "If you see what I mean. The tangibilities. People, he's not so good at understanding. And what a hell of a situation, just because he was a fool about that woman. I

don't think she came from much, if you take me. Very definitely not
out of the top drawer. It occurred to me that, as you say, she'd have
knocked around. Maybe several other people had some real reasons to
want her out of the way. I can see how it looks to anybody who
doesn't know Ray, but—"

"Isn't it the truth," said Jesse. "Very awkward situation. For him
and me too. Well, I'm glad to have your opinion—I'll poke around and
see what shows up."

"Anything I can do—"

"Yes, thanks very much."

Well, it was early to start feeling pessimistic: there were people to
look at, things to do. Dick O'Riordan, so nervous. That anxious extrovert Theo Grafton. Lee Davenport—who was "on the way up," and yet
condescended to let Tamar share the spotlight with him (or plan to)
at least once—Tamar, who evidently hadn't been much of a singer.
James Carlson.

Look at them all, maybe something definite would show. Ask about
Wednesday night. And try to trace Tamar back, to where she'd been,
what she'd done, who she'd known, in the past. Just in case that little
hunch was right.

At headquarters, Petrovsky was getting replies in from his impetu-
ous teletypes: Missing lists from all the major cities of the South. And
Clock was swearing at Petrovsky's half-cocked brainstorms. And the
police force of Cairo, Illinois, remained obtusely silent.

The corpse unearthed by the city bulldozer had been given decent
burial, but the furor its appearance had started went on. They'd never
get anywhere on it, barring a miracle, but a thing like that turned up,
you had to do all the routine on it.

EIGHT

Jesse descended on headquarters and bore Clock off for lunch. "You found that cab driver?"

"He came in this morning," said Clock. There were, of course, still odds and ends of collating evidence to clear up: formal statements from Pierson, the neighbors, the bartender, the cab driver. "He says he's pretty sure he picked Austin up on that corner, outside the apartment house. Or a door down. Austin hailed him. He took him straight to the hotel."

"What does he say about Austin's condition?"

"Same as the bartender. Very high, but not incapable. The fare was two-forty-five and Austin gave him three singles."

Jesse laid down the menu. "Have anything to say about the suit Austin was wearing?"

"It was dark on the street," said Clock. "He didn't notice, couldn't say."

"Well." The bartender's evidence about that suit bothered Jesse. It was such a meaningless lie: such a gratuitous lie. If it was a lie, of course. The bartender a complete outsider. (Was he? Just a few doors down from Tamar's apartment. But that was a wild idea.) The answer was that the bartender thought he'd been speaking the truth; and that made no sense either. "Most bars are fairly dark, the bartender could have been—"

"Not that one," said Clock. "Go and look. It's Nikki's Bar and Grill, a block down from the apartment. The grill side is well lighted, there's a barbecue pit, counter with stools, and it's not a big place, the light spills over."

"I still don't like it," said Jesse.

"I don't know what more you want." Clock was a little annoyed. "We do know how to read evidence, you know."

"Oh, granted," said Jesse. "But it feels all wrong, Andrew. That gun check out as the Lewis girl's? It did. Doesn't that make a little pattern to you, all that—saying that Wednesday night or early Thursday something happened, or Tamar found out something, that scared her—set her wanting to run? And Austin doesn't tie into that."

"You can read it that way," agreed Clock, "sure. But if that was so, it was probably something irrelevant to the murder. We said it could be that she knew a couple of smalltime pros, using the pro slang like that. So maybe she knew a little too much about one of them and he'd threatened her—something like that."

"And then right afterward Austin, who's known for his even temper, comes along and kills her instead?"

"Smalltimers don't—"

"How do you read it *was* a smalltimer?"

"I don't read that any way," said Clock, "damn it. Maybe she was worried about some other female who was jealous of her. What I do know is, she was smalltime herself—just a punk kid. And the evidence on Austin is clear as day."

Jesse sighed. "The cab driver know what time he picked him up?"

"He said between nine fifteen and nine thirty. Bartender says Austin came in about eight fifteen. You can't still be sold on him, Jesse. There's too much evidence."

"And very nice circumstantial evidence," agreed Jesse. "All the same, I have to work on it. Did she have an address book?"

"You know damn well I'm not supposed to let you look at exhibits," said Clock. "But all right, you can look at it. Not that there's much to it. You can be so damn stubborn."

"Runs in the family," said Jesse, and Clock scowled and said he knew that already.

There wasn't much to the address book. She'd just scrawled down a few names in a barely literate hand, some with only phone numbers attached. Grafton was there, Betty Lewis, O'Riordan and Jimmy Antropus, the number of Austin's hotel—no new names.

"Who's Antropus, by the way?"

"Vocal teacher," said Clock. "Also gives piano and guitar lessons. No evidence of any close connection. And now, if you haven't, I've got work to do."

"*Man is born to labor,*" said Jesse. "So have I."

He had this afternoon free; he should be looking over the statements on that Bauer suit, but it could wait. He had to be in court tomorrow—Mrs. Brisbie's divorce; that wouldn't take long, but he had appointments in the afternoon. He was curious to know about last Wednesday night, who had visited Tamar. Try to cover that this afternoon, in person or by phone—preferably the former, to get impressions of these people—ask about that. See James Carlson tonight.

That bartender—

He set off for his various quarry. By six fifteen he was feeling even more puzzled and curious, and he'd got exactly nowhere at all, except that he'd had a look at those people who'd been recent intimates of Tamar's. And he didn't find Jeanie Carlson, who was absent from the tiny apartment she'd just moved into, absent from her new job at a small department store.

Tony Rodriguez. At present unemployed, living with parents at home. A sullen-eyed twenty-year-old, wary and suspicious of questions. He had been at The Cygnet Saturday night, seen Tamar there. Hadn't seen her last Wednesday night; he'd been uptown shooting some pool with a couple of pals.

Dorinda Keller, who was another of the waitresses at the Plaza Hotel. Rather typical: shallow little blond-by-request. She'd been out on a date both Wednesday and Sunday nights.

James Antropus. Fine head for a sculptor there, Jesse had thought. An impressively elephantine old man with a curl of black hair round a glistening bald spot, and a rich baritone voice. He lived behind a neat sign, *The Antropus School of Music,* in one side of a bare pseudo-Spanish duplex on Normandie Avenue. He hadn't seen Tamar on Wednesday either; he had been giving little Jeanie Carlson a lesson between seven and eight, and had another pupil after that.

Rita Garcia, puzzled and suspicious behind the Kress cosmetic counter ("But why're you *asking?* Everybody knows her husband did it—an awful thing—and that was Sunday night!"), hadn't seen Tamar on Wednesday night.

Nobody who knew Tamar—by the information they had—had seen her or been in her apartment on Wednesday night. Or so they said.

Jesse went wearily home and told Nell all about it, interrupting himself to shove Athelstane's forequarters off his lap. He was absently eating the cocktail pretzels Athelstane was so passionately fond of, as he relaxed over a drink.

"Well, that seems to me," said Nell, "if Austin is sure she was expecting somebody, that it must have been somebody nobody here knew she knew. If you see what I mean."

"That," said Jesse, dropping a couple of pretzels to the floor where Athelstane inhaled them greedily, "is only because, like the dutiful wife you are, you're swallowing whole your woolgathering spouse's notion that Austin isn't guilty and that Tamar's behavior just before the murder is significant. It's a lot easier to think that whoever she was expecting just isn't admitting it. Maybe because he was an errant husband making a little time with Tamar. Maybe—if we still say she knew a couple of pros—because he or she was meeting a numbers peddler there, or a reefer peddler. Or—if my idea's halfway right—because something happened there on Wednesday night that—" He paused, and after a long moment said, "Yes. Yes. Something that, A, scared Tamar and sent her after a weapon and money to leave town, and, B, provided a motive for somebody wanting her out of the way."

"Why can't Andrew *see* that?" Nell was irritated. "He's not stupid."

Jesse grinned at her. "He's not married to me so he doesn't necessarily regard me as infallible."

"*And* neither do I," retorted Nell, "but you do get feelings about people. I know that. As for being infallible, I don't know what you did when you fixed that new switch in the bathroom, but whenever you turn it on now the hall light goes on and off like an advertising sign."

"I'm not an electrician," said Jesse plaintively. Athelstane leaned over the chair arm and slurped a wet pink tongue across his cheek, expectant of more pretzels. "I said we ought to call one." He got out his handkerchief.

"At the prices they charge now? But you haven't got anything to prove it, about Wednesday night. Where else can you look?"

"James Carlson," said Jesse. "Though I don't really expect there's anything to that. Have to look. It's that damn bartender I don't like. . . ."

"Well," and Nell got up, "dinner in a few minutes." Athelstane, having finished the pretzels, followed her kitchenward hopefully.

He hadn't really expected much of Carlson and he didn't get much. Carlson a big nice-looking young fellow, very frank and open. "See,

I'm ten years older than Jeanie, I feel responsible since Mom and Dad were killed in that accident last year. Hell, Jeanie always seemed sensible—we had it all planned, she was going to L.A.C.C., work her way through, be a teacher. And then she gets to know this no-good Frank Goldberg. I don't want you to think I'm prejudiced, Mr. Falkenstein—wouldn't matter if his name was O'Kelly or Smith or what, he's just no good. And he gets her in with this crowd at that place, and she goes off half-cocked about that girl. Look, hell, she's just a kid, she hasn't the judgment. I guess it looked sort of glamorous to her because it was all so different, know what I mean. I didn't like it, but it wasn't until this Lewis woman came to see me—"

Betty Lewis, it seemed, the down-to-earth straightforward type. Beating about no bushes. She liked Jeanie, thought Jeanie's only relative and guardian ought to know about the company she was keeping. So she'd retailed the story of the poor little Fielding kid, and Carlson had gone up in a sheet of flame. Had told the story to Jeanie, who refused to believe it, and issued orders that she break off relations with her low-class pals, especially Tamar, immediately. Jeanie, of course, had retaliated by moving out bag and baggage.

"Quitting school and all—getting this fool job as a salesclerk," said Carlson. "I had a hell of a time finding her, and I can't do a thing with her—" He ran a hand through his hair.

"Not the best way to've handled it maybe," said Jesse. "Nobody likes being ordered around, but especially seventeen-year-olds."

"Oh my God, I saw that afterward! I should've been—more tactful. Tried to reason with her. But the idea of Jeanie out on her own—like an unweaned kitten! I'm—"

"Did you ever meet Tamar Austin?"

"Just once." Carlson looked at him more alertly. "You aren't by any chance hunting around for somebody to put in her husband's place?" His jaw came forward. "My God, how wild can you get? That one's pretty obvious. I didn't like what I knew of her, no, what she was doing to Jeanie, but—for God's sake!"

"What do you think of your sister going around with Lee Davenport?"

"I don't think much of any of that crowd," said Carlson forcefully. "Davenport's an oddball. I'm trying tact now, but she's still mad at me. My own damn fault. I worry like hell about her—hope I can coax her back to school, back to using some sense."

"Understandable," said Jesse. "Mind saying whether you've got an alibi for Sunday night?"

"An—" Carlson looked angry, looked amused, laughed. "Sorry to disappoint you, Sherlock, but I have. I was on a double date with my fiancée and her sister and boy friend."

So that was that. Jesse looked at his watch as he came out of the old apartment house. It was only eight fifteen. That bartender . . .

He'd found out who the Fielding kid was—Anne Kathryn Fielding, living with parents at an address on Edgemont; but he'd got no reply at the house— A neighbor out watering his lawn had said they'd all packed up and gone off somewhere, couple of weeks ago.

Lee Davenport, thought Jesse. "Death and the Lady." "Here lies a poor distressèd maid . . . Whom Death now lately hath betrayed." He had the irrational feeling that that long grave mouth, those dreamy secretive eyes, hid some knowledge. . . .

Austin not the only case on hand, damn it. Ought to be looking over those statements; that suit would be coming up before the bench within ten days. Jesse swore, climbed into the Ford and switched on the engine.

It was the single apartment over a triple garage in the rear of an old, dignified house on Berendo Street. The drive was dark; Jesse felt his way carefully. There was a fenced yard, and a dog barked at him sharply: scurry of paws on cement, and a smallish dog at the fence, growling. Somewhere there was a guitar.

Full moon just rising. It showed him a wriggling black cocker inside the fence. "Nice dog," said Jesse. Three windows above the garage, the right-hand one lighted. A wooden staircase going up that side. He started to climb. The lighted window was partly open.

The guitar was louder now. And Davenport's strong golden tenor rang over it, compelling as before.

> "I courted pretty Polly the livelong night,
> Then left her next morning before it was light.
>
> Pretty Polly, pretty Polly, come go along with me,
> Before we get married some pleasures to see.
>
> She jumped on behind him and away they did go
> Over the hills and the valley below."

A pleasant, simple little tune. And the guitar suddenly talking in minor, and softer.

> "They went a little further and what did they spy,
> A new-dug grave with a spade laying by.

> Oh, Willie, oh, Willie, I'm afraid of your way—
> I'm afraid you will lead my poor body astray.

> Pretty Polly, pretty Polly, you've guessed about right,
> For I slept on your grave the best part of last night."

Jesse stood on the little landing and knocked sharply. The guitar was stilled.

"Why, evenin', sir," said Davenport with grave courtesy.

"Your mind seems to run on death, Mr. Davenport," said Jesse.

Davenport laughed under his breath. "Now shouldn't it do? With Tamar and all? Come in, sir. You wanted to see me? I do wonder why. You bein' that Austin's lawyer, I understand." He still carried the guitar; he laid it down carefully, faced Jesse smiling. He wore dark slacks, an open-necked white shirt.

"Well, I don't think Austin killed her, you know," said Jesse.

"Now don't you?" said Davenport. "Sit down, Mr. Falkenstein." He picked up the guitar again and struck a thoughtful soft chord. "Well, neither do I," he said unexpectedly.

"Oh?" Jesse sat down. It was a rather bare living room, but neat and pleasant: light, graceful, modern furniture, polished vinyl flooring simulating parquet: a stereo phonograph, a tape recorder on a table, a studio spinet. "What do you know about it, Mr. Davenport?"

"Don't know anythin'," said Davenport, emphasizing the second word. "And why'd you think I did, sir? I didn't even know her very well."

"I don't know," Jesse heard himself say honestly. "What do you guess, Mr. Davenport?"

"We can always make guesses, I suppose," said Davenport. "You made a guess about the period of that song. You a musician, sir?"

"Listener," said Jesse economically. "Like Bach myself. Everything dovetailing, nice and neat."

"And all very strict," nodded Davenport. "Good, but not the spontaneous thing. The honest-to-God thing." The guitar whispered under his fingers. "Straight from the guts."

"Maybe not," said Jesse. He felt you had to approach Davenport, somehow, in his own language. He was groping at it. "You didn't like Tamar, even if you didn't know her well."

"I was sorry for that one, sort of," said Davenport softly. "I was. Knew her enough to know what she was. You like Bach—all those boys?" The guitar, surprisingly, spoke more disciplined music. *"Komm, süsser Tod . . ."* and stopped. "You know what I thought of, looking at her there? You not up in folk music, you wouldn't know it. Modern Israeli thing—Bikel does it. That man—who can touch him? But I thought of it. Her lyin' there all broken, finished. It says—you won't know the Hebrew? no—

> A shepherd and shepherdess are in the hills,
> She talked to him, he talked to her.
>
> Two eyes glitter in love,
> They are aflame. . . .
>
> The moon gone down and the day dawns,
> Night is gone, the dream ended.

The dream ended. Like that. For that's a song without morals," said Davenport. "The crude thing. What you want this minute, and damn any thinkin' about five minutes ahead. That was her. The poor little not-so-nice girl."

"You didn't like her," said Jesse, "any way. You didn't think she could sing—your sort of thing."

"Ah!" said Davenport. "She was a nothin'. I've known the Tamars."

"But you were going to let her sing with you. At The Cygnet, anyway. Understand you've a little reputation, Mr. Davenport. As—on the way up. Why were you cutting her in?"

Davenport's expression closed even tighter. He said casually, "Any matter? Maybe little Jeanie asked." His fingers wandered over the guitar.

"You were," said Jesse, "down at the Ace-High on Central Avenue when Tamar was getting herself strangled. Sort of unusual, Mr. Davenport. The all-Negro places, they're pretty snobbish about letting whites in."

"So they are, sir," said Davenport dreamily. "But the boys with the music strong in them, they know each other from the inside, not the outside. Everybody down there knows me, we get along fine." And, thought Jesse, seeing in his mind's eye a row of closed, secretive black faces, when they have accepted a white man like that, maybe accepted him far enough to tell lies for him . . . Davenport looked up, for the first time, squarely at Jesse; his little smile curved. "Just why'd you want to see me, anyway? I don't know one thing about it, except what I've said."

"You said you knew the Tamars. And so you don't think Austin's guilty? Why not, Mr. Davenport? And if you had to make a guess, what would it be?" Jesse's tone was very soft.

Davenport looked thoughtfully at the guitar, touched one string to make a little thrumming. "Why, I'll tell you, sir. Just meetin' the man a few times, I don't think Austin's got enough blood in him to strangle anybody. You askin' for a guess what's behind it? Well, you know, sir, this Tamar, she came from somewhere and she'd been places and known people and found out things. So she had. The good Lord knows she could be annoyin', like all that kind, and maybe somebody just naturally got good and mad and reached for her blind, over the moment's thing." The guitar whispered. "But if I had to make a guess, sir, why, I'd say, just maybe, there was some big old ghost out of the years ago came knockin' on Tamar's door. She made a lot of harm for the time she spent here. This way and that—on account of how she was. But any new harm she'd been makin' wasn't enough—by the people connected. I'd say that. For murder. It was a ghost come knockin' on her door, tell her she'd made harm enough. . . ."

As Andrew had said, the bar was better lighted than most. A small place, scarcely a twenty-foot frontage on the street; and half of it given over to the grill, a narrow aisle of counter and stools. The garish fluorescent lighting from that side necessarily reached past the waist-high partition into the bar.

The bar, like the grill, was only about thirty feet long; there was just the one bartender. The same one, on duty from four to midnight here, three days a week. His name was Al Traynor. He was a big paunchy man about forty-five, dark, with a good deal of jaw.

Jesse climbed onto a stool. This much light, hard to see how Traynor could have been honestly mistaken. But, the complete outsider. Swearing that Austin had been wearing the light gray suit, when Austin swore it was the charcoal—almost black.

Hell's teeth, was he wrong? Was Austin guilty? All the evidence—

Jesse stared at the neat row of bottles lined on the long shelf behind the bar. Amber-topaz Scotch, carnelian-colored bourbon, pale vermouth, colorless gin and vodka and tequila, golden tequila, dark brown crème de cacao, pale tawny sherry, red burgundy and claret, pale greenish sauterne, rose Bols almond, Cherry Heering, glowing smoky brandy. The damn bartender . . .

There were only four other men in the place, all served. Traynor came up to him. "Bourbon and water," said Jesse absently. How to get at the man? He didn't look like one easy to persuade he'd been wrong about anything. Had he lied? Deliberately? Why the hell should he? Bribed? He didn't look very corruptible either.

Newcomers climbed to stools on his left, a man and a woman. Jesse stared into his bourbon, which told him nothing. "Scotch on the rocks," said the man. "What'd you like, darling?"

"Oh—I don't know," said the woman fretfully, "crème de menthe, I guess."

"Coming right up," said the bartender. He turned to the long shelf. He searched along it like a bloodhound, peering close to read labels; it was a good forty seconds before he took down the long-necked squat bottle of vivid green crème de menthe and uncorked it.

And Jesse swallowed bourbon and water without tasting it, stared at him and wondered furiously. . . .

NINE

By Wednesday afternoon Clock had handed over all the relevant documents to a man from the D.A.'s office. A perfectly straightforward business, it was without much doubt enough so the inquest tomorrow would conclude satisfactorily with a verdict of murder by Austin. Which would end Clock's part in it, to his relief. He had quite enough on his hands now.

He thought Jesse would be advised to try for a reduction to second degree. The damn fool, thought Clock, between affection and exasperation, just had too subtle a mind to understand the average homicide. This thing had been open and shut; it had turned out to be, as it so often was, the most likely person, and the nice evidence had shown and that was that. He wondered what kind of defense Jesse would try to dream up.

But thinking of Jesse naturally led him to think of Fran. Little harpy. He shoved her to the back of his mind and started to get on with the other homicides presently giving him headaches.

That damned corpse. And Petrovsky having that harebrained idea—well, halfway he saw the logic in it. "But there's nothing to say the matches were originally his," he pointed out. "It might have been the killer who'd just driven west. They might have been sharing a room or something."

"And I've had another thought," said Petrovsky. "Could be we're on a wild-goose chase, looking for tenants of that rear house. It might be that the corpse was buried in that garage when the house was vacant."

Clock rubbed his jaw. "By somebody around there who knew the property? I don't know, but I don't like that idea much. I don't think anybody would bury a corpse in somebody else's garage. And I don't think anybody hauled that corpse very far from where it got to be a corpse. Not natural. Of course we don't know because we don't know who he was, but what it looks like is the crude impulsive thing. You've got to use a little imagination, build it up. Say it was a couple of men entirely unconnected with the Manfred property. That they had a fight on the street somewhere nearby and one got killed. Or even in some house around there. I don't see the other one doing anything so elaborate as burying the body. If it was on the street, he'd just run, trust to luck. If it was in a house, sure, he'd dump the body somewhere, but I don't see him burying it. Why was the body buried? Because somebody in one of those two houses on the Manfred property got stuck with it, it had some connection to one of the houses. I think he must have been killed in the house—one of them—and more likely the rear house. Because of a couple of circumstances. First, the garage was nearer to that one. Second, Mrs. Manfred probably has a good skinful of *vino* by the time she goes to bed and sleeps like a log. But if it was her and somebody else—such as this Jack Battuck—who buried the body, they couldn't be sure the tenants wouldn't hear them."

"That's awful pretty deducing, Sergeant," said Petrovsky, "and where does it get us? We've found three of the five tenants who lived in that house that period of time. Nothing says yes or no on any of them. The Popes we can count out, I think. There's the Kellys, couple in their thirties with three kids—he's a clerk in a men's store on Main. Nothing shows on them, perfectly ordinary people—no sudden vanishings of rich cousins or in-laws. Then the Hoffs. He's a clerk in a liquor store. No kids, two poodles. Nothing funny in their background either. There could be, but it doesn't show. So where do we go from here?"

"Don't tell *me*," said Clock. "And meanwhile your brainstorm's given us all these new Missing lists to check. It was your idea—you can start on that." Petrovsky groaned.

The Austin inquest went just the way he'd expected. The coroner sat without a jury and took the full evidence, as they hadn't asked for an adjournment: no need, they had it all. Jesse sat beside Austin, but didn't try for an open verdict: he hadn't any ammunition for that. Austin was nervous, giving evidence; he sounded desperate. Clock didn't think the coroner liked him much. The other witnesses showed up well: the neighbors who'd overheard the quarrel, Pierson, the bartender, the cab driver, Davenport and the Carlson girl—who drew a fatherly beam from the coroner.

He didn't take long over a verdict—murder, and Raymond Charles Austin ordered held without bail. As he already was, of course.

And at that Clock felt sorry for Austin, poor devil. Some killers, a rare few, you felt a little sympathy with: once in a long while you could feel, There but for the grace of God.

He went over to Jesse, who stood frowning after his forlorn client, absently jingling coins in his pocket. Jesse's lean face, with its individual high-bridged nose and long jaw, wore an expression less amiable than usual. He looked at Clock and said, "So that's that. You'll have me hiring out as a private eye yet, Andrew."

"You're pleading him Not Guilty? More fool you," said Clock.

"Been said, everything has the defects of its qualities—words to that effect. You see so much of the crudities, you get out of the habit of looking deeper."

Clock laughed. "And I've been thinking that you lawyers deal in such picayune, tortuous businesses, you look for the subtleties where there aren't any."

"Could be," said Jesse. *"Wisdom went forth to reside among men and found no dwelling."*

"And where did that gem come from?"

"Apocrypha. Bit of Holy Writ the choosy Christians didn't like. Did you notice, by the way, that seen across the room our bartender Mr. Traynor has a pronounced limp?"

"Well, so what?" said Clock.

Jesse smiled. For an uncanny moment his irregular lean features reformed and it was Fran's one-sided impudent smile on his mouth. "I've got a little idea," he said, "that Mr. Traynor's limp is a point of great significance to my client. See you, Andrew." He turned and ambled off, briefcase tucked under one arm.

Clock stared after him suspiciously. Jesse (as he often admitted himself) wasn't up on his homework when it came to all the smart borderline-legal moves to rescue a client from the law; but on the other hand, Clock had never underrated him as the amiable easygoing fellow he looked. Not, anyway, after he'd got to know him.

Clock massaged his Neanderthal jaw, mentally recorded the fact that he needed a shave and wondered what the hell Jesse had meant by that. His mind went back to last June and that offbeat case: Jesse saying, Not guilty—such a hell of a clear case, such obvious evidence—and eventually proving an alibi and showing up who X really had been. . . . It couldn't happen again, of course. A freak set of circumstances was all. But Clock remembered uneasily that there the evidence had been stronger than this on Austin—hell, they'd had fingerprints. Well, mistakes like that didn't happen once in a blue moon. Not if you had a reasonably competent police officer on the job.

Which he thought he was.

With a little shadow of uneasiness still at the back of his mind, he went out of the courtroom, down the corridor toward the street entrance. The big bartender, Al Traynor, was standing at the top of the steps just outside, hands cupped trying to get a cigar alight in the slight wind. Clock stopped and assisted him with a lighter. "Er—excuse me, Mr. Traynor—personal question—but I notice you're limping. Little accident?"

Traynor laughed, unperturbed. "That's my peg leg, Sergeant. Hardly think of her any more, had her so long. Had my leg taken off by a streetcar back when I was only fifteen. Below the knee, and it hardly ever bothers me, I got so used to it, but naturally she's a little stiff. Thanks for the light," and with a nod he went down the steps, the left leg dragging a little.

Clock stared after him, shrugged, sought his car and went back to headquarters. It was four o'clock.

He was greeted by the news that they'd finally located Jack Battuck and brought him in. Clock's flagging interest in the unknown corpse stirred a little; he had Battuck brought up to his office.

Almost on first inspection, he absolved Battuck of any connection with the corpse. Battuck was a stout jolly-looking old fellow with a suspiciously red-veined nose, a hearty laugh, and childlike blue eyes, round and honest. He was a retired S.P. engineer. Clock sighed over his little record of assault: probably an argument over politics, or the superiority of Diesel to steam locomotives.

Battuck had just come back from a visit to his sister in Oakland: reason they hadn't found him until now. He was tremendously interested in the buried corpse; it never crossed his mind they had suspected him of being connected to it, or his old friend Helen Manfred, whose late husband had been a dear pal of his. He speculated interestedly on who could have put it there. Somebody who'd rented that rear house, maybe?

"We've thought about the tenants, of course," said Clock noncommittally.

"Well, might be I could help you more'n Helen could. See, she never paid much notice to 'em, not bein' a nosy woman, thank God. But while I was boardin' with her, I used to do any little fixin'-up needed to be done, you know, like washers in the faucets and that, and I guess I could tell you a mite more. . . ."

He did. The Royballs (and God knew whether the Cairo, Illinois, police were looking for them at all) had been a young couple. Ordinary young folk, said Battuck indulgently, and what if they did throw a party once in a while? Royball had had a job at a gas station, he seemed to remember, and she'd been kind of pretty. Dark. No, no kids. "But I don't guess they was more than about twenty-one or so, around there."

The Popes—Mrs. Pope had nagged her husband something awful, but otherwise— "Well, I don't see nasty-nice folk like that with a *corpse*." Neither did Clock. And the Kellys—they'd let the kids run wild, and one thing he did recall, Kelly didn't like cops. Something he'd let out once. So maybe he was kind of a crook, some way?

Clock sighed and wished it was so simple, black and white. A substantial reason why police work was as tiresome—and as dangerous—as it was, was that numbers of ordinary reasonably honest citizens had an unreasonable dislike and fear of uniformed authority, which they inevitably passed on to their kids. And what with progressive education and the way people didn't discipline kids any more—

And the Hoffs— Battuck cocked his white head at Clock and said, "You know, he asked if he could use the garage to store some stuff. Helen got five extra a month for the garage—some people wouldn't have a car. He didn't. But he paid for the garage. I dunno what he put in there, but he put a new padlock on the door. D'you reckon—" He looked excited.

That was interesting, though it might not mean a thing, of course. But they'd look a little closer at Hoff, just in case. Clock was pleased with Battuck; he'd given them a very little something more.

Battuck was very disappointed that they'd already buried the corpse. "I mighta recognized *something*," he said sadly.

Petrovsky was moaning over all those interminable Missing lists. But it had been his idea, and an idea of a sort: you never knew where you'd hit pay dirt.

Clock went home, wondering what Fran was doing tonight. Poring over her damn silly fashion sheets, or (just maybe) out with somebody more interesting than a thirteen-year veteran police sergeant with nothing much to recommend him except a nice clean record and the Police Medal for saving that baby when he was still in uniform. Feeling disinclined to get himself a meal, he finally went out to a nearby restaurant.

When he came back to the apartment, as he slid his key into the lock, the phone started ringing.

He got it on the third ring. "Would you mind," said Jesse, "if you can remember, telling me exactly what Lee Davenport and the Carlson girl said that morning they found Tamar's body? To you, I mean. And/or to each other."

"Why the hell?" asked Clock blankly. "Well, let's see—" He cast his mind back and repeated the conversation as best he could remember. "That Davenport—an oddball all right. I thought at first maybe he'd been smoking reefers."

Jesse sounded amused. "Only the practicing artist, Philistine. It's apt to be a funny breed."

"I believe you. I checked on him at Lockheed, and believe it or not they love the guy—said he's a very fine mechanic, for God's sake. *And* a musician? New one on me."

"Get *off* my feet, you monster," said Jesse. "Sorry, you know how curious Athelstane is about the phone. Yes? You should study palmistry, Andrew. Almost exact same kind of hands owned by musicians, mechanics, surgeons. That's all you remember?"

"That's it. Why? What've you got up your sleeve, anyway? About Traynor—he's got an artificial leg. Since he was a kid."

Jesse laughed. "Isn't that nice. I rather thought it'd be something like that. No, I won't say till I'm sure. Thanks very much."

"Somehow," said Jesse dreamily, "I thought I was being hinted at. But was this the specific hint? Doesn't seem so, though—"

"What are you talking about?" asked Nell.

"That Davenport," said Jesse, sounding thoughtful. Suddenly he unfolded himself from the armchair. "Sorry, I think I'll desert you awhile. Overtime." He went down the hall to the master bedroom, glancing with foreboding at the other three doors. Den and guest room, hell; she kept saying four, which was ridiculous, expenses what they were. Two at the most. But wives— Athelstane sat on his feet while he put on tie and jacket. He came out to the living room again and said, "Back in an hour or so, I think."

"From where?" asked Nell.

"*A silent woman is a gift from the Lord,*" said Jesse. "I'll tell you when I get back—if I get anything. No, you can't come," he added to Athelstane, who mourned.

Backing the Ford down the drive, he wondered. That Davenport. Hints? Try to read Davenport. He guessed something, but for some reason his hands were tied, he couldn't come out with it. Why? At first glance, you might see Davenport as the detached intelligence, the impersonal observer; but nobody who was capable of top performance in any of the arts was lacking in emotion. No. So what about Davenport? The first thought Jesse had was, Jeanie Carlson; but Jeanie had had a crush on Tamar, there wouldn't be anything to that.

Curiously, some of what Davenport had said echoed the funny hunch he had himself. "Some big old ghost—"

He was playing that hunch. Playing it to the hilt. And feeling a little foolish about it. He'd started the ball rolling by writing a polite request to the Bureau of Vital Statistics in New York, asking for whatever they had on Tamar Rebecca Adkins, reportedly born there some time in 1943. (Austin hadn't even known when her birthday was.) It was a place to start. Because, when you came to think about it, even grant that Tamar was one of those people who didn't like remembering her past, lived for today, it was just a little odd that more hadn't come out, to her friends, to Austin: little casual mentions of family, home town, school. Tamar only twenty-one, and probably she'd been away from home for some time, but all the same—

He didn't know what that might say, what he hoped to turn up. He was playing it blind. And he had an irrationally firm conviction that New York would be a dead end.

He parked the car, walked back to the entrance of The Cygnet. He passed through the little foyer to the main room and sat down at a table alone. There wasn't much of a crowd tonight, perhaps thirty people altogether.

A waiter came up at once. "Yes, sir?"

"Coffee, please. Is Mr. Grafton here tonight? I'd like to see him."

"Yes, sir, I'll tell him."

A lank young man in levis was occupying the stage, singing "Bar-

bara Allen" in a reedy tenor. Jesse looked around and saw Dick
O'Riordan sitting at a table alone, looking morosely at a glass of beer.
Jeanie Carlson wasn't there, or Davenport. Tony Rodriguez and Rita
Garcia sat together. No Betty Lewis.

He wondered again about Anne Kathryn Fielding. Ought to follow
that up. Just in case. A hunch was irrational, nothing to go on really. . . .

"Sir? You wanted to— Oh, Mr. Falkenstein!" Theo Grafton's smile
faltered for one second. He drew out the opposite chair, sat down. He
was again all in shades of fawn and beige, the earnest tubby little
balding man. He let the smile fade. "Isn't this the most *dreadful*
thing!" he said, lowering his voice. "I heard the result of the inquest
on the radio. To think of anyone— That poor child! She may have
been immature, greedy—" his fat little hands gestured—"but it doesn't
bear thinking of, a life cut off so young—and so violently! You are, er,
acting for Mr. Austin? A sad position— I can see, rather hopeless—"

"Oh, I don't know," said Jesse. The waiter came with his coffee.
"You never know what'll turn up. Hope you don't mind answering
some questions, Mr. Grafton?"

"I? But I'm afraid I couldn't tell you anything useful at all," said
Grafton sadly. "I barely knew Mr. Austin. And the last time I saw
Tamar was that Saturday evening."

"I was thinking of a while before that," said Jesse.

"Well, of course, any help I can give you—" Grafton sighed. "For
we must feel that the poor man was temporarily insane, didn't know
what he was doing. The kindest thing. I've never believed in that old
eye-for-an-eye business, Mr. Falkenstein. Why take two lives instead
of one? I daresay the poor fellow is full of remorse now. Anything I
can do—"

"Mmh," said Jesse. He added cream to his coffee and stirred it. "I
understand Mr. Davenport's known as a performer on the way up to
popular recognition? He's made a couple of records, has been on TV?"

"That's so," said Grafton, beaming. "A very fine young man, Mr.
Falkenstein. But what—"

"And Tamar Austin, by what I've heard from various people, had
ambitions to be a singer but wasn't at all talented? Even as an amateur?"

Grafton gestured deprecatingly. "Oh well, now, I don't like to— She
wasn't *trained*, of course—"

"You've answered the question," said Jesse. "So how come you pressured Davenport into planning to sing with her? He said it was your idea. He didn't like her much. *Or* her singing."

The lank young man had gone from the stage. In his place had appeared the poised young woman, tonight in a plain blue dress, and the young man with the lute; and to a rapt audience she again sang Campion, sweet, true and moving, with the lute speaking plaintive chords.

> "Come, my Celia, let us prove
> While we may the sweets of love,
> Time will not be ours forever,
> He at length our good will sever—"

"How," asked Jesse in a conversational tone, "did Tamar pressure you into persuading the great Davenport to cut her in? You know, I've got a little idea about the answer there. She had something on you, didn't she, Mr. Grafton? She knew—"

"I—" said Grafton. He went corpse-white, and sweat sprang on his forehead. "For God's sake, I don't know what you— What have you f-found—"

> "Why should we defer our joys?
> Fame and rumour are but toys—"

The clear soprano rose triumphant.

"It's obvious you did," said Jesse. "He didn't want any part of her—said so. But he agreed to let her sing with him. He said it was your idea. And you know why as well as I do, Mr. Grafton—"

"No," gasped Grafton. "Oh God—"

> "To be taken, to be seen,
> These have crimes accounted been."

The last chord held and died.

Grafton said tautly, "You can't prove anything—Lee would never— I thought— Oh God, if *you* could find out—" He blundered to his feet. "Just a lie," he panted, and turned and fled, stumbling among the tables blindly.

TEN

Clock was now mildly interested, or a bit more, in Henry Hoff who had rented the house at 2808½ Holland Street during July and August two years ago. Who hadn't had a car but had rented the garage for storage and put a shiny new padlock on it.

It just could be that, taking a closer look at Henry Hoff, they'd find some little lead. Come across, maybe, some nefarious side line Henry Hoff had been engaged in, possibly with a partner who had subsequently dropped out of sight.

"Go and take a look at him," said Clock to Petrovsky on Friday morning, and Petrovsky went. It made a welcome change after poring over all those Missing reports.

"I gave it a little thought," he said when he got back a couple of hours later. "No reason to ask for a search warrant, and if there is anything funny, or was, I wouldn't get anywhere just asking questions. But it just so happens I've got a cousin in the Fire Department. You know there's always a squad out spot-checking for fire hazards, just at random. So I asked Jim where to call, and went up and flashed my badge for co-operation. After all, just as likely there's a fire hazard of some kind at Hoff's place as anywhere else. So they sent a man out with me. He did most of the talking."

"You may pass the sergeants' exam someday after all," said Clock. "What's the setup look like?"

"They're living in a better district—Alta Vista Avenue, just below Third. Nice ordinary house, a lot better than the one on Holland. They rent it. Mrs. Hoff was home." Petrovsky settled his chunky figure into the chair and groped for a cigarette. "Home-dyed henna hair, about forty, ought to go on a diet and look who's talking, lot of costume jewelry, Brooklyn accent. Very anxious to co-operate with the authorities."

"That was nice."

"We saw through the house—some new furniture, modernistic type, and the kind of draperies that lie on the floor. My wife says they're unhygienic. I can't say I care for poodles much either. Silly-looking animals. They're both big black ones. The smoke-eater was nice and polite, but he even wanted to look in closets—I'd told him he did. She didn't mind, she said, all eager to co-operate. Quite a lot of new-looking clothes, fur coat and so on. But no fire hazards. So we went out in the back yard. They keep their trash all nice and tidy in big plastic cans. But there's a padlock on the garage door, and something across the window inside. By this time she was getting a little nervous—we were being pretty thorough. The smoke-eater asks why the padlock, and says he'll have to see inside, and she says, oh well, her husband has a lot of valuable stuff in there, power saw and so on, and she's sorry but she hasn't got a key. So I spoke up then and said all apologetic we'd really have to inspect the garage, and did she think her husband could drop home to leave the key and we'd come back about three this afternoon?"

"She was relieved," said Clock amusedly. Petrovsky's cunning little plots always tickled him, in contrast to Petrovsky's round innocent face and snub nose.

"As hell," said Petrovsky. "So we came away—" he looked at his watch—"and made a date to go back about twelve thirty. Just in time, I hope and trust, to catch Henry moving whatever the hell it is out of the garage. It just might turn out to be something incriminating."

"I'd almost take a bet on it," said Clock. "I'll try to suppress my curiosity for another two hours."

He went back to the paper work on that mugger they'd just picked up, went out for a hasty lunch and got back to his office just in time to take Petrovsky's call.

"I'm at the Wilcox Street station," said Petrovsky. "Waiting for a doctor. I collected a bullet." He sounded quite cheerful about it.

"What? What the hell happened? You—"

"Well, there was a little ruction," said Petrovsky. "Nothing serious, Sergeant—little twenty-two slug in my upper arm. Just be stiff a few days. It was liquor in the garage—about ten cases of the real bonded stuff, nothing but the best. When we came up, Henry—he's a big bruiser, shoulders like a bull—was loading it into the back of a station wagon. We went up, and the smoke-eater made a spiel about finding we had time to drop back then and was this Mr. Hoff. Talk about catching anybody flat-footed. I introduced myself then and asked about the liquor. She tried to talk fast about how he works in a liquor store and this is just stock he's storing, but he went to pieces and hauled out the gun. So I jumped him, that's all. We're all down here, her having hysterics and him handcuffed to a radiator. What else I called about— O.K., in a minute," said Petrovsky off the phone, and went on, "The place he works is the John Barleycorn Liquor Center on Spring Street—and I remembered on account of the name, it's a chain and they've had a lot of break-ins lately, I read about it in the paper. I thought maybe somebody down in Burglary might be interested in Henry."

"You're probably very right," said Clock. "Sorry about the bullet, Pete. You sure you're O.K.? Better take the rest of the day off."

"Oh, I'm all right," said Petrovsky. "Little action makes a change."

Clock was still grinning as he took the elevator down to Burglary and Theft. He told Sergeant Adam Hellenthal about Henry, and Hellenthal was pleased. "Isn't that nice?" he said. "You're the answer to a prayer, Andrew. That one's been a real mystery and a hell of a headache for almost a year. We like to think we're fairly bright, but we never tumbled to this. We had it figured for a gang. This John Barleycorn chain got hit oftener, but there were a few others too. So it turns out just one man. Oh yes, I see—smart little operation. For pretty sure, this Hoff . . . That rings a faint bell— We'll look and see if we've met him before." He used the inside phone to call Records and ask for a check.

"What was the mystery?" asked Clock curiously.

"Well, you see," said Hellenthal, "every time a place got hit, naturally the burglar alarm went off and alerted the nearest precinct house, and a car shot out there within minutes. To find nothing, but utterly. Smashed-in door or window and so much stuff missing that it'd have taken half a dozen men working at top speed to shift it in the time they had. So we figured, a gang. Now you give us Mr. Hoff, and thanks very much indeed, I can see his M.O. and a very nice one it was. Naturally he had keys to the store where he works, and he knew about the alarm system, how to switch it on and off. I wouldn't doubt —this is a new chain, and it's mostly got new buildings—that to save

FOUR BY EGAN

money they had all the same locks on the stores. Never crossed my mind to ask, or ask about employees, because it was so obviously an outside job—windows smashed or the back door forced. Yes, and the other places—probably he spotted them as having the same alarm system he was familiar with. Maybe he got impressions of the locks— must have. A very neat little operation," said Hellenthal almost admiringly. "And I hope we'll get out of him who was buying the stuff under the counter. Here and there in the county are a few restaurant owners not so averse to getting a case of the real stuff at cut rates."

"I don't see—oh," said Clock.

"He'd just quietly unlock the back door and walk in. Switch off the alarm system. Turn on a light just in the back, the stock room. Car outside in the alley. Take his own time about loading the stuff into his car. Then switch on the alarm, relock the door going out. And stage his fake break-in, smashing a door or window, and he'd be pulling out while the first alarms went off. I think I'll go right up to Hollywood and have a talk with Henry," said Hellenthal tenderly. "And it could be I'm jumping to conclusions, but I really do think you've solved our mystery for us, Andrew." He got up, but the inside phone interrupted him. He listened for a while, looking interested, and then asked, "What about De Graaf? Ever picked up since?" He listened some more, looking even more interested, and said, "Thanks very much. You may be pulling that file for the Homicide office."

"What's all that?"

"Favor for favor," said Hellenthal. "Hoff's in Records. He was picked up about five years back for another burglary. A supermarket. With him was picked up one Billy De Graaf, a juvenile—seventeen then. Wasn't enough on De Graaf to charge him along with Hoff, but he had some reefers on him and got sent to the sheriff's farm for a year. Hoff got a one-to-three, first count. He'd evidently just got out two years back when he moved into that place you're interested in. And I suppose nobody'll ever know now what he had behind *that* shiny new padlock. As for De Graaf—" he paused deliberately—"about six months ago Narcotics went to see him at his last known residence because somebody they picked up was a known associate. And what, Andrew, do you suppose Billy's mother told them?"

"I'll bite, Adam," said Clock. "What?"

"She said Billy'd gone off about a year and a half back, and good riddance, she hadn't seen or heard of him since and hoped she never would, all the trouble he'd made her."

"Now just fancy that," said Clock. "What did Billy look like?"

"I didn't ask. You will."

"As of right now," said Clock, getting up.

"Maybe we've both had a little break," said Hellenthal. "*Never depend on a miracle,* says the Talmud, but they do sometimes happen."

"For God's sake," said Clock, "don't you start throwing Holy Writ at me too!"

Jesse had been in his office ten minutes that morning when Miss Williams looked in and said a Mr. Grafton wanted to see him.

"Oh really?" said Jesse. "Send him in. . . . I was going to pay you another call sometime today, Mr. Grafton. Thanks for saving me the bother."

The Grafton who crept in and hunched in the chair beside his desk was very different from the affable, beaming little man who acted as host at The Cygnet. He looked miserable and defeated. He raised frightened, humble eyes to Jesse and said, "Please. I had to come and ask you—beg you— I don't know how you found out, maybe she told other people—but please, Mr. Falkenstein, if you just won't— I *can't* have my wife know. I just can't."

"I don't go around telling all I know," said Jesse cautiously.

"She's such a high-principled woman," said Grafton earnestly. "She'd leave me, I know she would. I'd rather kill myself than have her know. Please. It wasn't Lee told you, it couldn't—"

"No, it wasn't Davenport," said Jesse.

"I knew he wouldn't. Mr. Falkenstein, I was only nineteen, I'd never been in trouble before, please believe me. The police and the judge didn't believe me but it's so, I never knew what those other two were up to until— I didn't! And it was so long ago, sixteen years, I'd almost forgotten it, but— I don't know how she knew! I can't imagine—but she did, and my wife—such a very high-principled woman, she'd—"

"Tamar knew, and pressured you on it," murmured Jesse. He felt a little ashamed of taking advantage of Grafton; the man was such an easy mark.

Grafton nodded docilely. "I couldn't think how she knew. She just laughed and said—and said—she supposed I wouldn't like for anybody here to know—about the trouble I got into—back in Dyersburg. She knew—all about it. I don't know how. Oh, she was hard! I—I haven't liked this new element coming to the club, but how can I keep them out? She—she'd brought some of them. I didn't know what to *do*, Mr. Falkenstein. I don't know how you found out. Did she tell other people? Even when she'd promised—if I let her sing—if I got Lee to—"

"That's what she wanted?"

Grafton nodded miserably. "At first," he said, "I was so frightened— If Marcia ever knew, she'd leave me, I knew—she— People don't understand Marcia, but she's a woman of such integrity—"

"And you persuaded Davenport? That couldn't have been easy."

Grafton looked down at his tight-clasped hands. "Lee knew," he said. "He knew all about it—because—one of the others was his older brother. Half-brother. But you can trust Lee, I didn't mind, I didn't worry about that. And he didn't like the idea, but he'd do it—for me. That was all right. But with *you*—"

"Did she ever ask you for money?" asked Jesse.

"Right at the last." Now he thought Jesse knew all about it, Grafton was coming out with answers as meekly as a punished child. "On that Saturday. She wanted a thousand dollars. I didn't know what to *do*," said Grafton in agony. "I couldn't raise that and not have Marcia know! Oh, that Tamar, she was a hard one! No feelings at all—I tried to explain—but she just laughed. Said I'd have to get it somehow, that was all, she needed it. Oh my God—"

"What did you do?"

"I managed to raise six hundred, I pawned my diamond ring— I told Marcia I'd lost it—and a few other things she wouldn't miss— I was going to beg Tamar— She was coming to the club on Monday, it was then I was supposed to— Oh God, I was never so thankful in my life as when I heard—"

"Monday," said Jesse. "Sure it wasn't Sunday night, at her apartment, Mr. Grafton? You know, seems to me you had a pretty good motive for wanting Tamar out of the way. A better one than the motive of sorts the D.A. pinned on my client."

Grafton stared at him and went even paler. "You're saying—you think— Oh my God, no! No, I didn't do that— It was Austin, everybody knows it was Austin—I couldn't do a thing like that— Besides—besides, I was at the club then— I'm always there, evenings—"

"What time did you get there on Sunday night?" Jesse was remorseless.

"About—about eight thirty," said Grafton. "Maybe earlier, I couldn't—"

Fat little dimpled hands, thought Jesse, but a cornered rat will fight. Was this it? And how to prove it? And then, would Grafton—even temporarily demoralized—come out with all this so openly if he had been X? He leaned over the desk suddenly, forcing Grafton to meet his eyes. "It wasn't Austin," he said. "You look like a good substitute to me. Did you? Did she demand the full thousand, so you panicked and just went for her blind? That's the way it happened, wasn't it?" Probably Andrew would do this better, he thought.

Grafton shrank. "No— No, it wasn't, I didn't! I—oh God!" He stumbled to his feet. "Please," he said, "please don't tell, Mr. Falkenstein. Really, it wasn't me, I couldn't do such an awful thing—but I *can't* have Marcia know about—about the other. Please, Mr. Falkenstein." He fled, colliding blindly with the doorpost.

Jesse sat looking after him for a full minute, thinking. Then he got up and reached for his hat. He said to Miss Williams, "If I'm not back by eleven thirty, apologize to Mrs. Bancroft and ask her to wait. I probably will be." Downstairs, he headed the Ford for the San Fernando Valley.

There were a lot of questions and red tape. A form to sign. A special guide with a badge. Like kids playing G-men, he thought. Maybe it was all necessary, but it was irritating. Finally, after about half an hour, they parked him in a square cement-floored room with chairs and tables, a couple of couches, a Coke dispenser and a cigarette machine and a coffee dispenser. The sign on the door said EMPLOYEES' LOUNGE.

He waited for ten minutes and Lee Davenport came in. Davenport in a moderately dirty white overall, his strong spatulate hands grease-stained.

"Well," said Davenport. "Unexpected pleasure, sir. Somethin' urgent, you interruptin' work of national importance? I wasn't due for a coffee break for another half hour." He moved over to the coffee dispenser, fishing for coins in his pocket.

"Belatedly," said Jesse, "it penetrated my mind that you'd been hinting at me, Mr. Davenport. Obliquely. I ruminated a little and reached a conclusion. Upshot being, I've just heard a rough sketch of how and why our Tamar had been putting the bite on Mr. Grafton."

"Oh, *hell!*" said Davenport. His hand on the paper cup moved involuntarily, and the scalding coffee splashed his wrist. He set the cup down on a table, wiped his hand with his handkerchief. "My good God almighty," he said. "I never hinted about that to you. Never meant to. Goddamn it. That poor little man." His eyes were very serious, very blue, raised to Jesse's. "So you're castin' around to find somebody to put in your client's place. I reckon you're a pretty good lawyer, sir."

"Just perseverant," said Jesse. "Now the cat's out of the bag, what were the details? Armed robbery, burglary?"

Davenport sipped coffee; he said almost absently, "Gas station holdup. Piddlin' little job, and I believe Theo when he says he didn't know what the other two were up to. Bum a cigarette from you? I don't once in six months, but I think I'll have one now. Thanks." He drew on it strongly. "You can't think that scared little man killed Tamar. He'd as soon have tackled a she-bobcat. Crazy about that down-the-nose wife of his—D.A.R. member, cold as a fish, puritanical as all hell, but some reason, he's crazy about her. Poor little Theo. If this comes out, you know, he'd be like to kill himself. Poor respectable little man. You wouldn't do that, Mr. Falkenstein. Just damn silly to think Theo could do a murder."

"He seems to have had time to do it. If. He didn't get to The Cygnet until about eight thirty that night."

"You wouldn't do a thing like that, sir," said Davenport. "I know Theo. So maybe it wasn't Austin killed her—I don't think it was—but it wasn't little Theo." He smiled crookedly. "Maybe you'll recall what it says somewhere in the Bible, sir—*I desired mercy, and not sacrifice.*"

"It's a hell of a nice motive," said Jesse. "Somehow I got the notion you were dropping hints about Grafton."

Davenport looked at the paper cup, finished the coffee. "No, Mr. Falkenstein. I was hopeful that little business'd never come out, and I'm right damn sorry it has. Nothin' but grief and trouble, and doin' no good to anybody. I'll tell you how sure I am of Theo. You break this, I'll swear he was with me at the time, till he got to the club."

"That's very damn sure," said Jesse. "You'd go to jail for perjury, Mr. Davenport."

Davenport smiled. "I've seen the inside of a few jails," he said.

"Knocked around a little, sir. Among other things, got to know this and that about people. So you got the idea I was hintin' at you."

"Funnily enough," said Jesse, "even before that I'd had a small hunch that this was, just maybe, what you hinted at. Something out of Tamar's past catching up with her. So you didn't mean Grafton?"

Davenport put out his cigarette carefully in an ashtray. "I've been keepin' in the background here," he said, "part on Theo's account. And the little Jeanie—just a mouthful for one like Tamar, silly little kid. Lucky enough she went to hero-worshipin' the honest-to-God pro old Davenport. Soon or late I'll convince her back to her big brother and the college lessons." He smiled wryly. "Do-gooder, me. Sure. And what I know about Tamar—reason I maybe did hint at you a little—it isn't anythin' like what you cautious boys'd call legal evidence. But I'll part with it if you press me. For what it's worth. Maybe take your mind off Theo."

"Take it I'm pressing you," said Jesse.

Neither of them had sat down; they faced each other, not as duelists, and an odd wave of liking and respect flowed between them.

Davenport's blue gaze wandered to his hands. "Bum another cigarette? Thanks. It shook me, you know, and I might say it takes somethin' to do that. She'd been—tryin' to hook me, after she heard I'd got a little way up the ladder. I wanted no part of her, the Tamars I'd met before, but she was kind of persistent. This was a night about nine, ten months back, call it April. Nice spring night, and a full moon. Maybe it was the full moon. Anyway, there'd been a party—at Jimmy's place. Lot of people there. I never saw her get high before or since. She was no stranger to liquor, Tamar—hold it with the best. I don't take more than a couple, ordinary, so I was kind of bored at that party. I generally am, at parties. People actin' silly, talkin' loud. And Tamar for once high as a kite." His eyes were remote, seeing into the past.

"You're about to quote *in vino veritas?*" said Jesse softly.

"Could be, could be," said Davenport. "Jimmy asked me to take her home and I obliged. It did shake me right up, sir. She was laughin' and carryin' on, sayin' what a fine party it'd been. Don't think she knew who she was with, tell you the truth. Don't think she remembered anythin' about what she'd said, next day— Leastways, she never asked me about it. But there she was, that night, laughin' and talkin' about the party. And she said, 'Never had such a good time since the night we killed the old man. You ever killed anybody, honey?' And I didn't say anythin', and she said then—laughin' all silly she was—'We tied him up and Eddy slapped him around some till he told where the money was. Jeez, he was scared—and then Eddy cut him with his knife, and was there a lot o' blood, and then we poured kerosene on the fire and ran. It said in the papers, whole place burned to a cinder. It was awful excitin', that was— The other one wasn't near so much fun.'" Davenport stopped.

They looked at one another. "I tell you, sir, it shook me," said Davenport.

"I can see where it might," said Jesse.

"Laughin' away to herself," said Davenport. "I never said anythin' about it. And it's nothin' like evidence, even I can see. But I'd say maybe there's reason to think, there could be some ghost from years ago to come and haunt Tamar."

ELEVEN

All the while he was listening to the garrulous Mrs. Bancroft, and taking notes about her projected suit against the department store whose steps she had fallen down, Jesse was thinking about Tamar. *Never had so much fun since the night we killed the old man.* He could imagine how it had sounded, in a drunken babble, with the drunken laughter. He didn't wonder that Davenport had been shaken.

And, of course, no evidence there at all. Eddy. No Eddy had turned up in Tamar's recent past. Jesse hadn't a doubt that that old man had been killed, just that way, sometime, somewhere: and it might not even have been spotted as murder. But it was a big country, a lot of violent crimes got committed in it over any period of time, and he hadn't the ghost of a clue where to start looking.

Tamar's incoherent babble might give him (and Davenport) the cauld grues; but it didn't do much of anything else.

He probably wouldn't hear from New York until Monday. If then.

He got rid of Mrs. Bancroft eventually and sat thinking about Ray Austin out there in the county jail, and how much Grafton might be worth as a suspect, and about Tamar. And Eddy . . . But that might have been several years ago, and the Tamars drifted. Picked up friends, boy friends, and dropped them.

He remembered the once he had met her, that indefinable aura of wildness. Something outside the rules. Yes, indeed, there might have been ghosts to haunt Tamar. *The other one wasn't near so much fun. . . .*

The office door opened and old Mr. Walters poked his head in diffidently. "Don't want to interfere with any work. Just bein' in the neighborhood, I thought you might come out to lunch. Not much fun eating alone, and it's the maid's day out."

"You old sinner," said Jesse, "I feel better already. Come in."

Mr. Walters came in, sat down and hauled the inevitable bottle out of his inside breast pocket, beaming at Jesse. They'd acquired Mr. Walters in the course of that offbeat case last June; Nell claimed to have fallen in love with him, and Athelstane definitely had. Mr. Walters was short, fat, untidy and bald, with a straggling gray-white handlebar mustache and shrewd little dark eyes. "I had to see the dentist," he said now, pouring a couple of drinks into the glasses Jesse produced, "or I'd never've got off the leash. It does beat all how folk figure—even a man's own sons. Get to be seventy-five, eighty, all of a sudden you aren't considered responsible any more. Aren't supposed to be interested in anything except sitting around, maybe watching TV. Tchah!" said Mr. Walters, and drank.

Jesse regarded him with affection. "Maybe it's an omen, you dropping in. I've got another private-eye job on my hands. This Ray Austin. Read about it?"

"Oh? That one. You his lawyer?" Mr. Walters shook his head. "Not much of a mystery, is there? Way I read it, from the papers, he just lost his temper and went for her. Some women— I always have thought the character of the deceased ought to be admitted as relevant evidence, like they say. There was a buyer I hired once— Mitigating circumstances, you know." Mr. Walters renewed his drink placidly. "That's another thing," he added darkly, reverting to his own grievances. "How do they think I built up a successful business and retired with a couple million dollars, if I don't have good sense? At me every minute, Put on a coat, don't forget your medicine, don't stay out late. Think I was four years old."

"Annoying," said Jesse sympathetically. "But you've broken jail today, anyway. And I have too got a mystery. Listen to the story."

Mr. Walters listened, looking interested, and at the end said, "Now isn't that something! I see what you mean. It's all circumstantial evidence on him, but it mostly is in homicides."

"Quite valid." Jesse considered him. "Like to help me put a crack in some of it?"

"Anything I can do," said Mr. Walters obligingly.

"Fine. We start by me buying you a drink."

"Now that's an offer," said Mr. Walters, "I very seldom turn down."

Jesse laughed and stood up. "Come on." He shepherded Mr. Walters downstairs and into the Ford, turned right on Western out of the lot and headed downtown.

"We're passing a lot of perfectly good bars," said Mr. Walters at the Santa Monica Boulevard intersection.

"Heading for one in particular. Now listen. You've got on a new suit—"

"Not very. About six months old."

"Today it's new. We're going to talk about it. You're not sure what color it'd be called, dark gray or what."

"It's charcoal gray, anybody can see that. At least that's what the tailor called it."

"Ah, but there are wheels within wheels, same like Ezekiel saw," said Jesse. "Just back me up." He turned left on Beverly.

He had checked to make sure, dropping in there casually a couple of times, talking with Traynor. Traynor was on the night shift Sundays, Mondays and Tuesdays, the rest of the week on from ten A.M. to six. He hoped they wouldn't hit his lunch hour. A gamble any way you looked at it.

He parked and they walked back to Nikki's Bar and Grill. "Hole in the wall," said Mr. Walters.

There were eight or ten other men at the bar, and Traynor behind it. He recognized Jesse, grinned a welcome at him as they climbed up on stools, and came up smartly. "Yessir?"

"Bourbon and water," said Jesse.

"Same'll do for me," said Mr. Walters.

When Traynor came back with the drinks, Jesse was saying, "It's a good piece of material for the price, you got a bargain. Talking about my friend's new suit," he added for Traynor's benefit. "But the color seems a bit—what d'you think?" His tone was friendly, drawing Traynor into conversation.

"Oh, it looks fine," said the bartender. "Nice piece o' goods like you say." On invitation he leaned across the bar and felt of Mr. Walters' lapel. "Dacron or one o' these synthetics, isn't it?"

"It's the color I kind of wondered about," said Mr. Walters, blindly playing up. "Whether it's not too young for me."

"Well, I always say, a man's as old as he feels," said Traynor jovially.

"What fancy name did they have for the color, I forget," said Jesse.

"I'd call it a kind of gray, wouldn't you say? But they always have to dream up the fancy titles—bad as women's clothes these days."

"It was some kind of gray," said Mr. Walters, "I think."

"Well, it *is* gray," said Traynor.

"A kind of light gray?" Jesse insinuated softly.

"Yeah—anybody can see that." Traynor looked a little puzzled over all this talk about a suit; he went off to welcome a new customer, and Jesse smiled at his drink.

"I kind of thought so," he said in satisfaction. "It was indicated. Finish that and we'll find less of a hole-in-the-wall for lunch."

"You get what you were after? What? I don't—"

"I did. You see, that poor fellow lost a leg when he was just a kid."

"And what's that got to do with Austin in jail?"

"Fact that he's minus a leg," said Jesse, "automatically says he was excused from any military service, and he'd never try for any job where there was any sort of physical examination—requirements. But it is a little funny at that—I'd say he was about forty-five, wouldn't you?—that he's never found out."

"Found out," said Mr. Walters suddenly, looking at his sleeve, "that he's got some kind of color blindness. Sure. Calling this light gray. I'll be damned. You don't mean to tell me—"

"That's just what. He said in all good faith that Austin had on a light gray suit, when Austin swore he had on a suit about the same color as the one you're wearing—charcoal. But he was wrong. He couldn't tell the difference—*and he doesn't know it*. Looks like an honest enough fellow, think he'd have said he couldn't tell if he knew it. Different types of color blindness—some people can see some colors and not others, and some people, I understand, don't properly see any color at all. Funny nobody ever spotted it in Traynor, or that he didn't himself. Tell you another thing, I bet he's not married. Wife would have seen it."

Mr. Walters finished his drink and regarded Jesse avidly. "What you couldn't do with that in court, boy! Better 'n any TV drama. Paradin' somebody in a dark suit, and asking him what color— How'd you spot him, anyway? Going psychic?"

Jesse grinned. "I saw him hunting along that shelf for a bottle of crème de menthe—you see how that bright green shows up like a neon sign—having to read the label before he identified it. Q.E.D. This isn't the kind of bar where he'd get asked for these fancy drinks often, or probably he'd have put a label on it. Though of course he doesn't know he *is* color-blind, apparently."

"I'll be damned. *What* a courtroom scene that'd make—"

"Hoping it won't come to anything so melodramatic," said Jesse. He finished his drink, rattled the dwindling ice cubes in the glass. "If I can find enough to show definitely that Austin's not X, or that somebody else is, this won't come to a trial. Nicer that way. But—at the moment—rather doubtful. Oh, Andrew won't like this, or the D.A., but it's not enough to get Austin off the spot."

"Must say you convince me," said Mr. Walters. "Come on, let's go up to the Silver Dollar or somewhere with comfortable chairs. I want to hear all the details. Might be I'll have an idea or two."

"Mannings' is nearer—"

Mr. Walters looked at him in outrage. "It's got no liquor license!" he said indignantly.

When old Mr. Walters had regretfully taken himself off in a cab for the expensive Mar Vista home of his son and daughter-in-law ("Damn it, think I'd lost whatever since I had when I hit seventy—Like I tell Betty, I got to votin' age sixty years ago next month and I guess I can still be called an adult"), Jesse did what he should have done several days ago. He went back to Francis Street to the old apartment house. With his fingers crossed that the place hadn't been re-rented or left sealed by the police. But he didn't see any reason why it should have been.

He rang the manager's bell, explained to him frankly. "What exactly has been done? Anybody come for her possessions?"

Pierson, a big paunchy man, looked hesitant and worried. "So you're his lawyer, hey? Well, guess he needs one o' those all right. I been wondering about it, tell the truth—I was thinking of calling and asking that police sergeant. I guess, technically speaking, everything in the place belongs to Mr. Austin—I know the furniture is his—but naturally he can't do nothing about it, sitting down there in jail. You couldn't expect it. I see the funeral's going to be tomorrow, I suppose he couldn't even arrange that, somebody— And I never heard that she had any relatives here. But on the other hand, you understand that I'd like to rent the apartment. You're a lawyer— What had I ought to do?"

"Nothing's been touched since the police went through it?" His lucky day, thought Jesse.

"No, and I don't know what's right to do," said Pierson. "Never had this sort o' thing happen before."

"You'd better pack it all up and put it in storage," said Jesse. "In Austin's name. Let me know which company, I'll take care of the bill. Until we know something definite one way or the other, about Austin. But—"

"Not much doubt there, poor young devil."

"Yes, well, meanwhile I'd greatly appreciate it if you'd let me look through the apartment, Mr. Pierson. You see, I've got to build up a defense for him, and any little evidence of—well, what Mrs. Austin was like—"

"See what you mean," grunted Pierson, fingering his jaw. "Well, I guess there's no harm in that," looking Jesse over. "Long as you're his lawyer." But he still looked worried. He turned from the door, went to a desk across the room, got out a bunch of keys. "I'll take you up. You look it over much as you please—and—" He stopped on the first tread of the stairs and looked back at Jesse. "After, if you'd stop by and hand the key back, Mr.—what did you say—"

"Falkenstein."

"Mr. Falkenstein, there's something I'd like to ask you about. Just a little thing, but—well, since I recollected, it's been on my mind."

"Oh. Something—?"

"You take your look at the apartment," said Pierson stolidly.

He let Jesse in and went clumping away downstairs. The apartment smelled stale and dead, being shut up even this length of time, no windows open. Its dreary, sordid disorder struck him as oddly pathetic: so obviously the place of someone entirely ununderstanding of any of the amenities, someone who had lived minute to minute, without coherent plan or routine.

There was a faint lingering whiff of whatever fingerprint men used these days, and most surfaces were stained with a residue of it, powdery. Stain on the carpet: spilled beer, wine? The carton full of refuse. The furniture at crazy angles. Dust on everything.

He went into the kitchenette. Looked as if every dish and pan in the place had been dirtied, and just left. He wrinkled his nose at the mess. The refrigerator held only a quart of spoiled milk and a lone pork chop still in its sterile plastic wrapping. Cupboards, a few cans— a full bottle of Scotch, a half-empty bottle of vodka, six cans of beer.

There wouldn't be anything here. It was a very long chance indeed that there'd be anything anywhere here to give him the smallest lead. After all, Andrew's men had been through everything in this place with a fine-tooth comb. Anything remotely suggestive or interesting they'd have noticed.

At the same time, Jesse reflected—well, they didn't come any better than the L.A.P.D., but the human element entered in too. By the time the search of this apartment had been made, every cop on the case was aware that it looked pretty open and shut on the husband, Ray Austin; it was possible—no more than that—that some little thing, pointing subtly in another direction, might have got overlooked.

He went into the bedroom. Nothing had been touched here since the police had done their looking. Andrew said she'd been on the floor between the bed and the windows. Chalk outline still showed, where she'd been, and a stain on the carpet. Jesse looked from the stain to the walnut-veneer bedside table on that side of the bed. He thought he'd take a small bet that she'd had Betty Lewis' gun in that table drawer. Maybe the attack had begun in the living room and she'd got away, run in here to get the gun, and been caught before she reached it. Logical. And that just didn't sound like Austin. Any man might go berserk for thirty seconds, reach for her throat: but a sustained running fight—Andrew said she'd been pretty well beaten up.

They'd found Austin's prints in several places, but that was only logical too. Up to about a month before the murder he'd been living here, and by all the evidence Tamar hadn't been the type to go in for furniture polish and elbow grease.

Jesse opened the door of the old-fashioned walk-in closet. There weren't too many contents. He remembered O'Riordan saying, *When she was dressed up*— Four long evening gowns, scarlet, black, sapphire-blue, white. Chiffon, velvet, nylon. Not expensive, but—typical? —very fancy. He had an idea that Fran would turn up her nose at them and say, Main Street. High-heeled sandals, a pair of gold mules, cheap thong sandals. A couple of blouses, capri pants, fallen in a heap on the floor. A very fancy green nylon waltz-length nightgown hanging on a hook on the back of the door, with a lacy black slip.

He turned to the chiffonier, having felt along the closet shelf and found it empty of anything but dust. Easy to see the drawers had all been searched, though he didn't suppose Tamar had kept them any less untidy than the police had left them. She hadn't had much, that was evident—the few dress-up clothes, the few euphemistically-termed casual clothes. Here were torn lace panties, a couple of bras, a half-slip; more capri pants, a couple of pairs of shorts, three pairs of nylons, one with a broad run. In the two smaller top drawers, a little heap of costume jewelry, a few handkerchiefs.

He went into the bathroom. A wild disorder here: bottles and jars standing all around, jamming the open medicine cabinet. Creams, lotions, all sorts of cosmetics. A dirty towel on the floor, dirty face cloths and towels flung haphazardly on the towel racks. He shook his head at it and came back to the chiffonier. He turned over the heap of costume jewelry, and ran his hand all the way to the back of that drawer. There was something there; he drew it out.

He wondered if the police had found this, and what they'd made of it.

And what the hell was it?

A little bag. A very little bag, made of some kind of soft leather, a dull brown, with leather drawstrings. Whole thing only about an inch and a half square. He pulled the strings apart.

A very little mess of what looked like dried leaves, or grass, and a tiny scrap of something red. He sniffed. A faint aromatic odor.

Sachet? he wondered. But that was usually in little satin bags, wasn't it? Ask Nell. Nell always kept empty cologne bottles to put in drawers. Nell the parsimonious: her Norman peasant blood, probably.

He had a feeling that the small leather bag was of some significance. He dropped it in his pocket.

The second top drawer held another little pile of costume jewelry, just dropped in, tangled together, and among it was a small square box. A jeweler's box. He opened it. A ring box. In the slot was a ring with a smallish square blue stone. It looked like a good ring—he took it to the window. On the inside of the shank, turning it against the light, he made out the mark *14k*. White gold, and the center stone could be a sapphire. He put that in his pocket too, in its box.

He turned over the heap of jewelry. Mostly dime-store stuff, flashy, overlarge earrings and brooches, wide bracelets, the gold and silver colored metal already turning dark. But among that pile was a watch, lying loose. He picked it up.

It was a Hamilton watch, seventeen-jewel. There were sixteen small diamonds round the oval dial, and a white-gold band; one of those solid, inflexible bands, made like a bangle bracelet. He took the watch to the window and turned the band to the light, without much real expectation of finding anything.

Engraving on the inside of the band. Damn it, it was so small he couldn't— He turned sideways to let the light from the window fall on it.

Joanna from Eddy, 1962.

Well, well, thought Jesse raptly. Eddy.

—And then Eddy cut him with his knife, and was there a lot o' blood. . . .

Joanna?

One of Andrew's minions had slipped up a little here, thought Jesse. But it was understandable: such tiny engraving. He put the watch in his pocket. He thought he'd got more than he'd had a right to expect. He locked the apartment door after himself and went down the stairs to ring Pierson's bell.

"Thanks very much, Mr. Pierson," he said. "Very co-operative of you."

" 'S all right," said Pierson, taking the key.

"You said you had something you wanted to ask me?"

Pierson still looked worried. "Look," he said, "I don't want to get into trouble with the cops. My God, nobody's a walking encyclopedia, are they, Mr. Falkenstein? I mean, I see maybe a hundred, two hundred different people every week—who remembers everybody? Well, I didn't remember this guy, and then later on I did, but I hadn't before I told the cops what I knew about it. So what do I do now?"

"You remembered something—mmh—relevant afterward?" said Jesse.

"That's right. Look, the cops I know. They're so damn smart themselves. I go and say, sorry, boys, I just remembered this, and they get sarcastic about it. Hell, a man isn't *expecting* to get involved with a murder case, and I got enough to think about in the ordinary way—"

"Well, all the same, you'd better tell them," said Jesse. "What was it you remembered afterward?"

"How many faces do I *see* a week?" demanded Pierson belligerently. "Hell and damnation. I suppose I'll have to tell them. The damn smart-boy cops, saying are you sure and why didn't you say so before. Look, he'd only been here—for me to see him, leastways—a couple of times. Why should I—"

"Somebody you'd seen before? Who?"

"*I* dunno who," said Pierson. "Just, I'd seen him maybe three times, coming in or going out. Once with her. The first time—I was in the hall taking out my trash, he could see I come out o' the door marked MANAGER—he asked me which apartment Mrs. Austin had, so I knew who he was coming to see. Naturally."

"Yes. You remembered him later—how?"

"That Sunday night," said Pierson worriedly. "The night she got killed. I said how I come back downstairs from seeing her and Austin, about seven thirty. Well, it was a little later on, maybe not quite an hour later, I had to go up to Mrs. Bryant's, she said her kitchen faucets was leaking. And just as I come out o' my place, this guy was coming in the front door. He come up the stairs after me, but number twenty-two's the other way, in front, I didn't see which door he went to. Look, it doesn't really matter, does it? We know she musta been dead then because Austin'd gone before. So this guy doesn't get any answer and just goes away again, that's all."

"Someone who'd come to see Mrs. Austin before," said Jesse, keeping excitement from his tone. "You don't know his name? What'd he look like?"

"Oh, I'd *recognize* him," said Pierson. "Kind of a handsome young fellow, black hair and white skin, sort of Irish-looking—dressed sharp. But what the damn cops'll say—"

Dickie O'Riordan.

TWELVE

"Ever seen it before?" asked Jesse.

Austin looked at the ring in its box. "Yes, sure, it's hers. She never wore it but once or twice since I knew her, but it's hers." He took it out of the box. "Funny," he said. "It shows you what she was like. Just an ignorant kid. It's a good ring, that's a real sapphire, about two-carat I'd say, and there are a couple of diamonds as side stones. But Tamar thought it looked cheap, didn't like it, because the stone was so small. She liked—oh, you know, the flashy things. I remember, when we went to get the wedding ring, she picked out the biggest, flashiest-looking dinner ring in the case, wanted it for an engagement ring. It was priced at five thousand and something." Austin laughed unhappily. "And kept saying, 'Why can't I have it, Ray? I don't get it.'" He turned the sapphire ring over in his fingers. "She didn't like the set I finally persuaded her to get. That was expensive enough—" His mouth twisted; he said, "I'm still paying on it. I suppose there've been bigger fools, but—"

"Well, forget that for a minute. Have you seen this watch before? Hers too?"

"Yes, it is. But she didn't often wear that either. Time didn't mean much to her. I don't know where or when she got either of them, she had them both before I knew her. So far as I know," said Austin, belatedly cautious. "I saw the watch first when—when she was unpacking her things at the apartment—after we were married. I didn't see her wear the ring until, oh, maybe a couple of weeks later."

"Yes. She ever say anything about either the ring or the watch?"

Austin leaned back on the jail cot. "Funny," he said, yawning, "since I've been in this place I wish I did smoke. Gives you something to do. That first time I noticed the ring, I said how pretty it was, and she said, oh, did I think so, it wasn't very big. I looked at it then and saw it was quite an expensive ring. I should think it set somebody back around a thousand bucks, maybe more. I said that, and she was surprised, didn't believe it could be worth so much. I asked her where she'd got it, and she hesitated a minute and then said it had been her mother's."

"Oh," said Jesse. He took the ring back, looked at it meditatively. "It looks to me like a modern design." He was thinking of what she'd said to Davenport—of how horrified Austin would be if he knew that. *The other one wasn't near so much fun.* Implication that she and Eddy had got some money from "the old man." And had killed somebody else. Also robbing that one? He looked at the pretty sapphire ring. "And damn it, the box is no use. Why couldn't it have been one of those with the jeweler's full address? A lot have." The box was a jeweler's box all right, gray simulated-leather outside, lined with white rayon; but there was no name on it.

"It was too big for her," said Austin. "The ring, I mean. She had to wear it on her middle finger."

"Oh," said Jesse. "Now, I don't know if you can make it out in here, but there's some engraving on the inside of that watch band. Says, *Joanna from Eddy, 1962.*"

"What? That's funny, I thought—"

"Isn't it? Know anybody by either name?"

Austin shook his head. "I can't imagine— Do you—are you thinking she could have *stolen* it?"

"That could be," said Jesse. "And equally it could be her real name was Joanna." Austin looked stunned; he'd been disillusioned with Tamar, but not quite this far maybe. "But it all looks a little queer, doesn't it? Ever seen this before?" He produced the tiny leather bag.

"I never laid eyes on that in my life," said Austin. "What is it anyway?"

"No idea," said Jesse. "Well—do some ruminating on it, 's all. *To be patient is sometimes better than to have great wealth.*" He stood up. "Another thing I meant to ask you. Your mother and stepfather—"

Austin said miserably, "I've been thinking. *Hell* of a mess. And, my God, even if I get out of here somehow, if I could prove I didn't— Banks are pretty strict, I don't know whether Mr. Raglan'd take me back. But it doesn't look very hopeful that I will get out from under, does it, Mr. Falkenstein? It seems like a nightmare—me, Ray Austin, sitting here charged with murder—nothing that could really happen. . . . And what good would it do, write Mother and put her through that much more misery? The trial and so on. I don't know, maybe better wait until we know—one way or the other. While they're —all right, I mean Bruce is in business in Reading, insurance—well, they haven't all that to waste. She'd want to come right out, it'd be expensive. God, I don't know what to do. She'd think it was funny I didn't let her know, but—"

"Maybe you'd better," said Jesse. "Family support."

"God, I don't know," said Austin. He was silent, and then said, "Bruce is O.K., but he never thought an awful lot of me, because I didn't run with any gang in high school, or date much—like that. He always made fun of my going to the Y. You know. He's one of those big hearty fellows. I know just exactly what he'll say when he hears about this. That I always was a little neurotic, he's not surprised I went out of control and killed somebody. I really didn't, you know. And Mother, who's very sweet but not the world's greatest brain, maybe believing him."

"I see," said Jesse. "Well, up to you. You think it over. And we're not in the home stretch yet by any means, but one piece of news I've got for you—we know now why the bartender misled the police about your suit." He told Austin about Al Traynor.

"Oh my God, but that's wonderful! Won't it show them how wrong they are all the way, when—" Austin lit up with excitement.

"Take it easy. That's only one little link in their chain after all. They won't like it, but they won't come rushing right down to unlock the cell door. However, it's something. We'll hope to come up with something else." He didn't mention that O'Riordan had been seen in the apartment building after Austin had left, because in itself that said nothing. He couldn't be proved to have been inside Tamar's apartment. "Just keep your fingers crossed," he said. "Don't claim to be much of a detective, but I'll continue to poke around."

He went home, and found Fran and Nell discussing fashions over sherry. Athelstane came to greet him joyously. He kissed Nell and said, "Very enlightening," to her query about his day. "Nice little bit of evidence turned up in Austin's favor."

"Oh, really?"

"For heaven's sake," said Fran amusedly, "are you going to do Andrew in the eye again, Jesse?"

"Well, seems he's arrested the wrong man again. And I think I'll tell him about all this and let him do a little worrying." Jesse went down the hall to the phone. Athelstane followed him interestedly, sat down on Jesse's feet and stuck his big black wet nose against the mouthpiece.

"You monster," said Jesse. "Talk about indulgent bridegrooms, letting her saddle me with you!" Of course they hadn't known then that Athelstane was a mastiff; that horrid revelation had come later.

It wasn't quite five thirty; Clock should still be in his office.

He was. "Hello, Andrew," said Jesse. "*A natural love of learning,* so says the Letters of Aristeas, *is man's highest possession.* I thought you might like to learn a few new little things to ruminate on overnight."

"Oh, you did?" said Clock. "Such as what?"

"The bartender," said Jesse. "You know—Traynor. Who said Austin had on a light gray suit. 'Fraid he's out as a witness for the prosecution. He's got some kind of color blindness."

"What the hell d'you—"

"Heard him today, and so did a witness, say a charcoal-gray suit—nearly black—looked light gray to him. Funny thing, he doesn't seem to know he's color-blind. Never taken any thorough physical, such as military, et cetera—obviously, on account of the leg."

"I will be Goddamned," said Clock. "I will be—"

"Quite an honest fellow. You'll want to check him yourself. Expect it'll come as a big surprise to him—as well as you. Great relief to me. Thus vindicating my judgment of Austin."

"For *God's* sake!" said Clock exasperatedly. "So that's what— You're damn right we'll check it out. I will be—"

"Save the ammunition," said Jesse. "I have more." He went on to quote Davenport as to what Tamar had come out with after that party; there was silence at the other end of the line, and then Clock said softly, "Just fancy that."

"A little bit," said Jesse, "like those real-life killers in *True Detective,* Andrew? The ones it's a little hard to believe in—that there are people like that. Davenport said it shook him. Shook me. But for what it's worth—"

"What the hell is it worth? Here and now?"

"Nil. But continue to preserve patience, I have yet more." Jesse prodded at Athelstane, who was leaning so hard against him in an effort to get at the mysterious sounds inside the telephone that Jesse had to brace himself against the wall. Athelstane weighed some ten pounds more than Jesse did, which sometimes made discipline difficult. "One of your minions slipped up a little on the search of that apartment. I suppose you heard about the only good pieces of jewelry she had—a sapphire ring and a Hamilton diamond watch."

"I did. What about them?"

"She claimed the ring—which was too big for her—was her mother's. I think any jeweler'd tell you it's too modern a design, if the mother's supposed to've been dead any length of time. And there's some engraving on the watch band. It says, *Joanna from Eddy, 1962.*"

"You don't tell me," said Clock in a flat voice. "Damn it, I had that watch in my own hands and didn't—"

"I just looked on a very long gamble. Ordinarily you wouldn't expect it," Jesse comforted him. "But there it is."

"Yes." Clock didn't sound happy about it.

"You'll also be pleased to know that Theo Grafton had a very good motive to want her out of the way." He told Clock about that. "He didn't get to the club until about eight thirty that night. I wonder if he could prove an alibi somehow?"

"Oh, for God's *sake,*" said Clock.

"And another little item," said Jesse. "You'll be hearing about it from Mr. Pierson. He's just remembered. About an hour after Austin left on Sunday night, Dick O'Riordan came into the building. Pierson says, what does it matter, he didn't see him actually at the apartment door—assumption is, she was already dead, consequently didn't answer, and he went away. But he didn't tell us about it, did he? Said he was home all Sunday evening. Naughty boy. And maybe she wasn't dead, Andrew. Maybe every last word Austin told you was gospel truth, and he left her alive. And maybe she did open her door to O'Riordan."

Clock said tiredly, "Damn you." Jesse could see him massaging the prognathous jaw that, at this end of the day, would be showing a dark shadow of beard. "What am I supposed to do with this? It's out of my hands now."

"Know that. Also know you don't like to railroad people, however unintentionally. Just keeping you up to date with the facts. To, maybe, create the small doubt in your mind. Because it could be, as time goes on, I might want to ask you for some of your—mmh—facilities," said Jesse, "to check this and that. And if you're convinced there's even the possibility of a little mistake, you'd co-operate."

Clock was silent, and then asked, "You've built up a theory?"

"Hardly call it that. But I've got a little hunch it was a motive rising from something that happened in the past. And maybe you'll admit that, with this revelation about the night they killed the old man—and the other one not being near so much fun—Tamar had quite a little past. Even at twenty-one."

"I'm bound to agree with you there," said Clock dryly. He sounded tired. "My God. Listen, Jesse. You'd better drop that ring and watch off here tomorrow morning. Just for fun, I'll have an expert look at them."

"Good boy. I'll do that. And another little something too. O.K., I'll see you." Jesse hung up and said, "Get off me, monster." The mysterious sounds having ceased, Athelstane obliged. Jesse's left foot had gone to sleep. He limped back to the living room, declined sherry, went to the kitchen to build himself a drink, came back and sat down. He said, "Poor Andrew. Quite a conscience as a police officer. He'll be doing some worrying."

"Have you really turned up something to show that—?" Nell was excited. "It sounded so hopeless—"

Jesse told them what he'd turned up, fished out his exhibits. "But I can't believe in what Davenport said—that's just wild, Jesse! Nobody would—so utterly cold-blooded—"

"You'd be surprised," said Jesse. "What d'you make of those, Fran?"

"It's a nice ring," said Fran. "And almost new—quite a modernistic design. You know, it looks like the sort of ring that somebody'd pick out as an engagement ring for a girl who didn't want a diamond. Yes, some girls don't," to his lifted eyebrows.

"Well, a thought. What about this?" He dropped the little leather bag into Nell's palm. Neither of them made anything of that. "Well, nevertheless, all this is going to stay on Andrew's mind. Depending on what else I get, may reconvince him yet." He lit a cigarette and sprawled deeper in the chair.

"*Poor* Andrew," said Fran in her sweet high voice. "He's so *serious* about everything."

"And what's wrong with that?" asked Jesse a little coldly.

"Oh, I don't know—" Fran wandered over to powder her nose at the entrance-hall mirror. "I must get home, I've got that article on hair tints to look over. The heavy-handed superior male, that's all," she added, groping in her bag for tissue and wiping off her lipstick. "I'll bet when there isn't a female around he rants about crazy women drivers. Kind who'd like to ban all cosmetics and votes for women. Victorian."

"There are times," said Jesse, "when I think you didn't get smacked often enough in your tender youth. Sometimes tempted to make up the arrears myself. You know damn well he isn't—"

Fran laughed derisively. "Superior males sticking together. You and Father lauding him to the skies. I can't imagine why, when I've also got somebody like Gary Freeman chasing me—with goodness knows how many millions—"

"Oh my God, that polo-crazy lout," said Jesse with a groan. "If you marry him, Frances, we'll both disown you."

"I've no intention of marrying him," said Fran, "having a funny prejudice about having to send the second footman on a tour of all the bars every night looking for the master. I just *mentioned* it. As against that twentieth-century Neanderthal man down there at head-quarters."

Nell preserved a tactful silence, exchanging a private glance with Jesse.

"Listen," said Jesse, "I've heard you talk often enough about these predatory, shallow females you associate with in your damn ridiculous world of fashion. Kind whose sole interest in life is themselves—latest expensive clothes and make-up and so on. You didn't used to think much of 'em. *Or* sound much like 'em. But look at you!"

Fran looked in the mirror with apparent satisfaction: and with cause. At her small, slim-but-rounded person with sleek dark hair in the latest fashionable cut, her creamy complexion, brilliant dark eyes under heavy arched brows, scarlet mouth; at the latest Fabergé costume suit done in charcoal wool, and the gay little scarlet Corot blouse, and the one important costume brooch, and the big gold ear-rings.

"Look at you!" said Jesse. "Straight out of *Vogue*—or your own little bit of froth for light-minded females—and behaving just like all the silly females who never read anything else. Inclined to agree with Andrew about career women."

Fran turned and looked at him. "Did I—sound like that? Really? I didn't mean to, Jesse. I don't like that type any better than— Did I *really?* Maybe I ought to quit this job. I'm sorry, I know he's not exactly like—"

"Evidently still fairly sound of mind," said Jesse. "Just keep it in hand, Fran. And don't annoy Andrew—teasing at him. He's too good a man. If you don't want him permanent—and personally I think you'd be a fool not to jump at him—don't keep him dangling. Not fair on the man. And if you do—and personally I think it'd be the best thing that could happen to you—say so in plain words."

"Well, really!" said Fran, recovering herself. "We haven't quite reached that matriarchal stage yet. Well-brought-up girls wait to be asked. I'm off, darlings. See you."

"Career women," grumbled Jesse. "And at that, maybe not fair to Andrew, stick him with a flibbertigibbet like that. . . ."

Clock sat at his desk and felt depressed, uneasy and angry. That Austin thing. Jesse saying— But damn it, they couldn't have done anything else, the way all the evidence pointed. It looked so obvious. Austin placed there at the right time. So obvious a reason for him to lose his temper with her. A small woman, easily killed without intention. The bartender's evidence. The blood. The overheard, loud quarrel. The torn-up check.

What more could you ask for? And now, Jesse coming up with these odds and ends. Except for the business about the bartender, just odds and ends—nothing to say anything for sure. But—hints. Implications.

To say maybe, just maybe, they'd jumped the gun a little.

"Hell and damnation," said Clock aloud to the empty office.

Like any good cop, he very much disliked the feeling that there was even a possibility that he'd charged the wrong man. The L.A.P.D. just didn't do that kind of thing.

He wasn't by any means ready to start thinking they had, here—but he couldn't, now, help thinking about the possibility.

He passed a hand over his face. Go out and get something to eat, he thought. And then, to the County Jail to ask Henry Hoff some questions.

Not that he expected he'd get anything out of Henry, but it was part of the routine that had to be done.

They now knew that the corpse buried in the garage hadn't been Billy De Graaf. Billy De Graaf, according to his official description in

Records, was—or had been—five-seven, two hundred pounds, sandy in
coloring with blue eyes and rather lavishly decorated with tattooing: a
mermaid on left upper arm, a heart and arrow on left lower arm, *Sally*
enclosed in a heart, right lower arm and across his chest (said the file
discreetly) a nude female figure.

So? So, Henry Hoff hadn't buried Billy De Graaf in the garage floor;
but just conceivably he might have buried somebody else. Though
Clock didn't see it. Smalltime thieves didn't as a rule go in for violence.

He pulled himself to his feet tiredly. Ray Austin . . . Damn, he
thought, is Jesse right? Not only about that, but about veteran cops
getting a little blind to the subtleties? When they came along so
seldom?

He'd been a cop on this crack force since he was twenty-one: thirteen long years. He'd thought he was a good one. You looked at the
evidence and you acted on it, went the direction it pointed. That was
all.

God, had he jumped the gun on Austin?

Have an expert take a look at that jewelry. And get what? Probably
nothing. That O'Riordan: take a closer look at him?

The night we killed the old man.

God, thought Clock, *True Detective*, all right. The raw, the incredible realities any cop had run into. Oftener, a lot oftener, than the remotely subtle, complex thing.

Ray Austin, the incipient banker. Incipient stuffed shirt.

Eddy. Eddy, who had "cut him with his knife" . . . She had, everybody had said, been here about two years. Clock mentally reviewed
the homicides that had come through this department in that time,
and shook his head.

If there was any chance of a mistake—

Clock straightened and took a breath. Tired—this other damned
anonymous thing—but, have a drink before dinner, he'd be O.K. He
went out to the sergeant's desk in the anteroom. Sergeant Raven, on
the night shift, had just taken over. "Say, Gene," said Clock, "I know it
wasn't our territory, so skip that—but will you do some asking around,
other county forces, check Orange and Ventura counties, San Diego,
might as well. For a homicide, or it might've been put down as accident, where an old man was burned to death alone in a house. House

destroyed, evidently. Might've been a suspicion-of-arson on it. Within the last two years."

"Give me a night's work, all right," said Raven, scribbling notes. "O.K., I'll see if I can find it." He looked after Clock a little curiously as Clock took down his hat and went out.

THIRTEEN

On Monday morning Jesse sat at his desk and contemplated a brief letter which informed him that no listing of a Tamar Rebecca Adkins could be found in New York's vital statistics records.

He hadn't really expected there would be. Tamar, it emerged, had been chary of having anyone know much about her past. And how the hell to trace her back? She'd been in L.A. about two years, but before that, where? Her friends said vaguely, Chicago, Baton Rouge; but when? And—a sudden thought—had she come to L.A. alone?

O'Riordan said he'd had a vague idea she'd originally come from Maine or New Hampshire, somewhere up there. One of the New England states. And come to think, Andrew said that Tamar was an old Puritan name. Jesse rummaged and got out an atlas: sighed over it. New Hampshire had ten counties, Maine sixteen: so, write letters to all those bureaus of vital statistics? And it might have been another New England state, Connecticut or Massachusetts or— The hell with it. So he did start the long hunt, and eventually find out what her home town had been, what would it give him? A good chance, if it had been a smallish town, that somebody would remember when she left home, and maybe why, and maybe with whom. But nothing about where she'd been since.

He didn't know why, he just had the feeling he'd like to know where she came from: that it might be interesting to know.

He didn't have an appointment until after lunch: he could brood over it. What about Joanna, whoever she was? Ten to one the watch had been stolen. Tamar hadn't had any qualms about stealing Betty Lewis's gun. Probably the ring too. On the other hand, one of the names on the watch band was Eddy, and Tamar had once known an

Eddy. With a vengeance, thought Jesse. But then, Eddy wasn't such an uncommon name.

Where the hell could he look now? He hadn't located O'Riordan to get a new story out of him about that Sunday night; he might have better luck trying The Cygnet. Yes, and what would O'Riordan say? He could guess; and no way to disprove it. Hell.

He was pleased when the door opened to admit old Mr. Walters, who said, "Girl said you weren't busy," and plumped his solid person down in the chair beside the desk. "Ruminating on this, hey? So've I been. Altogether, it's a funny kind o' business. The sort of girl you make Tamar out, you can see how she'd hook some nice young fellow like Austin who hadn't been around much, sure. For a while, till he saw through her. But—" Mr. Walters set his bottle on Jesse's desk and looked at it—"what he said about her evidently thinking anybody works in a bank is rich, and so on—I make her out pretty ignorant. Naturally shrewd maybe, but ignorant, if you get the difference."

"Yes, but what does that say?"

"Now you're smarter 'n that, Jesse. It says to me, first, she left school pretty young, and second, she probably grew up in a small town, and third, in a kind of low-class family. You seem to be so set on finding out where she came from." He poured a small drink for himself.

"Query every record office in the New England states? And I don't know that it'd do us any good to find out. That's just a funny hunch. What could it tell us about here and now? She probably cut all connections, nobody there'd know where she went."

"That was just one o' the things occurred to me," said Mr. Walters. "Maybe I'll try writing a detective story sometime—this sort of thing's kind of interesting. Keep me from stagnating in my old age. Seems to me one awful important thing to find out is, how in hell did she know about Grafton being in jail?"

"He hadn't any idea. Why's it so important? She could have known somebody who knew him in prison, or—"

"Sixteen years back?" said Mr. Walters. "That's a long time to a girl like Tamar. Sixteen years back she was only about five. And anybody in the poky with Grafton then'd have to have been at least eighteen, which'd make him about thirty-four, thirty-five, now. And that's another thing—to a girl like that, anybody over twenty-five's ancient. I know 'em. Now, the next point is this. Just exactly where did Grafton get into trouble?"

"No idea. Wait a minute, he said Dyersburg."

"Well!" Mr. Walters set down his glass. "That's something. Been looking it up?" He picked the atlas off the desk.

"No, of course not, I—"

"No time like the present." Mr. Walters turned briskly to the index. "Dyersburg. Hum." He ran his finger down the lines. "Could be just plain Dyer, and he tacked on the burg—local term, maybe. Only Dyersburg's in Tennessee, but there's a Dyer in Indiana and Arkansas, a Dyer Brook in Maine, a Dwyer in New Mexico and a Dycusberg in Kentucky."

"Why not ask him?" said Jesse. "Simpler."

"So let's ask him," said Mr. Walters. "Don't you see, boy, that one way she could have known about Grafton is if she came from somewhere around the same parts?" He added a little to his drink. "Tell you what," he said, sounding adventuresome, "let's us go to that Cygnet place tonight, hey? Sounds kind of interesting. I like those old songs myself—remembered some my mother used to sing, maybe some those young folk wouldn't know. There was one about a frog—" He drank. "Like to take a look at some of these people for myself." He leaned forward conspiratorially. "Believe it or not, I'm loose. They've all gone up to Lake Arrowhead for a week, winter sports, nobody home but the maid, so I can come 'n' go as I please."

Jesse grinned at him. "It's a date, provided Nell doesn't mind—and you promise not to ogle all the young females."

"Not my vice," said Mr. Walters.

"But I warn you, it's only licensed for beer and wine."

"Tchah!" said Mr. Walters. "They provide glasses, don't they?"

Clock was feeling tired and out of sorts as he drove up Highland Avenue, parked in front of Fran's apartment, climbed stairs and pressed her bell. Fran opened the door and told him he was late and that she was starving. As usual, she looked like one of the slick cover models of her own magazine. Clock could never fathom why: it was a kind of magnetism, he thought gloomily.

"Your tie's crooked, Andrew."

"Damn my tie. You'll take me as you find me," he said irritably. "I'm in no mood to be criticized, Frances."

"I thought nothing shook the iron composure," said Fran, sliding into his new Pontiac. "Frascati's, please."

Clock bit back a retort. Why the hell and how the hell he'd ever fallen so hard for this female! Just on account of her charm—if she wasn't exactly beautiful, the big dark eyes with the unbelievable lashes, and— Everything in pants trailing after her since she'd learned to walk. So naturally she got spoiled. As hell. In spite of the other two Falkensteins having some common sense. Thinking she could order any man around. Little harpy . . . He liked nice old-fashioned girls who were interested in a home and kids.

He drove up Hollywood Boulevard, deliberately, to The Seven Seas. He wondered, not for the first time, why she kept on going out with him. Nothing in common at all.

"Male superiority," said Fran mockingly, getting out of the car. They went in, and heads turned as she passed, as usual. The head-waiter hurried up, bowing and smiling.

They ordered preliminary drinks—"Which I need," said Clock. "And also some nice feminine sympathy. Which I won't get from you. All this coming along at once—"

"Aren't I nice or feminine or sympathetic? Poor Andrew. What you want is some meek little woman to reassure you you're the big smart fellow."

"Damn it!" said Clock, scowling at his drink. "This Austin thing. It just could be— I'd hate like hell to think so, but it could be. This force doesn't have the reputation of railroading people. By God, if that's so—"

"The honor of the regiment!" said Fran brightly. "I *do* understand, darling."

Clock set his glass down and leaned across the table. "Don't you take that tone with me, Frances. Don't I know that bit—all men little boys to be humored. I'm not a little boy, I'm a full-grown adult male, and I don't like to be patronized. And don't say darling to me when it doesn't mean anything. Is that understood?"

"Goodness, on only half a drink. Yes, Sergeant. Sorry, Sergeant."

"Why the hell do you keep coming out with me?" asked Clock frankly.

Fran smiled at him and said lightly, "You make such a good foil for me. Beauty and the beast."

"I asked for that one," said Clock. The drink had relaxed him a little: he laughed. "Just bear it in mind, Fran, and if you don't mind, we'll drop in at that Cygnet place after dinner. That damned case—"

In fact, he thought, all the damned cases he had to cope with at the moment. That doctor's wife in Leimert Park. And not a smell of those elevator men who'd held up the liquor store and shot the clerk. And the routine still straggling along on the anonymous corpse, maddeningly because in the end it would all fizzle out and get filed under Pending and that would be that.

And now his uneasiness over this Austin business . . . So, it was out of his hands, but all the same it was his business when a witness lied to him, and he'd gone to see O'Riordan again.

It was a shabby, cheap apartment; when O'Riordan reluctantly let him in, he found Les York there too. He'd interrupted a card game; cards were scattered on a rickety old table.

"Well, the bloodhound's back," said York. "What you want now?"

Clock didn't sit down. "So you were at home all that Sunday evening, Mr. O'Riordan?" he said gently.

O'Riordan licked his lips. "What you mean? Yeah—I said so."

"That's funny," said Clock. "Then your astral soul must have been visiting Tamar's apartment. The manager noticed it. About eight thirty."

"Oh, hell," said O'Riordan miserably. "I might've known. Look, I—it was only natural I wouldn't say I was there, wasn't it? Until you tumbled it was that creep she married did it. I mean, nobody wants to get involved in a—" He looked from Clock to York, sullen and defiant. "I figured she was out, see? When she didn't answer the door. Wouldn't I? And I just come away. That's all. We didn't have a date, I just—dropped by."

The obvious thing, what Clock had expected him to say. And York said, sounding bored, "Worth anything to you, Dickie told me about it when he came in. Just like that. What the hell, you took Austin out of circulation for it, what's the pitch, working overtime?"

Clock surveyed the two of them. York hulking, confident, derisive; O'Riordan nervous, defiant. He had no comeback at all. Because who could prove any different? And Austin was the man charged—on adequate evidence.

But he felt even uneasier about it, looking at this pair. The casual pro slang. O'Riordan a punk if he'd ever seen one. York, what? A lout. Quite possibly a pro lout.

Well, they'd said maybe Tamar had known smalltime pros. So these were it. It didn't say anything about Austin: that Austin wasn't guilty.

"It's never a very smart idea to lie to the law," he said.

"Well, hell, Sergeant, I'm sorry, but you can see it didn't really matter—she must've been dead already then— I just didn't want to get *involved*—"

"Think twice the next time," said Clock. And that was all he could say. But he set Petrovsky to looking into backgrounds, on both O'Riordan and York. As well as he could. And in Records. Just for fun.

And then, Grafton. He'd done a little asking at The Cygnet, arousing the inevitable curiosity but that couldn't be helped: Grafton had come in late that Sunday night, about eight forty. So Clock had gone to his home address, and had a little surprise. A very classy house in a very classy neighborhood, on June Street: not a dime less than fifty thousand, he'd figure—and a uniformed maid answered the door. So, thought Clock, the wife had money: quite substantial money. Letting Grafton play around with his little club, which probably just about paid its way. Thinking of Davenport's reported words, he reflected cynically that Grafton had a better reason than true love for not wanting his better half to hear he was an ex-con. If she was so strait-laced.

He asked the maid if she remembered what time Grafton had left the house that Sunday. It wasn't much of a hope, but she did. She also asked suspicious questions. Clock said, "Oh, well, we had a bet, you see— I'm a friend of his, down at the club. I bet him he couldn't get to the club from here inside half an hour, and he claimed he did, and I—"

"Oh," said the maid, "I get you." Clock had spotted the racing form thrust hastily into her uniform pocket. "Well, it was about eight. They'd been to some fancy affair that afternoon, and the missus, she's a great one for dinner served all formal—he wanted to leave his usual time, but she made him stay all through, so he was late."

So that almost definitely put Grafton out of it, didn't it? June Street wasn't far below Third. He had about a mile and a half to go over to Western, and then a hundred and nineteen blocks, call it eight or nine miles, down to The Cygnet. He'd done damn well to make it in approximately forty minutes, through traffic. Clock couldn't see him tak-

ing even ten minutes out to stop off and murder Tamar: added to
which he'd have had to go a good distance out of his way.

All the same, he wondered how the hell she had known about Grafton. What with the discrepancy in their ages. And what with Jesse's
funny hunch that the murder had been triggered by something out of
the past. If you said Austin wasn't It, that could be so. If. Damn it, it
was perfectly adequate evidence on Austin. . . . That bartender. So
far unavailable to test for color blindness; he'd taken the weekend off
to go over to Vegas. Due back home tomorrow.

And then, just as he was thinking of checking out, running home
for a quick shave and a clean shirt before picking up Frances, the
Cairo, Illinois, police had broken silence.

"My God," Lopez had said, "they've actually got a teletype."

The Cairo, Illinois, police had apologized, but they were busy and
shorthanded. They were interested to learn that the L.A.P.D. was interested in the Royballs. They were interested too. Eben and Sarah
Royball, they thought, might have a number of police forces interested
in them. She had been picked up seven times for shoplifting during
their residence in Cairo, and the man for drunkenness, petty theft and
assault. No terms; just probation. Unfortunately the Royballs, who had
taken up residence in Cairo in October two years back, had moved on
the following September, no one knew or cared much where. Official
descriptions were appended.

"Well, there we are, or are we?" said Petrovsky sadly. "Assault. The
likeliest tenants of Mrs. Manfred's house to have left that corpse behind. Might have been anybody—drifter Royball picked up in any bar.
And what points to where they are now?"

"You're forgetting Uncle," said Clock. "Inquisitive Uncle in Washington. The man must be holding some sort of job, and his employer
has to pay in Social Security for him. Ask Washington."

"And wait six months for an answer," said Petrovsky, "by which
time they'll have moved on somewhere else. O.K., O.K."

"There now," said Mr. Walters disappointedly, "some of 'em knew
that frog song after all. But they haven't got the right tune."

A couple of untrained sopranos were harmonizing uncertainly on it.

"Mr. Frog went a-courting, he did ride, ah-hum!
Mr. Frog went a-courting, he did ride, ah-hum!"

"That's not right at all," said Mr. Walters, affronted. "It goes, With a roly-poly, gammon and spinach—"

There was a quiet laugh behind him, and Elliott Carey put a hand on the third chair at the table. "Mind? That's just another version, you know—they're both quite legitimate."

"All I know is, that's not the way I heard it," said Mr. Walters stubbornly.

Jesse introduced them. "I like to drop in here occasionally," said Carey, "on the chance of hearing one of the young pros like Davenport, or that extraordinary Libby Ford who sings Campion. Lovely voice. Davenport's here tonight—I hope he'll give us something."

"Something less macabre than what I've heard of him up to now," said Jesse.

Carey ordered coffee absently as the waiter came up. "Mr. Falkenstein—about Ray. Has anything shown up that might—? I mean, I simply can't believe that—"

"No. Neither do I. Working on it. Quite a few odds and ends have shown up, yes. Hope—with luck—to get him off. Playing detective," said Jesse with distaste. "Not my job. But, damn it, he's placed there, I can't hope to show an alibi, so what it comes down to, I'll have to make a stab at locating the real guilty party before anybody'll listen to me. Quite a little miracle needed."

"Well, you've got an assistant," said Mr. Walters, hauling out his bottle. He had disposed of the thin burgundy into a potted plant nearby, and surreptitiously replenished the glass. "Not to sound superior, but anybody who's lived to eighty-one, he's just naturally got his wits sharpened better 'n you young fellows—that is to say if he had any to start with. You're the folk-song fellow?" he added to Carey. "Doin' a thesis on it? Kind of interesting."

"Well, it is," said Carey. "I'm very glad to hear that— You think there's a chance for him? If there's anything I can do—I went to see him, you know, he's feeling pretty low."

"Not surprising," said Jesse.

"Offer you a real drink?" asked Mr. Walters.

Carey smiled. "No, thanks. There's Davenport."

Jesse watched him thread his way among the tables. Davenport, the little grave smile on his long mouth, his blond hair brushed neatly off his wide brow. Davenport, whom he'd so lightly dismissed—because he liked him. Davenport's half-brother had been in on that holdup with Grafton, all those years back: so, they came from around the same area? And maybe Tamar too—who had known about Grafton. Maybe the link? Davenport's secretive, unsmiling eyes . . . Davenport, down at the Ace-High listening to the blues. Oh yes? When they accepted a white man so far, far enough to lie for him. Maybe.

"Well, Lee," said Carey, smiling. "Got something offbeat for us tonight?"

"Evenin', sir," said Davenport in his soft voice. "Evenin', Mr. Falkenstein—" and he nodded, courtly, at the introduction of Mr. Walters, who looked at him interestedly. "Not so offbeat, no. A thing I like. Old tune and new words, but by somebody who felt the music the right way." He passed on, making slowly for the raised platform.

"My word," said Carey, "that's a stunning girl. New here."

Jesse turned casually and saw Clock and Fran just coming into the room. "Well, well," he said softly, and smiled. "So I did plant the seed of doubt in Andrew's honest heart. Three cheers." Carey looked a question at him; he shrugged and shook his head. "Remains to be seen what comes of it. Wonder if he's seen O'Riordan."

"That's young Fran," said Mr. Walters disapprovingly. "Got up to kill as usual and teasing at the current fellow in tow. Past time she was married to somebody like the sergeant who'd put up with no nonsense."

"And how right you are," said Jesse. "But on the other hand remember what old Rabbi Johanan said—*Follow a lion rather than a woman*. What a thing to wish on Andrew, coping with that twenty-four hours a day. But I still have hopes he may transform her into a respectable housewife."

Carey's eyes were on the stage, where Davenport stood under the spotlight. The hum of conversation was dying as he was recognized; there was a scatter of applause. He fingered the guitar, and it whispered in minor.

This time the strong golden tenor was subdued; it carried across the room, but softly, almost tenderly.

> "Down by the salley gardens my love and I did meet;
> She passed the salley gardens with little
> snow-white feet.
> She bid me take love easy, as the leaves grow on
> the tree;
> But I, being young and foolish, with her would not agree."

It was a simple, plaintive tune. He let the guitar carry it through once alone.

> "In a field by the river my love and I did stand,
> And on my leaning shoulder she laid her
>   snow-white hand.
> She bid me take life easy, as the grass grows on
>   the weirs;
> But I was young and foolish—and now am full of
>   tears."

The applause was slow, reluctant to break the little spell, and then enthusiastic.

"He *is* good," said Carey. "That's Yeats, isn't it?"

Jesse was looking around for Grafton. He wondered if Clock had seen Grafton too. And, damn it, nothing to get hold of, to suggest any new lead. He tried to catch Clock's eye, but Clock was leaning to Fran; they were talking absorbedly, gesturing at each other.

"You like that any better than the ones all about death, Mr. Falkenstein?" Davenport, surprisingly, drew out the fourth chair at the table and sat down.

"Yeats," said Jesse absently. "Very nice, Mr. Davenport, yes. Where's Grafton? I'd like to—" He looked at Davenport. "But you'd know, wouldn't you?"

"Know what, sir?" Davenport balanced his guitar carefully against a leg of the table and added, "Coffee," to the waiter.

Mr. Walters drank and said, "You're pretty good on that thing, aren't you? You let me ask him, Jesse. He's one you don't have to spell out things to. You're lookin' crosswise at him because you like him and you're thinking it could be he's mixed up in this. I don't figure he is. What we'd like to know, Mr. Davenport, is just exactly where it was Mr. Grafton got into his little trouble awhile back."

"Where?" Davenport looked very curious. "Now just what's behind that, sir? I don't rightly see that's anything very relevant."

"I'll tell you why," said Jesse. "Because, damn it, I swear to you—hunch or no—this thing had its roots in the past somehow. I don't know how long ago, or just how. But I've got this hunch that if I can trace Tamar back—find out where she came from—"

"Oh," said Davenport. "That's the notion in your mind." His eyes slid to Elliott Carey. "Not much trouble about that, I wouldn't guess.

I could've given you a good guess on that any time you asked, sir. What do you say, Mr. Carey? You're the one that's studied yourself into an expert on all the different versions and where they come from. She gave you a song. I heard that." He smiled at the coffee the waiter had just set before him.

"What d'you mean?" asked Jesse blankly.

Carey said, "You want to know where the girl hailed from originally? Well, I only talked with her a few times, and the Lord knows I'm not an expert on that subject, but you're bound to pick up this and that, as Lee just implied. I don't know, let me remember—you never get that z sound in *greasy*, for instance, much above southern Illinois, and I don't think I ever heard anybody say geetar for guitar above the Mason-Dixon line. And—"

"Accents," said Jesse. He looked from Carey to Davenport.

"You want to know where she grew up?" said Davenport. "Sir, I could pinpoint it for you. Drifted around quite a bit, so I have, down there—and other places. Couldn't say what use it might be to you, sir, because that one, I'd say she left the nest right early and she'd been to a lot of places and met up with a lot of people in those places since— but you want to find out where she started from, you have a look at west Tennessee. On up from Tipton county, maybe Lauderdale or Crockett county. Maybe on up north from there, but I'd say Crockett county. Somewhere along there. Me, I was born in Guthrie, Kaintuck', but we moved down to Gibson county later. But we broke up early, after Ma went. Somewhere around there, Tamar hailed from." He lifted his cup and drank.

FOURTEEN

"I don't think Andrew's feeling happy about it," said Jesse, hanging up his jacket. "Neither am I. Of course O'Riordan said she didn't answer the door and he just went away. What else would he say? Nothing says he didn't. Nothing says there was really very much between 'em." He unknotted his tie, slung it over the tie rack. He began to unbutton his shirt.

"Do you think Davenport's right about where she came from?" Nell was sitting up in bed, looking very tempting in a new topaz-colored nylon gown, her hair neatly braided for the night. Athelstane occupied the whole other half of the bed, and was producing gently whuffled snores.

"Alienation of affections," said Jesse, eying him. "*I* don't know. I guess he could be—he claims to be the expert. I've sort of fallen out of love with that idea. Where'd it get us? She probably left the home town at a fairly early age—knowing where she left from doesn't point to where she's been in the meantime or what's happened to her."

"Well, it just might, Jesse. Somehow. I think you ought to check on that area, anyway."

"Oh well, it couldn't do any harm, I suppose," said Jesse good-humoredly. He hung up his trousers, found a clean pair of pajamas, and got into his robe. "Anything to please you." He surveyed her approvingly. "Says somewhere in the Talmud, *The grace of a wife delighteth her husband, her discretion shall fatten his bones.* You're looking exceptionally graceful."

"Fatten his bones!" said Nell. "Of all the ridiculous— Maybe I'm not discreet enough. I try to feed you as well as I can, but if your bones are fattening it's not detectable from the outside."

"Have we got a map anywhere?" Jesse wandered out to the living room and presently came back with an old college textbook. "How do you tell when west Tennessee gets to be east, anyway? Impossible shapes they made so many states. I suppose on account of mountains or something. Yes, well, do it thorough or not at all. There you are. Eighteen counties." He found his pen and took notes of the county seats. "Union City, Dresden, Paris, Huntingdon, Dyersburg, Trenton, Lexington, Henderson—"

"I didn't ask for a list, darling," said Nell. "Just said you ought to check. You never know what's going to give you a lead."

Jesse put his pen down and closed the book. "No, but—I wonder what the hell he meant," he added to himself irrelevantly. "He usually means something."

"Who?"

"Our young-at-heart octogenarian," said Jesse. "Said he remembered reading somewhere that a straight stick points two ways."

"Well, and so it would," said Nell. "What had you been talking about?"

"O'Riordan, I think. But damn it, how could we tie O'Riordan in? There's no evidence that he was anything but a casual boy friend. Did I tell you she'd tried to pawn that sapphire ring?"

"*Had* she?"

"Thought she might have, when Austin said he'd told her it was valuable. I looked up the pawnbroker nearest her, and went and asked. He remembered it all right—she'd come in that Saturday morning. He offered her a hundred and fifty for it—of course you never get anywhere near the full value—and she got mad. Said, 'But he said it was worth a lot more,' and walked out. Well, sure it was. Evidently she didn't try another place, because there the ring was."

"She certainly wanted to raise some money in a hurry," said Nell thoughtfully, tickling Athelstane under one black floppy ear.

"To get out of this burg and head back for Chicago," agreed Jesse. He shoved Athelstane, with effort, far enough toward Nell so that he could sit on the edge of the bed, and lit a cigarette. "Since Wednesday night or Thursday morning. Also apparently scared about something—hence the gun."

"Yes. Nobody she knew admits to seeing her Wednesday night, but she implied to Austin that she expected somebody."

"Which is why I say now, what the hell does it matter where she came from? I'm still sold that the murder came out of something in her past, but the odds are it was something that happened after she'd left home and family."

"But that could be a starting place," said Nell.

He agreed morosely.

"Jesse. This O'Riordan. Davenport seemed pretty sure about the Tennessee thing, and even you said she sounded Southern. Why should O'Riordan say she came from New England?"

"Obviously," said Jesse, "because that's what she'd told him. She'd also said so to Betty Lewis and that Garcia girl, and probably others. She wasn't letting anybody know—" He stopped and looked at her.

"Exactly," said Nell, looking smug. "When you reason it out. Why wasn't she? What could it matter to her, here or now, that people should know she'd come from Tennessee or—or Timbuktu? Unless—"

"You may have a little something there indeed," he said. "Yes. Unless something had happened back there that—what? Think I'm reviving interest in finding what her home town was. Yes, she even lied on the marriage-license application, put down New York." He prodded Athelstane's solid hindquarters. "You've got a bed of your own, monster," he said absently. "Think I'll have a small drink—want one?"

"Just a little one, if you are."

Jesse went out to the kitchen. When he came back with two glasses, he said, "Anyway, Andrew saw O'Riordan again. And checked on Grafton. Thought he would. Conscientious as he is. He doesn't like it so well now, but he's not saying so yet. Grafton seems to be out of the running." He told her why.

"Oh. Jesse, I'm thinking about Lee Davenport now."

"Oh, so've I," said Jesse sadly.

"He seems to have grown up in west Tennessee too. And his brother knowing Grafton, and Tamar knowing about Grafton—"

"Well, look at the map, there's quite a lot of west Tennessee. And I'd guess he's been out on his own since he was just a kid too. He implied that. He's a good seven, eight years older than Tamar. Even if she— Look, a lot of people live over in Orange County, they don't all know each other."

"I just mentioned it," said Nell meekly.

Jesse prodded Athelstane some more; Athelstane sighed deeply and snuggled closer to Nell, his jowly lips smacking loudly as he hunted some dream quarry. "Fran," said Jesse, "collected the usual percentage of interested looks. I wish to God Andrew would act a bit more Neanderthal with her."

Nell laughed. "So you've worked that out? What Fran really wants, though she may not know it, is a man to get the whip hand over her and threaten the cave-man technique."

"Just threaten?" Jesse cocked an eye at her.

"Only she mustn't ever find out it was just threats," said Nell demurely. "We can't all be civilized like you and me."

"What Fran needs," said Jesse darkly, "is a good spanking once a week regular until she stops acting like a—"

"Oh now, there's a lot of good in Fran. She's really quite intelligent," said Nell, sounding amused. "Why does she keep on going around with him, unless—? Only she won't admit it to herself."

"You may have something there too," said Jesse thoughtfully. "You know, I think it might provide the impetus, so to speak, if Andrew was to get shot up a little—oh, nothing serious—by some hood. I mean, in the hushed hospital atmosphere, with him looking all wan and pathetic in his bandages—she just might—"

"Jesse," said Nell severely, "you've been smuggling Ethel M. Dell out of the library! If you don't succeed as an amateur private eye, you can always try your hand at fiction for the women's magazines. I can just *see* Fran—" She began to giggle. "*Or* Andrew! Were you thinking of ambushing him and shooting him yourself, to set up this romantic scene?"

"God forbid, probably kill him, not being used to lethal weapons."

Nell laughed and picked up her glass again. "But I wonder what he *did* mean?" she said suddenly. "Darling Mr. Walters. About a stick pointing two ways. What's that got to do with O'Riordan?"

"God knows," said Jesse. "Let's get this monster into his own bed."

Tuesday started out being a rather hectic day for Clock. Some new evidence came in on the Leimert Park homicide, and as Petrovsky and Lopez were both out, he had to check it himself. He'd sent a man out to collect Traynor the bartender for the color-blindness test, and got back just in time to be waylaid by the lab man who'd made it.

"Well, you spotted it all right, Sergeant—he's way off the beam, way off. It was a hell of a shock to him, too—he'd never suspected it. Like nearsighted people, you know—they just think everybody sees things that way. And just as more men have it than women, it's likelier men wouldn't realize it, not taking so much interest in clothes and so on. As a matter of fact, color blindness of one sort or another is much commoner than most people realize. You see, the layer of the retina closest to the chorioid—"

"Wait a minute. There are different types?"

"Oh yes. Not a great deal is definitely known about it, actually, but the most modern surmise is that the cones are responsible for color perception. The rods and cones are contained in the second level down from the retina—"

For some reason Clock found himself thinking about the mote in thy neighbor's eye. "Yes?" he said patiently.

"The first is the pigment layer, which contains the visual purple, which of course affects the ability of the eye to adapt to conditions of light and dark. The nerve cells known as rods and cones come next. The cones are believed to affect the vision in light, the rods in darkness. Now, there are three fundamental color impressions—red, green and violet. Hering's theory suggests—"

"Look," said Clock mildly. "All I want to know is, Traynor doesn't see colors normally?"

"Well, no. There are different types of the disability, you know, some mild and some very basic. Not too much is definitely known. But, no, of course he doesn't, when he even confuses dark shades with light. It seems to be a basic type of—"

"All right, thanks, let me have a report," said Clock. He went on into his office and found Petrovsky eating a ham sandwich at his desk. "What did you get on York and O'Riordan?" he asked.

Petrovsky made a derisive sound through the sandwich, swallowed and said, "Waste of time, Sergeant. I don't like this color-blind bartender either—nice piece of evidence gone blooey—but it's not the only evidence says Austin did it, after all. I grant you, they neither of 'em are exactly the ordinary honest young fellows they claim to be. Lessee. York said he'd been in Barstow on a job, didn't he? For his brother-in-law. Well, he wasn't. Been in the County Jail for sixty days, for letting a lot of traffic tickets accumulate—illegal turns, speeding, one drunk charge—and contempt of court. Fines amounted to nearly six hundred bucks. He finally paid up. He's got an almost brother-in-law—at least the guy's sister claims she's engaged to him—name of Fox, Thomas L. Fox, foreman of a construction gang for an outfit in Walnut Park. Otherwise, not much shows on him. Not much shows on

O'Riordan. One thing—neither of 'em's registered with Social Security."

"Yes. You want to bet? Smalltimers. Drifters. Picking up the eating money any way handy—gambling, petty theft, maybe break-ins here and there. O'Riordan not in Records?"

"Uh-uh." Petrovsky took another bite of sandwich. "York's traffic tickets go back about eighteen months. They've revoked his license, but he'd only got a California license about six months before that. Put down he was from across the line in Nevada, showed a Nevada license. It'd been issued the same year."

"Oh really," said Clock. What did that say? States varied in requirements and tests. Nevada was a hell of a lot of empty space with just a few people, a few towns—comparatively speaking. Pretty easygoing on its driving population. So, ask over there where York told them he'd come from? Why? York—and his pal O'Riordan—rather obviously the typical rolling stones, the smalltime drifters living lives without pattern. The kind who crossed over the line now and then, as he'd just said, but stayed smalltime. And they were on the outskirts of a case that was finished, damn it. Out of his hands. He had enough to do without worrying about cases he'd passed on to the D.A.

He'd really had no business sending that ring and watch, and the mysterious little leather bag, up to the lab. The case was over, as far as his office was concerned; that aspect of Tamar hadn't any connection with her murder at all. The fact that maybe she had stolen jewelry. Just maybe during the committing of a more serious crime. *The other one wasn't near so much fun. . . .* Tamar.

"You ever think about forms of justice?" he asked suddenly.

"Hardly ever," said Petrovsky around the sandwich. "Too abstruse a problem, Sergeant."

Abstruse was a hell of a good word, thought Clock. Here was this girl Tamar, ignorant, selfish, completely lacking in any empathy for any other human being, existing only for what pleasure, what possessions she could get out of life—demonstrably doing no positive good and probably a good deal of harm (there was "the little Fielding girl," and Jeanie Carlson—and Grafton). There was some good hearsay evidence that she had once been, at the least, an accessory to two murders, a robbery and willful arson. If she'd been caught up with on those counts, she'd at least have run a great risk of the gas chamber. Yet when a man—for whatever reason—lost his temper and choked her to death, he was legally guilty of murder too. Whereas the upright fellow at San Quentin who activated the lever that dropped the gas pills—

But of course you couldn't equate it; there was a clear-cut difference.

"What it comes down to," Petrovsky was saying, "there may be some laws on the books anybody with common sense wonders how they got there. But as long as they are on the books, it's our job to see they get kept. Simple." He finished the sandwich, said, "I should've gone out and got a salad or something instead, stick by that diet, but what the hell? You know something? There's one law still on the books I'd just love to see got kept. Set every patrolman in town enforcing it—with a stiff fine maybe, or a weekend in jail. One that says it's illegal to dress like the opposite sex. All those fat women in pants—" He looked wistful.

Clock laughed. "That'd be fun all right." He got up and told Sergeant Miller to send out for a ham sandwich on wheat and some coffee. It had just arrived when one of the minor great men of the force arrived on its heels, Philip Abrams himself, first assistant to the lab chief, seldom seen out of his own particular domain.

"Well, what brings about this honor?" asked Clock, sitting up.

Abrams had a little paper parcel in one hand. He was a short, broad little man with a round face, the square graceful hands of the technician, and he retained a childlike excitement and enthusiasm at helping the good guys play cops and robbers. He untied his little parcel with care and handed over the ring box and the diamond watch uninterestedly.

"The things you boys are sending us these days," he said. "Sorry to have taken so long, but I had to do a little research on it. Unusual research," he added. "Deadly dull job."

Clock grinned at him. "Go on, you know you love it. What've you got to tell me?"

Abrams collapsed into the chair beside the desk. "There's nothing to be got from that jewelry, what'd you expect? Like that fellow in those old-fashioned detective stories, use the microscope and find the different kinds of dust, so you know right off X lives on a street with a bakery at one end and a lumber mill at the other. Tosh. It's ordinary commercial stuff. The watch retails for three-eighty-five. Standard design. The ring was made by a big manufacturing jewelers' firm, Crown

—also a standard design, but not so many made because not so many people are ready to spend upwards of seven to eight hundred bucks for a ring. Either one might have been bought at any good jewelry shop in the country."

"Thanks so much," said Clock. "And?" He knew there was an "and"; Abrams was looking excited, his pale eyes bright behind his old-fashioned rimless glasses.

"You almost stumped me on this," he said. He unfolded the paper again and looked fondly at the tiny leather drawstring bag. "It's empty now," he said almost regretfully, "except for the teeth, of course. Hardly enough left to analyze of what was in it."

"Well, what was in it? What is it, anyway?"

"I had to do some research," said Abrams. "Me, graduate chemist, reading up on voodoo. Hell of a thing. This little thing, Sergeant, is sometimes called a juju. And other names, varying as to the locality. It is—or was—a personal amulet, a sort of protective talisman against ghosties and ghoulies and things that go bump in the night. Against old boogerman. They're usually made up by some old witch woman—somebody with that reputation. The stuff gathered at the dark of the moon or whenever the stars were right—you know. Want to know what was in it? There was some mountain-rowan leaf, and some mistletoe, and dried Spanish moss, and a small tooth which originally belonged to a dog, and the tail end—no pun intended—of what was left of a couple of rattlesnake rattles, and a piece of red cotton cloth, and a single claw from, I think, a bobcat—I'm not a zoologist—"

"Are you leveling?" asked Clock incredulously. "What the hell—"

"That's how I felt at first," said Abrams, smiling broadly. "But as I say, I did some research. It seems these things aren't so uncommon as you might think. A lot of people, even reasonably educated people, are superstitious." He tapped the little bag. "This is Negro superstition—uneducated Negro, of course—very prevalent through the South once and, so the authorities say, still to be found in remote areas and some not so remote. Protective white magic. How the hell does it come into one of your homicides?"

How the hell indeed, thought Clock. He looked at the little bag. He could see now, crudely tanned deerskin. Protective magic. Tamar's. Yes? Must have been. Yes, ignorant, selfish, childish Tamar. Negro?

Davenport down at the Ace-High. How wild could you get? Those boys down there, the Negro businessmen, professional musicians, were wise city boys long away from the witch doctor.

Tamar. And what Jesse said Davenport had told him about her origin. Could be, that sort of background—poor-white— She'd treasure such a little talisman. Well, it hadn't helped her much.

"I'll be damned," he said thoughtfully. "Well, I can see where it might fit in. Thanks very much. It tells me nothing useful, but thanks anyway."

Abrams said, "I thought you'd find it interesting. I did. The things you boys send us these days . . ."

Tuesday went on being a little hectic, and Clock didn't take much notice when a messenger came in with a cardboard carton, said, "Returned from Prints," and dumped it on the corner of his desk. He glanced at it and grimaced—that flotsam and jetsam gleaned from the earth near where the anonymous corpse had lain. He'd never expected anything out of that. Waste of time to send it in.

Those Royballs. The likeliest ones, as Petrovsky put it, to have left a corpse behind. And not one hope in hell of pinning it on them. Even when they located them. When they'd never found out who the corpse had been.

That was at two twenty, and Clock went on to question a very-maybe suspect in that liquor store holdup, and to more paper work. It was nearly four thirty when Reynolds from the Prints office called him.

"Don't you look at your mail, Andrew? I've been expecting you to call me all excited and offer to buy me a drink or something."

"What?" said Clock blankly. "I don't—"

"That stuff from your Holland Street corpse," said Reynolds amusedly. "I don't know how you expected there'd be any prints after all this time. But we're pretty fastidious down here, you know, don't like getting our hands dirty. We took the trouble to wash off a couple of your exhibits. Better take a look, Andrew. We felt sort of pleased with ourselves. Just one little word of gratitude—"

"Hold on," said Clock. He put the phone down and slid his swivel chair down to the end of the desk where the carton sat. The flotsam and jetsam—dog collar, yo-yo, half an ace of spades, the— There was a little cardboard box. And a note stapled to the carton, in Reynolds' sprawling hand: "Sorry to take this long, but you did say no priority.

And see what showed, just with a little elbow grease! Basic first principles—cleanliness is next to, etc."

Clock opened the box. Inside, on a bed of cotton, was the little St. Christopher medal. Once suspended from a fine silver chain: an inch of that still hung from it. It had been cleaned and polished, and was obviously sterling silver: the bas-relief figures of St. Christopher and Christ Child stood out plainly.

He turned it over, puzzled.

Engraving, clear and sharp.

G.E.T. And below that, *B.T. A-B—Prot.* And below that, *Wichita, Kan.*

"I will be Goddamned!" said Clock. "I will be—" And he lunged to rummage in drawers. "Pete! For God's sake where's that list, where'd you—"

"What's up?" asked Petrovsky, appearing in the doorway.

"The list, that first Missing— All right. All right, I've got it—"

And there it was. There, by God, it was. George Edward Tice, twenty-three, six-one, a hundred and seventy, hair brown, eyes brown —reported missing September 10, 1962.

Clock snatched up the phone. "Reynolds? Boy, I'll buy you a drink all right! I'll buy you enough drinks to give you the D.T.'s! I'll—"

Reynolds laughed. "It wasn't hard to find, Andrew. You boys ought to cultivate more hygiene, 's all."

FIFTEEN

The flyer had been sent originally to the Highway Patrol, and passed on in much abbreviated form. Now, when Clock got on to that office and took down the full details, it began to look as if they'd got somewhere.

George Edward Tice had left his parents' home in Wichita, Kansas, on August 28, 1962, driving a 1960 blue Chevrolet Corvette, license plate such-and-such; the car was registered in his name in California. He was a third-year student at California Polytechnical College, and was therefore heading for Pasadena, to the college boardinghouse where he lived during the school term. He had expected to arrive there, taking his time on the cross-country drive, on September first or second. When he hadn't shown up by the date the fall term began, the college registrar queried his home address, and he was eventually reported officially missing, by his father, on September tenth.

"Somebody did some work on this," said Clock, "and found out something. Joe, call down to Traffic—and check with the Highway Patrol—and see if anybody here ever picked up his car." He got on the outside phone and requested a call to Police Headquarters in Wichita. He was told he'd have to wait for it. Not long, said the long-distance operator soothingly.

He got on the inside phone and chased down Dr. De Villa. "Come up here and read a description, please. We think we've identified that corpse, want your confirmation." But that was really superfluous, once he read over the detailed information on that original flyer. All they'd had on Tice here was his name and a general description; this filled in a lot more.

Twenty-three, six-one, a hundred and seventy. Complexion medium-fair, hair brown, eyes brown. Appendectomy scar, scar fracture of right leg eight years old. Would probably be wearing sports clothes, a gold Bulova wrist watch on a gold flexible band, and a fourteen-karat gold class ring bearing the seal of the Wichita High School with, on its shank, his initials and the date of his graduation, 1959. Possibly also wearing a little-finger ring of gold set with a one-carat white zircon, and on a neck chain a sterling St. Christopher medal with his initials, blood-type and religion indicated on its reverse side.

Clock got up and paced, waiting for the doctor, waiting for the long-distance call. Petrovsky was reading the description. "Brother, talk about miracles! And we said it was a waste of time collecting all that stuff! I suppose the medal got torn off somehow when they—whoever—were burying him, and dropped a ways off. Well, you never know, do you? But how the hell did he get there? A nice clean-cut college boy—down on Holland Street? And those Royballs—listen, they'd already—"

"I know, I know!" said Clock. "Just gives us a few more problems." He stopped short, fingering his jaw, and then said abruptly, "I want Jack Battuck and Mrs. Manfred—no, skip her, get that other woman, one who lived next door, what the hell's her name—Mrs. Kale. She seemed a lot nosier, she may remember something useful. Go bring 'em both in, now. Apologize, but—you know the routine."

"Aye, aye, sir. I suppose I don't get to go home for dinner," said Petrovsky.

"You're on a diet anyway," Clock reminded him. He paced some more. Yes, how the hell had George Edward Tice ended up under the garage floor of 2808 Holland Street? Damn it, those Royballs had moved there in July, early in July, a good two months before. No indication that either of them had been away. Tice didn't sound the kind to have known anybody in that neighborhood. You could guess with fair certainty, substantial money, going to Cal Tech, driving a Corvette, the jewelry, the fact that he hadn't apparently been working his way . . . Various police forces would have done some work on this, and Clock wanted to talk to all of them.

He looked at his watch. Ten to five. It'd be ten to seven in Wichita; a lot of people just sitting down to dinner.

De Villa came in and he thrust the report at him. "Is this our boy? Looks a hundred percent to me."

De Villa looked it over and agreed. "So I was that far out in my guess—I wouldn't have said the body was that old, thirty months call it. Poor kid. Sounds like a decent kid too. How did he end up like that, I wonder?"

"We'll try to find out," said Clock, and leaped for the phone as it rang. He was answered by the night desk sergeant in Wichita; transferred to a lieutenant, who didn't seem to know much about it; transferred to a captain who said that the chief had taken a personal interest in that and he'd better talk to him, and gave him the chief's home number. Annoyed, Clock put through another long-distance call and eventually was connected with a heavy bass voice that identified itself as belonging to Chief Burroughs. Clock told him what they'd just come up with, and Burroughs said he'd be damned.

"I'd figured we'd never know any more about that one," he said. "God, it'll be a shock to his mother, bring it all back again—and she just lost her husband a few months back, too—stroke. Buried in a *garage?* I will be damned."

"I suppose the state police all across the country between looked," said Clock. "Do you know what conclusion they came to? Was there ever a spot pinpointed where he was last seen, or anything like that? You know what route he was taking?"

"Sure—sure, I can give you all that. My God, after all this time. Don't seem possible. Sure, but you'll want to talk to Captain Eden of our state police. He did most of the work on it. My God, Sergeant, you aren't asking identification after—? His mother—"

"The body's already buried. But it's pretty definite it was him all right. Where can I contact this Eden? . . . O.K., thanks, I've got that."

"My God," said Burroughs. "Well, I can tell you that when everything was in on it, as far as we could all make out, Captain Eden figured it was another o' those hitchhiker things. But you'd better talk to him. This is really definite? Because if so, I'd better go break the news to Martha—his mother. Poor soul."

"We've got that St. Christopher medal with his initials. From where the body was. And the descriptions tally exactly."

"Be damned," said Burroughs heavily. "Well. Thanks very much, Sergeant, but I don't relish telling Martha. After all this time."

"Was his car ever picked up anywhere?"

"Yeah, the police found it abandoned, about a week after he turned up missing—to show, I mean—in a town called Gardena, somewhere your way."

"Oh," said Clock. "Really. Well, thanks— We'll probably be in touch with you." He hung up, called long distance and asked for the number Burroughs had given him. Lopez came in and said Traffic didn't know anything about the car. "No, it was left down in Gardena," said Clock. "Get onto them and find out the details, will you?" Gardena was one of the towns within the big town that was incorporated, and maintained its own force. Lopez got on the outside phone, and Clock waited to be put in touch with Captain Eden.

Who, when he arrived on the line, sounded brisk and competent. And as incredulous as Burroughs. "I will be damned," he said. "After all this time. So it seems we were all wrong—he did get to California after all, not just his car."

"How did you figure it? Anything suggestive turned up at the time?"

"Quite a bit," said Eden. "Let me think back. Of course I'll look up all my records on it, but I can give you a rough outline. The Tices are fairly substantial citizens, money, you know, and we all put our backs into it. We knew which road he'd be taking, highway sixty out of Enid, through Amarillo, over to Globe, Arizona. And probably the alternate sixty-seventy across the California border. All those state boys were out looking and asking—Texas, New Mexico, Arizona. Three or four places—gas stations, restaurants—remembered the car. But you know how it is on any national highway, there're so many cars coming through—and we were asking a good two or three weeks afterward. Then when the car turned up in California, well, after we'd all heard what that Arizona rancher said, we figured—"

"What rancher?"

"Sorry, I should've told it in order. Far as I recall, it was somewhere outside a place called Superior. Lot of empty territory out there, I gather. Don't remember the man's name, it'll be on record. He heard the state boys were asking around, finally came in to tell his story in case it connected. Seems he'd been riding around his ranch one afternoon, and at a place where the road crosses it—a secondary road, not the highway—he came across this blue car. He didn't know much about cars, couldn't say what make it was, but he did say it was royal blue and a small car, with a long hood. Close enough? Anyway, there was a girl and a man in it, and he said the man was lying back as if he was asleep. He rode up closer, to ask if they were out of gas or something, and right away the girl got out of the car and said it was all right, they'd just stopped to look at a map, and she went back and started the car up in a hurry. That was all he saw, but he also said that about an hour later when he came back that way, he saw a blue car going down the road in the same direction, couldn't swear it was the same one but he thought so. Well, that made it look to all of us as if—"

"Sure," said Clock. "The same sad old story. The homicidal hitch-hiker. A *girl?*"

"Yeah, I know. But various people all across his trail remembered the car, and one place—a roadside restaurant in Arizona—several people said he was with a dark-haired girl. But if he was killed for his cash and car, well, no girl did that. Or hid the body so careful it never turned up. There might have been a man to help her—we don't know."

"Yes. And a Corvette—quite a little squeeze, three people. Did he have a habit of picking up hitchhikers?"

"Some conflicting testimony there," said Eden. "A couple of his close friends said he usually did pick up men in uniform. His mother said righteously he'd never do such a thing as pick up a *girl*—the class of woman who'd be *hitchhiking!*" Eden sounded amused.

"Oh," said Clock. "I see."

"That type," said Eden. "You get me. We didn't get much out of her, she's the sort goes hysterical in a crisis. It was a hell of a thing, all the same. You can see on a thing like that, there's never anything like definite evidence. But putting what we got—or didn't—together, it looked as if he'd been murdered—so there probably was a man—for what cash he had on him and the car. They hunted around the spot where the rancher'd seen the car, but hell, all that open country, you couldn't cover every inch. Never found anything to say he'd been murdered, but when he didn't turn up anywhere— I mean, he was a responsible boy. And now he shows up in L.A. after all. Be damned. Well, I guess you've got something on your hands, Sergeant. Not very likely you'll get anywhere on it this late."

"Maybe not," said Clock, "but I have to look. The name Royball mean anything to you? Well, do you know if the Tices knew anybody by that name?"

"No idea, we can ask."

"Yes. O.K., thanks— I'll be glad to see your notes on it."

It wasn't even sure, he reflected, that it should be his case. What that rancher said—young Tice might have been killed anywhere between here and where he'd picked up his passenger—or passengers. A girl. Well, if thirteen years on the police force had taught him anything at all, he thought, it should have taught him that when it came to good or bad character, capability for violence and so on, there really wasn't much to choose between. He dialed long distance and asked to be connected to the Arizona State Police office in Phoenix.

Jesse sat back in the deepest armchair and ruminated. The phonograph emitted the magnificent soothing mathematics of the Toccata and Fugue in D Major, he was comfortably full of dinner, a mild drink stood ready at his hand with cigarettes and Athelstane was sprawled asleep across his feet.

A straight stick pointed two ways. Too abstruse to figure, he thought. So what?

All right, take it point by point from the beginning, maybe some little overlooked thing would point a direction where to hunt a new lead.

Wednesday night Tamar had been expecting somebody. (Wait a minute. Austin said the bedroom door was closed on Sunday night, but open on Wednesday—as it usually was. Was somebody already there on Sunday night when Austin saw her? Well, think about that later.) She hadn't been much interested when Austin told her he'd seen a lawyer about a divorce. Had hurried him out. And no mention of money.

Yes. Something else on her mind right then. No clue as to what.

Thursday morning she went out and stole Betty Lewis' gun. Scared of somebody? Or just preparing for a possible emergency?

From Thursday on, she was urgently pressing Austin for money. She tried to pawn the sapphire ring. She demanded blackmail money from Grafton for the first time. Something had come up that made her anxious to get away, out of town. All that pointed away from Ray Austin; but the way the D.A. had set up the case, that could be quite irrelevant to her murder. The murder, as Andrew and the D.A. had built it up, had been committed impulsively, perhaps unintentionally, when Austin lost his temper.

Only it hadn't been. All that had something to do with it, must have. Something that had happened or something she had learned that Wednesday night, had triggered all that. Sure, maybe the murder had happened just that way, for little or no real motive, somebody losing his temper at her. But her need for money to leave town was somehow relevant.

The phonograph shut itself off, switched itself on and began to emit the solemn first Brandenburg Concerto. Jesse snuggled deeper into the armchair, eyes closed. He found Bach a definite aid to cerebration.

Well, that was valid. But how to reach any conclusion as to who she'd been expecting that night? Or why?

Tamar's immediate circle. She'd picked up people and dropped them. She had probably known a good many more people here than they'd found out about. The ones that showed, that Austin remembered. Everybody who'd known her wouldn't necessarily come forward to say so, and especially— Well. The crowd who frequented The Cygnet. Rodriguez, the Garcia girl, Jeanie Carlson (pity James Carlson had an alibi), Betty Lewis—they never had looked up that Frank Goldberg who'd evidently first brought Jeanie to The Cygnet: could he be tied in? No harm to find him and take a look at him, thought Jesse. And Grafton, and come to think he'd never tried again to check on Anne Kathryn Fielding. Just possibly some irate father, uncle, brother— Only that didn't jibe with the something out of the past. Davenport. Yes, Davenport of the golden compelling tenor, who had known— Some girl named Pat. The girls she worked with at the Plaza Hotel. And, of course, Dickie O'Riordan.

O'Riordan such a nice candidate, thought Jesse. The handsome weakling, black-Irish good looks. A boy friend of Tamar's—before and after she married Ray Austin. Dickie O'Riordan who'd been in the building an hour after Austin had left it. But no way to prove he'd done anything but knocked at her apartment door, got no answer and gone away.

Hell. Jesse took another swallow of his drink and put out his cigarette. The phonograph switched off, switched on and began the *St. John Passion*.

(Davenport said, "Good, but not the spontaneous thing, from the guts." *My name is Death, cannot you see. . . .*)

York. No. York wasn't one of the Cygnet crowd. Just O'Riordan's roommate.

That pair, said Andrew, drifters across the legal line. Very probably. But—O'Riordan? He looked and acted like something of a weak sister. Could you see him doing a murder? That murder?

Jesse thought gloomily that this would probably come to trial. He'd hoped like hell to come up with something to clear Austin definitely before that; he didn't like criminal cases; a very long chance that he could argue the jury into a Not Guilty verdict, claiming Austin as an unlikely killer, et cetera. Nothing to get hold of, damn it. But—

"What?" he said, starting convulsively at Nell's voice.

"I said," said Nell firmly, "that you promised to take me to see the new Disney tonight. At the Pantages. *Come* on. Do you good to forget all your problems for a while and have a good laugh."

"Oh hell," said Jesse plaintively. "Did I? Damn. Oh well. *Better a man's wickedness than a woman's blandishments* . . . I wasn't getting anywhere anyway. Vicious circle, damn it. Get off me, monster. Wait till I put on a tie."

All the state forces were very prompt and helpful; long teletypes had poured in overnight. They were about all Clock had; Battuck hadn't been found last night, and the Kale woman was visiting her daughter in San Diego, expected back today.

He was most interested in the complete statement, forwarded by the Arizona State Police, of rancher John Coleman. He read it over again thoughtfully.

It was Monday, September third. I had ridden out to the northwest border of my spread to— [Skip that. Here]: I saw this car. It was a kind of bright blue, not a very big car. I don't know nothing about them foreign cars, I thought that was what it was. There was two people in it, a man and a woman. As I come up closer, I saw the man was laying back in the seat like he was asleep. No, sir, I didn't see no blood but I wasn't in maybe twenty-five feet. I couldn't say what he looked like, but I got the idea he was kind of a young fellow, I don't know why. She got out like she didn't want me coming closer. I asked if they was out of gas and she said no, just stopped to look at a map, it was all right. She said I had a likely-looking horse. I was riding my quarter horse Billy, he's likely all right. No, sir, all this time the man in the car never moved. The girl, well, I don't know, she was maybe about twenty and dark-haired. I wouldn't call her good-looking, she looked as if she hadn't combed her hair in a week, and she had sort of queer eyes, like a cat's. She had on a pair of blue pants and a shirt without any sleeves. Yes, it was like she didn't want me too near that car. She got back in quick and started the motor. . . .

Clock thought that maybe all that said the murder had been done in

Arizona. By the girl? That savage dent in the corpse's skull. Well, a heavy enough weapon . . .

Why bring the body to L.A.? Maybe Coleman had scared her—or them—from dumping it? But the car had come back—if it had been the same car.

Clock wondered if there had been any cover around that spot, trees or bushes. Because, say there was a second man, he might have been around somewhere—digging a grave?—and so the girl had to come back for him after Coleman had gone. Which was pure imagination.

Petrovsky looked in the door. He wore a harassed expression. He said, "Sergeant, I'm sorry, but—"

He was jostled out of the doorway. "*Who* is in charge here? I must see the officer in charge—"

Clock stood up. She was a large, soft-looking feather bed of a woman, much made up, in dramatic black upon which diamonds glittered; her voice throbbed with emotion. "Are you the officer who found my poor fated boy? I must see him— I will never believe until I have seen the remains—all these months I've kept faith that he was alive somewhere, somehow, but they told me— Ah, I would know! A mother's—"

"Er—Mrs. Tice," said Petrovsky unnecessarily. "Seems she took the first plane out—"

"Yes," said Clock with a mental groan. "Won't you sit down, Mrs. Tice? Of course you have all our sympathy, but I'm afraid the body has been buried. You understand—"

"They told me it was definitely Eddy—but I would never be *certain* unless—a mother's intuition, officer— I came at once—"

"Yes, yes," said Clock soothingly. She subsided into a chair, still panting slightly, her diamonded bosom heaving.

"My poor darling boy—the best son a mother ever had, officer. They were all quite wrong to say Eddy would ever have taken *that sort* of woman into his car—a hitchhiker! Some wicked man, it must have been— My boy was the *soul* of integrity, officer, he never saw the bad in anyone. Never a *moment's* anxiety did he cause me, until this dreadful thing of course—not at all like his sister—my daughter Linda —quite rebellious as an adolescent Linda was, but Eddy—"

"I thought his name was George," said Clock.

The bosom heaved even more convulsively. "My dear, *dear* husband—named for him, but we always called him— I have tried to *be-*

lieve, all this long while, but when Mr. Burroughs called— Some wicked robber, it must have been. Not possibly— Why, he was engaged to a very sweet girl, a real lady, from one of the first families of Pasadena—she had been visiting us that very summer, during Eddy's vacation, and both Mr. Tice and I approved of her *highly*. Such a lady. Eddy would never—"

"Mrs. Tice—please—" said Clock helplessly. He was constitutionally allergic to matrons like Martha Tice, and understood Chief Burroughs' reluctance at having to break the news. Not all the detailed information had come in yet, and he tried to coax her into coherence by asking definite questions. "Would he have been carrying much cash on him? Do you know how much—"

She reared back indignantly, carefully wiping her eyes to avoid smearing the mascara. "Of course he had an adequate amount of money—simply for expenses on his trip, but to *some* low-class people I daresay it would seem like a fortune. He would have had—*as* I told Mr. Burroughs at the time—between two and three hundred dollars. For such a pitiful little amount—my darling Eddy! We had such high hopes of him—" She sobbed eloquently into her lavender-scented handkerchief.

"Yes, it's a tragedy," said Clock awkwardly, wishing that airlines had never been invented. "But as you say, crimes do get committed for really very little—"

She emerged from the handkerchief to fix him with a mournful eye. "*And* besides, there was Joanna's engagement ring. She had chosen it—at Magnusson's, our leading jewelers, but from their catalogue, it had to be ordered especially, and it hadn't come before she left for California. Such a sweet, ladylike girl. A large sapphire, officer, with several side stones, it cost over eight hundred dollars. And Eddy had bought her a Hamilton diamond watch as an engagement present, he had that with him too. You understand, all his grandfather's money had come to him—quite a substantial capital, if I do say so. It—"

Clock came slowly erect in his chair. "Joanna?" he said. "A Hamilton watch? A *sapphire*—"

"Miss Joanna Waverly," said Mrs. Tice with dignity. "Of one of Pasadena's *first* families."

SIXTEEN

"So now we know," said Jesse, "who the other one was. And we can make some pretty accurate guesses about a few other things."

"And just where does it get us?" demanded Clock. "I don't like this. I don't like it at all. Sure, so we can say it looks pretty sure that it was Tamar and some boy friend who murdered Tice. For the cash and the car. And buried him in that garage. Where do the Royballs come in, for God's sake? I don't see Tamar doing that murder alone, I think there must have been a man in it. But absolutely no lead to—"

"The Royballs," said Jesse. "Probably locate them eventually." He slouched in the chair beside Clock's desk and watched the third man in Clock's office, who sat very upright on another chair, glancing at Mrs. Tice's statement identifying the jewelry.

"Yes, but damn it, what about Austin? I—"

"I cannot see," said the third man, who was Lightner of the D.A.'s office, "that this has the slightest thing to do with our case against Austin. I grant you that, taken in conjunction with the reported remarks of Mrs. Austin—hearsay evidence, I remind you, and the woman was drunk at the time—we can postulate that she and some unknown man were responsible for Tice's murder. I agree that it was probably a man who actually killed Tice, and that she was accessory. But that was over two years ago, and has no relevance to the murder of Mrs. Austin herself."

"Oh, hasn't it?" said Clock. "Well, in my book it damn well could have, and I don't feel easy about it."

"The case against Austin is perfectly valid," said Lightner, examining his fingernails. "It's unfortunate about the bartender, but the rest of the evidence remains."

"And that's unfortunate too," said Jesse. "We've turned up some other evidence, how she was anxious to raise some money and leave town—how she stole a gun—and we can guess now what set her off. She heard that Tice's corpse had been found. It was in the papers, just a mention, but I think more likely she heard it on the radio that night. Little shock. Thought he was hidden till Judgment Day."

"And so?" said Lightner with a shrug. "She felt nervous about it turning up after all this time and decided to leave town. I still say that's irrelevant—"

"Doesn't make you think," murmured Jesse, "that maybe the fellow who did that kill was still here too? That maybe it was the Eddy she'd watched cut up the old man a little? Not too likely that Tamar'd joined forces with two such casual killers in her short life? And that, maybe, they'd quarreled or just gone separate ways since and now he, hearing about the corpse and seeing her nervous, maybe he got a little nervous too that she'd give them away somehow? And—"

"You've got an imagination, Mr. Falkenstein," said Lightner. "That's a lot of supposing."

"It sounds logical enough to me," said Clock. "Why'd she want a gun?"

"That," said Lightner, "is the only remotely valid point even to hint at Mr. Falkenstein's—imaginings. But there could have been a reason otherwise. Austin has denied it, but he may have threatened her."

"Oh for God's sake!" said Clock.

"Just a few points," said Jesse. "Austin's a quiet respectable fellow, never been in any trouble before. Reputation for never losing his temper. The one concrete thing you had on him, the blood on his suit, is nullified by the bartender's color blindness. Everything else is circumstantial—sure, quite good evidence as a rule, I'm just pointing it out. He's placed there at what could have been the time of the murder —though the doctor said eight to ten thirty, and Austin left her at eight. Bartender says he came in at eight fifteen, so it's not just his word. He admits slapping her, that's all. And Andrew here, taking for granted it was the usual crude thing, slipped up a little and didn't examine Austin's hands until—"

"Don't remind me!" said Clock, angry at himself. "I know I should have. We charged him two days after the murder, I didn't take a look until next day, and he wasn't marked at all then. But—"

"But," said Lightner patiently, "even though the woman was—er—

knocked around a little before she was choked, she was a small, light-weight woman. He could have marked her without doing much injury to his hands. That would show three days later."

"And she didn't try to fight back? That one would have, take a bet on it," said Jesse. "Didn't try to scratch his face, bite? I think whoever killed her would have got a little marked up, you know."

"Purely hypothetical," said Lightner. "And if you intend to try to introduce this at the trial, I warn you, Mr. Falkenstein, that we will contend formally that it is entirely irrelevant."

"My God, man, use some imagination!" Clock burst out. "Can't you see—"

"I hadn't finished, Mr. Lightner," said Jesse, sliding down a little farther in the chair and contemplating his long legs. "On the one hand, here's Austin, so upright and respectable—and even-tempered. On the other hand, here's Tamar—girl who's been mixed up in several felonies including two murders, along with a man named Eddy. A girl who had, without much doubt, been associated with other similar characters—people outside the law—kind of people who're apt to be unpredictable and dangerous. What are the odds, between a fellow like Austin and one like Eddy?"

"This Eddy is an entirely unsubstantiated individual. A name she mentioned once. There is no evidence—"

"—that there ever was an Eddy who used a knife on an old man, or just maybe killed and robbed Tice with Tamar's help, and is still somewhere around this neck of the woods, and maybe had a little dis-agreement with Tamar when she got nervous about Tice's corpse turning up, and in the course of argument got mad and strangled her. Sure," said Jesse. "But that makes a lot more sense to me than saying Austin did it."

"Austin," said Lightner, "is your client. The evidence—"

"What it comes down to," said Clock, "this doesn't shake you about the charge? You're still proceeding against Austin?"

"Yes, Sergeant. It's new evidence, certainly, but I can't see its rele-vance to the murder of Mrs. Austin." Lightner stood up and directed a cold glance at Jesse. "I'd make a guess myself that you might try to use all this—melodrama—to confuse the case and influence a jury. I'll warn you now that any such typical kike's tricks won't get past the bench, not with an honest judge."

Clock didn't bother to lower his voice as he said what Lightner was to the rigid back going out the door. Jesse slid down on the end of his spine and shut his eyes.

"Annoyin' little man," he said. "Makes just the opposite effect of what he intends. Somebody—one of the Pharaohs?—said awhile back, *Behold, it is a stiffnecked people.* Fellows like Lightner make me feel more so."

Clock swore. "Of course he's not representative—most of the boys in that office are reasonable, at least. I don't like it. I damn well don't like it. I tell you, if Austin gets convicted I'd feel uneasy about it the rest of my life. But there's absolutely no lead to—"

"No," said Jesse, "there isn't, is there? He's quite right, no evidence on it. Somebody else said, *In danger do not depend on miracles.* Take something like that to turn up Eddy, for sure and certain. Funny thing, coincidence. Eddy killing a namesake. But it's a common name."

"That's way out," said Clock, "at first glance. But I'm right behind you. With all this suggestive new stuff. My God, it's a familiar enough story to any cop—crooks falling out, or one getting cold feet and being a dangerous nuisance to another. And Austin's past record so clean. I can build it up." He was pacing angrily.

"No *terminus a quo,*" said Jesse. "We can guess the old man —whoever—was maybe their first venture. But where and when? Had they split up since, just got together again when they met Tice? Or what? I wouldn't take a bet that Eddy's among the friends of hers here who showed. Would you take a bet he's still here?"

"I'm not that big a fool," said Clock.

"Well—" Jesse unfolded himself from the hard straight chair. "So that's that. D.A.'s office being stubborn, maybe on the principle of the bird in hand. But you know—" he picked up his hat and looked at it thoughtfully—"somebody also said, *Is it not that Thou goest with us that we are distinguished?* Hypothetical supernatural powers might not deign to help out a mere Gentile, but me—" He opened the door. "The calendar's full, he won't come up for a while. Never know what might happen."

"Pollyanna," said Clock. "Damn that Lightner. No, I've got some imagination, I can see all that as well as you can. Old sins casting long shadows, so to speak. Eddy—but he's just a ghost, Jesse. We don't even know where to start looking."

"Know a few things," said Jesse. "Make a few more guesses. He was here somewhere—because when she heard about the corpse being found, she got in touch with him and she was expecting him that night. Hurrying Austin out. Also—"

"And O'Riordan came to see her," said Clock.

"I really don't think O'Riordan is Eddy," said Jesse. "That collar-ad minus any guts, knifing one man and banging another over the head? Uh-uh. Also, except for a big piece of luck, the odds were all against your ever identifying an anonymous body— Tamar needn't have been nervous about it. She was a callous little piece of goods, watch a murder done and laugh about it afterward, but she got worried when she thought her own neck might be in danger. Rather think Eddy saw clearer, told her not to be a fool, just sit tight, nobody'd ever find out who the corpse had been. Maybe Eddy got a little cross with her that Wednesday night? By what we can build up about him, he's not one to cross any way at all. Maybe that's why she wanted the gun. So—"

"That's a hell of a lot of maybes," said Clock. "So what, boy?"

"So maybe he's still here," said Jesse. "Didn't see any need to run. Especially after you hauled Austin off to jail. Tell Fran she's been neglecting Father lately, he's complaining. I'll see you."

Clock duly passed on the message across a table at Frascati's, and Fran looked contrite and said she knew, she'd go and see him soon. "It wasn't living our own lives or anything like that, I mean why neither Jesse nor I live with him. All those clocks—half of them in pieces, and Father tinkering with them. And mostly striking clocks. I felt like that Henry Irving thing, the bells, the bells, driving me mad."

"Yes," said Clock inattentively. "Let's go see him after dinner. I feel the need of his—er—perennial calmness."

"*Father?*" said Fran.

"I suppose it's dealing with company law," said Clock. "He makes you feel it's no good worrying. In due time destiny will hand down a decision. This damned thing. That damned Lightner. I wish to God they'd sent Waldon, you can reason with him. That Lightner, looking down his nose at Jesse—"

"Well, you should have listened to Jesse in the first place," said Fran tartly. "You and your circumstantial evidence."

"*On* the evidence, I couldn't have done anything else," said Clock, and unusually for him ordered a second drink. "Don't be arch at me, Frances. I tell you, I'd feel uneasy about it the rest of my life. This force doesn't charge innocent people. Or at least if we do, we don't hang on to them long, find it out. Eddy. Not one smell of a lead—"

"Except that one with the Irish name, what was it?"

"O'Riordan. But it can't be proved he did anything but ring her bell. And I'm with Jesse there, not likely he's Eddy. He's—too lightweight. I wonder if I went over Lightner's head—Douglas is no fool. But on the other hand he's bucking for re-election. Goddamn Alexander Hamilton," said Clock forcefully, and disposed of half his new drink.

"What? Darling Andrew, how many did you have before that one?" Fran was amused.

"Not kidding," said Clock. "Was it Hamilton who set up our legal machinery? Copied from the way Britain did it then—appointive jobs, elective jobs. The way our D.A.'s still are—making it the political deal. Britain got around to reforming that, and nowadays their Public Prosecutor's a civil servant with tenure, no political involvement either way. There's no pressure to yield to pull or the under-the-counter deals. Hell, I'm not saying Douglas isn't an honest man, but he's a politician—"

"Haven't you just contradicted yourself?" asked Fran.

"Maybe so," said Clock. "I didn't vote for him—not my party. But as D.A.'s go— He might listen. And again he might not. Jesse knows that much law, I guess—nothing to say legally this pipe dream is anything but that."

"Nell says she still thinks if you can find out something about where Tamar came from, something suggestive might show up. Jesse's written to all those vital statistics bureaus, I think. I rather think so myself."

"Well," said Clock dubiously, "remains to be seen. You're acting remarkably meek and friendly tonight. No baiting of the crude cop."

"Soothing the savage beast," said Fran placidly. "Besides, I can see you're worried about it, and I don't blame you. It's a queer sort of situation—and when you think of that girl, those two utterly callous murders—"

"Damnation. Yes. I think I will go see Douglas. Just on the long chance . . . Yes, let's go call on your father," said Clock. "Calming influence. And talk politics. He and I agree so well on politics, and somehow—after Lightner—I feel I'd like an evening of being agreed with."

"So you see where we stand," said Jesse gloomily.

Old Mr. Walters sat in the middle of the couch, Athelstane between his knees having his ears scratched, and swallowed bourbon. "Kind of awkward," he said. "I see that."

"Kind of!" said Jesse. "I can say it's easy to build up a story on it, one I told Lightner, counting Austin out. Obvious. Not obvious legally, and no place to start looking for evidence on it."

"I wouldn't say that," said Mr. Walters. He ran his hand down Athelstane's spine and Athelstane moaned happily, leaning against him. "Nice dog. Eddy was here. Might still be here."

"Sure. And I doubt very much that he's among the friends of hers we know about. And again, those two might not have laid eyes on each other since they—or Eddy—buried Tice in that garage. Even if she knew where he was."

"Now, not so fast," said Mr. Walters. "You young fellows go jumping to conclusions. We say this Eddy probably killed Tice because he'd already—according to Tamar—killed some old man, and it's not very likely Tamar'd have taken up with two men capable of that kind of murder. I'm with you there. We don't know where or when the old man was killed, but we know when Tice was killed—two years ago last September, approximate. Say even that they'd killed the old man just before that, maybe were on the run from that job. I somehow don't think so—I got a notion it was awhile before that—but they stayed together that long, anyway. It's pretty certain they landed in L.A. together, on account of Tice's car, isn't it?"

"Yes, but what does that—"

"Way I make out you're reading these two," said Mr. Walters, adding to his drink, "they're what Sergeant Clock calls drifters. Sometimes this side of the law, sometimes that. Line of least resistance. See a chance to get some easy money—like with Tice, poor fellow—no compunction at all, take it the easiest way. But she at least worked, on and off. I think maybe they both stayed here, not necessarily together but keeping in touch. You know. She evidently knew where to reach him when she heard about the body turning up."

"What I'd like to know," said Nell energetically, "is what on earth those Royballs have to do with it. The people who were actually renting the rear house on Holland Street. That just doesn't make sense to me at all. They'd been living there a couple of months, they couldn't be Tamar and Eddy under another name. It could be they were friends of either one—or both—but after all, you don't just walk into a friend's house and say, 'Excuse me, do you mind if I borrow your garage to bury this body I happen to have in the car?' To say the least—"

Mr. Walters smiled at her with kindly superior wisdom. "Now, Nell. Jumping to conclusions. Don't make it a harder problem than it is. I didn't have to do much thinking on that one."

They stared at him. "Oh, you didn't?" said Jesse. "*With the ancient is wisdom; and in length of days understanding.* So expound."

"First place," said Mr. Walters, stroking Athelstane's black jowls, "these Royballs don't seem to be just such very respectable people themselves, do they? Shoplifting and assault. Doesn't say they'd join in a murder. But then again, I got to thinking about their names, and I recalled a little quotation myself. About blood being thicker than water."

"Blood—" said Nell. "*But*—I don't see—"

"We figure that Tice actually got killed somewhere else, and they got scared off dumping the body or burying it, maybe kept looking for a likely place and then found they were too close to L.A. All right. They came to the Royballs' place, probably with Tice's body in the trunk of his car. Why'd they come there? Well, Mrs. Royball's name is Sarah." Mr. Walters retired into his drink.

Jesse struck himself on the forehead. "I'm going senile, maestro. And Tamar had a sister named Sally. *Mea culpa.*"

"Oh, of course!" said Nell excitedly. "Why didn't we see— But it still doesn't point any new way to look. We've just got to think of something, some way to—"

"Well, now, I can quote Scripture along with the devil. *If ye will not have faith, surely ye shall not be established.* I," said Mr. Walters, swallowing bourbon, "have got a hell of a lot of faith that the side of the angels'll always come out right in the end. That there's something working to see the good people win in the last draw."

"That's all very well to say," said Jesse. "We just sit and wait for Austin's guardian angel to materialize with some nice definite evidence on Eddy in his pocket?"

"Angels are neuter," said Nell.

"*I* don't know how it'll come," said Mr. Walters, "but somehow it's got to. Because we've all done our damnedest at this, so now we let the guardian angel take over, you want to put it that way." He reached for the bottle.

"Well, I can't see anything else we *can* do," said Nell.

"I don't know," said Jesse, "that I believe in guardian angels worth a single damn."

At five o'clock on Thursday afternoon he changed his opinion abruptly.

He'd been in court all day, with a tiresome client, an autocratic judge and a bumbling elderly attorney as opponent; when the bench adjourned court for the day he had an incipient headache and felt slightly bilious from the stale sandwich he'd snatched at two o'clock. The bailiff caught him at the courthouse door.

"Telephone, Mr. Falkenstein. It's your office."

"Yes, Miss Williams?" he said resignedly. Miss Williams would probably faint if he ever called her Margaret.

"He says it's important. This man, Mr. Falkenstein. He's a sheriff, he said. A Southerner of some kind. He—"

"A—is he still there?"

"Oh yes, he's been here about half an hour. His name's Ransome. He—"

"Hold everything," said Jesse. "Hang on to him. I'll be there in twenty minutes."

He made it in half an hour, even with the traffic on the freeway. When he came into his office, there was a tall youngish sandy-haired man sitting opposite Miss Williams' desk. He wore an ordinary dark suit and white shirt, but something said they weren't his usual clothes. His long sharp-nosed face was tanned and weatherbeaten, his sharp blue eyes friendly and curious. He stood up leisurely and showed himself as lank and tall as Jesse.

"Mr. Falkenstein? I'm Sheriff Dean Ransome, Lauderdale County, Tennessee." He offered a long bony brown hand. "You wrote a letter about Tamar Adkins. Came as a little surprise to us back home."

"Come into my office, sit down. Now—" Jesse felt a little excited.

"Saw it this morning," said Ransome, sitting down. Leisurely he got out a cigarette. "Bry Lamkin came over and showed it to me. What the hell, he says, lawyer in California wanting to know whether she was born here. He knows how I feel about that one. And I was just that interested, said to myself, I'm due a little vacation, 'n' I got the money in the bank, and why the hell not? So I went up to Ripley and bought a plane ticket. Quite an experience—all that way from home in

a few hours. These jets. And quite a sizable little burg you got here."
His wide mouth stretched. "Took a taxi from the airport. Town seems
to go on forever. Now just why in hell are you asking questions about
Tamar Adkins, Mr. Falkenstein?" He reached into his breast pocket.
"Got her birth certificate here, by the way."

"Dear God, are you the answer to a prayer?" said Jesse. "She's
dead, Sheriff. Strangled. And they've got her husband, who's a very
nice fellow and innocent as a tender babe, locked up for it. He's my
client. And I had a funny hunch that her murder came out of some incident in her past life, and I figured—"

"Now you don't say," said Ransome interestedly.

"She seems to have been involved in two murders—one of an old
man, and the—"

"I guess that plane ticket was an investment," drawled Ransome. "I
wasn't sheriff then, just a deputy—it was five years back—and Sheriff
Wagner, he said it was just a coincidence, them running off just after.
But then, he'd always been kind of sweet on Tamar's ma—she was a
good-looker—and then too, I do suspect he'd been in the habit of getting some bootleg from Jed Adkins. Me, I always figured it was Eddy
Scott accounted for old man Wrather—coroner said it wasn't the fire
killed him, but a knife. Eddy always carried a knife. Well, a lot of
men do down our way. Rumor was old man Wrather had a lot of cash
stashed away in his cabin. And maybe Bobby was in on it too— Bobby
Adkins. Tamar'd been running around with Eddy some. And when
they up and took off the week after— You say she got herself murdered? A real wild one, Tamar— Can't say I'm much surprised."

"Eddy Scott," said Jesse. For a moment he felt he stopped breathing. "You know him? Could describe him?"

Ransome looked mildly surprised. "Well, sure enough, Mr. Falkenstein. Knew all of 'em since they were kids. All the Adkins'. They're
back-hill people, ones to watch. Chancy ones."

"Chancy," said Jesse dreamily. "I believe you." He picked up the
phone and dialed headquarters downtown. "Homicide, please. Sergeant Clock there? O.K. . . . Andrew? Come to Papa, boy—we've got
a witness. With plenty to tell us, I think. . . . O.K." He put the phone
down and looked at Ransome. He said, "I never knew what a guardian angel looked like before. Try one of my cigarettes. Offer you a
drink?"

"I seldom say no to that," said Ransome.

SEVENTEEN

"I think the best way to open this ball," said Jesse, "is for us to tell Sheriff Ransome just what we've got and haven't got. And see what he can add to it. Take things in order."

Clock agreed. Ransome had acknowledged the introduction with interest and said now, "Fire ahead. Be interesting to hear how you boys set to work. Maybe I could see through your place while I'm here?—I understand you're just about the best they come."

"You won't say so when you hear how I messed up this one," said Clock. "But I hadn't any choice, it all looked— Well, here's the setup." He told Ransome about Tamar, Austin, the money, the gun and the color-blind bartender.

"Meanwhile," said Jesse to the ceiling, "he was also working overtime on an anonymous corpse."

Clock went on to that. "Eventually—when we did identify it, by a stroke of luck—on account of the date he disappeared, what the police work on it then showed, we pinned it down to the period when a couple named Royball was renting that house. And—"

"Now that's interesting," said Ransome, but didn't elaborate. "And then you started thinking, on Tamar, that maybe you'd jumped the gun?"

"Nothing definite. But when we heard what Davenport could tell, how she talked about this murder when she was drunk—" He told about that, and Ransome sat up a little in his chair, and a slow smile stretched his mouth.

"This I like," he said. "This I like very much. Brother, how I like it! I'll tell you a little bit more about that, but finish your story first."

Clock finished it. The identification of Tice, what investigation had turned up on that at the time, the guesses made about it. And his mother turning up, and inadvertently pointing straight at Tamar, identifying the ring and watch as in Tice's possession when he left Wichita.

"Uh-huh," said Ransome. "After the other, I can figure her in on a deal like that."

"Well, you can see how it looks now. Not likely she'd be running with two different men to do two similar murders—crude killings for profit. When it comes to a choice between Austin and this Eddy she mentioned, I know which logic says it probably is. But the D.A.'s office isn't playing. They've decided all this stuff is irrelevant to the case against Austin. And, damn it, technically they're quite right. And no evidence to say it isn't."

"And no lead at all to Eddy," said Jesse. "Except that he was here. Take an oath on it."

Ransome transferred his gaze to Jesse. "How'd you dope out the murder happened?"

Jesse shrugged. "Pay your money and take your choice. I think she got rattled when she heard Tice's body had turned up. Scared that he'd be identified, and that there'd be a lead back to her and Eddy. Just imagining what might have happened—she called him, say, and he came over to soothe her. No danger, the body'd never be identified, there couldn't be any way the cops'd find out. But she was nervous, said she was getting out. We don't know what terms they were on— Maybe he didn't want her to leave. Anyway, there was an argument, and maybe he threatened her. So next morning she stole that gun. Tried like hell, up to Sunday, to raise as much money as she could— And when she saw him again, Sunday night, said she hadn't changed her mind, she was leaving. So he got mad and there was a fight. Something like that."

"And that could be, if it was Eddy Scott," said Ransome. "Not one to cross when he's feeling mean. Hair-trigger temper I suppose he didn't show up among her friends here?"

"Not as Eddy Scott. Suppose we hear about him and old man Wrather now," said Jesse. "'Nother drink?"

Clock refused impatiently; Ransome accepted a refill, sat back with it leisurely and lit a new cigarette.

"My beat's some different from yours, Sergeant. Bigger for one thing, and a hell of a lot emptier. I've been trying to do a little modernizing since I've been sheriff—not to brag, think I'm a little smarter than old Wagner, and I've tried to bring in some smarter boys under me. Raise the standards some. We get some types to keep an eye on, down there, you wouldn't know about maybe. Like the back-hill people." He looked at his cigarette. "Lot of talk about progress—Federal aid, state aid, better schools and free clinics. A lot's been done, and some people have been helped a lot—take advantage of it. But some people, Sergeant, you just aren't going to change, like all of us know, havin' some common sense. People that just can't be reached.

"I suppose you'd call them hillbillies. But that's a kind of loaded word because it makes 'em sound comic, like the cartoon strips and the TV gags. And they're not comic. Not any way at all. They're a headache—to us, and to the people have to live in the same place, and you could say the Federal government. Ah, I suppose in a hundred years or so they'll have died off. Progress coming along, towns growing, and all. But at that I don't know. There aren't as many as there used to be, a lot have picked up and moved—got jobs in new industries and so on. But they don't change when they move to town.

"I guess most people know they come down from old-time settlers, mostly Scots-Irish, a couple hundred years back. Well, you look at how things were back then, you'll see that most of those people had no reason to love the law. They'd been persecuted by British law to a fare-you-well, and also they were just naturally independent, damn-your-eyes folk to start with and full of what the Bible calls sinful pride. Thing is, they haven't changed much that way. They've intermarried—and they're not just so persnickety about the legalities on that either—and they've degenerated some, but they're still very damned independent. About such things, as you've probably heard, as the liquor taxes, and sending their kids to school, and so on."

"The Adkins'," said Jesse, "were hill people?"

Ransome wasn't to be rushed. "Unless you know about it, it's a little surprising there should still be places and people like that in this country. We're not a very rich state, but we aim to provide as good schools as we can, see the kids get educated—white *and* black. Why, a colored boy right from Fort Pillow, Len Wilson, he got to be a lawyer, started his schooling in a one-room school. But it's just no never-mind, try to reach some of those people any way. They've always been like they are and they aim to stay that way." Ransome swallowed bourbon thoughtfully. "Tell you this. I live in a nice modern house like either of you might have—all electric kitchen, TV, power mower for the lawn and all. Take a daily paper. My wife works in the P.T.A., and my two boys know all about rockets and guided missiles like any kid here in your big metropolis. And forty minutes' driving away, say up the Wolf Hill Road, if I maybe got a heated radiator or ran out of gas, I wouldn't walk up to the nearest house and through the gate. No, sir. I'd stand a way back and announce myself and my business—if I didn't want a shotgun blast in my direction. Like it was seventeen sixty-four instead of nineteen sixty-four, and still Injun country. All intents and purposes, it still is seventeen sixty-four to them.

"But you want to hear something more definite. Sure. The Adkins'. Jed Adkins married again after his first wife died. Had four kids then, Sally and Jed Junior—he isn't right in the head, has fits—and Bobby and Tamar. Kids didn't get along with the stepmother. I know Jed— we all know him, including the state boys from Jackson—on account he's usually got a still operating somewhere, tucked away all cozy. He's served some time for it, and he'll probably serve more. On the surface, he runs a little farm up past Wolf Creek Junction.

"I've said these people are apt to be sort of careless about seeing the kids go to school. I can recall," said Ransome, "first year or so I was in uniform, we had to go up and talk to Jed about that. I don't suppose it did much good. Oh, they went enough to learn to read and write, that'd be about it. It was when she was at school that I first ran across Tamar. Be about ten, twelve years back, she was around eleven. See, the school's in town, Maple Grove, and coming into town Tamar'd pass the drugstore and the grocery and Miss Lacy's gift shop—" Ransome laughed without humor. "She started taking what she fancied. Candy at the drugstore, a pretty pin from Miss Lacy's and so on. She was a wild one even when she was just a kid. But maybe you don't want all these details—"

"Tell on, Sheriff," said Jesse. "All interesting background."

"She was in and out of trouble," said Ransome, "and usually Bobby trailing along after her. He's a year or so older but not what you'd call a strong character. The hell of it is, you see, it's practically impossible to pin anything on these people. So I'm pretty sure it was Tamar broke a window at Mrs. Coulter's dress shop and stole some fancy underwear, couple of dresses. Things she'd admired and said so. I go and ask, they all shut up like clams. I'm the law, and they don't like the law. Period. I get a search warrant, where does it get me? Nothing there. Things probably stashed away at some girl friend's, or in the woods somewhere. What do you do with people like that? And I suppose more important, what does it do to kids, growing up in a background like that? Tamar—she's a damn good example. A real wild streak there, you could see it. It doesn't surprise me any at all, hear about those murders. I hadn't figured her in on Wrather, but she evidently was. Does surprise me a little to hear she married this Austin. *And* that he married her, by what you say a decent fellow. Well, she had looks, sure. When she took the trouble to fix herself up. But she was pretty set on Eddy Scott."

"Let's hear about Eddy."

Ransome passed a hand across his mouth. "We don't," he said, "get an awful lot of juvenile delinquency, fancy words for it. Mainly a rural area, and the kids are too busy with their chores to get into trouble. But we get some. Got a good bit from Eddy Scott. It sort of, um, nullifies what the head doctors say, because he had a nice set of parents, had a good raising. Father's a real-estate salesman, nice fellow, goes to church regular. As you gather, a good long cut above the Adkins'. Me, I figure people just come equipped, good or bad. Anyway, Eddy was a wrong one from away back. Bullied the younger kids, stole anything he wanted that wasn't nailed down, you know how the chorus goes—from bad to worse. And a mean-tempered boy, Eddy is. I picked him up drunk one night, and spent three days in bed afterward—he's big, and fast, and tough.

"That's Eddy. The Scotts put up with a hell of a lot, never could see you can't change one like that. And they never go any direction but down. So we get to old man Wrather. Living alone in a cabin, outside a little town called Forbes. The usual talk that he's a miser, has thousands stashed away there in a box hung down the well or some place. So one night the cabin burns down, and there he is—what's left of him —burned along with it. But when we came to sort it out—Dr. Wayne's no man's fool—he didn't burn to death. Died of loss of blood—knife cuts. Sheriff Wagner said could've been anybody, escaped convict or a tramp—might even have been an accident. So it might. But when Eddy Scott took off for parts unknown a week later, along with Tamar and Bobby, I began to wonder. Because so far as anybody knew, Eddy was broke then, and Tamar and Bobby never had a chance at much cash. I mentioned it to Wagner, and Wagner said I was crazy, reaching on it. Eddy just a punk kid, he said. Well, there wasn't anything to do about it, if Wagner wouldn't go hunting 'em. Just the fix you boys are in, no evidence really. But I always have wondered, you know. Wrather was a nice old fellow. Used to feed the birds—he'd got them as tame as could be, all around his place. Gentle old man. I didn't feel kindly to whoever'd killed him. But I was just a deputy then, five years back."

"Nobody did anything about those three taking off? Girl was under age, wasn't she?" asked Jesse.

"Sixteen. Of age in Tennessee. Unofficially, that kind come of age damn early," said Ransome cynically. "What for? Jed didn't care—two idle mouths. Stepmother glad to be shut of them. The Scotts should've thanked God for good riddance of Eddy, but of course they didn't. Advertised, even hired a private detective in Memphis, but they never located him. He'd taken off with the family car. Sold it in Baton Rouge, to a car fence, and that was the last trace of Eddy. But maybe now you'll see why I was interested when Bry Lamkin showed me a letter asking if a Tamar Adkins had been born anywhere around my territory. Because I always had the idea it was Eddy accounted for old Wrather, and I've long wanted a little private talk with him on the subject. And it being a pretty hot affair between Tamar and Eddy, I figured the odds were where Tamar was, I'd find him somewhere close."

"Is that so?" said Jesse.

"I always figured they'd got married. No record anywhere in a couple of hundred miles, but that didn't say they hadn't. She'd told a lot of people they were going to. As for Bobby—well, he'd always tagged after Tamar, I suppose it was just habit. He liked Eddy too, and anybody Eddy could boss around, Eddy liked."

"That's all very interesting," said Jesse.

"Now you've told me an interesting story too," said Ransome. "And I can see Tamar and Eddy fitting into it just like a hand in a glove. I'll give you a little more. Tamar's sister Sally went off with a fellow named Royball six, seven years back—he came through selling vacuum cleaners or something."

"We had worked that one out," said Jesse. "Rather, one of my sharper minions had. Now, please, Sheriff, let's get to the grand-prize drawing. Let's hear exactly what Eddy Scott looks like."

Ransome obliged with a detailed, precise description of Eddy Scott and, for good measure, of Bobby Adkins. And Clock and Jesse looked at each other.

"So the light dawns," said Jesse. "And, by God, of course—'nother direction too. The straight stick. If A alibis B, it works the other way round too. My God, yes."

"So now we know," said Clock, and stood up. "Let's all go and see Eddy. If he's home. If not, we'll wait. And wait."

"You *spotted* him?" Ransome was on his feet in one lithe movement. "He's not calling himself Eddy Scott? Brother, if I could— Let's go!"

Jesse hadn't moved. "Just what are you going to say to him, Andrew?" he asked in a reasonable tone. "It's not a legal offense to use a false name, unless it can be proved it's for some ulterior purpose. You can't do that. You haven't got a single thing to accuse Eddy of."

Clock looked at him and rubbed his jaw.

"You've tied Tamar up to Tice, in a way. But, no evidence on Eddy. Or on—"

"People have been known to come apart when they're thoroughly questioned."

"I wouldn't count on it with Eddy," said Jesse. But he stood up too. "Have to try."

"You know right where to go?" asked Ransome curiously.

"After you told us. Where we'll get when we get there's something else," said Jesse. "Sure, you'll identify him. Sure, we'll ask questions— you and Andrew, the professionals. And just so long as he keeps saying, I don't know what you're talking about, we can't touch him. Absolutely nothing on him from the law's point of view. He didn't even abduct a minor, if sixteen's legal age in your state. So Tamar said he's the one took a knife to Wrather? Hearsay evidence—and she was drunk. I don't suppose his father would charge him with stealing the car."

"Hell!" said Clock. "I'll take him apart. A few hours of grilling—"

"He's not a Ray Austin," said Jesse. "On the other hand, there's— Well, we have to make a stab at it, of course. Come on."

Ransome followed them eagerly, his long nose almost twitching in excitement.

It was an old building, shabby and smelling of dust. They climbed stairs in silence, turned right down a narrow dark corridor. Jesse realized suddenly how hungry he was; in the excitement over Ransome's unexpected advent, they'd all lost track of time. He'd called Nell to say he'd be late, but he hadn't thought this late. He looked at his watch: it was seven forty.

Clock knocked sharply on the door. "Lucky if anybody's here," he said in a mutter. "Shank of the evening. I should have—"

But after a moment a step sounded inside, and the door opened cautiously halfway. "Forget your key? Oh—"

Clock shoved the door all the way open and they went in. The man fell back before them and said in a high frightened voice, "What do you—you can't—"

"Well, hello, Bobby," said Ransome in a pleased tone. "After all these years, quite a coincidence, run into you again."

The man they had known as Dick O'Riordan gave one sharp gasp, and then recovered himself to a degree, attempting the insolent attitude. "So all right," he said. "Is it a crime to use my mother's maiden name? I like it better. What the hell are you doing—"

"Where's Eddy?" asked Ransome. "Expect him soon?"

"I don't know what you're talking about. I haven't seen Eddy in two-three years. He and Tamar split up. They got married in Abilene, I guess, but then they split up." He spoke nervous and rapid; his eyes shifted.

"Is that so? So she wasn't legally married to Austin? Or did she get a divorce?" asked Jesse.

"I don't know. You can't come in here and—"

"We seem to be in," said Clock. "Did you see Eddy kill her, Bobby? You were there at eight thirty—and she let you in. Didn't she? She was alive then, wasn't she? What was the argument about? She'd got rattled when she heard we'd found Tice's body, hadn't she? She was so nervous she was going to run—leave town—and maybe Eddy didn't want her to? Was that it? Maybe you were a little nervous when that corpse turned up too— Were you?"

"No, I—don't know what you're talking about," said Bobby Adkins. But he took a step back, away from the three big men crowding in on him in the small room. He had gone white, and sweat broke on his forehead. He was the one who might break rather easily, the weak sister. "They split up," he said. "I haven't seen Eddy in— You've got no right to—"

"She talked about old man Wrather," said Sheriff Ransome conversationally. "Got a little high one night and talked. How Eddy cut the old man up till he told where the money was, and they threw kerosene on the fire. Were you in on that too?"

Adkins took another step back. He glanced from kitchen door to bedroom door, harried: no escape that way. "A lie!" he said breathlessly. "That's— I don't know what you're—"

"That's how it happened, didn't it, with Tamar?" said Clock. "She wanted to get away, said she'd raised some cash and she was getting out. And there was an argument, and Eddy got mad and—"

"I don't know what you mean," said Tamar's brother dully. He leaned on the shabby couch, licking his lips. "I don't know what you're talking about." He said it by rote, something he had been coached to say, over and over, if this moment of truth ever caught up to him.

Clock took a breath, but Jesse forestalled him. "That's a damn silly thing to go on saying," he said mildly. "Eddy was seen going into her apartment, you know. Maybe you didn't know that a nosy old maid lives across the hall. She saw him come—"

"No," said Adkins. "No. I don't know what—"

"—and she saw Tamar let him in. At about eight twenty, just before you arrived—"

"That's a lie, he was already— *Oh my God!*"

"He was already there, yes," said Jesse gently.

"*Eddy!*" said Adkins in a high whimper; and Clock whirled. "I didn't *mean*—" The slam of the bullet spun him around and he fell over the couch arm. The second slug took Clock in one arm before he could get his gun out. Ransome took off in a flying tackle, the third bullet hit the ceiling and Clock dived into the fray.

"All right, Sergeant, I've got his shooting iron," said Ransome, climbing to his feet. "Hello, Eddy. Just fancy finding you here, after all these years. Up, boy. You're going nowhere. Graduated to the big time since I threw you into a cell overnight as a drunk, haven't you? Packing the canister and all."

"Eddy, I didn't tell," gasped Adkins. "I did just what you said—"

The man who had called himself Les York got to his feet slowly. "You Goddamned bird-brained little squealer!" he said bitterly.

And that was to be the last useful word they got out of him. He stayed dumb even through the trial, and the last word he spoke was a curse to the hangman, ten seconds before the drop fell.

EIGHTEEN

But Bobby came apart and talked, and they heard the whole story. Quite a lot of it irrelevant to the murders, but it was interesting—as, Jesse said, a case history. It was, as Ransome said sadly, unprofitable to feel surprised or horrified about it. "Where would any of 'em come by feelings like that? Like in the song, they were just doin' what comes naturally."

They heard how, after Eddy and Tamar and Bobby had got old man Wrather's money, they'd driven to Baton Rouge and sold the car. Had quite a time for themselves as long as the money lasted, but it had only been about three thousand bucks. They were in Chicago when it ran out, and Tamar had got a job at a restaurant but she didn't like it much. Bobby and Eddy had pulled a few break-ins, but cash was hard to come by and they didn't know any fences there. Then on one of those jobs, Eddy got caught and knifed a cop—"not to kill him, but you know how they feel about that"—and drew a one-to-three. So Bobby and Tamar were on their own, and they found a swell way to do, some girl she knew put them wise to it. Pick up some well-dressed guy, you know, and get him to a hotel room, and then Bobby'd come in making like her husband, and shake him down. And Tamar worked on and off too.

They'd figured when Eddy got out they'd like to go to California. But when he did, he brought a pal back with him, guy named Brackett or something, and they had a deal all set up to hit this bank. Bobby was nervous about it, but Eddy said it'd be a cinch. Only it wasn't. Bobby was driving, he didn't go in with them, but the other guy got shot up and he and Eddy just barely got away, without any loot. That was when they'd changed their names, because the cops knew who Eddy was from his prints. "I guess sometimes Eddy wasn't just so smart as he thought," said Bobby sadly. And they knew who he'd been living with when he got picked up before, so Eddy said Bobby had to have a different name too. Only Tamar wouldn't, she said it was silly. She and Eddy had a big argument over that.

So they hopped another car because that one was hot, and started west. "See, Sally was living out here, she'd wrote home to Tamar before we left. Well, we got somewheres in Texas and the damn car gave out. It was pretty old, I guess. So Eddy picked up another one, a Dodge, but the cops had it on the radio pretty soon and—"

"Let's hear about Tice," said Clock.

"Sure, that was just it. *I* never had anything to do with the killings, honest! That was Eddy, see? We was in a town named Globes, Globe, somethin' like that, and Eddy says we oughta get shut of the car. There was this guy, at the same hamburger stand we were, and he was young and all. Eddy tells Tamar, Pick him up, ask for a lift, play like we're hitchin'. So she did, and he was going west O.K., only he just had a little car, there wasn't room. But when he paid at the counter, boy, did he have that wallet stuffed! So he looked like a good bet, see, so we lit out right off and got ahead of him and parked on the shoulder and Eddy got out and put the hood up like there's somethin' wrong with the engine. So when this guy came by he stopped, see. It was just about gettin' dark, I remember. Well, there wasn't much traffic—it's all awful empty out there in the desert—and Eddy kept him talking until there wasn't anything on the road— He'd got out some tools, see—and then he hit him with a wrench, I guess it was, and the guy fell down. So that was O.K., and we put him in his car in case anybody come by, and we took what there was. Only then it seemed like he was dead, Eddy hit him too hard, see. Well, we wanted that car. It was kind of awkward. But Tamar said she'd drive someplace and dump the body. Eddy went along too. I dunno exactly what happened, but they got chased off by some cowboy, and so we stashed the body in the Dodge's trunk and started west with both the cars. We went pretty fast on account we were nervous about the Dodge bein' hot, see. Well, then we got to Sally's place, we knew where she was livin' on account her and Tamar wrote letters to each other right along, and I oughta say, Sally and Eben never knew nothing about that body. It was still in the Dodge, and Eddy wanted to get shut of it bad. Said we'd been fools not to dump it in the desert somewheres, and I guess we should've. Only, you know how it is, we'd bought a couple cases of beer and I guess it just sort of skipped our minds till we was right in town."

At which point Clock exchanged an eloquent look with Ransome.

"That's all I helped on, honest. We had a party one night and Eddy and I pretended to go drink for drink but we didn't, and when the rest of 'em was pretty near passing out, we went out to the garage and— Sure never thought anybody'd find him there, four feet down! Or know who he was if they did. Eddy took all the stuff with his name on it, see, and put it in the trash."

They got along pretty good in L.A. for a while, he said, at this and that, only Eddy got to hitting the bottle pretty hard and he got sort of mean when he was high, slapped Tamar around some so she got mad with him. And then she'd get madder when he went off somewhere a month or two, knowing he'd probably picked up another girl. And she and Bobby went back to their badger game, him acting like her boy friend. "Other times too, on account she didn't really like anybody— that way—but Eddy, and so other guys didn't try to make up to her as much, thinkin' she was my girl."

And she'd gone off on this funny singing kick at that place. Some girl she knew took her there first. "Said there was a lot of money in it, there was kind of a fad for these old songs, and anybody knew any might make a lot. Anybody could sing old songs. Only, some reason, she didn't get to very often. *I* dunno the ins and outs of it. There was this Davenport guy, she made up to him on account he'd had parts in TV and made some records, only I guess he didn't fall for her. And—"

"How did you know about Theo Grafton's prison term, by the way?"

"Oh, that was just a kind of coincidence, like they say. See, I guess like they say you run into everybody in California sooner or later, and Eddy met up with some guy he knew in the pen back in Illinois. Older guy, must've been thirty-eight or forty, see. And one night he happened drop around, and Tamar wanted to go to that Cygnet place, so we did, and this guy—I forget his name, it was a foreign name some kind—he says, by God, there's this Grafton, he was in jail with him once, they got sentenced the same day, back in Dyersburg. I and Eddy didn't pay much notice, it was Tamar—see, she got the idea—"

"Yes, we know all about that," said Clock. "Now let's hear how Tamar came to get murdered."

Adkins stared at the floor miserably. "That was just awful. Sure. She could be pretty damn ornery, make you wild sometimes, but no call to *kill* her for it. Only Eddy gets sort of mean with any liquor in him. They'd had a big fight, just before she up and married that fellow Austin—because Eddy, he'd been running with another girl, see. And she met this Austin, and right away figured, some reason, he had a lot o' money. She made one hell of a play for him—part to get back on Eddy, too, I guess. And then it turned out—"

"Were she and Eddy legally married?"

Adkins looked vague. "There was something about a thing they call common-law," he said. "Eddy said. Said he reckoned they was legal man and wife. I didn't pay no notice. Anyways, Tamar and this Austin was, and then it seems he didn't have any money at all, and he made her mad, way he carried on, expecting her to cook and all. He turned out to be a real creep, that one. Try to throw a party or something, and he turned it all blue, sitting around like a mourner at a funeral.

"Well, anyways, then Eddy got in jail again, just the county jail—all the traffic tickets—and he'd just got out when, Jeez, that body turned up. And—"

"Tamar got nervous," said Jesse. "Said she was getting out of town, just in case."

"Yeah, she did, and she was trying to shake down Austin and that little creep Grafton, and— Well, you know, her and Eddy—I mean, he'd play around on the side but he always come back to her, and she'd always take him back. I reckon after a while in a cell again he was ripe for some hot boiler-makin' with Tamar, and he wasn't about to see her get away from him. We was both there that Wednesday night, he'd just got out and come hotfoot after her, and she'd called me—about that body. She was so worried Eddy couldn't reach her at all. She was bound and determined to light out, and she was still mad at him anyways. And he got mad and said he'd teach her if she tried to run out on him. But it didn't do no good, because once Tamar made up her mind, well, like I say she could be stubborn as all hell, see. Well, she called me on Sunday night, she sounded some scared—and Tamar didn't scare easy either—I knew Eddy'd gone to see her, I figured it was a waste o' time, but he thought he could talk her round. Anyways, she said this Austin had been there, but he didn't give her any money—she was mad about it—but she asked me to come, account Eddy was acting awful mean.

"Well, I went, only what she expected *me* to do about Eddy—I mean, once he starts acting up, take six guys to handle him! He'd knocked me around some before, on account all the time I forgot to call him Les 'stead of Eddy. And when I got there he was kind of steamed up. He had a bottle on him and he was working on it, see. *I* couldn't do nothing with him. Kept saying if Tamar tried to leave him, he'd kill her."

"And how come the neighbors didn't hear all this, the way they heard the quarrel with Austin?" asked Clock.

"Oh, that's Eddy's way, see— It's funny too, but the higher and meaner he gets, the lower he talks. Like kind of whispering." Adkins shivered involuntarily. "And it—it all happened so *fast*—" He gestured helplessly. "He hit her and knocked her down against the table, and she got up and started for the bedroom, but he got hold of her again and hit her— *I* couldn't do nothing, I tried to make him stop, but— And then she ran in the bedroom and him after her and—and when I got there he had her by the throat and—

"Well, it was pretty awful. He'd never do a thing like that in his right mind, he was right fond of Tamar. I mean, she could make you awful mad, but to *kill* her— But you see how it was, I mean, there she *was*, and neither of us was hankering to get connected to—"

"You just walked away with him?" said Clock. "From your sister's body? Stayed with him?"

"I—I didn't know what else to do," said Adkins. "He needed somebody look after him, like he was then. I got him sobered up some, and he was awful sorry about it, but he said likely they'd think that Austin did it. So— Well, she was dead. Couldn't nothing change that." He raised guileless blue eyes, smiled anxiously at them, trying to make them understand. He said, "Tamar or Eddy, they always told me what to do, and there was just Eddy left. But you can see *I* didn't have nothing to do with any o' the killings—"

"Oh, Lord," said Clock, "take him away and book him, Pete." And when Petrovsky had led Adkins away, he said to Ransome, "If that's the kind you breed down there, give me the big city any day. My God."

"People, they do come all shapes and sizes," said Ransome. "Like I said, all three of 'em just doin' what comes naturally. Come to think, Sergeant, I wonder how many other lives we've saved by catchin' up to them now? And they'll be small loss. At that, kind of wasted effort for you," and he grinned.

"Why? Oh—"

And Jesse laughed. "Too true. All your back-breaking routine at it goes for nothing, Andrew. Tennessee's going to claim prior rights, to avenge old man Wrather. Eddy won't get such a fancy death as the gas chamber."

"No, we're still old-fashioned enough to pay a hangman," said Ransome. "They won't hang Bobby—just stash him away. But Eddy—" He shook his head. "Nice parents, tried to give him a decent raising. Sunday School and all. Damn what the head doctors say, he just came equipped with the bad character."

Jesse stood up. "*A branch sprung of violence has no tender twig,*" he said wryly. "Sad and messy business. I trust you'll start the machinery to get my client out of jail, Andrew. Meditating on your sins meanwhile."

A couple of months after an extradition order had wafted Eddy Scott and Bobby Adkins back to Tennessee to stand trial for old man Wrather, Nell, leafing through the third section of the *Times* one morning, said, "Oh. Jesse, look at this."

Jesse looked. A one-paragraph announcement on the theatrical page that "the risingly popular young folk singer, Lee Davenport, starts a six-week engagement on Sunday night at Los Angeles' newest smart restaurant, The Cavaliers' Arms."

"Let's go and hear him," said Nell. "All of us. I'll call Fran."

"O.K.," said Jesse amiably. He liked Davenport.

"*Although,*" said Nell, belatedly cautious, "'newest smart restaurant'—it's probably horribly expensive."

"All you think about is money," said Jesse. "Haven't you heard all the rumors? You're the Gentile, I'm the one's supposed to be miserly."

"Like most rumors," said Nell, "greatly exaggerated. No, Athelstane! Down! You know you're not supposed to beg at the table. If you hadn't had the good sense to marry me, you wouldn't have a nice savings account at all. You didn't before we were married. All those L.P. records, and the latest stereo—"

"Yes, Mrs. Shylock," said Jesse. "I guess the exchequer will stand one evening out at a smart new restaurant. Maybe Andrew can afford it once too."

It was what was called an intimate place, a smallish room decorated with antique rapiers, crossed swords and sabers, with a fire flickering on a raised brick hearth and a small platform at the narrow end of the room. The four of them, hesitating on the threshold, were taken in hand by a brusque maître d' who led them toward a table midway from the stage; but Nell broke away to confront three men at a table just below it.

"And what on earth are you doing here?" she asked old Mr. Walters severely. "A respectable man of your age at a night club—"

"I had to put my foot down," said Mr. Walters, chuckling. "Let 'em know I'm not senile yet. As if I was four years old, not able to go round alone. You mind your own business, I said. Guess you know these two fellows."

Austin stood up and wrung Jesse's hand. "So nice to see you again, Mr. Falkenstein! So happy to meet you, Mrs. Falkenstein—Miss— Sergeant. Yes, well, you see, I've got to know Davenport a bit, through Elliott here—" Elliott Carey was smiling all around—"and we thought—"

"And so've I," said Mr. Walters. He sounded self-important. "Got to know some interesting people through you, Jesse—kind of a new lease on life. I gave Lee a song he didn't know, you know that? He's singing it tonight. Nice fellow. Remembered my old grandmother singing it— Lee was interested. O' course I had to come." He reached for his glass.

"Of course," said Fran gravely. A waiter grudgingly shoved a second table up; they all sat down and ordered drinks. Clock was yawning.

"I'm here under protest," he said. "This latest corpse—no ident on it yet, and—"

"*No* shop talk, darling," said Fran firmly.

"Don't call me—"

"Shh!" said Nell. "Here he comes."

Davenport strolled onto the stage, to a scattering of applause. There was a fair crowd for him; only three or four tables were empty. Jesse thought he recognized a few people here he'd seen at The Cygnet: the genuine fans. Davenport, his grave little smile fixed, seemed unaware of his audience; his fingers touched the guitar, and it spoke softly.

He sang, the strong golden tenor now tender, now ringing compellingly; and he got generous applause. He acknowledged it, smiling; and when the guitar struck two strong chords as a prelude for a new song, old Mr. Walters whispered importantly, "This is the one *I* gave him. He was interested. My grandmother—" And broke off to listen, rapt, to a melancholy saga in a minor key about a lass whose lover languished in Newgate Gaol.

Applause rose. They liked him, they were not ready to let him go, though the lights flared up to announce the end of the first show. Davenport stood smiling, made a little gesture of acknowledgment, and then as he touched the guitar to offer an encore, he spotted Austin at the table just below the platform. His long mouth lifted mischievously at one corner; the guitar spoke a sprightly tune.

"The devil he came to the farmer one day,
You owe me a debt and you've now got to pay—
With my whack fol-the-diddy,
Fol-lol the die-aye.

"It is not you or your daughter I want,
But that son of a bitch of a wife you have got.

"Oh, take her, dear devil, with all of my heart,
A-hoping that you and her never part!"

Clock muttered a laugh, next to Jesse. Austin looked a little taken aback: the incipient stuffed shirt. Carey was grinning.

"The devil he hoisted her up to his back,
And down to hell with her he did pack.

"Two little devils they hung in chains,
She upped with her foot and she kicked out their brains.

"Two more little devils was playing handball,
Said, Kick her out, Daddy, she'll murder us all!

"So the devil he hoisted her up to his hump,
And back to earth with her he did jump.

"So they say that the women are worse than the men,
They went down to hell and got chucked out again,
With my whack fol-the-diddy,
Fol-lol the die-aye!"

While applause still sounded, the stage went dark.

"Well!" said Ray Austin, but he sounded amused. "That was for me, I guess. Very appropriate."

"He's wonderful," said Fran, laughing. "*And* handsome, isn't he? Do you suppose he'll—"

He did. He appeared at the joined tables ten minutes later, let Mr. Walters buy him a drink. He said, holding up his glass reflectively, "I saw in the papers they convicted those two. Back in Tennessee. I guess you must be still blessing your guardian angel, Mr. Austin."

"And Mr. Falkenstein," said Austin. "My heavens, yes. It was like a nightmare. *Me*, accused of murder."

"It seems to come easy to some people, sir," said Davenport. "Such as Tamar." He drank.

"That one—" Fran shuddered. "You can hardly believe that kind of thing. So utterly callous."

"Not, unfortunately, so unusual," said Clock. "As any cop knows. People—"

"People," said Lee Davenport. "Still the most interesting thing there is around, aren't they, Sergeant? That pair. Does make you wonder. But the publicity did me a little favor. As you see. You want to stay on, I'm doing 'Death and the Lady' in the second show." He looked at Jesse and smiled. "You still prefer Bach. The laboratory mathematics, sir. Not the guts of the thing."

"Oh, expect you're quite right," said Jesse.

Davenport stood up. "That Tamar," he said. "She did shake me. You quoting Holy Writ. I sat through enough hellfire sermons to remember some—how does it go?—*He looked for justice, but behold, bloodshed.* . . ."

"Isaiah," said Jesse. "Yes, nice epitaph for Tamar and Company."

Davenport wandered off, and Clock said, "Well. I suppose he's good, but I need my sleep—this new thing—"

"Tosh, night's young," said Mr. Walters, beckoning a waiter.

"Oh, let's stay for the second show!" said Fran. "I *like* him. He's wonderful."

Clock looked at her suspiciously, and Nell and Jesse looked at each other with alarm.

"Develop a headache, quick," Jesse whispered to Nell. "A thick-headed cop is one thing, but I'll be damned if I'll have her chasing after Davenport. Little harpy. If Father'd spanked her oftener—"

"But he seems quite nice," Nell whispered back. "Not like Andrew, but maybe with some competition Andrew would—"

"Damn it," said Jesse, "the man's a musician—maybe a great one. Wouldn't want to see him upset. She would. She does. Could be, even, he's right about his kind of music. But the man's an artist, I don't want him upset. Any way. Develop the headache."

Nell said aloud that she had a headache. "What a shame," said Fran absently. "Go home and take some aspirin, darling. We'll stay for the second show and tell you about it. I think I'd like the Lobster Newburg, Andrew."

Clock looked at her even more suspiciously and resignedly signaled a waiter.

SOME AVENGER, RISE!

Rise from my ashes, some avenger, rise!

—Vergil, Aeneid

PROLOGUE

The man had a great deal of money, and the man had an obsession. The man had been and in most ways still was a very shrewd man: a judge of men, a judge of business affairs, and on the surface he was the same man, a sane man. But a conviction and an idea had taken possession of him.

He conceived that he had a vengeance to bring upon nine persons, and it mattered nothing to him at all how much of his wealth he spent to bring about that vengeance.

He had already spent a great deal, in this way and that. Some of the revenge was easy to attain, but then for others of the nine he had had to hire secret spies, and wait and plan for a long while before he found the way to reach them with his vengeance.

He had waited years, planning and brooding long, to start the doom moving, irrevocable and sudden as an avalanche, against one of the nine. This plan, unlike some of the others, did not demand of him personal violence; it had needed money to set up; and then it had needed the exact opportunity before the doom could be begun, before the first stone could be rolled, bringing the avalanche down.

The man had waited years for this. He had not minded the waiting, for he knew the day would come; it was sweet to brood on that. And the day had come.

And while he waited to bring down the doom on that one of the nine, he had planned and acted on others, so he had not minded the waiting. The man was seventy-two years old but he came of tough, long-lived stock; he knew he would live long enough—still shrewd and active—to accomplish his vengeance. And he had. This was the last one.

Smiling, he sat thinking about it, slowly sipping his afternoon high-ball. The first revenge taken—after it had come to him that the vengeance was due—that had been the crude, obvious thing. But it had been given to him to understand the better vengeance, and that was what he had brought to the others also.

Once it was finished, perhaps he could find peace.

It was April fourteenth, a Wednesday, a bright golden day, but the day of doom for the ninth one on the plotter's list.

He should be realizing it about now. It was five-thirty in the afternoon.

ONE

"They've got kind of resigned about it now, I guess," said old Mr. Walters cheerfully, swallowing the last of his replenished drink. "After all, they can't keep me locked up. Way they talk, you'd think I stopped having any sense when I hit seventy-five. But they've been a mite easier about my going out lately." Mr. Walters, ruddy and cheerful at eighty-one, was talking about his family.

Jesse Falkenstein grinned at him across his desk. "Couple of times," he said dryly, "you've made me feel I didn't have much sense."

"Tosh, you're still young, boy. Got any to start, you keep addin' to it, you know. You sure I'm not interruptin' anything?"

"Wish you were," said Jesse gloomily. It was getting on toward six o'clock, and he'd had a single appointment all day. "I could bear to pick up a few new clients. Just so long–" he knocked on the desk hastily–"as they aren't criminal cases. Often thought I'd have been a lot smarter to go in for the corporation side like my father."

"Business bad, hey?"

"What with the house payments and feeding the Monster," said Jesse, "I could do with–" And the office door opened and Miss Williams looked in agitatedly.

"Oh, Mr. Falkenstein–"

"Yes?"

"I was just about to leave when– I didn't know if you'd want–"

A man brushed by her in the doorway and came heavily into the office. He was a big man with heavy shoulders, rather untidily dressed in a mediocre dark suit; his dark tie looked as if he'd been pulling at it, hanging loose and crooked. He was not a good-looking man; he had big craggy features, a long prognathous jaw which bore a stubble of dark beard, and his dark eyes were bloodshot. He stood in the center of the room and looked at Jesse, and slowly Jesse unfolded his lank seventy-four inches and got to his feet.

"I didn't know if you'd want—"

"It's all right, Miss Williams," said Jesse. "You can go."

The newcomer just stood there, arms hanging, and Jesse and old Mr. Walters stared at him, for he was a man they knew. He was Sergeant Andrew Clock of Central Homicide, L.A.P.D.—but they'd never seen him looking like that before.

And Jesse felt one sharp pang of alarm, and he said quickly, "Fran? Andrew, is it—" Because he could think of only one thing that might make Clock look like that, some hurt or threat to slim, svelte Fran Falkenstein.

Clock shook his head. He went on shaking it, muzzily, as if trying to clear his mind. Then he said, "I thought—I could get you—but I don't know if they'd let me bring in a lawyer. Like the army. I don't know. Only I thought— Because, my God, my God, I don't understand it, it's not real, it can't be real, you know. It's just a nightmare, isn't it? I'm sorry, I didn't see you had somebody here. Oh, it's you." He looked at Mr. Walters. "Would they let me have a lawyer, do you think? I never asked the captain. Should have asked."

"You're not making sense, Andrew," said Jesse. "Sit down and let's hear what's wrong." But he had to prod Clock into the second chair beside his desk. Old Mr. Walters silently pulled out his bottle of bourbon and poured a hefty shot into his glass, shoved it over. He was watching Clock interestedly.

Jesse guided Clock's hand to the glass. "For God's sake, what's hit you?" he asked. "What do you need a lawyer for? Finally lost your temper with some stupid underling and clouted him over the head?"

Clock put the bourbon down in one gulp. "I needed that," he said. His voice was dull but there was something wild in his eyes on Jesse. "I—just don't understand any of this. It's like—it's just a nightmare, that's all. It's got to be. I'm sitting here in your office telling you—trying to tell you—but in a minute I'll wake up, and it'll have just been a nightmare. Because it's nothing that could happen, you know." He was asking them to tell him, reassure him, that it was just a nightmare.

"Andrew—"

"Thirteen years," said Clock. "I took the oath when I was twenty-one. A hell of a lot of times I've wondered why—thankless job to end all thankless jobs—but it's my job, you know. I never wanted to do anything else, and I'm a good cop, Jesse. You believe I've been a good cop, don't you? God knows I've tried to be. I saved that baby, that time—they gave me a medal for that: I told you that, didn't I?" Clock was talking dully, compulsively, his eyes anxious on Jesse. "I made rank three years after I joined the force, and that's pretty good going on this force. I was twenty-four. I was the youngest cop ever made rank, you know that? I was only in uniform three years. And no marks against me at all, you know that?"

"Andrew, what the hell's this all about?" asked Jesse. Something very wrong with Clock; something—

"He's had a pretty bad shock of some kind, boy," said Mr. Walters quietly. "Get another shot down him, maybe—jolt him out of it, hey?"

"Andrew—"

"I've tried, I thought I was— I was only thirty-two when I made sergeant," Clock was going on, earnestly. "And it's just crazy to think Starbuck could have had anything to do with that—with Skipper Arnold getting cooled, I mean—Starbuck's not a killer, I only brought him in to question because he *had* had an argument with Skipper, and you've got to be thorough. Just crazy. And I can't understand where— how— Look," he said. "Look, I get along with most of the boys just fine. We all get along. They're all good men—especially Pete Petrovsky. Oh, Dale's a little slow on the uptake sometimes, and I didn't recommend him for promotion, but, my God, Jesse, *Dale* couldn't— and besides, he wouldn't. I don't know who would. What?—oh, thanks." Automatically he emptied the glass again. "What's that one you quoted at me once—*every man's enemy is within himself*—enemies— But who *could* do it to me? My God, Jesse, my God, did I do it? Did I have amnesia or something?"

"Andrew, simmer down and tell it straight," said Jesse gently. "What's happened?"

Clock suddenly drew a long, long breath and held it, and let it out. He looked haggard, and there was both pain and fright in his expression. He said, "And how often, my sweet Christ, have I listened to them telling me—it's a frame, Sergeant—somebody framed me. How often—"

"Some kind of private trouble, Sergeant, you'd maybe like me to take myself off?" said Mr. Walters delicately.

"No," said Clock. "That's all right. I think maybe—the more heads we get on this the better." He sounded more rational. "And anyway, they're good, you know—and with no marks on my record, sure to God they won't just— But the way it *looks*—damn it, it doesn't make any sense!"

"From the beginning, Andrew," said Jesse. He sat down again. Whatever it was, it was something bad. He'd never seen the practical, efficient, dedicated-cop Clock like this.

Clock took another long breath. He said conversationally, "That liquor's hit me. I haven't had anything to eat since breakfast. I'm just not thinking. I should have asked the captain if they let you have a lawyer. Maybe it wouldn't look so good if I did bring a lawyer in. But surely to God it'd count for something, that I said right off, Look anywhere you want to? But when they— I just don't understand it." He looked at Jesse and came out with it then, abruptly. "I'm suspended," he said. "Pending fuller investigation. I'm supposed to have taken a bribe to cover up evidence against Paul Starbuck in that homicide. And I'm supposed—supposed to have taken it because I wanted the money for a— I told you it's crazy, it's just impossible—for this Helen Madden. I don't know the woman, I'd never laid eyes on her, Jesse. Anybody who knows me," said Clock painfully, brutally, "knows I haven't—seen another female—since I met Frances. I wouldn't—look twice at that one anyway. Never laid *eyes* on her. One of these rapacious little blondes—by request—with a beehive hairdo. Crazy. Her brother's an ex-con, he's been in Quentin. He did a one-to-five for armed robbery. Joe Madden. A punk—just a punk. And the girl—"

"What the *hell*," said Jesse stupidly. "But Andrew—"

"She said I gave her the money to buy a mink coat," said Clock. "You know I.A.—or maybe you don't. It was the editor of the *Telegraph* phoned Captain Thatcher. Monday. He'd had an anonymous phone call—all this about me—you know it was in the papers on Friday, Thursday too, I guess—about our questioning Starbuck, on the Arnold case. The editor wasn't about to stick his neck out and print it without checking—even if the *Telegraph* always does love to get hold of something against a cop. But then of course Thatcher and his I.A. boys went to work too. On me. Because Thatcher—Thatcher's a good man. Drops on anybody a little out of line—like lightning. You know this force. We're the top force anywhere. Partly on account of I.A. playing watchdog."

"Yes, but Andrew—how the hell could—"

"Hell, you keep the girl friend out past midnight, you're apt to get a lecture about it. Take three drinks instead of two, out to dinner somewhere, you get lectured. That's how I.A. was set up—damn puritanical. Cops setting an example and so on. I've never had a mark against me," said Clock. "But this—something one hell of a lot more than— Well, I see of course they'd *look*. Even on an anonymous tip, but—" He stopped, and said, "I need another drink. . . . She had a photograph on the mantel. In a frame. It was me. Me with her at some night club. She wouldn't let the captain have it, but it was me. Only it couldn't have been, could it? Unless I've grown a split personality and don't remember?"

"A photograph—"

"In a silver frame." Clock nodded. "And this punk, this Madden, he said it was so too. Never laid eyes on either of them. And Starbuck was scared to death—naturally—and he said, No, for God's sake, he hadn't given me any money, but my God, there's no way to prove that, about him. A pro gambler, they all carry around a lot of cash—and—"

"Slow down," said Jesse. "Let me take this in. The editor tipped off Internal Affairs and they went looking. All right. Evidence—of course circumstantial evidence is really the best kind. But, first thing strikes me, a pretty crude setup, isn't it? All of a sudden a good cop with no black marks against him veering such a long way off the straight and narrow? Didn't this Thatcher think twice about that?"

Clock finished the bourbon and looked up at him. "You're jumping in on my side blind, boy?" he asked softly. He looked, now, completely rational and sober. "You haven't heard—all they've got. You don't know. That teller— You don't ask me any questions at all, just take it on faith? My God, I'm asking *myself* if I could have lost my mind—my normal mind."

Jesse slid farther down in his desk chair. "Fellow named Bratzlav said a thing once. *Where reason ends, faith begins.* Man's got to believe in something. Figure I know you well enough to know you'd never turn crooked as a cop. There are things you'd do maybe puritans'd call wrong. Sure. But as cops go, I'd call you dedicated. As they say. Also figure your Captain Thatcher ought to be smart enough to read you."

Old Mr. Walters had poured himself another drink. "I'll go along with that," he said interestedly.

"Thatcher," said Clock dully, "doesn't know me. This is a big city force, after all. Sure, there's my record. But I guess among all your proverbs, Jesse, you could think of a few about how females get us tangled in their nets."

"So," said Jesse, "we do anything to stay tangled? Um. I want some more details. I.A. went looking. When and how?"

"Yesterday. Today. I didn't hear one damn thing about it until this morning. I was still working on the Arnold thing—I don't think we'll ever get anybody for it, but— The captain called, told me to come up to his office. I thought maybe one of the boys in the office was in trouble. I know Dale's a poker fiend, he might have— And then they threw this at me. This. Questions. Like a nightmare. And when I got it through my head what they were saying—that it wasn't some kind of damn fool joke—I blew up. I don't know if that was smart—I couldn't help it, Jesse. Me. Taking a bribe—running around with a—this cheap blonde. I said, for Christ's sake, look wherever you want to, I've got nothing to hide! Only then—then they looked. Sure. We all looked," said Clock tiredly. "And then they asked me a lot more questions. Thatcher and Lieutenant Clay. I don't know— I suppose they're good men, but that office, it's the watchdog, you know—it's their *job* to be suspicious, to keep an eye on every man on the force. And they don't know me, Jesse. Personally. When I made rank I was assigned to Wilcox Street in Hollywood. The detective bureau there. I was there until I made sergeant and got transferred downtown to Central. To Homicide. I never had a thing to do with I.A. before. I met Thatcher and Clay for the first time today. Seen them, heard about them. I guess they're good men. But what the hell *could* they think—all this evidence— I don't *understand* it."

"Tell me," said Jesse, "about the evidence, Andrew. One thing I'm supposed to know a little something about."

Clock looked down at his hands clasped tightly together across his lean stomach. They were big, capable, freckled hands. They had done this and that. They had saved that baby, so long ago. They had subdued a lot of punks and drunks and berserk men. They had, like Andrew Clock's body and brain and personality, been used—he had always liked to think—for good against evil. He hadn't any orthodox conviction about life except the blind conviction that there was this primal, eternal struggle between the forces of good and evil—between order and chaos—and he had chosen the right side. He had also a blind faith that a man on the right side had, essentially, nothing to worry about in life or death; the battle he might lose, but not the war. But today had shaken him, and shaken his faith. Since the moment the inside phone rang on his desk, and he picked it up and said, "Clock here," and a curt businesslike voice had replied, "This is Captain Thatcher in I.A. Will you please report to my office immediately, Sergeant"—not making a question of it.

He said, "They had seen that girl yesterday. They didn't get me up there until they'd— I just blew up. I said, for God's sake, they could look at whatever they wanted to—my bank account, my apartment— And they said they'd like me to see the girl. This—Madden woman. I'd never laid eyes on her before. And there was that photograph. I didn't believe it. I didn't— She called me Andy," said Clock numbly. "Nobody calls me— She—she did a good job on it, the bitch—hemmed and hawed and—you know—was arch at them. Word for it. Arch. What was wrong about her going around with a cop? Why shouldn't he buy her presents if he wanted to? Like that. And there was that photograph. I didn't believe it but—"

"Ways," said Jesse, "to make composites."

"Jesse," said Clock quietly, "it wasn't a copy of any photograph I've ever had taken. I knew that when I saw it. I haven't had many photographs taken—you know my father died when I was ten, and we didn't have money for things like that. I haven't got any family since my mother died, and God knows I haven't got the kind of face for anybody to want pictures of. It was a—a new photograph. Of me."

"There's a thing called a telescopic lens," said Mr. Walters.

"Oh, my God, tell it to Thatcher!" said Clock savagely. "So then we went to the bank. I was, Christ, being cooperative. I wasn't mad any more. I mean, I was, I was good *and* mad, but I was feeling kind of numb too, know what I mean—after that photograph. I said, whatever they wanted to look at—nothing to hide—"

His faith not shaken then. The honest man with nothing to fear, because in the end the man on the right side would always come out all right. This absurd, outrageous, unexpected charge would easily be revealed as the lie it was.

Brusquely authorizing the assistant manager to produce the records for Thatcher and Clay. The checking account, the savings account.

A sergeant on the L.A. force, the best-paid force anywhere, made a little over eight thousand a year.

Talk about thankless jobs.

But it was his job, and if it was taken from him he would lose a large part of his life. Of any reason for his life.

He knew what was in both accounts. A little under three thousand in the savings account, approximately eighteen hundred in the checking account.

Only, it seemed, he was wrong. The record said he had seven thousand, four hundred and seventy-two dollars in his checking account.

It was a lie. Somebody had made a mistake somewhere. He had not paid in the sum of five thousand seven hundred and forty-five dollars, on the previous Friday, April ninth. That he knew.

Only they identified the teller, by his initials on the deposit slip. And Clock was still staring at that slip when the teller came, called by the manager. Because it was Clock's own sprawling signature on the slip, the way he always wrote it. Which was another thing not to believe.

And the teller—a slender young man with wavy brown hair, a hand-painted tie and a deprecating manner—a young man named Walter Hendrickson—stared at Captain Thatcher, at Clock, and said, "Why, no, sir, you paid it in yourself, Sergeant—in cash. I remember that, even though we were busy—Friday, you know—because it was a little unusual. That much cash, I mean."

TWO

"—And then they went over my car. Back at Headquarters, I mean. That's where they found the tie clasp. That's what's supposed to be the evidence against Starbuck I found and covered up. The way I read it and the way they did too, I gather. It had his initials on it." Clock looked at his coffee cup and after a moment asked, "You still with me, Jesse?" But he looked at Nell.

"*The simple,*" said Jesse, "*believeth every word, but the prudent man looketh well to his going.* A tie clasp. They asked this Starbuck if it was his, and he denied it. Vehemently."

"Yes, sure," said Clock almost uninterestedly.

Jesse was absently fondling Athelstane the Monster's long ears. In an emergency, he knew he could always count on his Nell; Mr. Walters had regretfully declined an invitation to come along, and taken himself off reiterating demands that he be kept up to date on this, and Jesse had brought Clock home with him, to the house on Rockledge Road above Hollywood. Where Nell had taken one look at the two of them and said not one word about the three veal chops she had marinating, but produced in short order an enormous casserole of thick beef stew. Clock had just finished two platefuls of it which he'd consumed absently while still talking.

"What about Starbuck?" asked Jesse.

"Oh, for goodness' sake," said Nell, "he isn't important, Jesse. He's just the—the peg to hang it on. Even I can see that. Who you want to go after is that teller." She sat erect in her chair, his lovely elegant Nell with her gray eyes and her long brown hair in its severe chignon, and gestured impatiently with her cigarette. "It's perfectly obvious the teller must have been bought."

"You can say that," said Clock. "I can say it. A frame. But that's what's going to stick in Thatcher's throat—how could anybody in I.A. believe that? It doesn't make sense. Who would buy the teller, just to get me in trouble? How did anybody know the teller could be bought? I've only just started to think about this. God, I've had a day —but don't you see—"

Athelstane whuffled at Jesse, and Jesse absently fed him the last piece of his chocolate cake. "Also, not only the teller. Think about it. Nearly six thousand bucks gratuitously paid into your account. Gold tie clasp—fourteen-carat?"

"I don't know, it looked expensive. The initials were engraved. It was in the glove compartment of the car. Hell, the car's sitting in the lot most of the day—or when I'm home, on the street—there's no garage. Anybody—"

"Yes. The Maddens," said Jesse. "They're not in this just for the fun of bringing trouble to a cop. They're getting paid for their time. Other words, there's money behind this. Who might have a reason, Andrew— who's also got the money?"

"*Nobody*, damn it!" said Clock. "There's nobody like that. I'd know, wouldn't I? Listen, it's just wild. Sure, sometimes somebody you pick up comes out with the threats—I'll get you, cop. Like that. Punks— pros. They don't mean it, not once in a million times. About once in a million times one of them lays for one of us when he gets out—but that doesn't happen once in ten years. And if it does, it's just the crude assault. Nothing—nothing like this, for God's sake. I'm just an ordinary cop, I've never been mixed up with any melodrama that might lead to—this. It's just crazy."

"Has anybody ever threatened you at all?" asked Jesse.

"Yes, sure. Punks, like I say. Not one's ever done anything about it. Look, Jesse—just sitting here, trying to think about it, I can see how it looks to I.A. A frame? But anybody can see there'd have to be money behind a frame, and not hay either. That teller wouldn't risk his job for peanuts. The Maddens—how the hell did the Maddens get in on it? And who in God's name would lay out that much money just to—"

"But can't *they* see," said Nell impatiently, "that if you had done that, accepted that money, you'd have been an absolute fool to have shoved it into the bank so openly? Can't they—"

"Want to ask about that," said Jesse. "This Internal Affairs department—how do they operate? Gestapo bit? Snooping around every man on the force, alphabetical order maybe?"

"No, of course not," said Clock. "No, not like that. They—keep the eyes and ears open, is all. I guess you could say." He finished his coffee, Nell reached for the pot on its warming stand and he shook his head. "A police force is like an army—any organization—gossip gets around. Any little thing, somebody buys a new car, or moves—and then there are anonymous tips too, so-and-so's playing the races—and a lot of complaints from the public. I've heard they get around three hundred tips and complaints a year, mostly minor stuff, and they investigate every one, from complaints of impoliteness on up. Why?"

"Well," said Jesse, "just this. They don't go around taking official looks at the banking records of every man on the force as a regular thing."

"Well, my God, of course not," said Clock. "I don't— Oh."

"Yes," said Jesse. "With a perfectly clean record, why shouldn't you stick the money in the bank? That much money? You wouldn't keep it around in cash."

"But, Jesse," said Nell, "wouldn't they think it was funny that Andrew said right away they could look? When he knew— And didn't offer any explanation for it? I should think—"

"Couldn't say," said Jesse. "Not knowing Thatcher or Clay. Maybe they just figure they caught him—apologies—flatfooted. And he couldn't dream up an explanation offhand. What are they going to do now, Andrew? What's the position?"

"I don't know exactly. I'm suspended for two weeks—there'll be a hearing then, of some sort. They'll be taking a look at my—private life," said Clock. "At everybody I know. Asking questions. Find out what I've bought recently, where I go and what I do on my days off. They'll be questioning those Maddens, and, God, how do we know what more lies they'll tell, with what to back them up? I should think they'd want to take a closer look at that photograph. How the hell could that girl have it, Jesse? Say it's a composite—all right, I don't see how but say it is—my God, the lab could tell that but will the lab get it? With all the rest of this—evidence, it could be Thatcher'll just decide the thing's obvious, and not bother about the photograph."

"I thought you said they were on the ball."

Clock nodded slowly. "Yes," he said. "Yes, they are. Try to be. Like the rest of us. But, maybe you'd call it psychologically speaking, anybody gets hauled up before I.A. is on the defensive to start. And all this is so damn obvious—it sounds wild even to me, to say that some mystery man's framing me. Spending money like water to buy lies, just to ruin my career. There's nobody feels like that about me. I'd know, wouldn't I?"

Jesse contemplated the end of his cigarette. "Maybe not necessarily. Wild, yes? I suppose they'll be questioning all the men in your office too. Is any of them apt to—"

"Oh, my God," said Clock. "I've got to say I don't know. A thing like this— I'm not sure of anything any more. I always thought we got along just fine. Petrovsky, Lindner, Joe Lopez—they're all good men. I think the lieutenant would go to bat for me too, but—how can anybody get round all this evidence?"

Nell got up abruptly and said she'd try to get hold of Fran again. Clock just shook his head and said it didn't matter. Athelstane, who was fascinated with the telephone, departed hastily after Nell—and, the table being modernistically low, managed to upset Jesse's coffee cup with his tail as he got up. Athelstane—a fact they had not known when they acquired him—was an English mastiff.

"They'll be calling me up again too," said Clock. "I'm supposed to 'hold myself available.' I don't see—" he looked squarely at Jesse— "anything I—we—can do, but if I'm allowed to have a lawyer—I don't even know that—I'd better give you a retainer now."

"Touching faith," said Jesse. "There are things to do. *Woe be to fearful hearts and faint hands.* Not all that interested in your—um—ill-gotten gains." He thought about fate: it was a little remarkable, come to think. If Nell hadn't persuaded him to take that hopeless-looking case last June, they'd likely never have got to know Andrew Clock at all. And no man was infallible, but knowing Clock, Jesse found it quite impossible to believe this charge on him. The alternative, of course—the deliberate frame—was just as incredible. That was the trouble.

Nell came back and said Fran was still out. "We ought to find out more about that teller," she added energetically. "What did *he* do with the money? His bribe money?"

"Talk about touching faith," said Clock; but he smiled at her faintly.

"Just so," said Jesse, shoving Athelstane's forequarters off his lap. "*Forsake not a wise and good woman.* Quite agree with you."

"And that Helen Madden. That's something else. Look, anyone who knows you knows that—you've only been going around with Fran, Andrew."

"Um," said Jesse, putting out his cigarette. "Little idea there, that maybe your devotion to the job cuts both ways. Pretty big part of your life, isn't it? You don't have any hobbies that I know of. Quiet sort of fellow. Live alone—no near relatives. Like me, subscribe to the proverb, *In the multitude of words there wanteth not sin.* You ever do much casual talking about Fran, Andrew—to the men in your office, anybody else?"

Clock looked at him, slightly indignant. "Well, of course not, I wouldn't—"

"You know the sort of thing I mean. Happen to mention a girl you're dating edits one of these damn-fool fashion magazines. Or—"

"No," said Clock. "I see what you mean." He said it heavily. "I can say so, and you can say so, and Frances can say so, but it doesn't mean anything. I could also have been dating the Madden woman." He got up. "I guess we've said what there is to say. Except I haven't said thanks. To both of you."

"Oh, for heaven's sake, Andrew," said Nell crossly.

But when he had gone, her eyes were anxious on Jesse. "Is there any chance of proving it? So much— Jesse, it'd kill him. It's the only thing he's got, his work. Anybody who knows him knows that. The other men in his office—his record—"

"Character witnesses," said Jesse. "Evidence can be a funny thing sometimes. . . . I haven't kissed you properly since this morning. . . . Trouble is, the other answer is so damn fantastic. The frame. He should know if he has an enemy like that. Says he doesn't."

"Don't you *believe*—" Nell pulled away a little. "Jesse, you know Andrew wouldn't—"

Jesse traced her thick arched brows with one finger, gently. "*The way of men is froward and strange.* No, idiot woman, I don't think he's lying. But evidence I know a little about, and I can see that those boys playing watchdog aren't—probably—going to look beyond the nice clear evidence. Which I don't like. But the other way, it's so *damn* fantastic—sizable amount of money laid out just to blacken his name, get him fired from the only job he knows. It's crazy. And as for proving it—" He shrugged.

"But you're going to try?" asked Nell. "You told him to let you know what was going on."

Jesse smiled down at her, and Nell thought not for the first time how his smile transformed him. You thought him almost an ugly man, the high-bridged nose and long jaw, and then he smiled and was nearly handsome. Any way, of course, he was Jesse: reliable, deceptively mild—and deceptively shrewd—Jesse.

"Not so many clients clamoring for attention," he said. "And according to old Jeshu, *Idleness teacheth much evil.* I may as well poke around a little on Andrew's problem. I like Andrew too."

And Nell said explosively, "Oh, damn Fran! If she wasn't such a little flibbertigibbet she'd have married him months ago and this wouldn't— Oh, well, I guess it wouldn't have made any difference, at that."

When Clock parked in front of the old apartment house on Bronson Avenue, there was a darkened car parked ahead of his. He didn't glance at it; he was, suddenly, too preoccupied with his renewed rage, as he opened the door and the ceiling light went on, noting again the remnants of grainless powder on the dashboard, the glove-compartment door. Printing *his* car. As if he was—

A frame. They framed me, Sergeant. God, how often? The old weary tune.

Him, Andrew Clock. The dedicated cop. And why, why, why? And who? Money spent, just to—

But as he slammed the door, a light went on in the car ahead and a door opened.

"Waiting for you, Sergeant," said Detective Peter Petrovsky.

"Oh," said Clock. He felt confused, awkward, outraged; he didn't know how Petrovsky felt. He hadn't been back to the Homicide office since this morning, but he knew it would have got round, most of the story. Suspended. He thought suddenly how strange it would be, tomorrow morning: no office to go to. Nothing to do. He liked Petrovsky, he thought Petrovsky liked him, but after today he just wasn't sure of anything.

"Knew you'd be home eventually," said Petrovsky easily. Clock couldn't see details in the dark street, but he could conjure up the other man's stocky figure, round face and snub nose and mild blue eyes. "I thought maybe you'd like to hear what went on when those witch hunters descended on the office."

Clock was silent a moment and then he said abruptly, "Didn't you hear about the evidence they've got, Pete? Not from them, my God, I know. But—"

"Oh, the scuttlebutt got round," said Petrovsky. "Sure. Is that level, Sergeant, that bank teller saying—"

"It's level."

"Well, do tell," said Petrovsky thoughtfully. "That does make it very damn complicated, doesn't it? Fancy that. Of course they don't make much money, you can figure one of them happy to grab the extra loot."

Clock didn't know what to say to him. He didn't know. "Pete," he said, and he was frightened to hear his voice frightened, "Pete, I never laid eyes on the blonde chippie before. I never paid in that money. I don't know anything about it. Pete, you and Lindner were with me—when we searched Skipper Arnold's place. We weren't all together in every room all the time, but— Why the hell should I— I didn't—"

"Well, you better not come out with that to the Inquisition," said Petrovsky. "Because both Bob and I swore up and down we were all together all the time, Sergeant, so you couldn't have covered up any evidence. What good it did, who knows? Likely those damn watchdogs just figure we're trying to cover for you. You know how their minds work. I just thought I'd tell you so you wouldn't foul up the signals. And we also thought you might need a little cheering up, I've got a bottle of Scotch here. Don't know whether it's a brand you like."

Clock said, "Pete. You're supposed to be a trained detective—read plain evidence."

"So I am," said Petrovsky amiably. "But there's evidence and evidence, Sergeant. I've also worked with you for a couple of years. You might ask me in and offer me a drink, and I'll tell you what the witch hunters asked and what we said, hah?"

Wordlessly Clock got out his keys and turned up the walk.

"But I will say," said Petrovsky behind him, "if what I hear is so, it's complicated. The frame. You think about it, it must have cost somebody some money. Who'd want to frame you like that, Sergeant?"

"I don't know, Pete," said Clock helplessly. "It just doesn't make sense. I can't think of anybody with a reason. I don't know."

"Which just," said Petrovsky, "makes it more complicated."

"I don't see what all the fuss is about." She said it a little sullenly, a little fretfully. "So Andy's a cop. So what? I got an honest job, why shouldn't he take me out, he wants?"

Jesse contemplated Helen Madden with interest. He had found her by the simple expedient of looking in the phone book. She lived in a jerry-built new apartment building on Cole Place in Hollywood. She'd let him in without enthusiasm, but without protest, this Thursday morning.

"You're a lawyer?—Andy's lawyer? What's he want a— Oh, those men came with him yesterday. I guess he's in trouble of some kind, but I don't know anything about that. Well, look, am I going to turn down the money just on account I didn't know where it came from? Don't be silly, mister. I mention this sale on mink coats, he says go buy yourself one—how do I know he hasn't made maybe a lucky kill at poker or something? I like Andy, he's a nice guy."

She looked to be in her late twenties, and might be thirty-five. The standard product, Jesse thought: silver-blonde, provocative figure, latest fashionable make-up, pale lipstick and lots of eye shadow. Knit Capri pants and form-fitting blouse, bright green. And the expectable surroundings: untidy living room, magazines, overflowing ashtrays, cushions on the floor, a hi-fi set, a couple of abstract prints.

"I don't get all the big fuss," she said petulantly. "If Andy's in trouble it's nothing to do with me."

Helen Madden had a job; she was a hostess at the Cannibal Tavern, an expensive joint out on the Strip. She probably made good money— and spent it. She was, Jesse reflected, certainly no schoolgirl; and she was playing this very artless and very smart.

For how much extra take?

She was just sufficiently reluctant and just sufficiently revealing. He wondered if Captain Thatcher—and/or Lieutenant Clay—were smart enough to see that, or just took her at face value. Which it would be easy to do.

"If it's anything to do with you, I met Andy about six months ago at a poker parlor down in Gardena. Well, I was with Joe—my brother. I'm not so much for cards, but Joe— Well, for God's sake, mister, so he fell for me, he's not the first guy ever did that, and a girl's got to get by how she can—am I going to turn down the little presents?" She laughed. "So he gives me presents, I go out with him, so what? He's a nice guy, he takes me nice places. Why shouldn't—"

"The photograph, Miss Madden," said Jesse gently. "You mind if I look at it?"

"What—oh, that." The photograph was not in evidence, in its frame, on the mantel. "It got broken," said Helen Madden. "I'm sorry—it was a nice shot of me. Taken out at the Three Aces, nice place, we used to go there a lot. I—" And she glanced a little nervously at the second man in the untidy living room.

So, the photograph making a one-time appearance, maybe? Just for Captain Thatcher and Lieutenant Clay to see? Not for the lab to examine? Because I.A. could, of course—if they wanted to go to that length—get a warrant to seize the photograph. But what about the photographer at the Three Aces? Who might or might not remember taking one photograph. Or had he or she been bought too?

He looked at the man. "It got broke on account I broke it," said Joe Madden hardly. He'd been lounging in the doorway across the room: and he was expectable too. And interesting. He was about to become more so.

About thirty, Jesse thought. A punk, said Clock. It was a word for him. Not bad-looking, sandy blond, a sullen mouth, flashy sports shirt and slacks. Had done time in Quentin, said Clock, for armed robbery. "Goddamn cops," he said. "I told Helen she hadn't no business running around with a cop. Cops I don't like, mister, I say it to you or anybody comes asking—the cops shot my dad. *Our* dad. In cold blood they shot him, you think I forget that?" He looked at the woman with cold eyes. "Her taking up with a cop—argh! I told her—"

"Listen, Joe, he's a nice guy even if he— And I mean, well, a mink *coat.* Joe, why shouldn't I—"

"A *cop,*" said Madden. "I told her. Try to argue with females. Might have known it'd bring trouble. Guys come asking questions— more cops. I put the damn picture in the trash, and let her yell about it—and she's staying shut of that cop and all the rest from now on. And we both said all we're goin' to say, mister, see? You can just—"

"That's all very interesting, Mr. Madden," said Jesse. He meant it.

THREE

Not much use, reflected Jesse, to go and paw through the refuse cans lined up behind the apartment. He stood beside the Ford and lit a cigarette, ruminating. The photograph was window dressing; nobody was going to see it again. Assuming that Thatcher and Clay would have gone to the lengths of having the lab look at it, they weren't going to have the chance. And what a neat little play that had been!

All so very plausible. The vanishing of the photograph might have looked just a bit suggestive to Thatcher and Clay and whatever minions they had working under them: but a nice plausible reason for it. With characters to fit. Joe and Helen Madden. Joe, who didn't like cops, thought Jesse: the ex-con, the punk. Annoyed because Helen's keeping company with a cop; saying I told you so when more cops come down on them, playing Big Brother and telling her to get shut of her bad boy cop. Incidentally getting rid of the photograph. Presumably in the heat of argument. And Helen so plausible too, every way: a type a lot of men fell for. A type pretty obviously to take up with anything in pants who had money to spend. On the nice places, on Helen.

Very likely the I.A. officers had seen the mink coat. Would check on its purchase. Clock had told him how they'd go to work. Very quiet, no publicity: word would inevitably get round within the force, especially down at Central Headquarters, but the public wouldn't hear anything until I.A.'s decision was handed down, and it wouldn't be a crude firing: just a request for resignation.

He'd like to know about that mink coat himself. When and where.

Unless Thatcher, Clay and company could be convinced of the frame— If just one part of it could be proved a frame—

Jesse sighed and climbed into the Ford. He started for the bank

Clock used, and on the way he thought about Starbuck. Because after a little cerebration on this thing, this and that had occurred to him; as it probably also had to Clock, by now. Any way you looked at it, the frame was fantastic; but when you considered the timing, the timing from the minute Starbuck came on stage— Which led to an even more incredible conclusion.

No, there was some excuse, certainly, for Thatcher and Clay. Jesse supposed all the I.A. men had served apprenticeship in other offices, as ordinary cops. And if there was one thing any cop learned on the job, it was the axiom that what a thing looked like was usually just what it was.

They wouldn't buy the frame without evidence. And it looked as if that wasn't going to be easy to find.

Who had found the Maddens, that precious pair? Not unusual types, the Maddens, but so ideal for this setup. And then there was the teller, and there would be somewhere the photographer who had stolen the shot of Clock and probably made up the composite; and whoever had posed with Helen at that night club. And there was, of course, also the gold tie clasp. Anybody—the principal himself, X— could have made the anonymous phone call to the *Telegraph*. But you added it all up, it was something hard to swallow.

For anybody who didn't know Andrew Clock personally.

It did, of course, all fit together. Once you swallowed the initial premise . . .

The assistant manager of the bank was difficult. He didn't like upsets in routine, and he was annoyed at the implied criticism of the bank's staff. He didn't know anything about Mr.—oh, Sergeant, yes— Clock personally, all the bank records were confidential at all times, he really couldn't—

"Mr. Lanterman," said Jesse mildly, "apparently you don't realize that Sergeant Clock has been accused of serious misconduct, and could lose his job over it." Lanterman looked even more remote. "It's pretty clear" (cross fingers on that one?) "to anyone who knows him that he's being, um, framed for it. We're looking for evidence on that. I'm sorry to take up your time, but it's a question of a man's reputation, Mr. Lanterman. And irresponsible accusations can bring down any man. You, me. Somebody says you've been fiddling with the books, a little evidence shows up it's so, maybe you might feel a little bit irritated when the auditors brushed off your questions, hmm?"

"Oh," said Lanterman. "I didn't realize—" He looked indignant, and then interested, and then alarmed. He was a big solid man about fifty, with a large Masonic pin in his lapel. He sighed. "We really don't like to—"

"I've got a note here from Sergeant Clock, authorizing me to see all the records. But I want to ask some questions about this teller too. Walter Hendrickson."

Lanterman sighed again. "You can't expect me to like the implication that one of our employees is dishonest. In any way."

"Don't expect it," agreed Jesse. "But if he is, you'd prefer to know it, I suppose."

"Oh, hell," said Lanterman unhappily. "What do you want to know, Mr. Falkenstein?"

"To start with, how long has he worked for you?"

Lanterman stood up. "I'll have to send for his employment record. Miss Gleason—"

They waited, Lanterman in gloomy silence. "Just how d'you hire people?" asked Jesse. "This is a big chain. Central personnel office, downtown maybe?" He was thinking about the secondary conclusion the time-table had forced him to reach.

"What? Oh, no—no, each branch does that as needed. All our branches are fairly large operations, in a city this size. Mr. Jeffries handles personnel here. As a matter of fact, we have four new people training as tellers now. We train them on the job, you see. . . . Here's the file. Hendrickson." Lanterman frowned suddenly, opening the manila folder the silent secretary laid on his desk. "Oh, yes. He's been with us a little over two years. Since January of nineteen sixty-three."

Two years, thought Jesse. Well, well. "You just remember something about Hendrickson? When you said, Oh, yes?"

"I don't know what you— Well, I'm sure I don't know what it'd mean to you," said Lanterman stiffly, "but I do just recall Mr. Peterson—our chief teller—mentioning that he'd had occasion to—er—speak to Hendrickson. About his dress. That he should be—er—more discreet, if you take me. About his ties and so on. Which is nothing unusual, you know. Young men nowadays, especially in California, are— But we have to keep up a certain standard of—"

Banks, reflected Jesse, were nearly as persnickety about whom they hired as a good police force. It was not a comforting thought. He got out his notebook and wrote down the date. "All right. Did he have any recommendations?"

"No, he was just out of the army after doing his service and this was the first job he held. . . . He was twenty-two. . . . He graduated from high school—Hollywood High—and had two years of college at L.A.C.C."

"What's his address?"

"Really, Mr. Falkenstein—oh, well. Romaine Street." Lanterman added the number. "He hasn't any mark against him, apparently he's been quite satisfactory."

"What d'you pay him?"

"Really, this is— Well, I suppose there's no harm. We do *not* like to be publicly involved in any sensational—"

"Not likely to be," said Jesse. Unless, he thought, they did succeed in uncovering the frame—the fantastic frame—when the press would probably go to town on it.

"Well. Fifty-six hundred. That's before—er—withholding."

Jesse thought about Ray Austin, that case last month. Typical young banker: serious, ambitious. But take a young fellow with no particular aim or ambition, just holding a job for the money—two years of college, evidently not specially trained for anything—and it could very well be that (fifty-six hundred bucks—before withholding—not being what might be called a princely wage in this year of grace) such a young fellow would be open to a deal. A fast deal.

Find out about Hendrickson. If he was the kind might be open to a deal. Any year of grace, a lot of people would be. As old Jeshu put it, *Gold hath destroyed many, and perverted the hearts of kings.* How true.

Because there was that aspect of the frame too. That nobody was going to get hurt. Except, of course, Andrew Clock.

Nobody got stashed in jail for telling lies, when the lies weren't found out. Nothing would happen to Helen Madden for (presumably) dating Clock and taking presents from him—as she'd admitted doing—there wasn't anything illegal about it. Except, of course, that girls with ex-con brothers weren't the ideal dates for respectable upright cops. Joe Madden—his parole time up now—couldn't get into any trouble by backing her up that that was so, by doing a little acting. Walter Hendrickson wouldn't be in any trouble, unless it could be proved he'd lied, and that would be quite a little chore. Whoever had made up the composite photograph wouldn't be in any trouble; that was past praying for now, likely they'd never find out about that.

It must have looked like easy money to all of them.

"Any relatives?" he asked.

"A sister. She lives in Long Beach," said Lanterman shortly. "Mrs. George Herrick."

"I expect," said Jesse, "you do keep an eye, so to speak, on your employees. Realize it's a delicate subject, but after all banks—that is, you'd know if he bought a new car or a mink stole for the girl friend—"

Lanterman sniffed and said nothing, at last came out with, "Hendrickson has his own account with us. Perfectly open—nothing at all out of the way." He looked at the file before him. "I could tell you what rent he pays and what car he drives, yes, but I'm not going to. All I will say is that he is quite evidently living within his means, he's not in debt, and from everything we know about him he's a perfectly honest and honorable young man."

Nice, thought Jesse. Somebody being clever. Very, very clever. *Two years?*

A small snide thought whispered at the bottom of his mind, *Last June. You've really only known Andrew Clock since last June.*

And the first ten minutes I talked to him, thought Jesse irritably, I read him. The solid honest cop. Not clairvoyant: anybody could read him, knowing him.

Oh, yes? Thatcher and Clay—

Well, it looked like such solid evidence.

The alternative so very damned incredible.

He thanked Lanterman and went away, to find the handiest café and lunch. He had an appointment at one-thirty with a woman who wanted to make a will. Twenty-five bucks not to be turned down.

Even more incredible, the alternative, he thought over a sandwich and coffee, when you thought about it in detail and realized how delicate the timing was. Since Starbuck had triggered it off; well, triggered the opportunity. The timing said something at least twice as incredible, and he contemplated it unhappily.

The man with vengeance in his heart, the plotter who had brought down vengeance, strolled up a certain block of Sierra Madre Boulevard in Pasadena. He was well-dressed, he looked prosperous and content. He stopped before an old, large house set back from the street: an out-of-date house, three-storied, wide-eaved, from the days when large families had afforded servants. There was a tended lawn, flower beds; there were gateposts, and over them a discreet sign: THE SUNNYVALE REST HOME.

He turned and sauntered up the front walk, up the steps to the porch, and rang the bell. The house was well kept, freshly painted. The senior citizens who, senile or bedridden or otherwise incompetent, dragged out their allotted time in the Sunnyvale Rest Home, would pay high for the undoubted good care they received.

He removed his hat politely to the brisk, black-clad, corseted matron who opened the door. "Good afternoon," he said pleasantly. "I just wanted to ask—happened to be passing, I won't come in, thanks—how Mr. Teague is these days? Is he still with you? I'm a friend of his son's—"

"Oh, yes. Mr. Teague? That's a very sad case, isn't it, Mr.—? I'm afraid not too well. He hasn't any interest left, you see—he's been failing sadly lately. Won't you come in and see him, Mr.—"

"No, no, really I haven't the time, I just happened to be in the neighborhood. I'm very sorry to hear that. Sad, yes. Thanks so much." He shook his head gravely.

Strolling away, he smiled to himself. Good to know, to be so reassured. The better vengeance, yes. On those who deserved punishment.

The careless ones, the uncaring ones. Nine of them.

Thomas Teague had been one of them. A selfish, irascible old man— quite an old man even then—who, retired and comfortable in his old man's routine, half-childish perhaps, had had only one great interest and pleasure in life. The foolish, selfish old man—and his absurd television programs. The gibbering inanities on the screen. His only interest.

But, the better way had been revealed—the better vengeance—and so that had been taken away from the foolish old man. One night before Christmas, four years ago, as the foolish old man walked home along a dark street, he had been waylaid. His attacker had not wanted his well-filled wallet. No. His attacker had taken his eyes, with a little bottle of acid.

So the foolish, selfish old man dragged out his dreary days, blind and forlorn, in an impersonal rest home.

The plotter, the vengeance-bringer, was a little surprised he had lasted this long; but the longer misery, the better vengeance.

It was sweet to reassure himself.

It was Joe Lopez' day off, and Lopez was feeling miserable.

To start with, he liked Andrew Clock one hell of a lot. He respected him—as his senior, and as a man. And of course the word had got round. A lot of the details. The way I.A. worked, all so damn hush-hush, theoretically nobody but I.A. would know anything until the ax fell; in practice it was some different. For one thing, Petrovsky had phoned Lopez after talking with Clock last night; he'd also called Lindner. Which was natural.

And to go on with, Joe Lopez was a reasonably smart detective. He could reason from A to B to C. Knowing the specific details, he had: as had Pete Petrovsky.

As Joe Lopez, who had worked under Sergeant Clock and knew him, liked and respected him, he could make the instant, indignant, blind evaluation: a frame! And then as Detective Joe Lopez he looked at the facts, and he felt like hell.

It happened. God knew it happened. Not often, on this force, no. But there'd been those four men out in the Valley division, pulled those burglaries. And— A woman, they said. This Madden dame. The sergeant not much for looks, God knew, and a man could go off the rails—

And when you looked at it—at the timetable— That tie clasp and all.

"I thought you said you were going to fix that window," said his wife.

"Oh, all right," said Lopez dispiritedly.

"After all, we're not millionaires," said Teresa. "Things you can fix yourself—"

"I said all right," said Lopez. But while he was fixing the window quite suddenly he had an idea. An electrifying idea. So he put on a tie and called Pete at the office for the address and went to see if Clock was at home.

"Because I just had this idea," he said. "Maybe it's crazy."

Clock said heavily, "Joe, I appreciate— You know you're not supposed to contact me, any way. While the damn watchdogs are—investigating."

"Ah, the hell with it, Sergeant," said Lopez. "The hell with it. I know it. I talked to Pete last night. Heard the whole bit." He looked at Clock earnestly, his dark lean face serious. "I don't tell you I'm all that religious—Teresa hauling me off to Mass, example for the kid—but some things you've got to take on faith, Sergeant. Pete told me the evidence. But before I believe that, I'd believe—well, skip it. But you think about it, it gets what Pete calls even more damn complicated."

"Don't think I don't see it," said Clock.

"On account of the timing," said Lopez.

And Clock said again, "Don't think I don't see it, Joe. I've been doing some thinking too." He looked gray and tired.

"Because, you say, so it's a frame, you start to think how it was done. How it was built up. What had to be done, who had to be bought. The Madden dame and her brother. That bank teller. Maybe other people that'll show up. You want for some reason to frame a cop, the first obvious thing is to show he took a bribe, true?"

"True," said Clock.

"So, you buy the teller to tell a lie. But also," said Lopez painfully, "the average person we bring in to question, tied up to something, even if he's got money—which isn't usually so—he couldn't pay over any bribe without its showing some way—withdrawal from his bank account. Any substantial amount, and Pete says evidently they've got this pegged at ten G's."

"Way it's set up, it's to look as if I gave the Madden woman about forty-five hundred cash and banked the rest."

"Yeah. But a fellow like Starbuck—a pro gambler that usually keeps a lot of cash available—he could. So—"

"Joe, I'm seeing it."

"Resident of Nevada," said Lopez, fingering his jaw. "Over here on business—he says. Gets into a game with Arnold just by chance, poker house down in Gardena—has an argument with him, not important—but we automatically haul him in to question after Arnold's cooled. Starbuck's not important, except that he's the one man out of a thousand might have a nice piece of cash on hand to pay out. Which you'd know."

"All right," said Clock.

"Look what had to be done, Sergeant. We picked Starbuck up Thursday morning, week ago today. Nothing on him, we just questioned him. We'd gone over Skipper Arnold's apartment on Wednesday, after the manager found him shot there. It was in the papers we'd talked to Starbuck, on Friday. And Friday afternoon, as I get it, that cash was paid into your account. And Monday the *Telegraph* gets the anonymous call and contacts I.A. And by yesterday they find that damn tie clasp—supposed to be the evidence you'd covered up—and, hell, even that looks plausible. We had a seal on the apartment door and if Starbuck hadn't played along you could have supposedly gone back for another look and found it. It's just too close, Sergeant. What with engraved initials on the tie clasp and all. The times. You say it's a frame, then Starbuck must have triggered it—the chance to build a frame, see?"

"Don't I," said Clock. "Don't I."

"Because he could be supposed to have the cash on hand. So the framer, all of a sudden between Thursday and Monday, had to find the one teller who could be bought, had to find this Madden dame and her brother—and set that up, slip her the cash to buy the mink coat—get the cash to put in your account, get hold of that mono-grammed tie clasp and— It's just too much," said Lopez. "And you see what it says as well as I do."

"Oh, my God, yes," said Clock. "I just saw it awhile ago. The frame —that's incredible enough. I know. But when you think about all that, it must have been—set up—before. The Maddens. The teller. Just wait-ing an opportunity. Waiting for somebody like Starbuck to be in-volved in a homicide. I see it."

"Pete said complicated. By God it is. But Sergeant—"

"And who'd *believe* it?" said Clock desperately. He brought his fist down on the arm of his chair with a savage thud. "Who could be-lieve— And the money it must have—"

"Well, I had this idea," said Lopez. "I know it sounds crazy. But whoever'd do such a thing might *be* crazy. I mean, like having some kind of obsession. You know? My wife said something about million-aires that triggered it. I just remembered your saying something once —we were having lunch together—about your picking up that rich so-cialite fellow who tried to plant a bomb in his wife's bedroom. I seem to recall it made headlines—a long while back, of course. He got sent up to Atascadero, I think. Well, it's crazy, but somebody like that might hold a grudge. And men do get let out of Atascadero. I just thought—"

"You really reach," said Clock, "to make it a frame. All that I see. Just making it a lot more—fantastic."

"Sergeant," said Lopez, "I've worked with you. It was just a thought."

"Begley," said Clock reminiscently. "Begley? I'd almost forgotten that. I don't—" And the phone rang. He picked it up. "Clock . . . Yes, sir." He put the phone down. "Thatcher. They want to ask some more questions." He reached for his jacket.

"It was just an idea," said Lopez miserably.

FOUR

"So let's take it over from the top. When did you first meet Miss Madden?"

"Yesterday afternoon," said Clock. "When you took me to her apartment." He was answering questions automatically now; it seemed he had been sitting here, answering the same questions, for years. Sometimes alone, sometimes with other people. Starbuck had been here awhile ago, an uneasy Starbuck being bluff and hearty and man-to-man.

"Sergeant, that's not what Miss Madden says. Or her brother. Or—"

"Joe Madden's an ex-con," said Clock. "Are you going—"

"Wait until I finish, please," said Captain Thatcher coldly. "Or one of the waiters at the Gemini Inn on the Strip, who has made a statement that he has several times seen you there with Miss Madden."

Another one bought, thought Clock. Small fry, the waiter: makeweight. He just shook his head. "No, that's not true."

"Sergeant," said Thatcher, "look at me, please."

Clock did not want to look at Thatcher. He supposed Thatcher was a good man, and a good man to be in charge of this bureau, the watchdog of the force. A tall spare man, with steel-gray eyes and regular features, a neat and tidy man, small gold tie tack neatly centered on a dark tie. He sat behind an uncluttered desk, and Lieutenant Clay stood, or roamed around the office, or occasionally sat in the chair beside the desk. Clay shorter and stocky, and balding: less tidy, less good-looking. And they both looked at Clock with scarcely veiled contempt in their eyes, the natural contempt of good cops for a cop who has gone wrong, and thus degraded not only himself but every other man on the force.

He did not want to see their eyes. He had looked at bad cops like that himself. This couldn't be happening to him.

He looked at Thatcher and saw the contempt. He said, "Captain, I'm telling you the truth. I know about the evidence you have—think you have. I know how it looks. But all I can do is tell you the truth. I don't know that woman. She's lying. Madden is lying. The—"

"Bank teller is lying," finished Clay. "And the waiter. Why, Sergeant? What have they got against you?" He grinned mirthlessly.

"For money," said Clock. "For money."

Clay looked at Thatcher, who jerked his head. Clay went out. "I want you to listen to something, Sergeant," said Thatcher gently.

Clay came back in with Helen Madden. She was looking nervous, and a little frightened; Clock didn't know whether that was an act; he thought probably so, but there was so much he wasn't sure of any more. She was dressed to the nines, and she looked exactly like what she was, a cheap chippie. Main Street. The impossibly blond hairdo, sequined black dress a little too tight, spike-heeled pumps, too much costume jewelry. What the hell did they think of him, to think he'd— He thought of Fran suddenly, her utterly elegant and neat small person, the quick one-sided smile so uncannily like Jesse's, and he squeezed his eyes shut painfully for a moment.

Helen gave him one hard glance as she sat down. "I told you all you wanted to know before," she said. She sat on the edge of the chair, holding her big scarlet plastic bag on her knees and showing her legs which were, admittedly, very good legs. "If I'd thought I'd get into all this just because Andy happened to be a cop— I mean, honestly, dragged down here like I was a criminal or something."

"We'd just like Sergeant Clock to hear what you have to say," said Thatcher. His eyes were cold on her too. He sat back. Clay hoisted one hip onto the corner of the desk.

"Well, for God's sake!" she said. "If that's not the craziest, when Andy knows all about it anyway."

"About the mink coat. Miss Madden, when did you first mention a mink coat to Sergeant Clock?"

"Oh, well! It was about a week ago Tuesday. They were having a sale at Robinson's, I saw it in the paper, and I mentioned it to Andy that night—or it could've been Wednesday—when he came—"

"I was home both those nights," interrupted Clock desperately. "On

Wednesday, that Wednesday, I did some overtime on the Arnold case. I didn't get home until eight or so."

"Just listen, Sergeant. What time was that, Miss Madden?"

"Oh, it was late, I don't get home until after midnight and he knew that, naturally. Anyway, he laughed and said if he had the money he'd sure like to get me one, and—"

"Listen," said Clock, "how d'you suppose I'd ever be worth a damn on the job if I was chasing around half the night with—"

"Sergeant."

"Go on, Miss Madden. All about the coat."

"Well, I *told* you before! Andy came by the restaurant on Saturday. Where I work, I mean. He knew what time my break is, half past nine, he came then and we went and sat in his car in the parking lot. That's when he gave me the money. I'd never seen so much money all at once before. It was over forty-two hundred dollars, a great big wad of it. He was sort of excited. He said, There's your mink coat, baby, and you can imagine how excited I was— I said—"

"Did you ask him where he got the money?"

"Well, naturally, but all he'd say was, he'd made a lucky deal. And I ask you, how was *I* to know what kind of deal? I mean, it could've been at poker or something. *I* never knew anything about it, if he took it from somebody! How should I? He never told me, just gave me the money, and after all if a fellow wants to buy a girl a mink coat, who's going to turn him down? I didn't know where he got the money."

She was good, thought Clock. But then most women were natural actresses. He wondered how they'd known he didn't have an alibi for Saturday night at half past nine. Tuesday or Wednesday, pretty safe: a man working the eight-to-six shift, a man who lived alone, wouldn't be apt to have an alibi past midnight. But Saturday—had there, for God's sake, been a tail on him? To know that he'd been innocently sitting in his apartment reading a novel—because Fran had a deadline for some idiotic copy about spring fashions in make-up.

Fran.

"No," he said. "No."

"And I was nervous, I tell you, having that money—all that cash—at home over the weekend, but first thing Monday I went out to Robinson's and bought my coat. You saw it, goodness knows, pawed over it like— The saleslady was surprised about the cash too, but I just said I thought it'd be more convenient. Naturally I haven't got a charge account there, I couldn't afford it—and—"

"We have," said Clay conversationally to Clock, "a statement from the salesclerk. Apparently Miss Madden remarked to her that her boy friend had given her the money."

"Well, I was excited about it. I never had—"

Clock found he was shaking his head automatically; for a moment he had the panicky feeling that he couldn't stop it. He stopped. He said, "No. This is all—"

"Thanks very much, Miss Madden," said Clay.

"And if I'd known what I was getting myself into— Joe was right, all right, should have had better sense than to take up with a cop!" She got up, adjusting one nylon; she gave Clock a resentful look. "Even if I did get a mink coat out of it. Can I go now? Keep me here half the day asking silly questions—"

"That's all right now, Miss Madden," said Clay.

She started for the door, paused as she passed Clock's chair. "Well, I guess at that I'm sorry you got in trouble, Andy. But they can't say *I* knew anything about it." She shrugged. "Nice knowing you, lover—till you pulled the fast one." She went out quickly and Clay shut the door.

"I suppose you've got a tape going on this," said Clock.

"Why?" asked Clay. "We've got the statements. We're not the Gestapo, Sergeant. We—"

"I know what you are," said Clock. Much earlier, when Walter Hendrickson had been there, he had been afraid he was going to lose his temper. Any minute, with that deprecatory, polite young damn bank teller saying it all over again—*you paid it in yourself, sir, in cash* —any second, he was going to explode and smash these liars, these conspirers, these littly sly scheming men who were trying to prove that Andrew Clock was a bad cop. Trying to take his reputation, his career, his life and stamp them into the mud—to bring him, Clock, who'd tried all he knew how to be as good a cop as a man could be, down to destruction. Any second, he would explode—even as he knew instinctively it would be the worst thing he could do.

And then he had got to a place where he was in control. He had got past the point of doubting his own sanity, his own integrity, which the piling-up of evidence had brought him to. He knew that somehow, for some unimaginable reason, some secret enemy was doing this to him;

and he must stay sane and calm if he was going to meet the attack and show it for what it was.

So he looked now at Thatcher and Clay, a big man and very tired, but secure in his own integrity, and that sureness was in his slow voice, and he said, "I know what this department is, Lieutenant. You're one of the factors that make this the top force. Only one. This was the first police force anywhere to start to police itself with an Internal Affairs department, to keep an eye on its own men. And you've got some puritanical rules, and some of the boys resent you a little, but maybe it's necessary, to keep us the top force. I'm not going to remind you—" he was a little surprised they were listening this far— "of all the tests and standards and requirements the force uses to screen out the undesirables—were using when I joined. Men go wrong sometimes, you can't predict it. We've all seen it happen. I'm not going to remind you that I've never had a mark of any kind against me in thirteen years, or even that I've got promotion a lot younger than most men on this force. All I'm going to say to you is that I'm a career cop. I never wanted to do anything else, and I never intended to be the kind of cop who makes plainclothes rank, detective third, and stays there. All I've got to point to is thirteen years of my life. And then I'll say, if you think I'm capable of throwing that away—all of a sudden turning into an entirely different man and forgetting anything I ever believed about integrity—about my integrity as a police officer—all on account of that cheap little Main Street blonde— then all I've got to say is that you're goddamned bad judges of human nature." It had come out of him forcefully, even judicially; and as he stopped, for just one moment he saw something else in their eyes on him. Beginning doubt? Belated caution?

And then Clay smiled a little grimly. "Quite a little speech, Sergeant." Clay was remembering the solid evidence. "So you've been framed. The innocent boy."

"It's a frame," said Clock. "My God, I know how it looks. I can't explain why or who. But it's—"

"The Maddens," said Thatcher, "are lying. The bank teller, who has no possible connection with the Maddens and doesn't know you personally, is lying. The waiter, who doesn't know either the bank teller or Helen Madden, is lying. Is that what you're asking us to believe, Sergeant? Because they've been bribed to lie? The photograph of you and Miss Madden, that we saw in her apartment yesterday, must have been a fake? Somebody with some mysterious reason to get you in trouble has thrown away at least ten thousand dollars and—by your version—probably more than that, just to get you in trouble, spoil your reputation? Is that what you're asking us to believe?"

"Damn it, I know how it sounds."

"Does that seem very likely, Sergeant?" asked Clay.

"No, it sounds very damn incredible," snapped Clock. "But it's the only answer I come up with, because I know I didn't do any of that."

"The bank teller," said Clay, "is an ordinary bank teller. With nothing whatever against him, past or present. Good record with his employer. Somebody—this mysterious X—saw in a vision he'd be open to a bribe, to tell a lie?"

"I don't know," said Clock wearily.

"This mystery man picked the one waiter at that joint who'd be open to a bribe, to tell a lie?"

"I don't know. I only know—"

"Don't you have any suggestions—not even one—as to who this X might be? Maybe you stole somebody's girl once and he's bent on vengeance?" said Clay sarcastically.

Clock looked up at Clay silently, knowing how much use it would be to mention Begley. He understood what they were doing, and he understood how they felt. The evidence was so solid. To them, he was obviously the cop gone wrong, and the sooner they were done with him the better. The sooner they got him tangled in his answers, admitting this, admitting that, so they could hold the formal hearing—and he could see the ice in the chief's eyes now, the chief who was something of a personal idol to a lot of cops—and formally request the resignation, the better. And then try to counteract the bad publicity on it.

But didn't his record mean anything at all? Thirteen years— It hadn't been easy, always. During his mother's long illness, and the hospital bills— He could have made more, quitting the force for some other job. He was a qualified accountant; that was four years of night school. But he'd never wanted any other job, and now—

When they let him go, he got out of the building as quickly as possible, terrified he would meet a man he knew, maybe see the same contempt in his eyes. The anger was building again in him now, but a cold anger, a calm anger.

He found a public phone along Temple Street, where he'd parked, and dialed his own office. (Probably his own former office.) By the grace of God he got Petrovsky.

"Listen, Pete— Well, yes, it was a session—no good to kick it around. Listen, it's occured to me I'd like to know a little more about Joe Madden. The girl too, but she's got no record. Will you go poke around Records for me? And another thing—this is way out, but there was a guy named Begley, back in nineteen fifty-seven I think it was— Wilcox Street'd have details on it, but probably it's in Central Records too."

"Joe came in to tell me about that one," said Petrovsky. "Sure it's way out, but whatever's behind this has got to be. Obviously. And I will say, on the money angle, this Begley would have it to spend, I gather. O.K., I'll do some poking around. I already sent an inquiry up to Atascadero, ask if he's still there. Get you at home?"

"I don't know," said Clock. He gave Petrovsky Jesse's number. "Thanks, Pete. Have you seen the lieutenant?"

"Oh, my, yes," said Petrovsky, sounding amused. "He just got back from that peace officers' convention in Denver. He was calling the In-quisitors every name in the book—he was going up to see Thatcher, but—" his voice sobered—"he had to admit that the evidence—well. We turned up another possible suspect on Arnold, and we've got a new one—knifing over on the Row."

"That's nice," said Clock. "Well—"

"I'll be in touch," said Petrovsky.

When he got to Jesse's office, Miss Williams simpered at him and told him to go right in.

He went in to find Jesse lying slumped in his desk chair with his eyes shut, and old Mr. Walters placidly consuming bourbon in the cli-ent's chair. Jesse opened one eye and squinted at him.

"Man looks as if he could do with a drink, Edgar. You pour it for him."

Mr. Walters obliged. "This is kind of a mess, isn't it, Sergeant? I've had a couple of stray ideas, what Jesse's told me. First off, can you think of anything—any little incident maybe even years back—might have set somebody, and maybe a slightly crazy somebody, gunning for you? Because there's got to be some reason."

"Don't think I haven't been racking my brains!" said Clock. "I can't think of a damn thing. But Joe Lopez did." He told them about Begley.

"Well, well," said Jesse, straightening up very slightly. "Faint hope dawns. What exactly was your connection with Begley?"

"My God, it's a long time ago. I was a detective second at Wilcox Street. The call came in, it was the night shift as I recall, and I went out on it. With a squad-car driver. I don't remember much about it, except for the headlines—Begley was a stockbroker or a banker, something like that—wealthy anyway—and he'd gone off the rails all right. It was one of their servants called in. Begley was threatening to put a bomb in his wife's bedroom—he'd gone slightly berserk—the squad-car man and I put the cuffs on him and brought him in, that was all. I seem to remember the doctors said he'd had a stroke of some kind."

"Oh. Would he have known your name?"

"No idea," said Clock. "Wait. I testified at the sanity hearing. Sure. But whether he took it in— Look, it's wild. All that time ago. And all the cunning plotting?"

"Place to look," said Jesse, shutting his eyes again. *"Many have sinned for a small matter."*

"You and your Holy Writ," said Clock. "I thought the righteous men were supposed to come out on top every time."

"Not," said Jesse, "in the nature of things, Andrew. I'll offer you another one. *For a just man falleth seven times and riseth up again.*" He sat up and added a thimbleful of Mr. Walters' bourbon to his glass. "No harm to find out about Begley. Whether he's been released from Atascadero. Check out every idea. But more important, if we can show just one piece of the evidence was manufactured—"

"You've got more to check," said Clock, and told them about the waiter. "And that little bitch—she puts on a good act."

"Enjoying herself probably," said Jesse. "Ramifications to this. Somebody being clever."

"How the *hell* can you go on believing me?" asked Clock loudly.

Jesse finished his bourbon and gave him the sudden slanted smile that, so absurdly, made him look like Fran. "Second thought reassured me," he said. "Suddenly occurred to me, any man who'd fall so hard for Fran isn't within any human probability the man also to get involved with one like Helen Madden. Not reasonable, Andrew. If there's one constant in a man's nature, it's the type of woman he picks."

"That's one hell of a fine reason—" Clock began to laugh. "How true, how true."

"I," said Jesse, "after taking notes on Mrs. Gorman's will, went to sniff around where Walter Hendrickson lives. Modest apartment over on Romaine. Well within his means as a bank teller. Sure. But—*Prepare thy soul for temptation*, we're warned."

"You *got* something on him?"

"Here a little, there a little. Usual apartment tenants, don't know too much about each other. I was—um—an insurance investigator. He pays his rent nice and prompt. He's a nice polite young man. He doesn't—so far as anybody knows—have women visiting him, he doesn't give wild parties. Drives a six-year-old Ford. Has hay fever—the druggist on the corner told me that. Nobody knows if he has any special girl, but the manageress did tell me that he used to date one of the other tenants before she moved. One Marjorie Freeman. She—the manageress—gave me her new address. Want to see her. Want to locate some more of his friends."

"But you said you got—"

"Um. From the woman across the hall," said Jesse. "Who just happened to be going out when it was delivered. Maybe a little something. Hendrickson bought a new RCA color television last month. A console. Even at a discount house, not much less than seven hundred bucks."

Clock stared at him. "Last *month*? Last—"

"I said ramifications," said Jesse. "We can all see that, can't we? This wasn't a spur-of-the-moment deal. What did your man call it?—complicated. . . . Can't you think of *anything* else, Andrew? Any real or imaginary injury you might have caused somebody? Any time?"

Helplessly Clock shook his head. "Who makes enemies like that? Who'd go to the infinite trouble—"

"Well, any case, the who not as important as the how. If we can just prove one bit of evidence is a lie—" Jesse looked at Clock reflectively. "I think we go and lean on Hendrickson tonight. If we find him home. You look so nice and formidable—that jaw—very effective leaner."

Clock finished his drink and sat straighter. "Lead me to him, boy. I'll lean on him all the way!"

"Oh, Mr. Falkenstein—" the office door opened.

"Well, I might have known I'd find you all sitting around guzzling whisky," said Fran, marching in. "Nell finally located me. I was up north at a fashion show, getting photographs of the new hemlines, of all damn-fool things." She looked at Clock. As usual, she was looking more like a model for her own magazine than an editor, slimly elegant in charcoal wool sheath, one big gold brooch, the black star-sapphire earrings, nails and lips the newest shade of coral. "You do seem to have got into something, Andrew. But I expect Jesse'll manage to figure it out. At the moment what you need is a good solid meal. I've been sent to fetch you. Nell's got steaks waiting. Let's go."

FIVE

It was a middle-class apartment building, on a dark middle-class block: old red-brown brick, fading sign, THE ROMAINE ARMS. Cars lined the curb almost solidly; they had to park a block away. As they got out of Jesse's Ford, Clock said, "I'm not supposed to be doing this. Anything like this."

"No?"

"Uh-uh. When you're being looked at by I.A., you're supposed to sit home like a good boy, just waiting the summons for more questions, and trust the all-seeing Thatcher to come up with the truth." Clock laughed harshly. "Strict nonintervention. But hell, I'm in so much trouble now, what's a little more?"

They climbed the three cement steps to the little silent lobby with its rows of locked mail boxes on one wall. "Apartment twelve," said Jesse. He looked at Clock. "Shall we play cops and robbers? Heard about how you go on sometimes at a suspect. Two of you. One tough and mean, swinging metaphorical rubber hose, other one all gentle and nice making promises. Play it like that?"

"What have we got to lose?"

They climbed carpeted stairs. Apartment twelve was the second door down the dark hall. Jesse pushed the bell button; they waited.

When the door opened their ears were assailed by the raucous laughter of a canned audience from the TV. Directly across the room, catered to face the couch on the same wall as the door, stood the new console color TV. It was on, a panel show of some kind.

"Yes?" said Hendrickson, and then he recognized Clock. "Oh—" He was evidently relaxed for the evening, in rather gay blue nylon pajamas, a blue Chinese brocade dressing gown, leather slippers. Not at all a bad-looking young fellow, thought Jesse. Only about five eight, but well built: wavy dark hair, regular features, clear blue eyes. The mouth a little too small, a little—just a little—weak.

Clock, looming over him, put one hand on Hendrickson's chest and pushed him back into the room. Jesse followed them in, shut the door and thoughtfully went to shut off the TV. Canned laughter ceased abruptly.

"All right, you lying little son of a bitch, how much did he pay you?" demanded Clock loudly.

"What the—what d'you mean, walking in here—you can't—" Hendrickson spluttered indignantly. "Let go of me."

Clock shook him hard by the shoulders, terrier with rat. "How much were you paid to tell that lie?"

"I d-don't know what you mean. I—I—"

"Now take it easy, Andrew," said Jesse. He came to stand beside them. "I'm Sergeant Clock's lawyer, Mr. Hendrickson. Now all we want you to understand here is that you could be in pretty serious trouble, y'know. You could indeed. We know, of course, just as you know, that you lied about the sergeant paying in that money. Well, whatever happens about his job, Mr. Hendrickson, he's not going to let that go— Win, lose or draw, Mr. Hendrickson, we're going to prove that you lied, and sue you for everything you've got—including your bribe money." His tone was conversational.

Hendrickson stared at him, confused. "S-sue me? But what for? I don't—"

"Defamation of character," said Jesse. Lucky sometimes the average layman had very hazy notions about the law and the nature of evidence. "You can save yourself a lot of trouble if you'll just cooperate with—"

Clock shook Hendrickson back and forth again, violently. "I'm not interested in the lying bastard's money, for God's sake! Listen to me, Hendrickson!" He thrust his craggy grim face down at Hendrickson's. "If you don't give me some straight answers I'll beat you within an inch of your life!" He slapped the smaller man across the face, open-handed; Hendrickson's head snapped back.

"You lay off me, you big ape—you can't—" Hendrickson pulled away from him, and Clock's grip on the robe tore one lapel half across. "*Now* look what you— I'll call the police—you can't—" But the bank teller's eyes were frightened.

"The police!" said Clock, and laughed. "You dumb bastard, cops stick together, you ought to know that! Now who paid you how much to tell that lie?"

"It'd really be much easier on you to be cooperative, Mr. Hendrickson," said Jesse softly. "In the long run, that is. I don't suppose the bribe was enough to support you for the rest of your life—and when we've proved you lied, you know, the bank'll fire you and you might find it difficult to get another job. And don't think we won't prove it. I'm afraid the sergeant's a bit upset over all this."

"Damn right I'm upset!" said Clock. He took a step and slapped Hendrickson again. "You get this good, you little son of a bitch! Whatever happens down at Headquarters, you don't open up I'm going to catch you and give you the beating of your life! In fact, I think maybe I'll do it right now. Your own mother wouldn't know you when I'm done with you! *Who paid you to lie about me? Who?*"

"Now, Sergeant," said Jesse. "Catch more flies with—"

"Nobody!" gasped Hendrickson wildly. "I didn't—" He hadn't expected anything like this. He backed away from Clock, stumbled over an ottoman before the armchair and caught himself against the chair. "You can't do this."

"I don't like to do things that way, Mr. Hendrickson." Jesse sighed. "But if you're going to be stubborn about it, I suppose we can turn up the TV to cover any—er—noises. It'd be so much easier on you to cooperate with us. By the way, Mr. Hendrickson, where'd you get the money to buy the TV? The bank tells me you're not in debt—you paid cash for it? Where'd you get the cash?"

"I—" Torn between the two of them, Clock still menacing him, Hendrickson wet his lips, backed away farther. "I saved the money. What the hell difference is it to you? You can't come here and th-threaten me. I haven't done anything— I'll—"

"And that's quite an expensive robe," murmured Jesse, "I'd guess. Temptation, Mr. Hendrickson? Under strict orders—and of course your own common sense would tell you about that too—not to splurge, throw any money around. To create the hint of any suspicion. But you just couldn't resist starting to spend some of it—to enjoy in the privacy of the home where it wasn't apt to be noticed. Natural, maybe."

"I—don't know what you're talking about. Don't you touch me!" Hendrickson backed again as Clock moved toward him.

"You lying bastard, I'll get you!" said Clock. "Jesse, turn on the set. Answer me, punk! *Who paid you to tell that lie?*"

"I didn't—I didn't—you can't—" Hendrickson broke then, as Jesse moved leisurely toward the TV. He turned and dashed into the bedroom, slammed the door behind him and snicked the key in the lock. They heard frenzied activity as he pulled some heavy piece of furniture across the door—a bureau for choice, or the bed.

"Hell!" said Clock softly. "Is the phone in there? If he does yell for cops—"

"Leave it, Sergeant," said Jesse loudly. "The little man's scared to death. He'll break the next time we catch him—and he's got to come out sometime. He knows we know he lied."

"Damn it, let me take him now—"

"Not worth the trouble," said Jesse. "He'll come apart next time. Come on."

"The goddamn little liar," grumbled Clock as if reluctantly. They went out to the hall and stood a minute, but only silence emanated from apartment twelve. They started down the hall.

"More truth than poetry," said Jesse. "A physical coward, and he likes his nice clean-cut boyish profile. This may be easier than we think. You scared him all right. If he does come apart and admit it, that'd knock the props from the whole thing, and I expect your I.A.'d crack down on the Maddens then."

"God, I hope so. Yes, I think that'd do it, but would they look any further into it? Damn it, I want to know what the *hell* is behind all this."

"Have a little hunch it could be something interesting. And probably damn offbeat. One little thing we can guess at: our principal—whoever—thinks he's smarter than he is. Which same can be said of many criminal minds, true. A really smart operator never trusts accomplices. Especially paid accomplices. Anybody who'll take money for some nefarious act is so apt to take more to betray. And you can never be sure they won't talk in their sleep, or get drunk and talk too much."

"We keep after Hendrickson. Shall I go and glare at him in the bank tomorrow?"

"Useful idea, yes. I really think he might come to pieces. I'm a fool," said Jesse suddenly. "The deposit slips."

"I thought about that too, if—"

"That deposit slip presumably for the bribe money, you said it looked like your signature. Unless we assume, which is unlikely, that somebody mixed up in this is an expert forger, that's got to be a tracing. And, Hendrickson being involved, it's most likely a tracing from some former deposit slip—or of course a check—he could get hold of from your file, to hand over to X. Which means he had to substitute a deposit slip for the one he stole, and that one will be an obvious forgery. If we could locate that—"

"And it just could be," said Clock, "that after that one was used to trace the signature, he could have slipped it back into the file. And nobody, as you know, ever signs his name exactly the same way. If we could find the original slip, we could prove it was a tracing."

"I don't think a teller would have access to the back files—we can ask. Mostly girls who do the posting, isn't it? Well, back to the bank and the discreet Mr. Lanterman. But I do have hopes of Hendrickson. . . . Let's go see his erstwhile girl friend, shall we?"

She was, Marjorie Freeman, a nice girl. Perhaps a rather ordinary girl, but reasonably intelligent. She lived with her mother, and they'd moved from Hollywood to Pasadena when she got promoted; she'd been working as a file clerk at The Broadway, and got promotion to the job of assistant secretary to the personnel manager of the Pasadena branch. She now lived in a quiet middle-class apartment house, smaller than the one on Romaine, on Mentor Avenue, and she let them in after hesitation, looking rather bewildered. Her mother, she said, had already gone to bed.

She had a nice enough figure, smooth dark brown hair, brown eyes. She didn't quite understand what they wanted of her. "Is Walt in some trouble? A lawyer—"

"Well, he could be," said Jesse. "He could very well be, Miss Freeman. Er—I did say this is Sergeant Clock of the police?"

"Yes, you did." Her glance moved doubtfully to Clock. "Police? What on earth has Walt got to do with the police?"

"Well, we'd just like to ask you a few questions about him. Have you known Hendrickson long?"

"We went to high school together. Hollywood High. Only he graduated in nineteen fifty-nine and I graduated the next year. . . . Oh, well, we've dated on and off, I think mostly because we lived in the same apartment house for a few years, but it wasn't ever anything serious—you know. I like Walt all right, but not—not that way."

"Would you say he was a truthful man, Miss Freeman?" asked Clock.

"*Truthful?*" She stared at him. "Why, as much as most people, I guess. What on earth has he been doing, to have the police—"

"Be frank with you," said Jesse. "We think he's accepted a bribe to do something, call it dishonest."

"*Walt?*" she said.

"Strike you as all that impossible? You know him pretty well?"

"Well," she said slowly, "I've know him a long time. In a sort of casual way. I don't know—he was awfully sick of the bank, the last time I talked to him."

"When was that?"

"A couple of months ago, at Martha's. I was surprised he took that bank job, anyway. He was always—oh, well, you wouldn't be interested in—"

"Interested in anything you can tell us about him."

"Well, he wasn't ever the steady sort. You know what I mean. He didn't like routine. He had a lot of different part-time jobs when he was going to college, he couldn't seem to stick to anything long. Do you really want to hear? Well, he and his father used to live in the apartment on Romaine then, and he and I went around together a little. Just some. Then his father died, and he—Walt, I mean—was just out of the army so he just kept on the apartment himself. He was looking for a job then, he went to some employment agency, and then one day when he came home he said he'd got this job at the bank. To train on the job. It wasn't the kind of job I'd have thought he'd want, because banks don't pay too well, do they? An awfully, oh, secure kind of job, but— And he always seemed more ambitious. No, I don't mean that exactly, I mean ambitious to make money."

"Expensive tastes?" asked Jesse.

"Well, I guess, when he could afford nice things. But I couldn't tell you anything about it, if he did—do something wrong. I wouldn't know, he wouldn't say anything to me. Why'd you think I knew something?"

"We didn't, Miss Freeman," said Clock, "but you did go out with him, you know him. We thought you might know who some of his other friends are."

"Other girls? I wasn't the only one he went out with, I suppose—and he wasn't the only fellow *I* went out with. It wasn't—serious."

"Any of his friends. Other men."

"Oh. Well, he and Bill Dodd had kept up, I know. Bill was in school with us too. He married one of my best friends, Martha Simms, they live in Altadena. Walt and Bill both like to bowl. I don't think he had any special friends at the bank, I wouldn't know about—"

"When was the last time you went out with him?"

"Well, goodness, let me think. It sort of died a natural death after we moved, you know. As a matter of fact, I'm really going steady now with Bob Armstrong, he's a reporter on the *Herald*. Goodness, it must have been before Christmas—yes, it was just after Thanksgiving last year, Walt called and asked for a date, and I hadn't anything particular on that night so I said yes." Suddenly the brown eyes widened. "Why, yes, I do remember—"

"Mmh?" said Jesse encouragingly.

"Goodness, *has* he done something? Well, it was only," said Marjorie, "that he took me to Monte Blue's. And that's pretty exclusive and expensive, you know? I remember I was—well, like everybody else we've got to be careful about money these days, and the cocktails were a dollar and a half, and dinner nearly seven dollars, and I know a bank teller doesn't— Well, it was only, I said something about it, and Walt just laughed and said something like, you're only young once. But—Mr. Falkenstein—that was nearly six months ago."

"Mmh, yes," said Jesse. "So it was. Think of anything else, Miss Freeman?"

She shook her head. "Walt—I can't get over it. A *bribe?* Well—maybe I *can* just see it, at that. I mean—well." She was silent, and then said suddenly, "A lot of the kids at school didn't seem to think anything about that sort of thing, the way things seem to be nowadays—maybe I'm just old-fashioned. But he was awfully good at algebra, you know, and he used to do the other kids' papers for them for so much per."

"Oh, really?" said Jesse.

"If you want to know, I didn't hear about it until just the other night. I was at Martha's and Tom brought it up. I didn't know about it at the time. Anyway, even aside from Bob, I wouldn't have gone out with Walt again if he'd asked. If you want to *know*," said Marjorie Freeman.

"Unfortunately," said Jesse, "character doesn't constitute evidence."

"It constitutes a fair presumption of a tendency to weakness," said his sister tartly. She and Nell sat side by side on the couch listening to him. "You really are too scrupulous, both of you. All you have to do, obviously, is go back and beat the truth out of that rabbity little crook. A few good punches from Andrew and he'd come apart at the seams, by what you say."

Both Clock and Jesse looked at her with awe. She sat very upright, a glass of sherry poised in one long manicured hand, looking ultimately the sleek civilized female.

"*No wrath above that of a woman,*" said Jesse. "You want us both to go to jail?"

"Merely common sense," said Fran. "There's another quotation about bearing false witness."

"I really do think, Jesse," said Nell, "that it might be the quickest way to prove—"

"Look," said Jesse gently. "Basic principles, you two. Reason the third degree got abolished. Fellow like Hendrickson—some a lot tougher—you put him through enough, he'll say anything. Then next day, in front of the judge, he claims duress. I suppose you know what that means."

"Quibbling," said Fran largely. "And if you'll shut up for a minute— Our heavenly lamb Mr. Walters went home awhile ago, but he left a message. He wants you—" she looked at Clock—"to think back over your whole career and write down the names of everybody you've ever had contact with who, A, were at all queer in any way, or, B, had money. He said he's a lot more interested in who and why than how, and it's all very well for Jesse to try just to prove the frame, but it's more important to find out what's behind it. In the long view."

"My sweet Christ," said Clock, "am I a walking file case? How could I possibly—a cop meets a hell of a lot of funny people. Lunatics. Queers. Fanatics. Not so many people with money, but some." He shook his head. "I don't know—that old boy sometimes sees things, true enough. But what a job—I couldn't possibly—"

Jesse, having built himself a mild drink and handed one to Clock, sat down; Athelstane the Monster promptly came and sat on his feet. Absently, Jesse pulled one long droopy black ear. "Three pounds of meat a day," he said. "And all too few clients. And I waste my time trying to help an impecunious cop who'll probably renege on the fee."

"You're forgetting the unknown benefactor who handed me fifty-seven hundred bucks for nothing," said Clock wryly. "Do we go and lean on the Maddens now? That girl's tough."

"Most females are. Concentrate on Hendrickson, I think. That's the major lie, after all. If that comes unstuck—" The phone rang and he got up, went down the hall to answer it. Coming back, he said, "For you, Andrew."

Athelstane hurried down the hall after Clock and sat on his feet; Athelstane was fascinated with the mysterious voices inside the black box. Panting, and incidentally drooling on Clock's shoes, he eavesdropped unashamedly. Clock stroked the big broad head absently. "Clock."

"Joe Madden," said Petrovsky, "has a good reason—he thinks—to dislike cops. After seeing his record, I went down and talked to Sergeant Hellenthal in Robbery. He sent you his sympathy, by the way—nice guy, isn't he?"

"Yes, he is. Madden?"

"Yeah, well, he's got a little j.d. record, nothing much, but his dad—one John Joseph Madden—had a bigger one. Burglary, armed robbery. One night in April of nineteen fifty-seven, Daddy takes sonny-boy along on a job with him. Drugstore over on Rampart Boulevard. They hold up the place, collect what's in the till and are just walking out when, fate sometimes being on the side of the good guys, Patrolman Bill Drecker happens to walk into the store to get some aspirin, having a headache. The druggist yells, Stop thief, Drecker pulls his gun and both Maddens make a run for it, so Drecker naturally yells a warning, fires over their heads and then fires at Daddy's legs. He got him through the spine."

"Oh," said Clock.

"And ever since, Joe's been going around saying nasty things about trigger-happy cops who killed Daddy in cold blood."

"Oh, yes? So Joe'd be all too happy, maybe, to help get a cop—any cop—in trouble."

"Could be, could be. Especially if he got paid for it. He drew a one-to-five then, got out on parole in nineteen sixty-one. Nothing on him since, but somehow I doubt if he's reformed. Always a lot of muggings and purse snatchings we don't get anybody for. He's held jobs, oh, yes—gas-station attendant, that sort of thing. Not working now. Apparently living on sister."

"Yes. Anything on her?"

"Nothing. I asked around the tavern where she works. Not exactly a spotless reputation, but she's never been in actual trouble. Awhile back she lived for a while with a pro wrestler, name of Sam Spain. If that's his real monicker. You got asthma or something? I can hear—"

"It's the Monster," said Clock, "not me. What? No, no, it's a dog— never mind. Thanks, Pete."

"As Joe would say, *nada*. I got this and that on some known associates of Madden's. We're busy like always but Bob and I'll try to contact some of 'em, find out if he's maybe let out anything. I know, I know—hearsay, but maybe something."

"Pete, you know I appreciate—"

"Sergeant," said Petrovsky, "if they fire you, I'm next senior for your desk. It scares me. I don't want the responsibility. I'm just a dumb Russky." He hung up.

Clock found, absurdly, that he was looking down at Athelstane through a little blur.

He went back to the living room and relayed that. "See what turns up anyway. I'd better go home."

Fran finished her sherry and stood up, gracefully. "You can take me home first—my car's in the garage again." She picked up her scarlet stole.

"Yes," said Clock humbly. He never knew what Fran felt about him; but right now at least she wasn't baiting him or teasing him as usual.

As he got into the car after closing the passenger door on her, she said, sounding annoyed, "I simply cannot understand why they can't *see*— Those simple-minded damn fools."

"Don't swear," said Clock, turning the ignition key.

"I know, I know!" said Fran. "You don't like modern females who paint their nails and swear and drink cocktails. All *right*."

"What simple-minded damn fools?"

"This," said Fran disdainfully, "I.A. thing. Those—witch hunters. Anybody with a grain of sense can read you like a book."

"Is that so?" asked Clock.

"The complete dedicated cop," said Fran exasperatedly. "Maybe too dumb to be dishonest."

And then she didn't say anything more until Clock stopped the car in front of her apartment house and got out and went round and opened the door for her. Stepping out, she said, "Jesse and his quotations. You'd think we'd been brought up all religious. Andrew—"

"Well?"

"Nothing," said Fran. Suddenly she stood on tiptoe and kissed him, quick and light. "I can quote too, I guess. Like Holy Writ—*I have not seen the righteous forsaken.* Good night, darling." She tripped away from him, up the apartment steps, quickly, and Clock stared after her, bemused, still feeling her quick lips on his.

SIX

When Jesse got to the bank on Friday morning he found Clock already there, holding up a marble pillar. The pillar was directly across from where Walter Hendrickson stood behind his marble-and-brass-bars niche waiting on the public, at window number three.

"War of nerves?" said Jesse. "Not a bad idea." He glanced across at Hendrickson: Hendrickson very natty in a neat navy blue suit, a navy tie with a small light-blue pattern, a snowy handkerchief showing in his breast pocket. Hendrickson was aware of Clock; there was no one at his window now, and he glanced over toward Clock surreptitiously. "A weaker reed than our principal, maybe, thought. That's the trouble with paid accomplices—another trouble. By their very nature, they're so apt to get nervous and spill the beans. By the way, Andrew, why this bank? When you live in Hollywood?"

"Why—oh," said Clock, still fixing Hendrickson with a long-distance stare, "it's more convenient. I kept my account in Hollywood awhile after I got transferred, but it was impossible. A cop's apt to be a busy man. We get paid every two weeks, on Friday, and I'm usually on day shift. Well, that meant a lot of times I carried the damn check around for days before I had a chance to get to the bank—working down here until six, you see. So I transferred the account here—" this was the Bank of America at Broadway and Seventh—"and I can usually find half an hour to run over from the office."

"Mmh. Let's hear something about your financial habits. Usually deposit the whole amount? How often do you generally come into the bank?"

"I'm pretty methodical," said Clock apologetically. (Methodical men generally rather dull, he suspected Fran would think, and maybe

Jesse.) "I usually drop in to deposit the pay check on Friday every two weeks. Late afternoon as a rule. I usually stick about a hundred of it in the savings account, the rest in checking, and I keep out about thirty in cash. For the sundries."

"Yes. Paying for the larger items by check, the rest of the month."

"Yes, I pay the rent by check, and the car payments—that's actually a bank loan, not regular payments to a contractor. And—"

"Methodical let us say," said Jesse. "Andrew the brain. Cannily borrowing the price from the bank at six percent instead of paying anywhere from twelve to eighteen to the agency."

"Well, I can add two and two," said Clock reasonably. "And a civil servant's regarded as a good risk. I get in a supply of groceries once a week or so, and I pay by check for that. And I pay the gasoline credit card by check."

"You don't always go to any special teller."

"No, the one with the shortest line usually. At a guess—you don't notice all that much, and I'm generally in a hurry. I've gone to Hendrickson's window, oh, once out of four or five times."

"So, roundabout eight to ten checks a month, and two deposits."

"About that."

"Mmh. I don't think Mr. Hendrickson is enjoying his view," said Jesse. Across the width of the bank's main floor, Walter Hendrickson was again eying them covertly. A slatternly-dressed, middle-aged woman came up to his window; he pasted on a patently artificial smile.

"I don't think so either. I'm going out to lunch with him when he goes."

"I'm on my way to see Lanterman again. You'll be nice and available to do some more authorizing if he turns awkward."

But Lanterman was only resigned. "Deposit slips?" he said. "What are you looking for now? I don't—"

"Well, you see, if we're right, the actual deposit slip handed in on April ninth—by somebody—with the fifty-seven hundred bucks cash, had a traced signature on it. Quite probably a signature traced from some other deposit slip, though it could have been from a check. But I don't think so, because Hendrickson wouldn't have access to checks the sergeant wrote, except counter checks."

"No," said Lanterman. "At the end of the day, all the deposit slips, withdrawal slips, checks and so on from each teller's cage are collected and made up into—er—parcels for delivery to the girls keeping up the posting, next day."

"And after they're all entered, what happens to them?"

"Then they're parceled up again alphabetically and sent downstairs where eventually they're microfilmed for the permanent record."

"Oh," said Jesse, digesting that. "Then, if a teller wanted to abstract a slip for any reason, he'd have to do it the same day it was made out. And substitute another. I see."

"Really, Mr. Falkenstein, I can't believe that one of our— Oh, well. What do you want to see?"

"Let's start out," said Jesse, "with Sergeant Clock's file for three months back. How long are the actual checks, deposit slips and so on kept?"

Lanterman looked a little embarrassed. "Well, theoretically they're disposed of as soon as the microfilming is done, but we're usually behind on that. There's a good deal of paper work in a bank, Mr. Falkenstein."

"I believe you," said Jesse.

"In fact," said Lanterman gloomily, "a hell of a lot of paper work. Miss Gleason! . . . And what," he added, coming back to his desk, "with the half-educated girls we get— You wouldn't believe some of it. You really wouldn't."

There was quite a long wait until a breathless blonde with formidable statistics appeared with a topless cardboard carton. "I'm sorry, Mr. Lanterman. We couldn't find anything later than last November at first, and then we found that new records clerk—she's from South Carolina, you know—had put a lot of this Clock stuff in with an account under H. A. Clark."

Lanterman shut his eyes. "I trust you straightened *that* out."

"Oh, yes, sir. Mary's finishing it up now, checking by the account numbers."

"You see," said Lanterman simply, "what we put up with, Mr. Falkenstein. Clark. My God. Well, there you are."

Jesse dumped the contents of the carton onto Lanterman's desk and started to go through it. Methodical you could say Clock was; the deposits twice a month, and only one variation in this three-month record in the amount of cash he'd taken from deposited pay checks: on February nineteenth he'd taken fifty dollars instead of thirty. Fran's birthday was on the twenty-second: the extra twenty probably represented dinner and drinks at a slightly better restaurant than usual. . . . I wish to God, thought Jesse, the little harpy'd make up her mind to marry the man. . . . Checks made out in Clock's rather large hand to Ben's Supermart—to Mrs. Marguerite Keenan, probably the apartment manageress—counter checks to the bank, on the loan for the car—a check to a shoe store last month, the month before a check to a department store. It all looked in order. Jesse set aside the deposit slip which had accompanied the supposed bribe money; the signature on it looked entirely authentic, the large sprawled A and C of the capitals quite similar to other signatures, the writing slanted the same.

"So let's go back six months from then," he said.

Lanterman sighed. "I hope you realize I'm being very cooperative."

"Appreciate it."

"Miss Gleason . . ."

Apparently Mary had done her work efficiently; this time Jesse had the foresight to ask also for the statements to check, to be sure nothing had slipped by. As he examined the checks, the deposit slips, he thought uneasily that if this frame had been set up and waiting—a trap to be sprung—the sample signature might have been stolen quite a while back, the substitution—check, withdrawal or deposit slip— already been microfilmed and destroyed. He hoped to God not. More difficult.

But—nothing. "Any more actual paper down there, further back?" he asked.

Lanterman eyed the stack of documents. "We try not to let it accumulate more than a year back. I'll ask. Miss Gleason—"

There were the actual forms still there, awaiting microfilming, back to March of 1964. Jesse started through this last batch. Come to think, Hendrickson couldn't have stolen a check or a withdrawal slip: the necessary forgery of the substitution would have been spotted. It would be a deposit slip.

It was. A deposit slip dated May fourteenth. Not filled out in Clock's hand, but in a careless scrawl—the date rubber-stamped—just careless enough so it couldn't be said to be a real try at imitating his hand.

"How nice," said Jesse. He passed it to Lanterman. "Any rule about this? Actual signature demanded on a deposit slip?"

Lanterman looked at the slip and picked up another slip to compare. "No, of course not. Quite often people come in to deposit money in somebody else's account. You know—daughters to deposit Mama's pension check, and so on. But— I make out the initials on this as W. H."

"Oh, so did I," said Jesse, leaning back and staring at the ceiling. "I liked them quite a lot. Has Mr. Hendrickson gone to lunch yet?" It had taken some while to get through all the paper work.

"I'll find out," said Lanterman abstractedly. He went out of the office, the deposit slip in his hand. Jesse lit a cigarette and thought about several things. Just how long ago had the trap been set up? Longer ago than last May fourteenth, obviously. (Talk about incredible.) Because Hendrickson, under instructions, might have had to wait some time before Clock happened by window number three with a deposit slip. There was even another quite incredible thought about that. Had that been the first deposit slip abstracted? Because an individual's signature did tend to vary slightly as time went on. *Two years*, he thought. Since Hendrickson had applied for and got the bank job. A queer sort of job for him to take, said somebody who knew him fairly well.

Hendrickson under strict orders. Already sweetened with money, but ordered not to show any of it. (Where did he keep it?) Hendrickson, his salary augmented as long as he stayed on the bank job, ready and waiting to tell the one necessary lie, when the opportunity to spring the trap came along? And Hendrickson unable to resist the temptation to enjoy some of it anyway—how many other girls would he have taken out to the expensive places, how many times bought the little luxuries for himself that wouldn't really show?

Two years, thought Jesse. Oh, yes?

And he thought of Mr. Goldwyn's classic remark. *In two words, im-possible.*

Only nothing really was, of course.

But what about the Maddens? Joe Madden might have reason, or think he had, to dislike cops; which went for the girl too. But the Maddens were smalltime; quite aside from the money, it wasn't the Maddens who had set this up. How indeed had the Maddens been roped in?

Well, some suggested reason had to be shown for a veteran officer with a good record to take a bribe. Veteran officer suddenly goes off the rails over blonde beauty. Suggestion carefully offered (subtle, that one) that blonde beauty only took up with him for what he bought her, and was maybe on the point of breaking with him, on urging of big brother.

Jesse opened his eyes at footsteps in the anteroom. Lanterman came in with Walter Hendrickson. Hendrickson, thought Jesse, looked fairly demoralized, but that he put down to Clock, not Lanterman. An entire morning of meeting Clock's grim significant stare every time he looked up might well demoralize a tougher man than Hendrickson.

"This is Mr. Hendrickson—Mr. Falkenstein."

"Oh, we've met," said Jesse. "Haven't we, Mr. Hendrickson? Hope you're going to be more cooperative today." He smiled at the teller.

"Well, what's it about, Mr. Lanterman?" asked Hendrickson a little nervously. "If I've made a mistake of some kind—" He barely glanced at Jesse.

"I just wanted to ask you about this deposit slip," said Lanterman. "Your initials are on it."

Hendrickson took it and looked at it. "What—about it?" He swallowed unobtrusively, but his hand was steady on the slip.

"Deposit for Sergeant Clock's account," said Jesse sleepily. "But not in Sergeant Clock's writing. What happened to the original?" Lanterman the cautious banker shot him an annoyed glance for leaping to conclusions.

"The— I don't know what you mean," said the teller. "This was a long time back. I couldn't possibly remember the exact occasion. If I made this out instead of the depositor, well, a good many times people do overlook making out a slip and the teller does it automatically. That's why we have all the blanks in the teller's cages, you know that, Mr. Lanterman. That's probably what happened on this occasion. Or if the depositor hasn't got his bank book with him, you make out a—"

"In that case it would be stamped *Duplicate* and given to the depositor," said Lanterman. "I know that, Hendrickson. You don't remember anything about this?"

"Good lord, sir, it's nearly a year ago. How could I?" Very convincing, thought Jesse. Very natural. "That does happen oftener than you'd think—people endorse the check, but forget to make out a slip, particularly if they're in a hurry."

"So they do," said Lanterman, apparently thinking back to his apprenticeship as a banker. "But to save a teller's time, you're really supposed to give the depositor the blank to fill out himself. I should think—"

"Well, actually, sir, it's six of one, half a dozen of the other," said Hendrickson. "I find it just as simple to do it myself."

"Yes, I suppose so," said Lanterman.

"Funny," said Jesse. "Sergeant Clock a very businesslike, methodical fellow. Very odd he'd forget to make out a slip. Don't you think so, Mr. Hendrickson?"

"I don't know the man personally," said Hendrickson in a colorless tone. "I—"

"That's even odder," said Jesse. "Thought we all got pretty well acquainted when we called on you last night, Mr. Hendrickson."

Hendrickson's eyes shifted once. So he wasn't issuing any complaint: keeping quiet: no fuss, no publicity. But Clock had scared him. Interesting—and also suggestive. "I'm sorry," said Hendrickson carefully, "if anything I said—upset your friend, Mr. Falkenstein. But all I can do is tell the truth—about whatever I'm asked."

"Well, that's so," said Lanterman a trifle impatiently. "Well, Mr. Falkenstein—" He shrugged. "Whatever your theories, I'm bound to say Hendrickson's probably right. Tempest in a teapot. People do forget little things like that."

"I—excuse me, sir, but it's my lunch hour, may I—"

"Yes, yes, quite all right, thank you, Hendrickson. Well, Mr. Falkenstein—if you're satisfied—"

"Not quite," said Jesse. "I'd like to get this thing photostated, and I'd like a signed and witnessed statement from you as to the circumstances by which we found it."

"Oh, my God!" said Lanterman. "Lawyers! It doesn't mean a damn thing, I don't see—"

"Have a little notion," said Jesse, "it could be our first break."

He didn't, as he'd planned, help Clock trail Hendrickson to lunch. By the time he'd got the deposit slip photostated and Lanterman's signature on the statement, witnessed by the efficient Miss Gleason, it was after two o'clock. Hendrickson was back at his window and Clock was holding up the pillar again across from him.

Jesse relayed his news and Clock looked a little less gloomy. "By God, that could be— But it doesn't prove anything. I can swear I never in my life forgot to make out a deposit slip, but proving it—"

"Sure. But it got to Hendrickson. A little. I think we go on concentrating on him."

"I've been making him damn nervous," said Clock with a taut smile. "He doesn't like me hovering over him one bit."

"Few men with a guilty conscience would."

Clock grinned tightly. "I tailed him to lunch. He went to a hole-in-the-wall hamburger place on Broadway. I got the stool one down from him. The hamburger wasn't bad. Just before he finished his, the fellow sitting between us left, and I just leaned over and looked at him, all very much the screen tough, and said, 'Better not go out alone after dark, Hendrickson.' He put the rest of his sandwich down sort of sudden and left."

"Mmh, yes. He didn't, I don't think, expect quite so much interest to be taken in it. His little lie. Authority comes asking, he tells it—polite colorless young bank teller—and that's that. And that's funny too," said Jesse suddenly.

"What?"

"An enemy," said Jesse, "with sufficient reason—or what he thinks is sufficient—to go to so much trouble to frame you—who didn't expect you to fight back? Who—maybe—didn't know enough about you to know you'd fight back?"

Clock stared at him. "That's—well, far out, boy."

"You going to stick to him the rest of the day and night?"

"No," said Clock. "I'm taking Fran to dinner. She phoned me at eight this morning and told me I was. At—" he looked away—"the Gemini Inn."

The plotter, the vengeance-bringer, had been reassuring himself again that day. There had been nothing in the papers, but he knew that his vengeance was proceeding against the last of the nine. He had taken the trouble to learn something about that police force: books had been written about it; and he knew something of how the Internal Affairs department operated. That piece of vengeance would be going on successfully.

Reassuring himself, he had gone to look secretly at another of them he had brought the just punishment on: from time to time he liked to do that.

The taste of vengeance was very sweet.

The woman had moved, afterward; she had sold the house in Nichols Canyon and moved to an apartment in Hollywood, on Cahuenga Boulevard.

She had nothing in her life any more; he had seen to that, as she—among others—had seen that he had nothing in his life any more. What was the money? She had tried—he had found that interesting, if rather childish—to find something new, something to help, in one of these cultist religions: a thing called the Spiritual Light Association—she went to meetings regularly, he knew. But watching from a little distance, he was satisfied that the woman had found no reassurance, no emotional calm, no recompense. There were tired, bitter lines in her face, and her eyes were unhappy. She had nothing but the money, and the past sitting forever on her shoulder, the happy past that was forever gone. No happiness ever again: no recompense.

As he had none. So that was good.

He saw her come out of the building, and drive away in her car. Her clothes were expensive, but he saw her face and smiled. Her gaze passed over him remotely there: she did not, of course, know who he was, much less that his was the hand that had taken happiness from her in one fell moment.

Well, perhaps not all in *one* moment.

He had not expected that the husband, brooding and despondent, would blame her: would commit suicide. That had been a little bonus, on that one.

He remembered that he had not, then, been sure he could do that—bring himself to do it. Even to accomplish the needed vengeance.

A child. A little boy, not as— But it had, in the event, been very easy. And necessary, for the vengeance. The due punishment on the careless ones.

The beloved child. The child come so late to them, and so indulged. The Nichols Canyon house—so isolated, so convenient, no other house near, and just a little way down that road the steep curve, the hundred-foot drop off the hill. The maid's day off, Thursday. The woman sunning herself on the chaise by the pool. "Stay close, darling."

Quite easy. The car left far down the road. The child in the curving driveway—oh, he had had to wait for it, many dry runs, but eventually, naturally, the child straying. "I'm looking for my kitten, little boy, have you seen a kitten? A little white kitten? Well, will you help me hunt for her, please?"

Not quite three years old. Easy. He really had not minded at all.

The thing that mattered most. To all of them.

They had said, Accident. Naturally. It was intended that he bring the vengeance anonymously.

He watched the woman drive away, and he strolled home leisurely, enjoying (as much as his forever-numbed emotions enjoyed anything, now) the golden April weather. Precisely at six-thirty he was sitting in his own armchair in his well-appointed living room, looking out over the Hollywood hills, when the servant brought him his one before-dinner drink.

The ring of the telephone was unprecedented: the second telephone, the unlisted-number telephone that the servants had strict orders never to answer. Business, private business, he had said. It upset him for just a moment. He crossed the room and picked it up. He listened.

He said, "Nothing can go wrong, you fool. I told you— It makes no difference. Listen to me, I tell you nothing—"

But the little man would not listen. The little man was frightened.

Only, the plan could not go wrong. Not now. Every one of them must suffer the punishment. One little frightened man should not—

If it should be necessary, he had killed before. To bring about the better vengeance.

SEVEN

"This does not," said Clock, "look like the kind of place I'd pick to take a girl to."

"But presumably the girl was doing the picking," said Fran as they turned into the parking lot of the Gemini Inn. "It looks like exactly the sort of place one like the Madden girl would like."

The Gemini Inn was on the Strip. It was very modernistic in design, garishly beckoning with neon, and evidently attracted the late-late crowd; now at seven-thirty the lot was sparsely filled. An attendant in scarlet uniform hurried up to take the Pontiac from Clock.

Life-size bas-reliefs decorated either side of the front door: the traditional brothers, loosely draped in togas, of the zodiacal sign of the twins. In a discreetly lit small anteroom, they were met by an obsequious major-domo murmuring, "The bar first, sir?"

Clock acquiesced. The bar was, naturally, very dark: also sparsely filled. Little round tables and upholstered little round chairs. They did not, of course, know whether the relevant waiter would be on duty in the bar or the dining room.

"And I wish," said Fran, "we had a picture of the girl, Andrew. Though on the *other* hand—"

"A martini and a Scotch and water," said Clock to the waiter. "How did they find the waiter, I wonder. Thatcher and company?"

"That's why I said on the other hand," said Fran. "Because that just struck me. It was the girl, of course—even if they'd had time they couldn't have ransacked every night club in town asking. No, the girl threw off something like, He takes me to the Gemini Inn a lot, one of our favorite places, so they came and asked. And the waiter was— waiting."

"Yes," said Clock thoughtfully, offering her a cigarette. When the waiter came back with the drinks, he asked, "Are you by any chance the fellow a couple of police officers questioned the other day?"

"Police—" said the waiter. "You another cop?"

"Yes, I'm another cop," said Clock, hauling out his badge.

"Take your word for it, friend. Can't see a damn thing in here. As small as that. The cops asked all around, sure. Couple of people they're after, I guess. Showed pictures. It was Benny in the dining room'd seen the couple, nobody else remembered. What's it all about, anyways?"

"O.K., thanks," said Clock. The waiter shrugged and turned away. "See Benny, and then dinner some place else?"

"Um-hum," said Fran. "The Three Aces. Out on La Cienega."

"This is a waste of time," said Clock.

"Not so pessimistic. I think myself it's very likely that teller will break down, if you keep after him."

Clock swallowed Scotch and water, absently wishing it weren't so dark so he could see her properly—Fran even more eye-catching than usual in defiant scarlet silk, her sleek dark hair shining—and he thought about Walter Hendrickson, and wondered if he would break. And he wondered if, the chance arising, he would lose his temper far enough to beat up the little bastard. Unfair advantage. Hendrickson—

He had waited in the parking lot for Hendrickson, having spotted his car—the six-year-old blue Ford two-door. As Hendrickson came out of the bank at ten minutes past six, he had had to walk past Clock to reach his car, and Clock had given him a meaningful glare before turning toward the Pontiac. Hendrickson had driven straight home to the apartment on Romaine, but Clock had tailed him close all the way, and several times in halted traffic had seen Hendrickson watching him in the rear-view mirror. After parking on Romaine, Hendrickson had all but bolted for the apartment door, turning there to look back at Clock, a silent menace, sitting in the Pontiac watching him. . . . Fun and games: childish, Clock was thinking now. But if they could break Hendrickson, by any means—

They finished their drinks and went out to the anteroom. Clock was in no mood to be tactful; he showed the major-domo his badge and demanded Benny. The major-domo looked annoyed, looked alarmed, told him they were very busy and Benny couldn't be spared for long and went off reluctantly. Clock, waiting, stared at the badge in his palm. He'd had it a long time, he thought: he would miss it. Miss feeling it there, solid and hard whenever he pulled out his billfold. A thing which, in an important sense—only a symbol—told Andrew Clock who he was. Reassured him who he was.

It would, he thought, feel very peculiar not to be sergeant any more, just plain mister. Almost like—like being lost in a strange place among strangers.

He put the badge away abruptly.

Benny, when he came, looked at Clock there in the better light, and checked just slightly; for one fraction of a second alarm flickered in his eyes. He turned out to be Benny Giorgione, and he was brash, after that one moment: a stocky, dark, middle-aged man, his face scarred with old acne pits.

"Yeah," he said, "yeah, I told the cops that, mister. Why?"

"Sergeant," said Clock very gently. For a while yet, Sergeant. "You said you'd seen me in here. With a blonde woman."

"With Helen Madden," said Benny. "Acourse I dint know you was a cop. Sure. I did, so I said so." He smiled. "Why not?"

"You know Helen Madden, punk?"

"There ain't no need to call me names," said Benny, the smile vanishing. "I know Helen on account we useta work at the same place, when she was hostess at Rudy's out on Western. Which is the reason I notice her coming in here."

"And me."

"Sure. I—"

"You're a goddamned liar, Benny, and you know it," said Clock. "What was your rake-off?"

"There wasn't no—"

"I'm not," said Clock, "feeling like staying all legal about this, punk. And I'm a lot bigger than you, and a lot tougher. Sometime soon you're going to be telling some more cops you lied, and why, and how much you got for the lie. Or, just maybe, you're going to be over in the General wishing you had. You get me?"

Benny took a step backward. "What the hell, you can't—"

"Oh, but I can," said Clock. "Run along, punk. But look behind you now and then. I'll be attending to you, and soon. . . . And what did that accomplish?" he added as they went out, leaving Benny staring after them.

"Something," said Fran. She sounded as if she were smiling. "It afforded you some satisfaction, but also it tells us something. He's not just a waiter. He knows Helen Madden personally—or she knows him. Does your precious I.A. know that? Did he tell them that?"

"I don't know."

"Or did he let it out because he was nervous about facing you?"

"He wasn't nervous—he was brash."

"At first. So we can see how that was done. Jesse saying, That teller under instructions. So are—were—the Maddens. With the trap set up. So the opportunity happens along—Starbuck the pro gambler, big time, who could be supposed to have the cash on hand—so the instructions go out. Useful confirmation desired. And Helen buys Benny— probably showing him your picture. Naturally, so he recognized the picture the I.A. men showed him—and you just now. That photograph she had, Andrew—did it look as if it'd been taken with a telescopic lens?"

Clock shook his head helplessly. He tipped the attendant who roared up with the Pontiac—all normal parking lot attendants are frustrated racing drivers—and they got in. "I was so—shook, by then, I just saw it was a picture of me, Frances. I don't know. I'll tell you what really does shake me about this. Besides the—the impossible basic fact. It's that so many people can be bought. Oh, I know, the Maddens— and Benny—riff-raff. Sure. We've always got that type with us. But Hendrickson—an educated man, not a—"

"Does that really say anything?"

"I guess not," said Clock. "In a materialistic society." He thought of Marjorie Freeman saying, *Maybe I'm just old-fashioned.* "What can we find out at the Three Aces?"

"As a matter of fact I happen to know the place," said Fran. "The reason I want to ask about the photographer. Somebody took me there once, about six months ago." Some one of the really attractive men, with a lot more money than a cop, thought Clock, who were pursuing Fran Falkenstein. "It's—class. Expensive. Not a joint. So I wondered."

"What?"

"It's the kind of place," said Fran, "where the waiters all look like archbishops. I don't remember the photographer—we were there early, we were going on to a private party—but I'd as soon try to bribe one of those waiters as—as Winston Churchill."

It was, when they got there, all she had promised. The minute he stepped inside the hushed atmosphere, Clock began to feel apologetic about his seventy-dollar gray herringbone and the fact that he hadn't bothered to shave again. He also hoped the twenty-seven dollars in his billfold would cover the bill.

"You know I'm always considerate, Andrew," said Fran uncannily. "No drink, and I really only want the Caesar salad, or possibly the Dover sole. And you let me talk to the waiter. He might faint dead away if you showed him your badge."

She was charming to the waiter, who unbent slightly from his deathly grave poise. A photograph? Madam wished a photograph? The photographer did not ordinarily come into the dining room until after ten o'clock when the entertainment began. It was the after-theatre patrons who— Oh, Madam wished to speak to the photographer? Not, it was to be hoped, a complaint of any—

"Oh, dear me, no, quite the contrary," Fran assured him with her brilliant smile. "If I could just—that is, if the photographer *is* here now—"

The waiter unbent a trifle more. "Yes, indeed, Madam, that will be Miss Wills. I'll see, Madam, certainly." He laid enormous menus before them and tiptoed off.

"Entertainment?" said Clock. "I'd expect an organist and choir."

"But how perceptive. It's just an organist. On the electric organ. I understand he's brilliant at swinging Bach."

"If Jesse ever finds out you've set foot in such a place—" They both laughed. Suddenly Clock felt enormously optimistic: nothing was going to happen to him: it would all be all right, they'd break Hendrickson down and break the Maddens, and find out all about it, and it would be—

The photographer destroyed some of that false euphoria. The photographer turned out to be Miss Judy Wills, young and blonde and discreetly pretty, who was earning money for college in—admittedly—this somewhat unique way. "But I do take good pictures, and I'd be no earthly use waiting on tables," she said cheerfully. At Fran's invitation she sat down at the table, but declined a drink. "A picture of *you?*" she said to questions, staring at Clock. "Did I? I hope you're not going to say you want a copy of it."

"I would," said Clock. "Don't you remember?"

"Heavens, no. I take so many—after a while all the faces start to look alike. I try to pick the couples—or parties—who look as if they'd be interested, and I always ask. The manager's very strict about that, he doesn't want it the high-pressure deal. Like snapping the picture and then sort of shaming the man into paying for it, you know. The way a lot of places do—and then egging them into ordering copies. I charge five dollars."

"Do you do the developing?" asked Fran.

"Nobody does." Miss Wills gave them an impish grin. "I use a Polaroid. Delivery in one minute."

"And so no negative," said Clock.

"Well, no. It's just a kind of souvenir. You probably know you can get a gadget for the Polaroid to give you a neg, but this is strictly a one-shot deal. Once in a long while somebody asks about copies, and I explain, and if they really want one they'll pay for a second shot. But you don't find one couple in a thousand wants copies—the man buys it for the girl, you see. And even at five dollars, it's not overpriced, it really isn't—the film's so expensive, you see. Five dollars for eight shots— you've got to know what you're doing. Vic—the manager—he had me set it up like that, when we started offering photographs, just because he's deathly afraid of making it the high-pressure thing. The way a lot of places— No, I don't remember taking one of you at all, but I wouldn't. I take maybe twenty shots an evening, and I've been work- ing here eighteen months. . . . Oh, you're welcome, I'm just sorry I couldn't oblige you."

"You deduce anything from that?" asked Clock. "I think I do."

"I think," said Fran slowly, "that Helen Madden knew about that. Because—that was what made me wonder—in most night clubs where there's a photographer, you're pressured to order copies. I don't know how long they'd keep the negatives, but if that supposed photograph of you and Helen had been taken in a place like that— And I also think, because this isn't the kind of place Helen Madden would like, she doesn't know about it from the outside, so to speak—from having been here—but because she knows somebody who works here or has worked here. Apparently she's worked at different restaurants, she'd know other people in the business. Waiters, waitresses, hostesses, cashiers."

"Yes," said Clock. "She knew that, with her copy of the supposed photograph gone, there'd be no chance for anyone to get hold of an- other copy. Very plausible. Let Thatcher and Clay look at it once, and then ask around here—all very plausible why no copy is available. Anybody might guess that a photographer taking so many shots wouldn't be sure whether she'd ever taken one of a given individual. But it doesn't give us anywhere to go." He began to feel despondent again. "Damn it, we can figure out how it was done. How it was built up. What damn good does that do, when Thatcher won't listen? But in God's name, *why?* I ought to know, if I'd made an—enemy, God, that sounds melodramatic—like that. Somebody anxious to spend money like this to pull me down. Who, for God's sake?"

She looked at him soberly. "That's the big question. But I go along with Jesse, Andrew—the main thing is to get some evidence, to show it *is* a frame. If you can scare Hendrickson into admitting he lied—"

"And you know," said Clock, "even if we did, if we do, it could be he couldn't tell us one damn thing about X. This could all have been set up—anonymously. And by God, Frances, we will prove the frame—but I'm beginning to be one hell of a lot more interested in who and what's behind this. Because if he can frame one cop—"

"And that brings up something else," said Fran. "The motive, yes. Is it something to do with you as a cop—or just as Andrew Clock?"

Clock looked down at his big clenched fist on the table. "Frances," he said, "I tell you true, holding the badge there awhile back, I guess I don't feel there's much difference."

He left the Bronson Avenue apartment at seven-fifty on Saturday morning. To hell with Thatcher and Clay: they wanted to haul him in to ask all the questions over, try to break him down, let them wait. He —and Jesse—had succeeded in worrying Hendrickson, and he meant to worry him a hell of a lot more. If they could get Hendrickson—by threats, by persuasion, by any means at all—to admit he'd lied, that would do it. Maybe Hendrickson could tell them this and that about the principal behind it, or maybe not; but that would be something definite for Thatcher and Clay.

And he thought that, with evidence of the frame, I.A. would be interested enough to follow it up, find out who.

For God's sake, who? And why?

But obviously Hendrickson wasn't going to come apart very easy. He'd know the retribution he'd be letting himself in for.

Clock parked outside the Romaine Arms at eight-five. Hendrickson's blue Ford was sitting down the street. He had no idea what Hendrickson might do with his Saturdays; he meant to find out.

He waited until nearly nine o'clock before Hendrickson came out.

He was, this morning, dressed in sports clothes: gray slacks, a blue open-necked shirt. He looked, even at that distance, preoccupied. Clock let him get into the Ford, and started the Pontiac's engine; he swung out from the curb and fell in behind the Ford, making it very obvious. The Ford swerved suddenly and he saw Hendrickson's head snap round: good, Hendrickson knew he was there.

The Ford took off like a rocket then, down Romaine toward Highland, and took that left turn almost on two wheels: Clock swore and gunned the Pontiac. He had to wait for traffic, but saw the Ford ahead of him—four cars ahead. Hendrickson apt to get dropped on by a squad car, if one was around: he was jinking the Ford in and out of traffic, doing at least forty. Down to Beverly: to Wilshire: to Olympic. Clock had caught up a little now, two cars behind. The Ford turned on Venice Boulevard, right, and Clock breathed easier: a slow midway through town, traffic signals, a good deal of traffic. By the time they both stopped at the signal at La Brea, he was directly behind the Ford: on impulse, he tapped his horn, and Hendrickson turned in his seat and looked back at him. Clock waved at him genially.

The light went green; and with no warning signal, the Ford was wrenched over left into the turn lane and shot round down La Brea; oncoming traffic, just getting into gear, braked profanely. "Goddamn it to hell!" said Clock aloud, switched on his turn signal, had to wait for the traffic, made it around on the amber. He craned his neck: several blocks ahead, a blue car. He kept his eye on it when he could. Washington Boulevard, and goddamn it, he caught the light. He fumed. But straining ahead, he saw the blue car also stationary, two blocks ahead at Twenty-first. Green. He slammed his foot down: ahead, the blue car was under way again. He had a sudden foreboding. Twenty-third—and an entry to the Santa Monica freeway coming up.

The blue car slipped up and onto the freeway and was gone.

"Hell and damnation!" said Clock.

He drove the freeway all the way into Santa Monica, but never picked up the Ford.

The hell with it. Hendrickson heading for a leisurely day at the beach. Yes, but also a Hendrickson who'd been scared, nervous, maybe getting a little nerve back because he'd shaken the chasing cop. Hell.

Clock went home. Home to his notebooks. Because, when Fran had

SOME AVENGER, RISE! 591

relayed old Mr. Walters' message, he'd said, Am I a walking file case,
and only later realized that maybe he was.

He didn't like to admit it, but he was sentimental over this and that.
Could be—he vaguely remembered, that day way back in 1956, he'd
had a little vision of himself, lonely old man, poring over the record of
his life; anyway, that momentous day when he'd filled the last page of
the notebook, he hadn't—when the report was written up—thrown it
away. The first notebook he'd used as a plain-clothes officer, questioning people, taking notes. Foolishly, it had meant something to him, not
just a tool of his trade, and he'd put it away in a drawer. Had thought,
Maybe interesting, thirty years from now, read it over. Remember this
case and that.

Maybe even, if he ended up as captain or better, write his memoirs.

It had become habit, Clock the methodical man, and they were all
there, tucked away in an old shoe box on the closet shelf. All the ten
years' worth of notebooks. The routine. The leg work. The largely
uninteresting, uncomplex cases any cop met on the job.

And it was wild, because in those years he'd met the lunatics, the
simple ones, the violent ones, the few offbeat cases, the ordinary sad
and sickening police routine—the blood, the suicides, the homicides,
more of the punks, petty thieves and armed robbers—anything and everything every cop meets—but if he'd ever had anything to do with
such a cunning one as this one who had built the frame, conceived a
motive to build the frame, surely to God he must have recognized it at
the time?

Something to do with his career at all?

But Edgar Walters was a shrewd old boy. He saw things sometimes.
And if—

Clock started as the phone rang, and dropped the shoe box he'd just
taken down from the shelf. Thatcher again? Damn the pair of them—
"Clock."

"You know," said Petrovsky, "Joe Madden hasn't held a job in quite
a while. And both Bob and I agree that sister Helen isn't the kind to
go on supporting big brother indefinitely."

"I guess I'd go along with that. He living there?"

"Yeah. She pays one hundred and ten bucks rent. She gets paid four
hundred and forty per month—that's after withholding. And clothes
she likes, and cooking she doesn't like, they eat out most of the time.
More expensive."

"True," said Clock.

"Bob turned up something kind of interesting last night. One Frank Bayless. Old friend of Joe's—they met in Quentin—Bayless has a pedigree, one-to-three for assault. Like I say, we've been looking around for any associates of Joe's, and Bob was wandering around the bars down on Second and Third hoping to run into one of them, you understand, and came across this Bayless. Recognizing him from his mug shot. Bayless feeling no pain, so Bob claims to be also an old friend of Joe's, so Bayless gets a little confidential."

"Nice," said Clock.

"Bayless said, did Bob know what kind of deal Joe was into? Sure must be a dandy one, old Joe seemed to be making out fine, and no job or nothing, and he didn't think pulling off any jobs either. Old Joe setting them up for his pals here and there, pretty flush. Said he asked him awhile ago what he had going for him, hot dice or what, and Joe said he had a nice deal, that was all. Money for fun, Joe said. According to Bayless."

"Oh, really?" said Clock grimly. "For fun. For gunning for a cop."

"Could be. It says nothing," said Petrovsky sadly, "I know. But—something. And I had a little thought, Sergeant, about this Sam Spain."

"Oh?"

"That photograph you mentioned. Call it a fake—a composite—but somebody had to pose for it. With her. So somebody could transfer your face onto it. If just for the one viewing by the witch hunters. Well, Spain is a pro wrestler, it seems. And excuse me, Sergeant, but you're built kind of like that. Could be he was in the original photograph and they dubbed in your face? Just an idea. We're looking for Spain. And, Sergeant—"

"Yes?"

"That Begley got turned loose from Atascadero four years ago. He hadn't actually committed any crime, so he wasn't brought to trial. Released in the custody of his son. Son lives down at Balboa."

"How interesting," said Clock. "Pete, thanks. I don't know how—"

"I told you my motive," said Petrovsky.

EIGHT

Jesse got hold of Clock at ten-thirty. "Speaking of your ill-gotten gains, I think we ought to start spending some. I know a good private eye. Like to take a closer look—a twenty-four-hour look—at both Helen and Joe."

"Well—" said Clock. "Who'd you have in mind?"

"Tom Garrett Associates. I've used them a few times."

"Yes, they're all right—they're good. I met Garrett once, he was invalided off the force. All right, but what we might hope to—"

"If there's a pay-off set up, as there well might be, let's not miss it," said Jesse.

"Oh. There could be at that. O.K., go ahead. . . . I'm poring over my past life. All these notebooks." Clock expanded on that, and about Hendrickson. "I felt kind of superstitious about it at first—starting to look back over the whole record, maybe just as it's closing down. But it's a waste of time, there's nothing anywhere to indicate— All right, you hire the private eye if you want to. They might turn up something."

Nell came down the hall, dustcloth in hand, as Jesse finished talking to Tom Garrett. Athelstane as usual was sitting on Jesse's feet, big black nose thrust against the phone avidly. "Not until Monday? Hell. Well, if you can't you can't. O.K. . . . Yes, I know what it'll run to, you Shylock. Kind of life and death, so put some good men on it, mmh? Daily reports, please. O.K., I'll send you a retainer today. Thanks, Tom." He hung up. "Damn. He won't have the men free until Monday."

"You really think it's that important?" asked Nell. "I mean—what both of them were to do, so to speak, they've done. I should think—"

"True. But there could be a pay-off—a last pay-off—set up. Also could be that won't happen until Andrew's officially fired from the force." Jesse shrugged. "I just feel it'd be useful, might be, to know where they're going and who they're seeing. But, can't be helped. I'm going down to Balboa to take a look at that Begley. Who could be X. Hendrickson's taken off somewhere, we'll have to postpone the war of nerves until we pick him up again."

"Jesse—"

"Mmh?"

"Oh, nothing really," said Nell. "All right. I'll probably go out to the market, if I'm not here when you—"

"Mmh," said Jesse again, and went into the bedroom after his jacket. It was sometimes useful, thought Nell, that when he was really involved in a case, you could commit a murder in the next room and he'd stay blind and deaf.

Saturday, and Fran probably home. The minute Nell heard the Ford's engine start up in the drive, she sat down and dialed. . . . "Because he seems to think it's important, and I thought we might— Well, I *don't* know that the woman's home, or big brother, but we could go and *see*. And then if she— Any chance, after all . . . Wait a minute, Jesse said it was in the phone book." Nell scrabbled over the thin leaves—"Cole Place. That's somewhere around Wilcox, I think. Mmh. One-twenty-seven. O.K., half an hour."

Pleasantly infected with detective fever, she changed from her cotton housedress to the new lavender silk shirt dress, put on—after thought—a pair of low-heeled beige pumps (detectives tailing people sometimes have to spend time on their feet), powdered her nose, renewed lipstick, tucked powder puff and lipstick along with her wallet and keys and cigarettes into the beige handbag, and turned to find Athelstane regarding her sorrowfully from the door. He uttered a small questioning sound.

"I'm sorry, darling, you can't come this time," said Nell. "Come on, out to the back yard. Come *on*, you big lummox."

Athelstane mourned aloud, reluctantly came on. Nell checked that the gate was fastened and got into her baby Nash Metropolitan. Backing out, she had one last glimpse of the abandoned Athelstane, black nose squashed against the chain-link fence, watching his last hope of heaven vanish.

When she parked across the street from the apartment house where

Helen Madden lived, Fran was sitting in her yellow Dodge directly in front of the building. Nell locked the Nash, went over and got in the front seat. "Aren't we a bit conspicuous?"

"Out-of-towners puzzling over freeways," said Fran, who had a large Union Oil map spread out over the steering wheel. "I think she's there. Somebody, anyway. I got here ten minutes ago, and did some looking around. . . . Don't be silly, I had a story. I looked at the mailboxes, she's in apartment seven, and I went past the door—all these places built of plasterboard, you know, and somebody's there. The woman in the end apartment looked out and asked what I wanted, so I invented a name, must've been a former tenant, and came away. So now I suppose we sit here for the next three hours while Helen gives herself a shampoo or something."

"Maybe," said Nell. "It was just an idea."

That was at twenty past eleven, and they did sit there, talking desultorily, for half an hour; but then, down the open staircase at one side of the two-storied building came a blonde vision in sapphire-blue chiffon, rhinestone-heeled patent-leather pumps, and a much-sequined gold lamé stole, and turned up the driveway toward the garages in the rear. "That's got to be her," said Nell. "Fran, we *are* fools—we don't *know* that's her! But by all the descriptions—"

"For heaven's sake, get this map out of my way," said Fran, starting the engine. "Even in Hollywood, there couldn't be two such blonde tarts in an eight-unit apartment. My God, that dress— Strictly Main Street. That's her. What's she driving?"

Three minutes later a pink Volkswagen came down the apartment drive and shot down toward Santa Monica Boulevard. Fran made a reckless U-turn and went after it, a little slower. "For heaven's sake, don't lose her," said Nell. "If she spots us—"

"Bound to turn onto a main drag pretty soon," said Fran. "And in all the traffic— Wouldn't you *know* she'd drive a pink one!"

The pink one caught the light at Santa Monica, and waited, blinking its right-turn indicator. Fran put on hers, a car behind it. The light changed, and the VW shot coolly around the corner, narrowly missing a couple of pedestrians just stepping off the curb. "One of these damn fool women drivers," commented Fran, fuming as she waited for the pedestrians to cross. But Santa Monica is a slow main drag, liberally supplied through town with traffic signals and pedestrian crosswalks— and traffic; it was surprisingly easy to keep the pink VW in sight, now a little ahead, now some distance. Helen Madden was an erratic driver. All the way down Santa Monica they went, the VW edged well over into the right lane.

"She's looking for that turn onto Wilshire, I'll bet," said Fran. Which proved to be the case. As the colorful stack of the Beverly Hilton hove into view, on blinked the VW's right-turn indicator again, and the Dodge immediately behind now, they both swung onto Wilshire. The VW shot over into the extreme left lane this time. Fran managed to squeeze into the same lane behind an old black Caddy.

"This is easier than I thought," she said. "Does Jesse really think there's a pay-off coming up? But surely—"

"I don't know," said Nell distractedly. "Don't speak so soon. Where's she *gone?* Oh, Fran, you'll never—"

"I'll catch up." Fran put her foot down. The VW was four cars ahead, but the amber flickered on at the signal downhill. Fran slid over into the middle lane, and when the light changed made a quick start, flicking on her left-hand indicator, to beat two cars and catch up that far.

"Going all the way into Santa Monica," she said five minutes later; and five minutes after that, "so there you are. Meeting somebody for lunch."

The pink VW had swung into the parking lot of the Fox and Hounds.

"Well," said Nell. "I suppose we wait for her."

"And starve to death? Don't be silly, we may as well have lunch too as long as we're here. She doesn't know either of us from Eve, after all," said Fran firmly.

"Have we got enough money between us?"

That point settled satisfactorily, Fran went round the block and turned into the parking lot. An attendant came up for the car, and to his surprised interest Fran looked around the lot, spotted the VW and went over to peer inside. Coming back, she announced, "Well, at least we know we're chasing the right female. Hers, all right."

A quick glance from the entrance hall (the bar is situated conveniently at right angles to the main entrance there) confirmed that the quarry must be in the dining room. Fran tripped down the carpeted steps, looked around openly, and ignoring the headwaiter led Nell to a table against the right-hand wall.

"She's over there at a table in the middle," she hissed. "I can keep a casual eye on her, don't turn right away. She's with a man. Of course."

"What kind of man?"

"Looks like—oh—" Fran wrinkled her small nose—"junior executive of some kind. Only the sort who's only halfway important. Wind up getting a gold watch for fifty years' faithful service. About fifty. Kind of unimaginative, stodgy character who would fall for that type. Patting her hand now, and she's being coy."

"Honestly, Fran," said Nell.

"Well, I've got eyes, haven't I? . . . I'll have the shrimp salad, please, and coffee. . . . We'd better finish and just sit here over more coffee, no telling how long they'll linger."

But somewhat to their surprise, Helen wasn't planning the leisurely flirtatious lunch they might have expected. Toward the end of an hour, when she and her escort sat elegantly over brandy ("Really, at one-thirty!" said Fran), she started pointing to her wrist watch and smiling archly. By then Nell had got a glimpse of the man: a little paunchy, a little balding, well-dressed. When Helen finally stood up, Fran said, "Let's get out. We can lurk in the entrance if she stops to powder her nose."

The man dropped a bill on the waiter's tray and followed her out. She waited for him, patted his arm, laughed, all very girlish, and with a last smile tripped away toward the ladies' room. The man cast one fond look after her ("Honestly, men!" said Fran) and went on out.

"End of lunch date," said Nell. "Junior executive overworked, maybe—back to office. I wonder who he is."

"He may be known here. Jesse can ask later. Come on. Oh, damn, I haven't any change for the attendant—"

"I've got some."

Helen Madden came out at least fifteen minutes later. Fran and Nell, lurking in front of the restaurant, beckoned the attendant hastily; he produced the Dodge, and Fran had a good excuse to hesitate in the wide turn-in until the VW appeared in the rear-view mirror, behind them; traffic was thick on Wilshire.

"But we're *ahead* of her! How—"

"I have great faith in the—mmh—consistency of bad drivers," said Fran. "Just wait." She let the engine idle, pretending to fumble in her bag beside her, nervously scanned the oncoming traffic roaring past. The VW honked at her impatiently. A lull in the traffic left a wide gap; Fran, head down, ignored it; the VW honked again and then shot

round the Dodge, turned right on Wilshire and headed back toward
Hollywood.

"Maybe you ought to join the force," said Nell.

"Just imagination," said Fran. "Where now? I don't suppose she
goes to work until after six."

The VW led them, a little surprisingly, back into the heart of Hollywood, across town on narrow old Fountain Avenue with its many dips
and blind corners and, turning onto Kingsley, slowed down, started
up, slowed. "She's looking for an address," said Nell. This was an old
part of Hollywood, some blocks shabby, some fairly neat: old California bungalows, the cracker-box pseudo-Spanish stuccos of the early
twenties, brownish lawns, a few old four-family flats. The VW pulled
up suddenly in front of a single house, one of the frame bungalows. It
was freshly painted yellow with white trim, and the lawn was neatly
green—a place kept up well. Helen Madden got out of the car, showing most of her good legs, and hurried up the front walk, pushed the
bell. After a moment a man opened the door; she went in.

They sat across the street and waited. "Another assignation?" said
Nell. "Quite a girl."

"No money there," said Fran tersely. They waited another half-hour
before Helen came out again. Even from across the street she looked
tense and angry. The man followed her out onto the porch, talking to
her; she only shook her head at him, and hurried down to the pink car
at the curb. Fran started the engine of the Dodge.

And there the luck ran out. The pink VW led them up to Hollywood Boulevard, turned neatly left on the amber and vanished in
heavy traffic.

"Damnation!" said Fran, after a quarter of an hour's fruitless casting. "That's that. Well, at least—"

"Fran, let's go back to that place. On Kingsley. I don't think she'd
been there before, the way she looked for the address. It could be—oh,
I don't know! But let's. We could be—canvassers taking a poll or something. Maybe at least find out who lives there."

"Oh, well, it can't do any harm, I suppose. I'd like to know who the
junior executive is," said Fran moodily.

Back on Kingsley, they found the unpretentious old house, parked
in front of it. "Had we better go to some other houses first? Verisimili-
tude," said Nell.

"Are we TV pollsters or what?"

The man came round the side of the house, a trowel in his hand. He was a thin youngish man with stooped shoulders and a good deal of untidy dark hair. He glanced at the car, started for a flower bed at the side of the house and then hesitated, swerved and walked down to the car, bending to Nell's open window.

"Mrs. Roth?" he asked. He had an unexpectedly pleasant deep voice. Even in two words, it conveyed an extraordinary sense of utter integrity, of trustworthiness. Nell felt suddenly confused.

"No. No, I'm not—"

"Oh, I do beg your pardon. I just thought you—Mrs. Roth—might have mistaken the time, the appointment's not until four." The man had serious, rather sad dark eyes; he brushed back a lock of hair. "Are you looking for an address? If I can help you—"

Suddenly Fran got out from under the wheel and walked round the car. "I think perhaps you can," she said. "I'm Frances Falkenstein, this is my sister-in-law Mrs. Falkenstein. Would you—we'd be terribly grateful—tell us why—"

"Fran!" said Nell.

"—why Helen Madden came to see you awhile ago?"

The man stared down at her, at her small svelte person and brilliant eyes darker than his. "Madden," he said. "The two-o'clock appointment. Yes. But they tell me it's not ethical to talk about it. I've never seen why not. It's all interesting, what does come, and really the more we discuss it—" He brushed at his hair absently.

"What?" said Nell.

"Did you want a reading?" he asked. "I'm sorry, I assumed—"

"My God," said Fran, "I knew I'd seen you somewhere. You're Charles MacDonald. There was an article about you—and a picture—in *Fate* magazine."

"That's right. I don't care for the publicity, but—they said—to develop it, you know, I should try as often as possible. They want me to go back to Duke University—all those experiments—but I'm a working man, I can't leave my job." He shrugged. "I don't charge anything. I don't feel that would be right, but they tell me—so I take appointments on the weekends."

"Fran," said Nell, "what on earth—"

"MacDonald the sensitive," said Fran. "I remember the article. You —foretold where they'd find that little boy's body, didn't you?"

The thin young man shrugged again. "I don't know how it operates,

Miss—Falkenstein? Just, it does. I think some people— Well, sometimes it's more a cross than a gift."

Fran looked at him in silence and then said unexpectedly, *"Divinations, soothsayings and dreams are vain.* Mr. MacDonald, will you please tell us about Helen Madden? What she wanted of you? It's terribly important."

He smiled slightly. "That's the Apocrypha. I don't know much about it, Miss Falkenstein—philosophically. I beg your pardon, will you give me your hand a moment? Thank you." He shut his eyes for thirty seconds, holding her hand lightly, and then looked at them both and said, "You'd better come in. There's trouble, and maybe I can help."

Fran exchanged a glance with Nell. They followed him up the cracked walk. Nell thought, Very typical of the Helen Madden type, run to the fortunetellers, the quack astrologers, the gypsy card readers. Yes. But there is, there can be, occasionally, more than that to it. There is Hurkos and Croiset. There was Cayce. There can be—

It was an old house, old furniture in the living room, but all neatly kept. Charles MacDonald shut the door to the hall, on sounds of children presumably from the kitchen, and asked them to sit down. "How can I help you?" he asked simply. He looked like a simple man, Nell thought, in the sense that he was unsophisticated, direct.

"Helen Madden. What did she want?"

"People come to ask questions," he said. "Foolish questions. They hear about me somewhere, and they think I'm a—a fortuneteller. I only let them come because I'm told—people who should know about such things—tell me I should use whatever—gift—I have. But I can't always tell people what they want to hear. Sometimes I can't tell them anything." He looked at Fran seriously; Nell might not have been there. "Her name was Madden? I didn't— It was all very dark, you know. A dark matter. She wanted to know if the money was—safe, she said. Would come to her safely, with no trouble. That there wouldn't be a—a double cross, the way she put it. I couldn't see— I saw it was wrong money, from some wrong source, and I didn't see it giving her any happiness. Any permanent happiness. She was—is—not a very honest woman. I told her she was doing a wrong thing for this money, and in the end that always makes for unhappiness." He smiled ruefully; a quite ordinary young man, sitting knees apart on the shabby couch, his hands dangling, big square workingman's hands.

"Well, that's true anyhow," said Fran quietly. "Did she mention any names to you?"

He gave her a long slow look. "No. No. She only wanted to know about the money, and she didn't like what I told her. I couldn't help that." He shook his head. "I don't know how it works or what it is, you see, and nothing I do controls it. I've had offers—but I feel it isn't a thing that should be used for money. God knows I like money as well as anyone else, but— And all about that woman, I felt—I felt such a crude materialism—the money all she was interested in."

"And that's true too," said Fran. "Would you give me a reading, Mr. MacDonald? How do you—work it? A—"

He smiled gravely at her. "There's some trouble, I know," he said. "Let me have something of yours to hold, please."

"I remember—the article said you're a psychometrist."

"Words," he said. "I don't know anything about it scientifically, Miss Falkenstein. I'm an electrician working for the city."

Fran had her bag open. She said suddenly, "I thought I—" and brought out a heavy gold lighter. "That's Andrew's," she said. "I picked it up absentmindedly last night—must remember to give it back to him." She handed it to MacDonald. "Please."

He looked at the lighter. Clock had indulged himself last Christmas; it was the most expensive butane lighter Ronson made.

Nell looked at Fran, whose gaze was fixed on MacDonald. Well, *sometimes*, she thought. Among all the quacks and con-men and neurotics and hysterical mystics—

Certainly, what he'd said about Helen Madden—

"Trouble," he said, his eyes clouded. "Trouble and worry and deceit. He—he is greatly troubled, it's a question of money but more than that of—of—of name." They were silent, and MacDonald shut his eyes, holding the lighter. "There's a lot of violence. People being arrested. Trials. Men in uniform."

Fran glanced at Nell.

"And blood," said MacDonald. "Violence."

Nell sat forward without knowing she was going to speak. "Will we—" But Fran's voice cut across hers.

"What is the cause of this present trouble? The—the motivation?"

MacDonald was silent, now staring at the lighter. Then he said, "It's queer—there's a pear—a pear? I don't get that clear at all—but I do get the violence—blood—there was, you know, great passion—great emotion—it was terrible, all the blood—and I don't know what it means, but it was something—something to do—the arms of Ariadne."

He sat up straighter; he handed the lighter back to Fran. "I'm sorry if I haven't helped," he said simply. "I know there's great trouble."

"Fran, really," said Nell.

"So laugh. There are some—real ones. True ones. With second sight or whatever. *I* don't know. Only, he hit Helen, didn't he?"

"I suppose. But—the arms of Ariadne! I ask you. At least he didn't charge anything."

"And how typical she'd be one to run to—"

"I thought that too."

Fran started the engine. "Only he's not a—a fortuneteller. He's one of the real ones. I think. There *are* some, Nell, admit it."

"I do, I do. I can hear Jesse now. Are we going to tell—"

"I especially," said Fran ungrammatically, "am going to tell my darling lamb Mr. Walters. Nell, you never *know*."

NINE

When Clock came to the house on Rockledge Road on Sunday afternoon, only Jesse's Ford was in the open garage, the front door was open and past the screen emanated the hypnotic strains of the Toccata and Fugue in D Minor. The screen door was unhooked; Clock went in and was met by Athelstane in the entrance hall.

Jesse was lying supine in the biggest armchair, legs outstretched on the ottoman, eyes shut. "You come to any conclusion?" asked Clock, patting Athelstane.

Jesse opened his eyes. "Damn it, I'd just solved the whole thing—all beautifully clear—and now it's gone. Not a vestige."

"You were asleep," said Clock. Jesse pulled himself up and reluctantly shut off the phonograph.

"What are you doing here anyway? I thought you were chasing Hendrickson." Jesse eyed the cardboard carton Clock was carrying.

"Yes, well, that's something else again." Clock frowned. "The maestro said to meet him here. Called me this morning. He wants to see all these notebooks for himself, I don't know why."

"And have *I* been trying to reach *him!*" said Jesse. "He's due here? I don't need second sight to know who's responsible for *that*—for one thing, he's the only one who knows about this has any money—but if you don't think I had a shock when I saw it—"

"What?"

"In the *Times* this morning. My God." The Sunday *Times*, in all its hundred-page bulk, was stacked on the couch; Jesse picked up the first section. "Page four, and what it must have cost the old sinner I shudder to think. The *Sunday* paper."

Clock turned pages, looked, and had a little shock himself. It was the left-hand page, a bit below the middle; an eighth-page block ad, black-bordered, impossible to miss.

> ANY PERSON WITH ANY KNOWLEDGE OF
> THE GOLD TIE CLASP BEARING INITIALS
> P. S. MAY RECEIVE REWARD BY CALLING
> EITHER OF THESE NUMBERS COLLECT.

The two phone numbers were those of Jesse's office and this house.

"My God!" said Clock. "What it must have cost, Jesse—on Sunday, and—"

"It's none o' your business what it cost," said old Mr. Walters mildly from the door. "I got the money, and if I choose to spend it in pursuin' justice, so to speak, it's my own business." He came in and sat down, and Athelstane attempted to climb into his lap happily. "You got those notebooks for me?"

"But you shouldn't have—good God—"

"Did that Wednesday, soon as I heard about it there in Jesse's office. Thought it'd be best to get it in on Sunday when more people'd see it. I had to do quite some arguing, believe me! I guess they got the Sunday edition set up by about then. But I can be stubborn when I want to be."

"But why? I don't—"

"Well, to my mind," said Mr. Walters judicially, "that tie clasp is kind of the crux of the whole business—the frame, I mean. There's a couple of things about it I'll come to, but first and foremost, there's the fact that it had to be got hold of between Thursday and Monday."

"They didn't find it in my car until Wednesday."

"But the tip-off wouldn't have gone out to that *Telegraph* editor unless the frame was all set up ready to go, Sergeant. How often you look in your glove compartment?"

"Well," said Clock, "I'll give you that."

"Sure. Well, the way I see it, it had to be kind of a rush job getting those initials engraved on it. F'r instance, I got Betty this gold compact for her birthday—initials on it—took a week to get it back. And so I got to wondering. Our X couldn't have known what initials he'd want until that Thursday when Starbuck's name was in the papers, as bein' questioned—hey? Tie clasp or whatever, initials needed on it to mark it, hey? So somewhere around is going to be a jeweler, big or little shop, some place, who'll remember a rush job of engraving between that Thursday and Monday."

Jesse looked at Clock. "He does see things, doesn't he? Probably I didn't think of it because who can afford engraving on things?"

"So I just thought we'd better ask, in a kind of loud clear voice." The old man nodded at the *Times*. "Because, way you described it, Sergeant, these I.A. people keep it all hush-hush. Within the department. Even when—though it's not going to happen—they forced your resignation, little bit came out in the papers about it, they'd do all they could to keep back the details, you said—honor of the force—so it wouldn't be likely that some honest little jeweler in Azusa or Alhambra'd be reading all about a fourteen-karat gold tie clasp with the initials P. S. on it. Jesse, I could appreciate—"

"A drink," said Jesse humbly. "Coming up. *Honor the face of the old man.*" He went out to the kitchen.

"I don't know how to— I see, that could be—"

"Don't fuss about the cost," said Mr. Walters comfortably. "I've got interested in this business. Now we just sit back and see what turns up, on that. But there's a few other things. The average man isn't likely to be going around covered with monograms. Oh, I grant you the big-time gambler type like this Starbuck, maybe more than most— but we don't generally carry so much around that *can* be monogrammed, hey? Handkerchief—tie clasp—cuff links, maybe. That's about it. Oh, sure, shirt and tie, but they're not items a man's apt to drop accidentally and not notice. And I wonder, is a tie clasp either? Most of 'em—and an expensive one'd probably be more so—thanks, Jesse—" he took a glass from the tray—"have a pretty tight spring. And what I saw in the papers, this Arnold and whoever killed him didn't have any kind of fight?"

Clock shook his head. "Somebody just walked in and shot him, we think while he was—er—napping. Blind drunk, to be crude about it."

"So, not very likely the tie clasp'd fall off so easy. But there it is. The supposed evidence you were covering up for the extra loot. Just why in hell, Sergeant, should you have put it in the glove compartment of your car? Silly sort of place to carry it. A thing as small as that a lot safer in a pocket."

"Yes, but the implication is—rather vague, I guess—that I was going to set up a meeting with Starbuck, to give it back to him. Maybe in the car."

"Tosh!" said Mr. Walters roundly. "Nearly a week after you'd made the deal with him, got paid off, handed your blonde girl friend the cash for her mink coat?"

Clock shrugged. "Then I suppose another implication could be that I didn't intend to give it back to him, just stashed it there and forgot about it."

"I'm beginnin' to lose some respect for your I.A. officers," said Mr. Walters. "Should think anybody'd see Starbuck'd ask for it back pronto. If he did make a deal like that, it'd be favor for favor—the cash to you, you hand back the evidence to him. And even if you hadn't, Sergeant, why in hell would you keep it around? In case somebody ever did suspect, it was evidence against you."

"I don't know how Thatcher's building it," said Clock. "But it *is* evidence. And a cop who'll make a deal isn't usually a very smart cop."

"Well—we wait and see what that produces. Let's hope something." Mr. Walters retired into his drink.

"At least you're nice and logical," said Jesse. "Fran and Nell are coming unhinged. Babbling about psychic seers."

"Heard all about that," said Mr. Walters. "I had a long talk with young Fran last night on the phone. Me, the older I get the less I figure we know for sure about all that. And some mighty funny things happen. One reason I wanted to see all those notebooks of yours, Sergeant. Lucky you kept 'em all."

"I don't know if you'll be able to read half of it. I don't use shorthand, but abbreviations—"

"Have a stab at it anyway. The way I see this whole very funny business, there's two ways we can get you what they call vindicated, and I'll work on one while you and Jesse work on the other, see? We can take a short cut—if we're lucky—and find out for sure who. Or you and Jesse can turn up some real evidence it is a frame."

"We've got this and that," said Jesse. "That deposit slip— Oh, by the way, we can cross Begley off. I talked to the son yesterday. Old man's senile, practically bedridden, nurse with him all the time."

Clock sighed. "So. But there's something else. I remembered it just as I was going to sleep last night. When they were questioning me, Clay said that the waiter at the Gemini Inn hadn't any connection with Helen Madden. Whereas the waiter let out to me and Fran that he knows her."

"Only suggestive," said Jesse. "But something."

"And," said Clock, "I don't think Hendrickson came home last night." They both looked at him with interest. "I told you how I lost him on the freeway yesterday morning. He didn't even have a jacket on, just shirt and slacks. Well, he could have had a coat in the car, I suppose—but the nights are still cold. I went back to the apartment late yesterday afternoon—his car was still gone. I went back about nine and waited till after midnight—no sign of him, and no light in the apartment."

"Well, we saw we had him scared," said Jesse. "He could have taken the weekend off down at the beach, get us out of his hair. He could have gone to visit his sister, she lives in Long Beach."

"Sure. I just wondered."

"There's one thing," said Mr. Walters, thoughtfully replenishing his drink from his own bottle produced from his inside breast pocket, "about people like this Hendrickson. Way you describe him. Weak fella, sure. But it's the weak people who usually have the biggest damn stubborn streak of all. You said, Jesse, you figured Hendrickson hadn't thought there'd be so much fuss over this. If he didn't know what was behind it when he agreed to tell the lie, well, not bein' a moron he could guess what was behind it by the lie he was paid to tell. He thought he'd be asked, and he'd tell the lie, and that'd be that. No imagination. Or maybe he just figured to brazen it out whatever happened—no personal involvement, the lie couldn't be shown up. But either way, he knows he's stuck with it now, and like I say, your weak man is usually very damn obstinate along with it. Sure, a physical coward, but come to the point, I don't guess the sergeant'd really get down to using lighted matches on him." Clock laughed shortly and finished his drink. "And he knows if he admits the lie, he's in for trouble. No, he'll just set himself and go on saying it, and nothing but evidence'll make him change his story."

In which, time was to show, the old maestro was only half right.

"You're pessimistic," said Jesse.

"Uh-uh. So we just go find the evidence. I'm goin' to have a session with those notebooks. Where're the girls?"

Jesse groaned. "I was hoping you wouldn't ask. They've both got bitten by detective fever. They're out trailing Helen Madden again. Well, you never *know*—I'm the one wanted her tailed, *but* by a professional. . . . Mystic seers— God knows what they'll get mixed up in today."

In the event, it turned out to be more mystic seers. Helen had picked up a girl friend—"We don't know her name but here's the address," said Nell morosely—and gone on a tour of mystic seers, in fact. At a Spiritualist church in Hollywood, and then someone in Inglewood whose front-door sign announced him as Kozar, Hindu Mystic, and then, of all places, down to the Santa Monica pier to visit someone called Madame Blanche. In one of the stuffy little shops on the pier, where other mystic seers still abounded. There, of course, the two sleuths had had to leave the car and trail on foot; and the pier was so crowded that they had to keep fairly close, and the upshot of that was, Nell reported, that they'd got pushed right into the anteroom by a fat woman, and had to pose as clients. And of course, in that small space, Helen had got a good look at them, but it didn't matter now, the professionals would be taking over.

"And we couldn't just walk out, it'd have looked odd, you know. So we both had to have a—a reading. There were at least a dozen people waiting, two men. All talking about how good she is."

"At how much per? You do get into the damnedest things," said Jesse.

"Well, it was five dollars for a card reading and three if she read your palm, so I had that."

"My God!"

"She told Fran she'd get married in six months and have four children."

"I'm in favor of it."

"And she told me," said Nell, "I had a very autocratic husband but I have such a pure and noble nature I'm able to cope with him. We were only trying to *help*."

Clock called Jesse at his office at a quarter past ten on Monday morning. "I'm at the bank. Hendrickson is playing hooky. . . . That's right. I just saw Lanterman, and he wasn't opening up much, but he admitted Hendrickson hadn't called in with an excuse."

"You don't tell me," said Jesse. "I think I'd like to go and see if he's got a cold or what."

"I think so too. Now?"

"I've got an appointment at eleven-thirty. Meet you there in twenty minutes."

"O.K.," said Clock.

At the apartment on Romaine, they went upstairs as a formality and knocked at apartment twelve. Silence from within. Jesse said, "I do wonder. You know, I don't like this, Andrew. Was beginning to read Hendrickson just exactly the way Edgar does—stubborn little fool. I don't like this at all." He took three steps and pushed the bell of the door across the hall. In a moment the door opened and a middle-aged, pleasant-faced woman looked at them.

"Yes? Oh, it's Mr.—was it Falkenstein? You were here the other day, asking about Mr. Hendrickson."

"That's right, Mrs. Goodis. He seems," said Jesse, "to be missing. At least he doesn't seem to have been home since Saturday, and he didn't show up at his job this morning."

"Really?" She looked mildly surprised. "Of course I don't know him well, just to say hello to, like that, but a bank clerk, I should think he'd be the steady type. No, no, I haven't seen him in, oh, goodness, I don't know, a week anyway. But I wouldn't, you know. Very often. Him being gone all day, and I don't generally go out to market until after eleven, and by the time he'd be coming home— Well, you know how apartment people are." She smiled. "I know the Williamsons downstairs, but with both of them working we might not see each other for weeks. And really about the only time I lay eyes on Mrs. Furniss is when I pay the rent. But now I do think, I remember—I heard Mr. Hendrickson come in, on Saturday night."

"Oh," said Jesse. "It was late—after midnight?"

"How'd you know that? Yes, it was. I have trouble sleeping sometimes, and there was a full moon that night—that always makes me wakeful. I don't like to take things. So I was awake, it was after two, I know—and everything being quiet like, I heard him. These old places are pretty well-built, you don't as a rule hear your neighbors, but at night and quiet—I just heard the door open across the hall. The key in the lock and it opening and shutting. I remember thinking, Well, he's late, but of course it was Saturday night."

"I see," said Jesse. "Thanks very much."

She was looking at Clock inquisitively. "But if he's not at his job— oh, dear me, you don't suppose he could have been taken ill, there all alone, and can't— A young man, but it does happen."

"We'll try to find out," said Jesse. "Thanks very much."

"If I can be of any help—"

"Yes, thanks." Jesse headed for the stairs. "Manageress," he said tersely. "I don't like this at all."

The manageress was Mrs. Sheila Furniss (née O'Banion) and she was very firm with them. She was frank to say she couldn't understand what Mr. Falkenstein's interest in Mr. Hendrickson was at all, and she'd always found the best policy was not to bother tenants, unless of course there was a definite complaint, noisy parties or *women*. The late Mr. Hendrickson, God rest his soul, had been a fine man and she'd no reason whatever to suppose his son was any the less, lived here a matter of eleven years, first with his father and then alone, they understood, and a good steady position at a bank downtown after he'd done his rightful service in the army. He was a quiet young man who never bothered her with wanting new washers in the faucets or such, he'd always paid his rent on the dot *as* she'd told Mr. Falkenstein before, one of her best tenants and a boy she'd known half his life, and so she'd tell anybody came asking questions—

Not at home? Well, he wouldn't be on a weekday, what did they expect?

Not at his job? And hadn't phoned in an excuse?

"If he's as—er—steady a young man as you seem to think," said Jesse, "it seems a little odd, doesn't it? You know, he could have had a heart attack up there, or— We'd just like to make sure, Mrs. Furniss. You'll have a key to the apartment, of course."

Her face closed against him like a door shutting. Final. She was a little elderly woman with the cotton-white hair that tells of red hair in youth, faded blue eyes, a tight little mouth. She looked at them and said flatly, "Now that's just ridiculous, a young man like that. And if he's left his work, he'll have his own good reason, and it's not for me to pry. Young men, they chop and change around a lot, sometimes, before they settle down."

"Mrs. Furniss," said Jesse, "don't you think—just to be sure—"

"I do not," she said. "And what your concern in it is, is a mystery to me! Insurance investigator—likely, that is! And if you think my nose doesn't tell me that's a policeman alongside you, you've got another think coming! I've known Walter Hendrickson since he was twelve, thirteen, and he's a good boy—always polite, nice. Never could get enough of my raisin cookies, that boy. His father was a fine man. You can just take yourselves off now. If Walt's gone away, on a little vacation maybe, it's nobody's business but his, and if he wants to leave the bank it's his own business too."

When the spate was run and the door shut, Jesse drew Clock up to the stairs. "We've got to get in there," he said urgently. "Don't ask questions. Can you pick a lock? We've got to—"

Mrs. Goodis came down the stairs, shopping basket on her arm, and smiled at them. "Anything I can do, Mr. Falkenstein. I'll be back in a little while."

"Thank God she's out of the way. Come on!" Jesse took the stairs three at a leap. "We've got to—"

"Why all the urgency?" asked Clock curiously. "If he's run—though I'm bound to say I don't—"

"Maybe he hasn't," said Jesse.

It was a standard Yale lock. "Listen," said Clock, "I'm in enough trouble as it is, I can't—"

"Old apartments," said Jesse suddenly. "Back doors? Let's see." He went rapidly down to the end of the hall, where an outside door led to a rickety fire escape and a back yard lined with refuse barrels. The fire escape protested under their weight. In the yard, around the side of the building, were older wooden stairs leading to a long narrow balcony and doors giving on it.

"Second one from the front," said Jesse, starting up. "Thank God, Mrs. Furniss lives downstairs. I wonder if she knows something?"

"I don't *get* this," said Clock, climbing after him. "I don't—"

"I just want to be sure," said Jesse.

It was an old door, an old-fashioned four-ward lock. Jesse tried it with his safe-deposit key, longest on his chain, and fumbled for long moments. "Look," said Clock, "this isn't—I can't be a party to—"

"Damn," said Jesse, and turning out his pockets found a stiff little cardboard calendar, and applied it in the crook of the jamb.

"Where'd you learn about that?"

"I read *True Detective*," said Jesse; and the inner tongue snapped back and the door opened.

Clock went in after him gingerly. Breaking and entering—

The apartment was silent. It was also empty of humanity. A quick look through it—kitchen, dinette, living room, bedroom, bathroom— told that. Jesse pulled open the closet door: an old apartment, walk-in closet. Suits—three suits tidily on combination hangers. A pair of old slacks on a hanger. Two pairs of shoes, black and brown, on the floor, a pair of dirty tennis shoes. An old-fashioned painted bureau: he pulled open drawers. A sparse collection of white dress shirts: a couple of colored sports shirts. Knit cotton underwear. Socks. A few ties. Handkerchiefs.

The double bed was tidily made up.

Jesse charged into the bathroom again, opened the medicine cabinet. A much-squeezed nearly empty tube of toothpaste; an old toothbrush on the top shelf. On the bottom shelf, a double-edged safety razor in its box, a jar of shaving cream. Aspirin. A styptic pencil. A bottle of a nonprescriptive decongestant with two tablets left in it.

"Say anything?" asked Jesse. "To the experienced cop?"

"You aren't thinking—" began Clock. "Why, for God's sake?"

Jesse went back to the closet. At the very rear of it, behind the clothes hanging on the rod, stood an ancient battered suitcase of brown leather. It was empty.

"Why?" said Jesse. "My God, it just occurred to me, Andrew. He *was* scared, you know. You—and I—had scared him. Little man a coward to start with. Which same quite possibly X hadn't realized. The deal set up, sure, but Hendrickson hadn't expected you—or me—would kick up all this fuss. And you know, Andrew, the Maddens—that could well have been all set up anonymously, over the phone—or by mail—people like the Maddens, and Benny, don't look too far into motives—or people. But one thing we do know. That cash had to be paid into your account when the record says it was paid—on Friday, April ninth. On account of bank procedure. Somebody had to pay it in, and hand over the deposit slip with your fake signature on it. And I don't think our clever principal would have trusted either of the Maddens with that job. . . . We said Hendrickson's lie was the major lie."

"My God," said Clock.

"Yes. You see it too? If that's so, which it is, then the principal, X who built the frame, who like Starbuck somehow had access to a big wad of cash, paid in that cash in person, and handed over that deposit slip prepared beforehand. And therefore Walter Hendrickson must have seen him at least that once. Whether he ever had before. And even if he was disguised in some way—"

"My God, yes," said Clock. "And—"

"And Walter Hendrickson, I think," said Jesse softly, "was running scared. And considering the—the vindictiveness, the single-mindedness of this whole operation—X really out to get you, at any cost—well, if Hendrickson showed any signs of breaking, I don't think X would have let him stand in his way."

TEN

Jesse, slumped in his desk chair, was talking on the phone at one-thirty when Miss Williams tiptoed in and laid a card on his desk. He glanced at it, still talking, and grinned tightly. The card said austerely, Lieutenant Zachariah M. Clay, Los Angeles Police Department. "'Scuse me," said Jesse to the phone, and to Miss Williams, "Shoot him in."

He was still talking thirty seconds later when Clay came in. He swiveled around to look at him and gestured at the client's chair. "Well, we don't know about that. Realize you'd be upset, but— Mmh. Strong presumption, I'd say, but if you want to wait to report him— Oh, yes. No, you'd want the Wilcox Street precinct. But I'd be obliged if— Thought maybe you'd feel like that. Suppose I meet you there in an hour, O.K.? I think I can make it then. Right. Fine, see you then, and thanks." He put the phone down and surveyed Clay.

Zachariah. Quite a lot to a man who didn't take refuge in initials, he thought. Clay going bald, stocky, discreet tie, wedding ring, Masonic ring.

"I'm sorry to intrude on your time, Mr. Falkenstein," said Clay politely. "I'll try not to keep you. I believe you're acquainted with Sergeant Andrew Clock? To what extent—"

"Got round to me," said Jesse casually. "How well do I know, have I ever heard him discuss, do I know any other acquaintances, et cetera. Every hope he'll be my brother-in-law one of these days. Yes, Lieutenant, Andrew I know—little better than you. At the moment, also acting as his lawyer. Have a cigarette and relax, Lieutenant. Got quite a bit to say to you."

Clay frowned. "All I want to—"

"Lieutenant," said Jesse gently, "this is my office and I intend to do some talking. Very glad you dropped by—was coming to see you if you hadn't. Now—"

"I take it you're aware of the investigation," said Clay stiffly. "The sergeant had no—"

"Right to try to fight back? Just relax and listen, Lieutenant. I'll give you the little stuff first. Daresay you noticed the—mmh—notice in the *Times* about that tie clasp."

"We made inquiries at once," said Clay. "Interference— It appears to have been ordered and paid for by one Mr. Edgar Walters, the retired owner of a department store in—"

"Kind of a special consultant of mine," said Jesse. "So we start out with some of his deductions about that, Lieutenant." He outlined precisely the rather vague implications of the tie clasp: Glove compartment not very likely place for it. Why hadn't it been returned to Starbuck before?—at the time the supposed deal was made? Was it very likely that an expensive tie clasp with, probably, a strong spring— "You've seen it, Lieutenant, I leave that to you"—would have just fallen off unnoticed as its wearer entered an unlocked apartment, shot a sleeping man and walked out?

"Mr. Falkenstein, I'm not here to listen to theories. All I want—"

"Relax, Lieutenant," said Jesse. "You'll be hearing more than theories. At the time you questioned that waiter at the Gemini Inn, Benny Giorgione, he told you—or it was implied—that he didn't know either Helen Madden or Sergeant Clock. Now appears he does. He knows Helen Madden—reason he noticed her, he says—from when they both worked in the same place, Rudy's, out on Western. How'd you happen to pounce on Benny, Lieutenant? Let me tell you. The Madden female let it out the sergeant took her there a lot. So hey, presto, you go and ask, and turn up the obliging Benny."

Clay looked at him narrowly. "Have you evidence of that acquaintanceship?"

"Needn't sound so formal. You might not like the evidence—Benny said so to the sergeant and my sister Fran. Might deny it. But I rather think Benny's the kind might come apart if you leaned on him. Might not too. Listen some more. Looked up some known pals of Joe Madden's," said Jesse, glossing over Petrovsky's and Lindner's partisan activities, "and it seems Joe's told 'em—one of 'em anyway, one Frank Bayless—that he's got a nice deal going, money for fun. Joe not liking cops, leave it to your imagination what his notion of fun might be. He hasn't held a job in a while. Sister Helen, you might be interested to know, went to see a—well, call him a fortuneteller—the other day. According to him, she wanted to know if the money was going to come to her safely, that there wouldn't be a double cross. And—"

"Fortune— Really, Mr. Falkenstein, this says n——"

"Continue to take it easy," said Jesse. "Now I'd like you to take a look at this deposit slip, or rather a photostat of it." He produced it.

"You've been busy, Mr. Falkenstein," said Clay coldly. "I have seen the deposit slip. We have a photostat of it too."

"Not that one," said Jesse. "This one. Deposit slip dated May fourteenth, last year. By my reading, the one substituted for the one abstracted so X could use it to trace the sergeant's signature on the April ninth deposit slip. And I suppose the original May fourteenth one being gone with the wind, there's no hope of proving it was a tracing job. But just consider it for a minute. I looked for such a thing, Lieutenant. You didn't. Preconceived opinions, bad. *He who hardens his heart with pride softens his brains.* So the Talmud tells us. You can go looking back, all the time the sergeant's used that bank—and look at the records of his former bank in Hollywood—and I'll lay a bet you'll find that was the sole single occasion, supposedly, that he 'forgot' to make out a deposit slip and the teller did it instead. Quite a coincidence that teller, that May fourteenth, happened to be Walter Hendrickson. And now let's take a long hard look at the April ninth deposit slip. I had that photostated too."

"Our handwriting expert has confirmed that it bears Sergeant Clock's signature. This is a waste of time, and I must say—"

"You sit down, Lieutenant, and listen awhile," said Jesse without anger. "Also remind you, *Justice, justice shall you pursue.* Deuteronomy, if you're curious. This—"

"Mr. Falkenstein," said Clay, looking torn between amusement and anger, "I really don't—"

"As I say, original slip being unavailable, no way to show it *is* a tracing. But just look at it, Lieutenant. Think you'll agree the sergeant's a very methodical man. What goes on a deposit slip? Here are three blank lines to the left, hm, for name, address and date. Little box below with a hyphen all supplied, for the account number, which in this case happens to be one-one-four nine-seven-five. Then to the right there's a marked-off column where you're supposed to put, first, the number of the check or checks, the sum, and subtract any cash you want out of the total. With me so far? Fine. Here's the supposed deposit slip the sergeant—so Mr. Hendrickson blandly says—handed in with that fifty-seven hundred and forty-five bucks cash on April ninth. Here's his signature, looking all present and correct, on the top line— and every other blessed thing on it consists of figures. Lay another bet, Lieutenant, you can look back over his whole banking record and never come across another instance where he put the date in figures, like that—four-nine sixty-five. I've seen a lot of his deposit slips, which you haven't, obviously. Also would point out to you that the other deposit slip—the one that was abstracted by the teller who wrote a substitute for it—was for the sum of three hundred fifty-seven dollars and ninety cents, which same represents his two-week salary check, and incidentally contained in his hand all the figures needed to make out this April ninth deposit slip. People do make figures in funny ways sometimes—you see how he makes a five with the top bar a way above the rest of it. I only suggest—"

Clay leaned forward suddenly and took up both photostats. He stared at them. "Are you suggesting, not only that this is a frame, but that it was set up a *year* ago? That—"

"Probably longer," said Jesse. "Realize it sounds— Well. What with all the money expended and so on. Just asking you to consider it and— mmh—ruminate. On his record, to start with. On the character of the Maddens. On Benny, who I think was set up for you by Helen Madden. Set up on instructions—find another witness who'll lie for a little easy money. The frame had to wait, Lieutenant, for somebody like Starbuck to act as a catalyst, so to speak. As you'll see with a little ruminating. And maybe a lot of easy money was concerned, in Mr. Hendrickson's case."

"The bank teller has a perfectly clean record, and he's been there—"

"Two years, yes. He also has, I think you'll find when you take a look at the various girls he'd dated, a funny habit—for a bank teller—of taking them out to kind of expensive places. He also bought a big color TV console last month. Round about seven hundred bucks, I'd say. . . . You're not champing at the bit any more, Lieutenant? Interested in what I'm saying?"

"Go on," said Clay shortly. "If you've any more." He sat motionless, watching Jesse. His eyes didn't look cold, or thoughtful, or angry: just remote.

"So. Not having quite such a closed mind as you seem to, Lieutenant—" Jesse slid down deeper in his chair and folded his hands across his flat stomach—"I reacted to Andrew's tale of woe—I might say incredible tale of woe—with a little simple faith. *Thou hast made him a little lower than the angels*—Isaiah, Lieutenant—but on the other hand, don't like to think I'm that bad a judge of human nature. So I went looking, in my simple way, not for more evidence against him but for some to show it's a frame. And in pursuit of same I sized up Mr. Hendrickson. So did the sergeant. Now I realize he isn't supposed—you do have some damn funny rules down there, Lieutenant—to try to vindicate himself, fight back any—just sit quiet, good boy, and wait for the ax to fall. Like that? But you try it, Lieutenant. Let somebody tell your captain you're chasing around with a call girl, and let the evidence turn up to prove it, and you wouldn't say, Please, sir, it's a nasty lie, and let it go. Likely you—well, never mind. Occurred to both the sergeant and me it might be helpful to lean on Mr. Hendrickson a little, and maybe sooner or later get him to admit— Yes, yes, very reprehensible, Lieutenant, but what would you have done? Deprecating young man telling lies about you? Mr. Hendrickson didn't—doesn't—like either of us very much. Oh, do assure you, not a hand laid on him. Just—mmh—psychology. Mr. Hendrickson's a weak man, and something of a coward, and by last Saturday, which is the last time anybody saw him so far as I know, he seemed to be a little nervous."

"The last—"

"Oh, yes," said Jesse. "That's something kind of concrete, Lieutenant. Hendrickson last seen by the sergeant Saturday morning, scooting up the Santa Monica freeway. Woman who lives across the hall says she heard somebody enter his apartment about two o'clock Sunday morning—no guarantee it was Hendrickson. Well, you know, Lieutenant, I got to thinking about it. Bad habit of mine, maybe—exercising my imagination. Anyway, postulating this X who's gone to some trouble and expense to build the frame, one thing I saw clear. The Maddens are—at one remove. They could easily have been bribed anonymously, as it were. Small fry. Jump at the chance. But account of the way banks do things, that cash had to be paid in on April ninth just as the deposit slip says it was. And I think he would have done that in person, handing over that prepared slip with the traced signature. So Hendrickson would have seen him at least—even if he didn't know his name. Probably had some way to get in touch, just in case anything went wrong. And Hendrickson was nervous.

"So—never mind the details—I went and had a look through his apartment. Worried, you know. And you know what, Lieutenant? He's not there. Didn't show up at the bank this morning, didn't call in to say why not. He's left a lot of clothes, and a suitcase, and his tooth-brush and toothpaste, and his safety razor and shaving cream. Which seems a little odd, doesn't it?"

Clay stared at him. "The bank teller— Is that level?"

"Go and see," said Jesse. "I was talking to his sister on the phone when you came in. Mrs. George Herrick, down in Long Beach. She was upset to hear about it. Older sister—tries to keep an eye on little brother since Father died. Can't imagine why he'd go off like this. They're close, he's fond of her kids, comes to see her and so on. She's meeting me at his apartment in—" Jesse looked at his watch—"about twenty minutes, so I trust you'll excuse me. If she says nothing is miss-ing, she may want to report *him* missing." He stood up.

So did Clay. He laid the photostats on the desk. "The bank teller— Well, I'll say you've given me a thing to think about, Mr. Falkenstein. Really. Not that I can buy—"

"The frame. The fantastic frame," said Jesse. "Let's say not yet, Lieutenant, mmh? *Better is the end of a thing than its beginning.* That's Ecclesiastes."

Clay started for the door and turned back. "Mr. Falkenstein," he said, "we're really not fools. Evidence we can read."

"So go and read it, Lieutenant," said Jesse. Clay went out. "And I'd lay another small bet," he said to himself, "where you're bound for."

He would have won it.

The woman came walking her dog, every afternoon and every eve-ning, along the same route. Dog walkers fell into habit, which was lucky for the man waiting.

A quiet street of small apartment houses and homes, it was, little traffic, few pedestrians at any time.

She would come out of her apartment house, the dog on its leash, and turn right, and walk two blocks down and one block up, and then turn again to come back. It was a smallish dog; he didn't know any-thing about dogs or care; it was a little square dog with gray bristly hair and a square muzzle and a stump of a tail, and it frisked about the woman's legs on its red leash and she talked to it, fond and foolish, as a woman might talk to a baby. The dog couldn't be very old; it had been about eight months since he'd checked on the woman and killed the last dog.

He stood waiting, motionless, at the corner. There was a sign there, BUS STOP. He might have been waiting for a bus. He kept looking at his watch, impatient. You never knew, someone, some idle person, might be looking out of a window.

When he saw her come down the steps of the building, the dog leaping ahead of her, he fumbled in his pocket and dropped the chunk of raw beef. At the same time he dropped the glove he was not wearing, and bent to pick it up. Turning with a last impatient look at his watch, he strode rapidly away. The man had become tired of waiting for the bus; perhaps he was going to find a taxi, or get his own car.

But he knew when they came to the corner, the dog would pause to sniff at the bus-stop sign, and—being a dog—would swallow the chunk of beef in one gulp before he could be stopped.

It was fortunate, he thought, that it was not cats the woman kept. Tried to keep.

Cats, now— He had once tried to kill a cat. An obnoxious creature, owned by some neighbors: a black and white cat which came and sat on the sill of his study window and stared at him. If he had never cared for animals, he had not felt any active dislike; but he came to hate the cat. It looked at him with the detached interest of a scientist peering through a microscope: it looked at him—that was the awful, enraging thing—*as if it were superior.*

But for some reason he had not been able to destroy it. He had put poisoned meat on the window sill, and the cat had sniffed at it and with one disdainful gesture pushed it over to the ground, leaped down and covered it with dirt. He had tried that several times, but the cat had never— He had even taken a shot at it from the window, but missed. Queer to think he had found it so easy to kill a man with that gun, but not a cat.

The cat— Some of the naked red rage he had felt for it came back now.

He had almost reached the corner when he heard the woman begin to scream. He glanced back.

The dog had, of course, run true to the nature of dogs. It had found the beef and gulped it down even as the woman would have said, peering, "What's Precious found? Oh, you mustn't—"

The dog was in violent convulsions on the sidewalk. Strychnine did its work quickly. Before the first door opened in response to the screams, the dog would be dead.

And the woman again bereft.

As he was bereft.

It was indeed the better vengeance.

Smiling, the man walked on.

"I don't understand any of this," said Wanda Herrick, sounding frightened. She had sounded like a woman of character on the phone, and turned out to be just that in person. Got all the character baby brother didn't get, thought Jesse. She was a woman about thirty-five, a good-looking woman with curly dark hair, a generous mouth and probably normally a good figure: she was about six months pregnant.

She had overridden the scrappy Sheila Furniss magnificently, demanding the key to the apartment, and she stood now in the center of the living room, having been over the whole place.

"There's nothing missing as far as I can tell, Mr. Falkenstein. Of course I haven't been here very often—Walt usually came to see us, I've got the children and all. I didn't know he'd bought that great big TV. But I do recognize all the clothes here. I couldn't be positive he hasn't taken *some*, but it couldn't be many. I don't *understand* it. I know he hasn't liked the job at the bank, I was surprised he stayed with it so long. I was glad, thought he was settling down. And I don't understand what *your* interest is, how—"

"Kind of a long story," said Jesse. "Don't want to upset you any more, Mrs. Herrick, but the implication seems to be that your brother got involved in a little wrong deal. That he took some side money to tell a lie about one of the bank's clients, and—"

"*Walt?* What on earth do you— Oh, my God!" she said. "You mean he's run away? You mean he got found out and—"

"We don't know, Mrs. Herrick. Does that strike you as—mmh—possible? You think he might do such a thing?"

"Oh, God," she said. She sat down on the couch as if her legs had suddenly given way. "Walt—I don't *know*, but— He always—always wanted everything all at once. He's—impatient. As if anybody stepped into a top job at—at twenty thousand a year all at once! I tried to tell him that—but he was only twenty-one when Dad died, and a young man all on his own—I tried to talk to him, make him see, about that job with the printing firm—it was a *start*. So he was only a salesman, you have to start somewhere—he could have worked up. But it was the same story, like when he worked at the stationery store, and before in the market—why should he work like a slave, the boss didn't like him, wasn't fair. I guess in a way the job at the bank was fine for him, I hoped so, not *hard* work, you know, and he likes to dress well and look nice, and—"

Jesse sat down opposite, giving her time, listening.

"Jim always said, smart-aleck—about Walt. Oh, he likes him all right, he understands how I feel—my own brother. I tried to help him. That time he got caught—it was his last year in high—doing other kids' papers for them for pay—he's got a very high I.Q., you know—they weren't going to let him graduate, but I persuaded the principal— After all he was only eighteen."

"Mrs. Herrick. Do you think—"

"What's he *done*?" she asked. "You said, a lie—and, like a bribe? What *about*?"

"Little involved," said Jesse. "Point is—you know him—you feel it's a thing he might have done?"

She drew a painful breath. "He—he's always been so—impatient—to be on the top. With money. I guess I've got to say he's a little—lazy. About working for things. I guess people with high I.Q.'s— Well, he— I don't mean he's *crooked*. It wouldn't have looked that way to him, do you see? If he's—done something wrong, like that—oh, I know Walt!—he'd argue to himself it was really all right, just sort of stretching a point. He wouldn't realize how wrong it was, if—"

"See what you mean," said Jesse. That type. Plenty of them around. Why shouldn't I, when everybody else is getting his? "Mrs. Herrick," he said, "your brother could be in worse trouble than that. You've seen that most of his clothes are here, toothbrush and razor and so on. If he'd meant to run away—"

She stared at him. "What—what are you trying to *say*?"

"It wasn't necessarily Hendrickson who came here at two A.M. Sunday morning. We don't know. But that's thirty-six hours ago. And the job at the bank was at least a job—that he'd want recommendation from anyway—but he hasn't called in with any excuse for being absent. Don't you think you ought to report him as missing? As his nearest relative?"

"I—suppose—so," she said draggingly. "I just can't imagine—"

"The Wilcox Street precinct."

And on the way downstairs she said, "It's just—he was the cutest baby! I was ten when he was born, you know. Dad and Mom hadn't expected— And I guess Mom spoiled him. Some. But—"

Clock turned up about eight o'clock and demanded a drink. "Have you had anything to eat?" asked Nell.

"A hamburger, awhile ago. My God, have I had a session with those— You sure as hell stirred things up, Jesse. I'd gone back to the bank to talk to Lanterman, I—"

"And the lieutenant descended on you both," said Jesse sleepily. "Had a bet with myself he'd make a beeline for the bank. Hearing about Hendrickson. What'd they do?"

"My God, it was a madhouse," said Clock. Suddenly he began laughing. "Bankers. My God. When I got it across to Lanterman—how Hendrickson was definitely gone somewhere—he turned absolutely green and started summoning minions and giving orders. Because naturally, the first thing that occurred to him was, bank teller missing, had he taken any of the loose cash along with him? I'd guess they're still feverishly examining the books and counting the greenbacks. And Clay called in some minions too, and—"

"I have," said Jesse, scattering cocktail pretzels on the rug for Athelstane, who swooped them up like a vacuum cleaner, "lost a little respect for banks. Thinking of the new record clerk from South Carolina. Don't think they're anywhere near as businesslike as they claim to be. But figure I did give Clay something to think about."

"I don't know about that. Oh, thanks, you shouldn't—" Clock accepted the tray Nell offered him. "They hauled me down for more questioning. This time about what were my relations with Hendrickson, what had I said to him— And they didn't like some of what I had to answer. They left some men at the bank—"

"That's encouraging. Maybe looking at all your past deposit slips. Maybe apropos—*Better is the curse of the righteous man than the blessing of the wicked.* Any rate, things should begin to move a little now—Hendrickson officially missing, and the private eyes loose on the Maddens. See what more shows up. And I wonder what Edgar's making of your notebooks. . . ."

ELEVEN

Jesse walked into the Wilcox Street precinct house in the middle of Tuesday afternoon. It was an old, dreary-looking building, built of tan brick which had darkened with time. The desk sergeant on duty was very much in contrast to the building: a crew-cut blond in uniform who didn't look old enough to be out of high school, his uniform immaculate, his manner very formally courteous, his enunciation impeccable. Clearly, a young man who was out to make his mark as a career officer.

"Yes, sir? What can I do for you?"

"Sergeant Southby around? Like to see him."

"Yes, sir, I'll see." The sergeant picked up the phone. "Excuse me, sir, what name? Falkenstein, yes, sir. And what was it about?"

"Missing man—that Hendrickson. I was here yesterday with his sister when she reported it."

"Oh, yes, sir, I'll see if the sergeant—"

Eventually he was directed upstairs to the Detective Bureau. You'd think, he reflected, they'd at least paint the place; the old wooden stairs creaked, and in the room at the head of the stairs one window was propped open with a stick of wood.

"You'd be Sergeant Southby?"

"That's me. What prompted you to ask for me, Mr. Falkenstein? I'm not specially on that missing case." Southby smiled at him. He was a big man in his mid-thirties, starting to go bald; also starting to put on weight, probably fighting it; he had friendly blue eyes, a nose that had got itself flattened somewhere along the line and a good jaw. "We don't divide ourselves up into different divisions, like the boys downtown—take anything that comes along."

"So I understand," said Jesse, dropping into the chair beside Southby's desk. "Andrew Clock gave me your name, Sergeant. Said you were a pretty good friend of his."

"Well, be damned. Haven't seen Andrew in a month of Sundays, how's he doing? They keep you busy down at Central. Did— Say, I know you!" said Southby, looking amused. "The lawyer, sure. And it's your sister Andrew's fallen for so hard—he told me a little about it. Just a little—you know Andrew! Matter of fact, my wife and I ran across them some place one night, just before Christmas it was. I'm bound to say she's a damn good-looking girl, Miss Falkenstein. Seems like a nice girl too—think he's got a chance there?"

"Couldn't say," said Jesse. "Hope so, but Fran— Well, I didn't drop in to gossip, Sergeant. You heard any rumors over the grapevine about an investigation going on by the I.A. men downtown?"

Southby's eyes narrowed. "Why? I didn't—"

"Daresay you have. Few little rumors. Well, it's Andrew, Sergeant. Being investigated. Somebody, for God knows what unimaginable reason, has built a tight little frame on him, and some of us are out trying to prove the frame. Because—"

Southby looked very astonished and then very angry. "The hell you say! A— On *Andrew?* For God's sake, what are they trying to—"

Jesse began telling him. He'd got to Helen Madden, the mink coat and the cash Hendrickson said Clock had paid in, when Southby let out a muffled roar of profanity and said, "For God's sake, this is ridiculous! *Andrew?* With his record? For God's *sake*, we were at the Academy together. I'd as soon believe *I'd* done such a—"

"But you see it is evidence. And the I.A. men don't know him personally."

Southby was up, pacing. For the moment this office was empty of other men, though several more desks stood about. "Evidence," said Southby in a quieter voice. He stared at Jesse. "But my God, the money— I can't believe this—"

"Tell you all the details," said Jesse, and went on. Southby listened, biting his lip, chain-smoking.

"Good point about the date on that deposit slip," he interrupted once; and, "The girl asking that fortuneteller about money—looks very suggestive to me." When Jesse finished he swore again. "That's the most fantastic—all set up like that waiting for the chance—who in *hell*— Yes, yes, I see that, more important to prove it *is* a frame, but—

Hell, yes, we've heard rumors, but those damn rule makers keep everything so quiet. *Andrew.* I can't— Why'd he send you to me? Sure to God, anything I can do to help, but—"

"Well, Wilcox Street is on it now, see. Hendrickson. Technically he disappeared from your jurisdiction, and his sister reported it here. Yesterday. Obviously, I expect, you're going to have I.A. on your necks about it—don't suppose they're exactly indifferent to it, even if it hasn't changed their funny ideas about Andrew—but they're not going to be telling me or Andrew anything about what you find out. Andrew just thought—if you'd be so obliging—you could keep us up to date on what shows."

"Oh, sure, I see that. I wasn't briefed on it, but Dean told me something. I can tell you right now, we picked up his car. Hendrickson's. Early this morning, I think." Southby stepped into the hall and called, "Dean—see you a minute?"

Dean was a younger man, not quite handsome, with alert eyes and a humorous mouth. "What's up, Sergeant?"

"Mr. Falkenstein—Detective Dean. What about that guy reported missing? You said you found his car—where?"

"Ogden Drive, above Santa Monica. Woman called in and reported it had been there since Sunday, in front of her house, so of course we chased a car out to see if it was hot. It wasn't, but it was registered to this Hendrickson. All the squad cars have got that plate number too, so we hauled it in. It's in the garage now, but there wasn't a thing in it, I mean, to suggest anything. I had the lab boys go over it right away."

"No blood, nothing to indicate a struggle? No—"

Dean looked at Jesse curiously. "Not a thing, why? Not very clean inside—dust, dirt, litter bag full—but nothing unusual. Maps and whisk broom in the glove compartment. Dirty handkerchief on the front seat, and that's about it. Why?"

"Tell you later," said Southby. "Yeah, you know Clock too, don't you?"

"Why, sure, he was here up to— What's Clock got to do—"

"Tell you later. *Hell* of a story," said Southby. He looked at Jesse. "How d'you figure it, with this Hendrickson? He must have been bought, sure. You said you and Andrew had leaned on him a little. How was he reacting?"

"Nervous. Maybe—just maybe—running scared. But little fellows like that can also be awful damned stubborn."

"They can," agreed Southby thoughtfully. Dean looked from one to the other, puzzled.

"But Andrew had scared him, I think. Physically."

"Which also figures. You think he's run?"

"Well," said Jesse, "if he has, he's evidently run in the clothes he stood up in, didn't take his razor or toothbrush or, so far as we know, what money he had—the supposed bribe money. We don't know where he kept that. I've been back to the bank—" he grinned mirthlessly—"figure that Lanterman wouldn't have been so forthcoming if he wasn't still growing an ulcer over one of his tellers taking off like that. Anyway, he did part with the information that Hendrickson didn't rent a safety-deposit box, and his bank account looks just like what a respectable teller's account should look like—about four hundred in a savings account, little over a hundred in a checking account."

"Still, it seems to me," said Southby, "if he was going to run of his own accord, he'd try to take that. Five hundred bucks—"

"But we don't know how much more he had, do we? He could have bought a safe and stashed it in the back of his closet or under the bed. You've got to remember, apparently money no object in this caper. Ten thousand bucks that we know of— I don't doubt that the Maddens got another chunk, and who knows what Hendrickson's cut was? But—" Jesse put out his cigarette—"there's another way to read it too, isn't there? Hendrickson running scared. Hendrickson probably having seen X at least once. Probably having some means of getting in touch with him. Just in case. Getting in touch, all nervous about the big cop breathing down his neck, likewise genial lawyer threatening lawsuits—and X maybe seeing Hendrickson either running—to bring suspicion on him anyway—or breaking down and telling the truth. Or —well, build it how you want, X has gone to some lengths to ruin Andrew's career, blacken his name, and he might go to more."

"To *what?*" said Dean.

"Tell you later. You think he's dead?" said Southby bluntly. "That this— God, who in *hell* could have any reason— You think he's murdered Hendrickson?"

Jesse shrugged. "*For the imagination of man's heart is evil from his youth,* so it says in Genesis. Rather imagine that could apply to this joker. Don't know. You are, I suppose, checking all unidentified bodies against Hendrickson."

Southby looked at Dean. "What the hell is this all about, anyway?" asked Dean. "Bodies—yes, sure. There were only two. Within the time limit. First thing we did, sure. But the man hasn't been gone long, you know. Early to report it, I'd have said. Neither of the new corpses was Hendrickson. Both older men. One died of acute alcoholism, down on Skid Row. Other one was a user, took too big a dose."

"Look, Mr. Falkenstein," said Southby. "Wouldn't that be very damn suspicious right there—make it pretty sure Hendrickson was mixed up in something crooked—if he got himself murdered?"

"*Needs must when the devil*— Not," said Jesse, "if he happens to get found tomorrow or tonight in a cheap hotel, hanging from the shower rod by his own belt. Or, possibly, quietly in bed with an overdose of sleeping tablets in him. Or even with a bullet in his head and the gun beside him, the untraceable gun. Doesn't take much but elementary logic and caution to set up a suicide." He leaned back in the chair and shut his eyes. "So, no note, but they don't always. And the reason? Well, daresay a couple of people at the bank could say he'd been acting nervous—upset by having to make the statement to the police and all—and the I.A. officers do know that Andrew and I've been trying to do what we can on it. Who's to say—not me—that Andrew didn't see him alone, threatened him all very convincing? Nervous little fellow, Hendrickson, they'd say all severe—I can hear Clay now—look what you went and did!"

"Oh," said Southby. He passed a hand across his mouth. "You see it like that. Bound to say, you've got an imagination, Mr. Falkenstein. I suppose that could be. You do think he's dead. And no damn clue whatsoever to who— God! I've only just started to take it *in*. Andrew."

"Don't know," said Jesse. "Will say this. Hendrickson had some bribe money. No knowing how much, but it wouldn't have been peanuts and he couldn't have begun to spend it all. He didn't keep it at the bank so he kept it some place else. Say in a safe under the bed— damn fool thing to do, sure, but what *could* he do with it? Banks keep an eye on their employees' accounts, just naturally. He didn't have a safety-deposit box—possibly he was afraid the bank would secretly examine one of those. Anyway, somebody came to his apartment at two A.M. Sunday morning—needn't have been him. Just somebody with his keys. After the rest of the money? Because if a big wad of money was found there, it'd give the show away with a bang right there. At least I didn't see any money. Did you?" he asked Dean. "Assume you went over it."

"Yes, sure," said Dean mechanically. "No money, no. Nothing there to say—just like the car—whether he'd taken off voluntarily or what. It does look funny that he didn't take even such basic things as a razor and a toothbrush, but he could have bought new ones."

"Mmh," said Jesse. "I'm just thinking of possibilities. And if he was running, why leave the car? At the very least, it'd be worth something as a trade-in on another." Slowly he unfolded himself from the chair and found he towered over Dean.

"What about that—that girl?" asked Southby. "How in God's name they could buy that— His whole record—"

"*Many have perished through the beauty of women,*" said Jesse, "*and her love has been as a fire that burns.* Not that I'd class Helen Madden as quite such a *femme fatale,* but so much depends on the individual viewpoint. Got some private eyes looking at the Maddens. See what turns up. Anyway, Sergeant, no objection to—er—keeping us briefed?"

"My God, no—I want to see Andrew," said Southby. "This—who in *God's* name—"

"Or Satan's," said Jesse softly. "Yes. Got a special consultant working on it, Sergeant."

So they'd hear what Wilcox Street came up with on Hendrickson. Lucky, reflected Jesse, Andrew had an in there: men he'd formerly worked with.

Helen Madden, indeed . . . And Joe. The first report from Garrett Associates had come in this morning, on the Maddens. There wasn't much in it. She'd gone to a beauty salon in the afternoon, after staying in all morning, gone back to her apartment, gone to her job at six o'clock; home at half-past one, lights out. Joe had mainly spent the day playing pool downtown, had a few beers here and there, gone to a movie and at seven o'clock picked up a girl named Amy Krepps at her apartment, taken her out to a steak house, come back to her apartment. Fun and games? Very likely. Joe driving a 1957 two-door Chevy. And where'd he got the money for it? Hadn't held a job in a while. When he was working, not making big money—or saving it, probably. Garrett Associates promised to have more on the Krepps girl, and whether Joe had paid cash for the car or was buying it on time, in due course.

Jesse wondered if the reports tomorrow might have something a little more interesting to say.

Fran had dropped in last night while Clock was talking about his latest session with Thatcher and Clay, and said they weren't doing *enough*. I've been thinking about this Madden bit. The type I know, Jesse. Emotional. Selfish. Immature. Look at her going to all those idiotic fortunetellers. Which Mr. MacDonald is *not*, and you needn't laugh. *I* think she could be scared quite easily, maybe into doing something silly and giving it all away. If you—"

And Nell agreeing emphatically, the upshot had been that the four of them had gone out to the Cannibal Tavern on La Brea.

And what a place that was, thought Jesse. Jungle atmosphere. Fake palm trees. Tables fake upended tree trunks. Waiters all Negroes in fake zebra-skin costumes. Incongruously two groomed Hollywood blondes in shimmering evening dress as hostesses. One of them Helen Madden.

Artificial bright smile glued on, sheaf of menus in hand, ready at the door to the darkened dining room with its fake tribal fire crackling (courtesy of natural gas) along the rear wall. "It'll be a few minutes, sir"—"Four, sir? Right over here"—"If you'd like a drink while you're waiting—"

She had checked on seeing Clock, but she had, you could say, carried it off. Then. A cool smile, a comprehensive glance at Fran: Fran very *soignée* in her favorite charcoal chiffon— And at Jesse, her gaze dismissing Nell as, of course, impossibly old-fashioned with long hair, the severely cut plain beige sheath.

"My God, that dress," said Fran. "Whole bit very nineteen-fortyish. . . . I don't know that I'll trust you two to make a job of it. I'd better come too."

"You will sit here quiet with Nell and discuss fashions," said Jesse.

They had timed it. She'd said in Clock's hearing that her break was at nine-thirty. Half an hour after they'd entered the place, Jesse raised his eyebrows at Clock and together they went out to find her in the entrance hall. Talking animatedly to the other hostess—"And she was just wonderful, you really ought to go see her, dear—she knew all about me, honest! And she said—"

"Like a little talk with you, Helen," said Jesse conversationally; and

Clock swung her around by one arm. She faced them with a little indignant gasp.

"What—here, you let me go, you can't—"

"What, acting so coy when we've been such good friends?" said Clock, smiling. "Just a little talk, Helen." He drew her toward the door. "This is time for your break anyway, isn't it?"

The other hostess just stared after them.

Outside, in the cool spring night that still, in California, was somehow mild, they backed her up against the face of the building a little way down from the door. Red neon flashed on and off above them, showing her expression in sudden moments.

"What do you want?" she demanded angrily. "I don't want a thing to do with—"

"That's gratitude," said Clock, "for the nice mink coat. Didn't they teach you any manners, Helen?"

"Daresay you don't want anything to do with us," said Jesse, "but that's life, Helen. Here we are. Just to deliver a little warning."

"What do you—"

"Suppose you don't know Walter Hendrickson, Helen? No. He was the other half of the frame. Also took the nice money to tell a big fat lie about Sergeant Clock. Was it nice money, Helen? Or haven't you had all of it yet? Well, anyway, the sergeant isn't the man to take all this without fighting back, Helen, and he got Mr. Hendrickson to feeling very nervous. So nervous, Helen, that Mr. Hendrickson was maybe at the point of breaking down and admitting he'd told the lie. You following me?"

She stared at him, at Clock. "I don't know what the hell you—"

"And you know what happened to Mr. Hendrickson, Helen? He's disappeared. Fact. Didn't take any clothes with him, or his razor or toothbrush. In fact, we're afraid that Mr. Hendrickson is maybe dead some place."

"Because," said Clock, "it doesn't seem to be very healthy to get nervous around this X who built up the frame on me. You're already wondering whether the rest of the money'll really come, aren't you? Worried about a double cross? It all seemed a little too good to be true, maybe? Well, you better worry some more, Helen. It begins to look as if this smart boy you threw in with is a kind of chancy guy. Maybe he isn't going to want any of you around—to be able to admit you lied. Hendrickson was the bank teller, you know. He's gone. Who knows where? Look in the paper tomorrow and you'll see he's been reported missing."

"And it just could be," said Jesse, "X is figuring on all of you going missing. You and Joe and Benny and the photographer who made up that fake picture, and—"

"You're trying to scare me," she said contemptuously. "I don't know what you're talking about! Let me go."

"Didn't you ever stop to think, Helen," said Jesse, "it was a kind of crazy deal? Just to spoil one cop's good name? All the money—all the time you had to wait? To set up the frame? He's a nut, Helen—he's overdue for room and board at Atascadero—because who but a nut would want to do that? Spend all that money, wait all that time, just to—"

She put a hand to her mouth. "I don't have to listen to you."

"But you'd better think about it, Helen," said Clock. "He's way off the rails—and Hendrickson's gone already. What's he got in mind for the rest of you who helped him—just for all the nice money?"

"And didn't the mystic seer tell you, Helen," said Jesse softly, "and he saw true—wrong money, from a wrong place, and it'll never do you any good. Think about it, Helen."

They stood there isolated: the on-and-off slash of neon flashing monotonously over their heads. For some time no new customers coming past, the door opening. Flash: the white oval of her face lit up pink: flash, off.

"*How did you—* Oh, God!" she said with a little sob, and turned and ran from them. Back into the restaurant she fled, her lamé dress glittering as if she trembled as she ran, and when they came into the foyer she was gone.

"Scared?" said Clock heavily.

Jesse shrugged. "Think so. See what happens."

"You really think Hendrickson's dead?"

"Who knows? But it's useful to scare Helen with. Just possibly Joe."

"I know," said Clock, "that the—the imminent thing is to prove it's the setup deal. But, Jesse, I keep wondering—I can't help it—just *who* in hell? And *why?*"

"Don't look at me. Our special consultant working on that angle. You heard from him?"

"Not a word."

FOUR BY EGAN

So Jesse was wondering whether something more interesting might show in Helen Madden's movements on Tuesday. If she had been scared sufficiently. And if the Maddens had some way to contact X.

Preserve the soul in patience, he thought. He had a four-thirty appointment: expectably, another automobile damage suit. Money was money, what with the Monster, and Nell hopefully planning a family.

He went back to his office.

At nine-thirty on Tuesday evening, some fifty-five hours after he had retired into silence with Clock's old notebooks, Mr. Walters reached Clock at his apartment.

"Clock here."

"It's me. Listen, do you remember—"

"Oh," said Clock. "Don't tell me you've found anything significant in that stuff. I just can't imagine— I'd have known if—"

"I'm the one wants to ask questions," said Mr. Walters plaintively. "You remember anything at all about a Mr. and Mrs. Rodney Bayne?"

Clock thought and said no. "Doesn't ring a bell. Bayne. Bayne? Was it a case? Well, after all, maestro, in ten years as a detective I've been on a hell of a lot of cases. What about the Baynes?"

Mr. Walters sighed audibly. "No, don't suppose you'd remember 'em all. August sixteenth, nineteen fifty-seven, Sergeant. Young couple, I gather—got to quarreling. Over something."

"Wait a minute," said Clock. "Bayne. I seem to—"

"He ended up shooting her and then himself. Remember?"

"Kind of vaguely," said Clock. "I couldn't have said the name. Just one of those things. No, I don't remember any details, but they'd be in Records, if— It wasn't, for God's sake, anything mysterious. Not even the only case of that kind I was ever on. It's a thing happens. Husband or boy friend gets to drinking maybe, quarrelsome, suspicious— or the other way round—and if there's a gun handy— Just a routine case, the little I do recall about it. Why'd you pick it out?"

Mr. Walters sniffed. "Guess I can quote as well as Jesse. *Is Saul also among the prophets?* They had some money, by the—" he sniffed again—"the address."

"Oh," said Clock. "That strikes me as way out. I mean, I'm very much obliged to you for—but I just don't see— As far as I remember, it was just the routine thing. And eight years ago—"

"Um-hum," said Mr. Walters. "So I got another question for you, Sergeant. Oh, by the way, no calls on that ad in the *Times*?"

"No," said Clock. "Seems odd, if some jeweler *had*—but of course not everybody in L.A. County does see a Sunday paper. I guess that's a washout, two days after—and what it *cost*—"

"Never you mind about that," said Mr. Walters austerely. "There's a Yiddish proverb—*Money answers all questions*. May yet. Um—L.A. County, yes. Well, Sergeant, how about this fellow named Disbrowe? Who got shot? December first, nineteen fifty-nine. You were on it. Kind of reading between the lines in your notes—oh, I've been decipherin' 'em handy enough—you felt kind of strong about it."

"*Disbrowe!*" said Clock, and from six years' time he felt again the shock, the outrage and anger, they had all, at Wilcox Street, felt then. Disbrowe—Francis William Disbrowe. And what a completely anonymous kill that had been! "For God's sake," he said, "what brings that up, maestro? Disbrowe I can tell you about, sure—no cop ever forgets anything about another cop getting killed."

TWELVE

Having dropped into his office on Wednesday morning to pick up the Garrett report on the Maddens, Jesse fumed inwardly at having to spend the rest of the morning in His Honor Justice Botts's court. Justice Botts was difficult at the best of times, and was apt to be especially tiresome over divorces; possibly he was a disbeliever in the whole process. The Galen divorce didn't get called until after eleven, and when it did Mrs. Galen made a poor showing, agitated and incoherent; Justice Botts regarded her disapprovingly, and her witness with an even more jaundiced eye, but eventually granted the divorce and recessed at twelve-thirty.

Then, of course, Jesse had trouble getting away from the client. "You've been *so* kind and understanding, Mr. Falkenstein—I'll never forget it—don't know how I can ever repay you."

Jesse resisted the impulse to assure her that money would be just fine with him, and finally escaped. Over a ham sandwich and coffee he reread the private eyes' reports.

Helen—possibly—scared and unnerved on Monday night. What had she done Tuesday? Apparently nothing much. She'd left the apartment about noon and driven, in the pink VW, to a nearby supermart, brought home a lot of groceries and stayed home. Tuesday night was her night off. At seven o'clock a black 1963 Caddy had pulled into the drive of the apartment, its driver had gone up to Helen's apartment and after an interval they came out together. Appended description of escort: middle-aged man, executive type, well-dressed, partially bald. "Was subsequently able," added the report, "to investigate registration of Cadillac. Is registered to Norman V. Ball, Rodeo Drive, Beverly Hills." Ten to one, thought Jesse, the same lover-boy she met at the Fox and Hounds on Saturday. So. Mr. Ball had taken Helen to the Travelers' Inn, which was a newish roadhouse (featuring nightly dancing to Eddy Ainsworth's band) out on the Malibu road up the coast. Very likely the private eye had investigated the Caddy as it sat in the parking lot. They had stayed at the Travelers' Inn, presumably wining, dining and dancing, until one-thirty A.M., when Ball had driven Helen home, arriving at Cole Place at two-twenty-eight A.M., seeing her to her door and leaving immediately. Damn fool, thought Jesse, evening like that bound to catch up with a middle-aged gent. Probably went home, took some bicarbonate and fell thankfully into bed.

Joe Madden, on the other hand, had had a busy day—doing what? He had gone hither and yon, he had met these people and that, but from eight-thirty when he left the Cole Place apartment up to five-forty, he had repeatedly tried to place a phone call. Apparently. "On several occasions," said the report, "I was in a position near enough to subject to see or hear that the phone call was not completed. A total of nineteen phone calls or attempted same was made." Jesse paused to admire the private eye's grammar. "It is quite possible that some of these were calls to different numbers, but the number of occasions when to my certain observation the call was not completed, led me to deduce that subject was calling same number and finding it impossible to reach intended party."

Which was very interesting, reflected Jesse. Of course Joe, bored with Amy Krepps, might merely have been hunting up some old girl friend. On the other hand—

Joe had, yesterday morning, made a beeline for territory probably more congenial to him than middle-class Hollywood: downtown L.A. Third Street. He'd made his first frustrated phone call from a public booth in a bar there. From there he'd hit Sam's Pool Hall on Main, two more bars (but no drinks), a greasy-spoon café on Second (belated breakfast) where he'd used the public phone again: back to Sam's, where he'd played a few games with other customers and again used the public phone. And so on—the only thread running through the report the repeated use of public phones. And then at five-forty, at a bar on Fourth where for the first time that day Joe had had any drinks—three beers, said the report—apparently he had connected. "For the first time in my observation subject succeeded in getting answer. He talked for some time, several times appearing angry and/or excited. I could not hear anything of what he said as booth is sound-proofed. After approximately ten minutes' conversation, during which the party called did not seem to do as much talking as subject, subject hung up phone violently and came out of booth. Finished his third beer and then re-entered booth and made another call. During this call, subject's expression guarded, and he did more listening. Subject then—"

Well, what it came down to, had Joe been trying to contact the principal? To, possibly, demand a final pay-off, or even up the ante? Be interesting to know, thought Jesse.

He finished his coffee and sought a public phone booth himself, dialed Garrett Associates. He was passed around some, finally made contact with Garrett. "Listen, I've got the feeling this little business of mine is getting hot. Has your boy trailing Joe Madden reported in?" Operatives were supposed to when they could, he knew.

"Just a second, I'll check," said Garrett. "I don't do everything around here, you know. . . . Jay! You got anything in from—"

Jesse waited. Garrett came back on the line. "Yeah, he just called in ten minutes ago. He's with Madden out on a Hundred and Sixty-fifth Street. Madden's in a café there. . . . How should I know what Madden's doing out there? That's all that was reported. Routine. As to where they are."

"Who's the tail, anybody I know?"

"Miller—Wes Miller. Don't know if you know him."

"I do—met him over that nasty Brookhill divorce bit. Where exactly is this café?"

Garrett sighed and read the address to him. Jesse called his office to check; he had an appointment at four-thirty again but nothing else; however, he should of course be catching up on the inevitable paper work. The Crossley suit would be up in court next Monday; and there was this new damage suit. The hell with it for the moment. He sought the Ford and, tediously in traffic, drove across town, to hell and gone, out to the café on 165th.

It was, when he got there, a hole-in-the-wall café called Gertie's. So small that no self-respecting tail would attempt to share it with Subject. Jesse parked half a block away and strolled back, and after a little search spotted Miller sitting in his car across the street ostensibly reading the *Times*. He jaywalked across and opened the passenger door.

"Remember me?"

Miller, startled, turned quickly and after a second relaxed. "Mr. Falkenstein. Take another five years off my life. What are you doing out here in the wilds?"

"Hunting you. I'm the one—rather, eventually, client of mine—hiring you on the current job. Anxious to find out what, if anything concrete, has shown up. What's he been up to today?"

"Oh," said Miller, "that so?" Like his employer, Miller was an ex-cop; a bad accident had invalided him off the Arizona State Police. He was a man in his late forties, already gray, with a lean humorous face and shrewd dark eyes. "Climb in and shut the door. He's an ex-con, isn't he, this Madden? Thought so. Just something about him. Well, I won't stick my neck out and make any guesses, Mr. Falkenstein, but it looks kind of suggestive, if you get me. Suppose you've seen my report on his meanderings yesterday. All the phone calls—attempted ones. Well, he slept late this morning, maybe. Anyway he didn't show until about nine o'clock. He dropped into a Mannings' coffee shop on Sunset for breakfast—scrambled eggs, bacon and toast—and then he headed in this direction. I don't think he's got any remote notion there's a tail on him, no. He seemed to know just where he was going. He parked round the corner on Virginia, and walked up to the post office. You noticed the post office? On a Hundred and Sixty-fifth, up in the next block. I couldn't follow too close, it's not a big place and there weren't many customers that early. But he didn't stay long. He came out—this was—" Miller sighed—"at five of eleven. Took us awhile to get here, you know, from Hollywood. And he's been hanging around ever since. He went back to the post office at a quarter to twelve, came out and took himself a brisk six-block walk. Just killing time. He found a tavern over on Lakewood and had a sandwich and a beer. Then he came back and—"

"Went into the post office again," murmured Jesse. "O frabjous day, is this going to come unstuck? Don't tell me."

"What is it, a pay-off?" asked Miller. "I couldn't go asking any questions, but I've been a detective awhile. A post-office box?"

"I'd take a small bet. And I don't think," said Jesse, "I go asking any questions either. He knows me. He's still in the café?"

"Lessee, I called in about one-twenty, when he got settled there. I don't see how he can stay much longer, even playing the juke box. It's now two-forty. I should think he'd be showing pretty soon. If he knows your face, Mr. Falkenstein, get away from me."

"Will do. Thanks very much. I'll lurk. Want to see if he picks up anything." Jesse slid out of the car. Up at the corner on this side of the street was a dilapidated-looking independent drugstore. He strolled up there, picked a yesterday's *Herald* off the rack, paid for it and stood leaning on the building with the paper spread out before him.

It was a warm, sunny, clear day—clear for once. A troop of elementary-school youngsters came marching past, bound for home, trailing sweaters along the sidewalk, the little girls giggling together, the little boys running and whooping. Four, Nell said: my God. What with the Monster and the house payments—

Hendrickson. Was he dead, for God's sake? Or—

The frame. The impossible— Even his notorious imagination couldn't supply him with any motive, lunatic or otherwise. But it almost had to be lunatic, didn't it? The cunning, obsessive, lunatic-shrewd lunatic?

At three o'clock the door of Gertie's café opened and Joe Madden came out. He was wearing a garish Hawaiian sports shirt and brown slacks. He started quickly up toward the next block, toward the U.S. Post Office. Jesse watched Miller slide out of his car, folding his newspaper tidily under his arm, and wander in the same direction on this side of the street.

Ten minutes later, Miller came back. He was in a hurry, no pretense this time. He glanced around, spotted Jesse and made one small gesture, hand at waist-level, thumb and forefinger circled. He got into the car, started the engine and came up to the intersection of Lakewood, engine idling, and thirty seconds later turned the corner and took off. Presumably after Joe.

So. Joe had picked up whatever he had been waiting for. Jesse folded his *Herald* and went into the drugstore. There was a public phone. He dialed Clock's number.

"Thank God you're home. We've got something hot, and I need your badge. It's still impressive outside of Central jurisdiction, hm?" He outlined the situation rapidly. "I can't stay—it's three-thirty and it'll take me best part of an hour to get back across town, I've got an appointment. But you chase down here and follow this up."

"I'm on my way," said Clock energetically.

Clock got to the post office on 165th at four-ten, which was good going through traffic.

It was a smallish post office, with a kind of foyer where the locked boxes ranged along the rear wall, and double doors at the left leading into the main room, bisected into two unequal portions by a long counter. Two clerks on duty, one old and one young, both wearing the regulation white short-sleeved shirts with u.s. post office on the pockets. At the moment there were no customers in the place.

Clock went up to the older clerk and displayed his badge, creating instant feverish curiosity and a fervent offer of cooperation. The boxes? Well, he wouldn't know anything about— Some people paid by mail, some came in personally, but as to the actual renting of boxes, Mr. Ferguson was the man in charge of that. And what was it all—

"Then I'd like to see Mr. Ferguson," said Clock.

"Yes, sir. If you'll just step out to the foyer I'll let you in the back by that door, sir."

Ferguson, a rather pompous fellow near retiring age, was also cooperative. But while it added, it didn't add quite far enough. Still, it was something: another something.

A produced list of the renters of post-office boxes at this particular station turned up exactly one with—of course, of course, thought experienced-cop Clock—the initials J. M. The little small-time punks, how lacking in imagination they were. . . . Ferguson didn't remember anything personally about this John Maddingley, no. The records showed that Maddingley (and at that I.A. ought to think twice about this, for God's sake, they were experienced cops too) had rented the post-office box first in September of 1963.

Clock looked at that a little incredulously. But that was what it said. Box rented for this caper or another? Why?

The record also showed that the box rent had always been paid promptly in cash. Quarterly: the usual arrangement.

There wouldn't be any record, of course, of how often mail came addressed to the box: or what kind of mail. Unless one of the clerks remembered something. The sorters would just automatically put aside mail for the boxes, resort it later and put it in the boxes. "We can ask Mr. Pullen if he recalls anything," said Ferguson. Which they did. Mr. Pullen vaguely recollected that there had, he thought, been a letter addressed to that box today, but he couldn't recall at all whether it was local, address typewritten or otherwise.

And just how to use this? wondered Clock. If it had been a case he was working with the other boys— God, God, would he ever be peacefully back at his own familiar desk, doing the thankless job that was his job?—he'd have put a stake-out on it. With a warrant. That would make it so nice and easy. He couldn't do that here and now. The private eyes wouldn't have the authority to look at mail addressed to that box.

And in any case, it was ten to one the box wasn't used much. And in any case, Joe Madden had already picked up what he'd been waiting for this time. The pay-off?

But it was another something to put up to the I.A. officers. It was indeed. They weren't fools, after all.

The only trouble was—as it had always been—it was all such a hell of a tall story to swallow.

Nell called Jesse as he was taking notes from the indignant ramblings of a stout woman who was instituting a personal damage suit against a savings-and-loan firm which was too assiduous about keeping their floors polished, so she said. "A *most* severe back injury, the doctor said I may never fully—"

"Jesse? Have you seen our octogenarian today?"

"Not hide nor hair of him, why?"

"Oh, well, his daughter-in-law just called. The son he lives with, I mean—the son's wife he— Wondering if we had. They do fuss about him so. After all, he's entirely sane and sensible."

"Eminently," agreed Jesse. "I haven't laid eyes on him since Sunday. And nothing showing up from that *Times* ad. . . . Wonder what he's up to, if anything. Wonder if he—"

"He's usually up to *something*," said Nell.

At that precise moment, old Mr. Walters was looking for a taxicab. He was also feeling a trifle excited and awed. One part of his mind was dwelling thoughtfully on mystic seers. You couldn't get away from it: funny as it was, that sort of thing was *there*. Fact. Ninety-eight percent of it pure emotional idiocy: the rest—something else.

Very damn funny, he thought.

He stood on the curb outside the *Times-Mirror* building, absently brushing cigar ash off his rumpled jacket, and looked for a cab. Damn

D.M.V. had taken his license away when he turned seventy-five. He thought wistfully of his last car.

Of course it *could* be a coincidence. They did happen. But—counting in the mystic seer—it all kind of dovetailed. Only he didn't see— Oh, well, do a little, what did they call it, leg work on it and maybe—

He also thought about Disbrowe. Did Disbrowe come into it at all? What the sergeant told him, something kind of offbeat about Disbrowe, and you could sure as God say there was something offbeat about this frame on the sergeant.

Francis Disbrowe. Patrolman on the force, four years. Twenty-eight, married, a new baby—a boy. Good man, good record, nothing against him. Ordinary young officer driving a squad car around Hollywood. Lived in one side of a duplex on Harvard Avenue. So one night his wife Sandra goes out in the family car to visit her mother, who'd been sick, over on Gower, and when she comes home at ten o'clock and lets herself in, she finds Disbrowe dead on the living-room floor. Shot. With one slug—a .32-caliber, for pretty sure a Smith and Wesson Masterpiece. But no gun there; he didn't own a .32. And nothing stolen; nothing disturbed; baby sound asleep in the next room.

So, had he let somebody in? Somebody he knew, or a stranger? Nothing showed in his private or professional life, anybody with any reason to kill him. Wife definitely clear: not only all broken up, but the coroner said he died between seven and nine, and she was alibied. No strange fingerprints: not a clue.

They'd never got anybody for it. They'd looked—sure as hell they'd have looked hard, but nothing had ever showed up on it.

Funny.

Did Disbrowe come into this?

Mr. Walters finally picked up a cab (persecution he called it—still as fit to drive as he'd ever been, they seemed to figure anybody over seventy or so just had to be senile) and rode up to Hollywood.

He was putting one hell of a lot of blind faith, he thought, in the mystic seer. Well, young Fran had been impressed, and young Fran had her head screwed on tight. He sometimes thought tighter than Jesse.

Hendrickson, he thought. As if a ten-year-old couldn't— Well, Jesse had an imagination.

He paid off the cab, surveyed the apartment building, went in and found the superintendent.

"—So you're writing a book about it? Well, just imagine," said the superintendent, who was a fat motherly-looking woman.

It seemed to be the standard excuse people in books used for asking questions: as good as any other. To get people talking.

"—Wasn't here myself then, of course, but I suppose there was a lot of excitement about it. There would be, of course—a thing like that. Beg pardon? Oh, Mrs. Stuyvesant, she was manager here then. I didn't know her, no, sorry. . . . Oh, well, she's dead, you know. And this is a good neighborhood, too, but *these* days—well, even *then*, you just don't know what can happen. You really don't. All these delinquents. Coming home from the movies she was—that was back in the spring of nineteen-sixty—and of course it's pretty dark back there down the drive, *I* think they ought to put up a spotlight—some *hood* like they say waiting, and when she drove in—stole her purse and jewelry, and they found the poor thing laying there next morning, dead as a— I tell you, I put it down to all this progressive education like they call it— and mothers working, not taking proper— Beg pardon? I've only been here since June of nineteen-sixty, that's right. But—"

Mr. Walters asked patient questions and got copious answers.

"I don't suppose *that* poor old fellow would remember much to tell you—but, let's see, there was Mr. and Mrs. Norwalk, and Miss Far-quhar—*she* didn't move till last year—and old Mrs. Garden—Mrs. Geral-dine Garden, Mrs. she was but talk about old-maid gossips! Nice woman, you know, but *curious*. And *talkative*. Well, I expect I could give you—I seem to recall it was a rest home, after she got out of the hospital—after she broke her hip she couldn't—"

Mr. Walters figured he ought to have kept the cab. Scarce as hen's teeth up here in Hollywood. Damn D.M.V.

He wondered if there was anything *to* this. If so, very damned offbeat you could say.

He found a cab. He gave the cabby the address and said, "Son, you ever do any ruminating about human nature?"

"My God, dad," said the cabby, "in my job? What else is there to do? I ask you. I'll tell you the trouble with human nature, dad. There's just too damn much of it floating around. Now you take—"

"Now that's a way to put it," said Mr. Walters. "You like to pull over a second, I'll offer you a drink." He got out his bottle. He felt in need of a drink himself.

"Which I will not turn down," said the cabby. "You seem like a reasonable fare, dad. And a good brand too. My thanks to you. Now speaking of human nature, you take my mother-in-law—"

Mr. Walters put his bottle away and stroked his luxuriant mustache.

If he *had* anything, it was one *hell* of a thing.

But who? And, come to the point, why?

He rather liked this cabby, and asked him to wait. "Anything you say, dad." He walked up the steps of the St. Mark Episcopalian Rest Home. Looked like a nice, expensive place. But no rest homes for him, no, sir. Senior citizens, who the hell did they think they were fooling? You got old, well, you got old.

Only some people gave up sooner than others. He reflected comfortably on Grandfather Jonathan Walters, who had married for the fourth time at eighty-three, and asked the matron if he could see Mrs. Garden.

"What say? No, I'm not a relative—is there some rule?"

"Oh, no, sir. No. We just—she'll be *delighted* to have a visitor, sir. Such a nice old lady. And so *bright*. Mind as clear as can be, you know, and she just loves to talk."

Just exactly, thought Mr. Walters, what he wanted. At this stage of the game. Bright gossipy old lady.

"You can wait in the parlor, sir," said the matron.

Mr. Walters waited with some anticipation. He wanted to find out about this. Not just because he liked the sergeant, felt sorry for him. He wanted to find out the truth. There was a vague recollection in his mind—Jesse and his quotations—couldn't think where it came from, and he wasn't sure he had it right—something about, *There is nothing so curious or beautiful or interesting as the truth.* Was that it? You could also say, as human nature. People. And all his life Mr. Walters had been passionately interested in the endless vagaries of people.

If he *had* anything here—

It was six-thirty when he got Nell. "Jesse there?"

"Where've you *been?* Your relatives checking up on you. No, not yet. Any minute—"

"That Betty. Think I was four years old. Tchah. Well, maybe you can tell me. I just want to know who the private-eye is Jesse said was a good one."

"Oh. Garrett Associates. *Why?* Have you found out something? Jesse said—"

"Something. Don't know. I guess offbeat, you could say. If. Just occurred to me—lot of potential leg work involved—might as well hire it done. By somebody competent."

"Don't tell me," said Nell, "you're feeling your age?"

"Tchah!" said Mr. Walters.

"*Have* you found out—"

"I don't know. Maybe. Somethin' very funny, Nell. If. Just say to you—in the end, *Above all things truth bears away the victory.* However," said Mr. Walters, "however offbeat the truth may be."

THIRTEEN

"They wouldn't listen to me," said Clock heavily. "I don't think they paid any notice at all." He stood in the doorway of the dining room where Jesse had led him and did not apologize for interrupting the meal. "I don't think they'll think twice about it."

"Sit down, Andrew," said Nell. Athelstane, who had naturally accompanied Jesse to the door, whuffled as if in sympathy and pressed against Clock's legs. "Have you had dinner?"

"I don't want anything, thanks," said Clock; but he sat down at the table.

"What happened at the post office?" asked Jesse, picking up his fork.

Clock told him. "It looked straightforward enough to me. Cause and effect. My God, even the private eye guessed it was a pay-off! I thought— I went downtown, it was after five but I thought somebody would be in the I.A. office. They both were—Thatcher and Clay. I told them about it. I had to tell them about the private eyes, of course. They didn't like that, but I went on about all Joe's phone calls yesterday and then his hanging around that post office, and the John Maddingley box and so on. And all I got was a harangue from Thatcher about how I had no business to investigate on my own, I was officially suspended and the theory—"

"I thought," said Jesse, "you said they weren't making like the Gestapo."

"—How the theory I'd offered," Clock went on dully, "was mere leaping to conclusions, just trying to pretend—my God. I didn't think they were, Jesse. This is a good force. I'd never had anything to do with I.A. before. I don't—to give the devil his due—I don't think they *think* they are. Being unfair. If you get me."

"No, I don't."

"Well, most of the complaints and tips they investigate are minor, I gather. Nothing like this thing. And most of them are—justified, in some way. Not all, of course. But I figure that they've got used to being on the right side of the argument every time, maybe it's gone to their heads some. It's the only way I can— I mean, they're cops too, Jesse. They didn't start their careers in the I.A. office. But I don't think they half listened to me, for God's sake." Clock looked at the plate of ham, mashed potatoes and asparagus Nell set before him and absently began to eat. He looked very tired.

Jesse put down his fork and knife tidily parallel across his plate. "You do not tell me," he said. "Yes. Faithful sergeant making excuses for the witch hunters. For my money, friend, that's exactly what they are. Gestapo. So we're leaping to conclusions? You don't have a right to defend yourself? Somehow I seem to recall from my college days that the original legal system in this benighted nation was based on a slightly different precept."

"Jesse—" said Nell.

"I think," said Jesse, "they are beginning to make me mad, friend. Good and." He stood up abruptly and went away down the hall. Athelstane hurried after him. They heard him talking on the phone.

"I don't know," said Clock abstractedly, "that I've ever seen him good and mad."

"About once in five years," said Nell. "And I think I'm beginning to agree with him. That was all they said?"

"That was all. They didn't like the private eyes. I think they stopped listening after that."

Jesse came back. He said, "Finish your dinner. Seems to be a little time on hand. We're going to call on Joe and Helen. Funny—she's stayed home, didn't go to work tonight. Both tails sitting outside the apartment. I am now wondering whether it *was* pay-off money in the envelope Joe picked up today."

"What more have we got to say to them?" asked Clock. "You know you told a nasty lie, that's not right, hadn't you better own up? So they laugh in our faces again and we go away."

Jesse lit a cigarette, pacing the room. "There are several things I should very much like to say to Captain Thatcher and Lieutenant Clay," he said. "And I may do so soon." His voice sounded remote.

But when they pulled up behind a car parked across the street from the Cole Place apartment, he was outwardly himself again. "Take a bet that's Miller," he said, and walked up to the dark car and peered in. "Thought it was you. They both still in?"

"Mr. Falkenstein," said Miller. "Waiting for my relief man. Meet Ben Gates—he's on the girl. Yes, they're both up there. Wonder why she didn't go to work?"

"I'm making a few guesses about it. See you," said Jesse, and he and Clock walked across the street.

"A waste of time," said Clock.

Jesse didn't say anything. He rapped sharply on the door of apartment seven. They could hear voices raised which stopped abruptly. Then Joe Madden's voice said, "Who is it?" and the door opened a crack. His heavy, sullen face appeared briefly, drew back. "What the hell do you want?"

"Let us in," said Jesse, and shoved at the door. He shut it behind them, leaned on it and added, "You been doing a little thinking, Helen? About what we told you?" Both he and Clock looked at her with interest.

Something had shaken Helen, all right. She hadn't retouched her make-up in some time, and she'd been crying; mascara had run, grotesquely, down one upper cheek, and her silver-flax hair was disheveled. Minus the sophisticated veneer, it was a frightened baby-face, the immaturity showing through—and fright.

"We got nothing to say to you," said Joe Madden tautly.

"And you're feeling a little bit uneasy too, aren't you, Joe?" said Jesse. "You didn't find what you expected when you opened that envelope out of P.O. Box three-eleven at the Gardena post office, did you?"

Madden took a step back, obviously much startled, and nearly fell over one of the plastic chairs. "What the hell—"

Jesse smiled at him. "I think not. Helen's been feeling a little suspicious of the nice deal—after she heard about Hendrickson vanishing away. The other paid liar, you know, Joe. Urged you to contact the principal, get the rest of the money and maybe make tracks out of here for a while. Just in case. You reached him, but he didn't send you what you expected, did he? Nasty threatening letter, maybe?"

Neither of the Maddens said anything. Jesse looked back at Helen. "Told you he was a lunatic, didn't I? Lunatic kind of deal. And they'll do anything, and you never know exactly what they will do, do you?

Take a notion into their heads—and if he thought you might turn spady on him—"

"*No!*" she cried. She put her hands to her mouth suddenly. "I wouldn't— Crazy, sure— I told Joe, get *out!* I always thought—a real kooky setup, anybody who—"

"*Helen, shut up!*" said Madden. He took two strides and shook her violently.

"I—I didn't say anything, Joe," she faltered. "I wasn't—"

"Neither of us got anything *to* say," said Madden coldly to Jesse. "Especially to you." He ignored Clock.

And Jesse ignored him. "Some very nasty threats maybe, Helen? Showing he is the lunatic? Yes. You got yourself into a thing this time, Helen. Even afraid to go to work? *Because you don't even know what he looks like*—if he decides to—"

"Oh, my God!" she said. She began to sob. "Crazy—just crazy—like he wrote he'd use acid—and neither of us ever laid eyes on—"

"*Shut up!*" said Madden, and struck her backhanded, hard, with his left hand. She fell back onto the couch, still sobbing. Madden swung around to Clock and Jesse, and his eyes looked wild. "She—she got this threatening letter from an old boy friend, see, it's kind of shook her. Now listen, I ain't got a thing to say to you. You get out of here. You—"

"Joe," she said. "Joe. I didn't mean anything. I'm sorry. I won't—"

"That's right. Out!" said Madden, and opened the door. Helen crawled off the couch, went slowly into the bedroom. She didn't look back at any of them.

On the landing, Jesse looked at Clock. "And isn't it a pity that we didn't fetch along a tape recorder. Damnation. Just for a minute there she was all set to break it. Try to relay that interesting little scene to Captain Thatcher, don't suppose he'd listen to a word. Hearsay. *And,* damnation, the hell of it is if a couple of cops hauled her down to headquarters and worked on her, I think she'd come apart. But—"

Clock didn't say anything. He just stood there, a big tired worried man, and he looked ten years older than he was. He shook his head then and said, "They wouldn't believe us, and Madden'll see to it she doesn't talk any more. It's no good, Jesse."

"It will be," said Jesse. His eyes looked cold. "Go home, Andrew. Or go see Fran. You can't have one damn thing to do with the rest of tonight's activities."

"What—are you going to do?"

"Something maybe I should have done yesterday," said Jesse. "Yes. *Tell it not in Gath, publish it not in the streets of Askelon.* Andrew, go away. Go see Fran."

The *Telegraph,* the past ten days, had been itching to get some details. No official report, even that an investigation of an L.A.P.D. officer on serious charges was under way, had been made; but the *Telegraph* knew *something* was going on, and naturally other reporters had got a faint wind of it.

The *Telegraph,* of course, not the media Jesse wanted. The *Telegraph* would automatically take the position that here was another thing that only proved over again what a brutal, corrupt police force it was. But the *Herald,* now—the nice conservative logical *Herald*—

Jesse found a public phone along Santa Monica Boulevard and looked up Marjorie Freeman's number in the Pasadena-area book. He crossed his fingers that she'd be home.

She was. "What? Mr.—oh, yes, I remember."

"You said you were going steady with a reporter on the *Herald.* Mind telling me his name?"

"Yes, I—Bob Armstrong. Why?"

"Mind giving me his number? I've got a hot story for him."

She hesitated a little, finally parted with it. Still keeping his fingers crossed, Jesse dialed it and got a perky-sounding elderly woman who told him Bob was on nights now, and read the number to him without being asked.

Listening to the phone ring at the other end, Jesse looked at his watch. A quarter to nine. The *Herald* was an evening paper; also had an afternoon edition. He hoped he was in time to get this in the early afternoon edition. . . . "Mr. Armstrong? You don't know me—my name's Falkenstein. Lawyer. I've got a hot story for you. You've been hearing some vague rumors that an L.A. police officer is under investigation by the department for something serious."

"Oh," said Armstrong cautiously. "As a matter of fact—Falkenstein, did you say? You the lawyer that was involved in that funny murder case around six weeks ago? Yes, well, about the rumor—there was just a line in the *Telegraph,* but of course the *Telegraph*—"

"Saw it. Not so cautious—you've heard the rumor. Well, let's break it open. I'm going to give you all the details on it, and I think your editor'll want to print it all. I'm the officer's lawyer, Mr. Armstrong."

"Whee," said Armstrong. "Is this an exclusive? Is it really—"

"Think you'll find it newsworthy," said Jesse dryly.

"Wait a minute, let me get the news editor. O.K. if he listens in?"

"Quite O.K. Like to make it clear—I'm doing this without the consent or knowledge of the officer in question, and I'm not giving you his name. Got that? O.K. Now, there's been a fantastic frame set up on this man, and one part of it—one cog—is that bank teller who went missing a few days ago. Walter Hendrickson . . . No, you won't get any change out of the bank, but the way I read it, Hendrickson was paid to swear falsely that the officer had paid in some cash which he didn't. Bank teller bought. And it just could be the bank teller's since been murdered. And—"

"Oh boy oh boy," said another voice on the line. "All this and murder too?"

"—And you don't get this blonde's name either, or you'd pester her until you got the officer's name. Nix. But I saw her tonight, and you can say that she's in a—mmh—highly nervous state, having by her own implication just received a threatening letter from the X who set up the frame. . . . And the officer in question isn't going to like all this, but I figure in the long run it'll help expose the frame. . . . And this pro gambler Starbuck—"

"Listen, Mr.—what did you say, Bob—Falkenstein, will you come round and—after all, a thing like this, we like to verify—"

"Anything you say," said Jesse. And he thought a little grimly, *Before all your people will I do marvels.* Oh, yes? Well, it couldn't do much more harm.

They broke it in a special afternoon edition. They printed his long statement *verbatim;* gratuitously they gave him some nice publicity, recalling his involvement in those murder cases. As he'd foreseen, the suggested nature of the incredible frame was just so incredible that it had captured the editor's imagination, and all the details got mentioned: Jesse's reasoning on the deposit slips, and a broad hint at the essential character of the female involved, the fact that her brother was an ex-con who hated cops; there was a long paragraph about Hendrickson, and they'd even chased somebody down to Long Beach for an interview with Wanda Herrick, who had come out with a few of the same remarks she'd made to Jesse before. Bank Teller Sold

Brains in High School, said a minor head. And, Lawyer Fears Foul Play; Says Only Obsessive Lunatic Could Be Responsible. Where is Walter Hendrickson?

The edition hit the streets at three o'clock. At three-thirty Jesse began getting reporters from every other sheet in town. By four-thirty Miss Williams was so utterly demoralized that he put her in a cab and sent her home.

He talked to all the reporters, withholding only Clock's name and the Maddens'. He was giving a statement to the *Times* when old Mr. Walters walked in and sat down to listen.

"You can say that I certainly feel the Internal Affairs department has turned a deaf ear to all the suggestive evidence which points to a frame, I would hazard because of the very incredibility of such a frame. But, gentlemen, fantastic things do happen. I'd consider it only fair—indeed imperative—that some consideration should be given to this officer's character and record. I'd like to underline that he doesn't agree with my feeling about I.A.—he has shown complete loyalty to the L.A.P.D., which he has faithfully served for thirteen years. The—"

"I think," said Mr. Walters, "you got more company, Jesse."

Jesse looked up. Lieutenant Zachariah Clay stood in the doorway of the inner office. The *Telegraph* and the *Citizen-News* were still pre-empting Miss Williams' desk and phone; he ignored them, and the *Times*.

"Well, I've been expecting you, Lieutenant," drawled Jesse. "Come in. What delayed you?"

Clay walked up to his desk and stared down at him with arctic, remote anger. "Just what, Mr. Falkenstein, do you hope to gain by this—this Roman holiday of publicity?"

Jesse stood up, and he topped the other man by six inches. "I'll answer that question happily, Lieutenant. I expect to gain a public hearing. When I was in law school, Lieutenant, they told us that under the law of this land any man is to be presumed innocent until proved guilty. You don't seem to believe in that precept, Lieutenant." All the reporters had flocked up eagerly. "The officer in question—and I, as his lawyer and his friend—have tried to find evidence of his innocence, of this admittedly fantastic frame. We've offered you a number of suggestions. Only yesterday we discovered, and immediately told you, that the brother of this woman he is accused of giving part of the alleged bribe to—an ex-convict—maintains a postal box under an as-

654 FOUR BY EGAN

sumed name, which certainly seems at least suspicious and obviously suggests a means whereby he—and she—could receive a secret pay-off. We could have told you, Lieutenant, that both the officer and myself heard this woman admit that she'd been a party to a 'deal,' and is now frightened of the principal agent in that deal. After seeing your attitude on the other matters, I didn't suppose you'd even listen. The officer an interested party and inferentially I wouldn't be acceptable as a witness. You have not taken into consideration any—"

"Mr. Falkenstein. There *is* no evidence of a—my God—a frame. As a police officer, don't you suppose I know what constitutes evidence?"

"Lieutenant," said Jesse gently, "as a lawyer I know a hell of a lot more about it than you do. And as a reasonably intelligent man I also know when the nice legal evidence stinks to high heaven."

A thin white line grew around Clay's mouth. "You are not aware, Mr. Falkenstein," he said, "in the midst of your ridiculous allegations about Mr. Hendrickson, that the manager of the bank has received a letter from him? A letter of resignation. On Wednesday. Far from being the victim of 'foul play,' Mr. Falkenstein. Mr. Hendrickson was so upset by his irrelevant involvement in this—unpleasant business, and I might add by the physical threats made by—the accused officer —that he has resigned his job and—"

"Fled," said Jesse. "I was not aware of it, Lieutenant. Nor was the officer. Why not? He has a little stake in this, isn't he entitled to know the facts? Why wasn't that given to the press? And do you really believe that an honest man, only telling the honest truth, could become so 'upset' as all that?"

"The signature on the letter has been verified as Walter Hendrickson's. I do not condone—"

"And what was the postmark? Have you made any effort to find Hendrickson in person and question him again? As to exactly why he got so 'upset'? You don't choose, in fact," said Jesse, "to give the accused officer any vestige of fair play. You believe the word of an ex-con, a probably immoral woman, against that of one of your own men with not a single mark against him in thirteen years on the force? You lecture him because he dared to fight back, to try to vindicate himself. You don't even consider the possibility that he might be telling the truth? We've given you leads to follow up in your so-called investigation, Lieutenant. At some expense—because you won't do it—we've hired private detectives to look harder at these nice respectable, believable witnesses. The ex-con. The woman. And a weak, lazy, irresponsible man—Hendrickson—who is so lacking in common integrity that he sold his scholastic talent to the highest bidder, for pocket money, in high school. Is that the kind of witness you choose to listen to exclusively, Lieutenant?"

"Oh, brother, smite 'em hip and thigh," said the *Herald, sotto voce.*

"I would like to make a statement," said Clay loudly, as if he'd just realized the presence of the reporters. "The Internal Affairs department exists to police the police force itself, to insure that only the highest type of officer remains on the force. It is a scrupulously fair office, and in this case the evidence presented to it was almost incontrovertible. It is always a matter of deep regret to the department when a formerly upright—"

"Lieutenant," said Jesse, "you're not campaigning on the party ticket for mayor." The reporters laughed. "You've been a little too long up in Internal Affairs, Lieutenant, playing God. You pin your faith to the on-the-surface evidence, and you forget any common horse sense maybe you once had. *Woe to him who builds his house by injustice."*

"The evidence in this—"

"Two paid-for lies!" said Jesse contemptuously, and Clay turned on him, goaded into fury at last.

"Just trying to confuse the issue with these ridiculous— Of all the *incredible—* Typical lawyers' tricks! For God's sake, you think we're congenital idiots, to believe anybody would— Suggesting that over two years ago some— Goddamn it, do you think we *like* it?" shouted Clay. "This is a top police force, we take pride in— Do you think we *like* it when a man goes wrong? Can't you for Christ's sake let us deal with it in decent privacy, in—"

"No, Lieutenant," said Jesse. "I can't. Private justice is so often too damn private. Private hearings are so often the beginning of tyranny. Can't *you* even let a man's character and record be a witness for him?"

"Character be damned—the evidence is there! I—"

"So his record counts for nothing! You're ready to damn him on the word of these—to say the least—highly doubtful witnesses? Witnesses! Before God, Lieutenant, I'd hate to face you on the bench in any court! But by God, Lieutenant, I'm going to prove to you just what your witnesses are worth. *God will not cast away an innocent man.* You—"

"Oh, for *God's* sake—all the Bible-quoting in the—"

"Get out of my office," said Jesse, not raising his voice. "Now, you know, you've made me mad, Lieutenant. If you'd been willing to listen, just to listen—but you've played God too long. You need a lesson maybe, and maybe I'm just the man to give it to you. Get out."

"I don't have to take—"

"Justice and injustice my people know something about, and wasn't it truly said, *Behold, it is a stiffnecked people.* So I am, Lieutenant, when it comes to forms of justice—and ordinary fair play."

"Listen, damn it, all I'm saying— I never meant to imply—"

"Get *out!*" said Jesse hardly.

"I—" Clay cast a harried, angry glance around, and went.

"And the rest of you," said Jesse. "That's all. Good-bye."

The *Times* lingered, looking at him thoughtfully. "What chance have you got of proving it—if it's so?"

Jesse shook his head. He had the beginning of a headache. "I don't know," he said.

It was Mr. Walters who spoke up, surprisingly, in a mild voice. "*So shall my righteousness witness against me hereafter,*" he said, not to the reporter. "Little matter of faith, Jesse, that's all."

The reporter grinned and went out. "I wonder if Miss Williams has any aspirin in her desk," said Jesse.

"Don't know as I've ever seen you so wrought-up before. Thing to rile a man all right—them shutting their minds to anything that says maybe 'tisn't so. Why?"

"Playing God," said Jesse. "Nell said— Have you got something on this, boy? Something—concrete?"

Mr. Walters looked in a distressed way at the drink he'd just poured. "Don't know yet. I told 'em—those Garrett Associates—make it a fast deal. For the extra money. I don't know, Jesse, it looks—well, a funny business. Funny-peculiar like they say. And, hell, I only took it up because of what young Fran's mystic seer said. Sounded awful damn unlikely, you know."

"Took what up? I guess this'll do as well as the aspirin." Jesse poured himself a drink.

"The arms of Ariadne," said Mr. Walters, staring at his own drink. "Very damn funny. Young Fran—she mentioned that magazine. *Fate*. Picked up a copy. Very interesting. Can't deny, some very goddamned funny things do happen. This ESP—and poltergeists and such. And there is that fellow Hurkos—sees things. He's helped the police a lot of times."

"What the hell are you talking about?"

"Well, just— I came across it in the sergeant's notes, see. I'm just following it up. Talk about blind faith. But what that Garden woman said— Naturally she had all the details still in her mind, nice gossipy female like that. And there was the story in the *Times*, too. I kind of like that. Continued on page eight, and right in the next column— Could be coincidence, sure. Only—"

"Edgar," said Jesse, "you are maundering. What are you talking about?"

"Don't like to say until we get a report from these Garrett people. I just don't know," said Mr. Walters. He sounded worried.

At a sound in the anteroom Jesse looked up, and then stood. Wanda Herrick paused in the doorway.

FOURTEEN

"Are you going to castigate me too, Mrs. Herrick?" asked Jesse. "Come in. Meet Mr. Walters. Mr. Hendrickson's sister, Edgar."

"How do you do," she said absently. "Mr. Falkenstein, something has to be done about this. I didn't *realize*—"

"Couldn't agree with you more," said Jesse. "Sit down."

"I didn't realize—you didn't say much—what it was all about. But when I saw the paper—I'd just come out of the doctor's office when I caught a glimpse of the— This is an awful thing, if it's so." She looked at him miserably, hands clasped across her bag in her lap. "And it's a dreadful thing to say, but it's exactly the sort of thing Walt would do. Arguing himself into believing there wasn't anything really so bad about it—if he was getting money for—"

"Mrs. Herrick," said Mr. Walters, "you have any idea where he might have run to?"

She turned to look at him. "We don't know—" began Jesse.

"You stop exercisin' your imagination. Of course he's run—line of least resistance, like all his kind. Hadn't expected all the fuss, hadn't expected the sergeant'd come down on him. Figured he'd done his part as agreed—and just could be too, Jesse, same like the Maddens, he tried for the final pay early and got a little scared by the principal like you call him. Decided easiest, safest thing to do was take the cash and— Get out from under. Lie low awhile. I saw that. He didn't take the car because he didn't specially want to be traced through it. He isn't actually wanted for anything, after all—the police have got his statement. And you talkin' about safes under the bed. Just because he didn't rent a safe-deposit box at that bank doesn't say he didn't rent one some place else. Security-First or somewhere. And he stayed away from his apartment that Sunday to keep out of the sergeant's way. Mrs. Herrick, do you know anything about that letter?"

She nodded. "They—a Captain Thatcher—called and took me down to that big police building, on Wednesday afternoon. They had it there. I guess the bank manager had called them about it. They asked me if it looked like Walt's signature, and— I guess they were having, you know, experts look at it."

"At least doing a little wondering," said Jesse. "Did you see the postmark on the envelope?"

"No, but they said it was mailed Monday in Hollywood. I—"

"So there you are," said Mr. Walters, bringing out a cigar. "Decided to run like I say—just leave the trouble behind—only he couldn't get into his safe-deposit box till Monday. When he could, he just scooped up the cash he'd been hoarding and took off. Unless this publicity turns up somebody who sold him a car, I expect by air or train. Doesn't your imagination tell you, boy, that when he couldn't resist the big color TV and the nice restaurants for dates, he'd also for pretty certain have bought himself the electric razor, the electric toothbrush—latest gadget you got to have to be anybody—the nice clothes and, probably, when he knew he was running, a couple of nice suitcases?"

Jesse struck himself on the forehead. "*Mea culpa.* I was being melodramatic. *The hoary head is a crown of glory.*"

"It's exactly what he would do," said Wanda Herrick. She sat bolt upright, looking worried and angry. "Walt's not *bad*, Mr. Falkenstein. He'd never do anything cruel or mean—oh, I mean that he could *see* was cruel or mean! But I've got to say he was spoiled, and he—rationalizes about things. I know all the rest of it sounds just incredible —what you said about somebody spending all that money and time just to ruin that policeman—but if it's so, well, knowing Walt I can believe he did that. Took the money too— He didn't like that bank job particularly, but he stayed. I hoped he was settling down, but— Mr. Falkenstein, do you think he was *paid* to stay? It—it looks that way, doesn't it?"

"It does."

"I got a notion," said Mr. Walters, "could be he was paid to take it. The deal set up cold, then. All the more likely, you know. Just one little lie he'd have to tell, at some unspecified time—just one time abstract the deposit slip and mail it somewhere, likely—just once take in that wad of cash and stash it in the sergeant's account. Money for jam, like the English put it."

Wanda Herrick nodded. Now she was just looking angry. "I believe it. He's done things just like that—rationalizing—only nothing ever as bad as this. He's got to be punished for it. Maybe that would— I don't know. But I can *see* it."

"He got any favorite place he'd be likely to run to, Mrs. Herrick?"

"I think," she said, "it's quite possible he's up at Lake Tahoe. He likes it up there, always spends his vacations there. And if this is so, I suppose he'd have enough money to—just stay quiet up there—quite a while."

"Probably," said Jesse. "Also, far enough away that this—mmh—local news wouldn't be in the northern papers. And the police *have* got his statement. I don't suppose Thatcher and Clay are going to chase him up again in person. I rather think—"

"*I* rather think," said Wanda Herrick abruptly, "that I'm going to chase him up, Mr. Falkenstein. He can't be allowed to get away with this, no matter what trouble he gets into. He's got away with too many things, all his life—little things—and maybe some of it was my fault too, because I started out making excuses for him. But this is—really bad. And, you know, I could always get the truth out of Walt eventually. Mother never could—she'd believe anything he said—but even when we were kids, I guess because I am so much older, he'd eventually break down if I—backed him into a corner. It wouldn't be any good for you to go and look for him up there, but I can get the truth out of him." She opened and shut her bag, obviously planning. "I can park the kids with Jim's mother, she'll understand, and fly up there to-morrow morning. This has got to be straightened out."

"It'd be a long step toward that if you can get him to open up," said Jesse. "Guess you can see that."

She nodded shortly, standing up. "If he's there, I'll find him. I think he will be. And I'll get the truth out of him, and make him come back. I will say—" she smiled a little wintrily—"Walt respects me. And this time he's got to be—caught up to. Whatever trouble it means for all of us. I'll let you know. I'll be in touch." She went out quickly.

"Lay a bet she'll do it," said Mr. Walters. "Nice tough female—character."

"God, I hope so. God, it would give me great pleasure to watch those witch hunters listening to Hendrickson confess he lied! And I agree with you, she—" The phone rang and Jesse picked it up.

"This is the first chance," said Tom Garrett, "Miller had to call, and let the record show I'm calling you five minutes later. The Maddens have run."

"Oh, *hell!*" said Jesse. "They're gone? What—"

"Keep your shirt on. Miller took over again this morning, just in time to take after 'em. With a fellow named Batsford who's on Helen. They took both cars and made tracks. Luggage in Joe's car. Made one stop for a late lunch and pulled into Vegas about three o'clock. Miller—"

"For God's sake. Have they holed up? Thank God your boys kept on them."

"Yes, but I've got no license to operate in Nevada," said Garrett dryly. "I'd like some instructions, please. They can't stay on it, Jesse. Joe and Helen have taken rooms at a motel. A fairly ritzy motel, the Top Hat, outside of town. It appears they're going to stay a little while anyway."

"Yes," said Jesse. "Running, same like Hendrickson. Get out from under. And they too are not actually wanted for anything—way they'd figure. Damn. But I've got—pray God—a little hunch this is going to break wide open soon, and we'll want to hear their little piece of truth. Can't lose track of them. You know any competent private eye over there?"

Garrett thought and said, "There's Jim Byrd. He's not bad. Just a small agency, but he could be relied on to keep track of people at least."

"Good. Shall I call him or you?"

"I'll save you the phone bill," said Garrett. "Miller's calling back in half an hour for instructions. I'll tell him to pass them to Byrd. You'll get off a retainer?"

"In tonight's mail. Give me the address. . . . O.K., thanks, Tom." He relayed that to Mr. Walters, who had found a glass and poured himself a drink as soon as Wanda Herrick had left them.

"Just so," said Mr. Walters thoughtfully. "Grace of God, we can keep track of 'em. Got a notion—you couldn't expect it of the Maddens, but like Hendrickson they hadn't the imagination to look ahead and see what was likely to happen: that the sergeant would fight

back, and the fuss be made. Got in a little deeper than they thought.
And you know, Jesse, I also think that's so about X. I'd kind of like a
psychiatrist's opinion on one like that—not that I put just so much
stock in 'em, but you get one who's retained a little common
sense, they're right about some things. Kind of think this X has got a—a
megalomania, some kind—sure, the obsession like you say too, but that
he's got to a place where he feels like God. That he can do anything—
because anything he wants to do is right. Like—like Hitler and company. Pathological. Clever up to a point, but he's—lost touch with
things as they are, see? He could see what he had to do to build the
frame, but on account of this—losing touch, like—he never took into
account the fact that little people like the Maddens and Hendrickson
are so likely to break down."

"True," said Jesse. "Can't tell you how relieved I feel— That Mrs.
Herrick. If Hendrickson *is* up there—"

"Like I've been since it started," said Mr. Walters, "I'm a lot more
interested in what's behind it. But I think we got a good chance of
breaking it, now. A hell of a funny business. You better go home,
Jesse, Nell'll be having a fit. Nearly seven. Suppose I better go home
too or they'll be calling the police about me."

Clock got Jesse at home at eight-thirty. He had only just, belatedly,
seen the *Herald*, having spent an aimless afternoon watching an old
movie. "What the *hell* you think you're doing—you've just made it
worse!" he said bitterly. "Why—"

Jesse attempted to soothe him, attempted to explain. "They'll be
wild," said Clock. "They'll—"

"Oh, they are. Had a little set-to with Commissar Clay. Never mind,
they're going to be eating their words, boy. Listen to this." He told
Clock about Mrs. Herrick. "Bet you she'll do it, too. Come to the
point, I gather, Big Sister can always march him up to the principal's
office and make him 'fess up the truth."

"If he's at Tahoe," said Clock. "That's just fine and dandy. But all
these headlines, my God—they'll never forgive—"

"Preserve faith. Publicity never did any harm to the truth. And let's
hope when the truth comes out, it'll now be with such a bang that the
witch hunters will remember the lesson for a long while," said Jesse
grimly. "*Justice has but one form, evil has many*."

Clock was still up at midnight when the phone rang. He started at the loud jangle in the silence of his old apartment; and he wondered if this presaged some unimaginable new disaster descending on him. He moved slowly to answer it.

"Clock."

"Sergeant," said Detective Peter Petrovsky, "I hope I didn't wake you up."

"No, I wasn't—"

"But even if I had, I knew you'd forgive me. I told you I was just a dumb Russky. Kind of belatedly it suddenly occurred to me that the witch hunters might feel just a little bit shook up in their minds if we *could* come up with whoever really did kill Arnold. And/or, if you take me, come up with an alibi for Starbuck. I mean, while they haven't got the legal evidence to prove it—*now*, according to them—their whole case is that Starbuck was It, and paid you to cover it up. If Joe Doakes should confess he'd cooled Arnold, well, why should Starbuck get so scared of possible involvement when he knew he was innocent? We don't railroad people in this town—which Starbuck knows. We couldn't, for God's sake, bring him to trial on the tie clasp. He's got no pedigree. But just in case—I was sort of hopefully thinking, you understand—we did come up with the real killer, and the witch hunters went on maintaining that Starbuck did so, too, bribe the bad cop because he was afraid of being involved— You following me?"

"On your heels."

"—Well, I thought it'd be nice to find an alibi for Starbuck. Not so easy, either job. Reason you haven't heard from us. We've been making like bloodhounds eighteen hours a day. And you may not believe it right off, Sergeant, but we got both. Just today. Which I knew you'd want to hear, so—"

"The hell you— But Pete, if Starbuck had an alibi why didn't it—"

"Show. Yes. Well, I've cost the department quite a little money running it down. The Arnold thing just looked hopeless—you said that—one of these anonymous deals, could have been anybody. Arnold a smalltimer, a drifter, pick up with anybody. But on Starbuck—well, Arnold got himself shot, the coroner said, sometime between midnight and two A.M. on Tuesday night the sixth of April. Starbuck, who we just questioned casually because he'd had a little argument with Arnold that afternoon, said he went up to his hotel room about eleven-thirty that night, read for about an hour and went to bed. Alone. As you know he was—still is—at the Beverly Hills Hotel. Well, one thing you can say about me, Sergeant, I'm persistent. I got the names of everybody who had rooms in that wing that night, and I've been chasing 'em down."

"My God, persistent," said Clock.

Petrovsky laughed. "Yeah, a job. Some of 'em clear across the country now—that's the hotel for professional people of all sorts traveling on business. But point is, I finally found this Jefferson Coates. He's a representative for some manufacturing outfit in Kansas City. He had the room on the left of Starbuck's from the first to the sixth—checked out that Wednesday morning. And he says he does remember hearing somebody go into that room about eleven-thirty that night, just as he was going to bed. And he says that there's a connecting door to that room, locked of course then, and the bed faces it, and he was bothered by a line of light under the door till he fell asleep. Places the night because he left next morning."

"Well, as an alibi—"

"One of those circumstantial things. But a hell of a lot more than we had before. Then this morning, by one of those beautiful irrelevant flukes that fate sometimes sends our way, we got the gun that killed Arnold." Petrovsky was enjoying himself. "We do try to be so thorough, and you know when we get something on a murder gun, like we got on that one—that it was a Colt Trooper twenty-two—we spread the word around every department, if anybody comes across one in the daily routine, let's have Ballistics look at it."

"Yes."

"So last night about midnight a squad car picks up a D. and D. down on Main and they throw him in the tank overnight, only among other things he's got a Colt Trooper twenty-two on him, and no permit, so they take the gun away. And a fairly bright desk sergeant down there vaguely remembers there'd been a call out on that make and model from Homicide, so he sends it up to Ballistics. And it turns out by the comparison slugs to be the gun that was used on Arnold."

"How very, very nice," said Clock. "Was the D. and D.—"

"No, oddly enough," said Petrovsky. "He's just another drifter, name of Skiffington. He was scared to death when we hauled him up to question. Said he bought the gun from a guy he knows, yesterday, because he was planning a trip to Mexico and was afraid of bandits.

That's right. Guy named Kemsler—Harry Kemsler. Told us where he lived. So we went and picked up Kemsler—eventually, he didn't show until four o'clock—and we've been at him in relays ever since. Well, until about an hour ago, when he finally came apart and gave us a statement. Confessing he'd shot Arnold because they'd been after the same girl, a comely bit by the name of Marie who's a waitress in a bar on Fourth."

"How very, very nice indeed," said Clock. Sure to God I.A. would think twice about *this?* Starbuck about as far outside the Arnold case as— "Pete, you did it all according to Hoyle? So the smart-boy lawyers can't—"

Petrovsky chuckled. "Don't fuss, Sergeant. I remembered all the rules and regulations the ivory-tower boys so damn concerned for the poor criminal's rights have foisted on us. First thing I said to him was he had the right to have an attorney present. He asked me what the hell an attorney was."

Clock laughed; suddenly (and remembering Wanda Herrick too) he felt fine. By God, they were going to—

"That's really something, Pete," he said. "They'll have to think about this, won't they? Did you—"

"Sergeant, I'm damn tired and what with all the teletypes and leg work and pawing through Records I've scarcely seen my wife in three days, but *that* I had to do," said Petrovsky. "I had the stenographer type up an extra copy of Kemsler's confession and the entire session of questioning. I put that and the original teletype from the K.C. boys, who took the statement from Jefferson Coates, in a big manila envelope and I wrote on it *Special Attention Captain Thatcher,* and I took it up to the I.A. office. Which of course was closed, the witch hunters being eight-to-six boys, but I fastened it on the door with Scotch tape, and I only wish I could see the captain reading the contents tomorrow morning."

"Pete, thanks," said Clock. "I don't know how to say thanks. I'll sleep tonight. God, they've got to—"

"But, Sergeant, we're still no nearer guessing who and for Christ's sake why. I don't—"

"We may even be that." Clock felt suddenly very tired; he hadn't slept much last night. "We may break it sooner than we think. You'll be hearing—"

The plotter, the man who brought doom, was very angry. He had never expected anything like this: nothing like this, in all his plotting and conniving, had ever happened. He had brought the inevitable vengeance, because it was intended he should: he was above other men, above the little laws regulating other men. No other man had the right, as none had the power, to challenge *him:* to circumvent the necessary vengeance!

And that little man afraid, and running away. Dangerous? Why? Why could it happen?

It never had. The vengeance brought, and the taste of it so sweet, so sweet. Inevitable as doom—as *he* had made it. As he had the right, the terrible necessity, to bring it.

He was the omnipresent, destined to bring the vengeance. *He* could not be challenged. *He* could not be foiled.

A lawyer. The long columns in the newspapers. First yesterday, but more today, all the papers. It was like a nightmare, every point made —they had seen how—they had imagined—

No! The little ordinary men could not, could never fathom *his* all-cunning plans! It was unthinkable.

In blind fury he crumpled the newspaper and flung it across the room.

And the mind, still shrewd, but having fed on its terrible irrational obsession so long, the obsession that told him— *But there must be someone to blame, someone left to punish, someone to bear the blame and to bring revenge on*—the mind began to turn, then. The curious, intricate, still-mysterious, unfathomable mind that can never be mind alone but co-existent with spirit, and that is turned by the second's vagary to good or evil—the mind began to falter.

He was omnipresent. His great plans could not—could not— It had been intended! It had been divine will, and his the executing mind to bring it.

But another man (no!) had dissected the cunning plan, piece by piece, and the little men—

The little ordinary people—only useful as pawns in the planning— *No!*

"Jesse," said Nell, "what *do* you suppose he's found? He simply won't say."

"I know." Jesse lay back in the armchair and studied her through half-shut eyes. "He was maundering on yesterday about some story in the *Times*, continued on page eight. . . . Not a word from Andrew. I wonder if they did any thinking at all about all that Petrovsky handed them." Clock had called him first thing this morning about that, had been hoping to hear from Thatcher. "I hope to God those private eyes in Vegas don't let the Maddens slip away. I've got a hunch, by God, that Herrick female is going to—mmh—give us Walter's head on a salver, and—" The phone rang. Athelstane, who had been sound asleep on the hearthrug, whuffling in his sleep, sprang up and followed Jesse down the hall.

"Is this," asked an anxious male voice, "HO one-three-four-nine-seven?"

"That's right," said Jesse.

"In Los Angeles? The number that was—er—in the Los Angeles *Times* on Sunday the eighteenth? The—er—advertisement about the gold tie clasp?"

"*Yes*," said Jesse fervently. By God, was it all going to come unstuck at once? "Who is this, please?"

"My name is Fearing, sir—Thomas J. Fearing. I decided that I had *better* call, even though it was Los Angeles, because it did not seem that coincidence could quite explain— May I ask who I am speaking with?"

"My name's Falkenstein, I'm a lawyer. If you have any information to give us about that tie clasp, we'd be extremely—"

"Ah. Just so. Well, Mr. Falkenstein, it's a very curious thing indeed, and it does make one wonder about destiny. I am a Methodist myself, and I realize that the Church does not accept the precept of—ah—predestination, but nevertheless things do happen which make one wonder. You see, today happens to be my birthday, Mr. Falkenstein."

Athelstane was leaning against Jesse's knees listening earnestly. Jesse almost held the phone away to stare at it. "Mr. Fearing, if you have any—"

"Oh, I do beg your pardon." It was a pedantic, old-but-not-elderly voice, and Jesse's imagination presented him instantly with the picture of a scrawny, earnest fellow in his sixties with a prominent Adam's apple and a fanatic regard for the letter of the law. "That is not irrelevant. You see, my daughter Margaret lives in Los Angeles. Actually in Brentwood Heights—she married very well, a well-known surgeon—and naturally, she always sends me a birthday present, Mr. Falkenstein. In this case, it was a very charming Majolica vase—I collect china, you see—an antique, of course, as Majolica ware is no longer produced. And it was, also naturally, very well parceled up with a good deal of crumpled newspaper. Er—Los Angeles newspapers, of course. I am happy to say it came through quite safely. I—"

"Mr. Fearing, if you—"

"Dear me, yes, I must come to the point. Well, Mr. Falkenstein, I'm afraid I'm a rather precise man—my profession, you know—and I carefully flattened out the newspapers so that they wouldn't take up too much space in the refuse can—and *that* is how I happened to notice the—er—advertisement. About the tie clasp with the initials P. S., you understand. The parcel, you see, Margaret mailed last Monday—it arrived here yesterday, but I'm afraid I'm a *rather* sentimental person and I waited to open it until my actual birthday. And it was natural that Margaret had used the Sunday paper to pack the parcel. But it does make one wonder. About—er—destiny and such. I would take it that it is an important matter, such a prominent—and doubtless expensive—advertisement."

"Very important," said Jesse. "What do you—"

"Well, I have wondered and worried over it all day," said Mr. Fearing, "and finally decided to call. You see, Mr. Falkenstein, it is possible that I engraved those initials on that tie clasp. Quite possible. Even though the distance—but I believe by jet these days—"

"You—" Jesse swallowed—"you're an engraver?"

"I am a skilled jeweler, sir. I have my own shop, on Market Street. I will tell you—"

Jesse did hold the phone away. "Market— Mr. Fearing, where are you calling from?"

"Why, San Francisco, sir. This very convenient new direct dialing—I know the advertisement said, Collect, but I could not reconcile it with my conscience—if it should prove to be a coincidence. I felt that if what information I had to offer was—er—relevant, reimbursement would be— By God's grace I've done quite well, Mr. Falkenstein, very successful in a modest way, and I felt—"

"What do you know about the tie clasp?" Jesse kept his voice down with effort.

"Oh, yes. Well, I have the record, of course, in my accounts. I looked it up especially to be sure. It was on Thursday the eighth of this month, a gentleman came into my shop and picked out a tie clasp and made a request for an urgent job of engraving on it. He said it was to be a birthday present, and he must have it within a couple of days. The initials were P. S. I have a note of it. As luck would have it, I had no engraving jobs outstanding, and I was able to let him have it on Saturday—that would be the tenth. Yes . . . No, sir, he had never been in the shop before, I did not know him. His name he gave as George Latham. . . . That's right. . . . Oh, I could *describe* him to you, he was—"

"Can you identify the tie clasp?" Jesse found his hand on the phone slippery with sweat.

"Oh, yes," said Mr. Fearing. "Easily. It'll have an identifying mark on it—its manufacturer, you know."

"Mr. Fearing, can I ask you—this is a *very* important matter—if you'll get the first plane down in the morning? You'll be reimbursed for your time and— We'll need a witnessed statement from you—it's a police matter, Mr. Fearing—and formal identification of the—"

"Oh, dear *me*." Fearing sounded pleasantly flustered. "Dear me, yes —as important as all that? I did wonder—such an expensive advertisement it must have been. Dear me! And a Saturday, when business usually— But my conscience would not allow me, if it is as important as you say. If you will kindly give me your address, sir, I'll wire you which plane I am able to—"

Jesse put the phone down. San Francisco, he thought. The happenstance of an April twenty-third birthday. The staunch Methodist.

"You know," he said to Athelstane, "it *is* enough to make a man believe in destiny."

FIFTEEN

"Oh, yes," said Thomas Fearing briskly. "Yes, indeed, that's it." He let his jewelers' loupe fall from his right eye and looked up, smiling, around the little group. "This is the tie clasp I sold on April eighth to this George Latham. "There's no doubt at all."

Mr. Fearing had turned out, unlike Jesse's mental concept, to be a portly, friendly little man, meticulously dressed, who was very excited and interested at the notion of helping the police. As Jesse explained to him, it wasn't so much a question of that as of helping one policeman: which in no way damped Mr. Fearing's interest. He had foresightedly brought along his account books.

It had not, of course, been a matter of walking into the I.A. office and asking for the captain. Even the uniformed desk sergeant in the anteroom had given Jesse a cold stare on hearing his name; Jesse had given him a note for Thatcher, which stressed the fact that not only had he some important and definite evidence to offer, but the witness with him had kindly taken time off from his business and hoped he could tell his story as soon as possible. They had waited in the anteroom nearly an hour before the sergeant intimated the captain could give them fifteen minutes.

"So kind of him," said Jesse. "I think it'll be a bit more." He had met the twin cold gazes of Thatcher and Clay sardonically and introduced Fearing. "Let him tell the rest of it. Only maybe you'd better look at his identification first, or you might—mmh—leap to the conclusion that I'd paid him to tell you a tall story."

Fearing had looked shocked. "Oh, indeed I'd be most happy—" and he'd proceeded to lay out on Thatcher's desk an impressive array of identification, all the way from a photostated birth certificate, a library card for the San Francisco Public Library, a driver's license and a membership card in the National Association of Retail Jewelers, to a card announcing that he was donating both corneas, upon death, to the Estelle Doheny Eye Foundation. About then Thatcher resignedly told them to sit down; Clay remained silent in a corner, eying Jesse moodily and smoking.

Fearing had plunged into his story happily, mentioning destiny again and veering off to describe the antique Majolica vase, but eventually he'd got to the tie clasp and George Latham, and Thatcher, who'd been fiddling with a pen and staring out the window, sat up and began listening.

And now, Fearing, having minutely examined the tie clasp, was saying, "Oh, yes, that's the one. I recognize my own work, of course, and the clasp itself. I can show you my books—there's the maker's mark on the clasp, a brand I carry, but I recognize the individual—"

Thatcher stared at him. A Thatcher, thought Jesse with deep satisfaction, suddenly humanized by utter confoundment. "How can you possibly—"

"Well, if I could point it out—there's a tiny flaw just here on the underside. I noticed it at the time I was— And I *do* know my own work, after all, sir. This is the same clasp." Fearing looked at them. "What's the trouble, gentlemen? Don't you believe me? I assure you—"

"The gentlemen," said Jesse dryly, "have just relearned the truth of the old proverb that to err is human. Let's get it all perfectly clear. On Wednesday the seventh of April, a man was found murdered in his apartment, and Sergeant Clock and his minions naturally searched the place. It's alleged that during the search the sergeant found this tie clasp, recognized the initials on it as belonging to a man who had, if barely, known the dead man—a man who, being a professional gambler, might be supposed to have large sums in cash to pay out. So the sergeant secretly pocketed the clasp, intending to demand payment for its concealment. This *is* the tie clasp that was subsequently found in the glove compartment of his car? Yes. Well, it now appears that on that day, the seventh of April, this self-same tie clasp was, in fact, sitting innocent of any initials in Mr. Fearing's showcase. That, in fact, it sat there until the next day—you remember what time, Mr. Fearing?"

"It was in the late afternoon, roundabout four or four-thirty."

"Yes," said Jesse. "The news stories about the murder mentioned that Mr. Starbuck had been questioned. Just that. Nobody ever thought he was involved in it—he'd met the dead man very casually that afternoon in a Gardena poker house. But Mr. Starbuck has, on occasion, been in the news himself—when he built that five-million-buck casino over in Vegas not long ago, for example—and he's known to be a successful pro gambler. Sort who habitually carries a lot of cash. So the chance had arrived to spring the trap set for Sergeant Clock, gentlemen. And the principal—I think he took care of that himself—took immediate steps to obtain the alleged piece of evidence, so carefully initialed. You can get to San Francisco in fifty minutes by jet. Elementary precaution—just in case anything definite ever was made public about the nature of the evidence. If it ever was, it would probably only be locally, and a San Francisco jeweler—"

"Really it does make one wonder about destiny," said Fearing.

"In any case," said Jesse, "this kind of breaks the whole thing to pieces, doesn't it, Captain? This is the same identical tie clasp, and you really can't have it both ways. If it was sitting all bare of initials in Mr. Fearing's shop until Thursday the eighth, Sergeant Clock wasn't finding it in Mr. Arnold's apartment the previous day and marking it as incriminating evidence against Starbuck. House of cards, Captain!—and with this evidence you've got to admit it."

Thatcher closed his open mouth, but didn't say anything. "I also understand," said Jesse, "that you've been sent on some relevant material from Homicide. Relating to that murder, and to a nice circumstantial alibi for Mr. Starbuck. As a lawyer, I do sympathize with your liking for circumstantial evidence—nearly always the best kind." He divided a slow smile between Thatcher and Clay.

Thatcher said at last, in a low voice, "I will be damned. I will be *damned*." He picked up the tie clasp and looked at it. "Mr. Falkenstein, we owe you an apology. But I never would have—in a thousand years I never—"

"Think you owe one more to Clock," said Jesse.

Thatcher humanized himself some more by running fingers through his gray hair. "Most certainly," he said. "But— My God! Who could have believed—"

"Incredible, all right, we've all said it," said Jesse impatiently. "But you've got to see it now. The frame. And I think another thing you've got to see, the next indicated thing to do is gather in the Maddens and Hendrickson, I've got, er, minions working on that—and go through the intensive-questioning bit. I think they'll fold. Always so dangerous to count on the hired hands."

"Yes—but I can't—who in God's name would—" And suddenly Thatcher began to look very angry. "Such a—"

Clay came up to the desk. He had put out his latest cigarette. "I guess an apology you could say," he said gravely, looking down at Jesse. "But I'd like to remind you, Mr. Falkenstein, that we haven't been—call it emotionally detached—ourselves. We're the watchdogs of this force. We know from experience just how much harm it does when a cop goes wrong. Harm to every other man on the force—to the force itself—to every other force. It sickens us and it makes us mad. And here—you've got to admit—it all looked so damn clear because who would have suspected—" He rubbed his jaw. "I can see it," he said, "but I can't bring myself to believe it! The money alone—"

"That aspect of it we tackle next, Lieutenant. Expect you'd like to know the whole story, even though this clears Andrew. . . . I realize all that. Only natural. But seems to me, Lieutenant, you were almighty quick to disregard his whole previous record and character. Know how it looked—how silly it sounded, claiming a frame. But you see how it turns out. By the grace of God the evidence showing up—"

"And I really do believe that," said Fearing earnestly. "The grace of God indeed. If it were not my habit to fold newspapers neatly for disposal—"

"All I'm saying," said Jesse, "is, if you're going to set yourselves up as a tribunal, Lieutenant, you ought to keep in mind that the bench is supposed to be impartial. To listen to all sides of a thing. *A court may not permit one litigant to sit and compel the other to stand, one to speak all he desires and the other to be brief.*"

"That's very true indeed," said Fearing. "Who said that, sir? A quotation?"

"Old Rabbi Judah in the Talmud. Which is mostly concerned, do realize that, with hairsplitting legalities," said Jesse. "Those old fellows awfully good at that. Argue some little damn fool point all day. But sometimes, Lieutenant, I'll also say, you've got to forget all the rules of evidence and use a little common sense."

Clay kept staring at the tie clasp. "Be damned—I still can't— The Maddens, yes—" He looked at Thatcher. "George, this is pretty definite. We've got to—"

"They're over in Vegas," said Jesse. "I've got a private eye on them.

You'll want to have them picked up and shipped back. Hendrickson's sister has gone to find him and haul him home. She thinks he's up at Tahoe."

"Yes," said Thatcher. And suddenly, as if he was galvanized into action, the shock wearing off as he realized the need for action, he banged one fist on the desk and snatched up the phone. "Hank, get me the chief of police in Las Vegas. Right now! Urgent business . . . *Tahoe?* Why'd the sister think— Hank? After you've got Vegas on this line, put through a call to the chief in Lake Tahoe—oh, hell, it'd be the sheriff, I guess, that's a wide place in the road, don't suppose they'll have a— All right." He put the phone down. "I've got to do some thinking on this. That crazy story about the deposit slips. You mean to say—"

"Only way it could have been done," said Jesse.

"And, hell, that photograph— I only saw it *was* a picture of Clock, didn't examine it in detail, but—"

"We'll never see that again. Probably a shot stolen with a telescopic lens, Clock's face dubbed into a picture originally taken of Helen and her ex-boy friend Sam Spain. If you can find him, maybe he'll remember the picture being taken. Think you'll have better luck with Helen."

"And that bank teller—by *God*," said Thatcher, seeming to swell, "I'm just *seeing* it. Of all the goddamned, impudent, outrageous—"

"So now you know how the rest of us have been feeling," said Jesse. "Got one small suggestion to make to you."

"What?" said Thatcher.

"Let's, please, locate Andrew and tell him he's off the hook. Reinstated without a stain on his character. You know, he hasn't been feeling very—mmh—emotionally detached either, Captain."

"Oh," said Thatcher. "Oh, my God, yes." He snatched up the phone again, but before he could speak the sergeant's name, that worthy opened the door a crack and looked in.

"Excuse me, Captain." He wore a disapproving expression. "Sergeant Clock is here with—er—a couple of— He says it's very urgent, and he seemed to know that—er—" his gaze moved remotely over Jesse —"was here, and I—"

"Send him in, send him in!" said Thatcher. "I want him!" He stood up.

The sergeant looked faintly astonished, stepped back and opened the door wide. Clock came in looking strangely disturbed and excited, followed by a tall distinguished man looking urbane, and bringing up the rear was old Mr. Walters, looking exactly the same as always, fat, untidy and bald, with cigar ashes on his vest, his mustache drooping, and the bulge of the bottle in his breast pocket.

"Sergeant—" began Thatcher. It was, Jesse conceded, a handsome apology. But oddly, Clock seemed to listen to it impatiently. He accepted Thatcher's offered hand, he thanked him, he thanked Fearing.

"But, Captain—we've found out— Oh, hell, I shouldn't say we, it was—" he looked around and made absent introductions. The tall man turned out to be Dr. Aarons.

"Sergeant, I'm afraid I don't—" Thatcher looked at these invaders of his office in some bewilderment. "What—"

Mr. Walters had characteristically found a chair for himself and pulled it around to a position where he faced the captain's desk. "So this is your I.A. office," he said. "See, Jesse, no Iron Maidens. I figure, you show any reasonable man evidence, he's bound to listen in the end. All the same, I'm kind of relieved Mr. Fearing turned up. Thought that ad was bound to turn up something, though it was in a kind of queer way. Must say, Jesse, when you called me about that last night *I* did some wondering about destiny. Anybody mind if I smoke?" He pulled out a fat cigar. "To tell you the truth, I'm a mite relieved I didn't have to spring this story on Captain Thatcher before he got convinced he was wrong about the sergeant. Oh, yes, we've got the whole story now. I—"

"The *hell* we have! Who—maestro, how—"

"You let me tell it my way, or you'll never see it. You see—"

"Sergeant," said Thatcher, "who are these— Mr.—er—Walters? Just what is your interest in this, if I—"

"Kind of special consultant of mine," said Jesse hastily.

"Well, I appreciate that, Jesse," said Mr. Walters. "My interest, Captain, is, I would say, sort of legitimate. I'm a taxpayer in this city— my Lord, *am* I a taxpayer!—and I've got a vested interest in this police force. Help to pay your salary—and the lieutenant's—and the sergeant's. Didn't at all like to see a good man like the sergeant getting railroaded. On the other hand, like Jesse here, I did see that it had to be a hell of an offbeat thing, and you wouldn't believe it until it was proved. After thinkin' about it, you see, I somehow got the notion the reason for it, this frame, had to be tied up to something in the sergeant's past, and most probably somethin' to do with his job. So, as he couldn't remember anything—but naturally he's been on a lot of different cases—I started looking over all his old notebooks." Mr. Walters coughed and looked a little uneasy. "Now I came across this one thing—back in nineteen fifty-seven it was—and I decided to follow it up. I went back to where it happened and asked a few questions around and I finally—"

"Why?" asked Jesse interestedly. "Why'd you pick that one case?" Mr. Walters shot him an indignant glance. "Oh, no special—"

"No, tell them," said Clock. "*That's* really fantastic. You've got the evidence, they'll have to follow it up, and besides I think Helen will talk if she's pressed. But the mystic seer—" He shook his head. "I know some funny things happen, but I never put much stock in that sort of thing before. I'll think twice about it from now on."

"The— You mean that fellow MacDonald," said Jesse, "that Fran and Nell—"

"Oh, hell," said Mr. Walters. "Well, all right. They'll have to look at this, whatever they think of the seer." He told Thatcher about that; Thatcher looked amused and incredulous, and Clay laughed openly. "So, I'm looking at the sergeant's notebooks, and I come across this thing. This old case. And I looked twice, because," said Mr. Walters, "it happened at an apartment house called the Ariadne Arms. On Sunset Boulevard."

"My God," said Clock simply. "I did vaguely recall the case but I'd completely forgotten the name of the place. Naturally. Can you *beat* it? I never—"

"My God indeed," said Jesse. "Fran will never let us forget it."

"So I looked at it," went on Mr. Walters doggedly. "It's a big expensive place—rented two hundred and up then, probably a lot more now. It was a Mr. and Mrs. Rodney Bayne—young couple. They'd been quarreling a lot, neighbors said afterward. Gave noisy parties, but seemed like that was mostly Mrs. Bayne, because the husband apologized to the manageress. There'd been gossip. A lot of the other people living there are older people, see—and most of 'em disapproved of the Baynes. Bayne worked for a brokerage downtown—rich family— and the girl, she'd been brought up with money too. Knew how to throw it around."

"Mr. Walters—"

"I'm gettin' there," said the old man serenely. "So, quarreling. People said—I gather both of 'em kind of raised their voices in the process —people said, about her two-timing him with other men. People said she was a wild one. Four-five times before this particular night, either the manageress of the place—a Mrs. Stuyvesant—or one of the neighbors on their floor had called the police to complain about the noise from the Baynes's place. Either loud quarreling or loud parties. So, this particular night, about eight o'clock, the manageress gets complaints from a Miss Chesney who lived in the next apartment to the Baynes, and she calls the police. She also tells Miss Chesney she guesses they've all had just about enough of this sort o' thing, and she's going to ask the Baynes to move. The call went in to the Wilcox Street station. Sergeant Clock was working the night shift then—he wasn't a sergeant then, you know, plain detective—and he went out to answer the call along with a squad-car man named Disbrowe. Francis Disbrowe."

"Disbrowe!" said Clay, and sat up with a jerk. "That was—"

"They got to the place, and found a lot of the neighbors on that floor standing round the open door of the Baynes's apartment. I heard all this, case you're wondering, from somebody, a gossipy old lady named Garden, who heard all the details next day. She lived there too but she was in the hospital at the time. Mrs. Stuyvesant went visitin' her next day to tell her about the excitement, see. Mrs. Stuyvesant had gone up there before the police came, try to quiet 'em down, and she said the girl was half-drunk, and him not so far behind. All in all it brought out the neighbors on that floor. I'll tell you who they were." Mr. Walters brought out a folded sheet of paper. "There was this old bachelor, Thomas Teague, retired banker, lived alone. This Miss Doris Chesney. A Mr. and Mrs. George Cranston—he was retired too— money—great social people they were, elderly but always on the go, church work, bridge clubs and so on." Nobody was impatient now, since Disbrowe had been mentioned. Dr. Aarons sat listening interestedly. "Mr. and Mrs. John Norwalk, people in the late thirties—he was a top executive with a local cosmetic firm. Mrs. Stuyvesant of course—and then Patrolman Disbrowe and Detective Clock. You got that? Well, the police officers came and talked to the Baynes, and got them quieted down, and it seemed it was all over so they went back to the squad car and the neighbors went back to their apartments. The sergeant made a couple of notes for the report he'd type up on it, and

Disbrowe took him back to the station. 'Nother reason," said Mr. Walters parenthetically, "I carried on with this, his notes mention Disbrowe's name, and later on of course he helped investigate when Disbrowe got shot. Well, about two hours after this shenanigan, everybody gets a hell of a shock when six shots are fired in the Baynes's apartment. Everybody dashes out again, the manageress comes running and the police get called again. And it seems that Bayne, who'd evidently got to drinking some more and brooding, ended up shooting the girl and then himself. Both dead when Sergeant Clock came the second time, with some other men. Perfectly straightforward business —murder and suicide. I've been back over the newspaper stories about it at the time. And now," said Mr. Walters, "I'm goin' to tell you a little story. A sad little story about human nature, gentlemen.

"There was this man, and he was mighty successful in life. Far as money went. He inherited a lot, and he made a lot. He was a stockbroker. Associated with a big firm downtown. He got married the first time when he was twenty-one, but his wife never had any children, and she died of cancer when she was only thirty. Well, he got married again in nineteen thirty-three—he was forty years old then—and next year, that wife had a little girl. And you know how that kind of thing is—this man was just crazy about the baby. Like they say, the sun rose and set on this daughter. Especially as the second wife turned out sort of a bad lot, and he divorced her and got custody of the little girl. Dawn, her name was. Pretty girl—pretty as all get-out. I guess I can just outline this part, because," said Mr. Walters sadly, "we all know how that situation goes. Couldn't deny her anything, girl pampered every way, never punished for a thing, buy her anything she wanted."

"So very foolish," said Dr. Aarons suddenly, "and unfortunately so very human."

"Isn't it," said Mr. Walters. "Girl turns out wild as a hawk, like you might expect—maybe took after the mother some, too. He never could see any wrong in her. Expect, to him, she was just—gay. Vivacious. All young people like to have a good time, he'd say. Oh, I heard about it. . . . He used to keep a big house in Bel Air, he gave it up after— But I scouted around, asking old neighbors, and I found this exhousekeeper who was with him good many years—got a lot from her. She—the girl—she was just his darling, and nobody else understood her—she never meant any harm, just young and gay. Guess we all know how the words and music go on that. He was pleased when she got married—liked the young fella fine—and it was a big splashy society wedding. Girl was twenty-one then.

"He was in England when it happened, you see. When Rodney Bayne shot her and committed suicide. He wasn't mentioned much in the newspaper accounts—only, 'Mrs. Bayne's father was prostrated upon hearing of the tragedy and is reported to be in a London hospital.' Like that. Seems he had a heart attack or a stroke or something. I wouldn't be sure which, doctors'll probably tell you. Didn't even get home for the funeral, so he wasn't around while the official investigation was going on. This chatty ex-housekeeper tells me when he did get home, he had to spend almost two years in a sanitarium afterward. Private place up north near Sacramento, and I guess you'll want to talk to the doctors there too. Well, I got to thinking about what his state o' mind must've been, you see. I been talkin' it over with Dr. Aarons this morning—heard him give a lecture once, figured him for a sensible fellow, so I hunted him up."

"A rather classic pattern," nodded Aarons gently. "The need to blame anything but oneself. And also, I think, in these circumstances, the fact that the actual murderer was beyond further punishment. There was, in fact, no one left to punish for that death which took from him all he held dear—the only thing of importance, emotionally, in his life. You see the—er—single-minded reasoning, if we may call it that."

"Yes, well, fancy language but that's about it. Had a long talk, like I say, with this housekeeper. You'll want one too. Mrs. Martha Camber, down in Manhattan Beach. Pensioned off now. Innocent old soul, and she doesn't read the papers much—not that I suppose any of the rest of this got much mention. She said, even after he came home from the sanitarium, he couldn't seem to get over it. He retired from business then. She said, many's the time she'd heard him say, Why in God's name were all those people so careless, so selfish?—just going away and leaving her with that murderer. They should have known, should have seen he was dangerous. And the police of all people should have known, taken him in the first time they came. It was really all their fault—all those selfish people so bent on their own concerns they just went away and left her—to be killed."

"The need to fix blame somewhere," said Aarons, adjusting his glasses. Thatcher was listening, expressionless; Clay with incredulity; Fearing avidly.

"And then there was Disbrowe," said Mr. Walters. "It looked funny, when I read about that. Just shot, that way. No reason, seemingly. I just thought, you know, he was the other officer with the sergeant on that case. He was—like the sergeant—one of the people who'd gone away and left her. And I just thought it'd be kind of interesting to know about the rest of 'em. What had happened to them, since. I'd already heard that Mrs. Stuyvesant had been killed. Apparently some hood who jumped her in the apartment garage when she came home late. Purse rifled, and so on. You never got anybody for that."

"My God—" Clay looked startled. "You don't mean—"

"'S why I got the private eyes on it. Looking up all those people. I expect, you know, he did the same thing. Some of them still living there by the time he—started operations, some moved away. I wouldn't doubt, if you look, you'll find some agency around got commissioned to look up those people. How'd they know what he had in mind? Anyway, you know about Disbrowe. And the manageress. The Cranstons, they were out at a bridge party one night, parked their car across the street, and as they walked toward it they both got hit by a big car that didn't stop. I don't know if he meant to kill 'em—probably —but I figure, and Dr. Aarons backs me up, that's what kind of gave him the better idea. How to, you know, get his real vengeance on 'em all. Because neither of the Cranstons was killed, but it did, you could say, ruin their lives—any happiness they'd had. Both crippled, so they couldn't enjoy the gay social life any more, can't get around."

"It would be a symbol, you understand," said Aarons. "A most interesting case. As he had lost the only thing of emotional significance to him, the one thing in life that mattered, so must they. Once he had become fully obsessed with the idea that they were entirely to blame."

"Now, Miss Chesney," said Mr. Walters, and he looked very angry, "unmarried woman, fiftyish, inherited money—about the only thing she had, you could say, were her pets. Dogs, she likes. She had a little beagle, then—it got poisoned some way. Then she got one o' these Scotty dogs—nice little dogs. It got poisoned too. She's had six or seven dogs since. They all went the same way. Latest one, one o' those little Schnauzers it was, he got poisoned just the other day, on the street—something he picked up, with strychnine in it. Poor lady's just heartbroken."

"For God's sake!" said Jesse. "What a diabolical— Yes, I see. I do see, Edgar. For God's sake."

"This Teague fella. Old fella—kind of crotchety, maybe. Kept to himself. About his only interest was watchin' TV. You know what happened to him? He got assaulted one night and blinded by acid. Senseless attack—police figured some hophead, maybe mistaking the man for somebody else. Poor old man's in a rest home now."

Thatcher had half-risen; he was looking horrified and as incredulous as Clay now. "You're saying—"

"Look it all up for yourself, Captain. Dr. Aarons is interested—explains it better than I could. And you can say, a long time for a man to go plotting like that—eight years—but the doctor seems to think that'd kind of add interest to it, for him. Brooding on what he was going to do—had done. I figure, you see, he started out just crudely taking their *lives,*" said Mr. Walters earnestly, "because that was what his Dawn had had taken away. Till the Cranstons maybe showed him a kind of even better way. To take from 'em what was most important in their lives. The Norwalks. That was—well, it *could* have been an accident, but—" Mr. Walters shook his head, making a grimace. "They had a baby, you see. Been married fifteen years and given up any hope of a family, and then she had this little boy. You can maybe guess how they both loved that baby. They moved away—bought a house up in Nichols Canyon. Police record says the boy wandered away and fell off a cliff. I kind of wonder. And Norwalk, he got to blaming her for being careless, and finally committed suicide."

"*My God!*" said Thatcher. "This—"

Mr. Walters looked at his cigar. "Could be this'll turn out to be a kind of nine days' wonder, hah, Captain? When you sort it all out. Don't know what sort of evidence there'd be after all this time. Likely not much. Maybe you don't need to be told, once you look at it the right way up. Sergeant Clock, well, I guess anybody knows him could say about the most important thing to *him* is his job. . . . The fella probably spent a lot of time nosin' around on this, you know—as well as paying private detectives to find out. A little time spent watching the sergeant from a distance, say, 'd tell anybody he's pretty wrapped up in his career. So that was what he had to lose. That was why, Captain. Way me and Dr. Aarons read it."

"For the *love* of—" Thatcher stood up so suddenly his chair rocked.

And Jesse heaved a deep, deep sigh. "That was a point that had puzzled me," he said.

"You go down and have a look," said Mr. Walters, "at the first news story about the Bayne case—next day, in an afternoon edition of the *Times,* Captain. It's kind of interesting. He—her father—'d have gone there to see it too—when he got home. Before he had to go to the sanitarium. Probably brooded over everything published about it, in every paper. But in that one, the story's continued on page eight. And right in the next column, there's a little two-paragraph story telling about how Joe Madden had just got sentenced to a one-to-five term for armed robbery—and how he lashed out in court about the trigger-happy cops shooting his dad in cold blood. It mentions his sister too—'svelte blonde,' it says—bein' in court to hear the verdict. So our fella would have known maybe both the Maddens pretty ripe to join in a plot against a cop. Any cop, Captain. Especially if they got paid for it. And of course all the way through, the money's been no object to him. At least a mink coat for Helen, probably more." Mr. Walters suddenly looked tired. He put a wistful hand, absently, to the bottle bulge in his breast pocket.

"For *God's*— What's his name?" asked Thatcher in a deadly quiet tone.

Mr. Walters leaned back in his chair. "Charles Edouard Beauchamps," he said. "Out on Loma Vista Avenue in West Hollywood."

SIXTEEN

But before they took him there were things to be done. They were busy doing them the rest of Saturday and Sunday.

The Maddens, picked up by the local police in Las Vegas and confronted with Clay, who'd flown over immediately, agreed after a short session to return voluntarily. Joe wasn't talking, but Helen came out with quite a lot. In detail. It was about what they might have expected from Helen, Clock said afterward; they let him sit in on it.

"It looked sort of funny, but after all it was a good deal—Joe said. I mean the way it *started* was funny. This guy on the phone. Just a voice, like. Said he wanted to pay off a grudge, how Joe got it, and was willing to pay if we'd— Joe was all for it, it wasn't anything we had to do, see, nothing at all really—money for nothing you could say, a long time. Gee, I don't exactly remember when that was. Joe would maybe —nearly two years ago, I guess— He said, the guy, it just had to wait for the right chance to do it, see. I didn't understand that part of it— but the money came on the dot every month, to that post-office box he told Joe to rent. The money was to pay us to stay right here, see, ready and waiting for the time he'd start to do it. Of course Joe was all for it, chance to help do something to a cop. It seemed kind of funny to me because, gee, you got a grudge on somebody, you pay a couple of hoods to beat him up and that's that. I said it was all kind of kooky, but Joe, he always knows it all, he said No, the guy was just being subtle. Subtle, my God. And the money was fine, sure. I began to think maybe the guy'd never—you know—tell us it was starting to happen, so we'd be ready to do all like he'd planned out.

"Oh, well, he asked if I had a picture, any kind, with a boy friend— this was right at the first, see, and all over the phone—and I had that one of me and Sam, only not from where I said it was taken—another place. He told us—the guy—to send it to him, it was another post-office box somewheres—and awhile after that he sent it back, with like instructions. Only it wasn't Sam in the picture any more, his face I mean. It was—" she nodded once at Clock—"him. The cop. I was supposed to get a frame for it and when the guy called and said it was all starting, I was to put it out somewhere in the living room for anybody to see. For you cops to see—once—and he said— He'd *promised* about the mink coat. Gee, imagine—I mean, just to pay off a grudge! Well, it was a *deal*. And when he did call, that Thursday it was, he said the money—it'd be cash, he said—'d be in that post-office box Saturday and when anybody asked me—the cops—I was supposed to say the cop'd given it to me on my break Saturday night, and I was to go buy the mink coat first thing Monday and say to the saleslady my boy friend gave me the money. . . . What? Oh, well, that was awhile back, he sent a note about that—written on the typewriter it was—he said did I or Joe know anybody would say he'd seen me and the cop together, like at a big restaurant, see, and when it started I was supposed to get somebody like that, for some extra money, see, and sort of let out to you cops where—and all like that. So you'd— It was an extra five hundred bucks and I thought of Benny right off, because he always needs money, got a big family and he's a nice guy, and it wasn't anything—well, real *bad*, you know! I wouldn't have done n——anything real *bad*, it was just like telling a couple little fibs, and gee, if the guy was willing to pay just for *that*—

"But then, after, I got to feeling kind of nervous. All the big fuss made over it. You hauling me down here, all the questions and all. And that lawyer, and the cop himself, and they said—all about how the guy must be crazy, do anything like that, and I'd felt all along it *was* a crazy deal, only who's going to turn down the side money for such an easy— But I got to feeling more and more nervous, especially after I went to that Madame Blanche and she saw a dark aura all around me—and that other one, the man, only he can't be very good because he doesn't charge anything. It made me feel— Well, I said to Joe, let's just get out, is all! See, we was—were supposed to get five thousand bonus when it all worked and the cop was kicked off the force, and that hadn't happened far as we knew yet, but I pestered Joe till he called the guy—he'd give us a number we could call, see—and asked for the money then on account we didn't like all the cops around and I was nervous and all and I guess he sounded kind of tough because finally the guy said O.K., but when Joe went to the post-office box next day—" her face crumpled tearfully—"oh, Jesus, that letter! Like he'd use acid on me—and if we ever— Listen, you *do* know who he is? You're gonna arrest him, put him in jail? Because I—"

Thus Helen. Madden still wasn't talking.

They would, eventually, go back over all the other cases besides Clock's, and find no usable evidence at all. Except on one. It was maybe—possible—uncertain. But there was such a thing as moral certainty. And they took a long detailed statement from Mrs. Martha Camber, the ex-housekeeper, all of which made interesting reading.

Jesse had a wire from Wanda Herrick on Saturday night: RETURNING AT ONCE WITH WALTER CONTACT US LONG BEACH. So they set up that interview on Sunday afternoon in Jesse's office, with both Thatcher and Clay present.

Big Sister had backed Walter Hendrickson up against the wall. He was by turns deprecating, anxiously self-excusing, and sullen. . . . "I didn't think at first it was anything so awfully bad. I mean—well, and it was a lot of money. I— Well, it sounded just crazy. Look, I thought he was maybe a little nuts, because it *sounded*— Well, it was one day I'd been at the employment agency. Most of the afternoon, talking with some other fellows there, you know, and one of the clerks. They hadn't had anything to offer me that was really suitable—that I wanted, I mean—"

"Any soft job with big pay," said his sister. He looked uncomfortable.

"Oh, Wanda, it wasn't exactly— Well, anyway, this fellow called me on the phone that night. Crazy. He said was I interested in making a lot of money just for doing him a little favor some time. I listened, who wouldn't? I could always turn him down if I— Well, he said he'd been at the employment agency that afternoon—there were a lot of people there, I hadn't noticed anybody watching me—but he said, well, he thought I had just the—the qualifications he wanted."

"And wasn't he right," said Mrs. Herrick.

"Look, how was I to know *then*— He said all he wanted me to do was apply for this job at the bank. That bank. There'd been an ad in the paper, he said, for trainees, and I was to apply. I'd probably get the job, just out of the army and two years' college. He said he'd pay me the same salary the bank did—extra, you see—all the while I stayed

there, just waiting for when I could—could do the favor for him. Well,
I—"

"You didn't ask and he didn't tell you exactly what the favor was?"
asked Jesse.

"Well, he said something about—that he had a little grudge to pay,
and he just wanted me some time, when he told me to, to say somebody'd paid in some money when he hadn't. Well, my God, it didn't
sound like much of anything, how should I— And look, when he called
me again that time and told me to keep back that deposit slip, make
out another one, and send the original to him at this post-office box,
I'd already had a lot of the extra money, and I didn't feel I could—"

"Honest hired hand," murmured Jesse, and shrugged. "Didn't
worry you any that the—er—apparent victim was a police officer?"

Hendrickson looked sulky. "I didn't know this Clock. I never heard
anybody call him sergeant until after—well, after it all happened. *I*
didn't know. All it said on his bank books was Andrew D. Clock, how
should I know? Well, that was all, things just went on like always, I
didn't especially like the job but it wasn't hard work and as long as I
stayed I got the extra regular as could be every month. In cash, sure.
Sent to the apartment. Well, I wasn't fool enough to put it in my account at the bank—they always keep an eagle eye on their own employees, I found that out—and I didn't know but what they had some
way to look in a safety box too. So I took a box in the Citizens' Bank
up in Hollywood. I kept it there. What I didn't— Well, of course he
said that and I knew it—I shouldn't throw it around. People—the bank
—would wonder, and get suspicious. But I spent some—just on things
that wouldn't, you know, *show*. Well, after all—"

"And when he told you what you were to do that Friday, you didn't
have any suspicion of what kind of plot it was? You still didn't know
that Clock was a police officer? Be careful, Hendrickson," said
Thatcher coldly. "You called him sergeant yourself."

Hendrickson wriggled sullenly under their eyes. "Well, I—I did
know then. Parker mentioned it. He usually had the cage next to me.
Well, I guess I sort of half realized what it *could* be about—money
paid into his account, and I had to swear he'd paid it in himself—but—
well, I'd taken all that money because I'd *said* I'd do what he asked,
and I didn't feel— Well, after all I don't know the sergeant personally,
and for all I knew he *had* done—something, and this man— How
should *I*—"

"You really are a prize, Walt," said his sister grimly.

"Had you ever met this—benefactor?" asked Clay.

"No. Not until—if it was him—the money was paid in. That Friday."

"Everything you remember about it," said Thatcher. "Please."

"I don't know if it was him. He didn't say a word. It was a busy time. This man just stepped up to the counter and laid down this bundle of cash and a deposit slip. I counted the cash first and then I automatically asked if he had his book with him and he just shook his head. Then I looked at the deposit slip and saw it was made out to Sergeant Clock's account. Well, yes, I guess you could say I'd been expecting it, the— He'd called me the night before and told me to. Told me just to act natural and take it in quick as I could. Well, the—"

"Happen to notice," asked Jesse, "that the deposit slip had a replica of Sergeant Clock's signature on it?"

"I didn't take any notice, how should I? It was just a deposit slip. I wasn't— And he'd said, afterward, I was to be ready to swear the sergeant paid it in. So I guess I knew *something*. But after all it wasn't anything to do with *me*, and I'd agreed to—and I'd *had* the money— and how should I know but what—"

"Mr. Hendrickson," asked Thatcher abruptly, "could you identify the man who paid in that cash to the sergeant's account?"

Alarm flashed in Hendrickson's eyes. "I'm not sure," he muttered.

"Oh, come now. It's not so long ago."

"Well, I—it was only the once, and really I— Look," said Hendrickson in a burst of frankness, "I don't want one damn thing to do with that guy! I tell you. How did *I* know what I was getting into? What kind of a—an inquisition it'd be? I didn't like it. I said what I was supposed to say, but— And then that big ape of a cop and this smart-boy lawyer barging in, getting me all confused. I didn't know what that cop might *do*, and I— Well, the thing *was*, he'd said when I'd done it, and it was finished, he'd give me a bonus and I could leave the bank if I wanted. I've got—I had—nearly seven thousand bucks saved of that extra money. Well, I got to feeling, just, I wanted out. And I had a number where I could call him. I did and I said I'd done my part and what about the bonus? And he got— Well, I guess for the first time really I got to wondering about him. It really was, you look at it, a crazy deal. All that money—a grudge— And he sounded really nasty. I can't explain it exactly, only I— Well, I just thought I *had* done what

I was paid for and I tell you, I wasn't liking him any better than I liked that sergeant then, and I—"

Thatcher sighed, stood up and stretched. The police stenographer stopped scribbling shorthand and waited stolidly. "At least," said Thatcher, "we've got Fearing. To identify him."

"Oh, well," said Hendrickson hastily, "if you've *arrested* him and he's in jail, I guess I—"

They went to pick up Charles Edouard Beauchamps on Monday morning. They let Clock go along.

It was a new apartment building, exclusively modernistic, not too big: three stories, perhaps nine units. Big apartments. About six hundred a month, thought Clock.

A tailored manservant opened the door to them: Clock had thought the breed was extinct. Correct and colorless: "Whom shall I say is calling?"

Thatcher gave him a card. "'Kyou, sir." He would have left them in the entry hall, but they followed him. He paused, turned, surprised and uncertain. "We'll announce ourselves," said Thatcher. "Where is he?"

The manservant looked suddenly frightened. "What—" he said, sounding more natural, and glanced at the card, and swallowed, and gestured. They went into the living room.

He was sitting in an armchair by a window overlooking the near Hollywood hills. An old man, but still physically alert. Well-groomed and obviously prosperous: as obviously used to authority, and he looked at them and stood up slowly, not alarmed but annoyed. "Who are you and what do you want?" he demanded arrogantly.

"Police," said Thatcher. "We want you, Mr. Beauchamps. For a number of reasons."

The man drew himself up. "I don't understand you," he said coldly. "You have no business here. Go away."

"Look, Mr. Beauchamps," said Thatcher—and they were all feeling oddly awkward, for the man looked eminently sane on the surface, but they knew he was not sane, and he was an old man and they did not want to use force. "Helen Madden has talked. We know all about it. We can guess about all the rest. Of your—your vengeance. Is that how you thought of it? Disbrowe—the Cranstons—Mrs. Stuyvesant—the Norwalks' little boy? You felt it was—due vengeance?"

Beauchamps just stared at him; and then, in a moment, his eyes began to turn inward, blank. "No," he said. "No. Mine was the hand but it was destiny for the vengeance to be brought. No man can know, no one was to know, I—"

"Mr. Beauchamps, you'll have to come with us now," said Clay. He put a hand on the man's arm.

"Take your paws off me, peasant!" snarled Beauchamps. He jerked away. "*I* am not to be touched. No man can know the depth of my mind, my—" Clay's hand tightened on his arm and he lashed out suddenly, wildly, and his voice rose to a scream. "No—no—no—you *cannot* know! No man—it was divine destiny the vengeance the better vengeance given to me to see I only the executioner their fault their fault the selfish blind careless ones leaving her leaving her my darling no man can fathom *my* great—"

They had to use some force after all.

"Right over the line," said the doctor at the new jail facility on Alameda downtown. "I'm no psychiatrist but I don't need to be to see that." He grimaced. "Words of one syllable, when you caught up to him he cracked. Megalomania, some kind? Thought he was so far above the common herd, both from the standpoint of being justified in whatever he wanted to do, *and* being so clever he'd never be caught up to." He shrugged. "May be some physical damage too—strokes that affected the brain. You'll want the full examination, encephalogram and so on. I doubt if you'll ever bring him to trial."

They doubted it too. But there wasn't any doubt either that Beauchamps would be stashed away in Atascadero, the place for the criminally insane; and considering his age and his present condition, it was doubtful if he'd ever get out—to stand his trial for murder.

Because they found some evidence in the West Hollywood apartment.

They found a .32 Smith and Wesson Masterpiece.

And the Ballistics office is as neatly and precisely run as an efficient housewife's home; the records were there, and the slug filed away for, hopefully, comparison.

The .32 was the gun that had killed Francis William Disbrowe six years before.

So they could mark that file closed. Even if they couldn't send him to the gas chamber for it.

Which for pretty certain showed that (damn evidence) all the rest of it was his work too. The little boy. The dogs. The hit-and-run. And—

Close the book. Forget it. It was done. He'd be stashed away for keeps. The press would wring it dry: nine days' wonder. Clock would be offered a tempting sum by a true-police magazine for the story of his strange ordeal. Jesse would get some nice publicity out of it. Thomas Fearing would have an exciting tale to retell the rest of his life. And the press, and the public in general, would harass Charles MacDonald a lot more—MacDonald the sensitive, who was just an electrician who worked for the city and didn't know at all how his psychic gift worked.

"It was—" Clock shook his head. "You can't feel sorry for him, but almost you can't help it. Way off the rails, now, as the doctor said, as soon as he was caught up to."

"What I can*not* get over," said Fran, "is MacDonald. It just shows you—some of them *are*. Do you remember, Nell, he said, 'pear—pear,' and he couldn't understand it. You *see* what it was? *Père*. And Beauchamps of French ancestry. Really it does make you think."

"Said she'd never let us forget it," said Jesse. "Hope she isn't going off on a psychic kick now. Refill, Andrew?"

Clock shook his head. "*I* will," said Mr. Walters. He was sitting ensconced in the middle of the couch—the guest of honor, Nell said fondly—with Athelstane between his spread knees and Mr. Walters' free hand rubbing Athelstane's exposed stomach.

"What's going to happen to the Maddens and Hendrickson, Jesse?" asked Nell. "And that Benny?"

Jesse added a little to his drink and passed the bottle to Mr. Walters. "Charge of conspiracy—that covers so many things—wouldn't take a bet on what they'll get, if anything. Kind of vague, legally. No man's land. Any case—" he laughed shortly—"there they are, that kind. You can't cure 'em."

"But," said Nell thoughtfully, "all of it so—random. Wanton. All those people—and that poor child—just because of one man, with an irrational obsession. A lunatic obsession. It makes you wonder—"

"About destiny maybe," said Clock, nodding slowly. "Tell you— what with that MacDonald—sets *me* wondering. Just how much free will have we got?"

"Well, thing that struck me about it," said Mr. Walters, "it was all in the name of love. Which same is a very damn funny thing sometimes. Bible says somewhere, *Love is the fulfilling of the law*. But this and that I've seen these eighty-one years, I figure sometimes Satan goes to using it for his purposes too."

"*Love covers all transgressions*, also says," said Jesse dryly.

"Well, anyway, the sergeant's got an awful good story to include in his memoirs," said Mr. Walters philosophically. "It's been interesting, you can say. Like people always are, hey? Like fingerprints—no two of 'em alike. I never can make out why anybody can get to feeling—you know—bored with life. Hey? When there are all these people—milling around, cause and effect, things happenin' every minute, to somebody, somewhere—maybe to you 'n' me, next minute. Something always going on, with people. I guess about the most fascinating thing there is. Bad ones, sometimes, sure, tragic things happening. But in the long run, I guess there are more good ones. A lot of foolish people, but even most of them mean well mostly. If that says anything. Destiny? Well, it's a thing to wonder. That MacDonald fella—" He shook his head. "Funny." He retired into his drink.

They looked at him with affection and respect. Jesse said, "*All these things shall be laid bare in the scales and in the books on the day of the Great Judgment*. Which I sometimes wonder about too. . . ."

And Nell said, "For a man who claims to have no religion—"

"I," said Clock, rousing himself, "had better be getting home. It's late. Fran?"

"Um," said Fran, and stood. "I think I'll subscribe to that magazine. *Fate*. Very interesting, all that. When you *think* about it—"

"We'll never hear the end of it," said Jesse with a groan.

Clock held Fran's coat for her. "Come on," he said. "It's after eleven, and I've got a job to go to in the morning." And he thought that over, and added, "And, by God, I've never in my life been so glad to remember it!"